SAINTS

THE BOOK OF BLAISE

SAINTS

THE BOOK OF BLAISE

CREATED BY
SEAN LEWIS & BENJAMIN MACKEY

WRITER
SEAN LEWIS

ARTIST
BENJAMIN MACKEY

LETTERING/DESIGN
BENJAMIN MACKEY

IMAGE COMICS, INC.
Robert Kirkman – Chief Operating Officer
Erik Larsen – Chief Financial Officer
Todd McFarlane – President
Marc Silvestri – Chief Executive Officer
Jim Valentino – Vice-President

Eric Stephenson – Publisher
Corey Murphy – Director of Sales
Jeff Boison – Director of Publishing Planning & Book Trade Sales
Jeremy Sullivan – Director of Digital Sales
Kat Salazar – Director of PR & Marketing
Branwyn Bigglestone – Controller
Sarah Mello – Accounts Manager
Drew Gill – Art Director
Jonathan Chan – Production Manager
Meredith Wallace – Print Manager
Briah Skelly – Publicist
Sasha Head – Sales & Marketing Production Designer
Randy Okamura – Digital Production Designer
David Brothers – Branding Manager
Olivia Ngai – Content Manager
Addison Duke – Production Artist
Vincent Kukua – Production Artist
Tricia Ramos – Production Artist
Jeff Stang – Direct Market Sales Representative
Emilio Bautista – Digital Sales Associate
Leanna Caunter – Accounting Assistant
Chloe Ramos-Peterson – Library Market Sales Representative
IMAGECOMICS.COM

SAINTS: THE BOOK OF BLAISE TPB. First printing. SEPTEMBER 2016. Published by Image Comics, Inc. Office of publication: 2001 Center Street, Sixth Floor, Berkeley, CA 94704. Copyright © 2016 Sean Lewis and Benjamin Mackey. All rights reserved. Contains material originally published in single magazine form as SAINTS #1-9. "SAINTS," its logos, and the likenesses of all characters herein are trademarks of Sean Lewis and Benjamin Mackey, unless otherwise noted. "Image" and the Image Comics logos are registered trademarks of Image Comics, Inc. No part of this publication may be reproduced or transmitted, in any form or by any means (except for short excerpts for journalistic or review purposes), without the express written permission of Sean Lewis and Benjamin Mackey or Image Comics, Inc. All names, characters, events, and locales in this publication are entirely fictional. Any resemblance to actual persons (living or dead), events, or places, without satiric intent, is coincidental. Printed in the USA. For information regarding the CPSIA on this printed material call: 203-595-3636 and provide reference #RICH–703272. For international rights, contact: foreignlicensing@imagecomics.com. ISBN: 978-1-63215-696-9.

I grew up a first generation Irish Catholic in Upstate
New York. So, the Saints were fodder for bedtime
stories. My grandma would tell me about Saint George
slaying dragons, Saint Blaise and the boy he saved who
had choked on a bone, the Shroud of Turin, and more and
more. There isn't much to do in Upstate New York, so you
either conform and go to football games and VFW
barbecues, or you try to find simple ways to rebel. My
uncle was eight years older than me. He looked for an
identity in heavy metal music. I'd go to my grandmother's house and I would steal through his comic book
collection and his albums. There I found a whole new
world open up. *Swamp Thing* comics suddenly had an Iron
Maiden soundtrack. Downstairs my grandmother lit candles
and prayed rosaries. The mystical seemed to be all
around me.

As a child you make your own myths. Abandoned houses
become haunted in your mind, their backstories long
urban legends that you and your friends contribute to.
My mind was now filled with two things: religion and
comic books. And metal. Metal scared me back then. This
was before Ozzy Osbourne was a huggable reality TV star
and still was a mad man who ate a live bat onstage.
Years later, obviously, I could see the ridiculousness
in some of the posturing. But I also saw the need. We
need to believe in things, and one of those things is
our own personal power. People turn to metal for power.
They do the same with religion. They do the same to
stories.

Me? I am a worshipper of story above all else. My
ability to tell one is where I try to assert myself; for
my Uncle it was loud guitars, and for me it's precision
pens. SAINTS came about as a way to marry all the things
that obsessed me in my youth, all the things that scared
me and amused me. In the end it wasn't the hope of
making a scary book or a funny book, but to make a book
that I recognized myself in: balancing the horrific and
hysterical of life at the same time; unsure of what I
believe in even after committing myself to it; and above
all, searching for a way to be good in a world where
that gets more increasingly complicated and difficult.

The Saints are imperfect creatures, like you and me.
They are humans searching for a higher sense of
themselves and the world.

And so, the story begins…

-Sean

I

COMPULSION

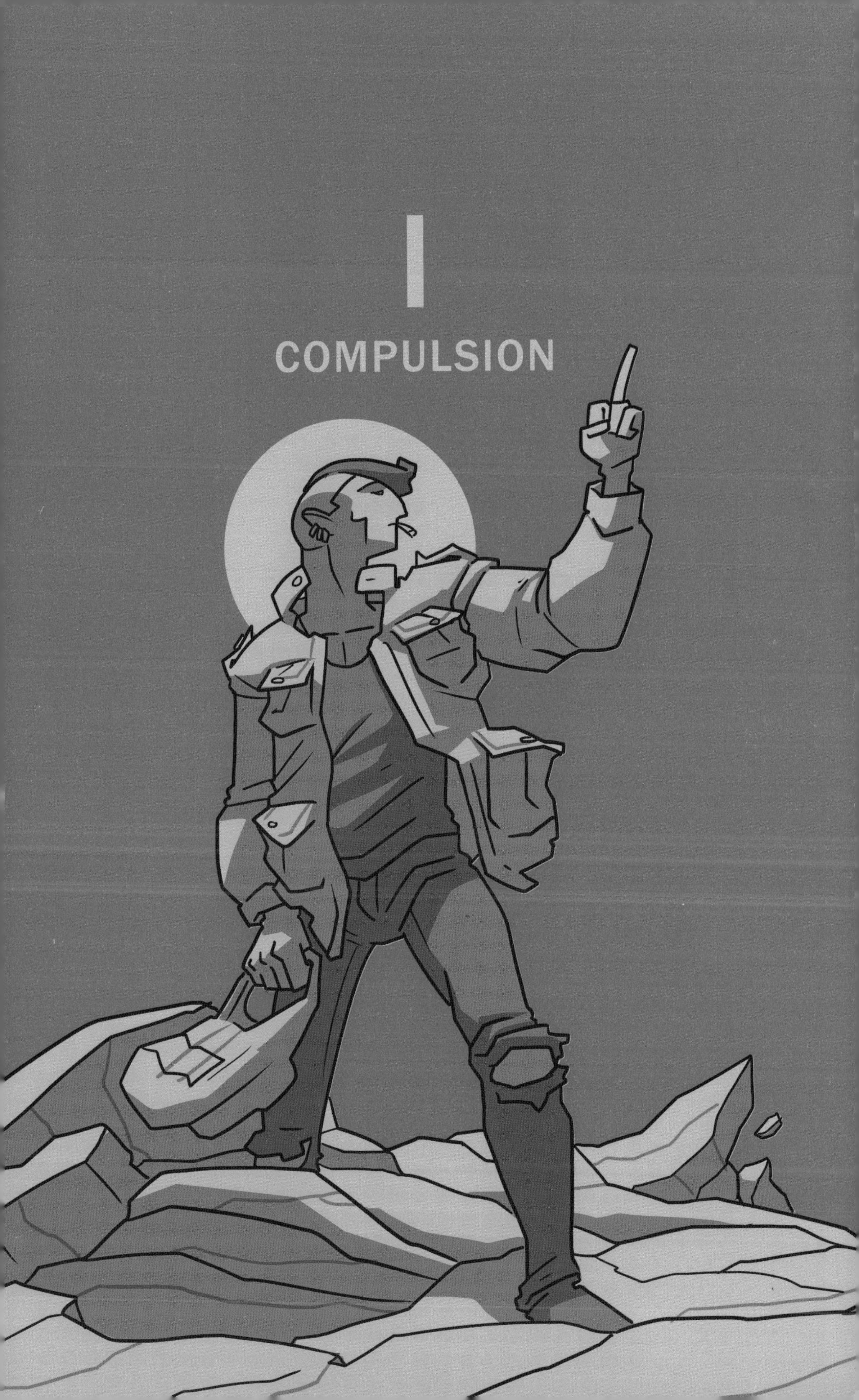

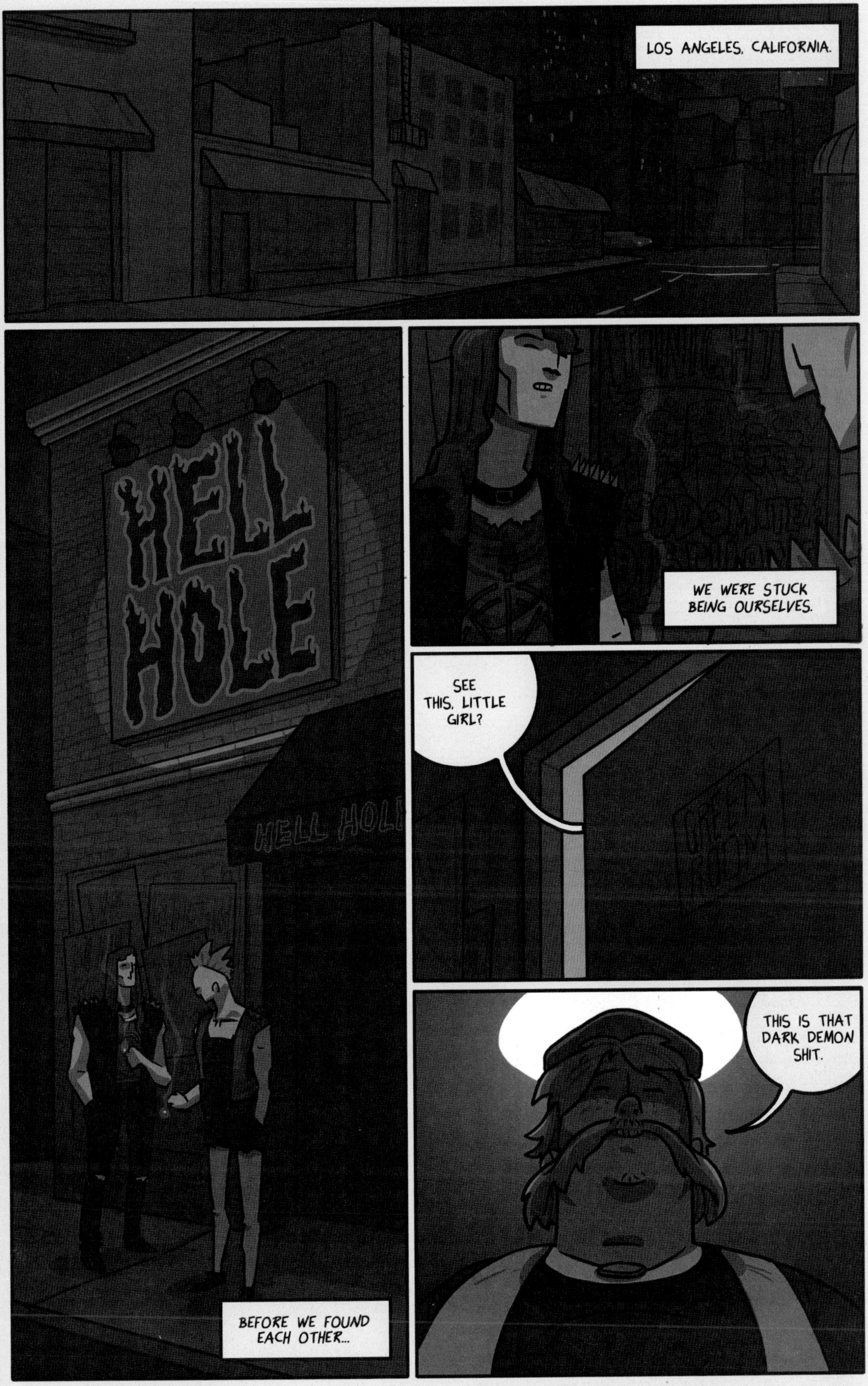
LOS ANGELES, CALIFORNIA.
HELL HOLE
BEFORE WE FOUND EACH OTHER...
WE WERE STUCK BEING OURSELVES.
SEE THIS, LITTLE GIRL?
THIS IS THAT DARK DEMON SHIT.

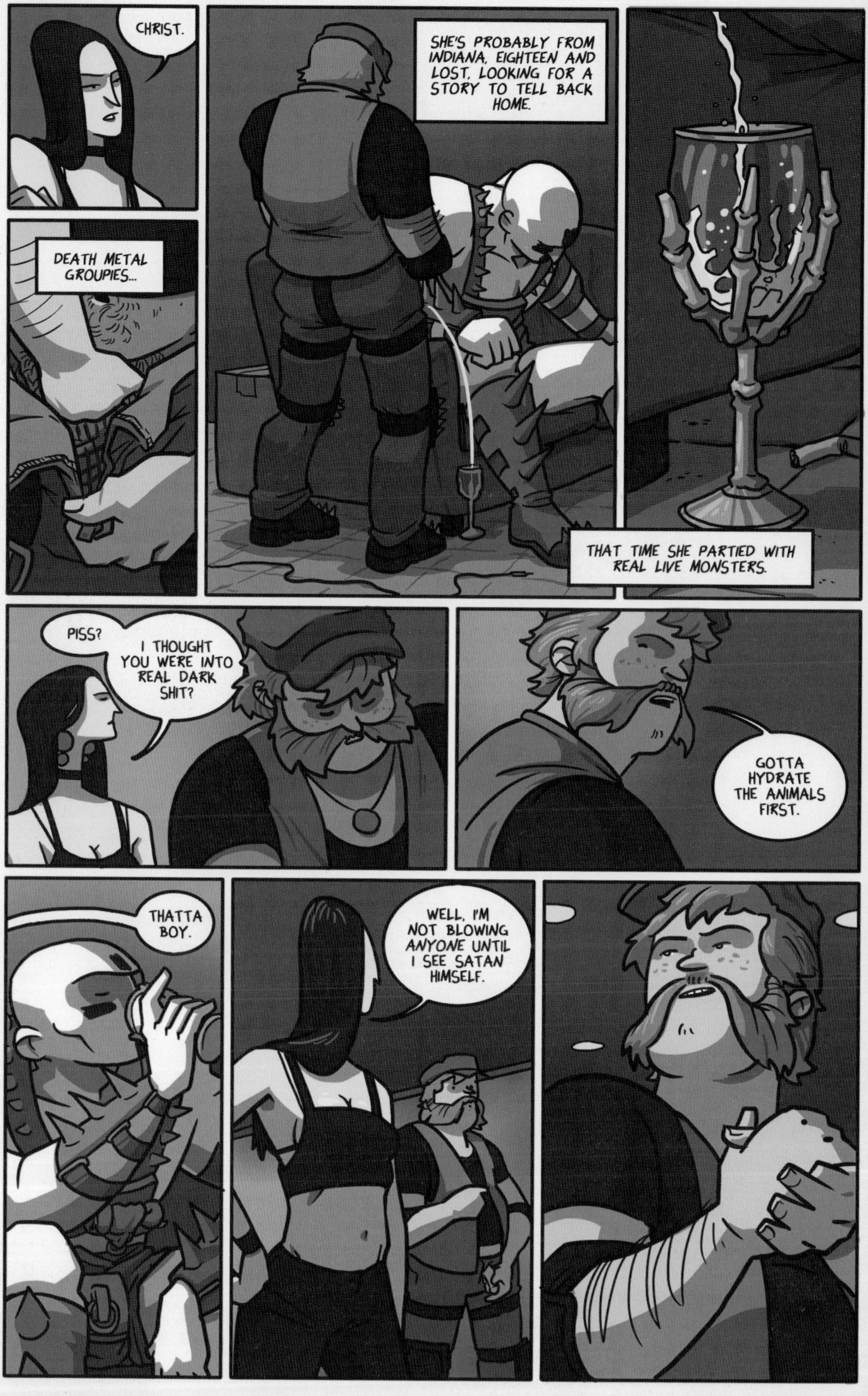
CHRIST.
SHE'S PROBABLY FROM INDIANA, EIGHTEEN AND LOST, LOOKING FOR A STORY TO TELL BACK HOME.
DEATH METAL GROUPIES...
THAT TIME SHE PARTIED WITH REAL LIVE MONSTERS.
PISS?
I THOUGHT YOU WERE INTO REAL DARK SHIT?
GOTTA HYDRATE THE ANIMALS FIRST.
THATTA BOY.
WELL, I'M NOT BLOWING ANYONE UNTIL I SEE SATAN HIMSELF.

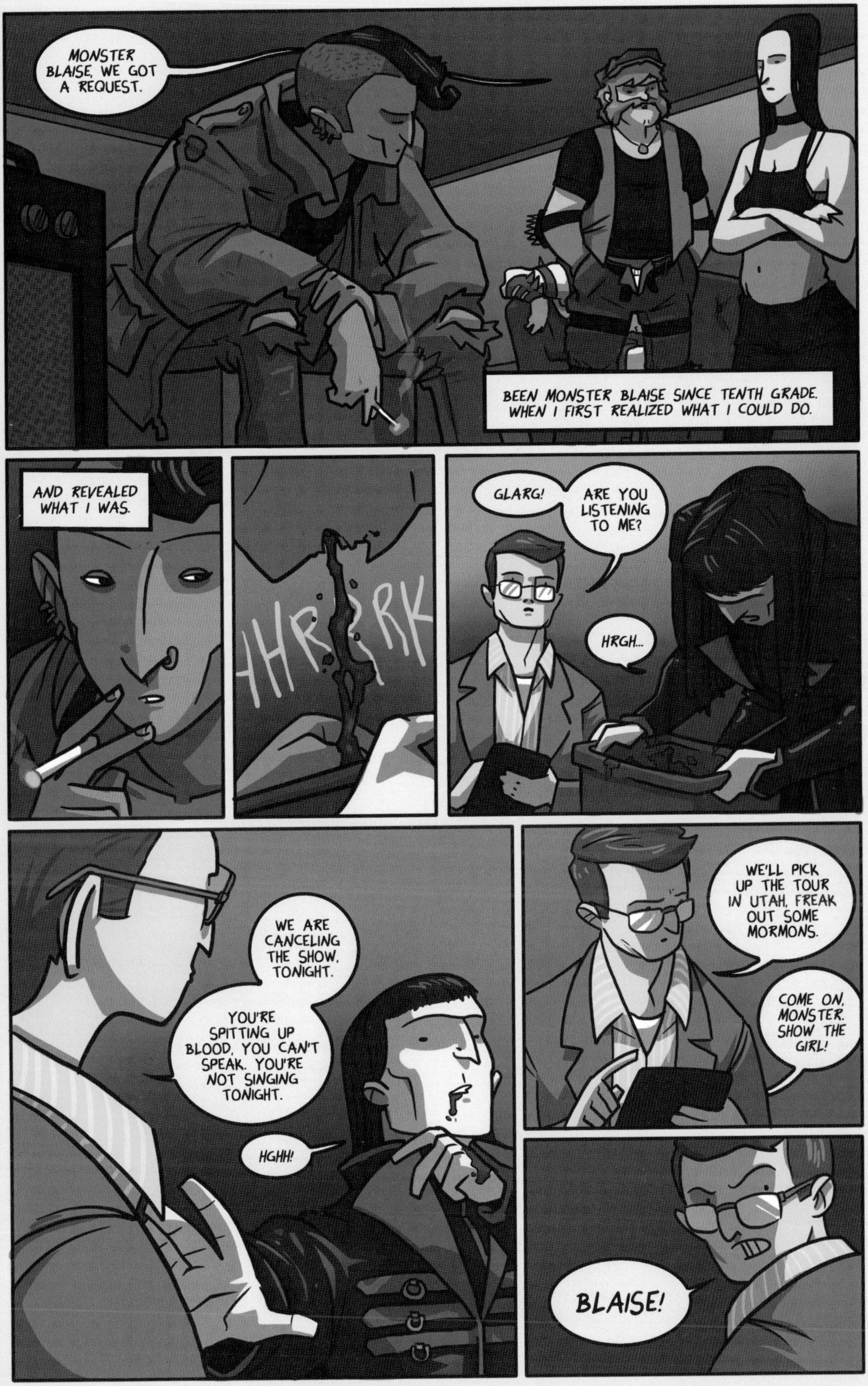
MONSTER BLAISE, WE GOT A REQUEST.
BEEN MONSTER BLAISE SINCE TENTH GRADE. WHEN I FIRST REALIZED WHAT I COULD DO.
AND REVEALED WHAT I WAS.
HHRRRK
GLARG!
ARE YOU LISTENING TO ME?
HRGH...
WE ARE CANCELING THE SHOW, TONIGHT.
YOU'RE SPITTING UP BLOOD, YOU CAN'T SPEAK. YOU'RE NOT SINGING TONIGHT.
HGHH!
WE'LL PICK UP THE TOUR IN UTAH, FREAK OUT SOME MORMONS.
COME ON, MONSTER. SHOW THE GIRL!
BLAISE!

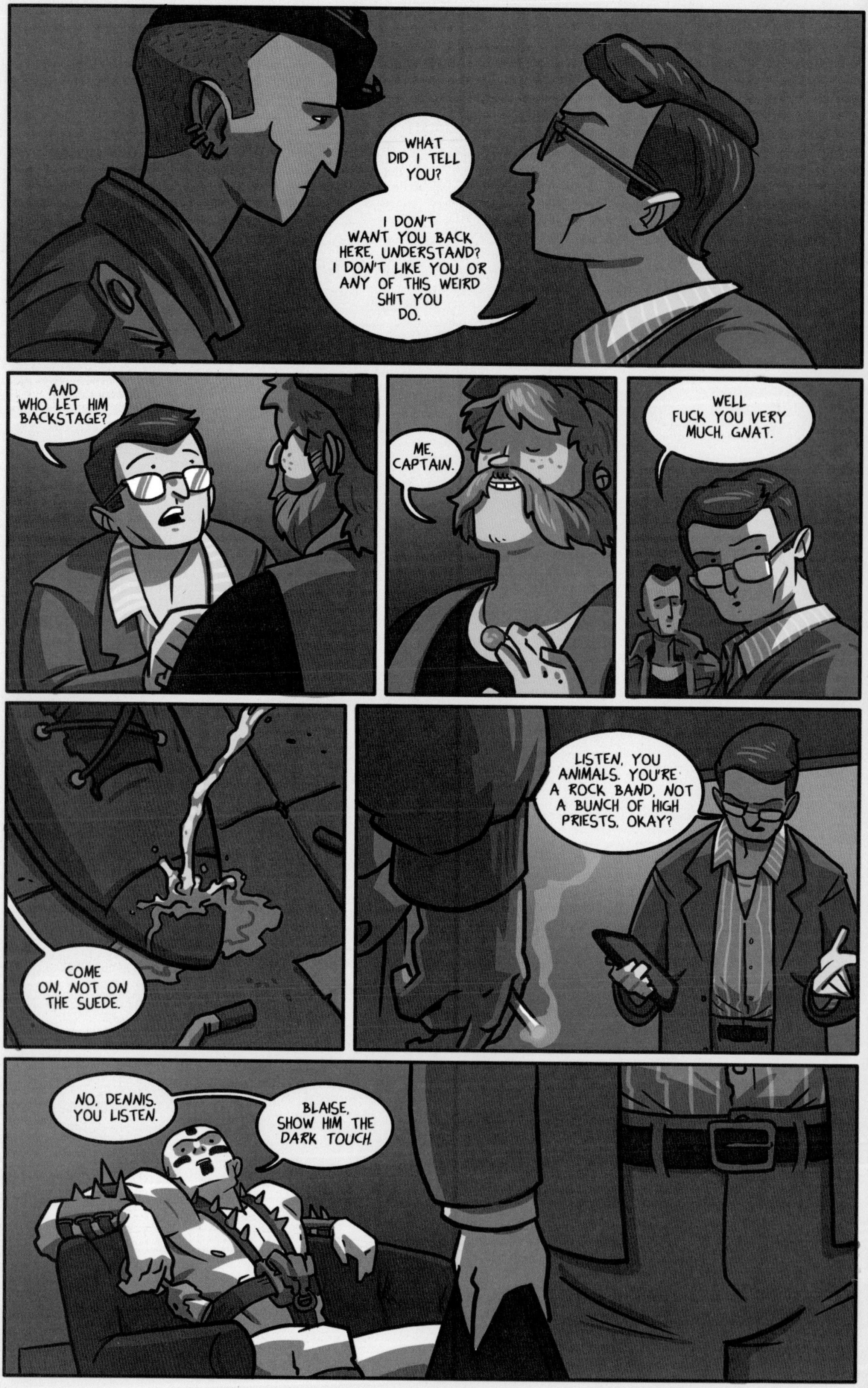
WHAT DID I TELL YOU?
I DON'T WANT YOU BACK HERE, UNDERSTAND? I DON'T LIKE YOU OR ANY OF THIS WEIRD SHIT YOU DO.
AND WHO LET HIM BACKSTAGE?
ME, CAPTAIN.
WELL FUCK YOU VERY MUCH, GNAT.
COME ON, NOT ON THE SUEDE.
LISTEN, YOU ANIMALS. YOU'RE A ROCK BAND, NOT A BUNCH OF HIGH PRIESTS, OKAY?
NO, DENNIS. YOU LISTEN.
BLAISE, SHOW HIM THE DARK TOUCH.

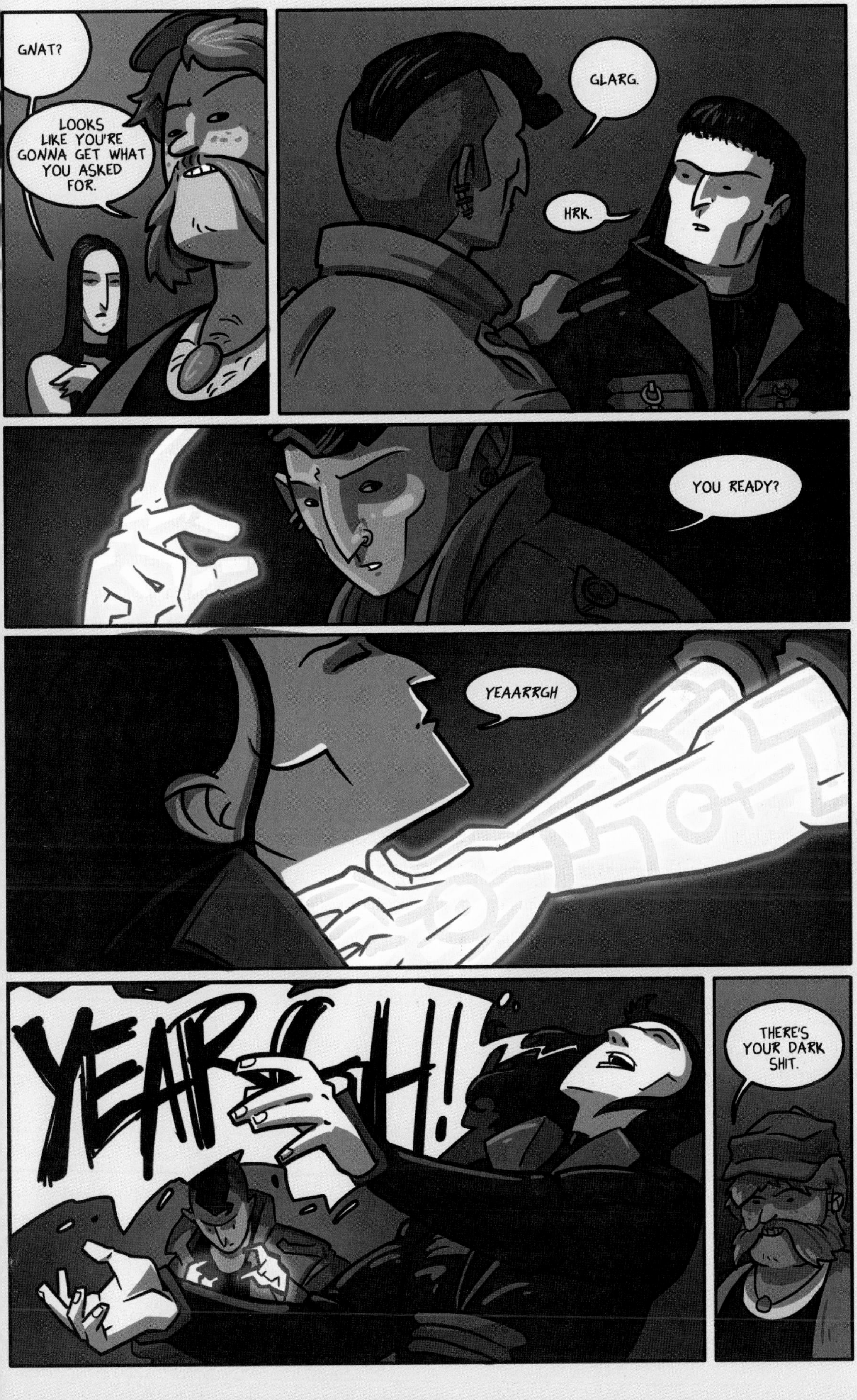
GNAT?
LOOKS LIKE YOU'RE GONNA GET WHAT YOU ASKED FOR.
GLARG.
HRK.
YOU READY?
YEAARRGH
YEARGH!
THERE'S YOUR DARK SHIT.

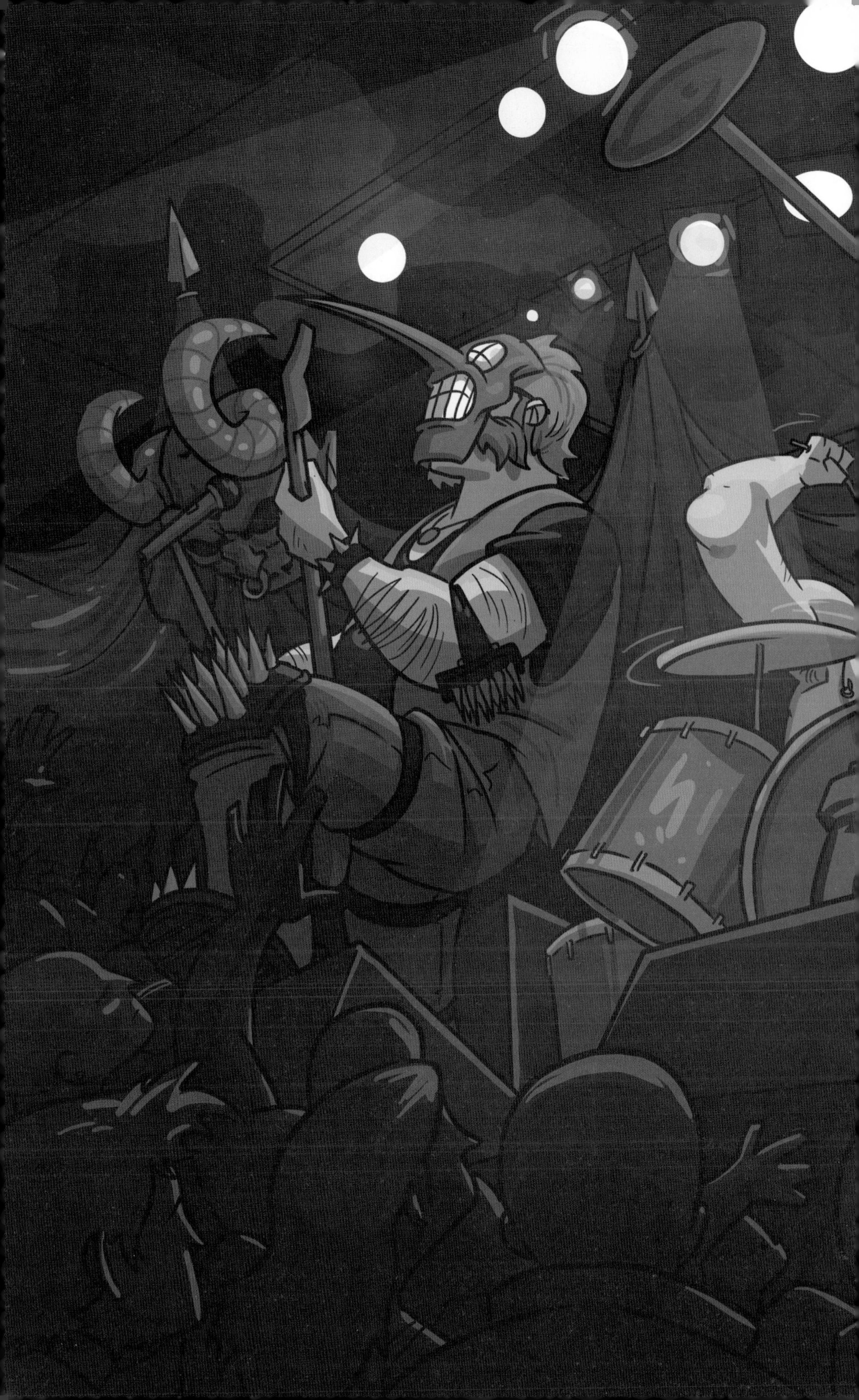

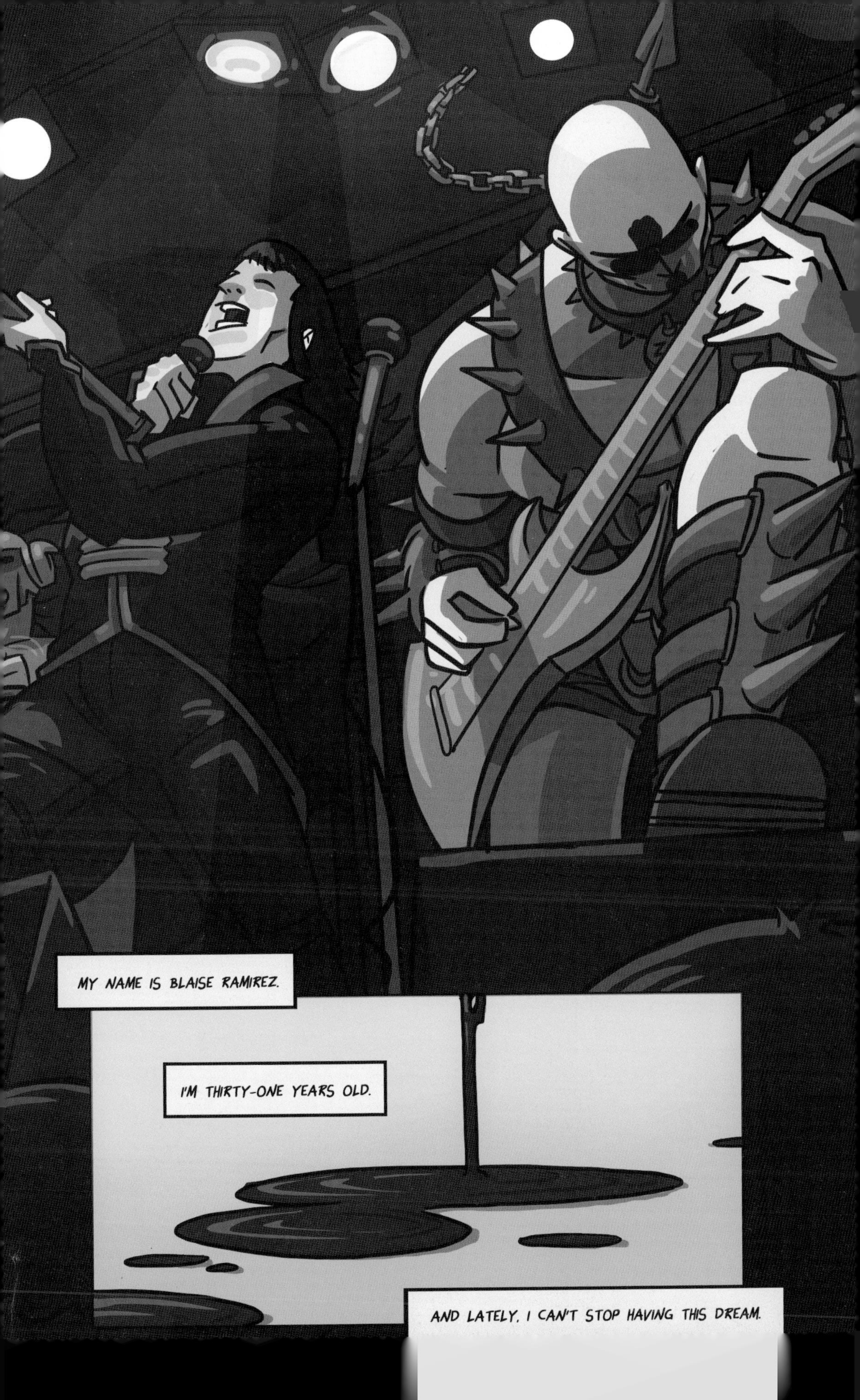
MY NAME IS BLAISE RAMIREZ.
I'M THIRTY-ONE YEARS OLD.
AND LATELY, I CAN'T STOP HAVING THIS DREAM.

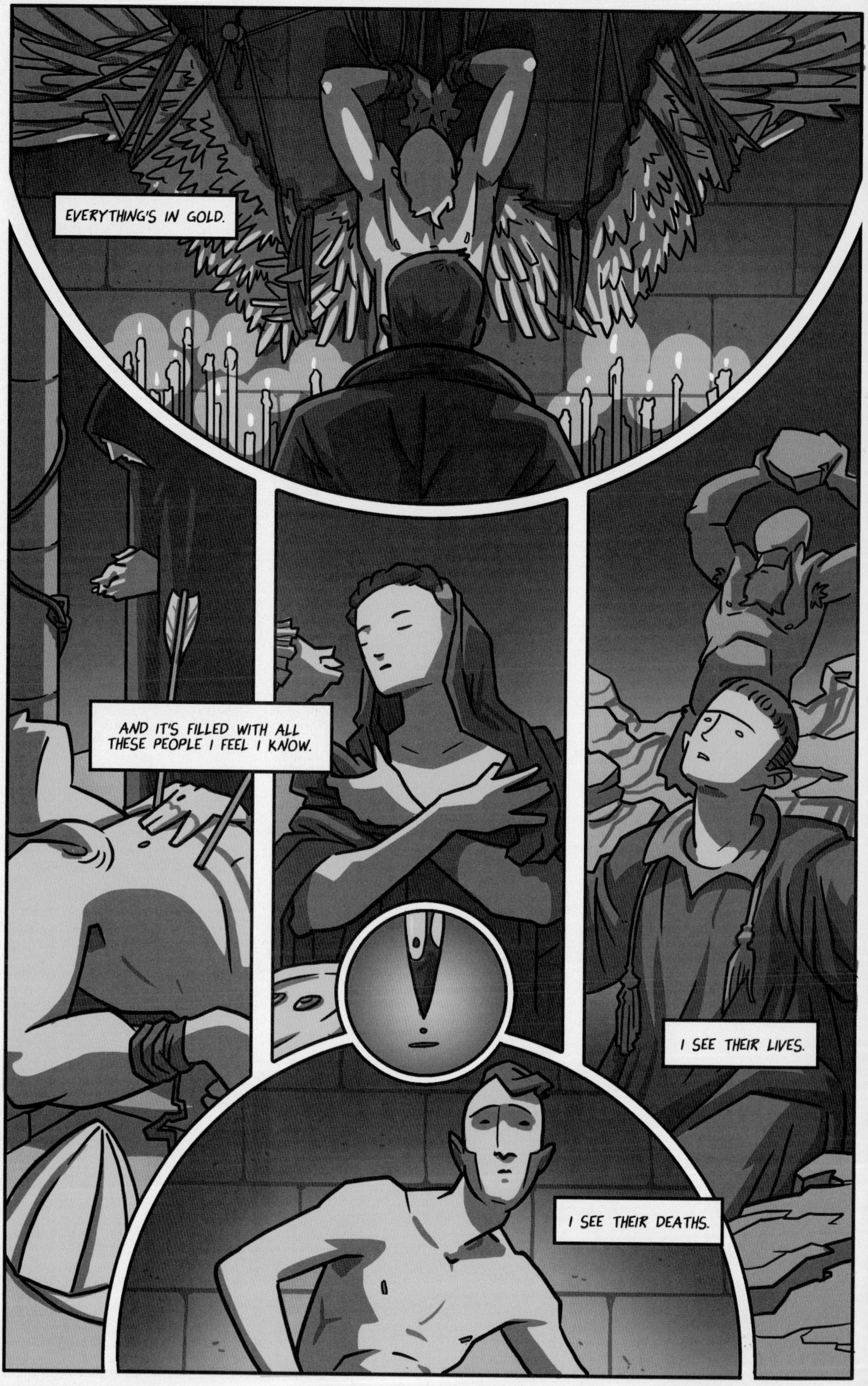
EVERYTHING'S IN GOLD.
AND IT'S FILLED WITH ALL THESE PEOPLE I FEEL I KNOW.
I SEE THEIR LIVES.
I SEE THEIR DEATHS.

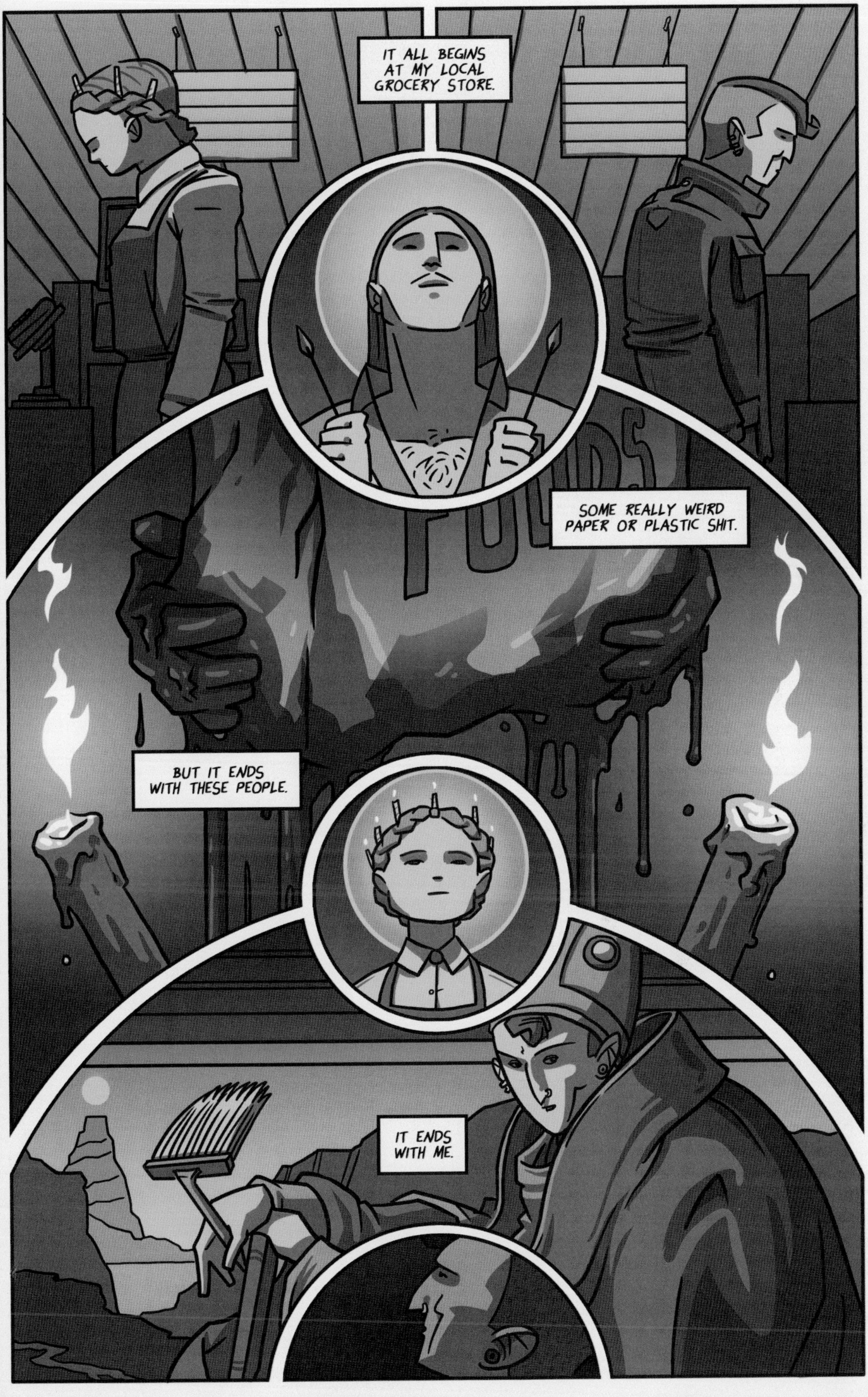
IT ALL BEGINS AT MY LOCAL GROCERY STORE.
SOME REALLY WEIRD PAPER OR PLASTIC SHIT.
BUT IT ENDS WITH THESE PEOPLE.
IT ENDS WITH ME.

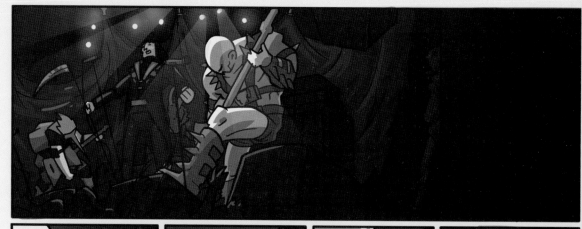

SO...

SO?

SO.

THOSE HANDS THE ONLY PART OF YOU THAT'S EVIL?

I'VE ALWAYS LOVED INDIANA.

BUT IT SEEMS I'M NOT THE ONLY ONE ENJOYING THE SHOW.

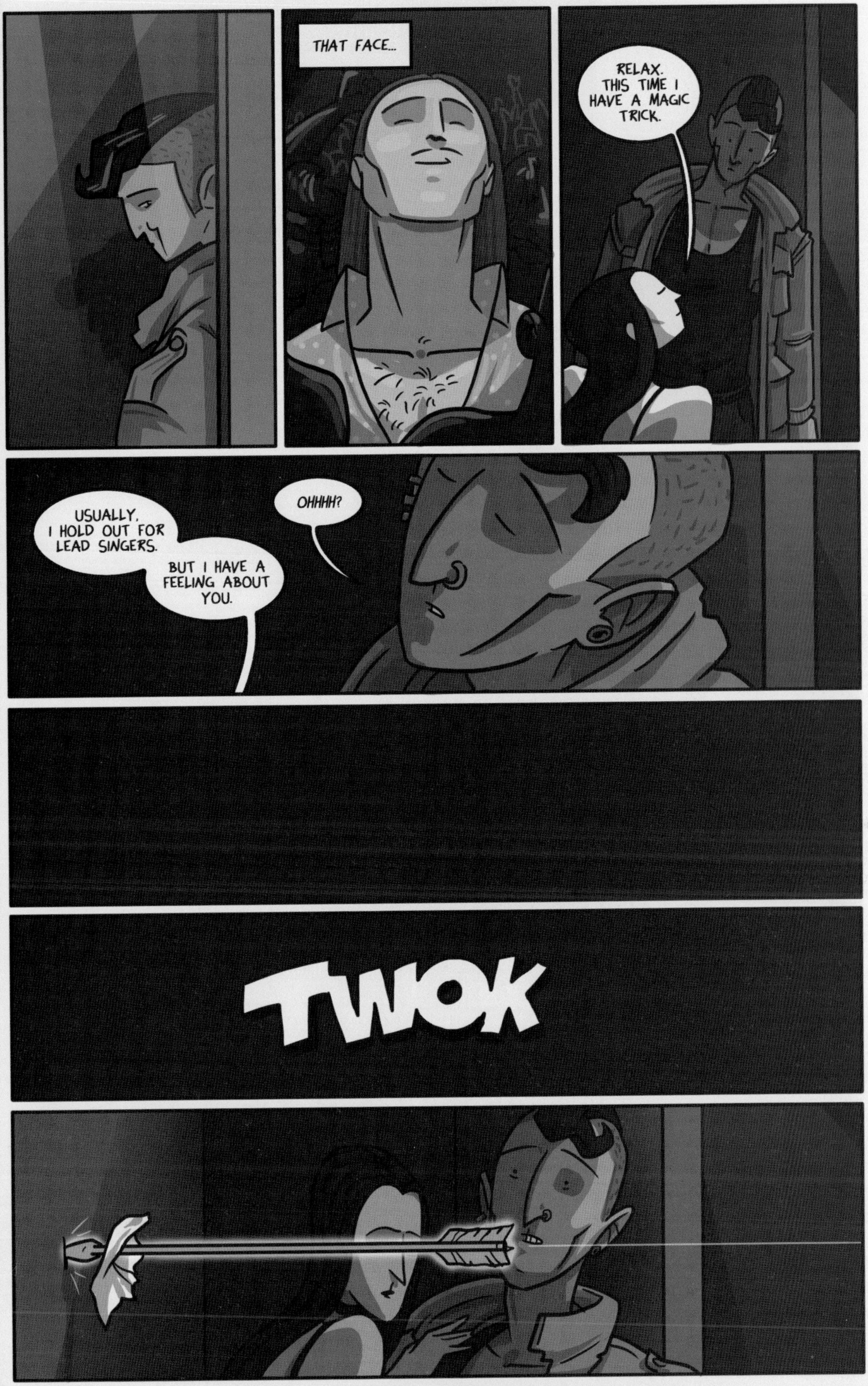
THAT FACE...
RELAX. THIS TIME I HAVE A MAGIC TRICK.
USUALLY, I HOLD OUT FOR LEAD SINGERS.
BUT I HAVE A FEELING ABOUT YOU.
OHHHH?
TWOK

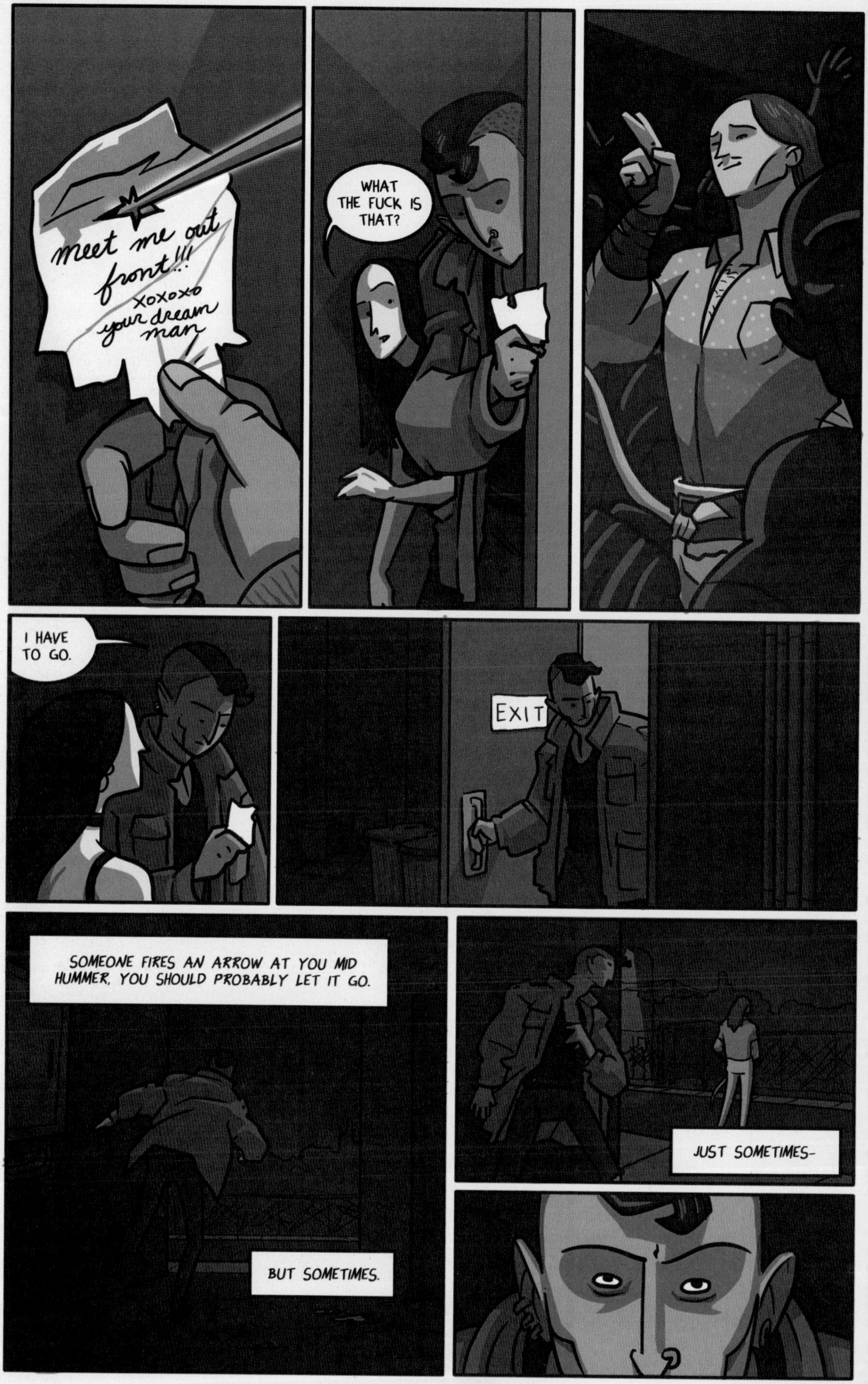
meet me out front!!!
xoxoxo your dream man
WHAT THE FUCK IS THAT?
I HAVE TO GO.
EXIT
SOMEONE FIRES AN ARROW AT YOU MID HUMMER, YOU SHOULD PROBABLY LET IT GO.
BUT SOMETIMES.
JUST SOMETIMES-

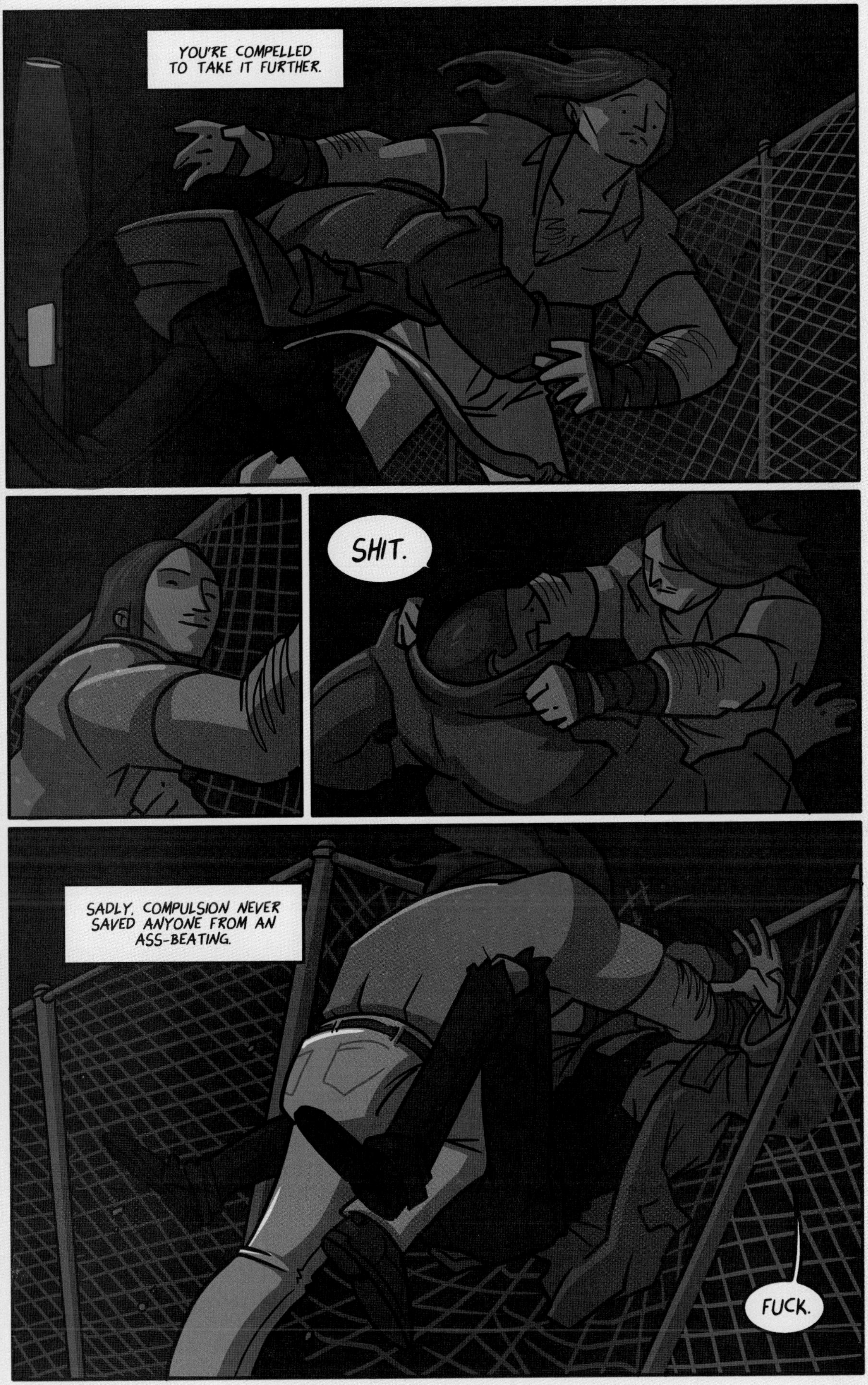
YOU'RE COMPELLED TO TAKE IT FURTHER.
SHIT.
SADLY, COMPULSION NEVER SAVED ANYONE FROM AN ASS-BEATING.
FUCK.

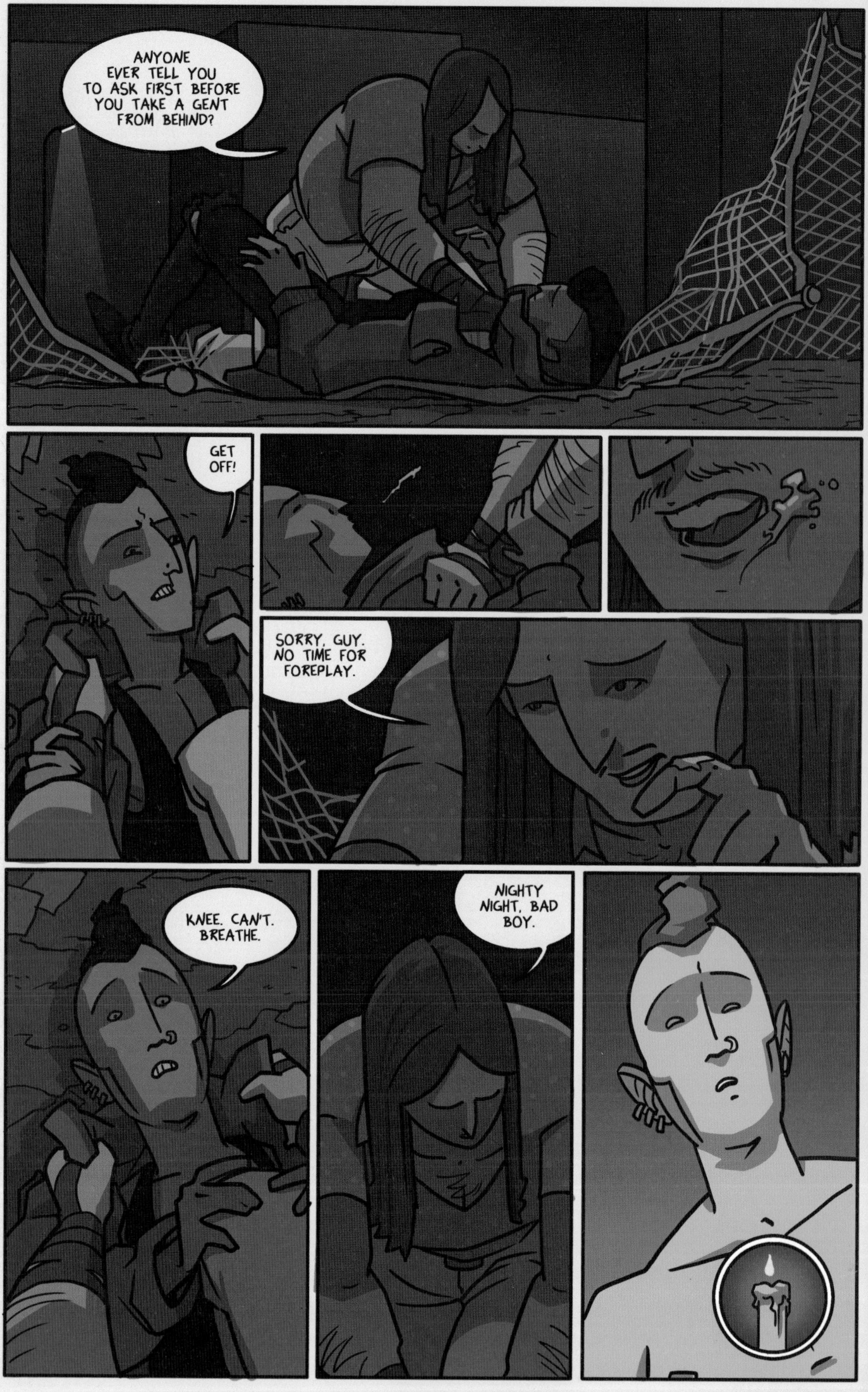
ANYONE EVER TELL YOU TO ASK FIRST BEFORE YOU TAKE A GENT FROM BEHIND?
GET OFF!
SORRY, GUY. NO TIME FOR FOREPLAY.
KNEE. CAN'T. BREATHE.
NIGHTY NIGHT, BAD BOY.

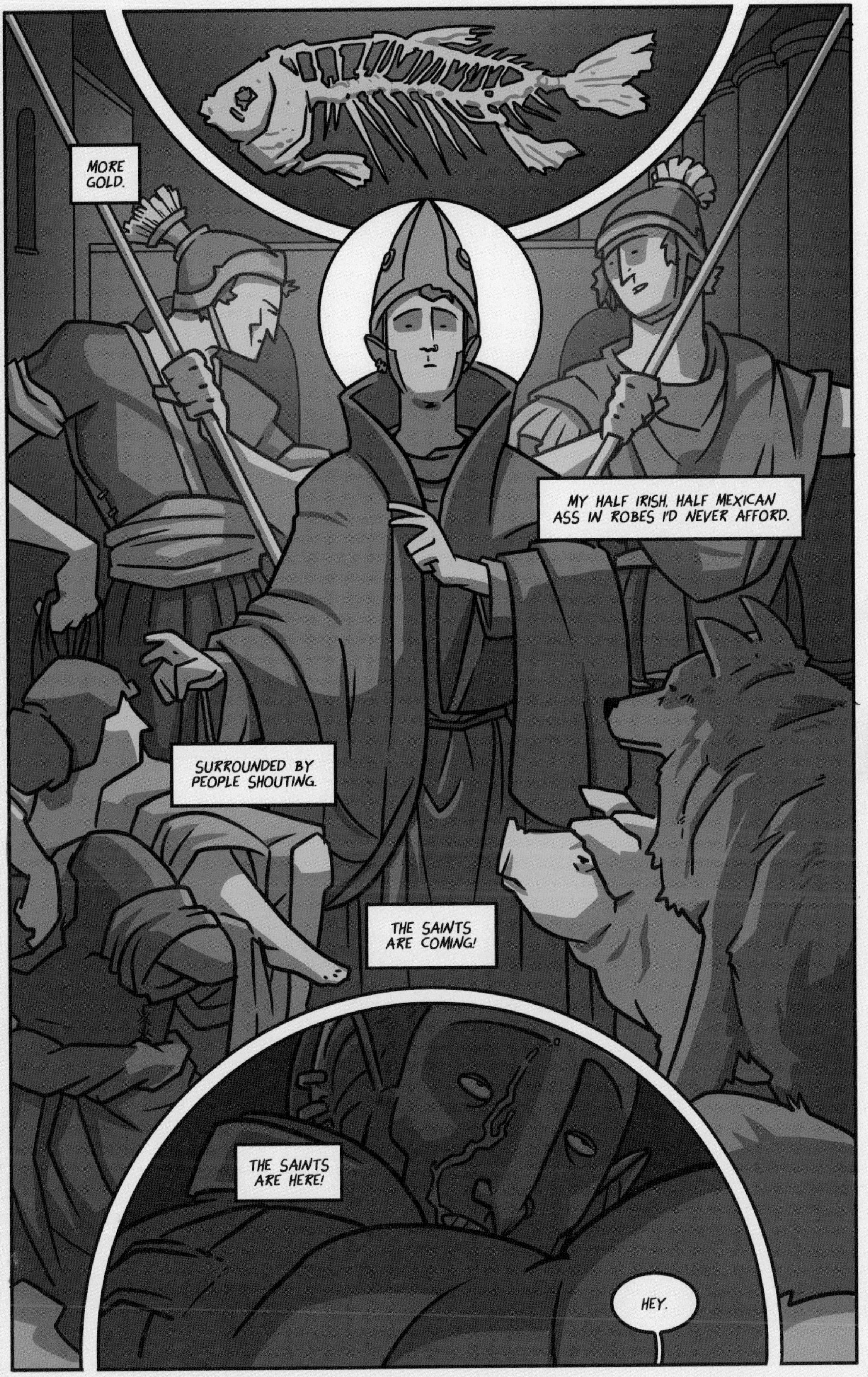
MORE GOLD.
MY HALF IRISH, HALF MEXICAN ASS IN ROBES I'D NEVER AFFORD.
SURROUNDED BY PEOPLE SHOUTING.
THE SAINTS ARE COMING!
THE SAINTS ARE HERE!
HEY.

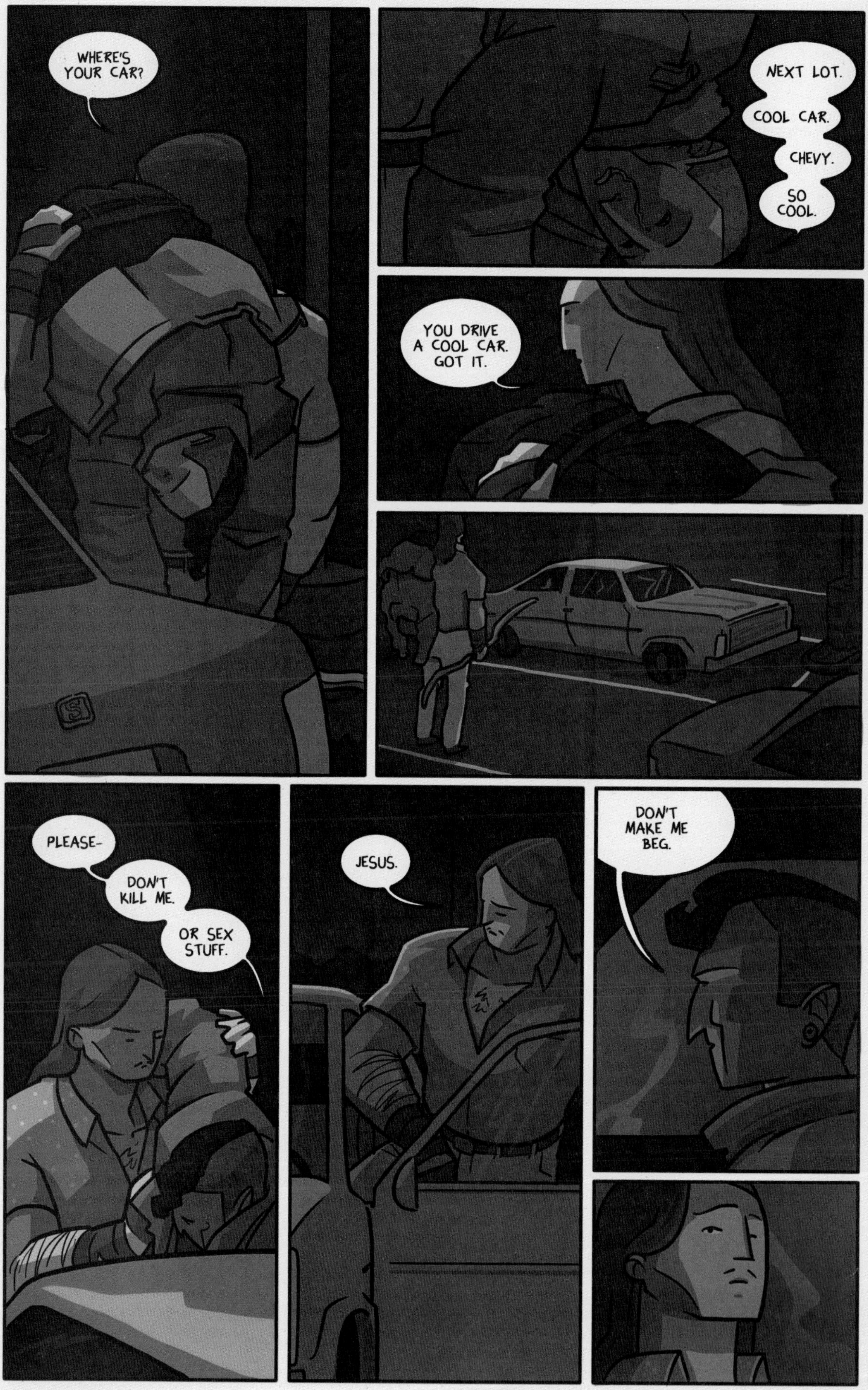
WHERE'S YOUR CAR?
NEXT LOT.
COOL CAR.
CHEVY.
SO COOL.
YOU DRIVE A COOL CAR. GOT IT.
PLEASE-
DON'T KILL ME.
OR SEX STUFF.
JESUS.
DON'T MAKE ME BEG.

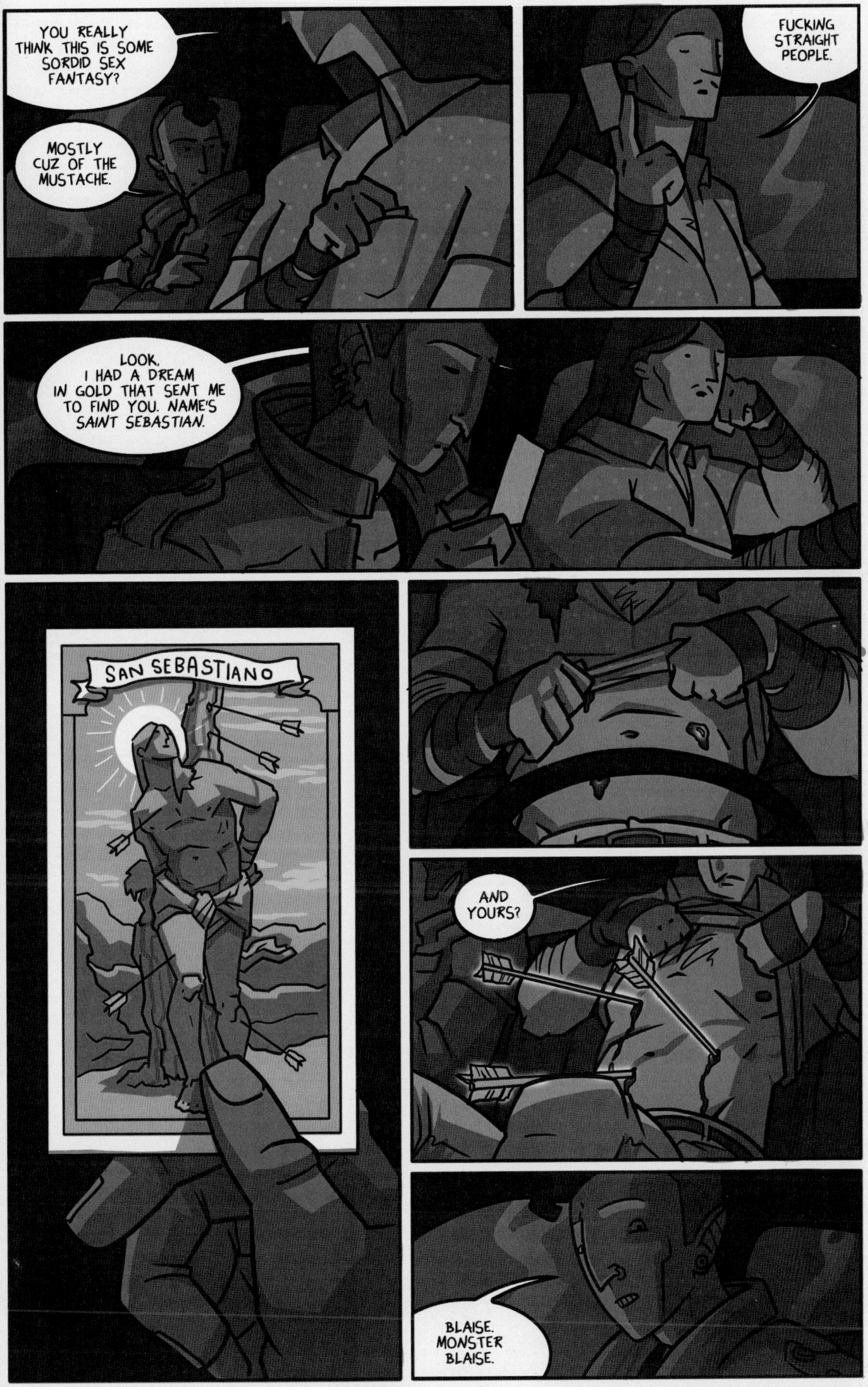
YOU REALLY THINK THIS IS SOME SORDID SEX FANTASY?
MOSTLY CUZ OF THE MUSTACHE.
FUCKING STRAIGHT PEOPLE.
LOOK, I HAD A DREAM IN GOLD THAT SENT ME TO FIND YOU. NAME'S SAINT SEBASTIAN.
SAN SEBASTIANO
AND YOURS?
BLAISE. MONSTER BLAISE.

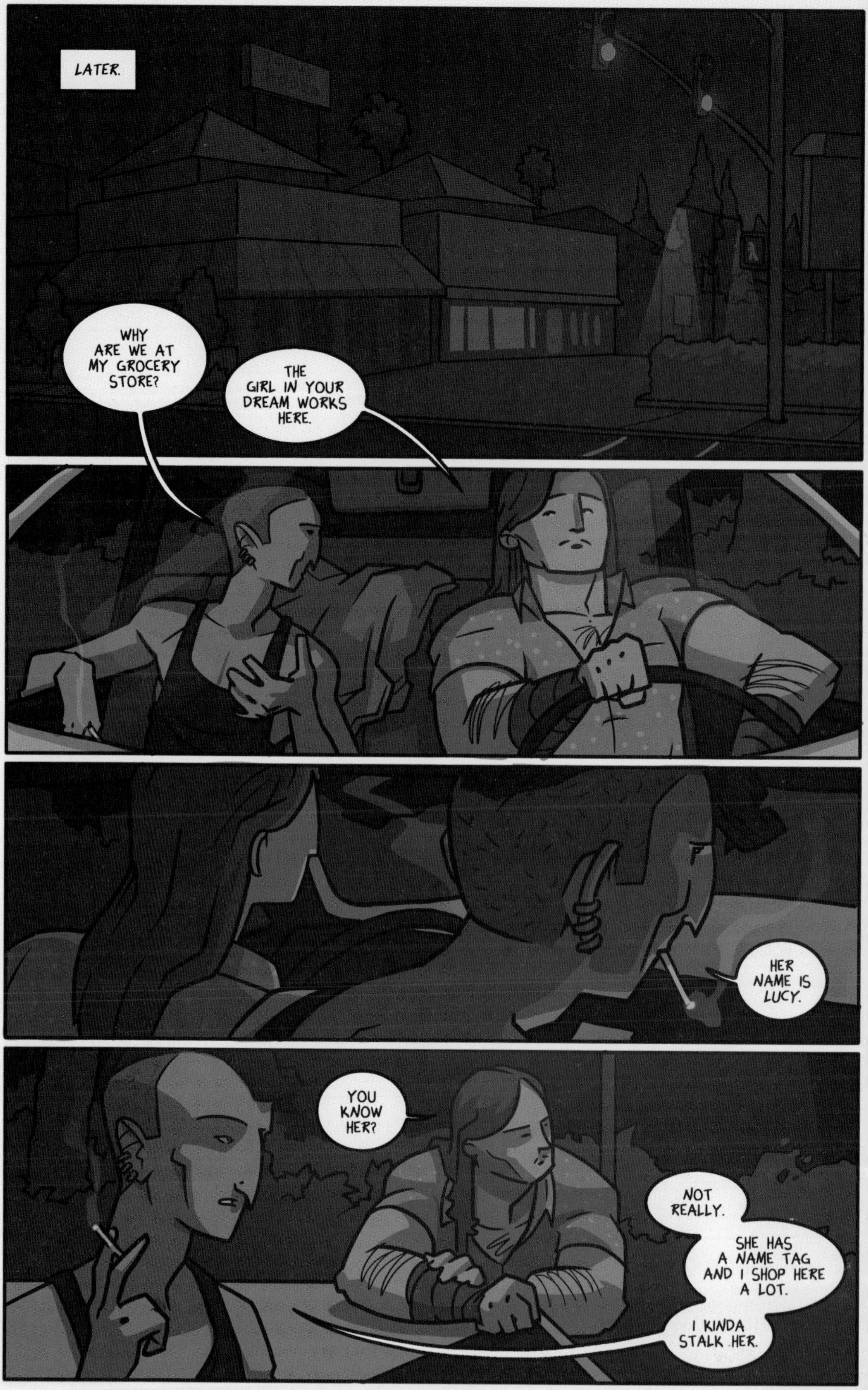
LATER.
WHY ARE WE AT MY GROCERY STORE?
THE GIRL IN YOUR DREAM WORKS HERE.
HER NAME IS LUCY.
YOU KNOW HER?
NOT REALLY.
SHE HAS A NAME TAG AND I SHOP HERE A LOT.
I KINDA STALK HER.

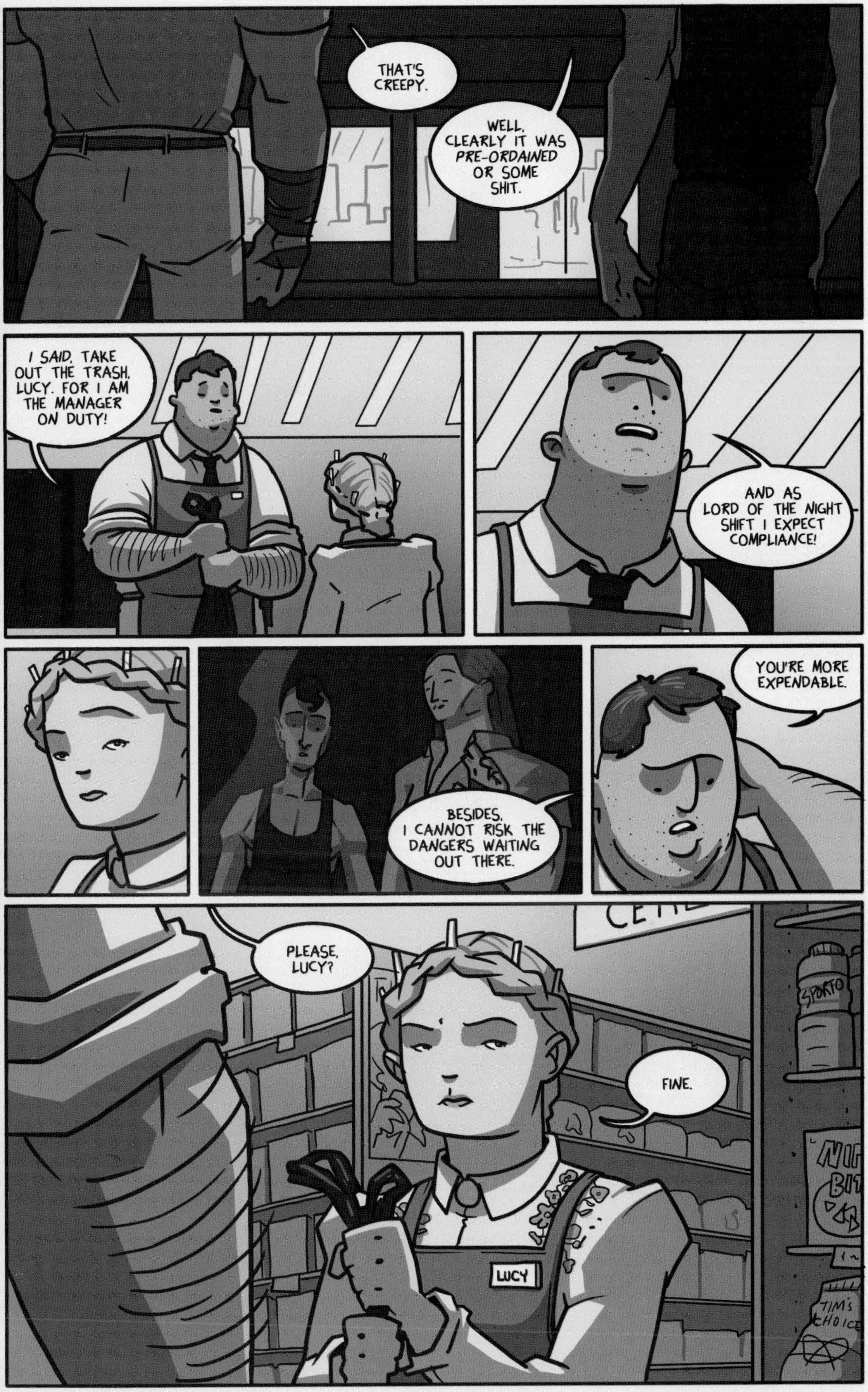
THAT'S CREEPY.
WELL, CLEARLY IT WAS PRE-ORDAINED OR SOME SHIT.
I SAID, TAKE OUT THE TRASH, LUCY. FOR I AM THE MANAGER ON DUTY!
AND AS LORD OF THE NIGHT SHIFT I EXPECT COMPLIANCE!
BESIDES, I CANNOT RISK THE DANGERS WAITING OUT THERE.
YOU'RE MORE EXPENDABLE.
PLEASE, LUCY?
FINE.
LUCY
SPORTO
TIM'S CHOICE

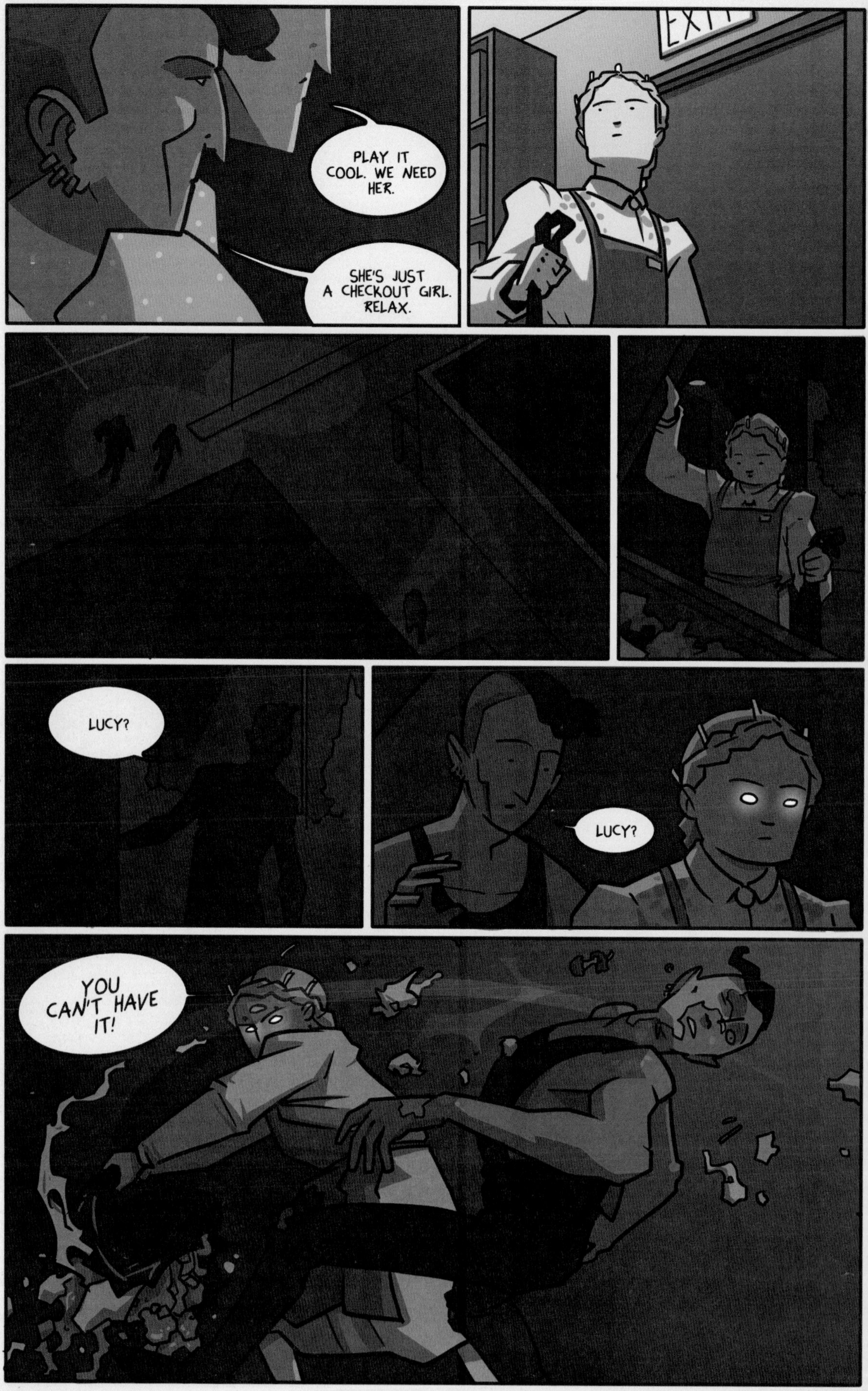
PLAY IT COOL. WE NEED HER.
SHE'S JUST A CHECKOUT GIRL. RELAX.
EXIT
LUCY?
LUCY?
YOU CAN'T HAVE IT!

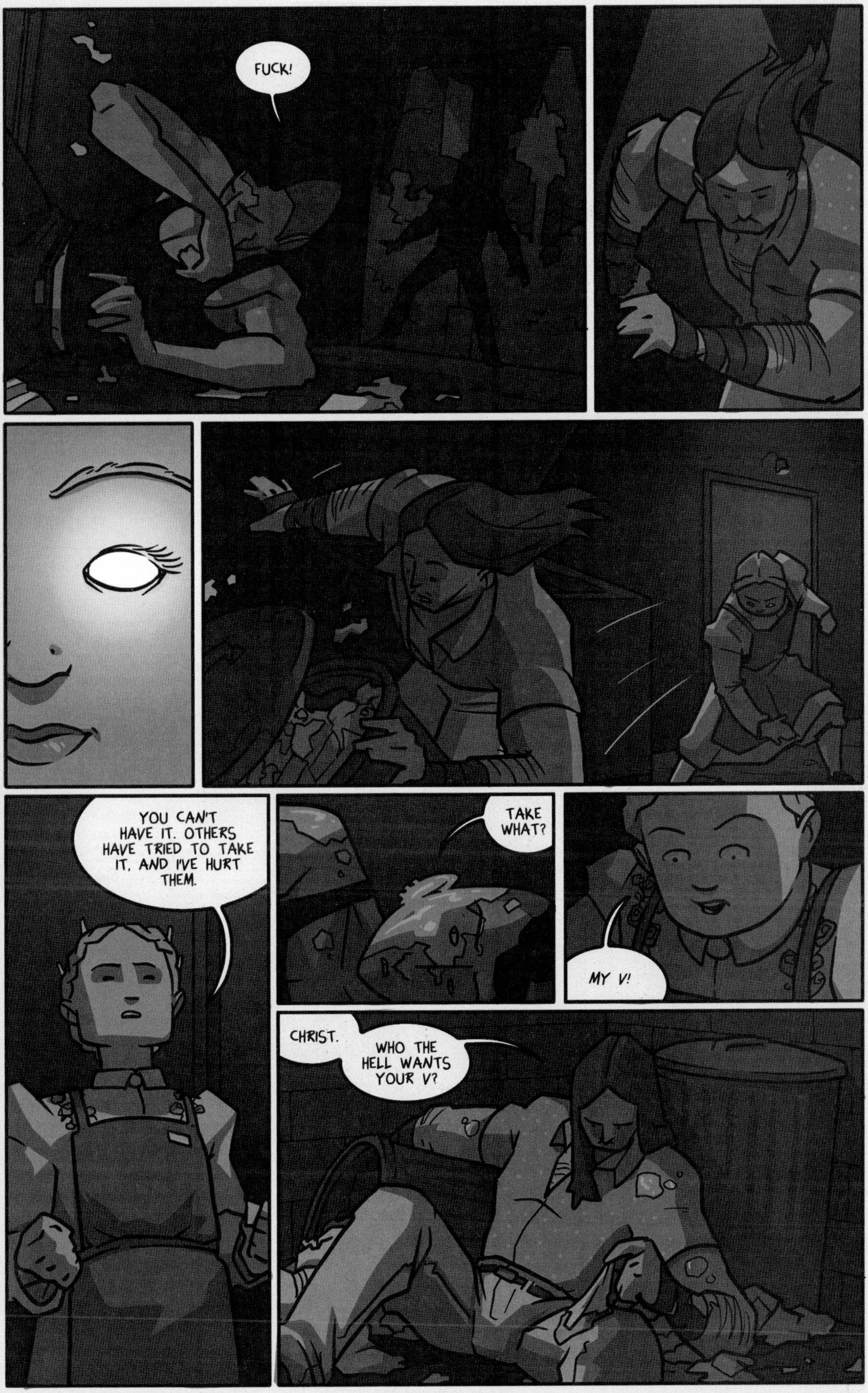
FUCK!
YOU CAN'T HAVE IT. OTHERS HAVE TRIED TO TAKE IT, AND I'VE HURT THEM.
TAKE WHAT?
MY V!
CHRIST.
WHO THE HELL WANTS YOUR V?

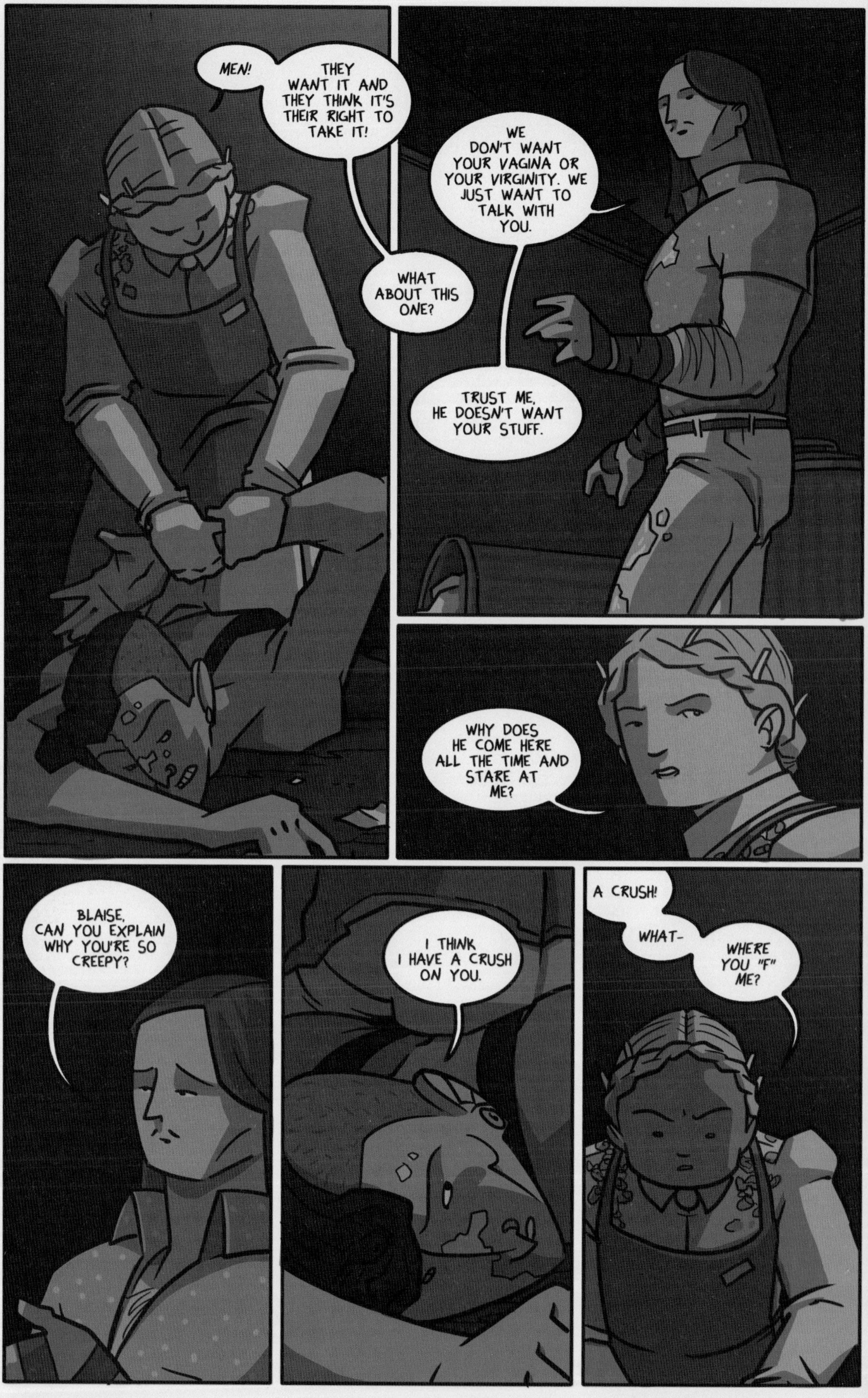
MEN!
THEY WANT IT AND THEY THINK IT'S THEIR RIGHT TO TAKE IT!
WHAT ABOUT THIS ONE?
WE DON'T WANT YOUR VAGINA OR YOUR VIRGINITY. WE JUST WANT TO TALK WITH YOU.
TRUST ME, HE DOESN'T WANT YOUR STUFF.
WHY DOES HE COME HERE ALL THE TIME AND STARE AT ME?
BLAISE, CAN YOU EXPLAIN WHY YOU'RE SO CREEPY?
I THINK I HAVE A CRUSH ON YOU.
A CRUSH!
WHAT-
WHERE YOU "F" ME?

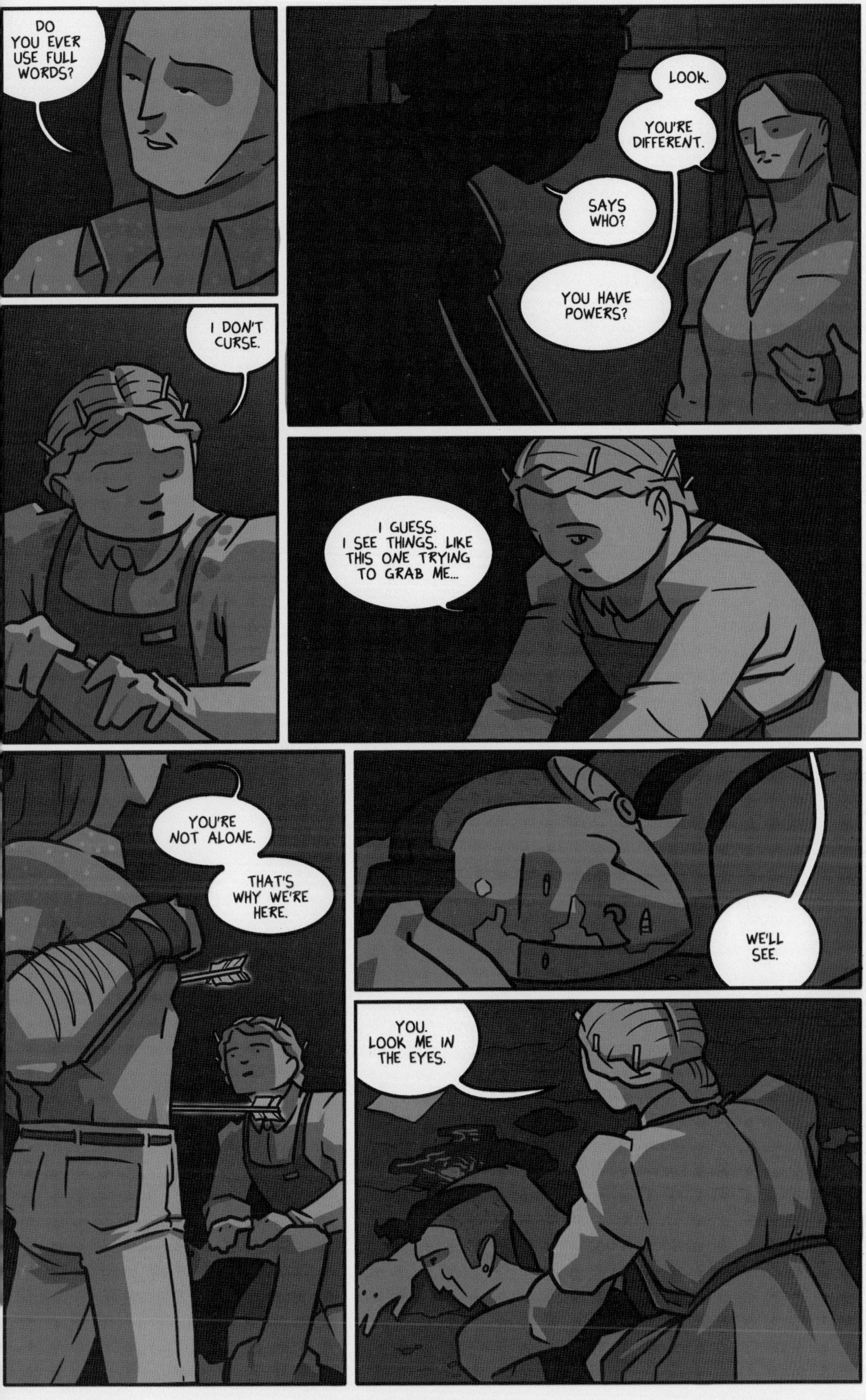
DO YOU EVER USE FULL WORDS?
LOOK.
YOU'RE DIFFERENT.
SAYS WHO?
YOU HAVE POWERS?
I DON'T CURSE.
I GUESS. I SEE THINGS. LIKE THIS ONE TRYING TO GRAB ME...
YOU'RE NOT ALONE.
THAT'S WHY WE'RE HERE.
WE'LL SEE.
YOU. LOOK ME IN THE EYES.

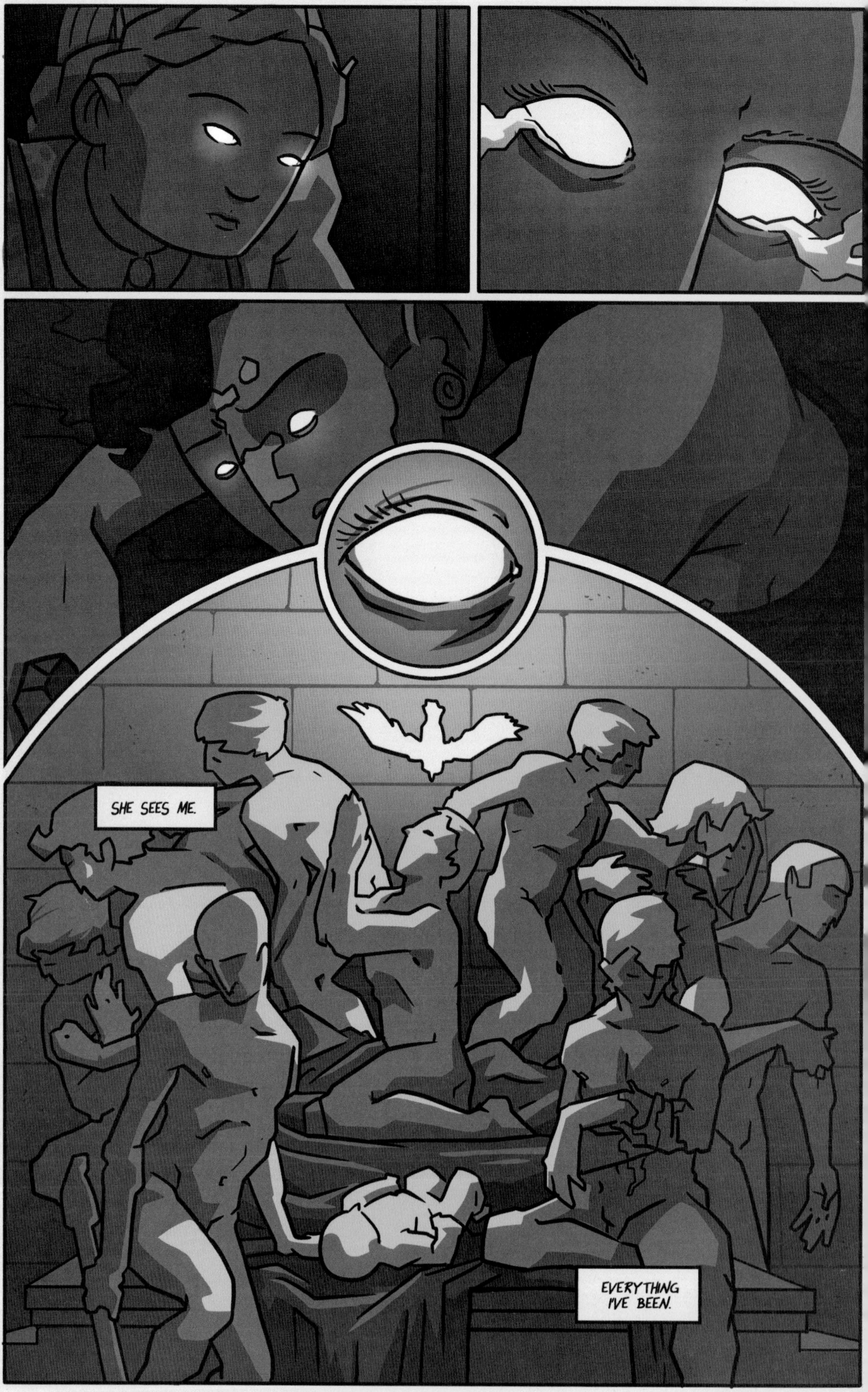
SHE SEES ME.
EVERYTHING I'VE BEEN.

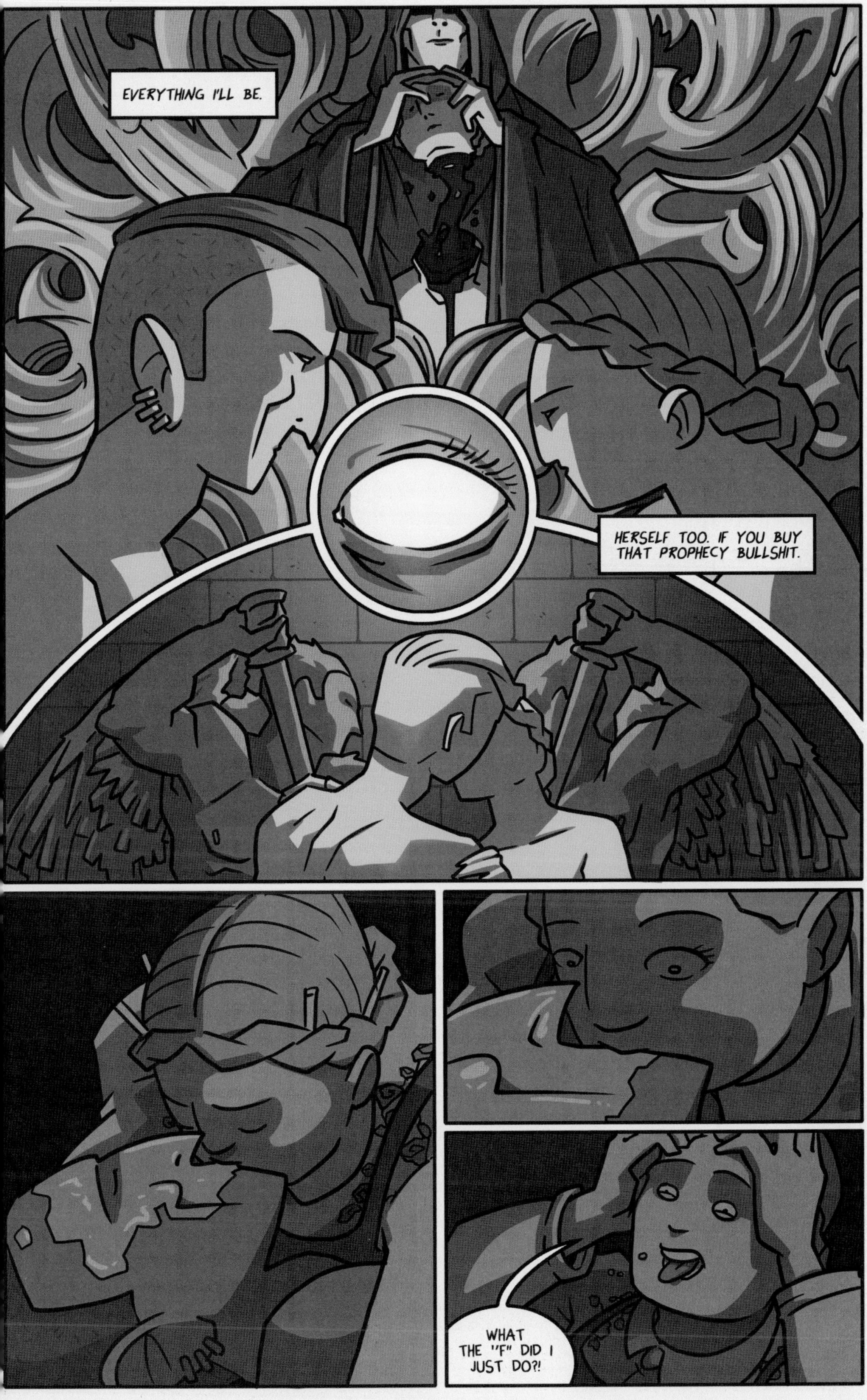
EVERYTHING I'LL BE.
HERSELF TOO. IF YOU BUY THAT PROPHECY BULLSHIT.
WHAT THE "F" DID I JUST DO?!

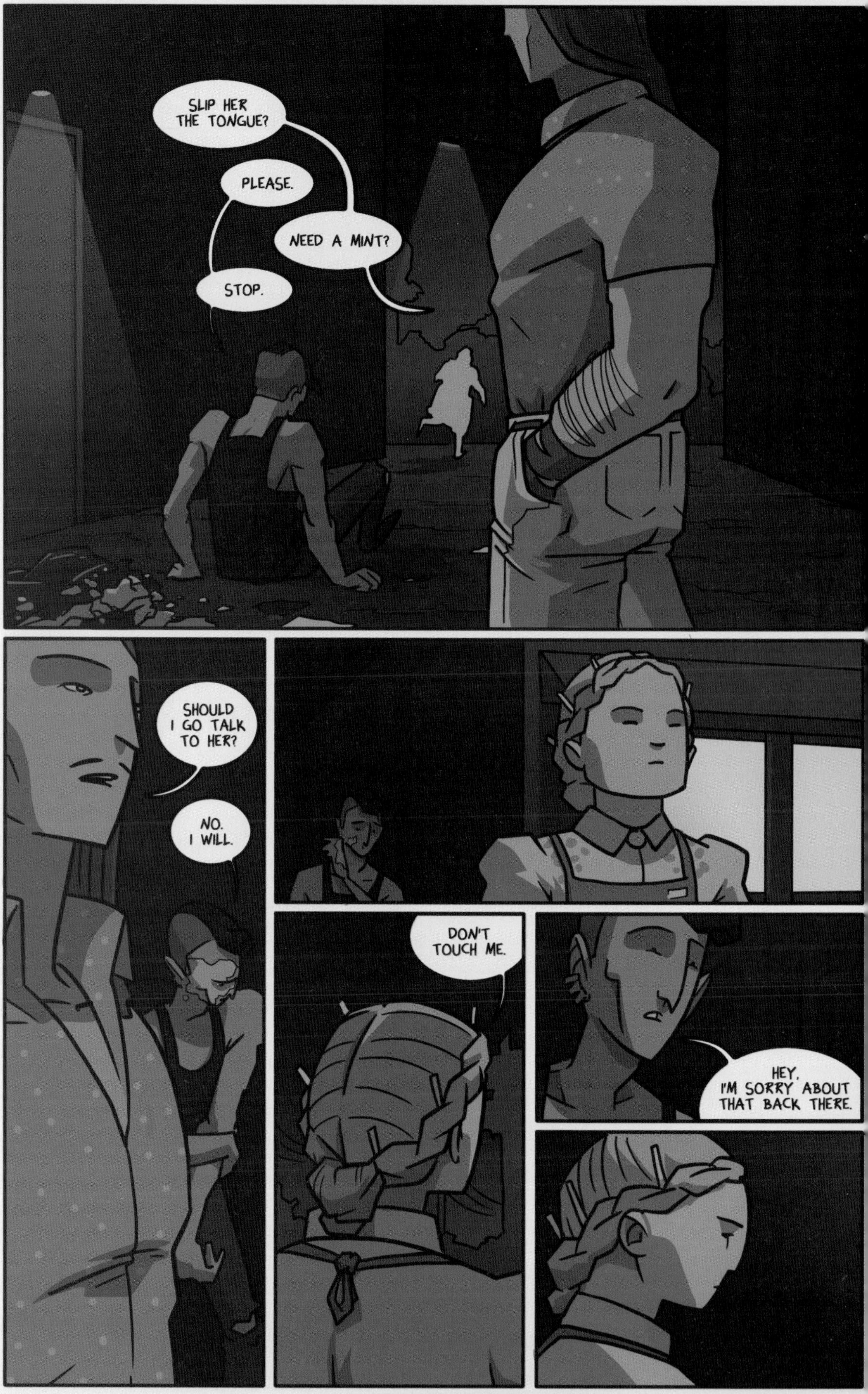
SLIP HER THE TONGUE?
PLEASE.
NEED A MINT?
STOP.
SHOULD I GO TALK TO HER?
NO. I WILL.
DON'T TOUCH ME.
HEY, I'M SORRY ABOUT THAT BACK THERE.

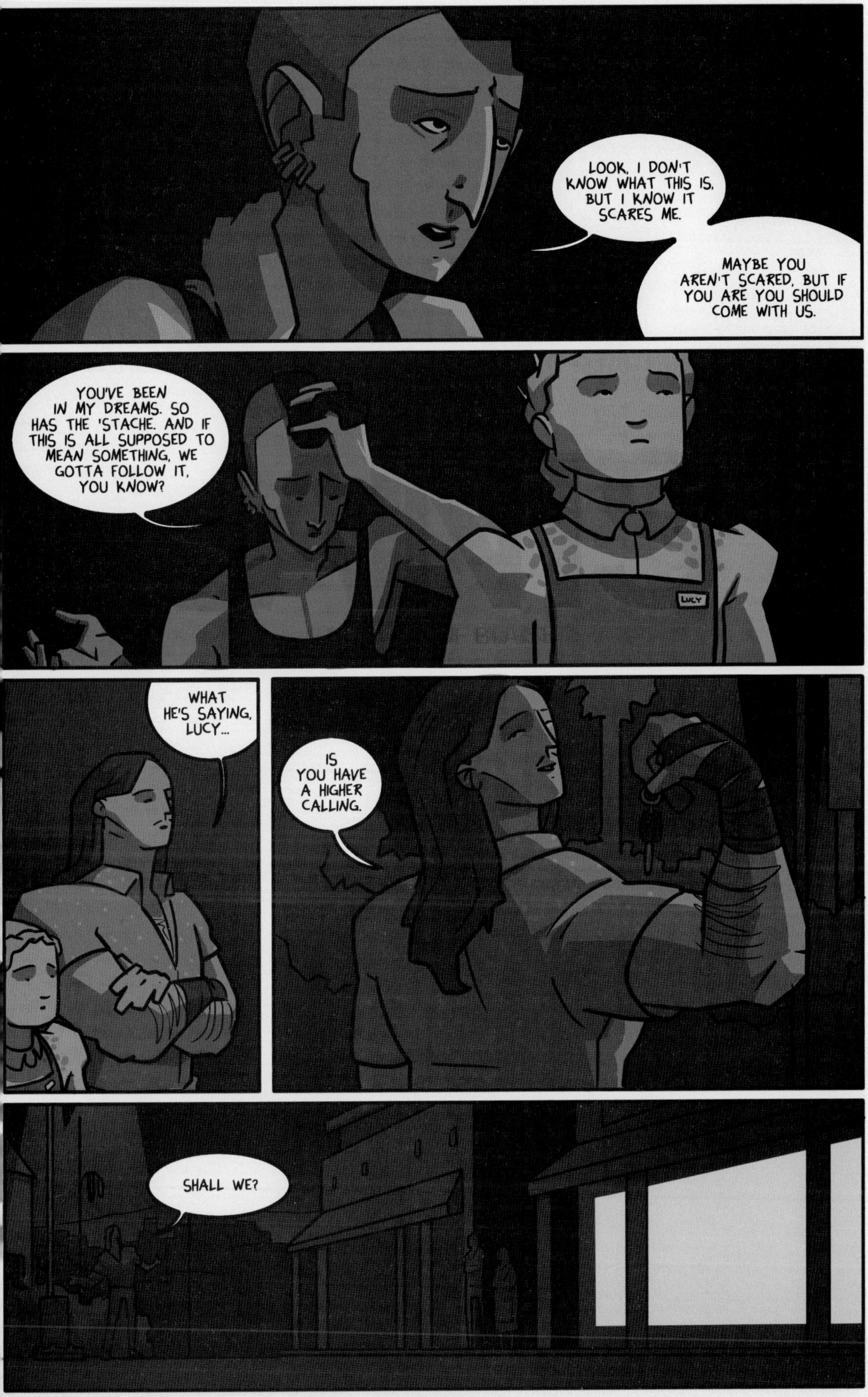
LOOK, I DON'T KNOW WHAT THIS IS, BUT I KNOW IT SCARES ME.
MAYBE YOU AREN'T SCARED, BUT IF YOU ARE YOU SHOULD COME WITH US.
YOU'VE BEEN IN MY DREAMS. SO HAS THE 'STACHE. AND IF THIS IS ALL SUPPOSED TO MEAN SOMETHING, WE GOTTA FOLLOW IT, YOU KNOW?
LUCY
WHAT HE'S SAYING, LUCY...
IS YOU HAVE A HIGHER CALLING.
SHALL WE?

I DON'T KNOW WHAT THIS IS.

BUT I MEANT WHAT I SAID—

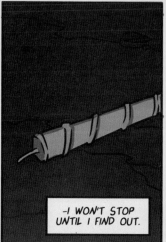

—I WON'T STOP UNTIL I FIND OUT.

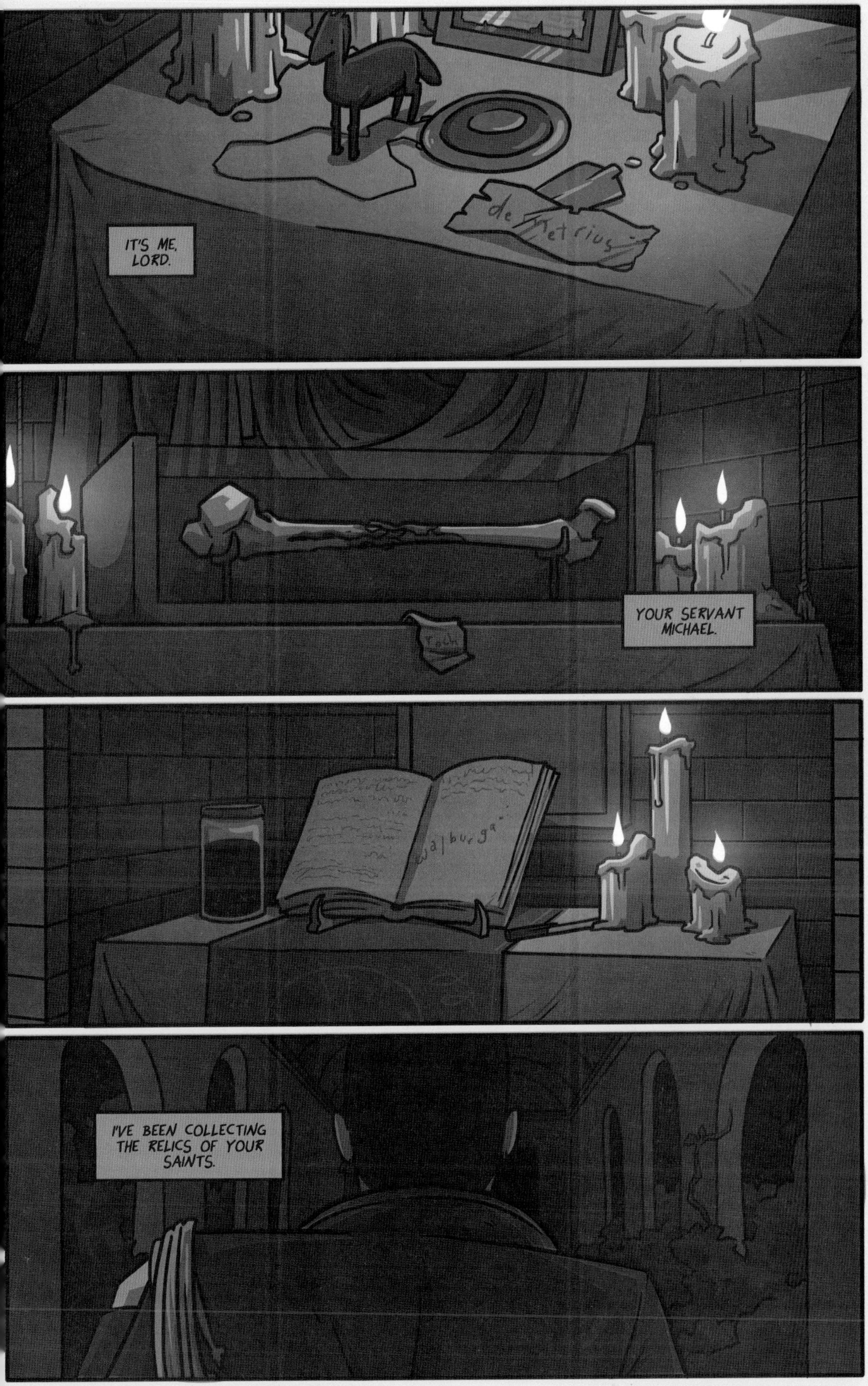
IT'S ME, LORD.
demetrius
YOUR SERVANT MICHAEL.
walburga
I'VE BEEN COLLECTING THE RELICS OF YOUR SAINTS.

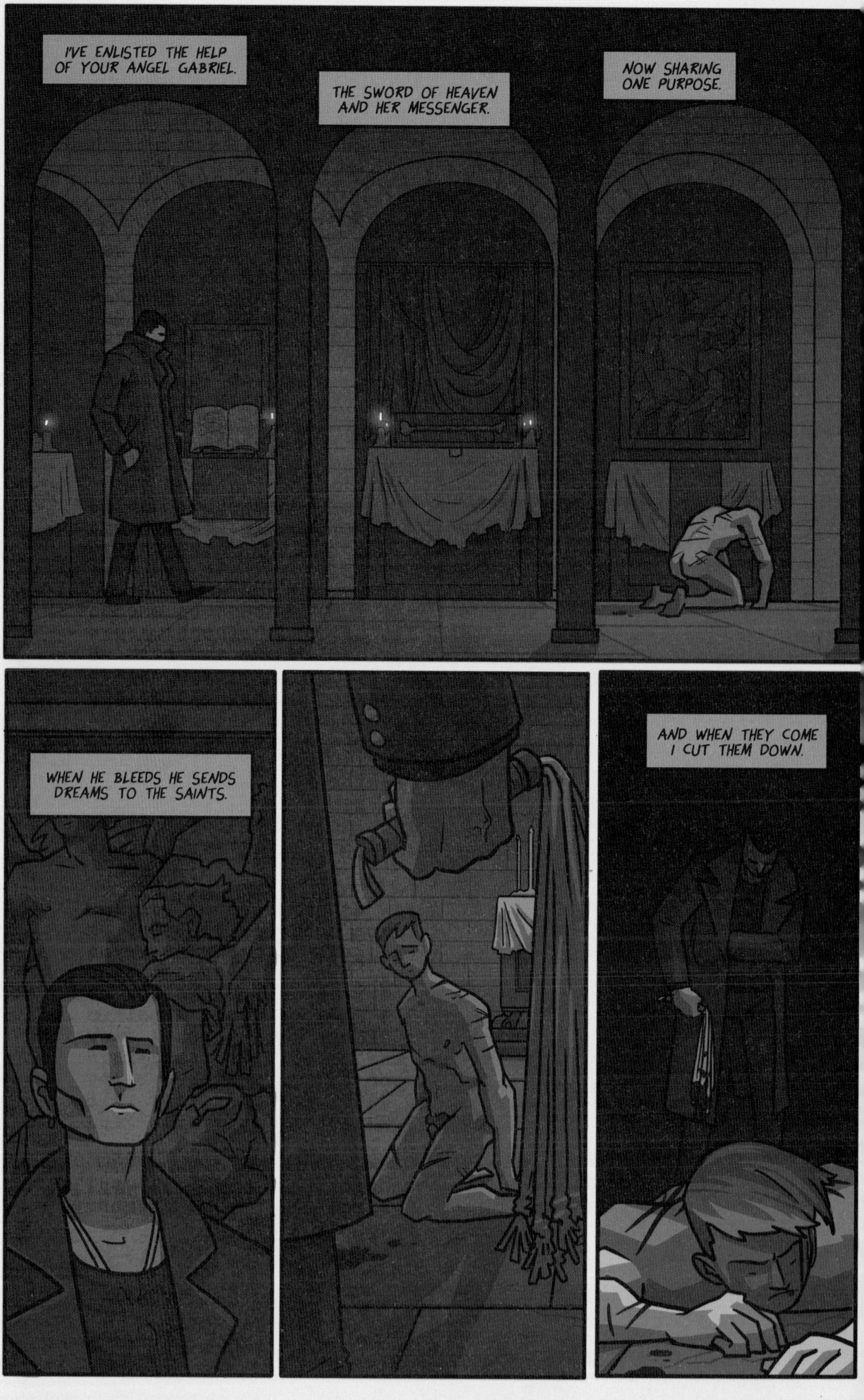
I'VE ENLISTED THE HELP OF YOUR ANGEL GABRIEL.
THE SWORD OF HEAVEN AND HER MESSENGER.
NOW SHARING ONE PURPOSE.
WHEN HE BLEEDS HE SENDS DREAMS TO THE SAINTS.
AND WHEN THEY COME I CUT THEM DOWN.

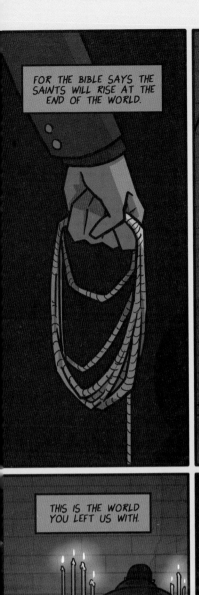

FOR THE BIBLE SAYS THE SAINTS WILL RISE AT THE END OF THE WORLD.

BUT I WON'T GIVE THEM THE CHANCE.

THIS IS THE WORLD YOU LEFT US WITH.

THE WORLD YOU ABANDONED.

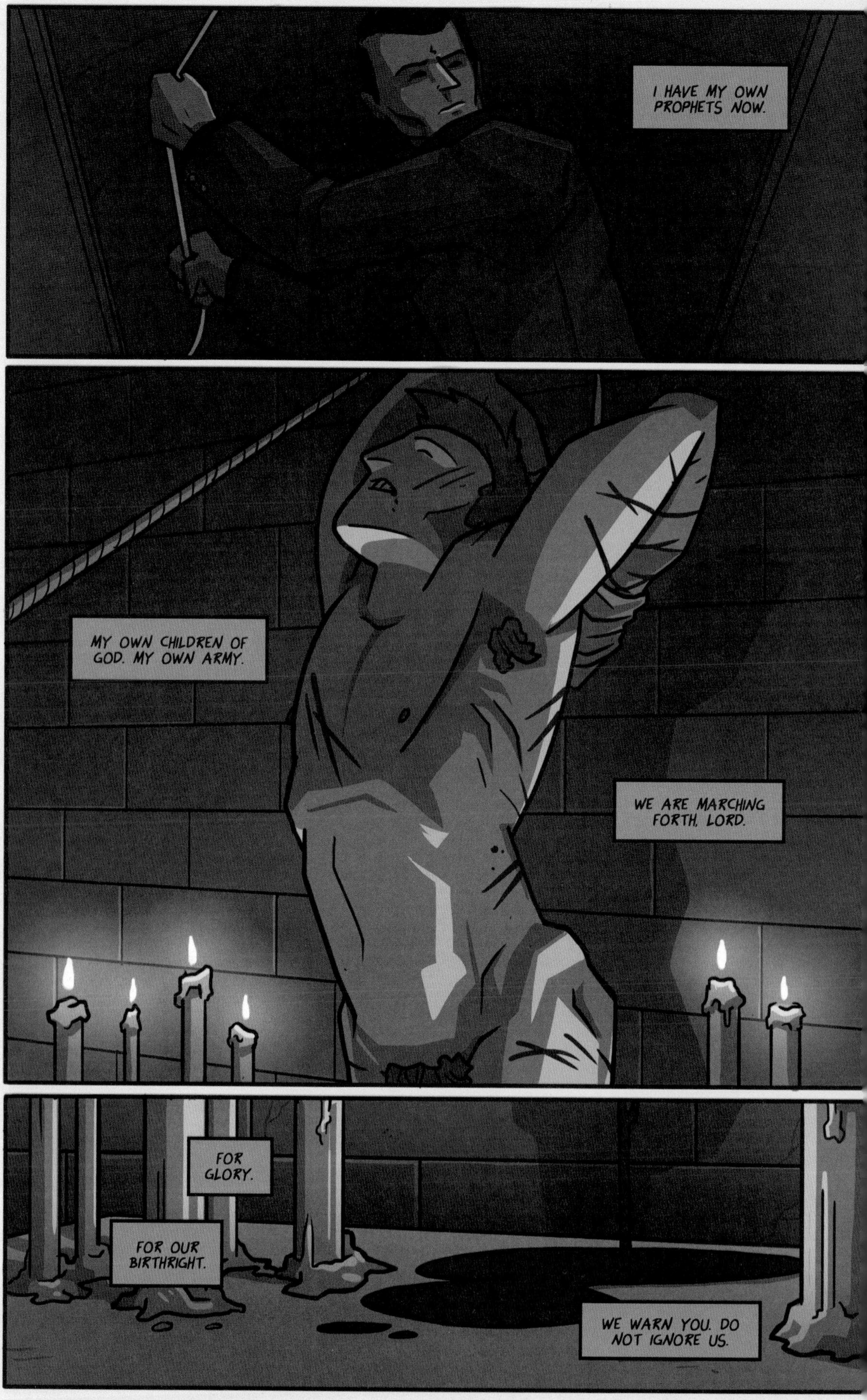
I HAVE MY OWN PROPHETS NOW.
MY OWN CHILDREN OF GOD. MY OWN ARMY.
WE ARE MARCHING FORTH, LORD.
FOR GLORY.
FOR OUR BIRTHRIGHT.
WE WARN YOU. DO NOT IGNORE US.

II

COMMUNION

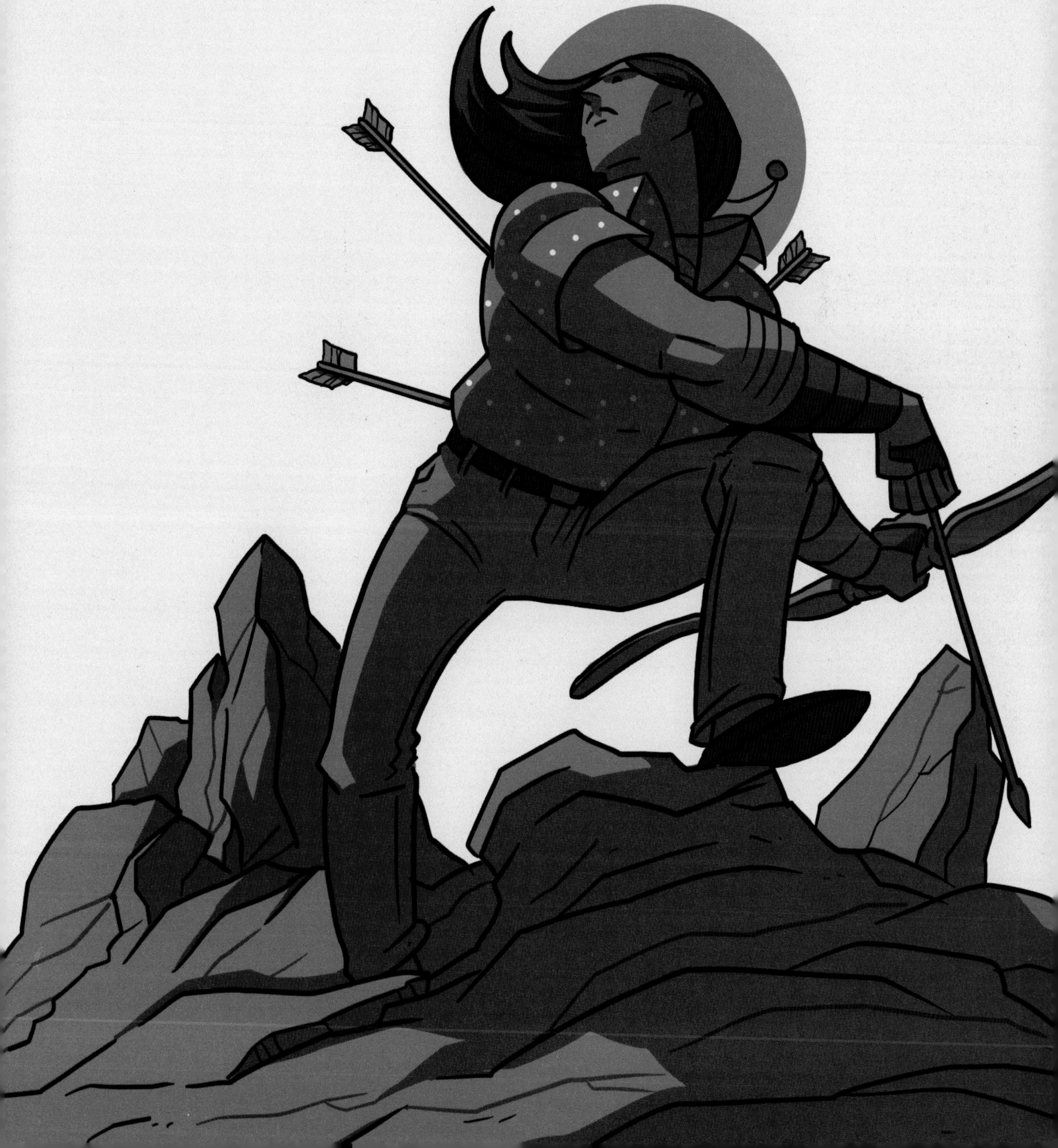

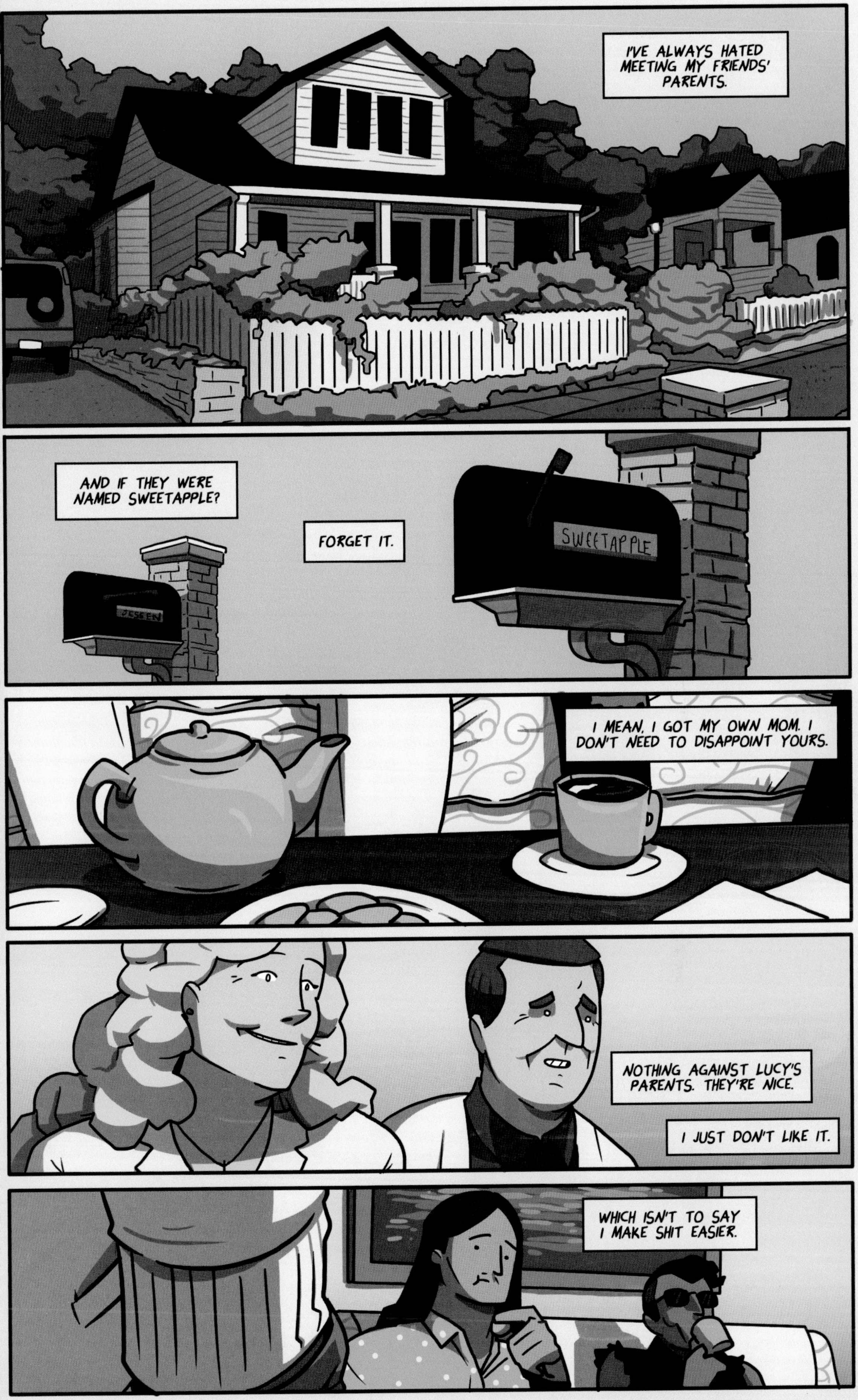
I'VE ALWAYS HATED MEETING MY FRIENDS' PARENTS.
AND IF THEY WERE NAMED SWEETAPPLE?
FORGET IT.
SWEETAPPLE
I MEAN, I GOT MY OWN MOM. I DON'T NEED TO DISAPPOINT YOURS.
NOTHING AGAINST LUCY'S PARENTS. THEY'RE NICE.
I JUST DON'T LIKE IT.
WHICH ISN'T TO SAY I MAKE SHIT EASIER.

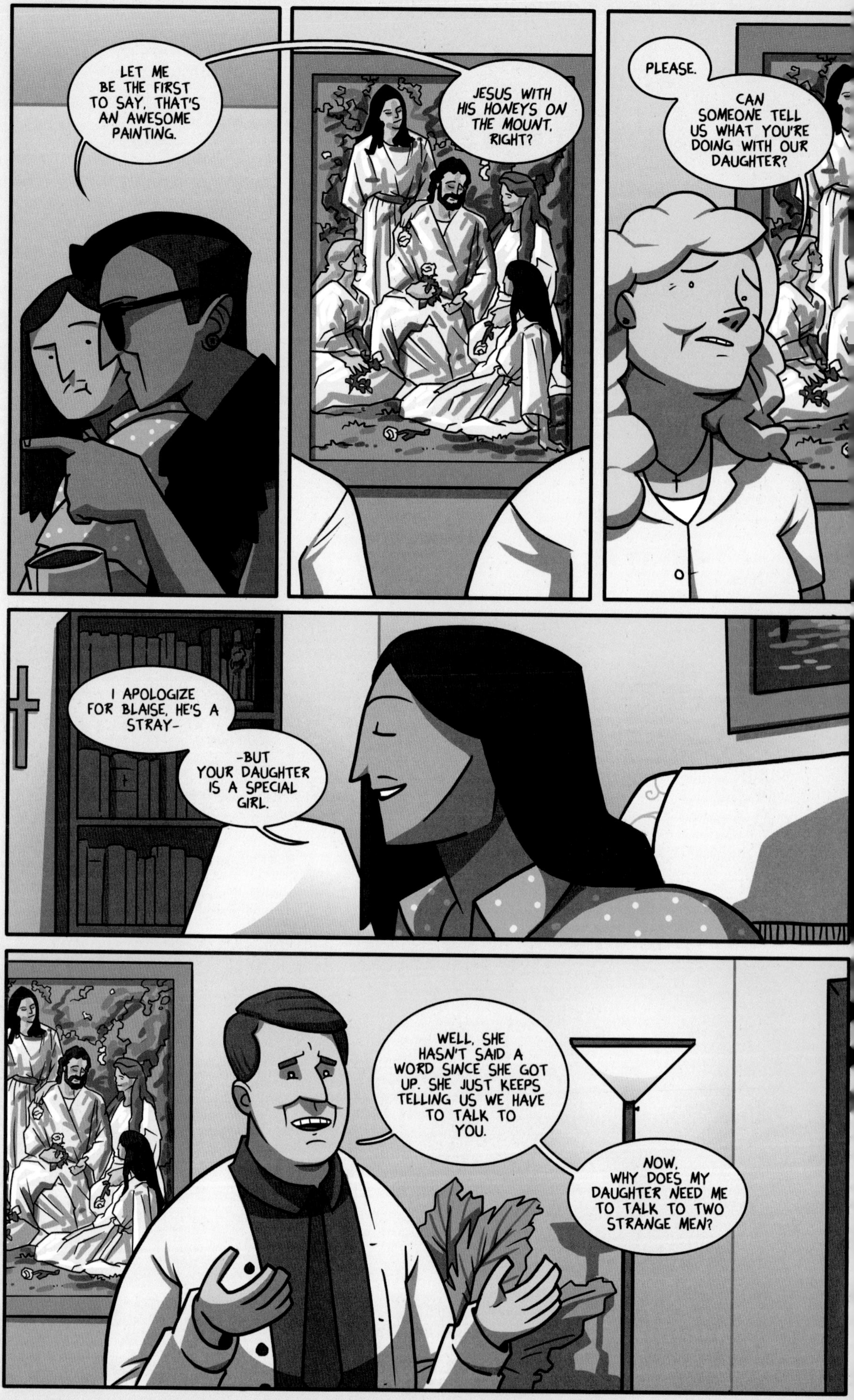
LET ME BE THE FIRST TO SAY, THAT'S AN AWESOME PAINTING.
JESUS WITH HIS HONEYS ON THE MOUNT, RIGHT?
PLEASE.
CAN SOMEONE TELL US WHAT YOU'RE DOING WITH OUR DAUGHTER?
I APOLOGIZE FOR BLAISE, HE'S A STRAY-
-BUT YOUR DAUGHTER IS A SPECIAL GIRL.
WELL, SHE HASN'T SAID A WORD SINCE SHE GOT UP. SHE JUST KEEPS TELLING US WE HAVE TO TALK TO YOU.
NOW, WHY DOES MY DAUGHTER NEED ME TO TALK TO TWO STRANGE MEN?

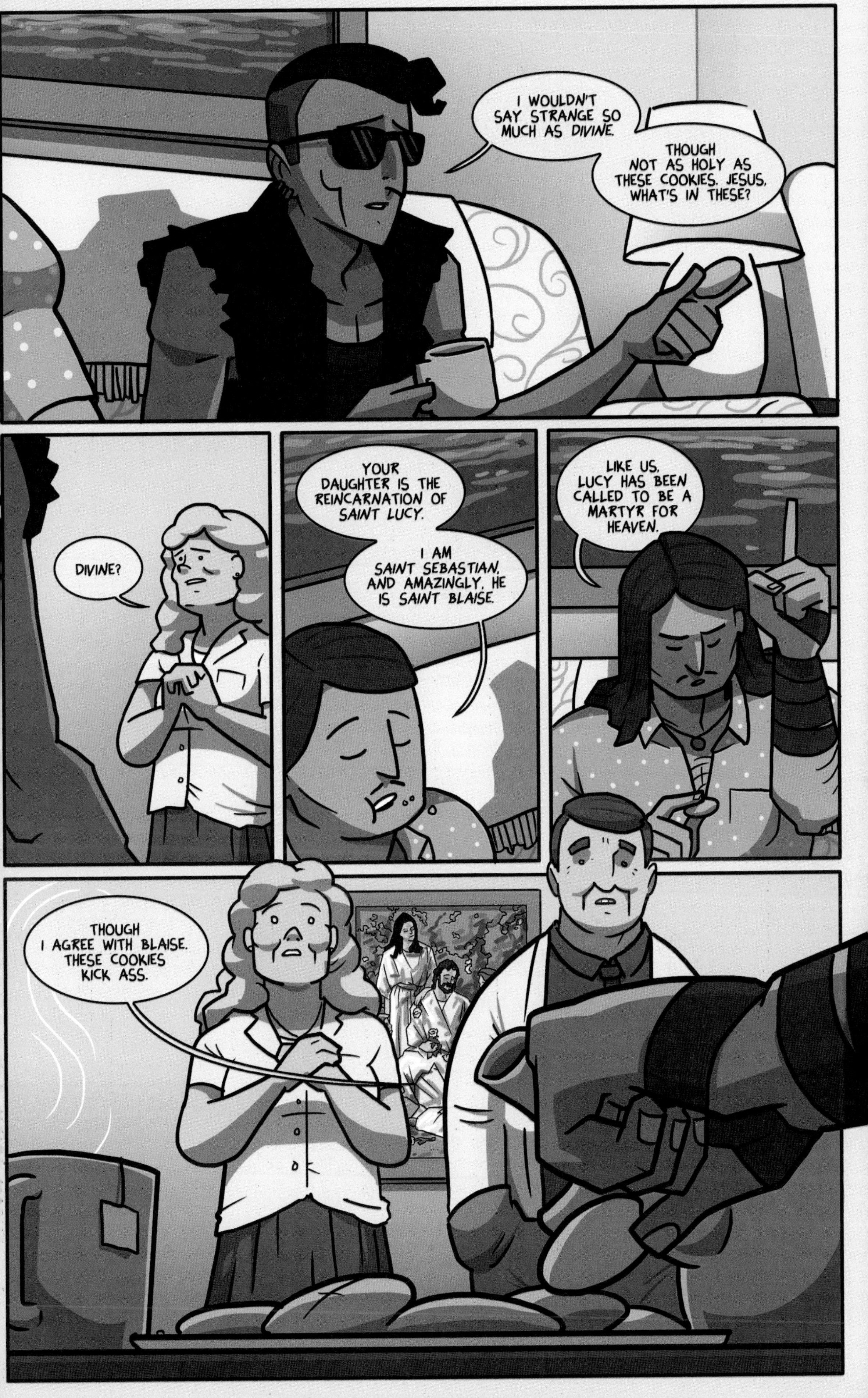
I WOULDN'T SAY STRANGE SO MUCH AS DIVINE.
THOUGH NOT AS HOLY AS THESE COOKIES. JESUS, WHAT'S IN THESE?
DIVINE?
YOUR DAUGHTER IS THE REINCARNATION OF SAINT LUCY.
I AM SAINT SEBASTIAN, AND AMAZINGLY, HE IS SAINT BLAISE.
LIKE US, LUCY HAS BEEN CALLED TO BE A MARTYR FOR HEAVEN.
THOUGH I AGREE WITH BLAISE. THESE COOKIES KICK ASS.

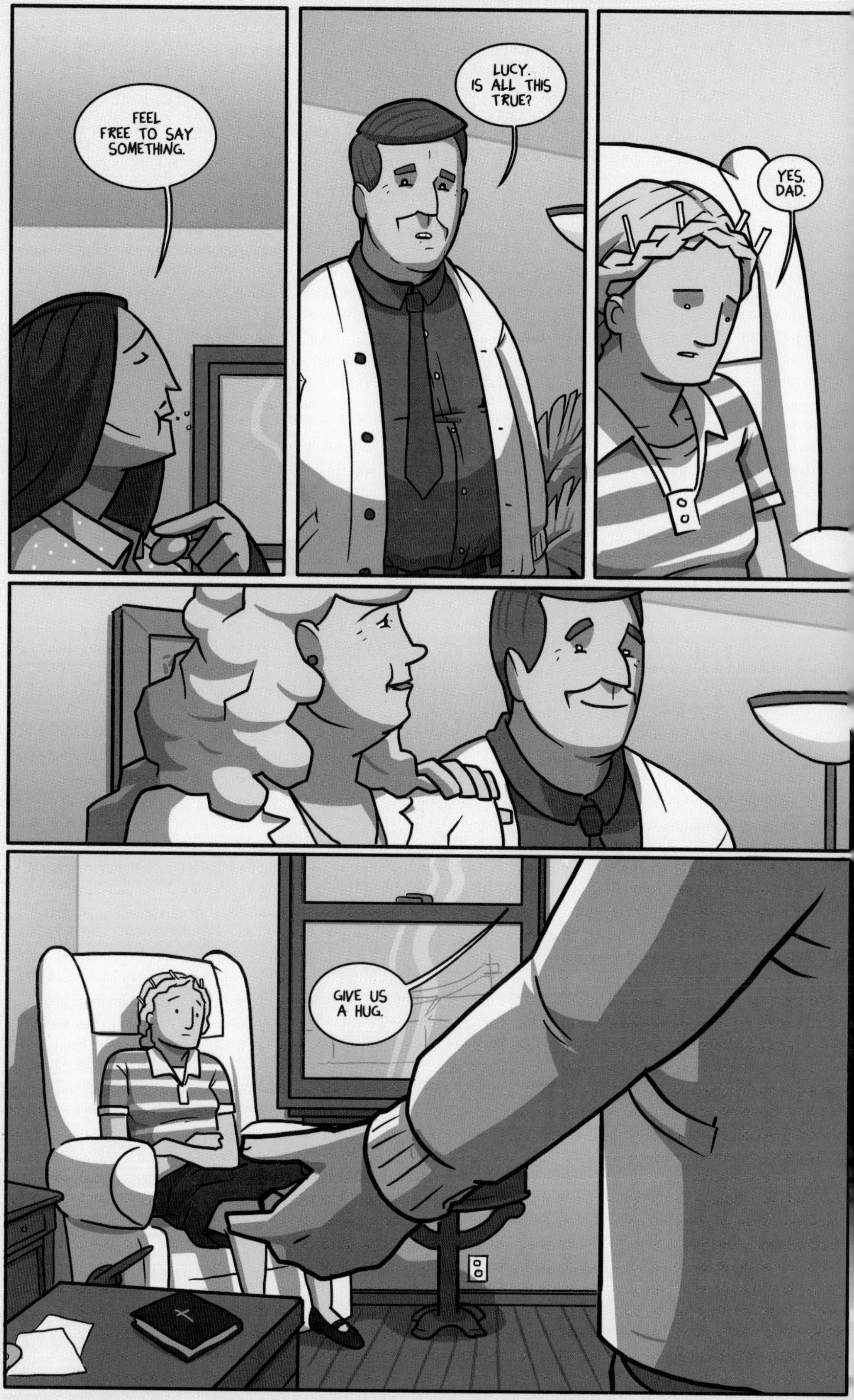
FEEL FREE TO SAY SOMETHING.
LUCY. IS ALL THIS TRUE?
YES, DAD.
GIVE US A HUG.

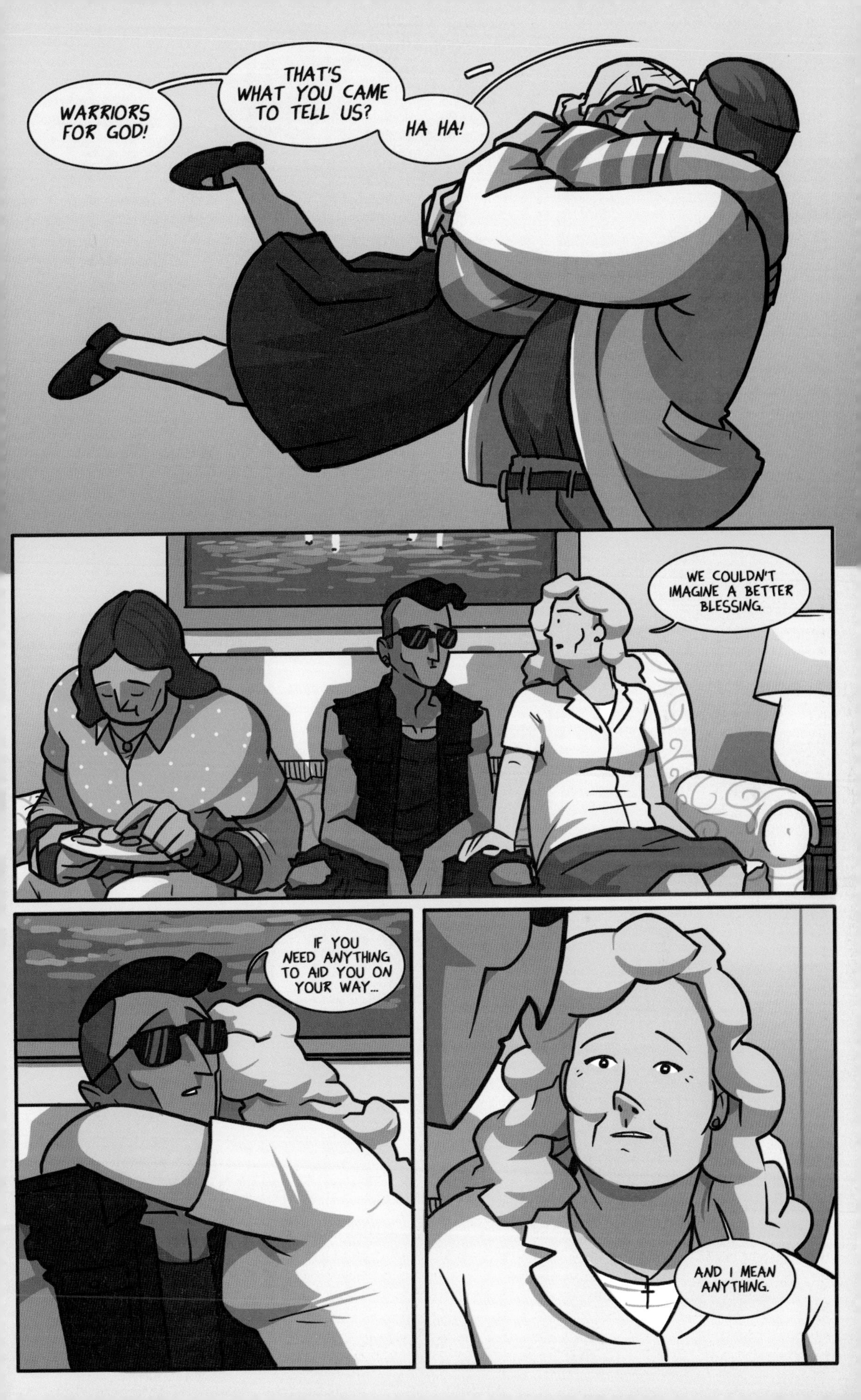
WARRIORS FOR GOD!
THAT'S WHAT YOU CAME TO TELL US?
HA HA!
WE COULDN'T IMAGINE A BETTER BLESSING.
IF YOU NEED ANYTHING TO AID YOU ON YOUR WAY...
AND I MEAN ANYTHING.

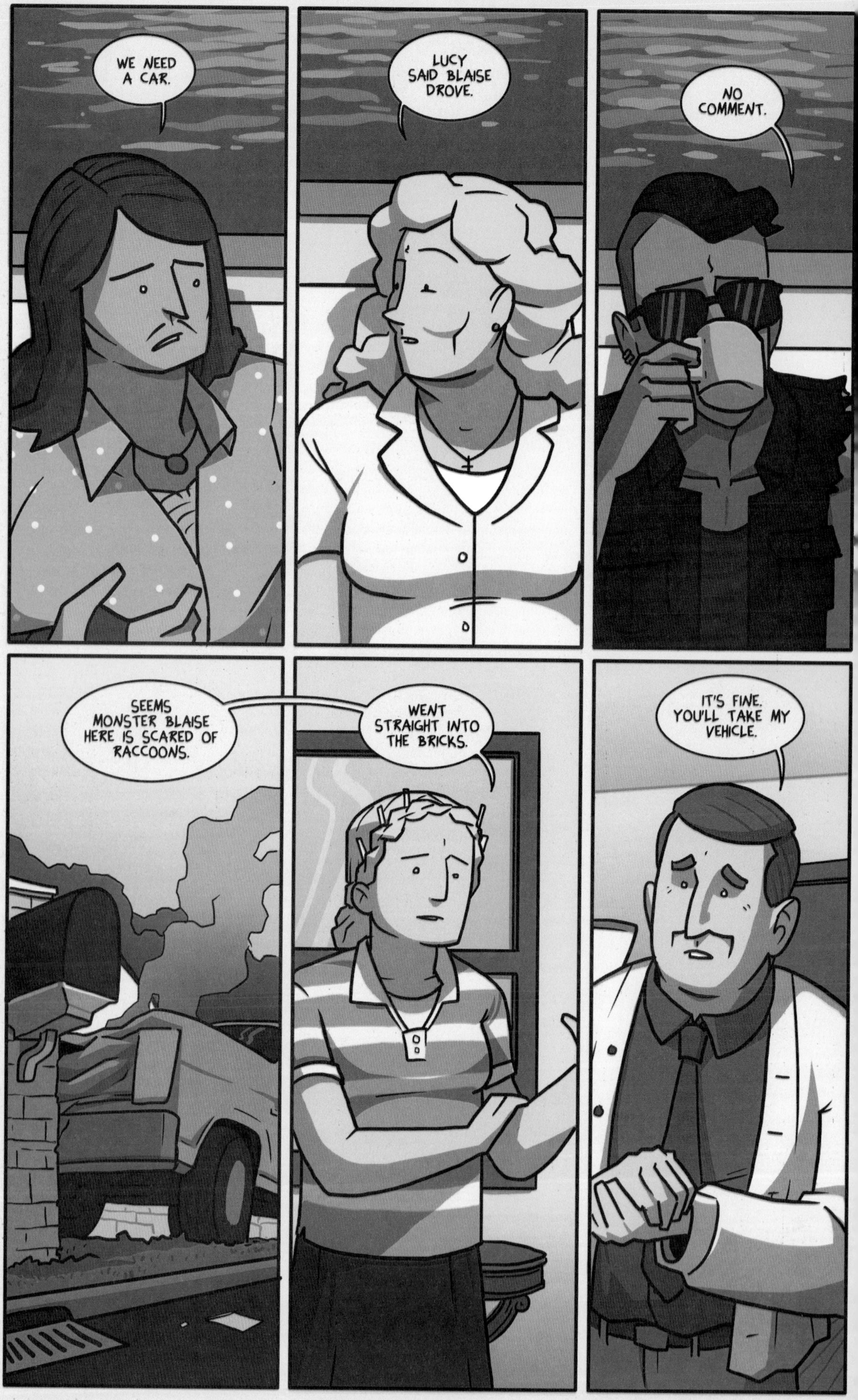
WE NEED A CAR.
LUCY SAID BLAISE DROVE.
NO COMMENT.
SEEMS MONSTER BLAISE HERE IS SCARED OF RACCOONS.
WENT STRAIGHT INTO THE BRICKS.
IT'S FINE. YOU'LL TAKE MY VEHICLE.

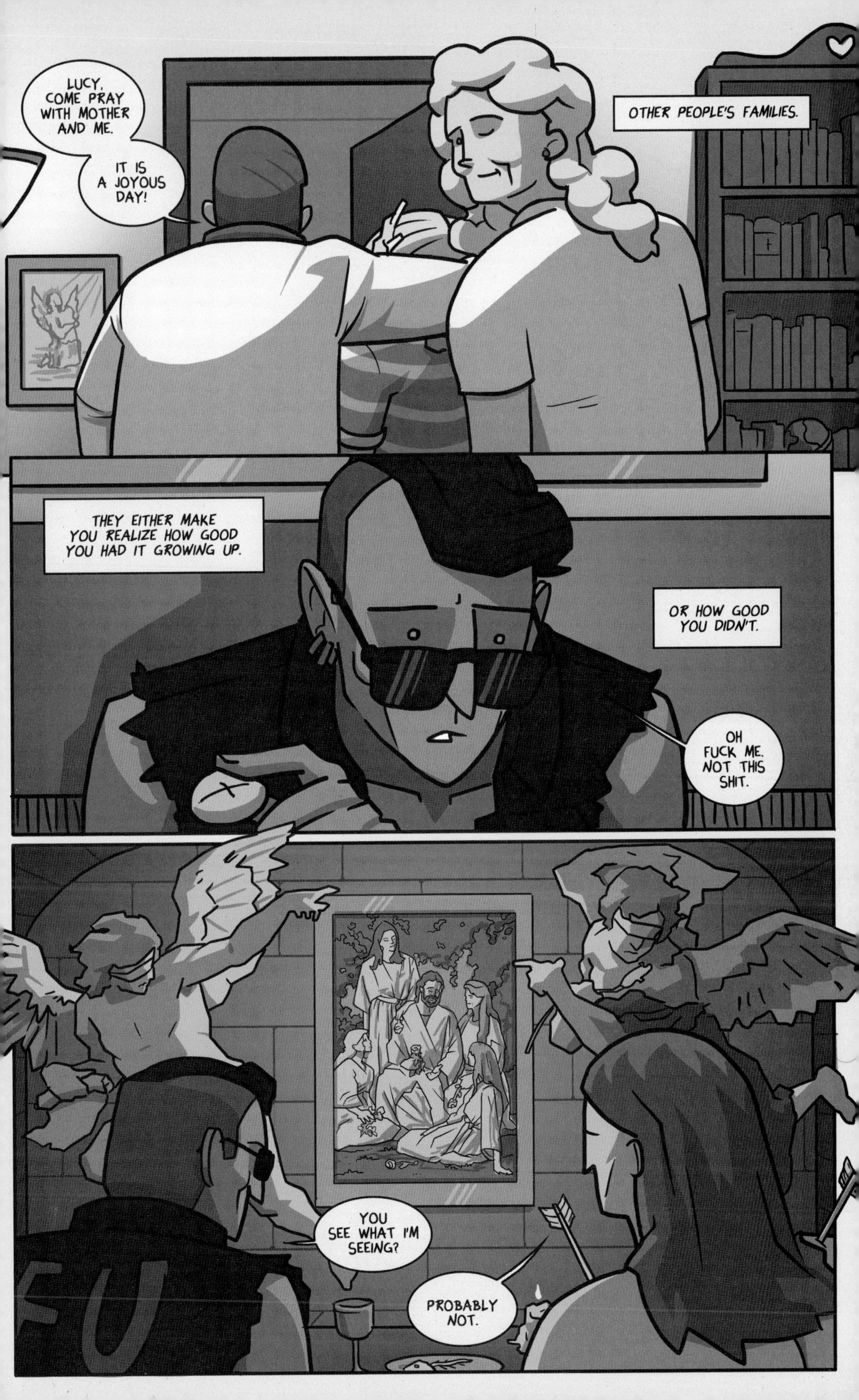
LUCY, COME PRAY WITH MOTHER AND ME.
IT IS A JOYOUS DAY!
OTHER PEOPLE'S FAMILIES.
THEY EITHER MAKE YOU REALIZE HOW GOOD YOU HAD IT GROWING UP.
OR HOW GOOD YOU DIDN'T.
OH FUCK ME. NOT THIS SHIT.
YOU SEE WHAT I'M SEEING?
PROBABLY NOT.

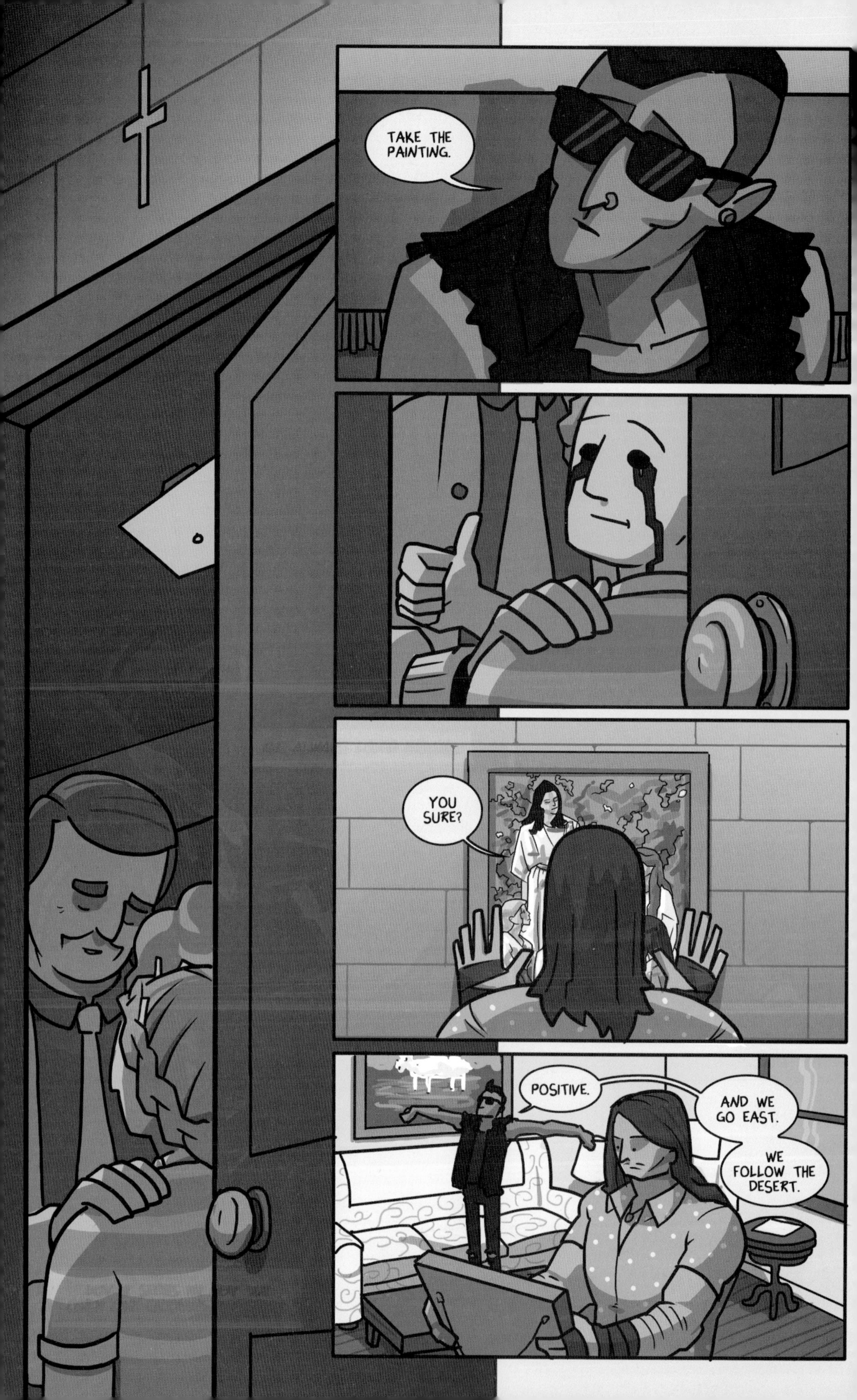
TAKE THE PAINTING.
YOU SURE?
POSITIVE.
AND WE GO EAST.
WE FOLLOW THE DESERT.

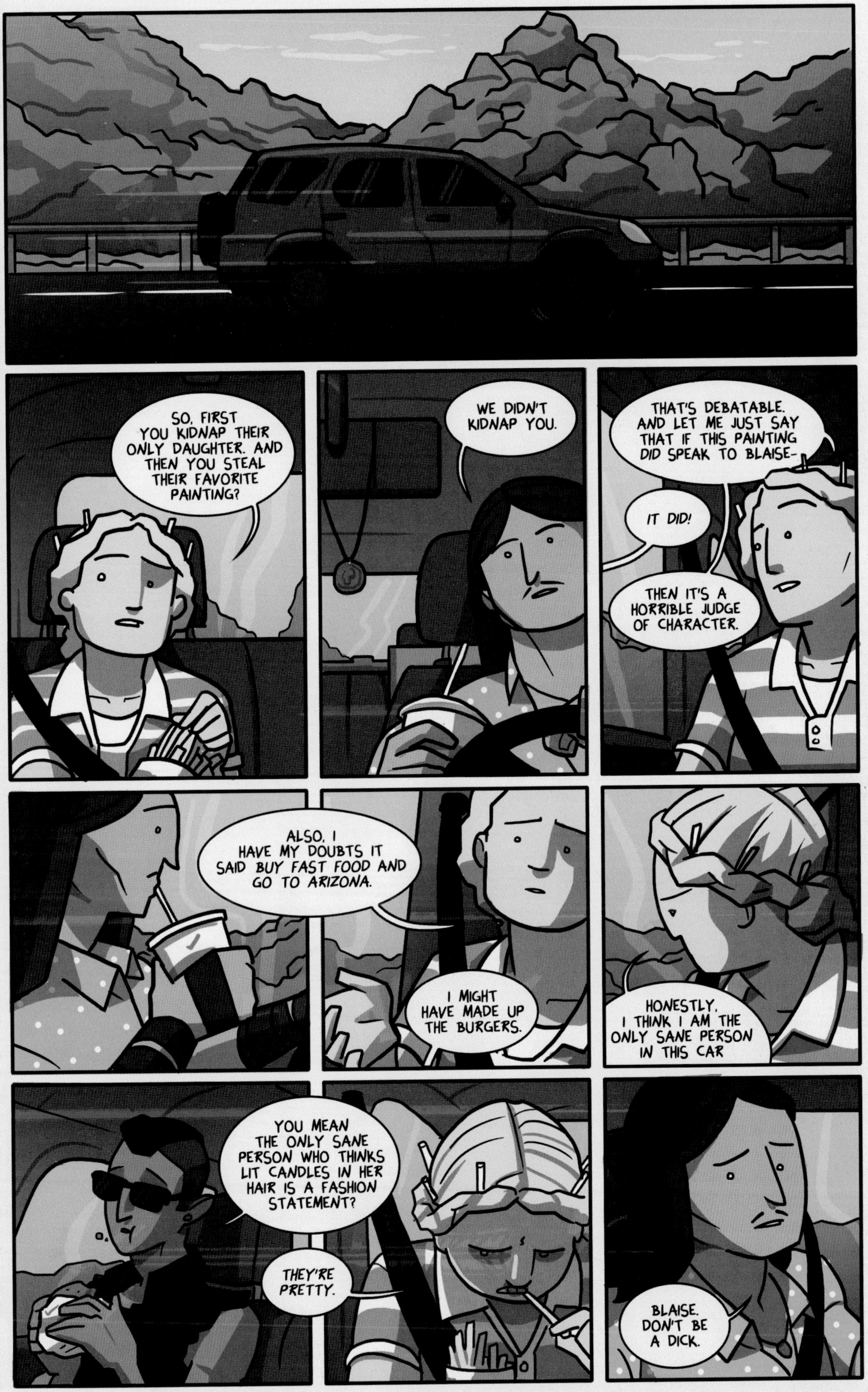
SO, FIRST YOU KIDNAP THEIR ONLY DAUGHTER. AND THEN YOU STEAL THEIR FAVORITE PAINTING?
WE DIDN'T KIDNAP YOU.
THAT'S DEBATABLE. AND LET ME JUST SAY THAT IF THIS PAINTING DID SPEAK TO BLAISE-
IT DID!
THEN IT'S A HORRIBLE JUDGE OF CHARACTER.
ALSO, I HAVE MY DOUBTS IT SAID BUY FAST FOOD AND GO TO ARIZONA.
I MIGHT HAVE MADE UP THE BURGERS.
HONESTLY, I THINK I AM THE ONLY SANE PERSON IN THIS CAR
YOU MEAN THE ONLY SANE PERSON WHO THINKS LIT CANDLES IN HER HAIR IS A FASHION STATEMENT?
THEY'RE PRETTY.
BLAISE. DON'T BE A DICK.

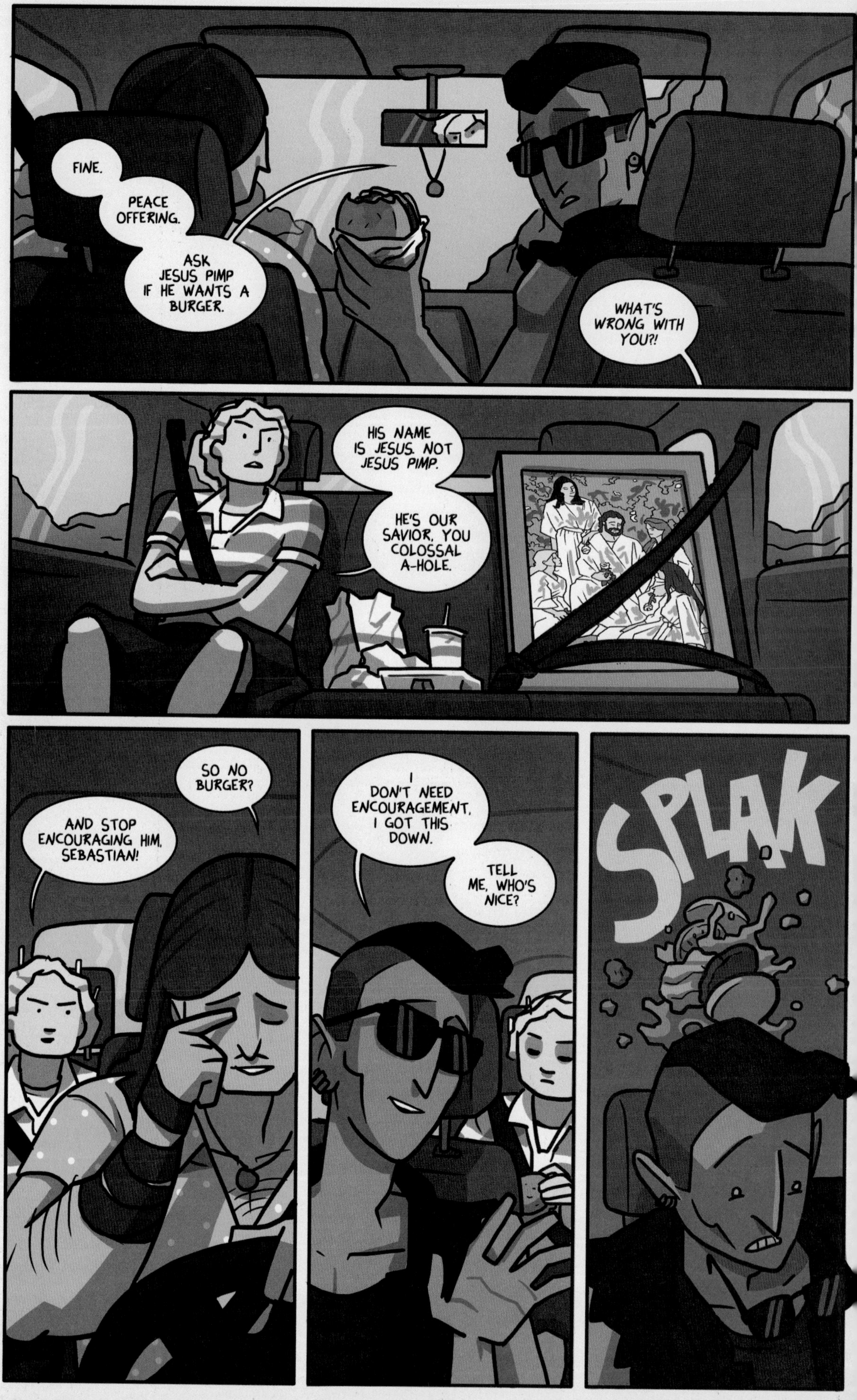
FINE.
PEACE OFFERING.
ASK JESUS PIMP IF HE WANTS A BURGER.
WHAT'S WRONG WITH YOU?!
HIS NAME IS JESUS. NOT JESUS PIMP.
HE'S OUR SAVIOR, YOU COLOSSAL A-HOLE.
SO NO BURGER?
AND STOP ENCOURAGING HIM, SEBASTIAN!
I DON'T NEED ENCOURAGEMENT, I GOT THIS DOWN.
TELL ME, WHO'S NICE?
SPLAK

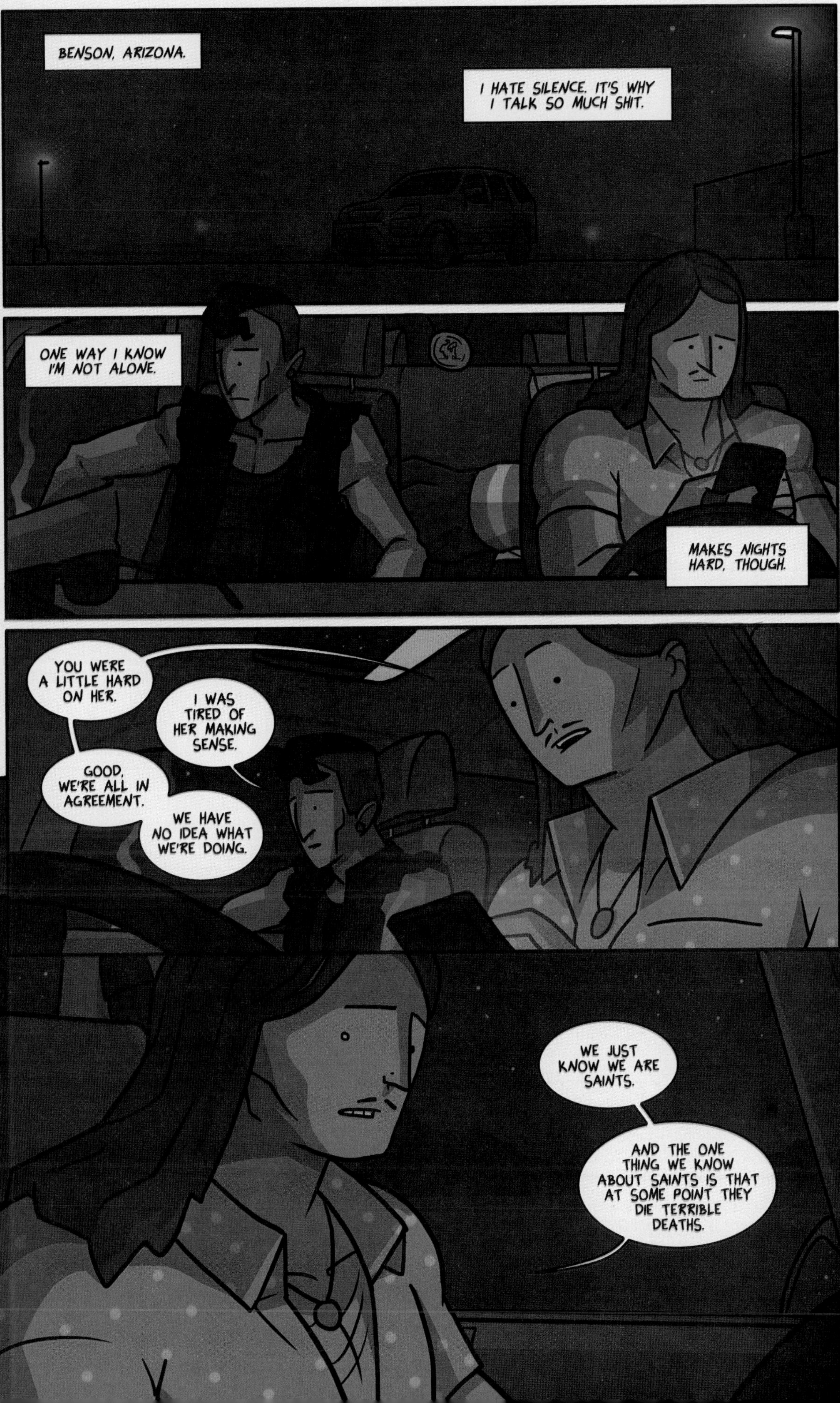
BENSON, ARIZONA.
I HATE SILENCE. IT'S WHY I TALK SO MUCH SHIT.
ONE WAY I KNOW I'M NOT ALONE.
MAKES NIGHTS HARD, THOUGH.
YOU WERE A LITTLE HARD ON HER.
I WAS TIRED OF HER MAKING SENSE.
GOOD, WE'RE ALL IN AGREEMENT.
WE HAVE NO IDEA WHAT WE'RE DOING.
WE JUST KNOW WE ARE SAINTS.
AND THE ONE THING WE KNOW ABOUT SAINTS IS THAT AT SOME POINT THEY DIE TERRIBLE DEATHS.

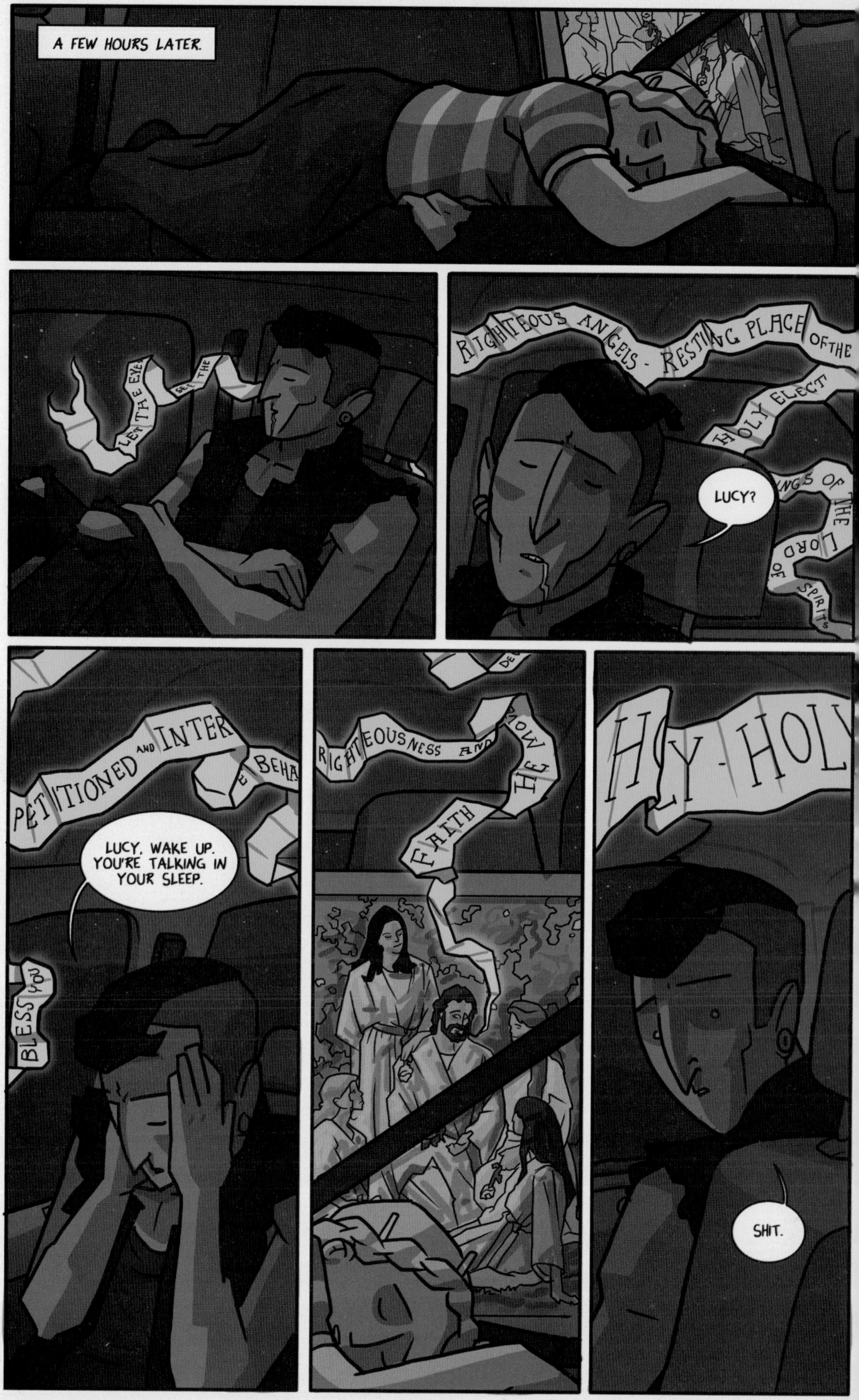
A FEW HOURS LATER.
LET THE EYES SEE THE
RIGHTEOUS ANGELS - RESTING PLACE OF THE HOLY ELECT
LUCY?
OF THE LORD OF SPIRITS
PETITIONED AND INTER
BEHA
LUCY, WAKE UP. YOU'RE TALKING IN YOUR SLEEP.
BLESS YOU
RIGHTEOUSNESS AND
FAITH
SHIT.

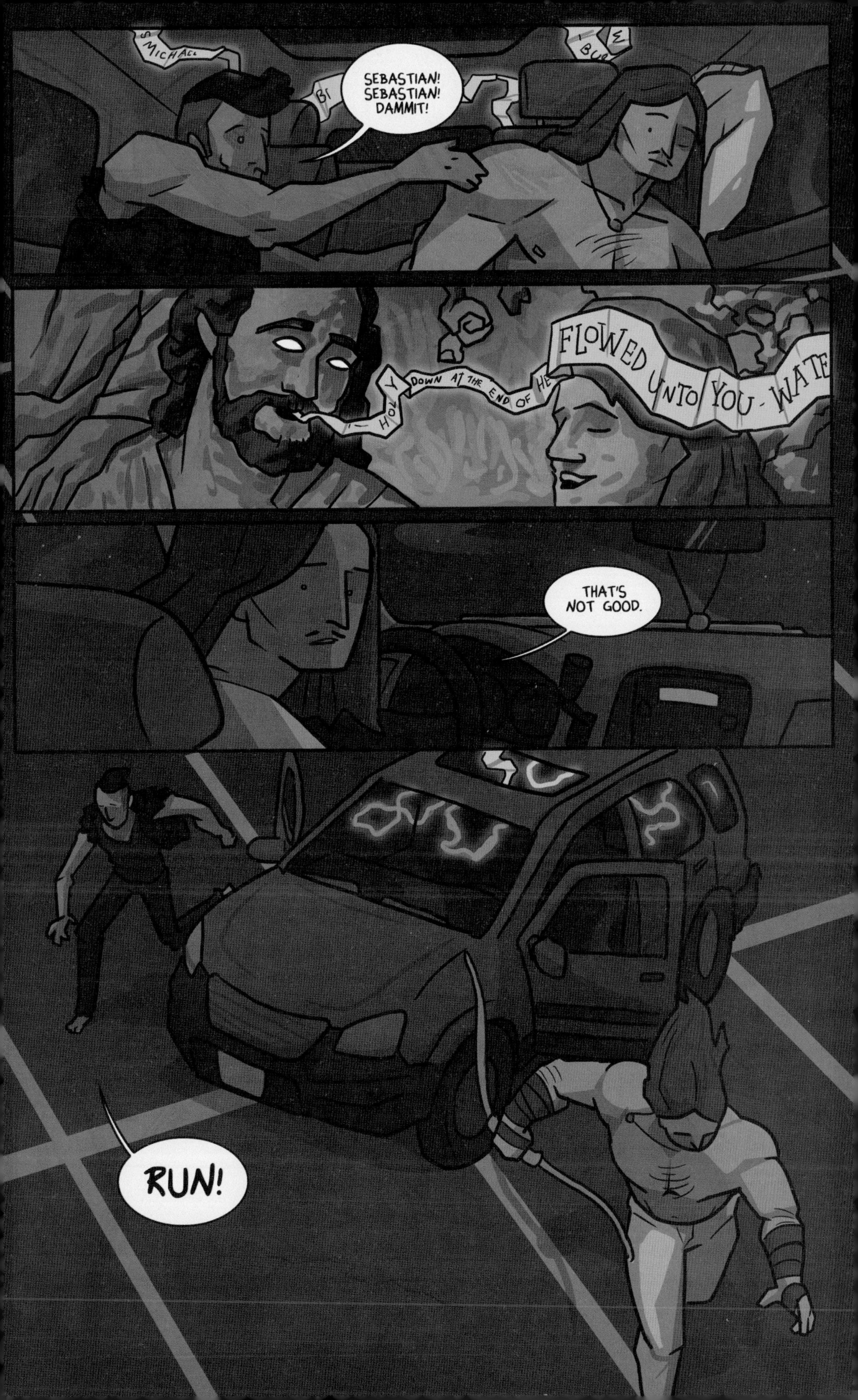

SEBASTIAN! SEBASTIAN! DAMMIT!
I — HOLY DOWN AT THE END OF HE
FLOWED UNTO YOU - WATE
THAT'S NOT GOOD.
RUN!

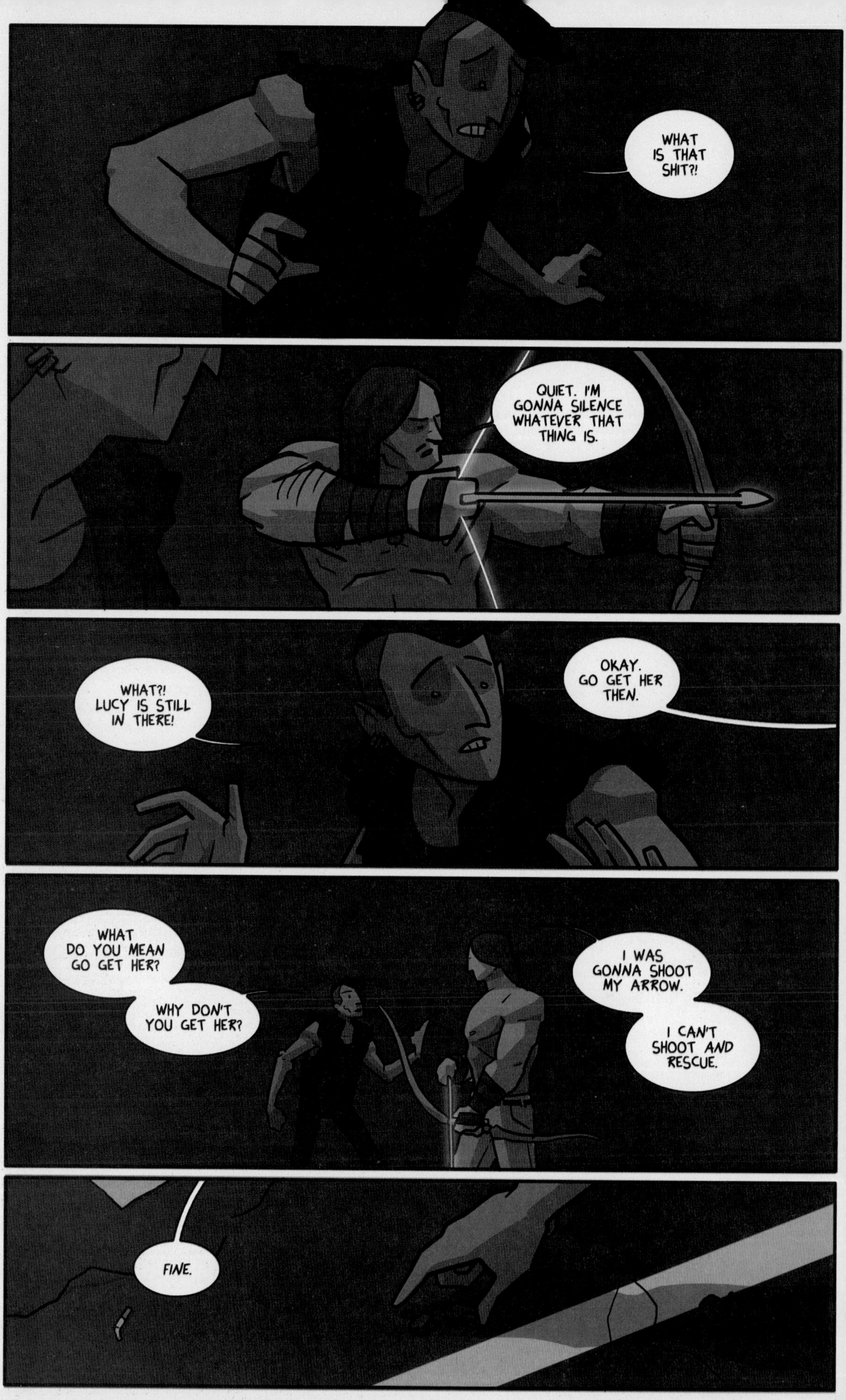
WHAT IS THAT SHIT?!
QUIET. I'M GONNA SILENCE WHATEVER THAT THING IS.
WHAT?! LUCY IS STILL IN THERE!
OKAY. GO GET HER THEN.
WHAT DO YOU MEAN GO GET HER?
WHY DON'T YOU GET HER?
I WAS GONNA SHOOT MY ARROW.
I CAN'T SHOOT AND RESCUE.
FINE.

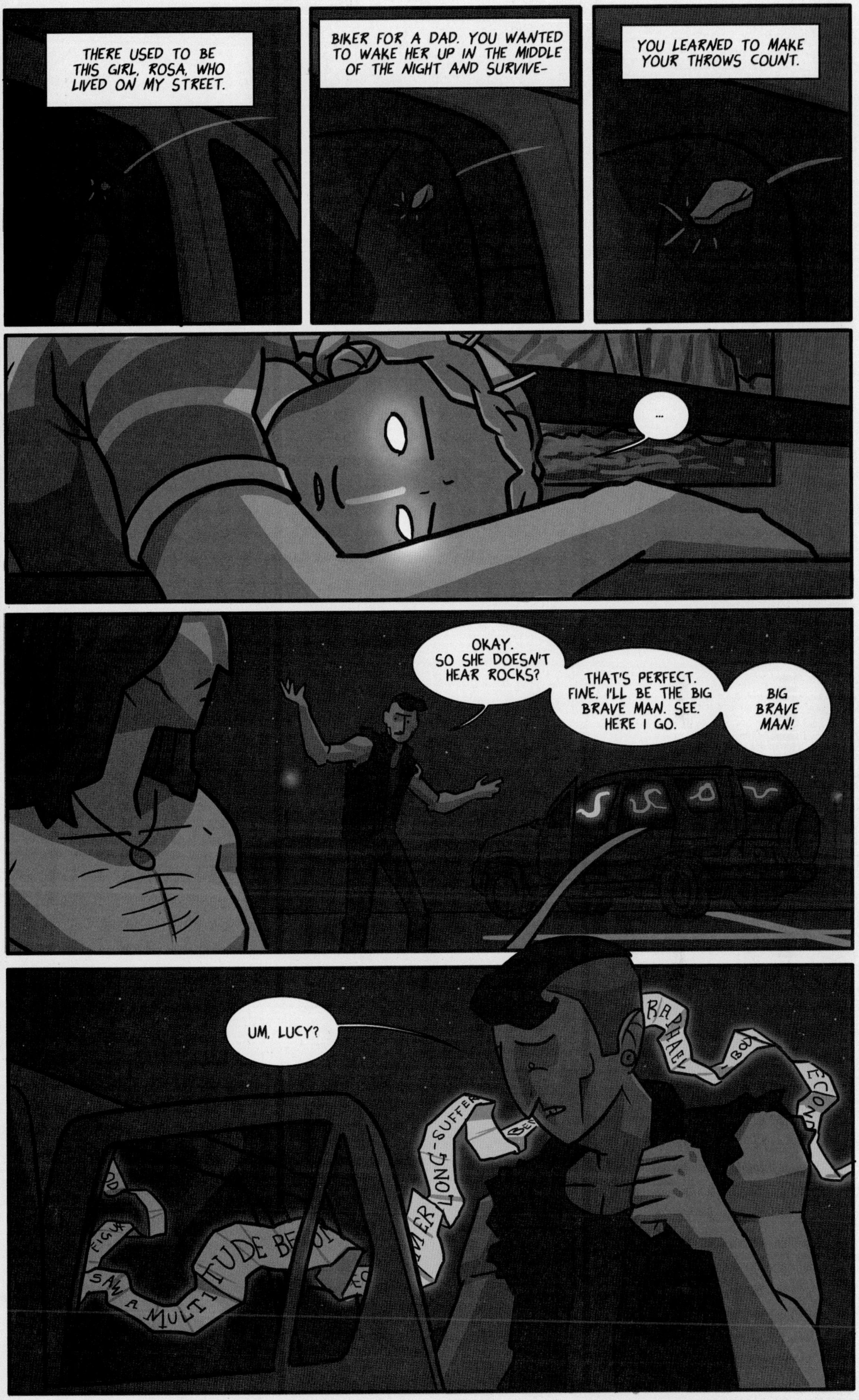
THERE USED TO BE THIS GIRL, ROSA, WHO LIVED ON MY STREET.
BIKER FOR A DAD. YOU WANTED TO WAKE HER UP IN THE MIDDLE OF THE NIGHT AND SURVIVE-
YOU LEARNED TO MAKE YOUR THROWS COUNT.
...
OKAY. SO SHE DOESN'T HEAR ROCKS?
THAT'S PERFECT. FINE. I'LL BE THE BIG BRAVE MAN. SEE. HERE I GO.
BIG BRAVE MAN!
UM, LUCY?

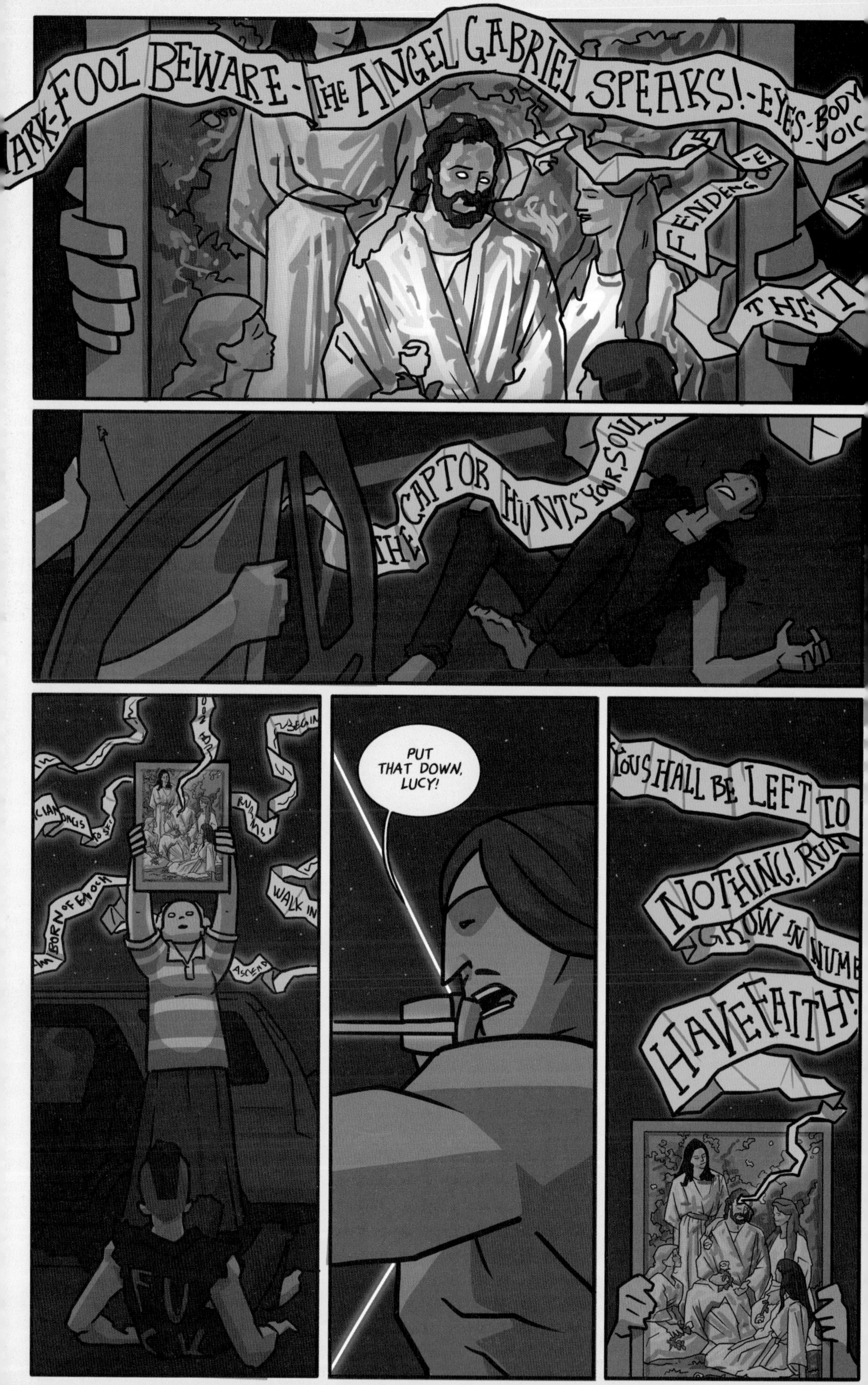
ARK-FOOL BEWARE-THE ANGEL GABRIEL SPEAKS!-EYES-BODY
THE CAPTOR HUNTS YOUR
BORN OF ENOCH
WALK IN
ASCEND
PUT THAT DOWN, LUCY!
YOU SHALL BE LEFT TO NOTHING!
HAVE FAITH!

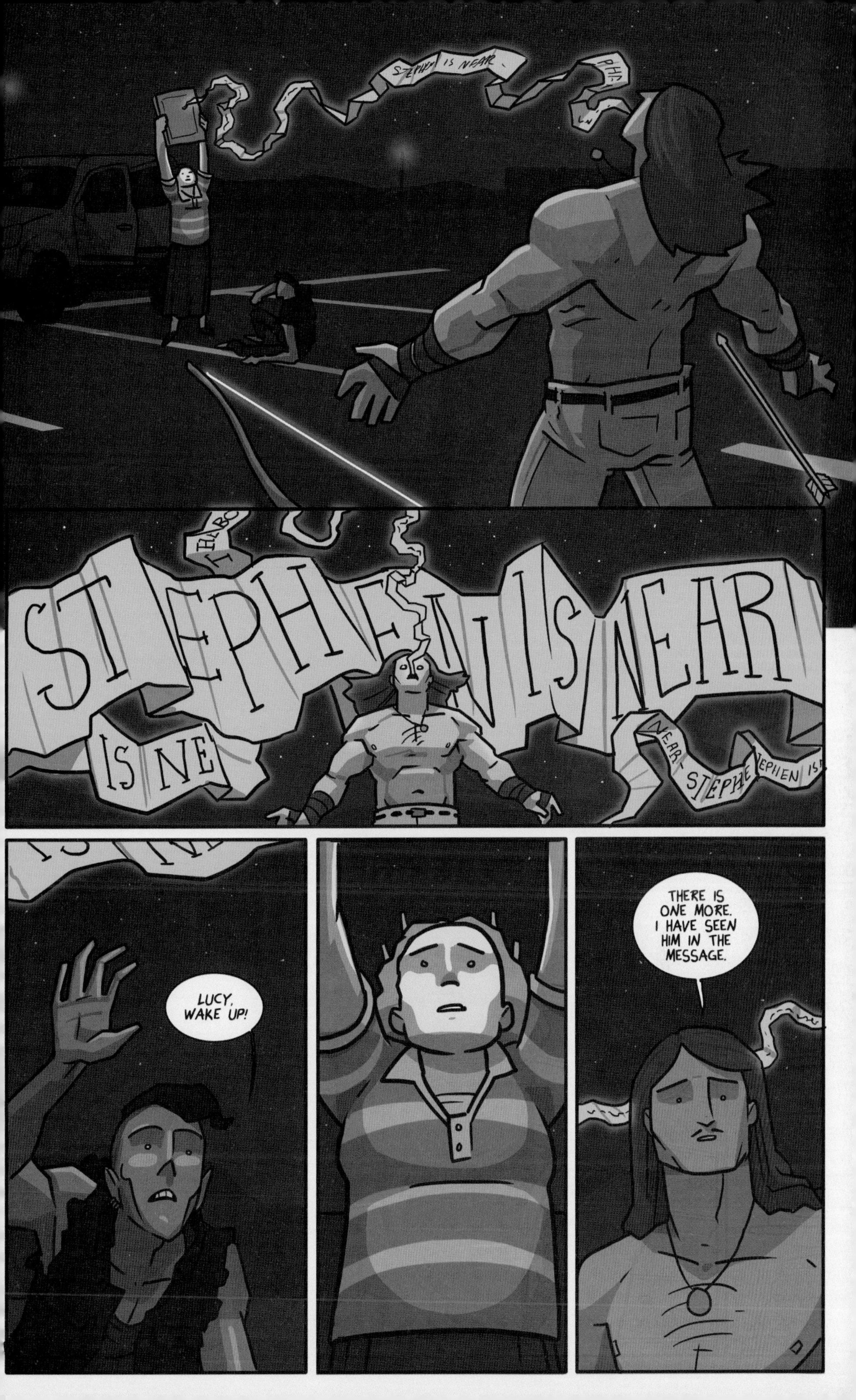
STEPHEN IS NEAR
STEPHEN IS NEAR
IS NE
NEAR STEPHE
EPHEN IS
LUCY, WAKE UP!
THERE IS ONE MORE. I HAVE SEEN HIM IN THE MESSAGE.

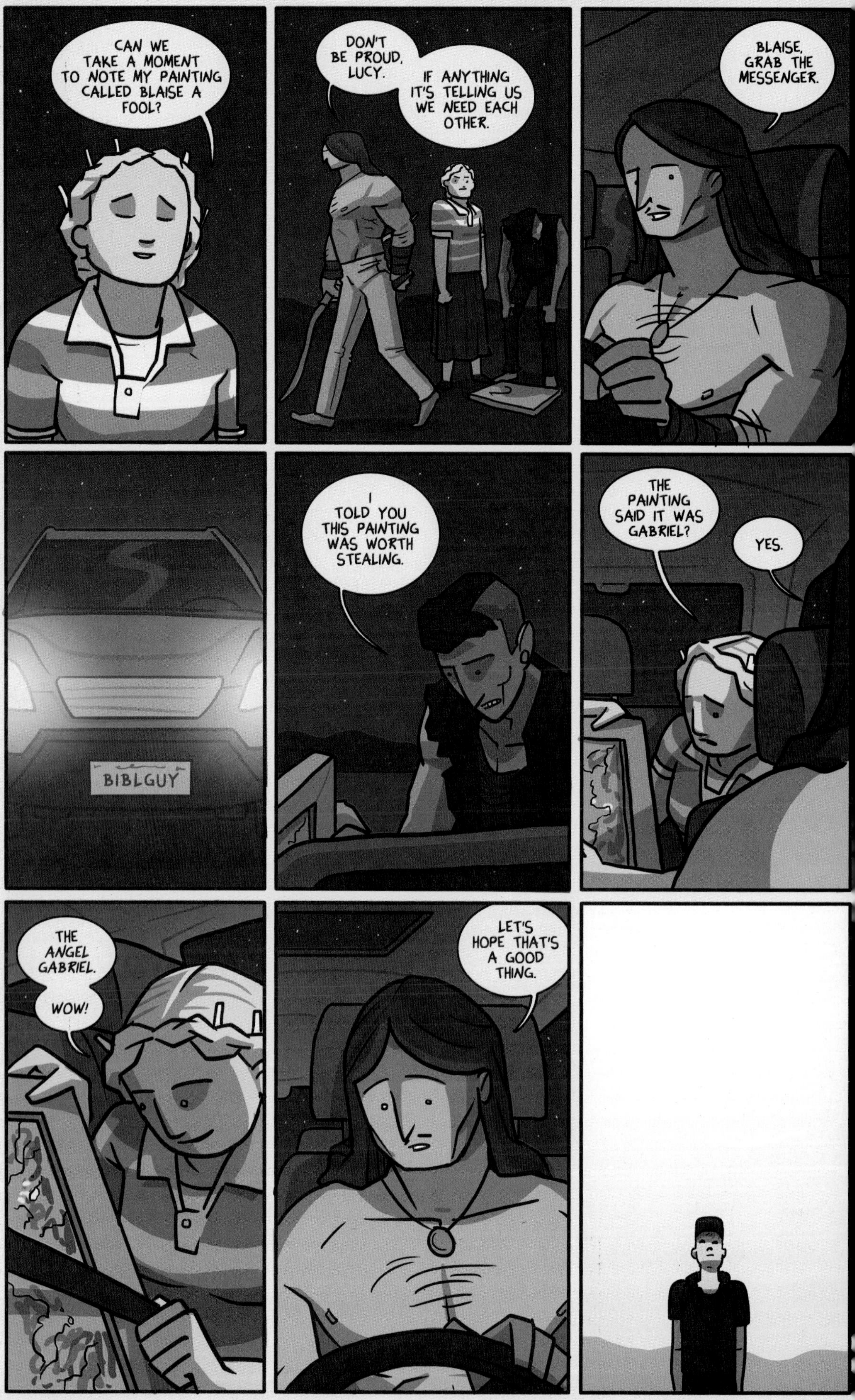
CAN WE TAKE A MOMENT TO NOTE MY PAINTING CALLED BLAISE A FOOL?
DON'T BE PROUD, LUCY.
IF ANYTHING IT'S TELLING US WE NEED EACH OTHER.
BLAISE, GRAB THE MESSENGER.
BIBLGUY
I TOLD YOU THIS PAINTING WAS WORTH STEALING.
THE PAINTING SAID IT WAS GABRIEL?
YES.
THE ANGEL GABRIEL.
WOW!
LET'S HOPE THAT'S A GOOD THING.

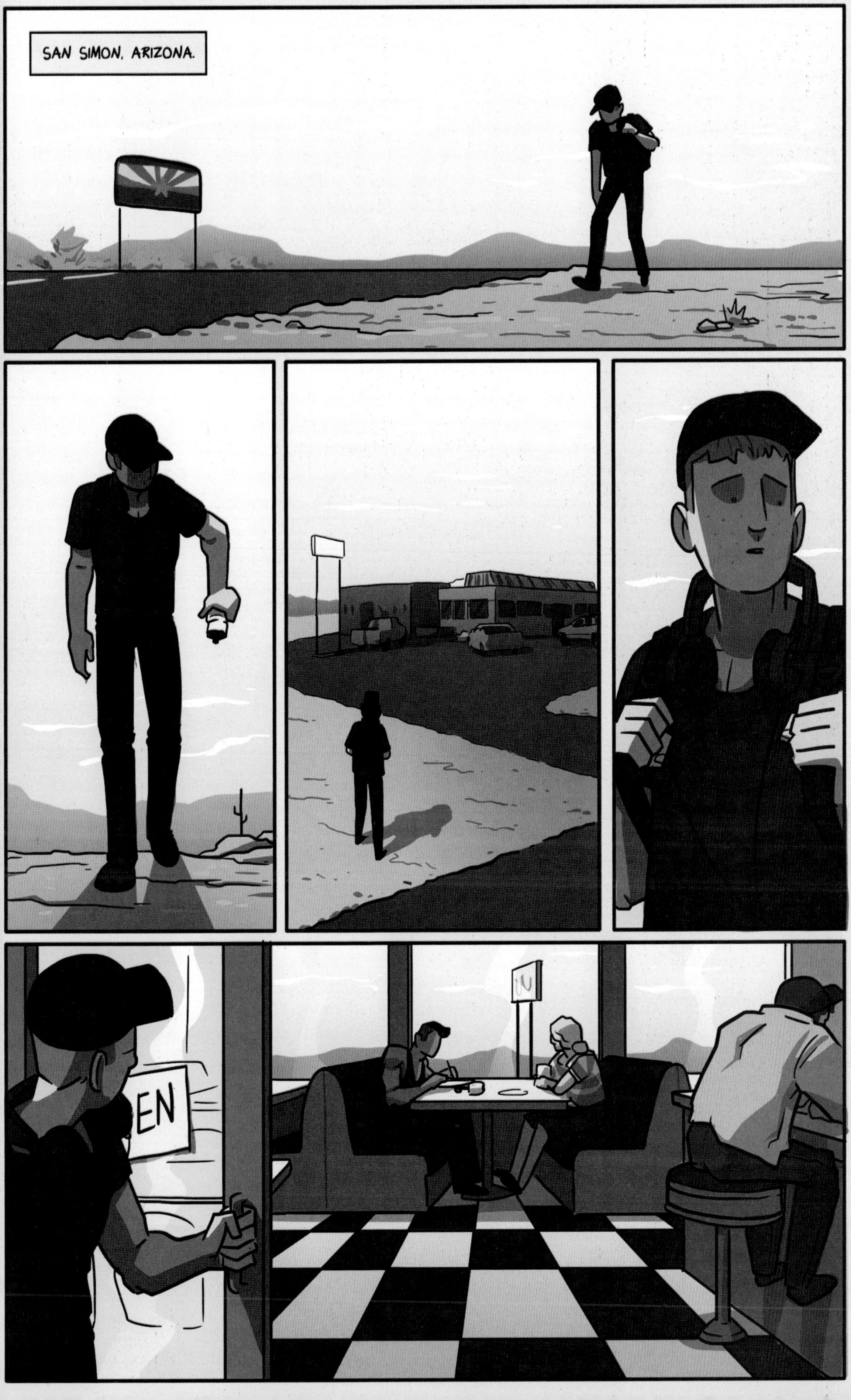
SAN SIMON, ARIZONA.
EN

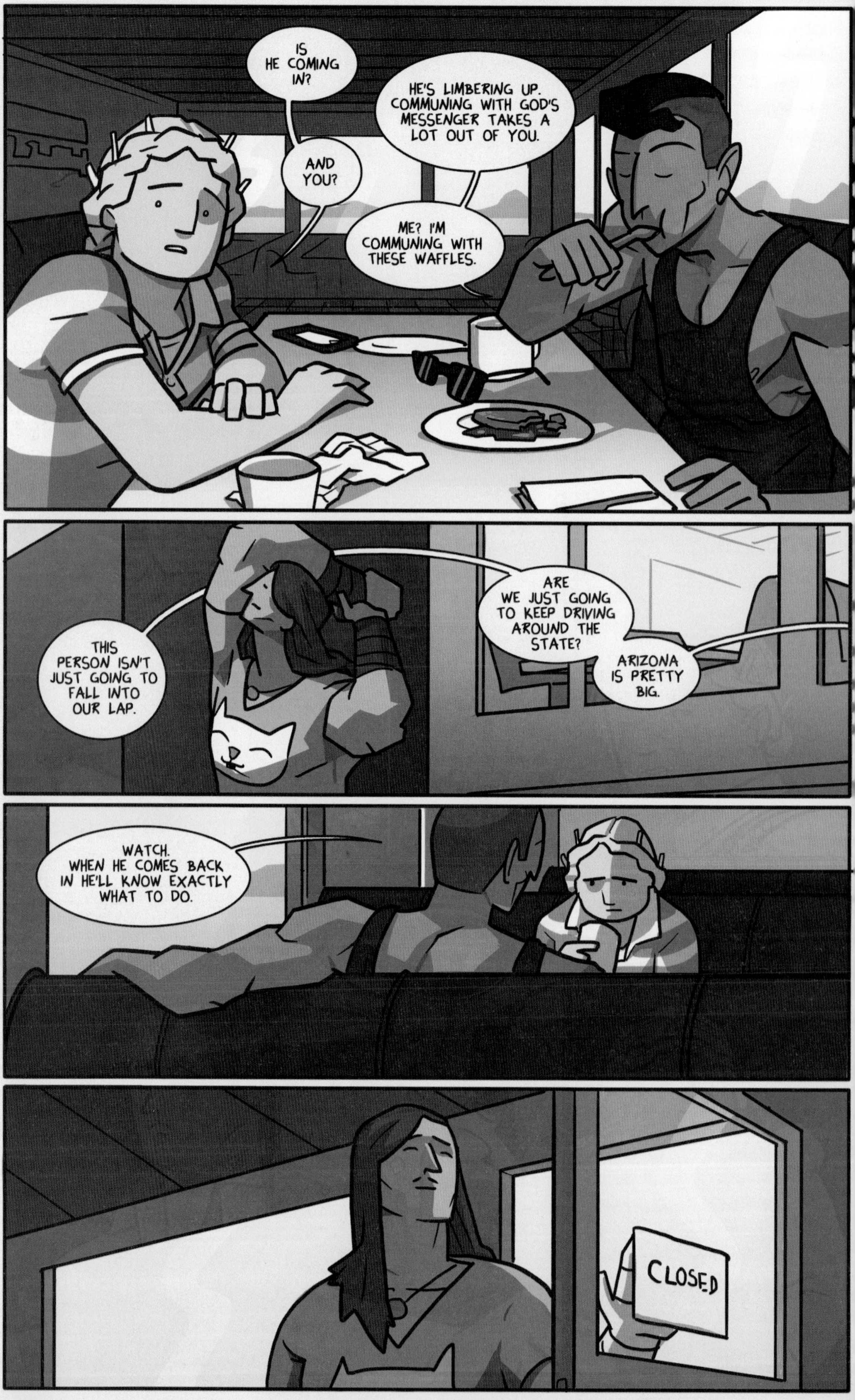
IS HE COMING IN?
HE'S LIMBERING UP. COMMUNING WITH GOD'S MESSENGER TAKES A LOT OUT OF YOU.
AND YOU?
ME? I'M COMMUNING WITH THESE WAFFLES.
THIS PERSON ISN'T JUST GOING TO FALL INTO OUR LAP.
ARE WE JUST GOING TO KEEP DRIVING AROUND THE STATE?
ARIZONA IS PRETTY BIG.
WATCH. WHEN HE COMES BACK IN HE'LL KNOW EXACTLY WHAT TO DO.
CLOSED

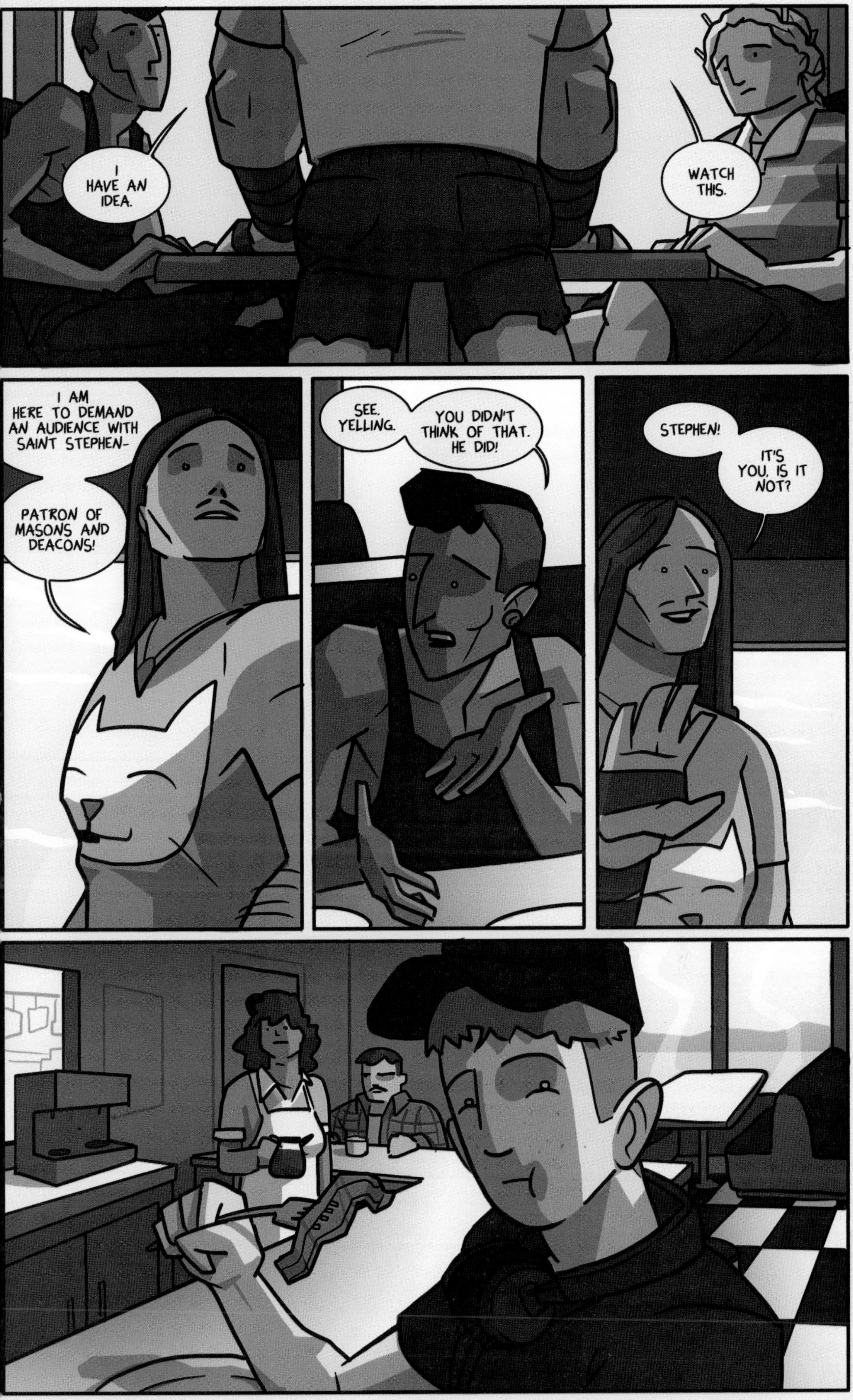
I HAVE AN IDEA.
WATCH THIS.
I AM HERE TO DEMAND AN AUDIENCE WITH SAINT STEPHEN-
PATRON OF MASONS AND DEACONS!
SEE. YELLING.
YOU DIDN'T THINK OF THAT. HE DID!
STEPHEN!
IT'S YOU, IS IT NOT?

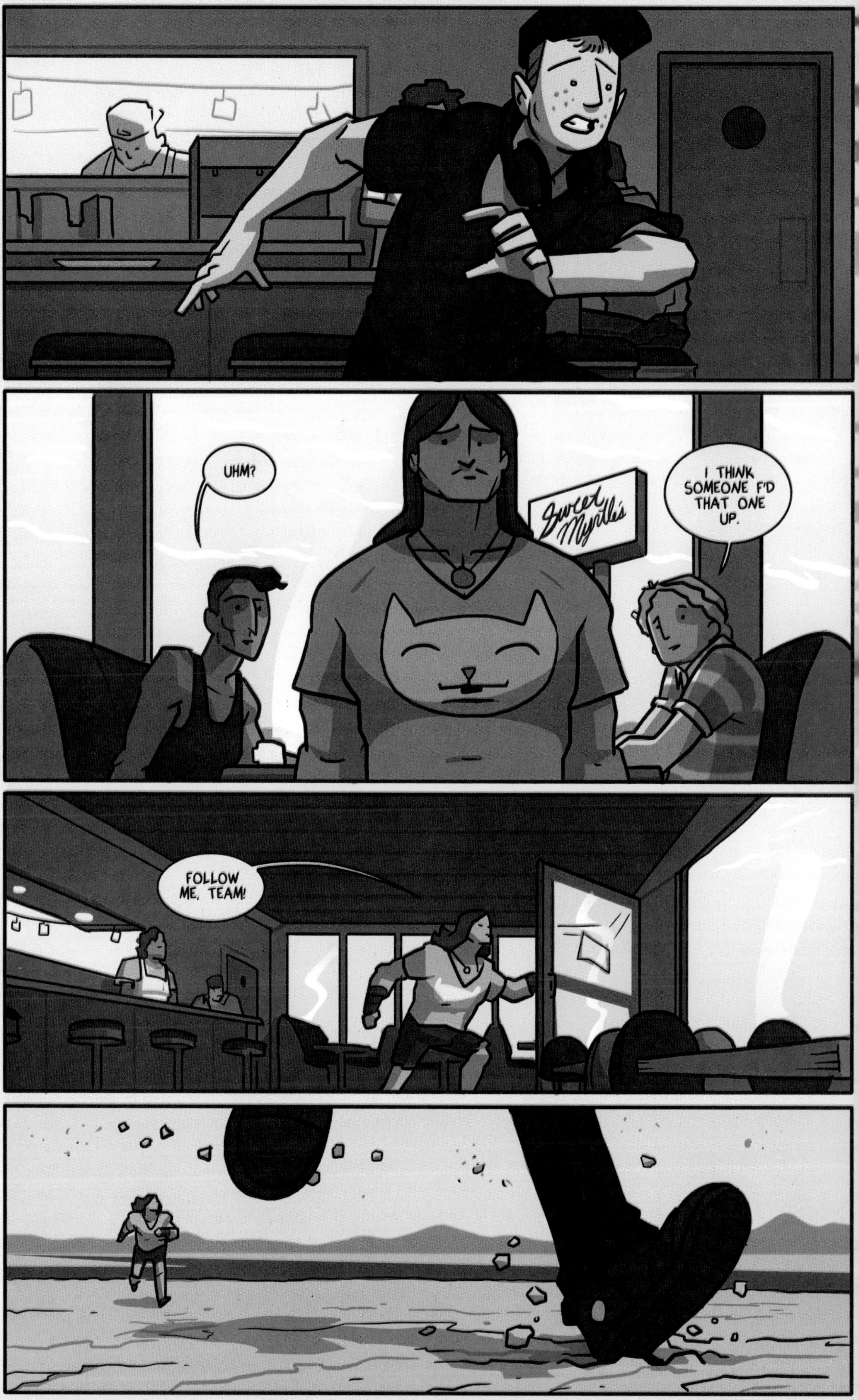
UHM?
I THINK SOMEONE F'D THAT ONE UP.
FOLLOW ME, TEAM!

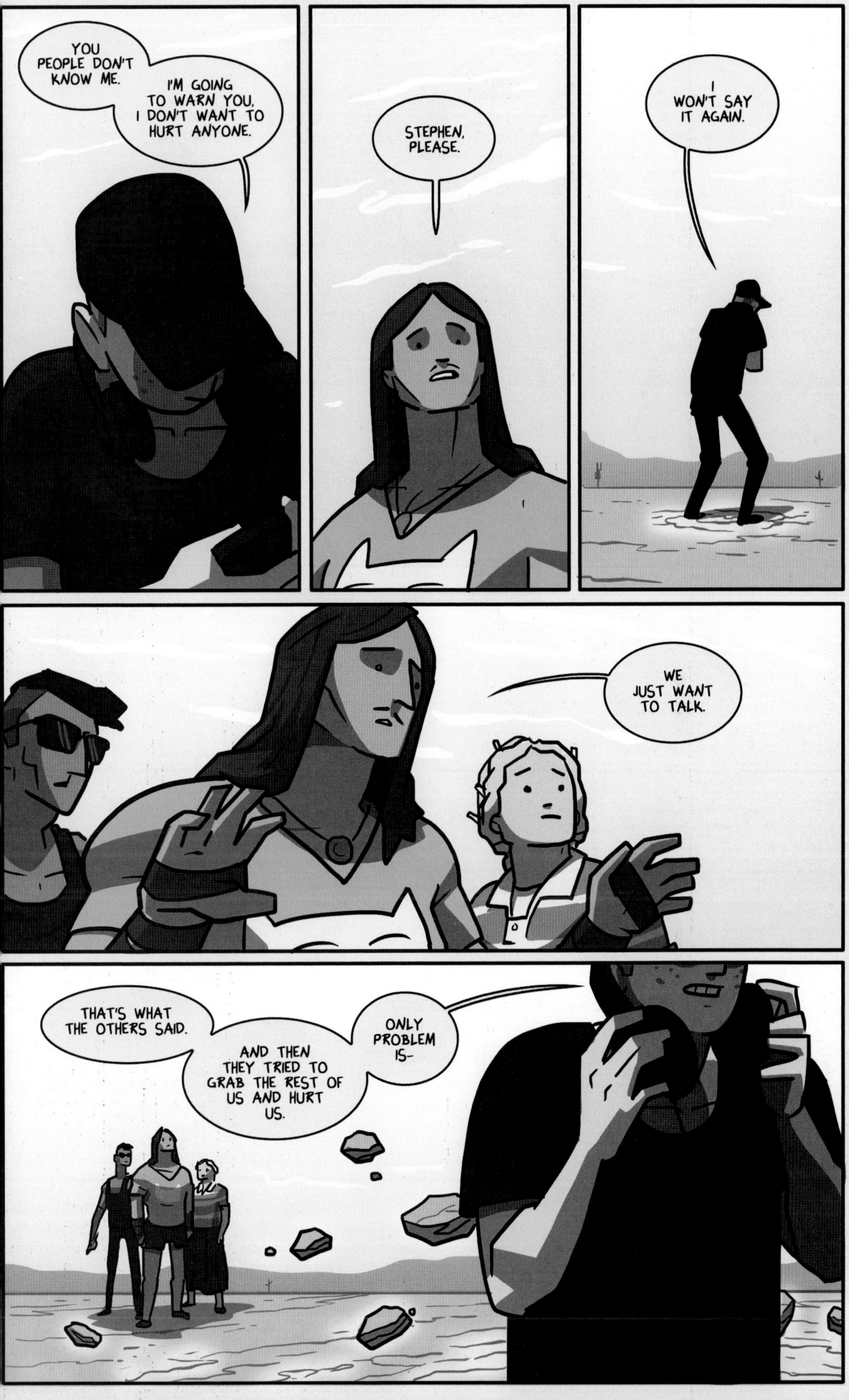
YOU PEOPLE DON'T KNOW ME.
I'M GOING TO WARN YOU, I DON'T WANT TO HURT ANYONE.
STEPHEN, PLEASE.
I WON'T SAY IT AGAIN.
WE JUST WANT TO TALK.
THAT'S WHAT THE OTHERS SAID.
AND THEN THEY TRIED TO GRAB THE REST OF US AND HURT US.
ONLY PROBLEM IS-

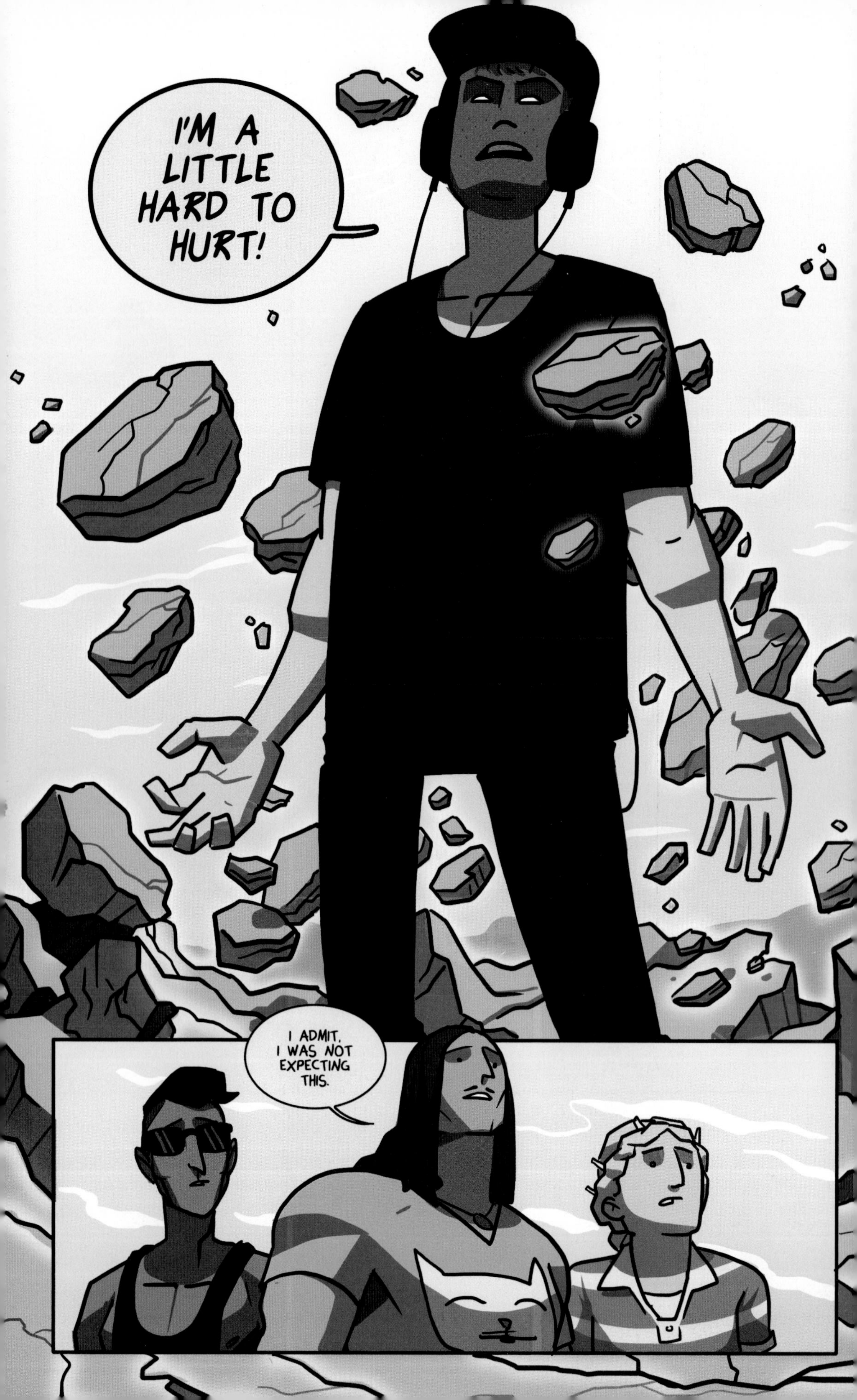
I'M A LITTLE HARD TO HURT!
I ADMIT, I WAS NOT EXPECTING THIS.

III

OFFERING

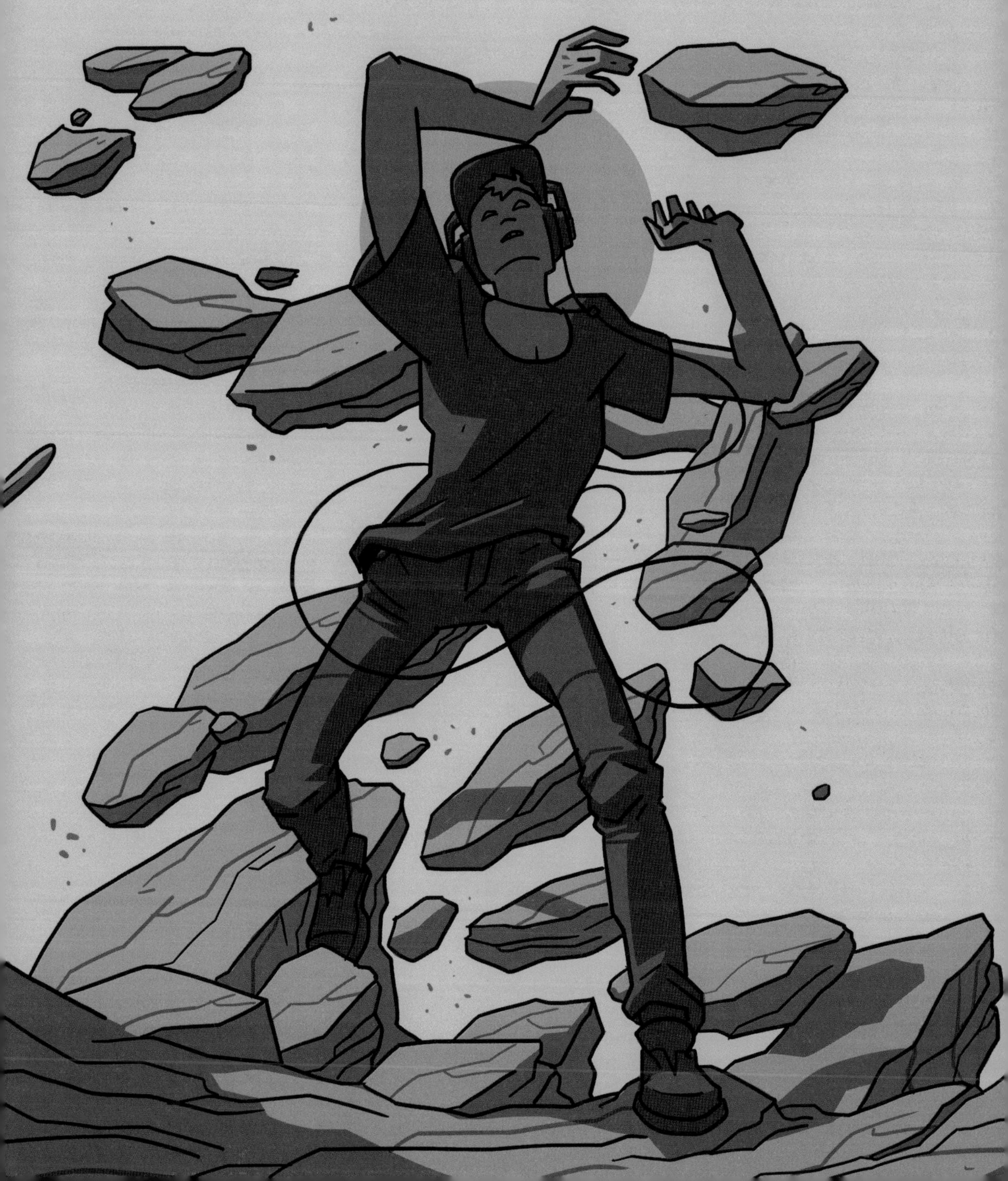

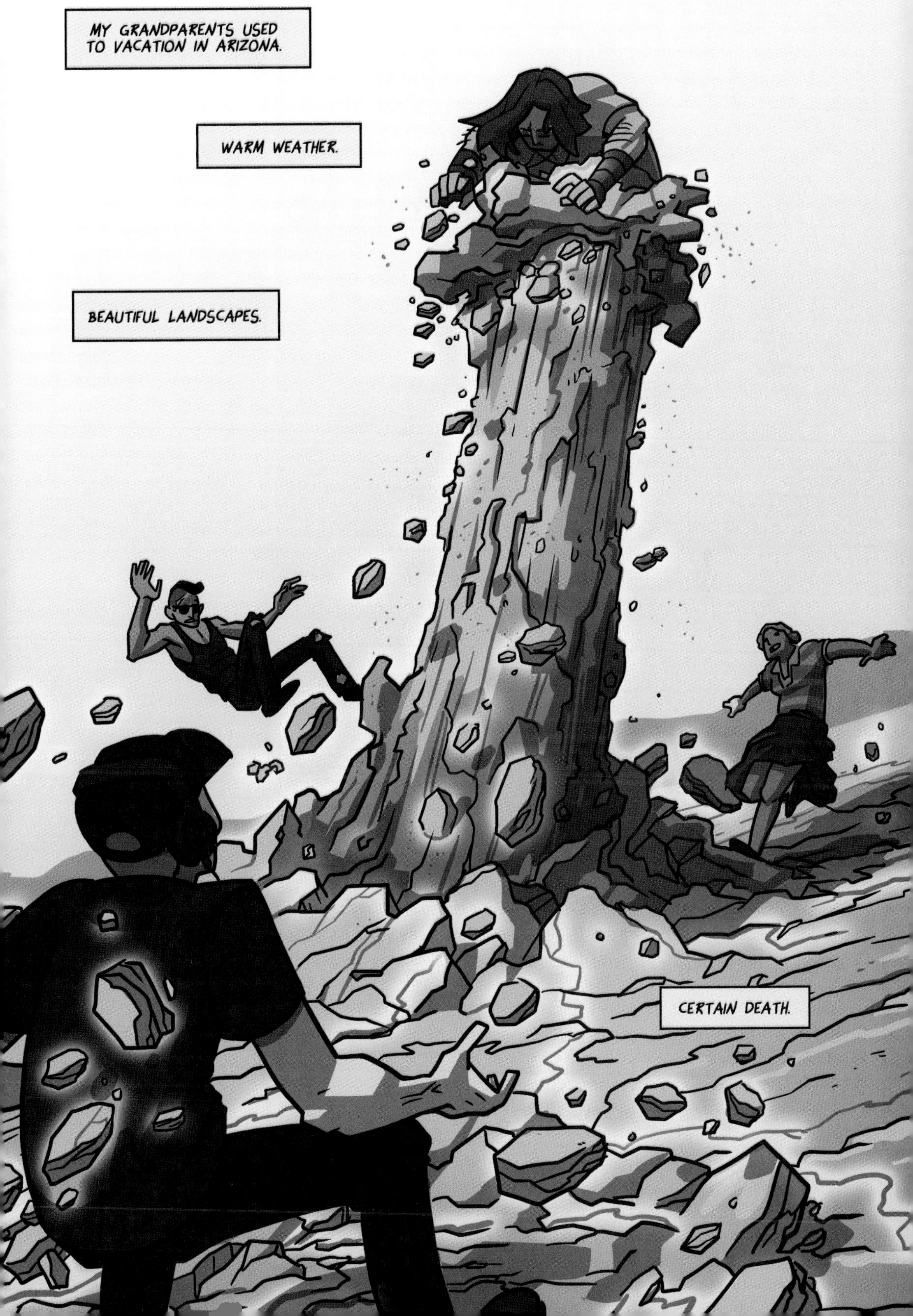
MY GRANDPARENTS USED TO VACATION IN ARIZONA.
WARM WEATHER.
BEAUTIFUL LANDSCAPES.
CERTAIN DEATH.

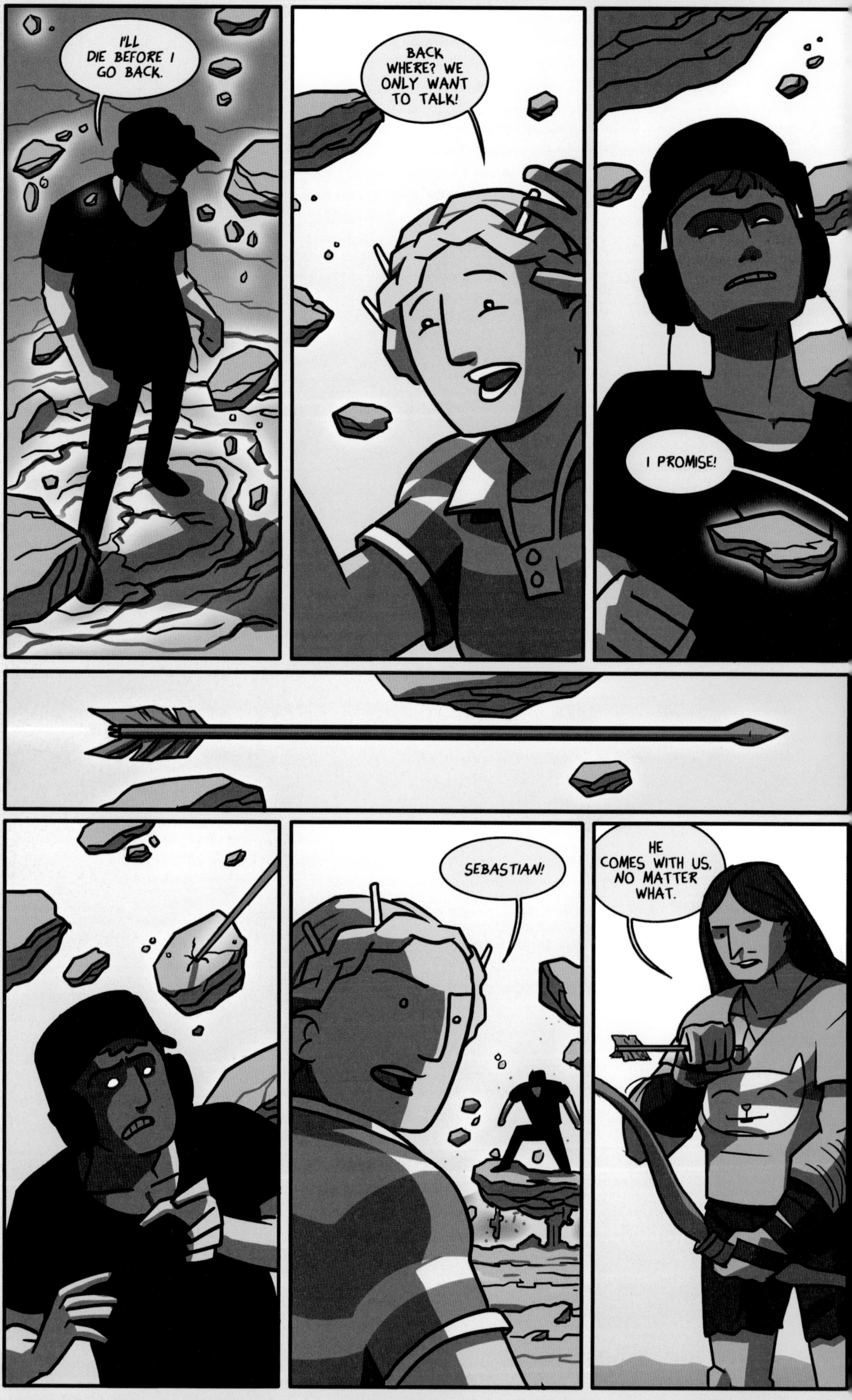
I'LL DIE BEFORE I GO BACK.
BACK WHERE? WE ONLY WANT TO TALK!
I PROMISE!
SEBASTIAN!
HE COMES WITH US, NO MATTER WHAT.

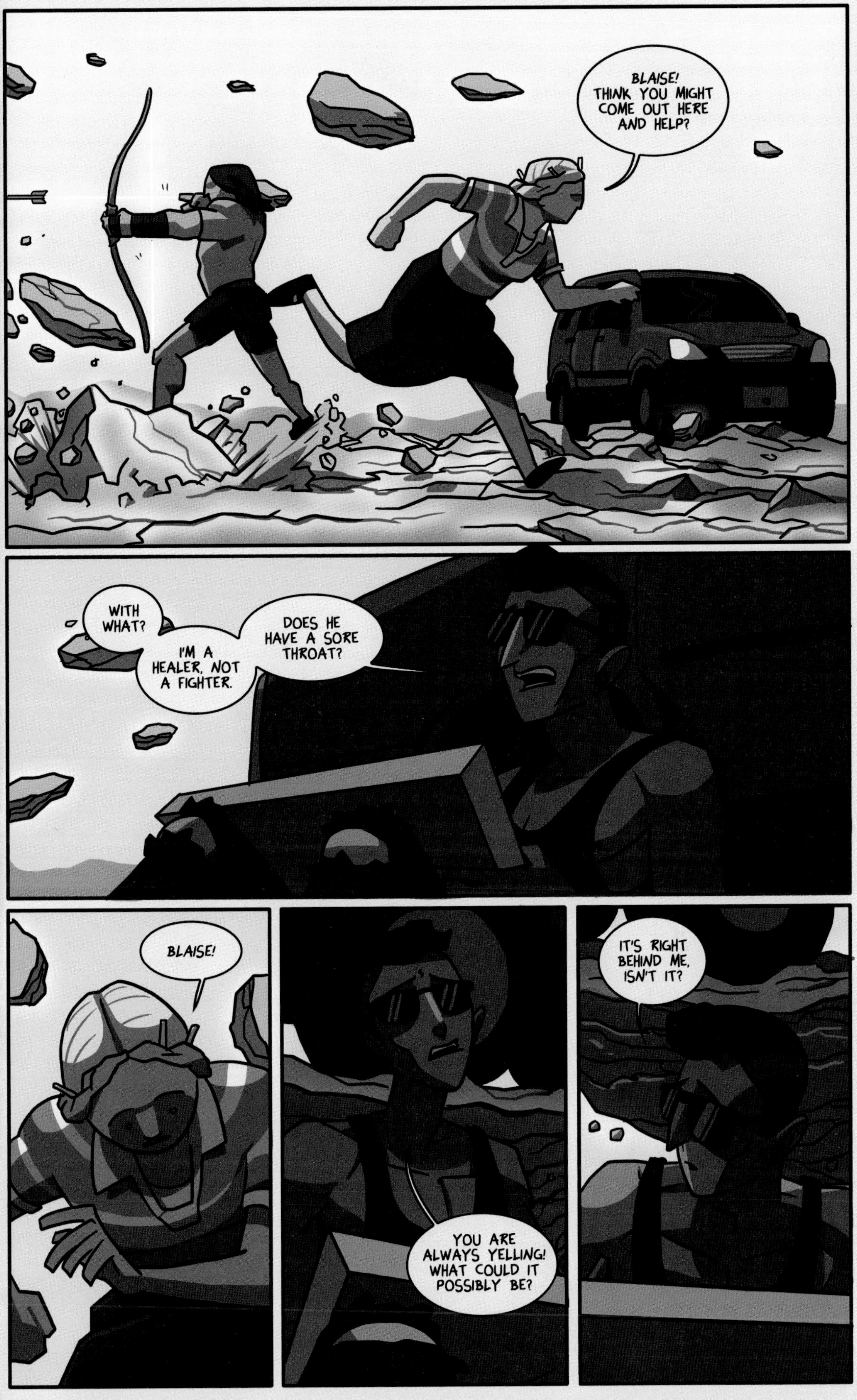
BLAISE! THINK YOU MIGHT COME OUT HERE AND HELP?
WITH WHAT?
I'M A HEALER, NOT A FIGHTER.
DOES HE HAVE A SORE THROAT?
BLAISE!
YOU ARE ALWAYS YELLING! WHAT COULD IT POSSIBLY BE?
IT'S RIGHT BEHIND ME, ISN'T IT?

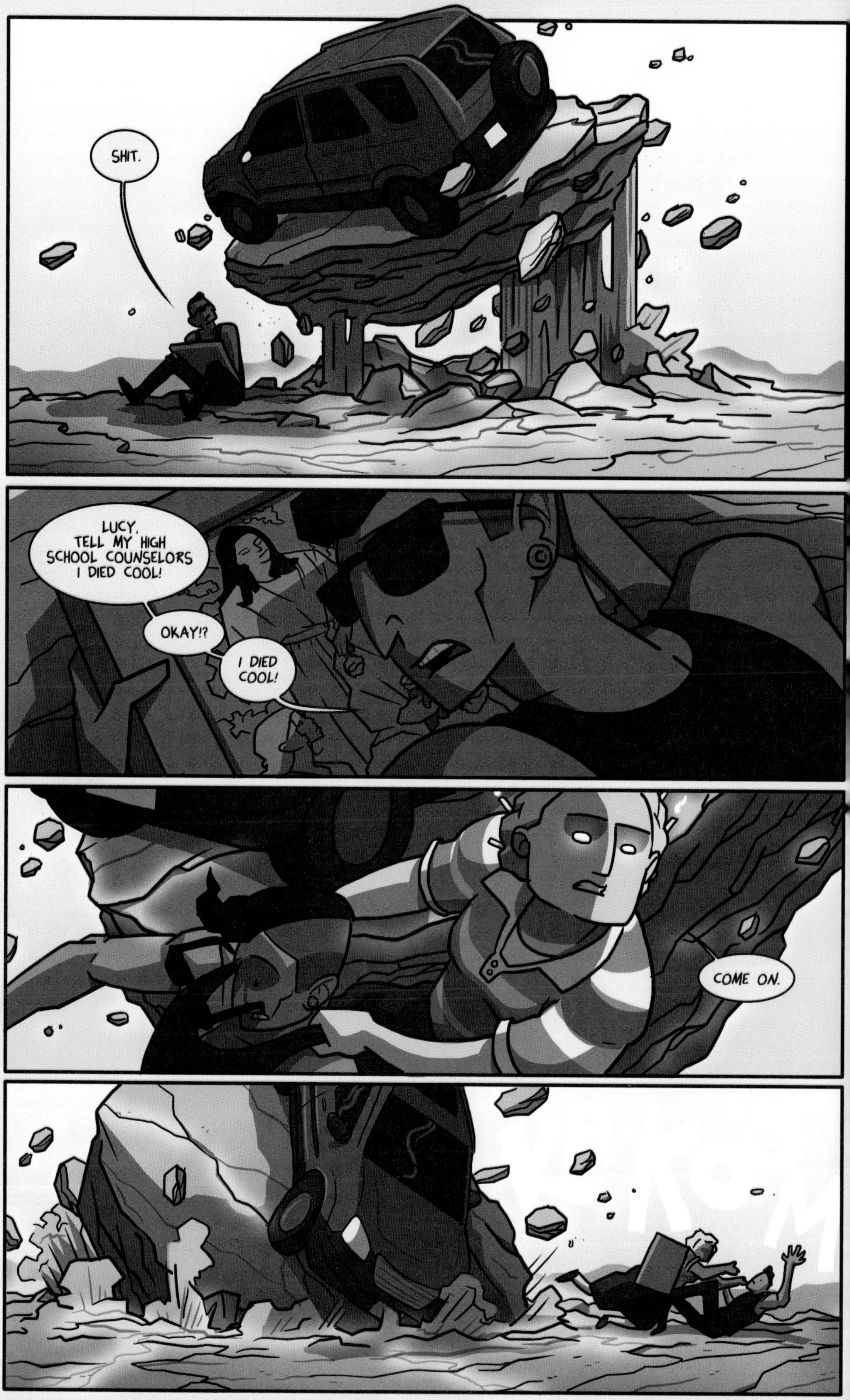
SHIT.
LUCY, TELL MY HIGH SCHOOL COUNSELORS I DIED COOL!
OKAY!?
I DIED COOL!
COME ON.

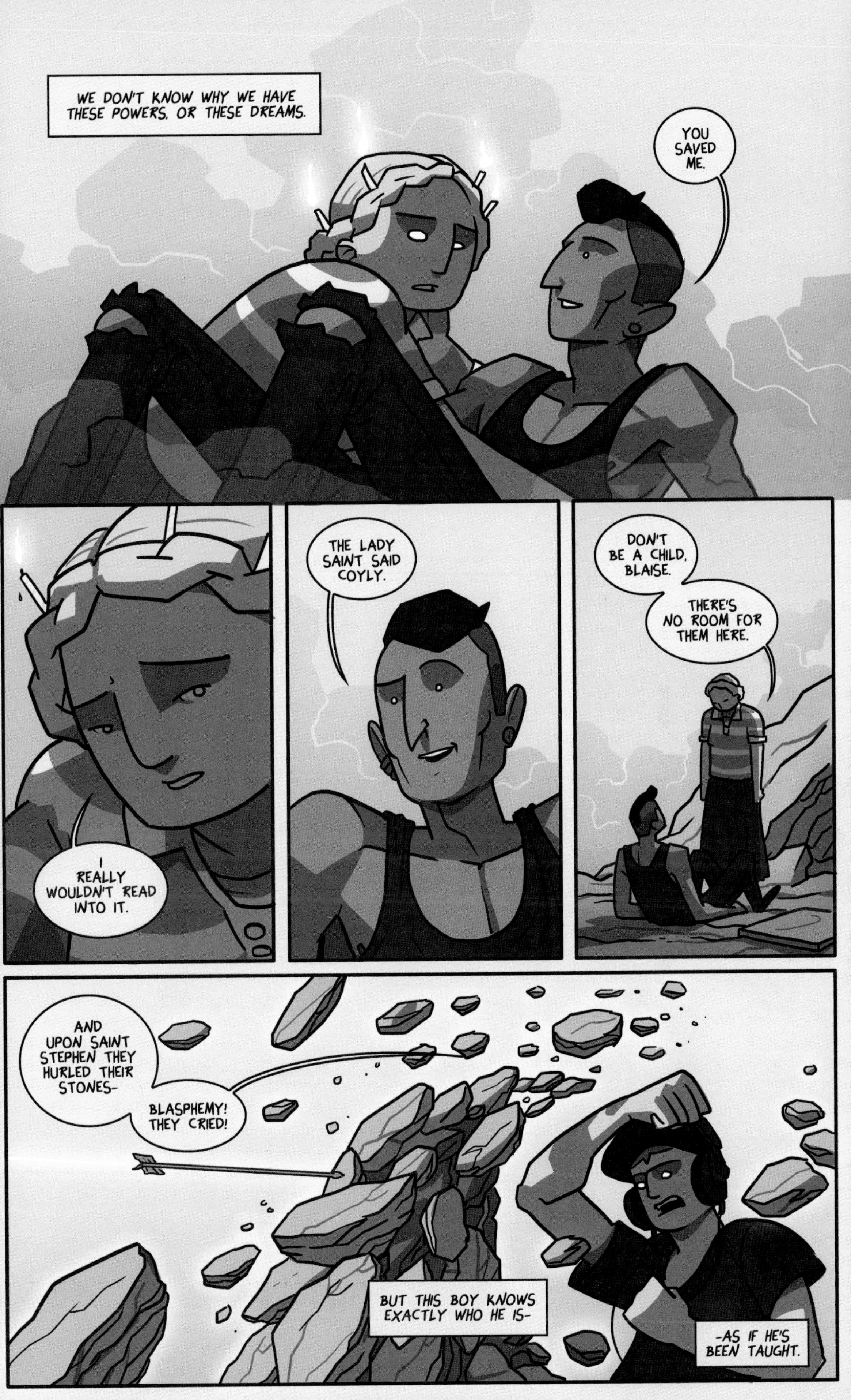
WE DON'T KNOW WHY WE HAVE THESE POWERS, OR THESE DREAMS.
YOU SAVED ME.
I REALLY WOULDN'T READ INTO IT.
THE LADY SAINT SAID COYLY.
DON'T BE A CHILD, BLAISE.
THERE'S NO ROOM FOR THEM HERE.
AND UPON SAINT STEPHEN THEY HURLED THEIR STONES-
BLASPHEMY! THEY CRIED!
BUT THIS BOY KNOWS EXACTLY WHO HE IS-
-AS IF HE'S BEEN TAUGHT.

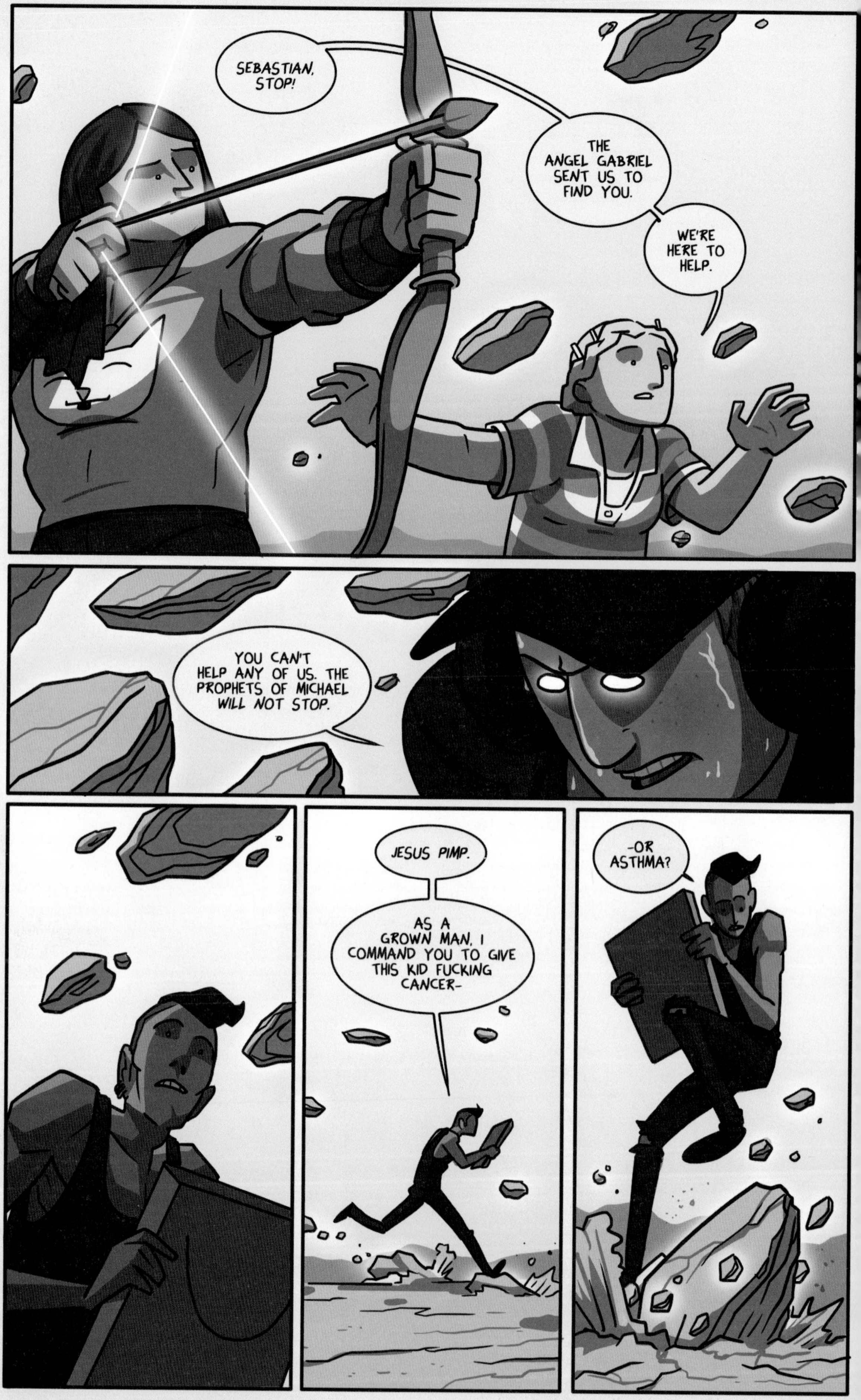
SEBASTIAN, STOP!
THE ANGEL GABRIEL SENT US TO FIND YOU.
WE'RE HERE TO HELP.
YOU CAN'T HELP ANY OF US. THE PROPHETS OF MICHAEL WILL NOT STOP.
JESUS PIMP.
AS A GROWN MAN, I COMMAND YOU TO GIVE THIS KID FUCKING CANCER-
-OR ASTHMA?

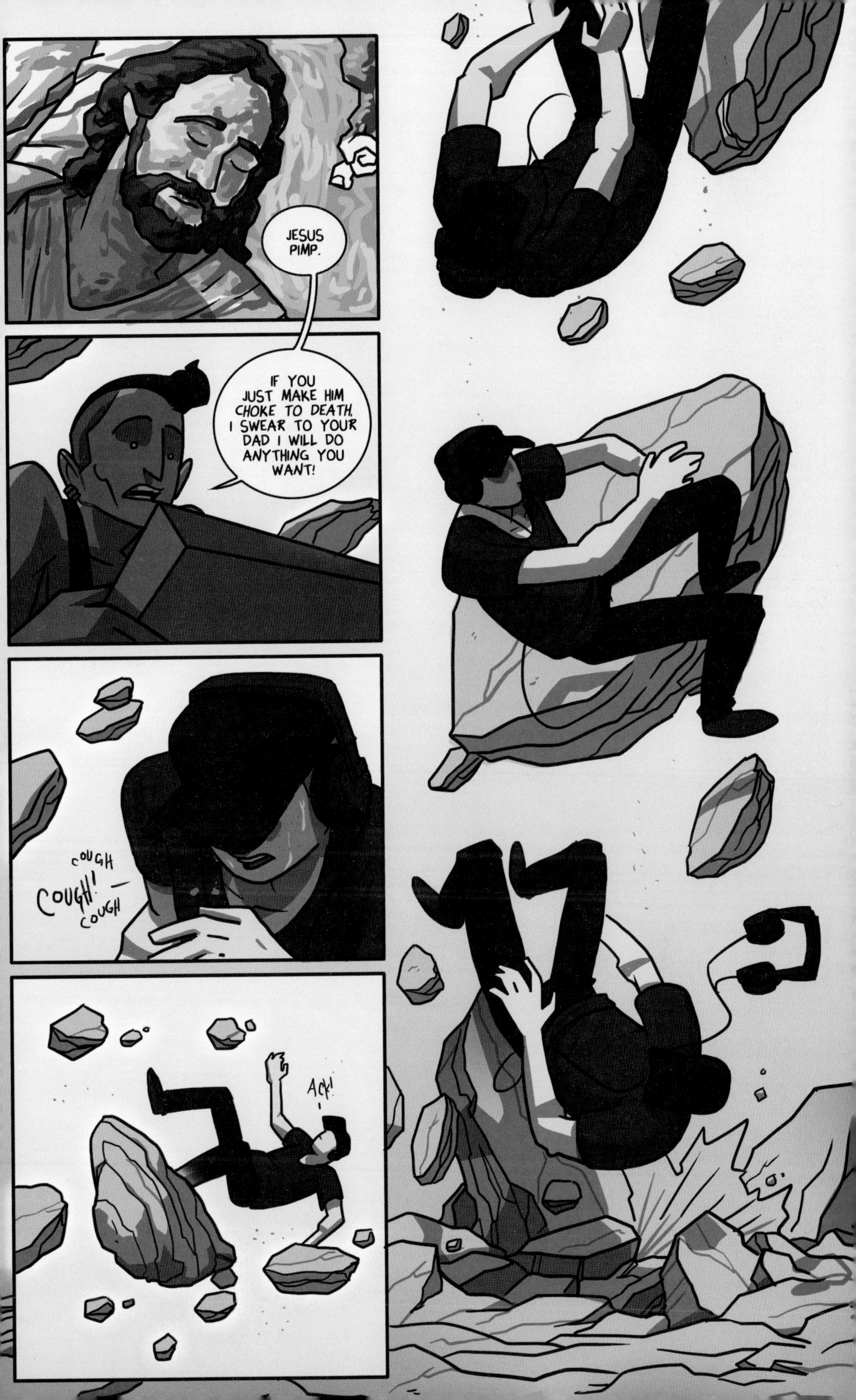
JESUS PIMP.
IF YOU JUST MAKE HIM CHOKE TO DEATH, I SWEAR TO YOUR DAD I WILL DO ANYTHING YOU WANT!
COUGH
COUGH!
COUGH
ACK!

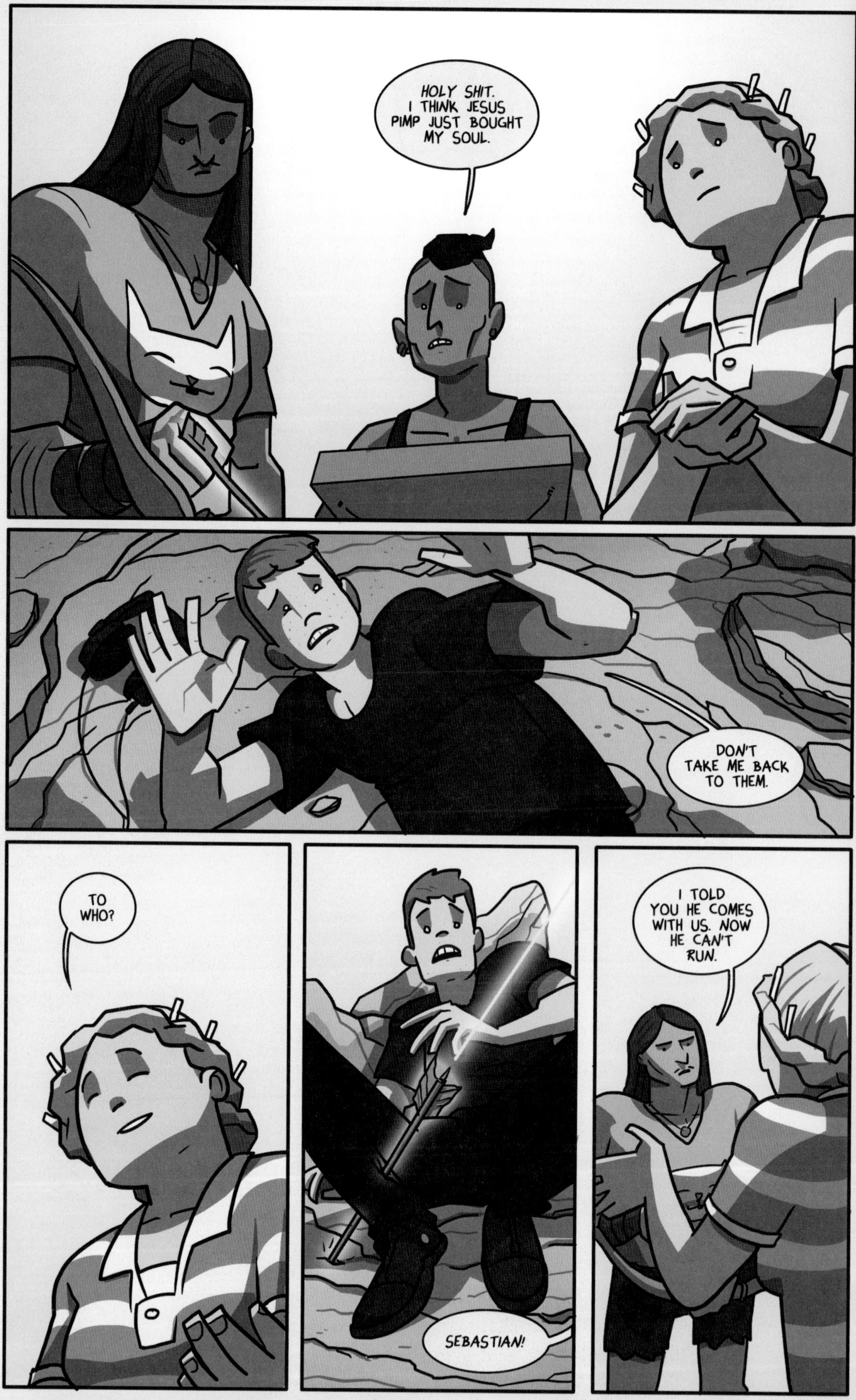
HOLY SHIT. I THINK JESUS PIMP JUST BOUGHT MY SOUL.
DON'T TAKE ME BACK TO THEM.
TO WHO?
SEBASTIAN!
I TOLD YOU HE COMES WITH US. NOW HE CAN'T RUN.

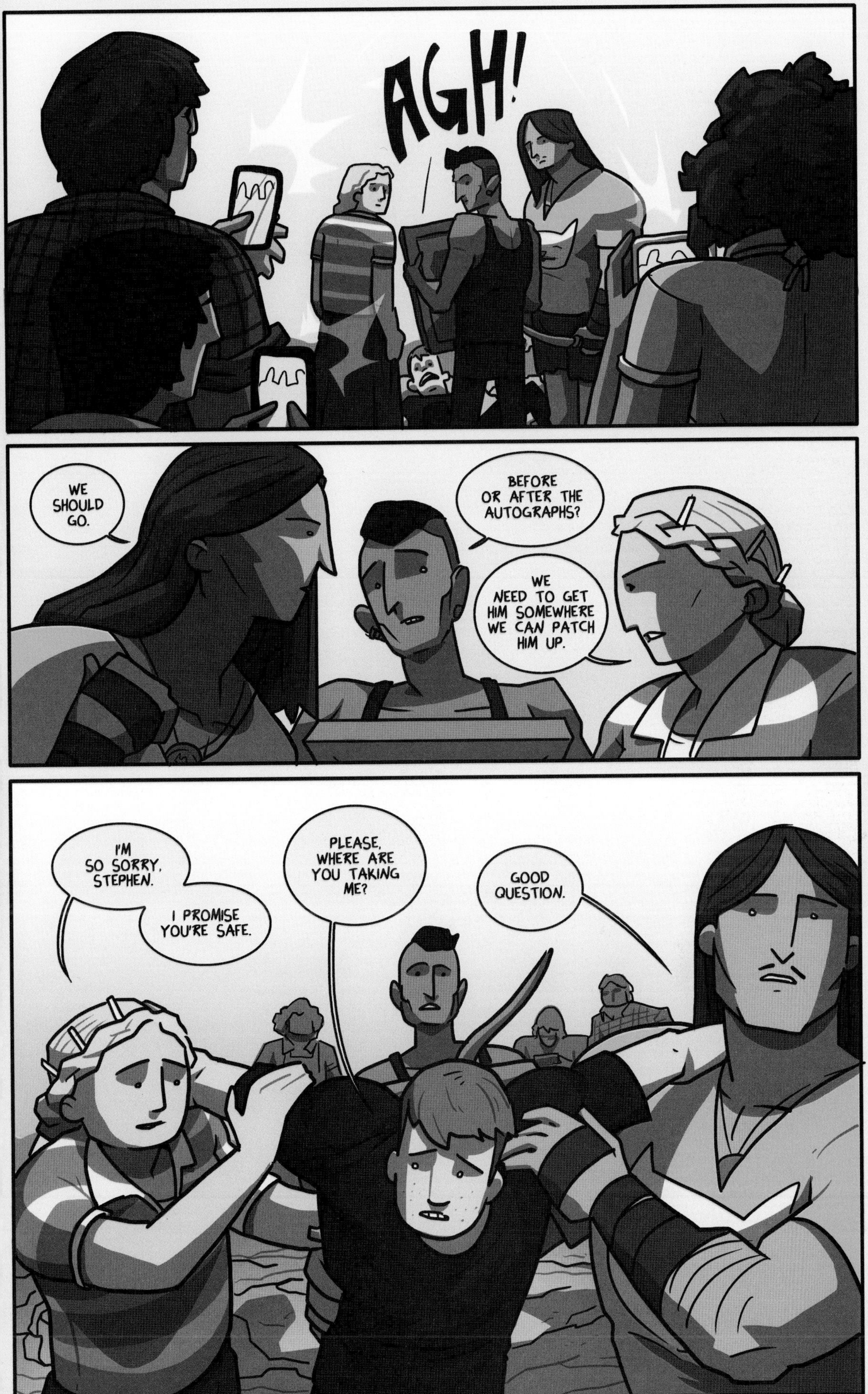
AGH!
WE SHOULD GO.
BEFORE OR AFTER THE AUTOGRAPHS?
WE NEED TO GET HIM SOMEWHERE WE CAN PATCH HIM UP.
I'M SO SORRY, STEPHEN.
I PROMISE YOU'RE SAFE.
PLEASE, WHERE ARE YOU TAKING ME?
GOOD QUESTION.

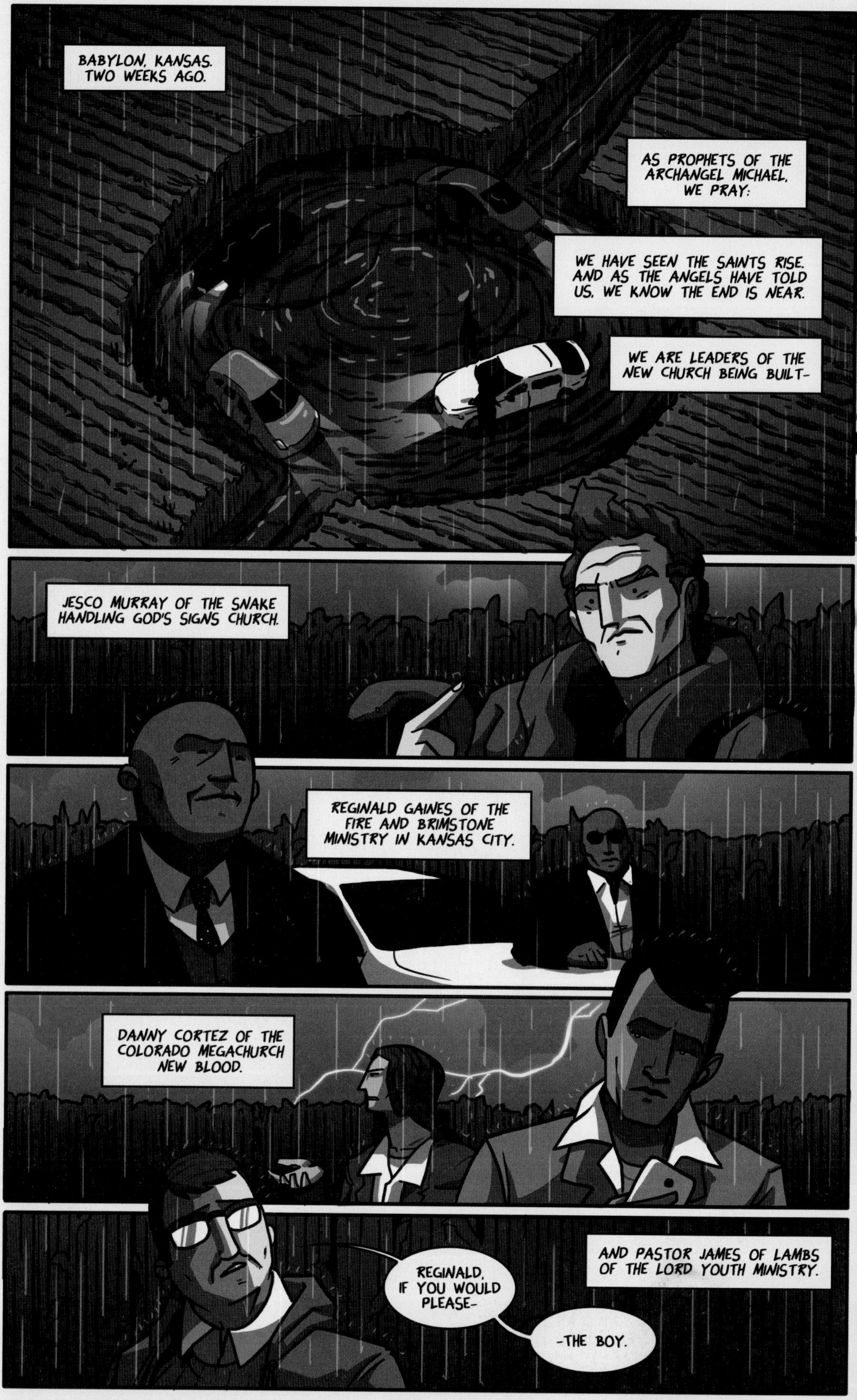
BABYLON, KANSAS. TWO WEEKS AGO.
AS PROPHETS OF THE ARCHANGEL MICHAEL, WE PRAY:
WE HAVE SEEN THE SAINTS RISE. AND AS THE ANGELS HAVE TOLD US, WE KNOW THE END IS NEAR.
WE ARE LEADERS OF THE NEW CHURCH BEING BUILT-
JESCO MURRAY OF THE SNAKE HANDLING GOD'S SIGNS CHURCH.
REGINALD GAINES OF THE FIRE AND BRIMSTONE MINISTRY IN KANSAS CITY.
DANNY CORTEZ OF THE COLORADO MEGACHURCH NEW BLOOD.
AND PASTOR JAMES OF LAMBS OF THE LORD YOUTH MINISTRY.
REGINALD, IF YOU WOULD PLEASE-
-THE BOY.

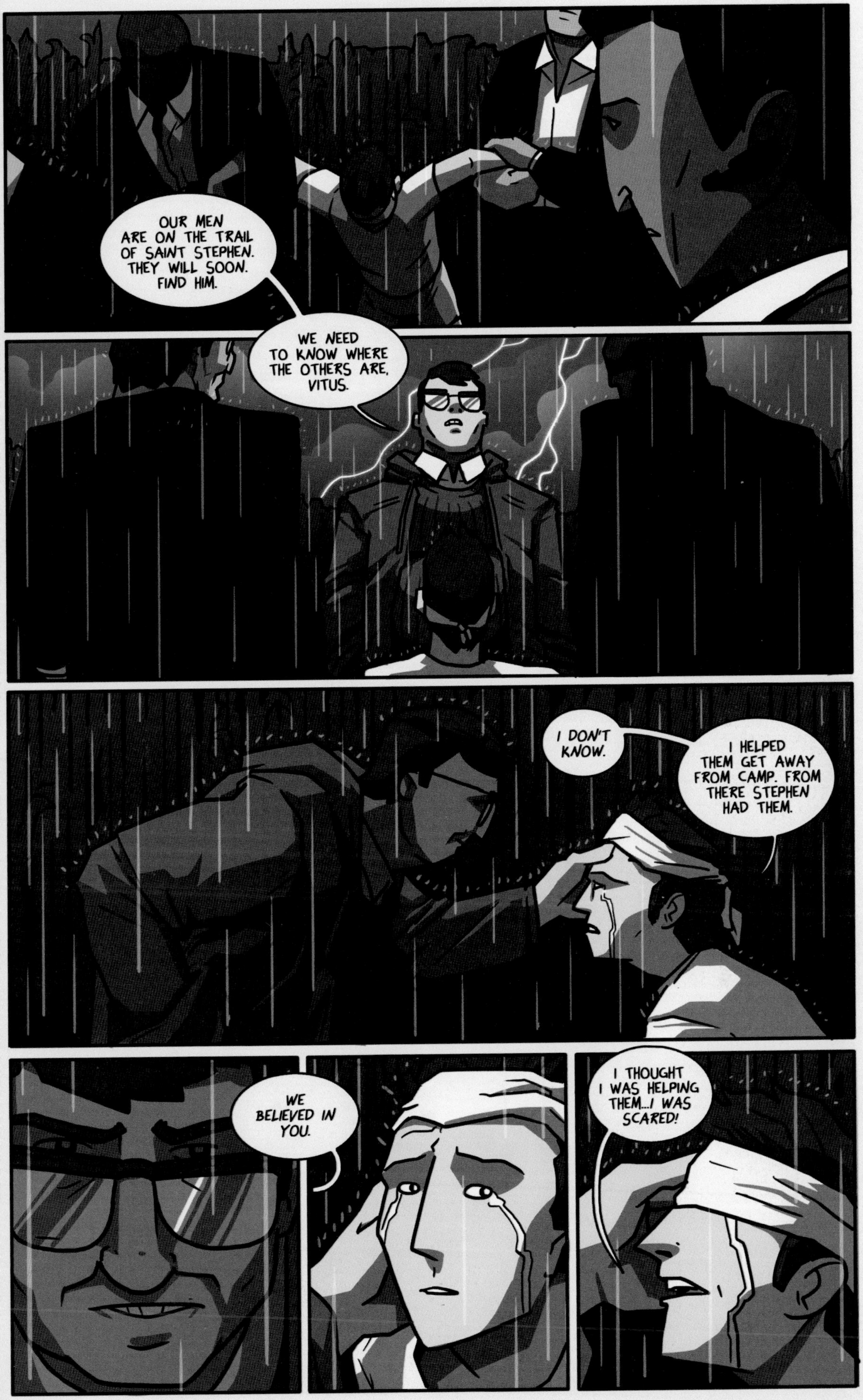
OUR MEN ARE ON THE TRAIL OF SAINT STEPHEN. THEY WILL SOON. FIND HIM.
WE NEED TO KNOW WHERE THE OTHERS ARE, VITUS.
I DON'T KNOW.
I HELPED THEM GET AWAY FROM CAMP. FROM THERE STEPHEN HAD THEM.
WE BELIEVED IN YOU.
I THOUGHT I WAS HELPING THEM...I WAS SCARED!

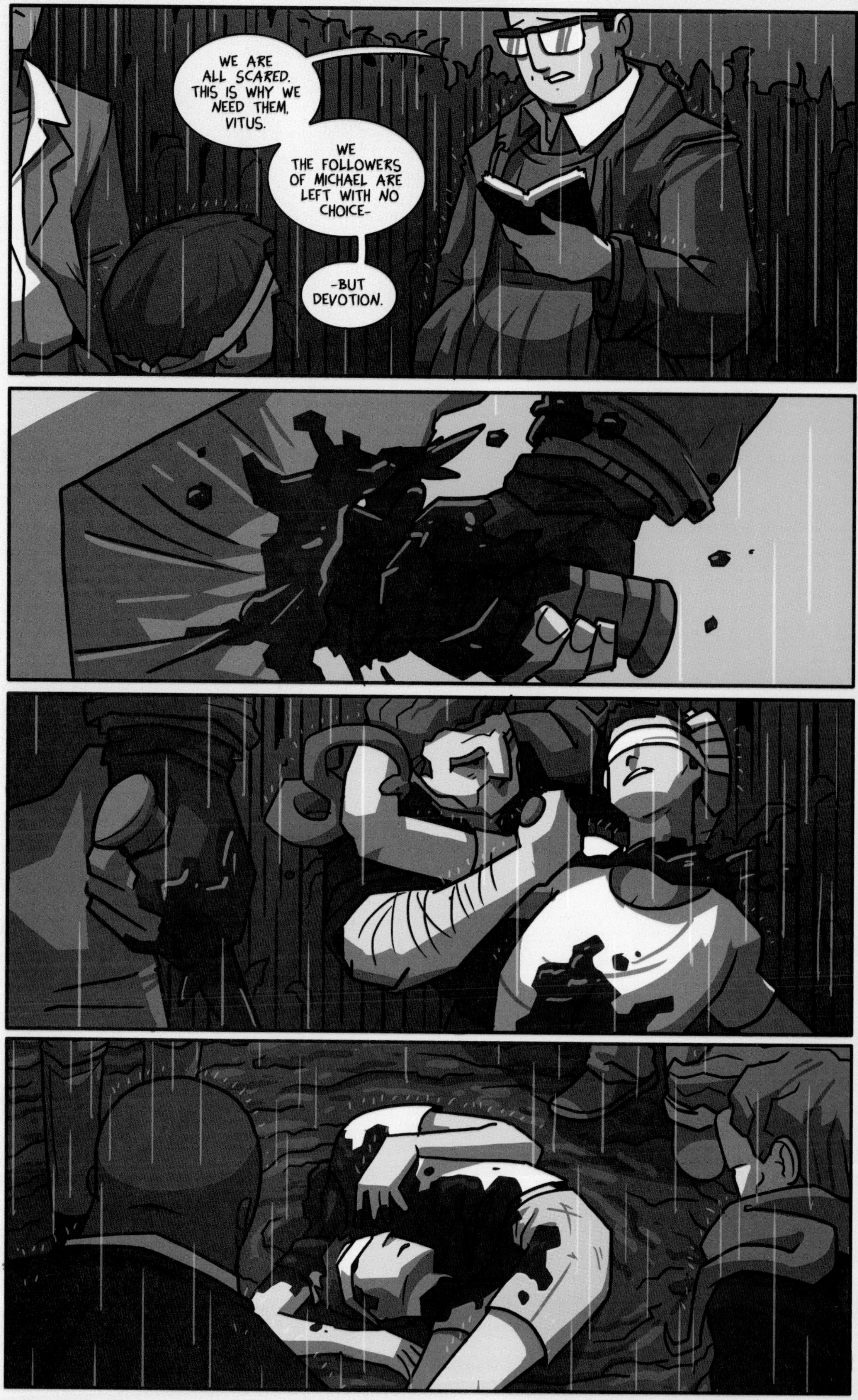
WE ARE ALL SCARED. THIS IS WHY WE NEED THEM, VITUS.
WE THE FOLLOWERS OF MICHAEL ARE LEFT WITH NO CHOICE-
-BUT DEVOTION.

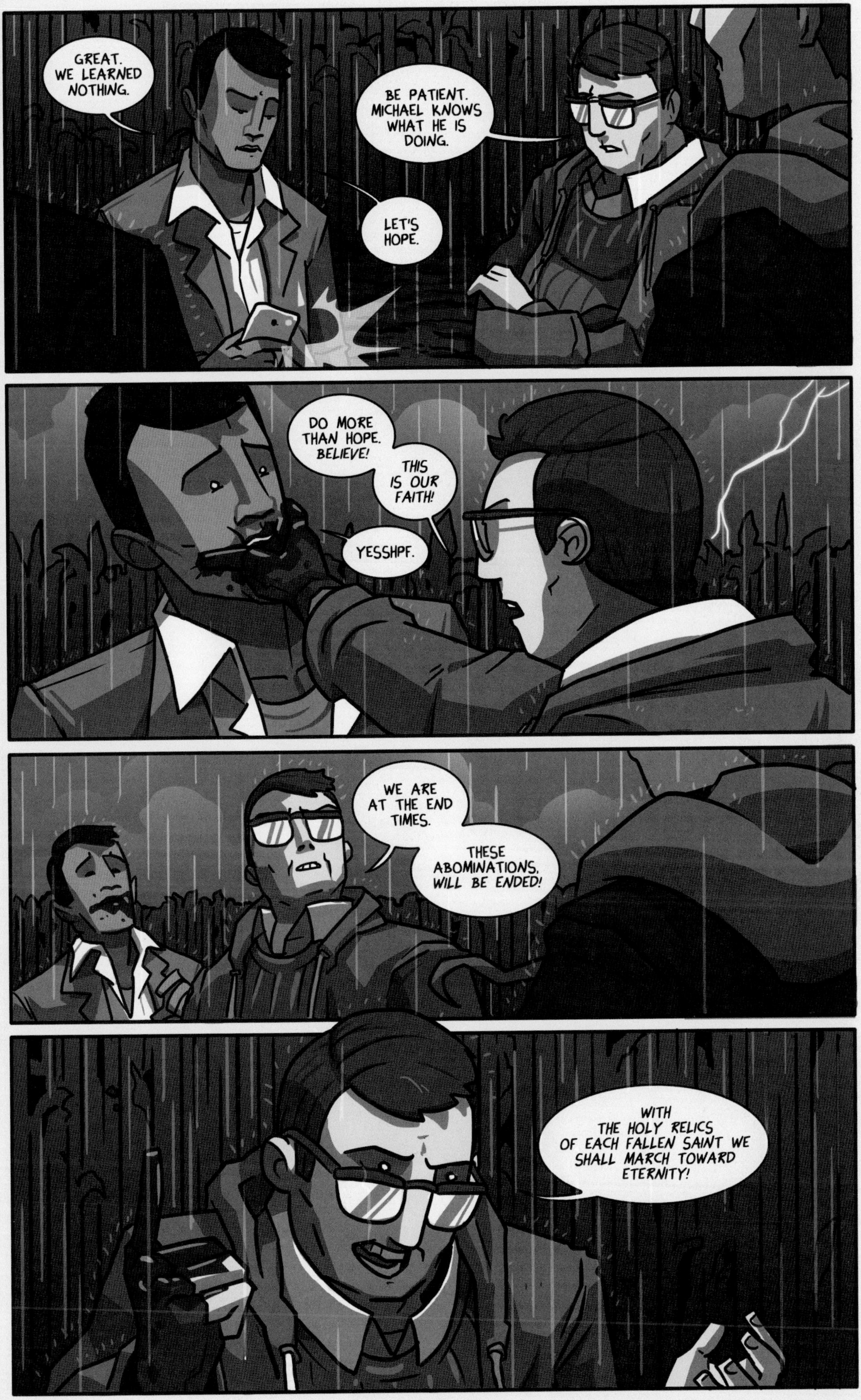
GREAT. WE LEARNED NOTHING.
BE PATIENT. MICHAEL KNOWS WHAT HE IS DOING.
LET'S HOPE.
DO MORE THAN HOPE. BELIEVE!
THIS IS OUR FAITH!
YESSHPF.
WE ARE AT THE END TIMES.
THESE ABOMINATIONS. WILL BE ENDED!
WITH THE HOLY RELICS OF EACH FALLEN SAINT WE SHALL MARCH TOWARD ETERNITY!

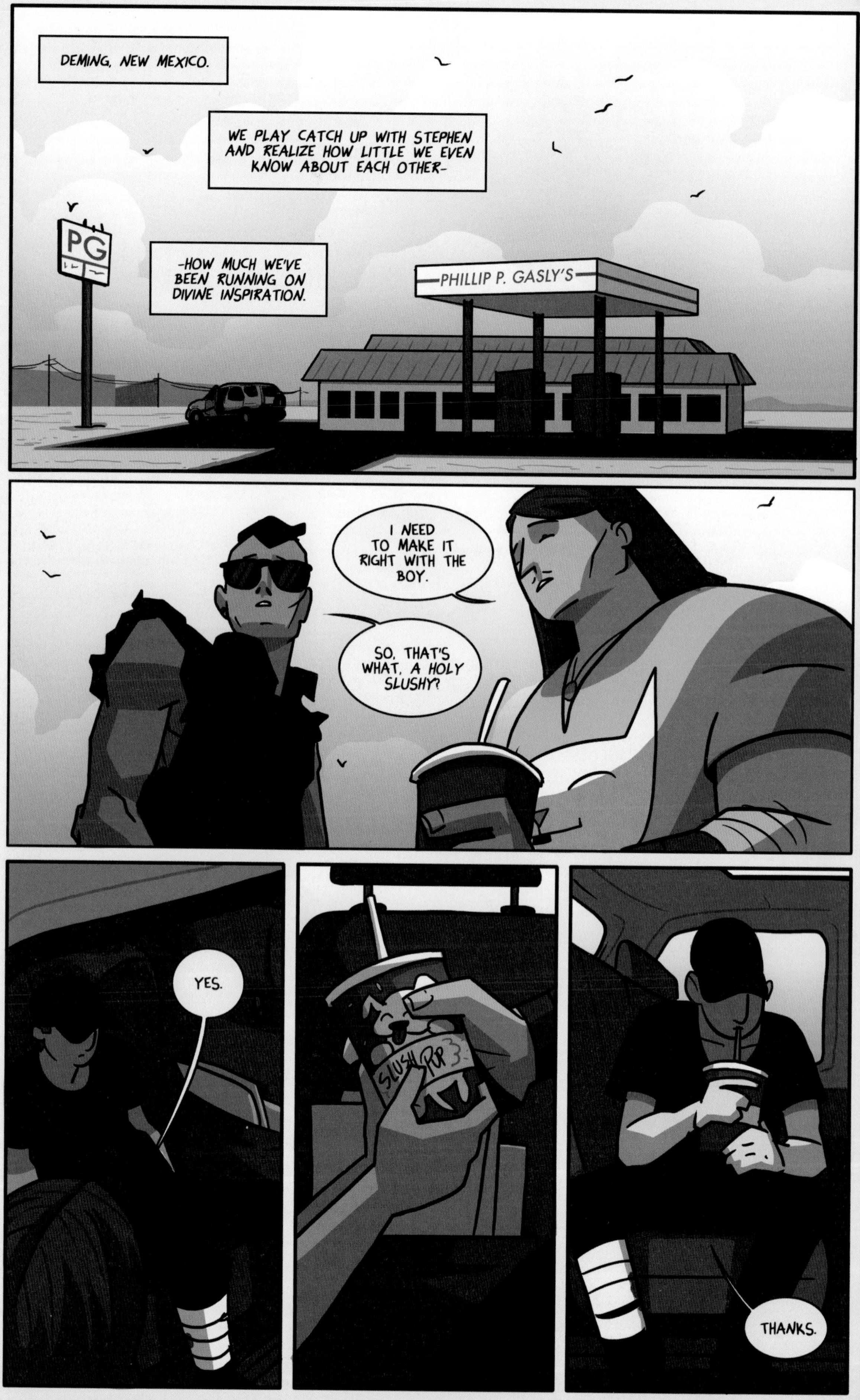
DEMING, NEW MEXICO.
WE PLAY CATCH UP WITH STEPHEN AND REALIZE HOW LITTLE WE EVEN KNOW ABOUT EACH OTHER-
PG
-HOW MUCH WE'VE BEEN RUNNING ON DIVINE INSPIRATION.
PHILLIP P. GASLY'S
I NEED TO MAKE IT RIGHT WITH THE BOY.
SO, THAT'S WHAT, A HOLY SLUSHY?
YES.
SLUSH POP
THANKS.

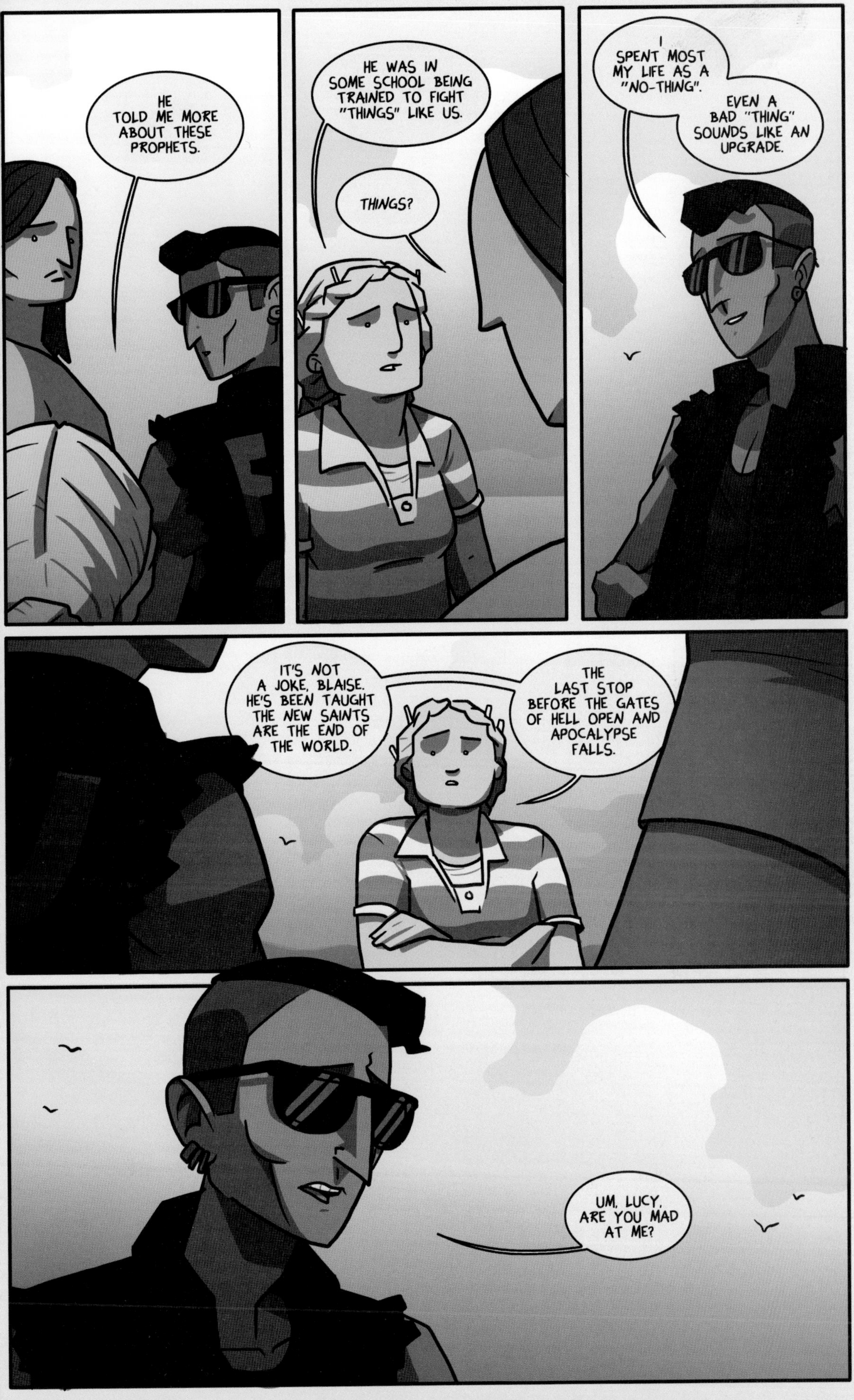
HE TOLD ME MORE ABOUT THESE PROPHETS.
HE WAS IN SOME SCHOOL BEING TRAINED TO FIGHT "THINGS" LIKE US.
THINGS?
I SPENT MOST MY LIFE AS A "NO-THING".
EVEN A BAD "THING" SOUNDS LIKE AN UPGRADE.
IT'S NOT A JOKE, BLAISE. HE'S BEEN TAUGHT THE NEW SAINTS ARE THE END OF THE WORLD.
THE LAST STOP BEFORE THE GATES OF HELL OPEN AND APOCALYPSE FALLS.
UM, LUCY, ARE YOU MAD AT ME?

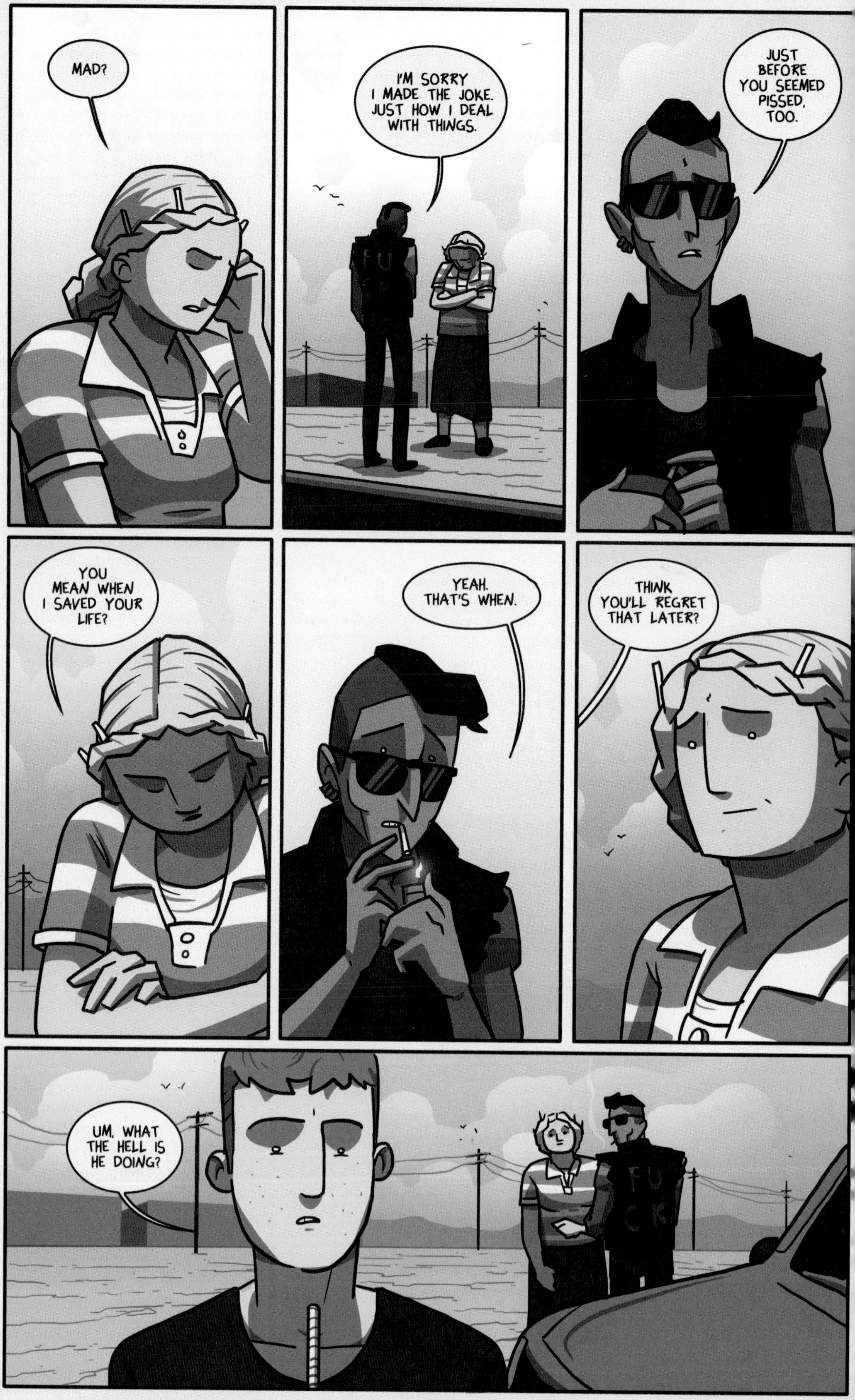
MAD?
I'M SORRY I MADE THE JOKE. JUST HOW I DEAL WITH THINGS.
JUST BEFORE YOU SEEMED PISSED, TOO.
YOU MEAN WHEN I SAVED YOUR LIFE?
YEAH. THAT'S WHEN.
THINK YOU'LL REGRET THAT LATER?
UM, WHAT THE HELL IS HE DOING?
FU
FU CK

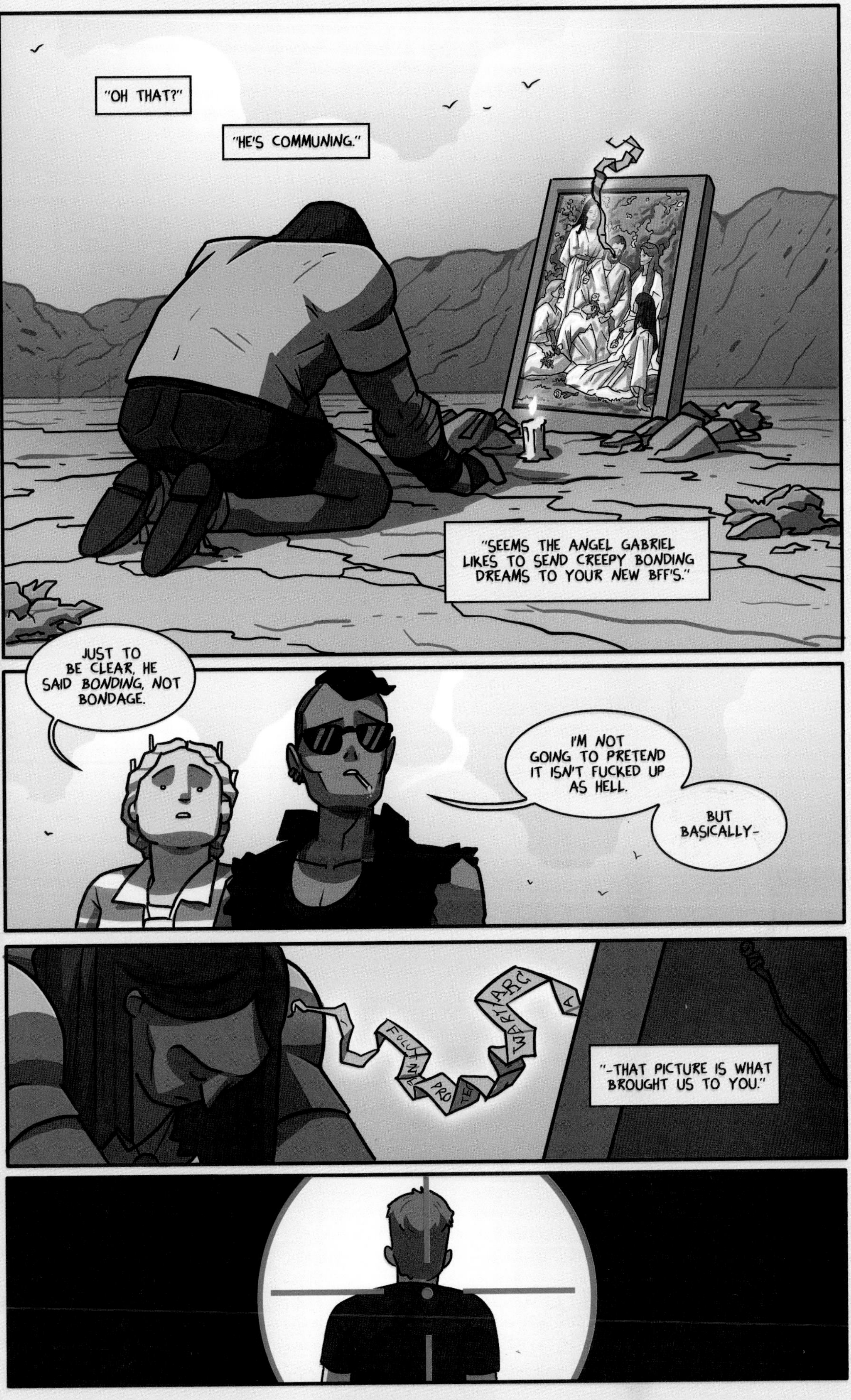
"OH THAT?"
"HE'S COMMUNING."
"SEEMS THE ANGEL GABRIEL LIKES TO SEND CREEPY BONDING DREAMS TO YOUR NEW BFF'S."
JUST TO BE CLEAR, HE SAID BONDING, NOT BONDAGE.
I'M NOT GOING TO PRETEND IT ISN'T FUCKED UP AS HELL.
BUT BASICALLY-
"-THAT PICTURE IS WHAT BROUGHT US TO YOU."

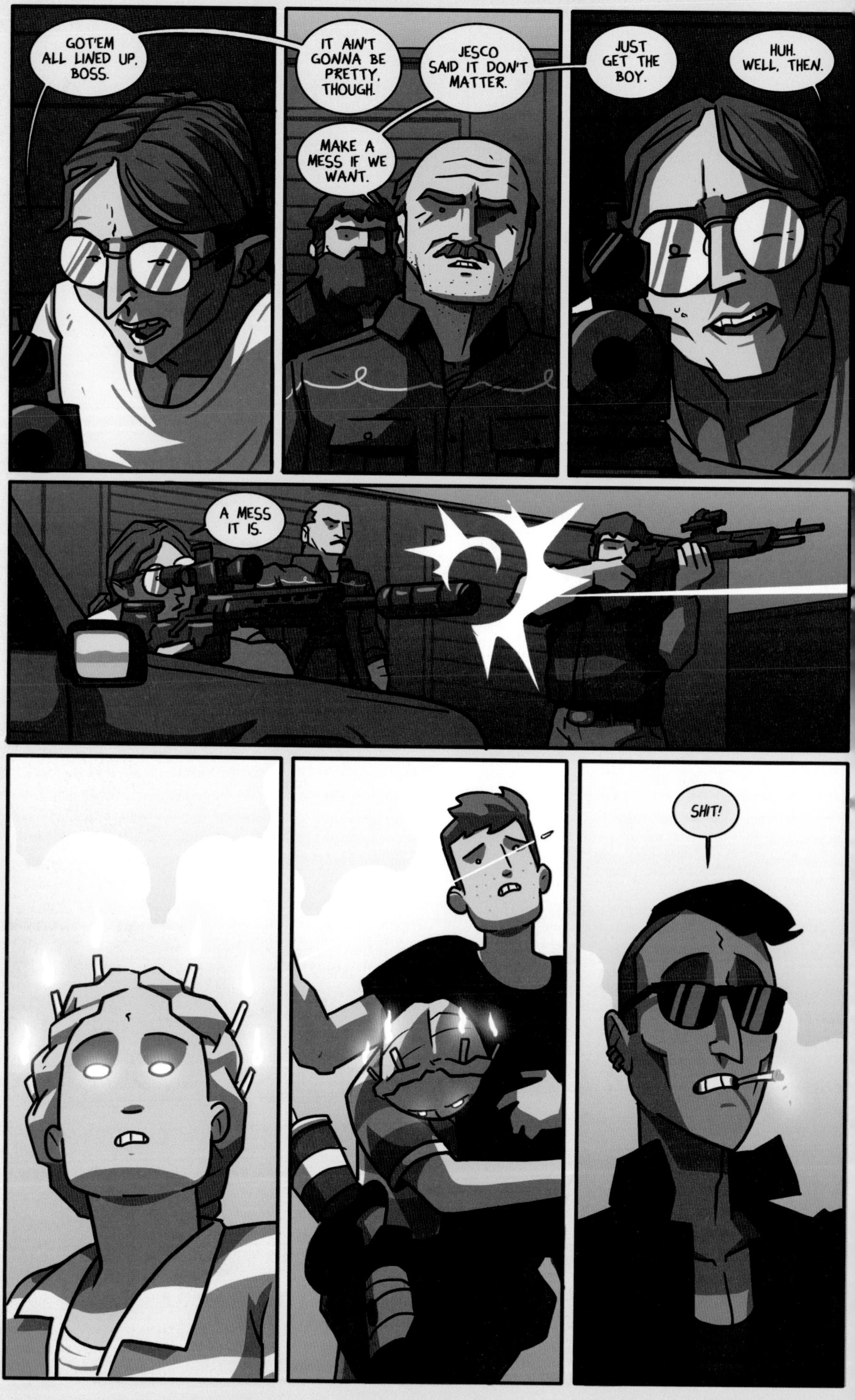
GOT'EM ALL LINED UP, BOSS.
IT AIN'T GONNA BE PRETTY, THOUGH.
JESCO SAID IT DON'T MATTER.
MAKE A MESS IF WE WANT.
JUST GET THE BOY.
HUH. WELL, THEN.
A MESS IT IS.
SHIT!

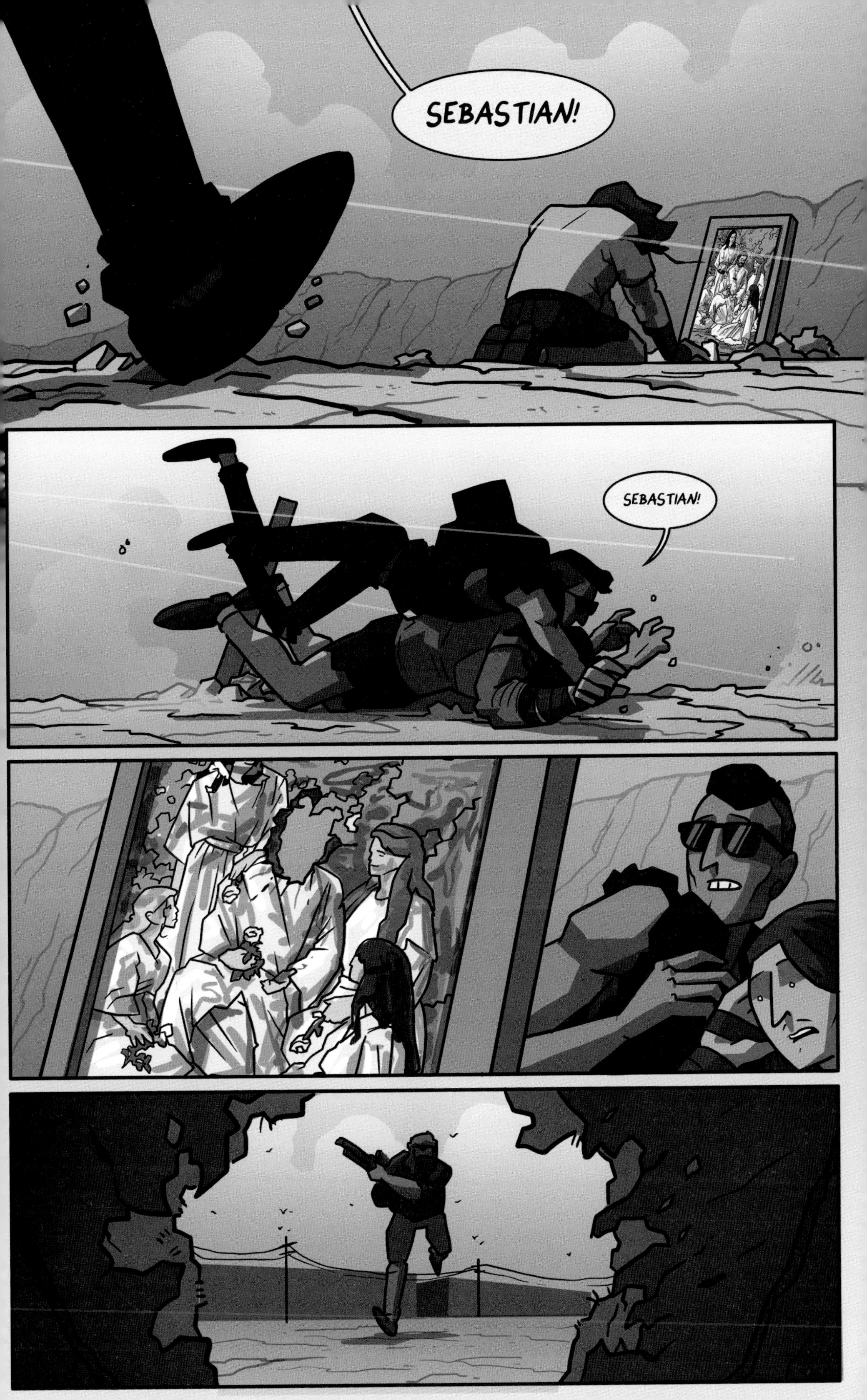
SEBASTIAN!
SEBASTIAN!

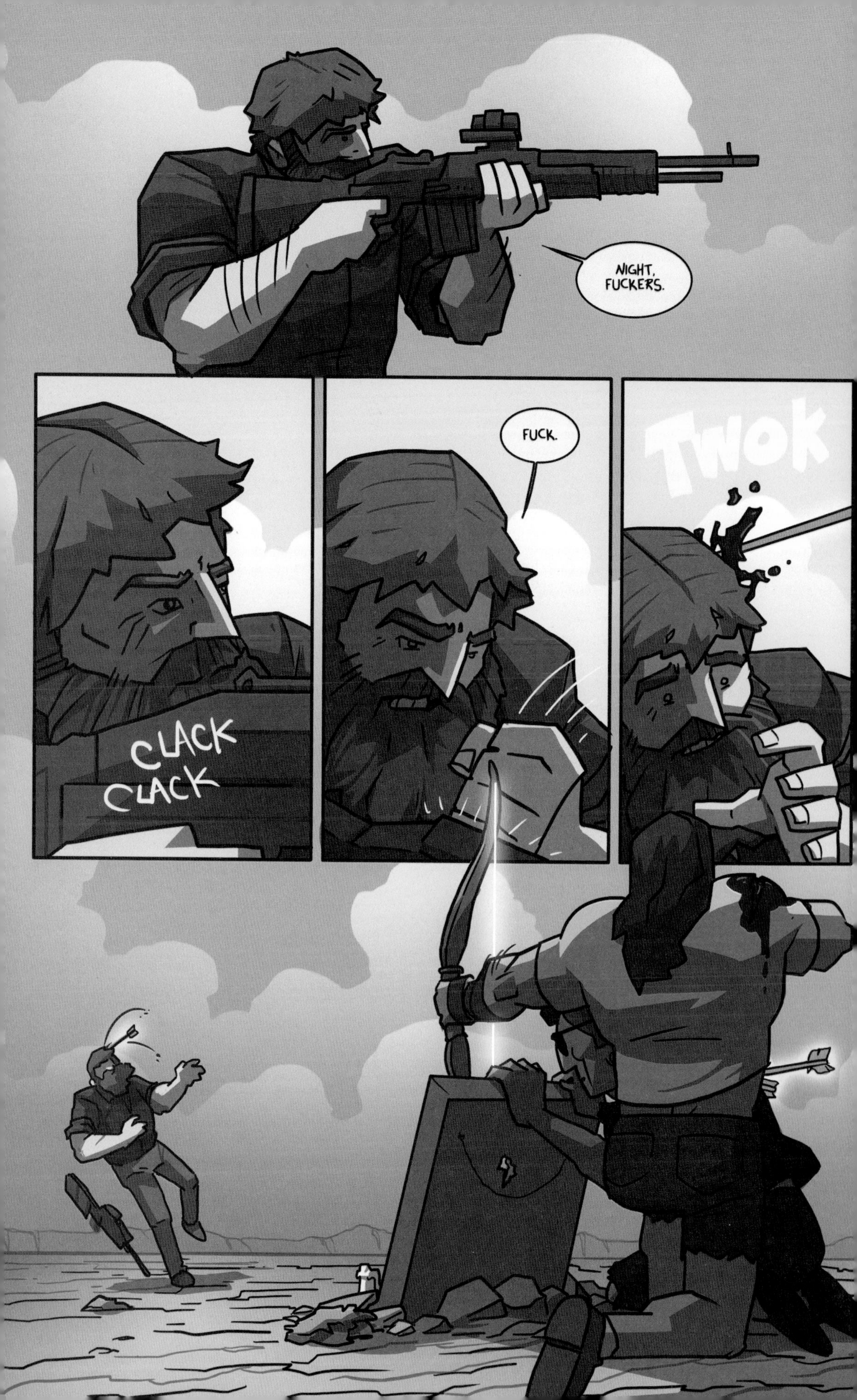
NIGHT, FUCKERS.
CLACK
CLACK
FUCK.
TWOK

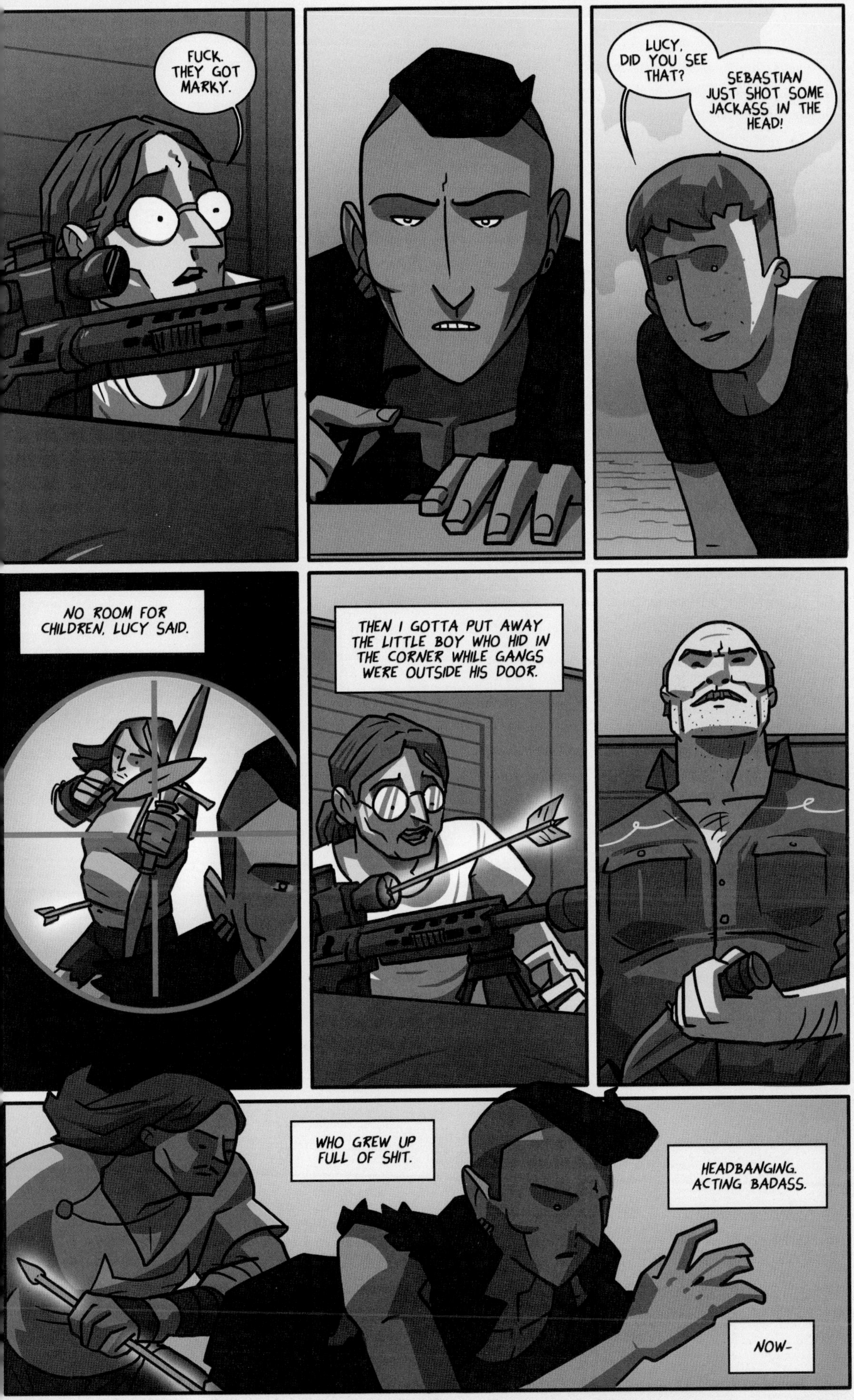
FUCK. THEY GOT MARKY.
LUCY, DID YOU SEE THAT?
SEBASTIAN JUST SHOT SOME JACKASS IN THE HEAD!
NO ROOM FOR CHILDREN, LUCY SAID.
THEN I GOTTA PUT AWAY THE LITTLE BOY WHO HID IN THE CORNER WHILE GANGS WERE OUTSIDE HIS DOOR.
WHO GREW UP FULL OF SHIT.
HEADBANGING. ACTING BADASS.
NOW-

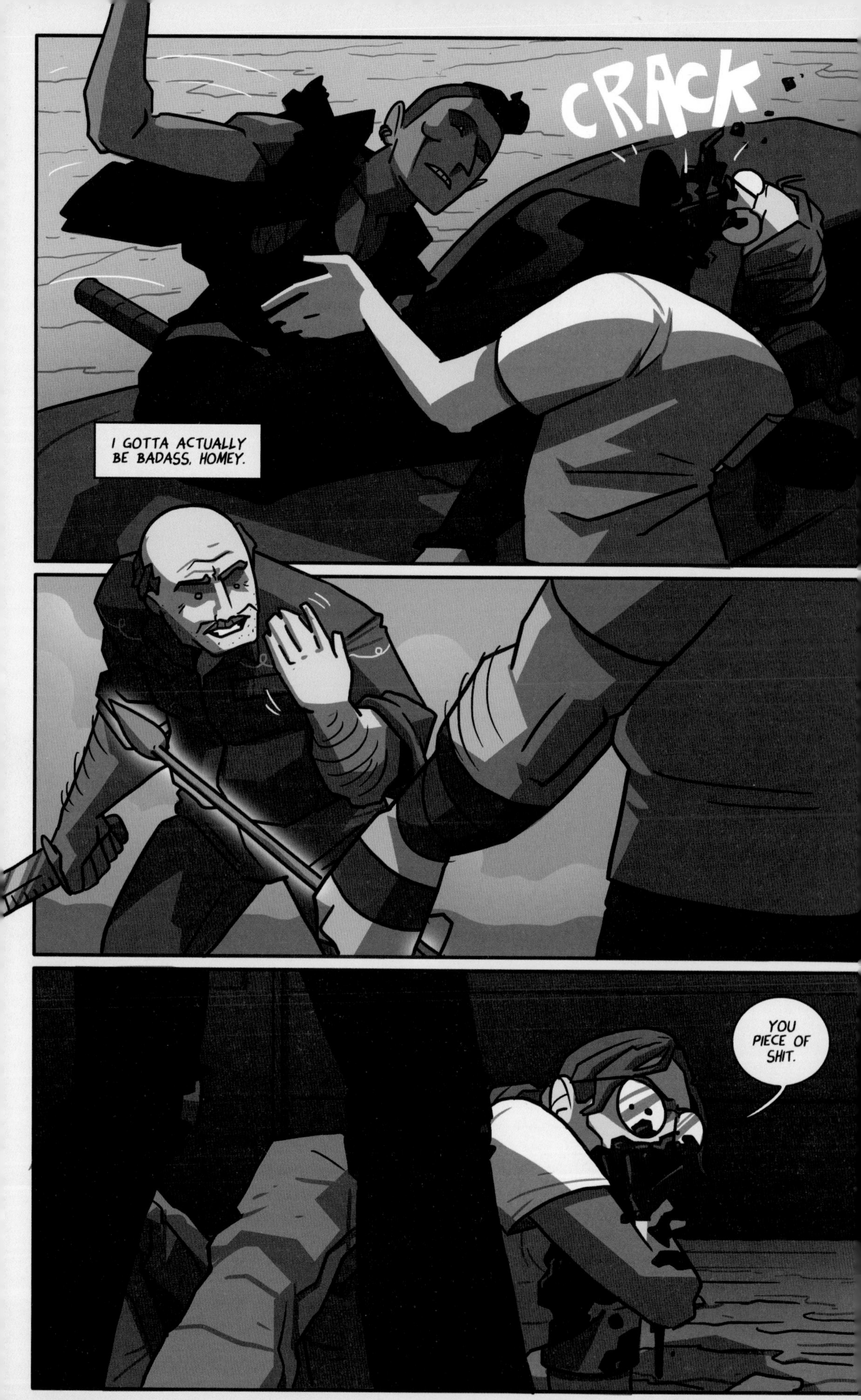
CRACK
I GOTTA ACTUALLY BE BADASS, HOMEY.
YOU PIECE OF SHIT.

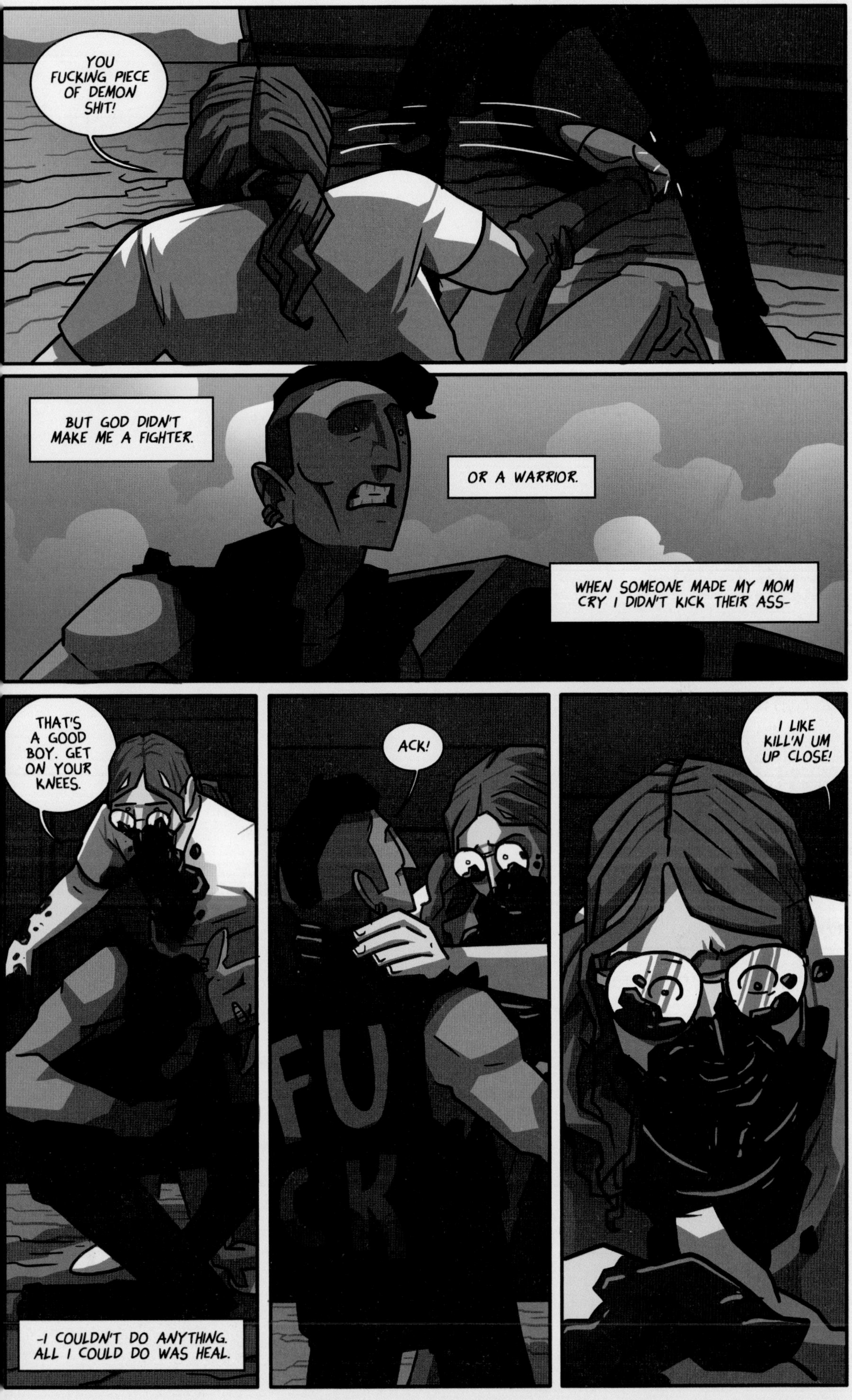
YOU FUCKING PIECE OF DEMON SHIT!
BUT GOD DIDN'T MAKE ME A FIGHTER.
OR A WARRIOR.
WHEN SOMEONE MADE MY MOM CRY I DIDN'T KICK THEIR ASS-
THAT'S A GOOD BOY. GET ON YOUR KNEES.
-I COULDN'T DO ANYTHING. ALL I COULD DO WAS HEAL.
ACK!
FU CK
I LIKE KILL'N UM UP CLOSE!

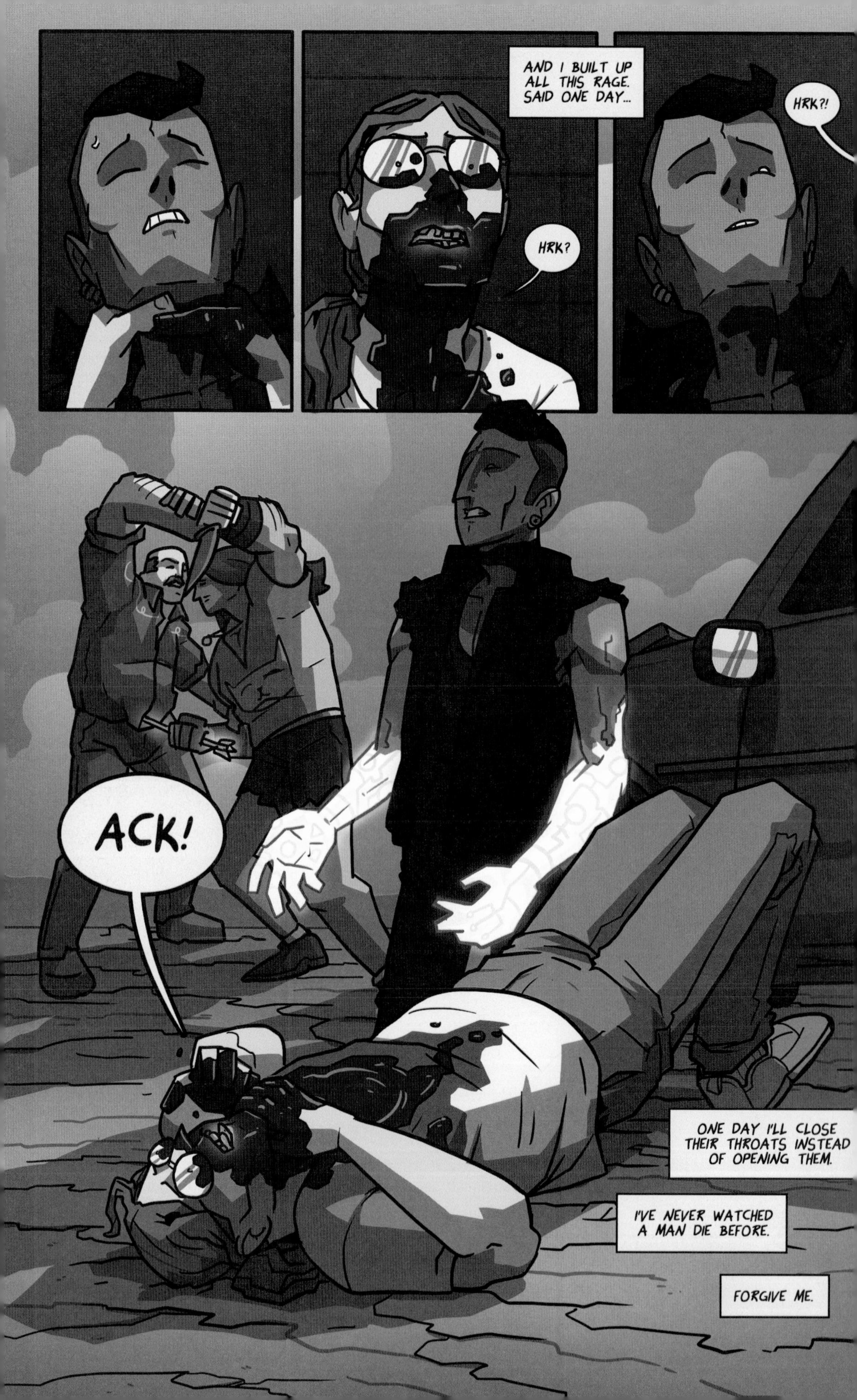
AND I BUILT UP ALL THIS RAGE. SAID ONE DAY...
HRK?
HRK?!
ACK!
ONE DAY I'LL CLOSE THEIR THROATS INSTEAD OF OPENING THEM.
I'VE NEVER WATCHED A MAN DIE BEFORE.
FORGIVE ME.

IV
SUMMONING

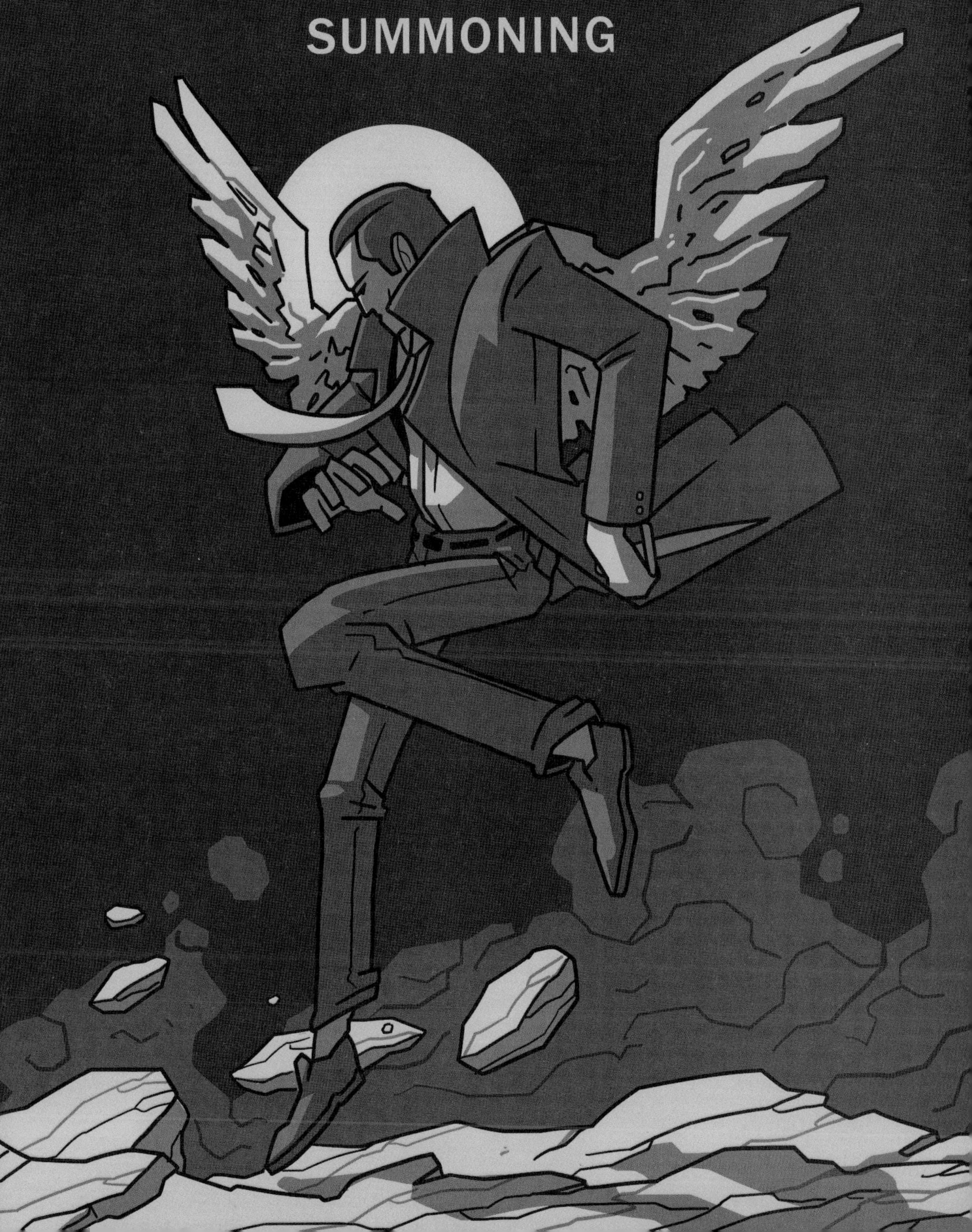

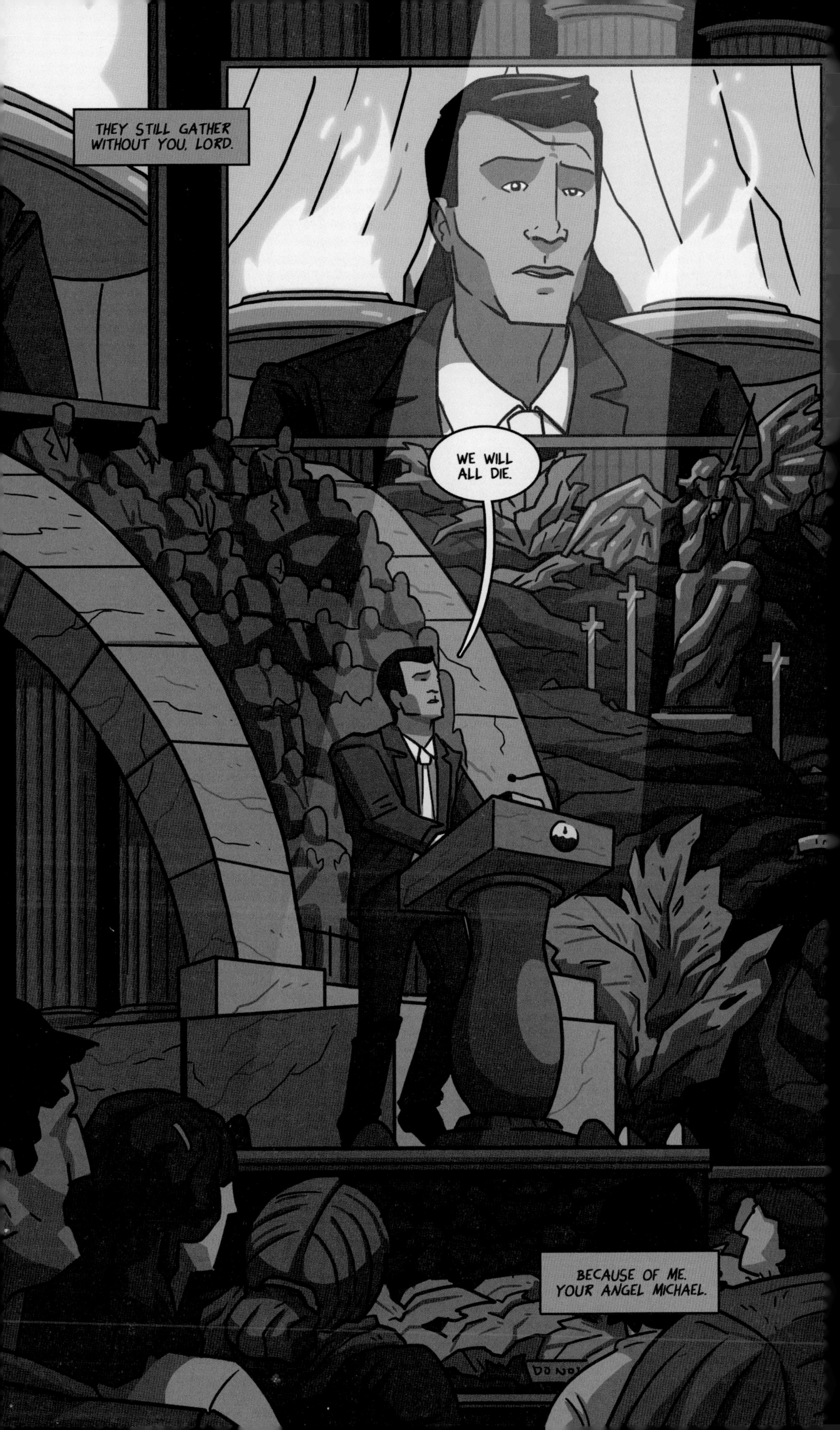
THEY STILL GATHER WITHOUT YOU, LORD.
WE WILL ALL DIE.
BECAUSE OF ME. YOUR ANGEL MICHAEL.

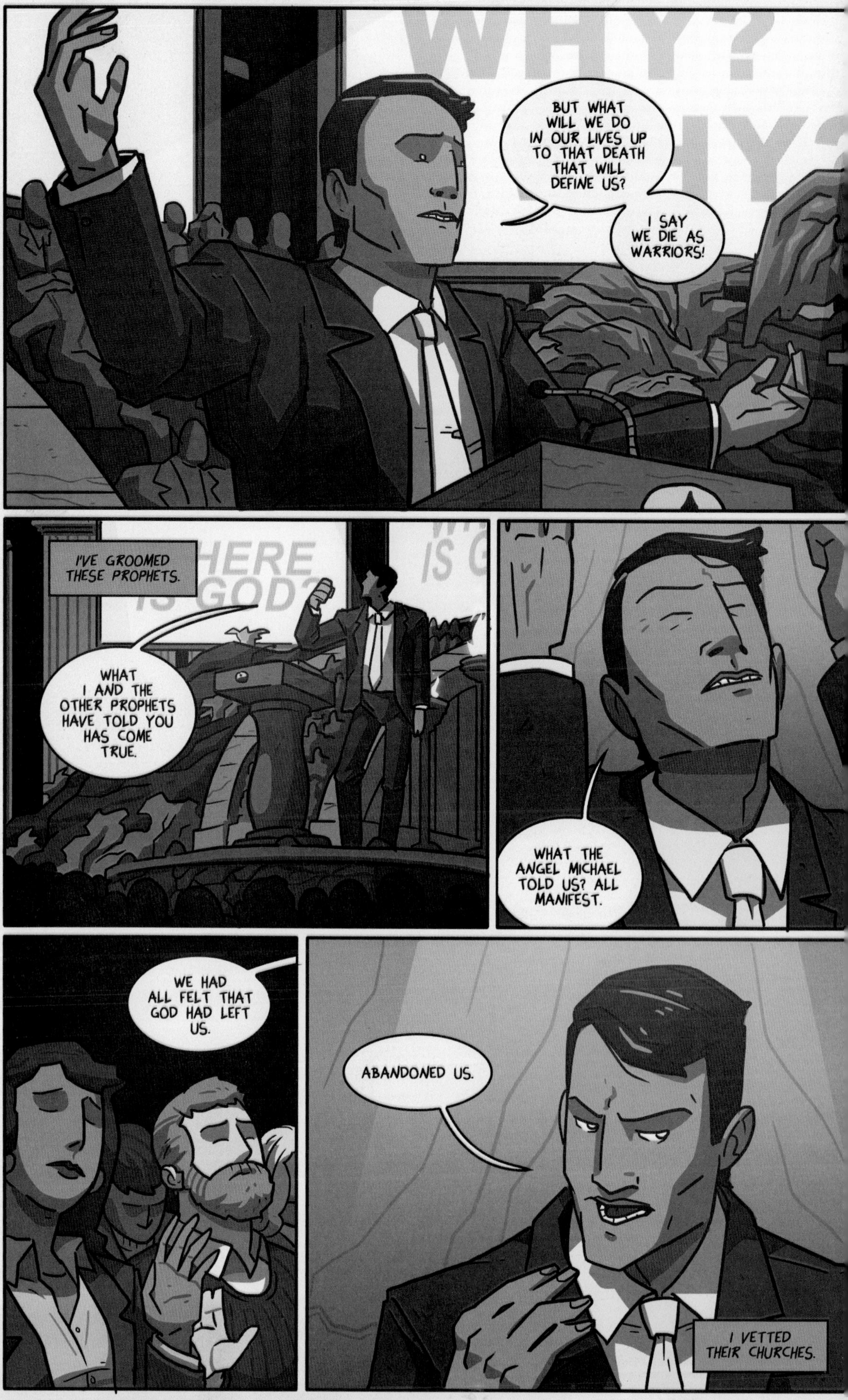
WHY?
BUT WHAT WILL WE DO IN OUR LIVES UP TO THAT DEATH THAT WILL DEFINE US?
I SAY WE DIE AS WARRIORS!
I'VE GROOMED THESE PROPHETS.
WHAT I AND THE OTHER PROPHETS HAVE TOLD YOU HAS COME TRUE.
WHAT THE ANGEL MICHAEL TOLD US? ALL MANIFEST.
WE HAD ALL FELT THAT GOD HAD LEFT US.
ABANDONED US.
I VETTED THEIR CHURCHES.

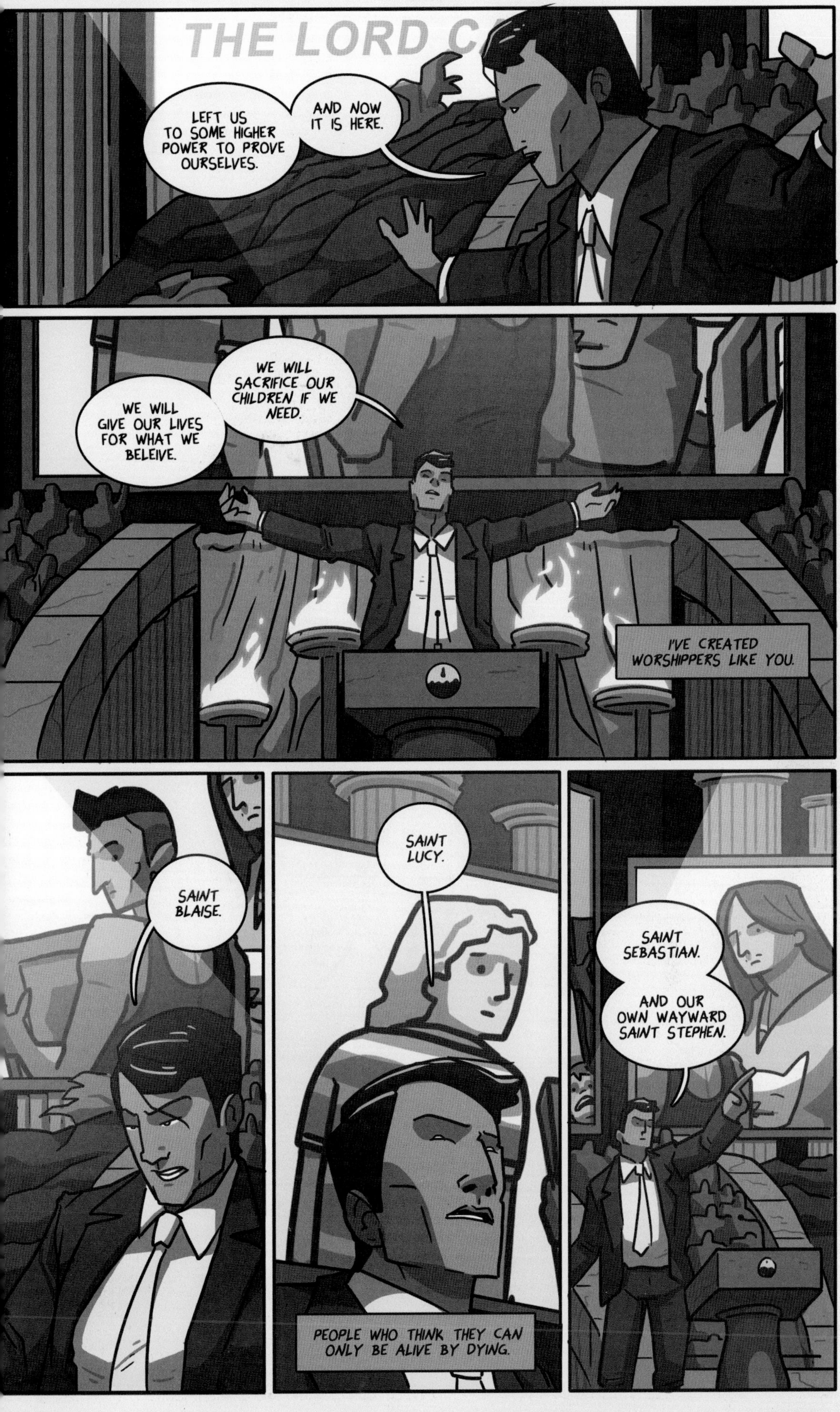
THE LORD C
LEFT US TO SOME HIGHER POWER TO PROVE OURSELVES.
AND NOW IT IS HERE.
WE WILL GIVE OUR LIVES FOR WHAT WE BELEIVE.
WE WILL SACRIFICE OUR CHILDREN IF WE NEED.
I'VE CREATED WORSHIPPERS LIKE YOU.
SAINT BLAISE.
SAINT LUCY.
PEOPLE WHO THINK THEY CAN ONLY BE ALIVE BY DYING.
SAINT SEBASTIAN.
AND OUR OWN WAYWARD SAINT STEPHEN.

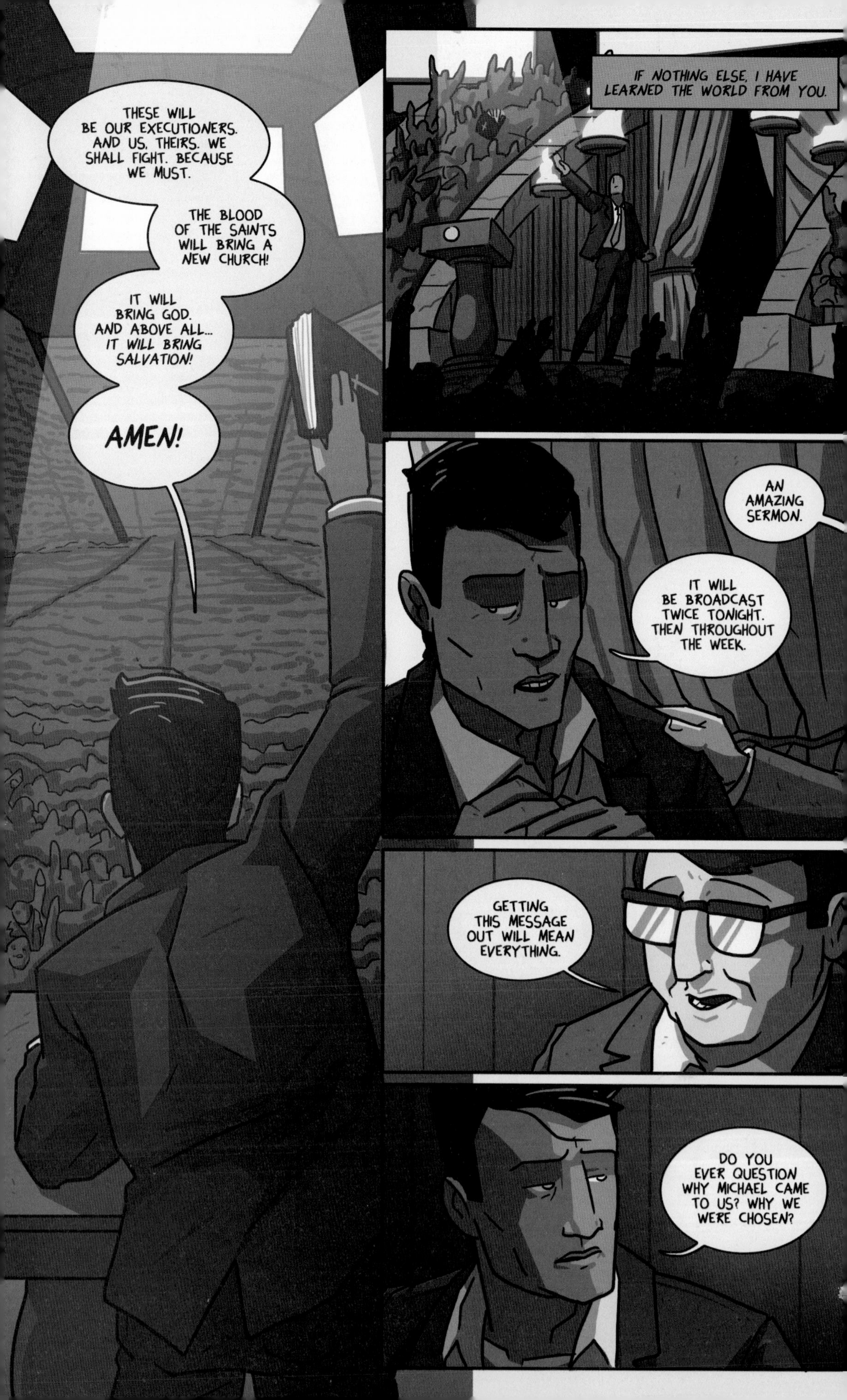
THESE WILL BE OUR EXECUTIONERS. AND US, THEIRS. WE SHALL FIGHT. BECAUSE WE MUST.
THE BLOOD OF THE SAINTS WILL BRING A NEW CHURCH!
IT WILL BRING GOD. AND ABOVE ALL... IT WILL BRING SALVATION!
AMEN!
IF NOTHING ELSE, I HAVE LEARNED THE WORLD FROM YOU.
AN AMAZING SERMON.
IT WILL BE BROADCAST TWICE TONIGHT. THEN THROUGHOUT THE WEEK.
GETTING THIS MESSAGE OUT WILL MEAN EVERYTHING.
DO YOU EVER QUESTION WHY MICHAEL CAME TO US? WHY WE WERE CHOSEN?

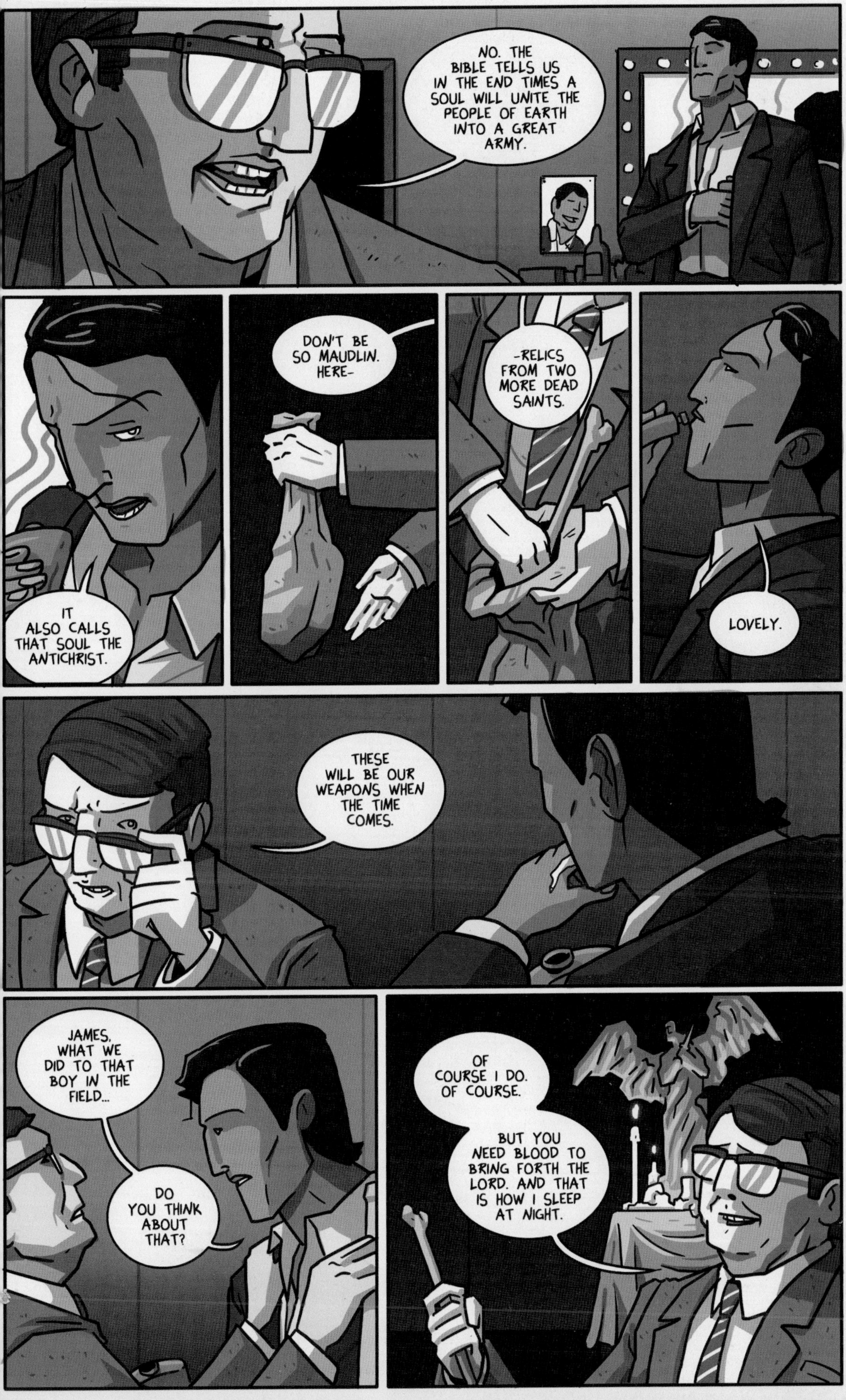
NO. THE BIBLE TELLS US IN THE END TIMES A SOUL WILL UNITE THE PEOPLE OF EARTH INTO A GREAT ARMY.
IT ALSO CALLS THAT SOUL THE ANTICHRIST.
DON'T BE SO MAUDLIN. HERE-
-RELICS FROM TWO MORE DEAD SAINTS.
LOVELY.
THESE WILL BE OUR WEAPONS WHEN THE TIME COMES.
JAMES, WHAT WE DID TO THAT BOY IN THE FIELD...
DO YOU THINK ABOUT THAT?
OF COURSE I DO. OF COURSE.
BUT YOU NEED BLOOD TO BRING FORTH THE LORD. AND THAT IS HOW I SLEEP AT NIGHT.

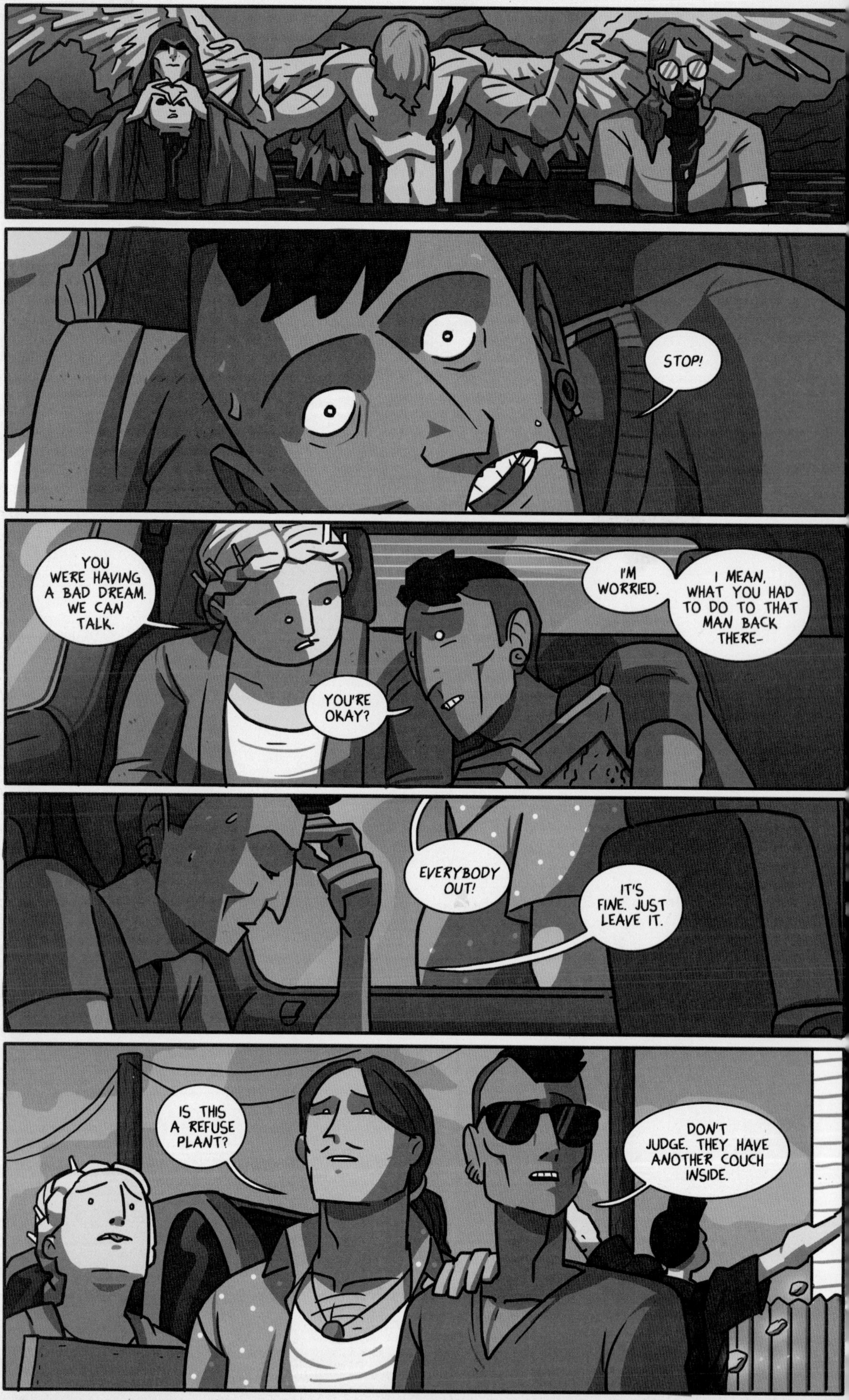
STOP!
YOU WERE HAVING A BAD DREAM. WE CAN TALK.
I'M WORRIED.
I MEAN, WHAT YOU HAD TO DO TO THAT MAN BACK THERE-
YOU'RE OKAY?
EVERYBODY OUT!
IT'S FINE. JUST LEAVE IT.
IS THIS A REFUSE PLANT?
DON'T JUDGE. THEY HAVE ANOTHER COUCH INSIDE.

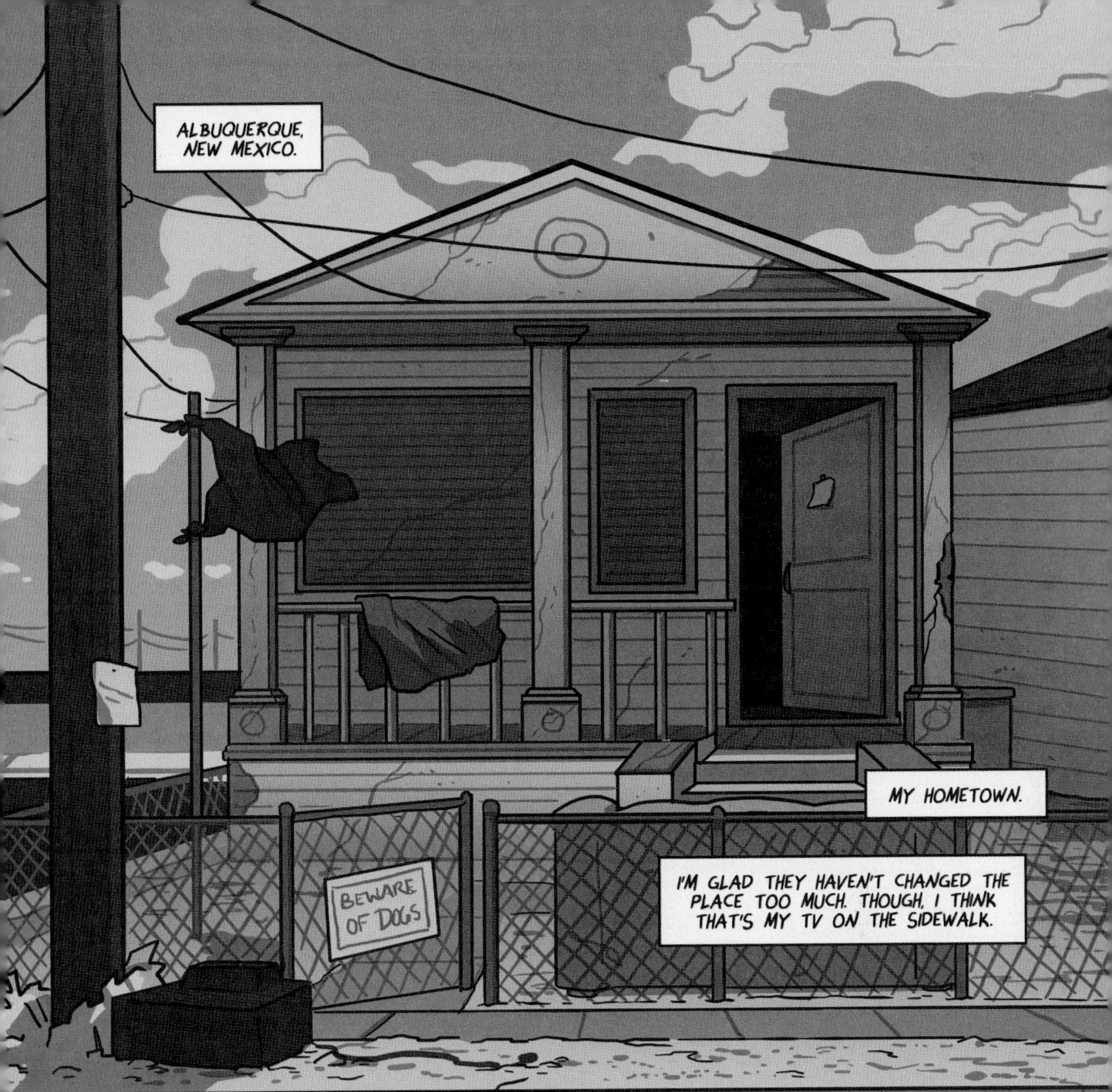
ALBUQUERQUE, NEW MEXICO.
BEWARE OF DOGS
MY HOMETOWN.
I'M GLAD THEY HAVEN'T CHANGED THE PLACE TOO MUCH. THOUGH, I THINK THAT'S MY TV ON THE SIDEWALK.

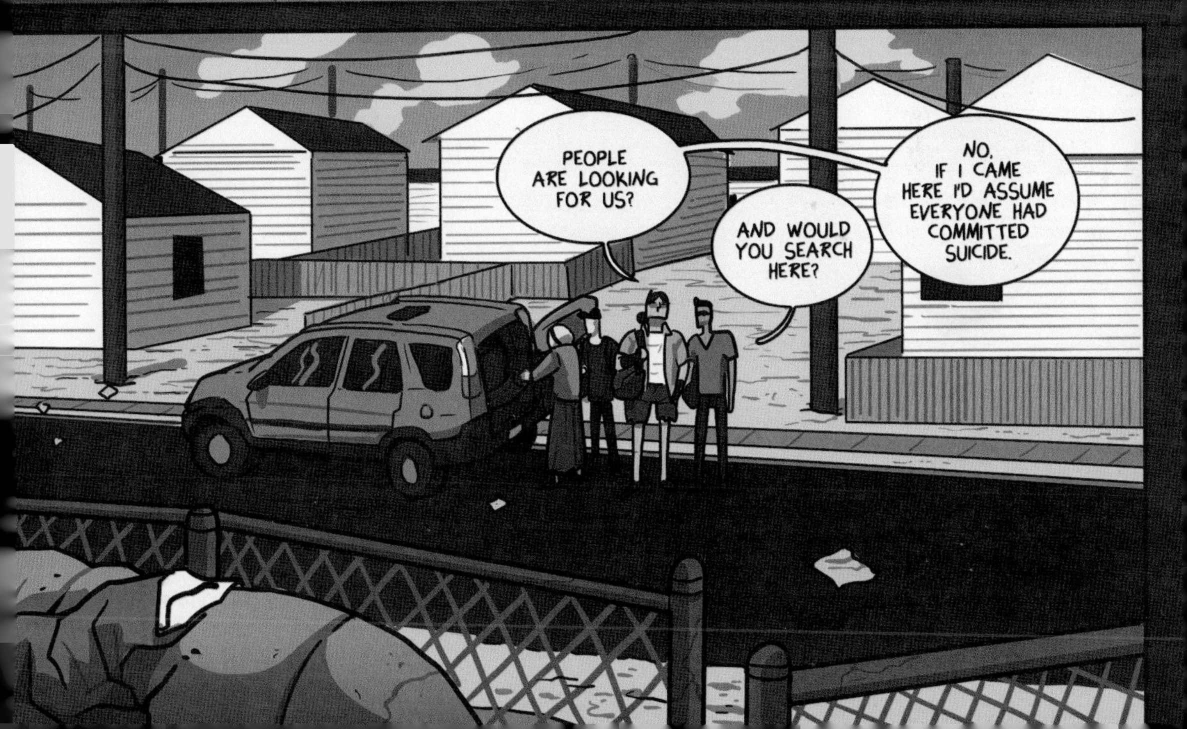
PEOPLE ARE LOOKING FOR US?
AND WOULD YOU SEARCH HERE?
NO, IF I CAME HERE I'D ASSUME EVERYONE HAD COMMITTED SUICIDE.

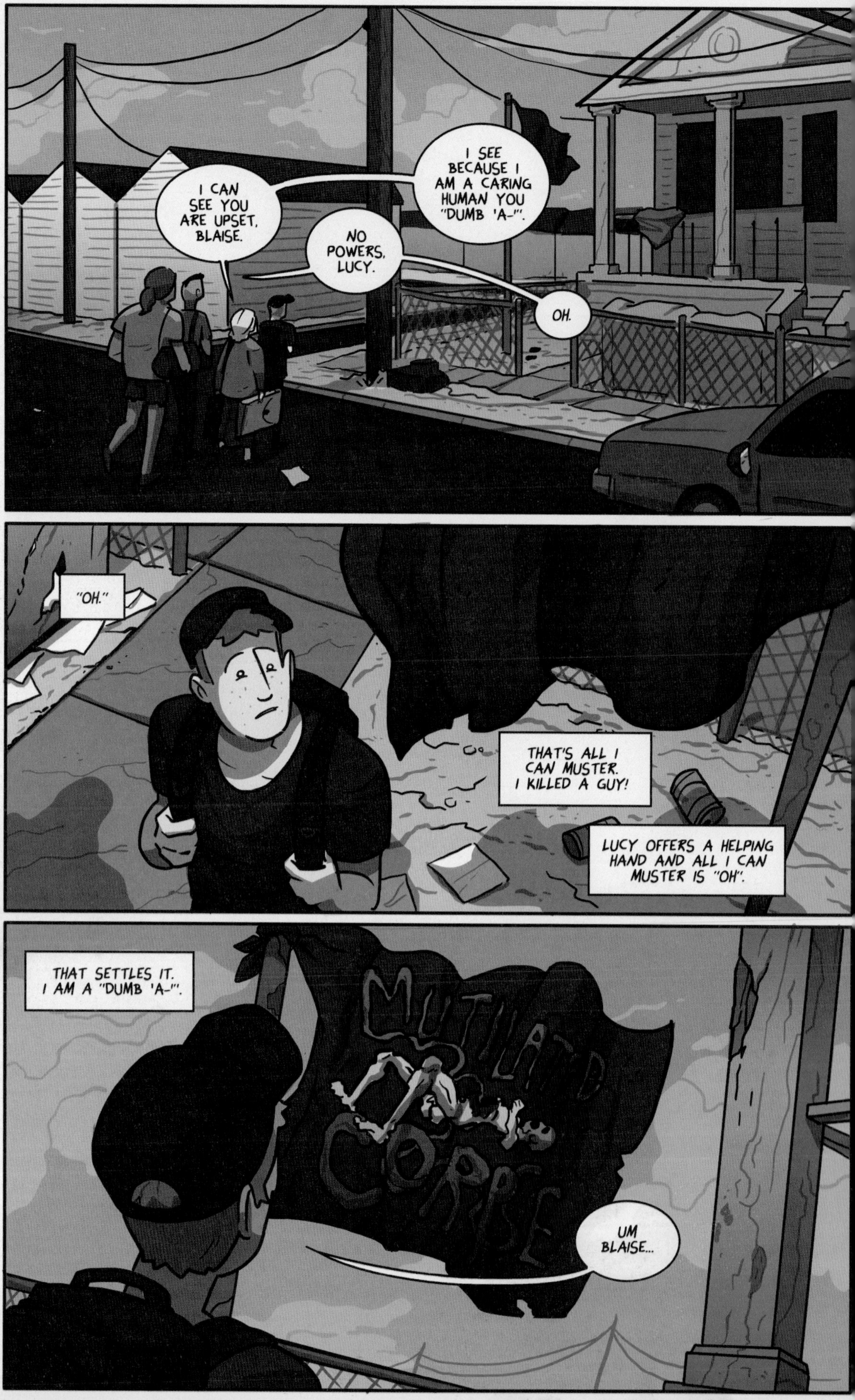
I CAN SEE YOU ARE UPSET, BLAISE.
NO POWERS, LUCY.
I SEE BECAUSE I AM A CARING HUMAN YOU "DUMB 'A-'".
OH.
"OH."
THAT'S ALL I CAN MUSTER. I KILLED A GUY!
LUCY OFFERS A HELPING HAND AND ALL I CAN MUSTER IS "OH".
THAT SETTLES IT. I AM A "DUMB 'A-'".
UM BLAISE...

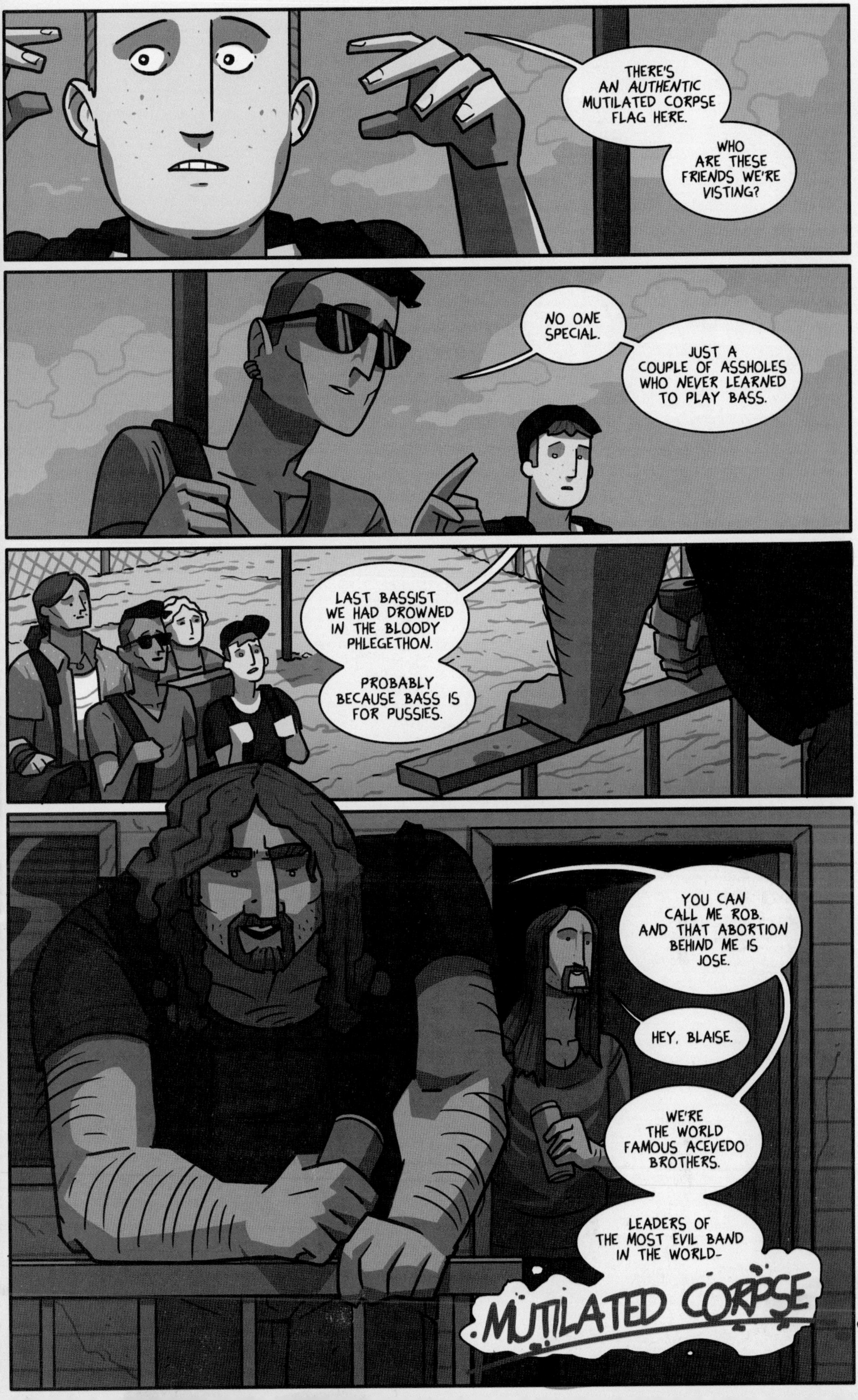
THERE'S AN AUTHENTIC MUTILATED CORPSE FLAG HERE.
WHO ARE THESE FRIENDS WE'RE VISTING?
NO ONE SPECIAL.
JUST A COUPLE OF ASSHOLES WHO NEVER LEARNED TO PLAY BASS.
LAST BASSIST WE HAD DROWNED IN THE BLOODY PHLEGETHON.
PROBABLY BECAUSE BASS IS FOR PUSSIES.
YOU CAN CALL ME ROB. AND THAT ABORTION BEHIND ME IS JOSE.
HEY, BLAISE.
WE'RE THE WORLD FAMOUS ACEVEDO BROTHERS.
LEADERS OF THE MOST EVIL BAND IN THE WORLD-
MUTILATED CORPSE

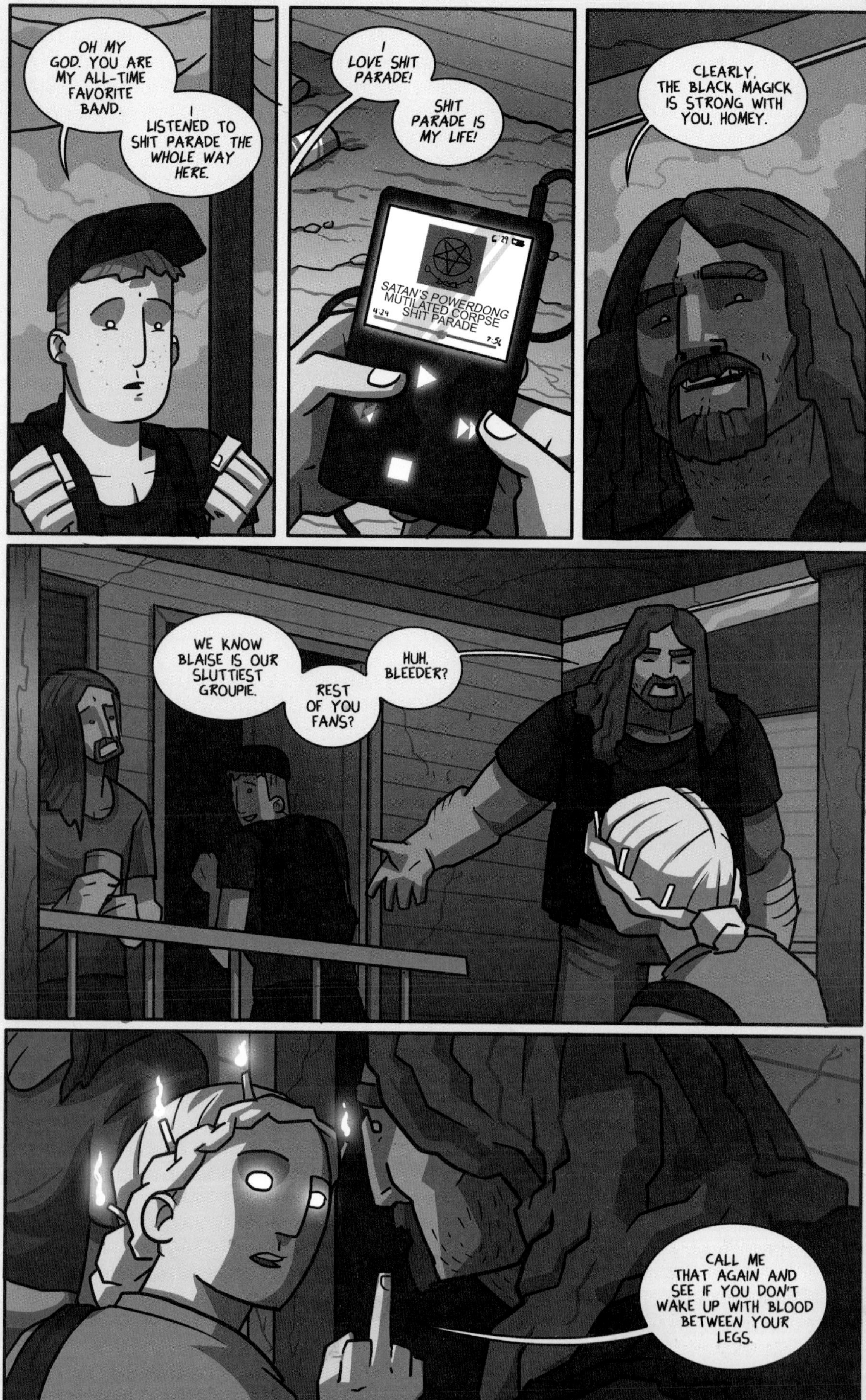
OH MY GOD. YOU ARE MY ALL-TIME FAVORITE BAND.
I LISTENED TO SHIT PARADE THE WHOLE WAY HERE.
I LOVE SHIT PARADE!
SHIT PARADE IS MY LIFE!
SATAN'S POWERDONG
MUTILATED CORPSE
SHIT PARADE
4:24
7:56
CLEARLY, THE BLACK MAGICK IS STRONG WITH YOU, HOMEY.
WE KNOW BLAISE IS OUR SLUTTIEST GROUPIE.
HUH, BLEEDER?
REST OF YOU FANS?
CALL ME THAT AGAIN AND SEE IF YOU DON'T WAKE UP WITH BLOOD BETWEEN YOUR LEGS.

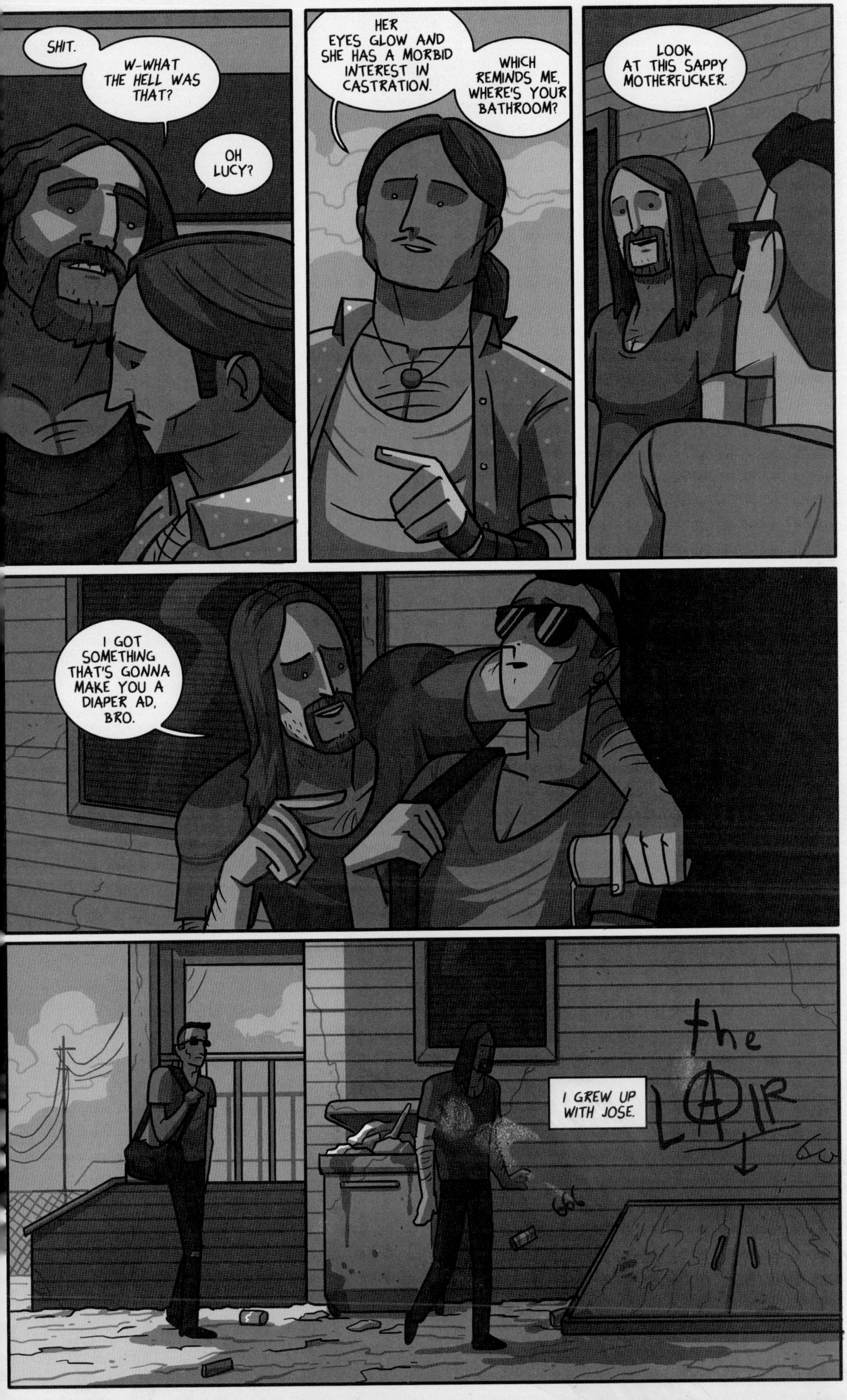
SHIT.
W-WHAT THE HELL WAS THAT?
OH LUCY?
HER EYES GLOW AND SHE HAS A MORBID INTEREST IN CASTRATION.
WHICH REMINDS ME, WHERE'S YOUR BATHROOM?
LOOK AT THIS SAPPY MOTHERFUCKER.
I GOT SOMETHING THAT'S GONNA MAKE YOU A DIAPER AD, BRO.
I GREW UP WITH JOSE.
the LAIR

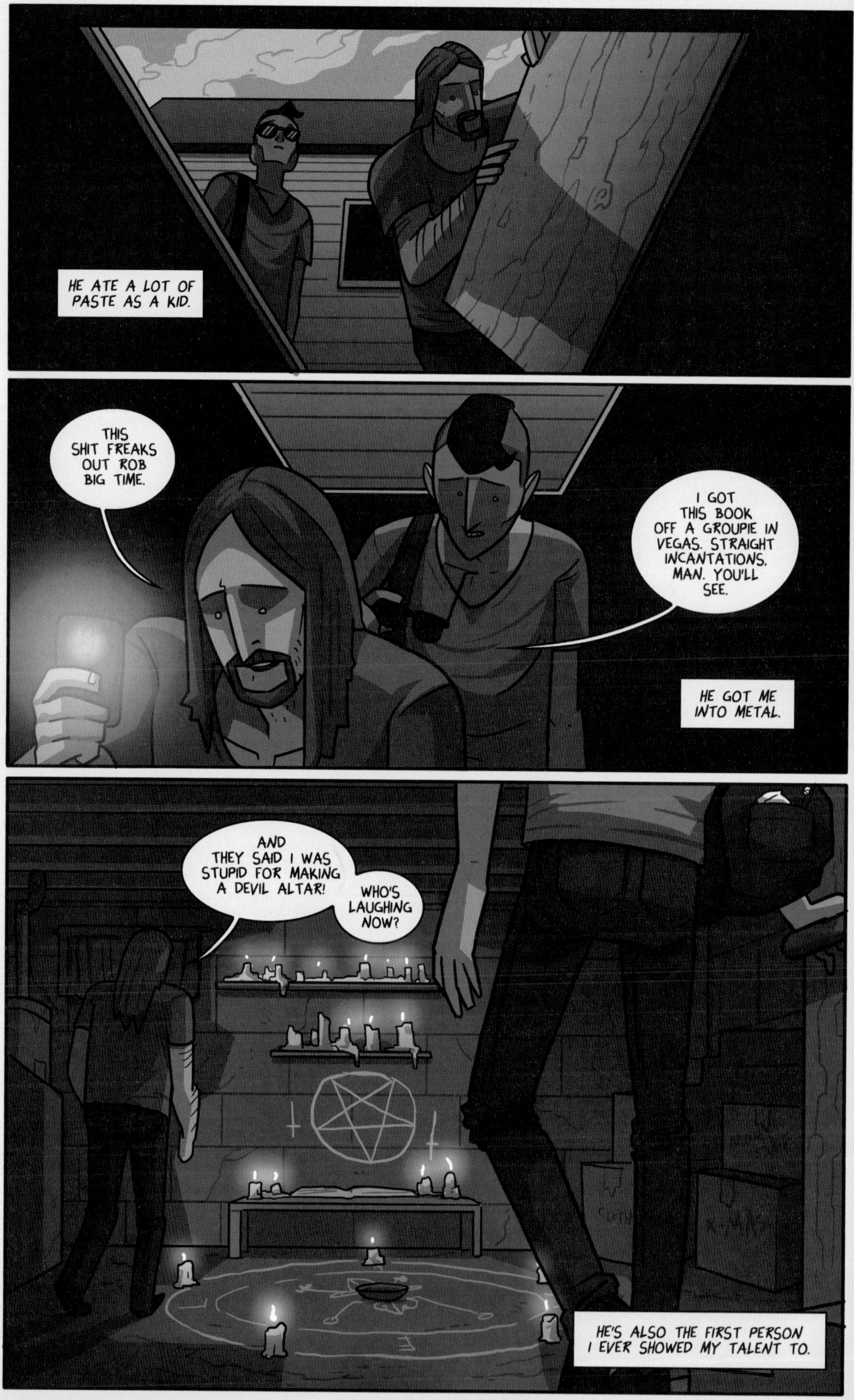
HE ATE A LOT OF PASTE AS A KID.
THIS SHIT FREAKS OUT ROB BIG TIME.
I GOT THIS BOOK OFF A GROUPIE IN VEGAS. STRAIGHT INCANTATIONS, MAN. YOU'LL SEE.
HE GOT ME INTO METAL.
AND THEY SAID I WAS STUPID FOR MAKING A DEVIL ALTAR!
WHO'S LAUGHING NOW?
HE'S ALSO THE FIRST PERSON I EVER SHOWED MY TALENT TO.

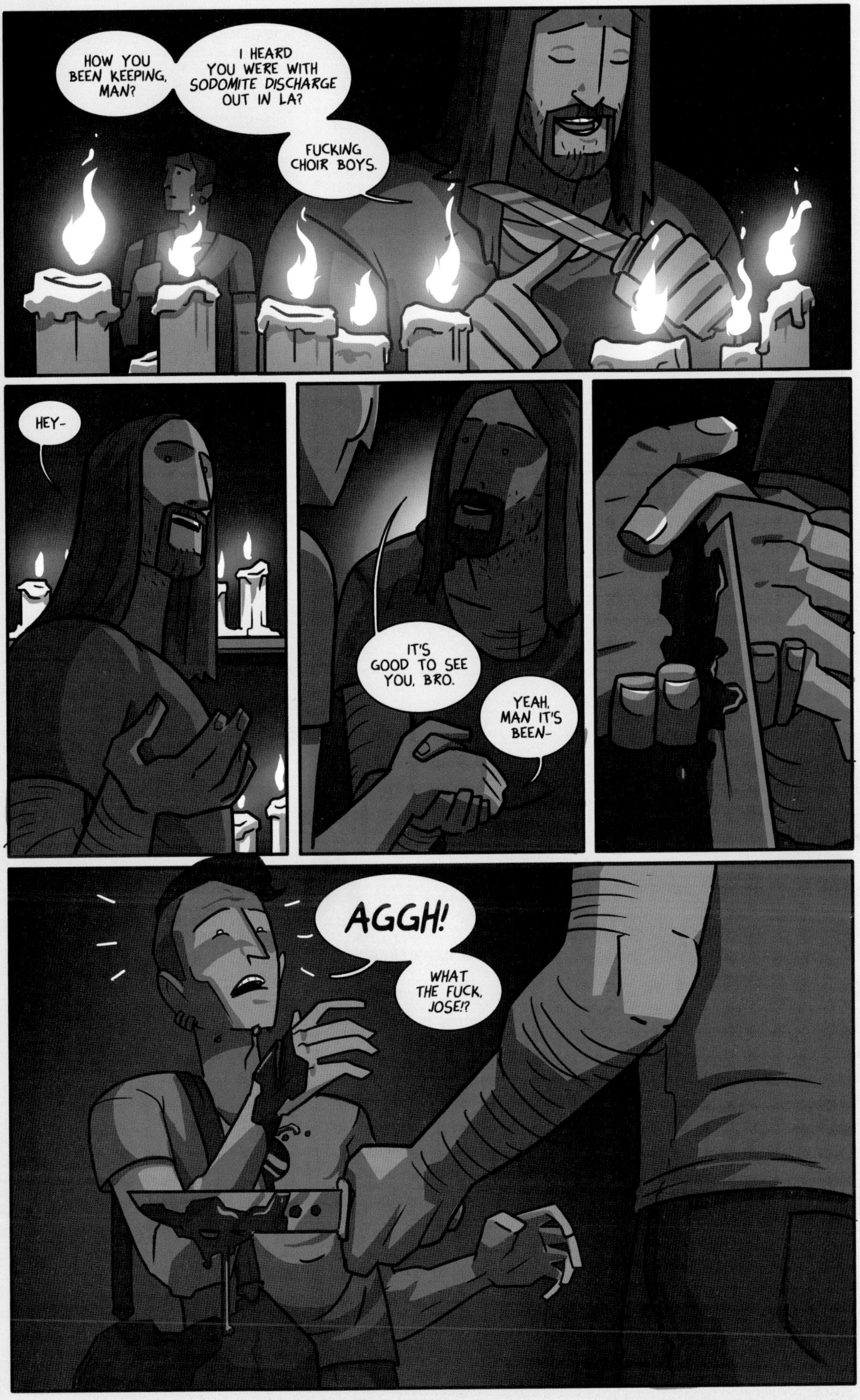
HOW YOU BEEN KEEPING, MAN?
I HEARD YOU WERE WITH SODOMITE DISCHARGE OUT IN LA?
FUCKING CHOIR BOYS.
HEY-
IT'S GOOD TO SEE YOU, BRO.
YEAH, MAN IT'S BEEN-
AGGH!
WHAT THE FUCK, JOSE!?

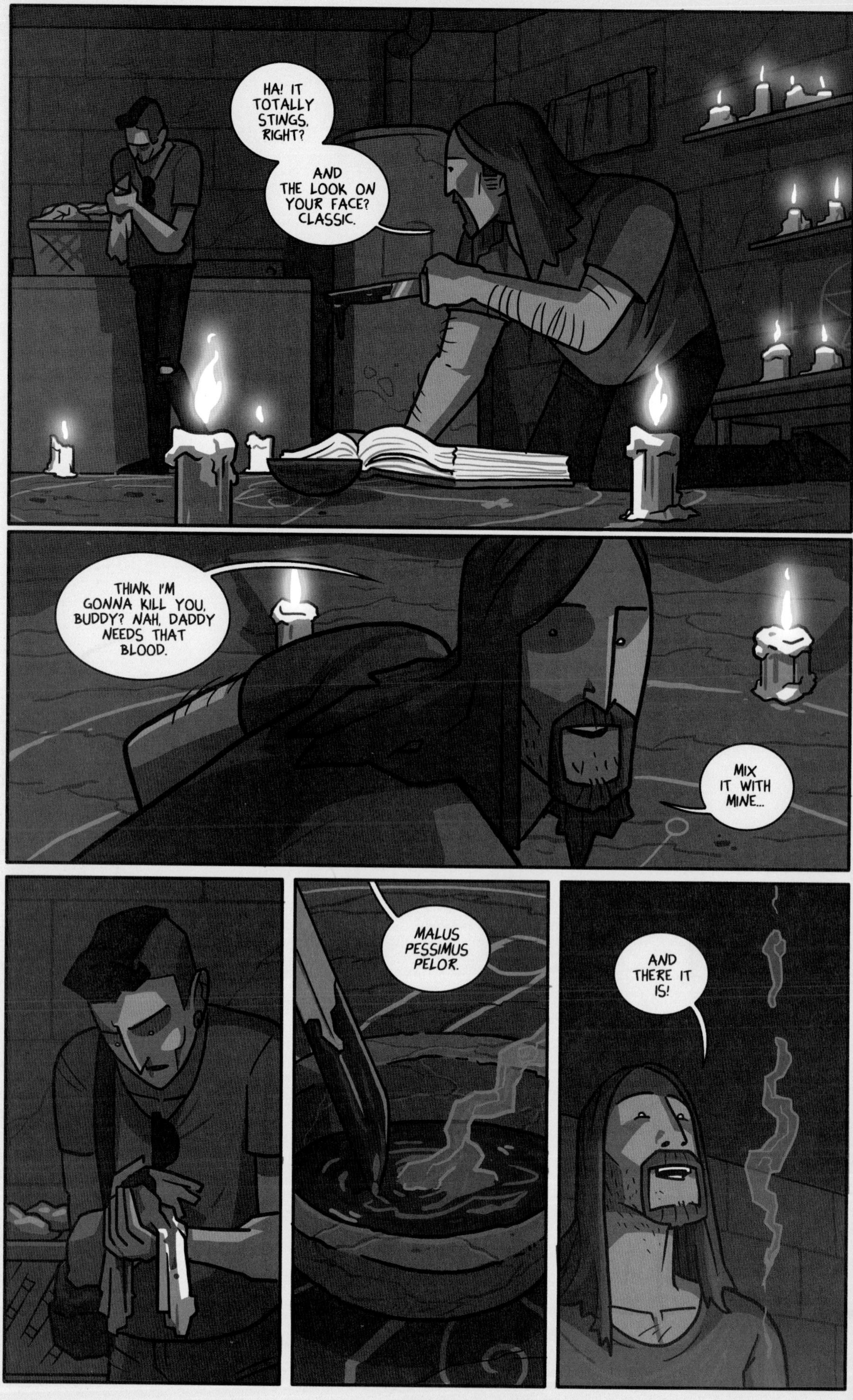
HA! IT TOTALLY STINGS, RIGHT?
AND THE LOOK ON YOUR FACE? CLASSIC.
THINK I'M GONNA KILL YOU, BUDDY? NAH, DADDY NEEDS THAT BLOOD.
MIX IT WITH MINE...
MALUS PESSIMUS PELOR.
AND THERE IT IS!

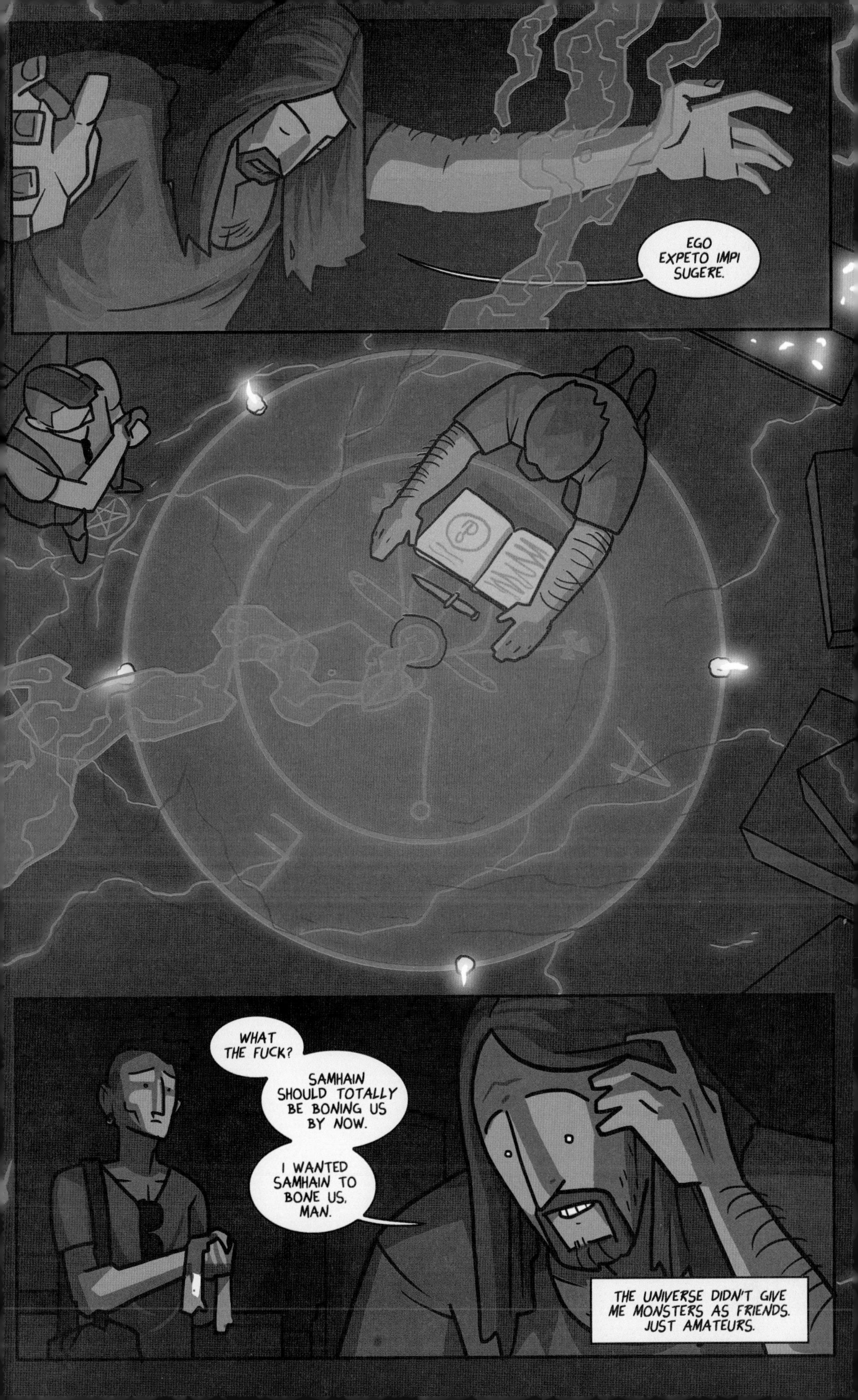

EGO EXPETO IMPI SUGERE.
WHAT THE FUCK?
SAMHAIN SHOULD TOTALLY BE BONING US BY NOW.
I WANTED SAMHAIN TO BONE US, MAN.
THE UNIVERSE DIDN'T GIVE ME MONSTERS AS FRIENDS. JUST AMATEURS.

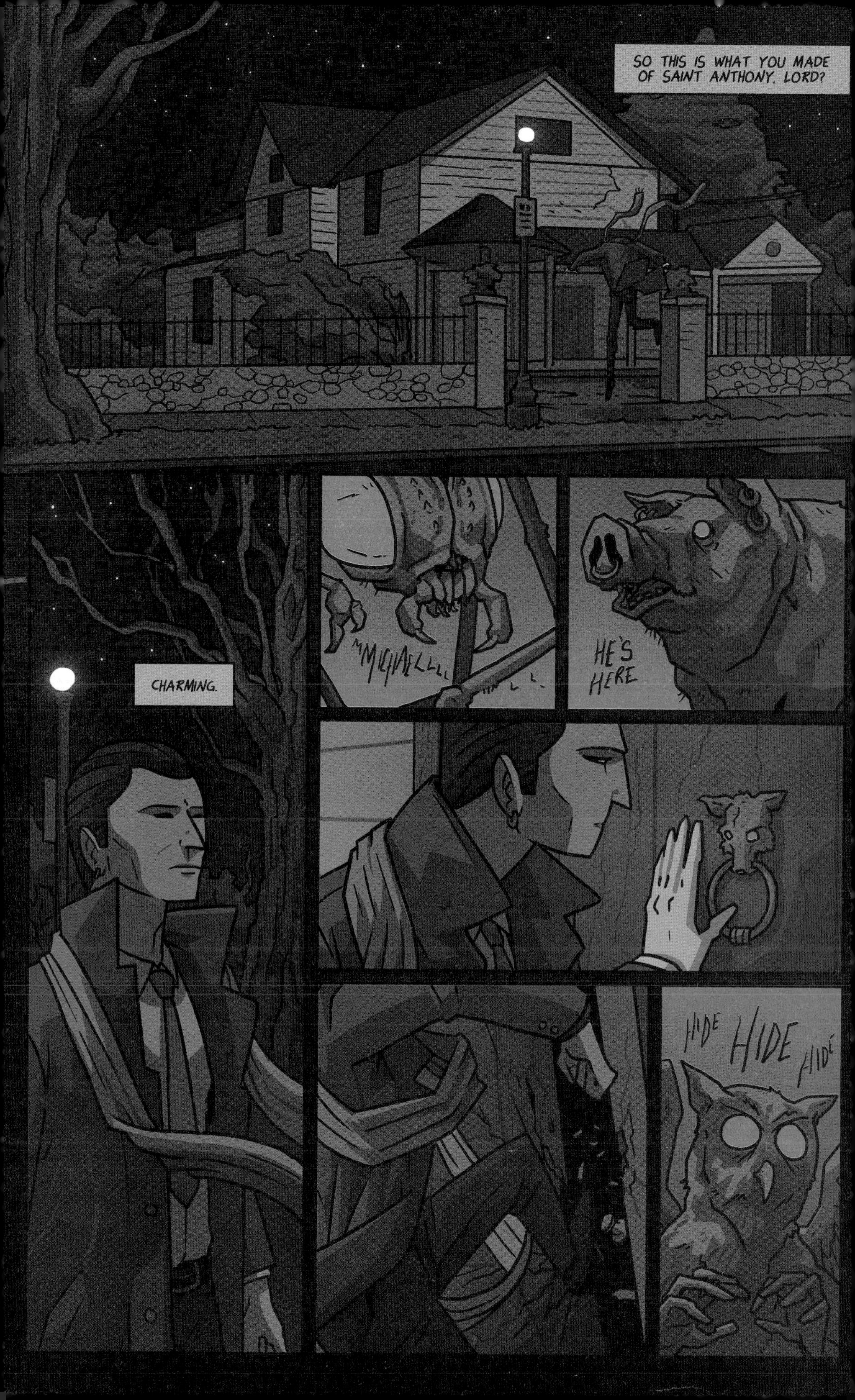
SO THIS IS WHAT YOU MADE OF SAINT ANTHONY, LORD?
CHARMING.
MMICHAELLLL...
HE'S HERE
HIDE HIDE HIDE

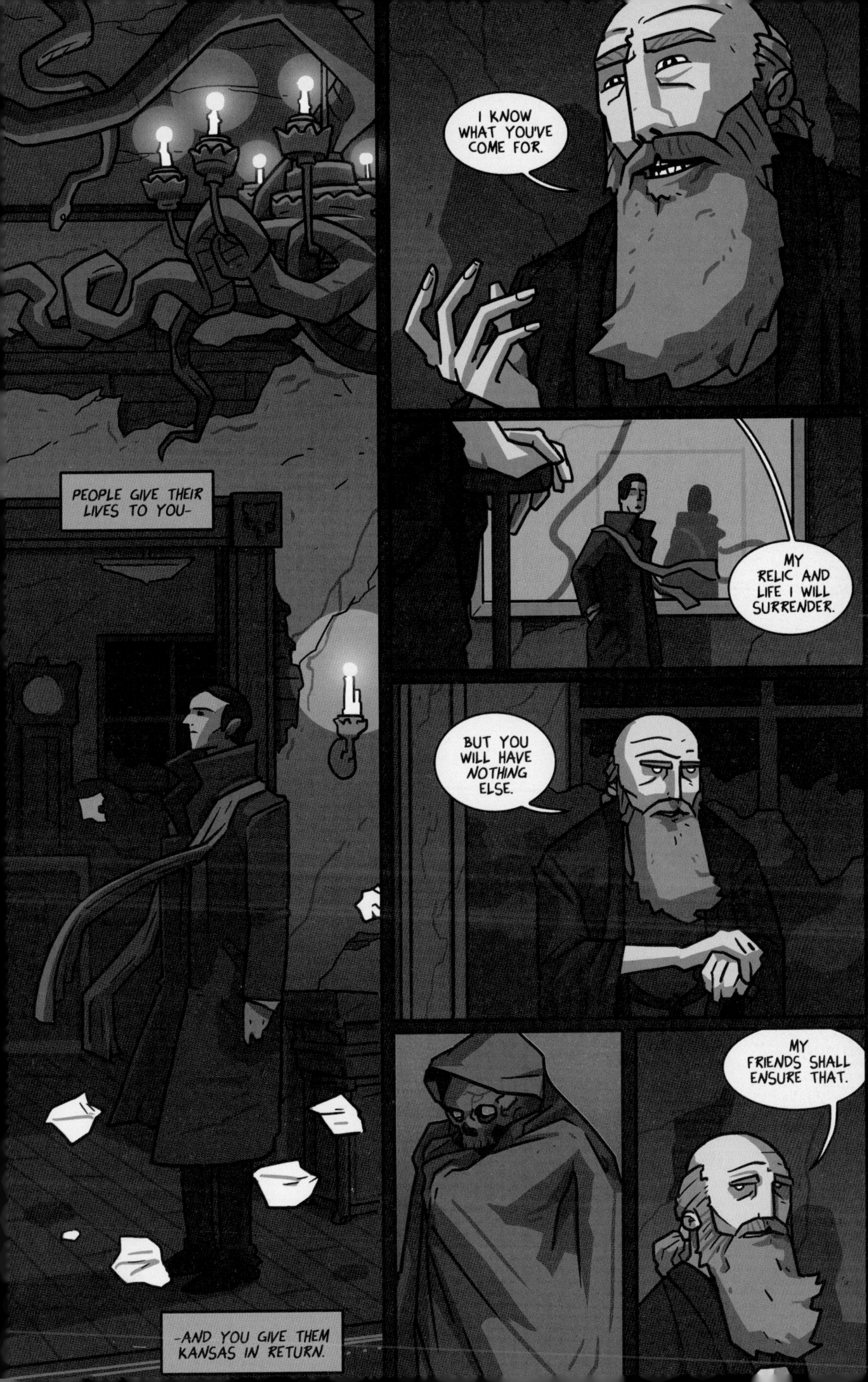
PEOPLE GIVE THEIR LIVES TO YOU-
-AND YOU GIVE THEM KANSAS IN RETURN.
I KNOW WHAT YOU'VE COME FOR.
MY RELIC AND LIFE I WILL SURRENDER.
BUT YOU WILL HAVE NOTHING ELSE.
MY FRIENDS SHALL ENSURE THAT.

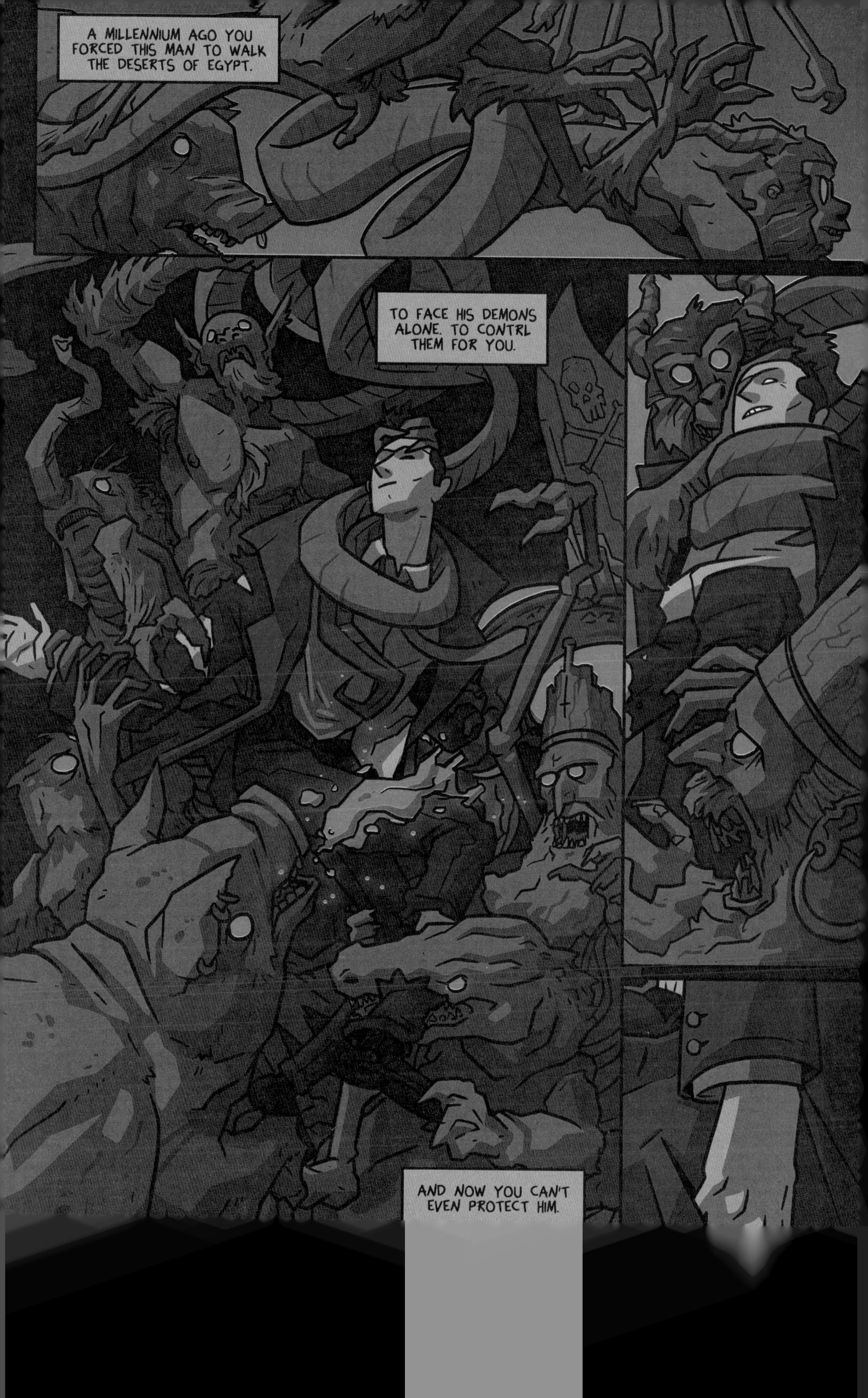
A MILLENNIUM AGO YOU FORCED THIS MAN TO WALK THE DESERTS OF EGYPT.
TO FACE HIS DEMONS ALONE. TO CONTRL THEM FOR YOU.
AND NOW YOU CAN'T EVEN PROTECT HIM.

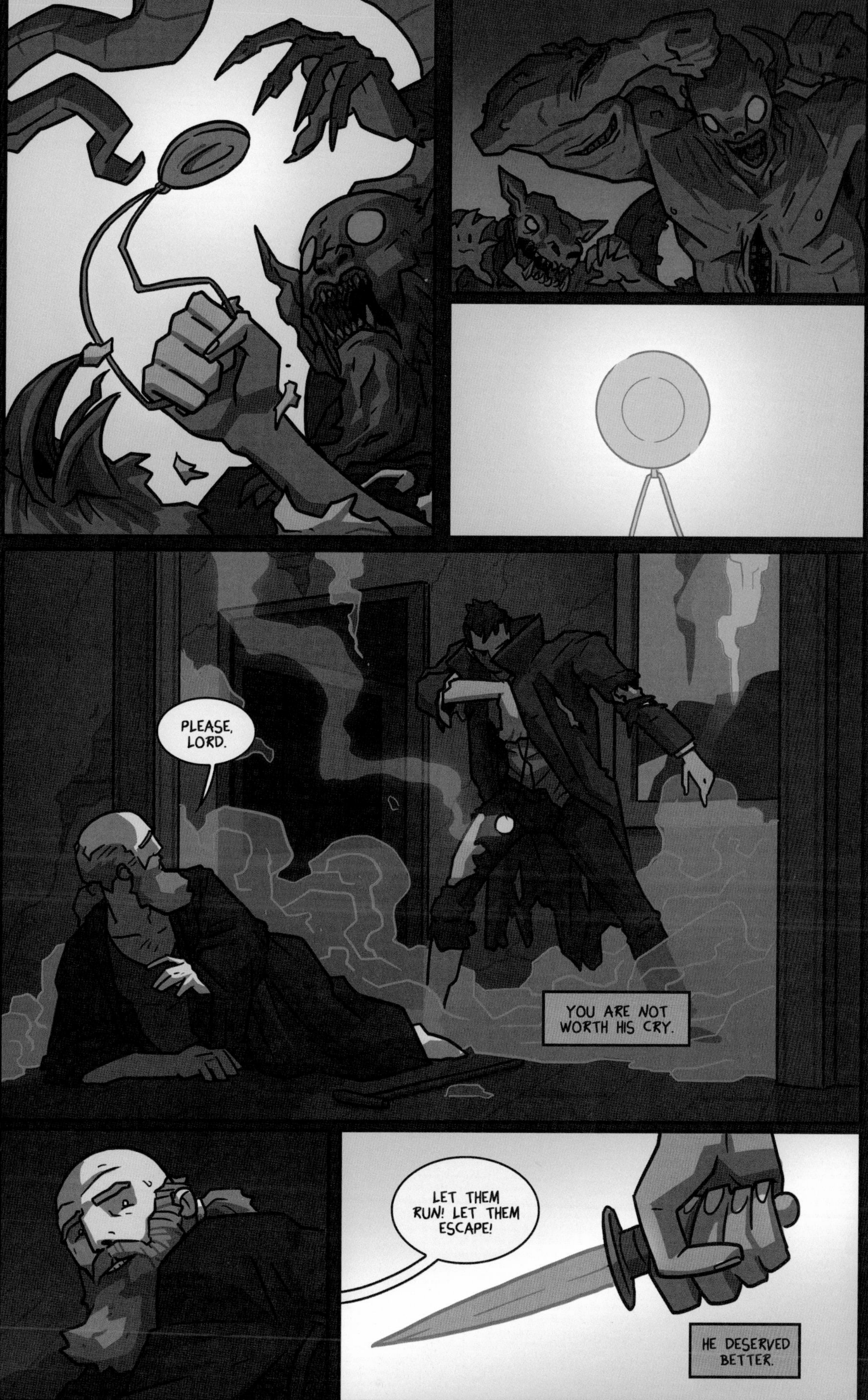
PLEASE, LORD.
YOU ARE NOT WORTH HIS CRY.
LET THEM RUN! LET THEM ESCAPE!
HE DESERVED BETTER.

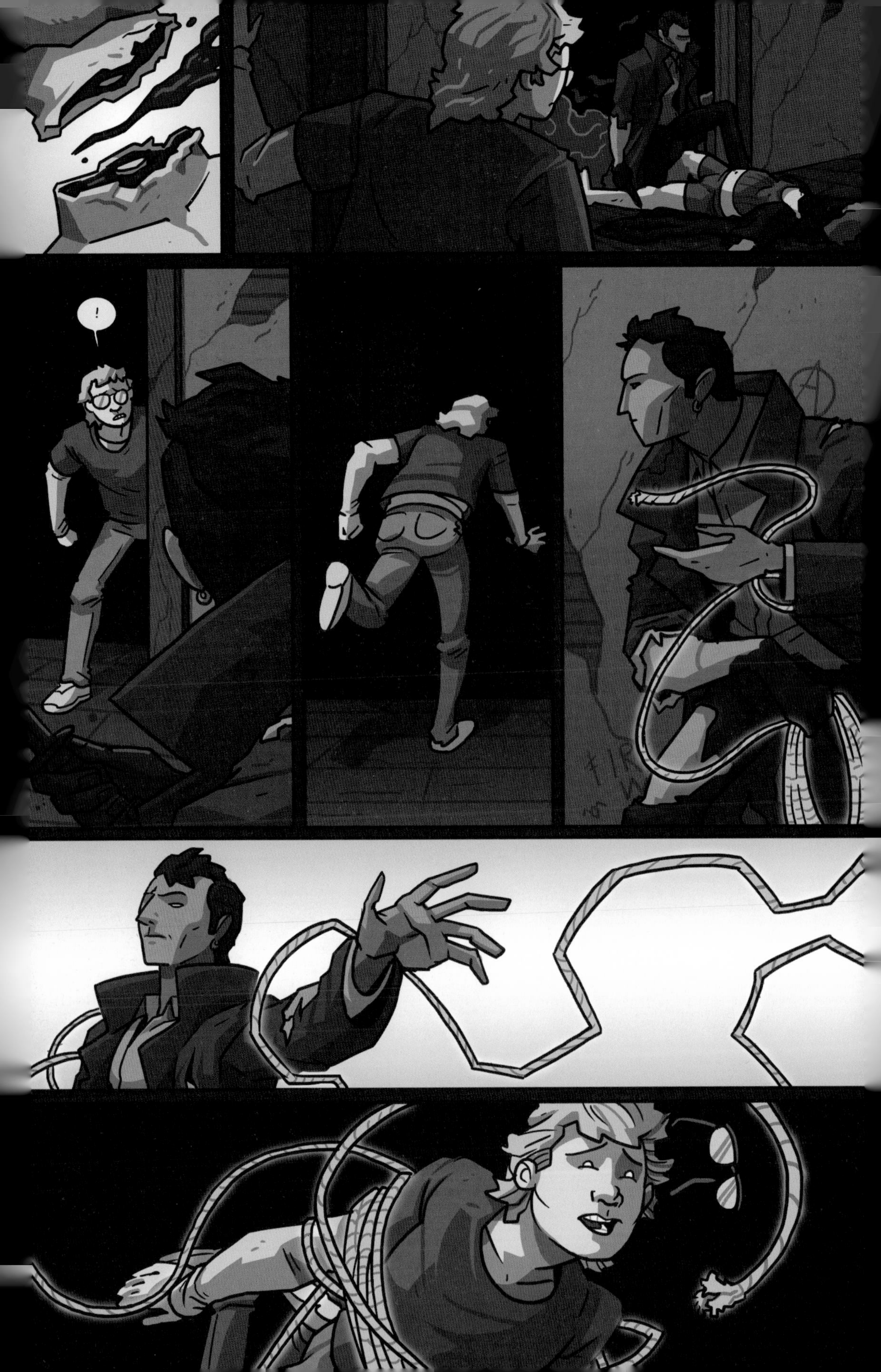
!

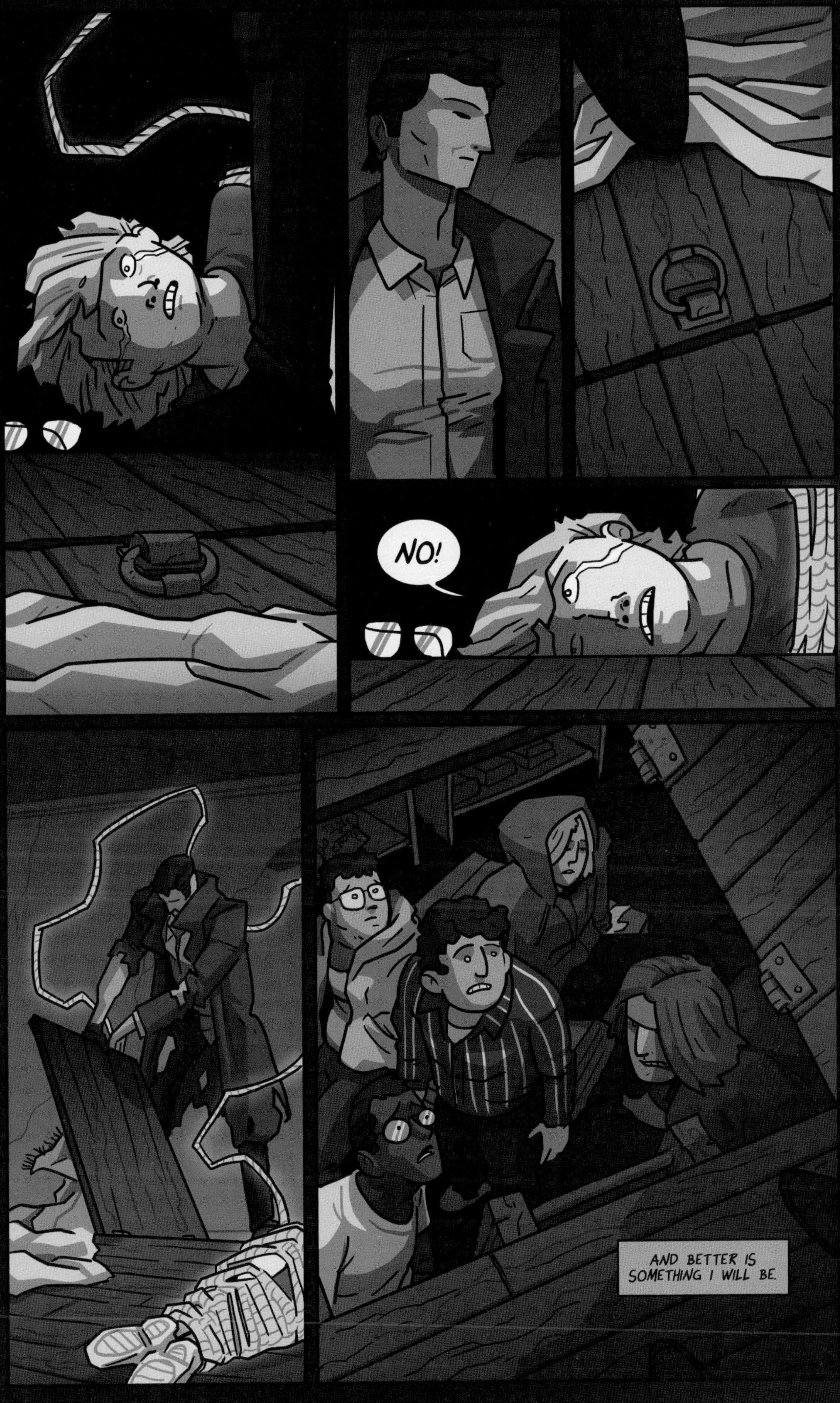
NO!
AND BETTER IS SOMETHING I WILL BE.

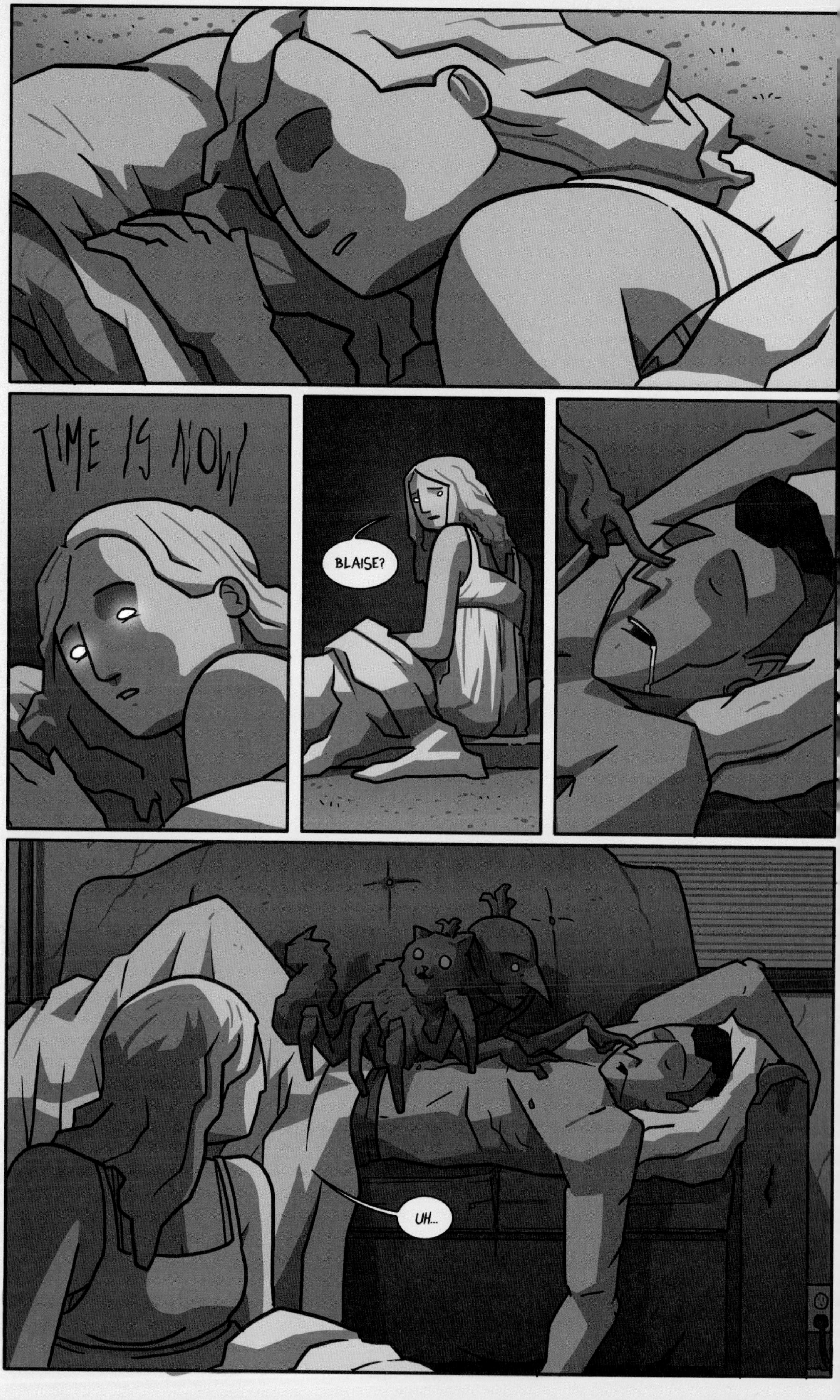
TIME IS NOW
BLAISE?
UH...

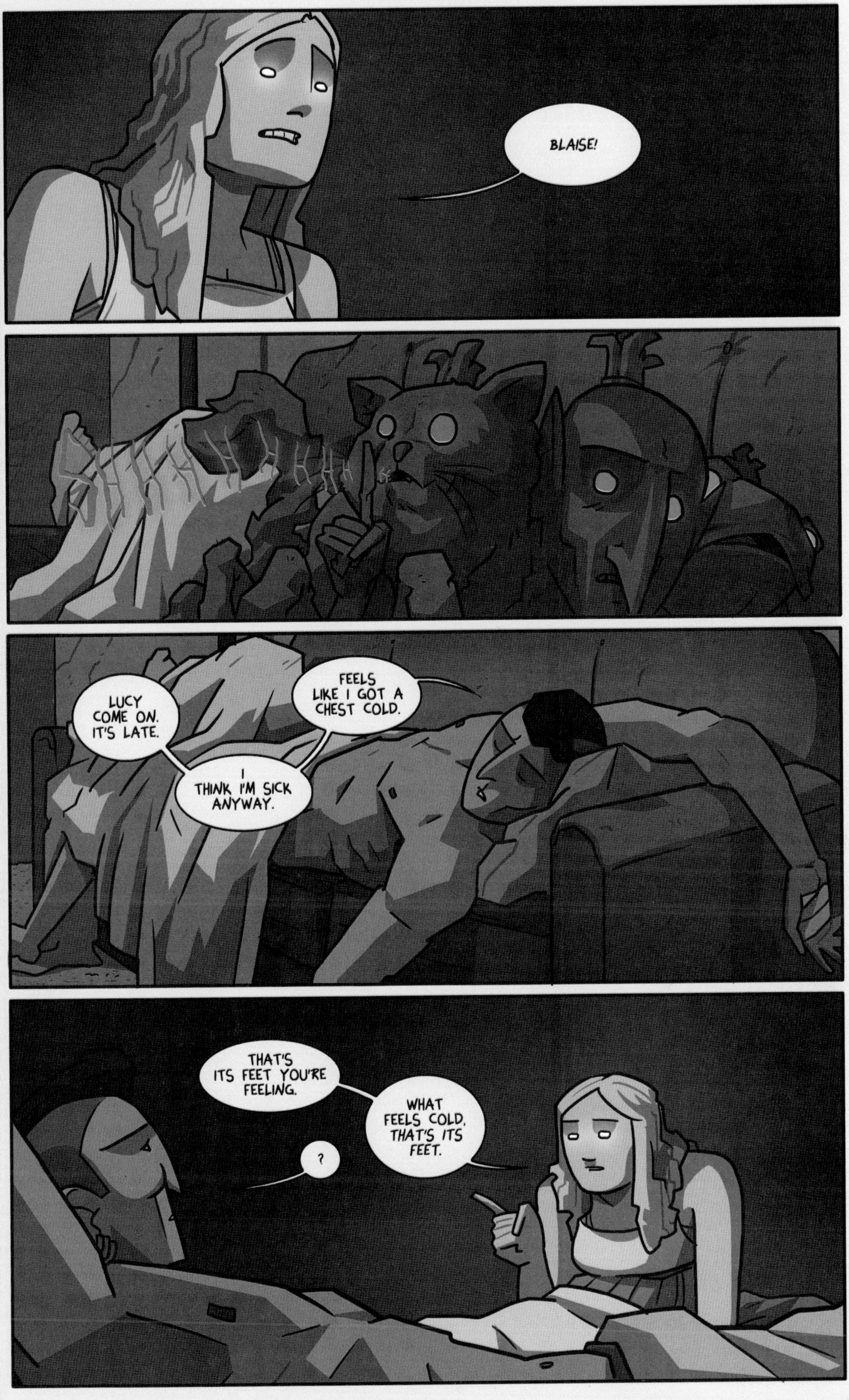
BLAISE!
LUCY COME ON. IT'S LATE.
I THINK I'M SICK ANYWAY.
FEELS LIKE I GOT A CHEST COLD.
THAT'S ITS FEET YOU'RE FEELING.
WHAT FEELS COLD, THAT'S ITS FEET.
?

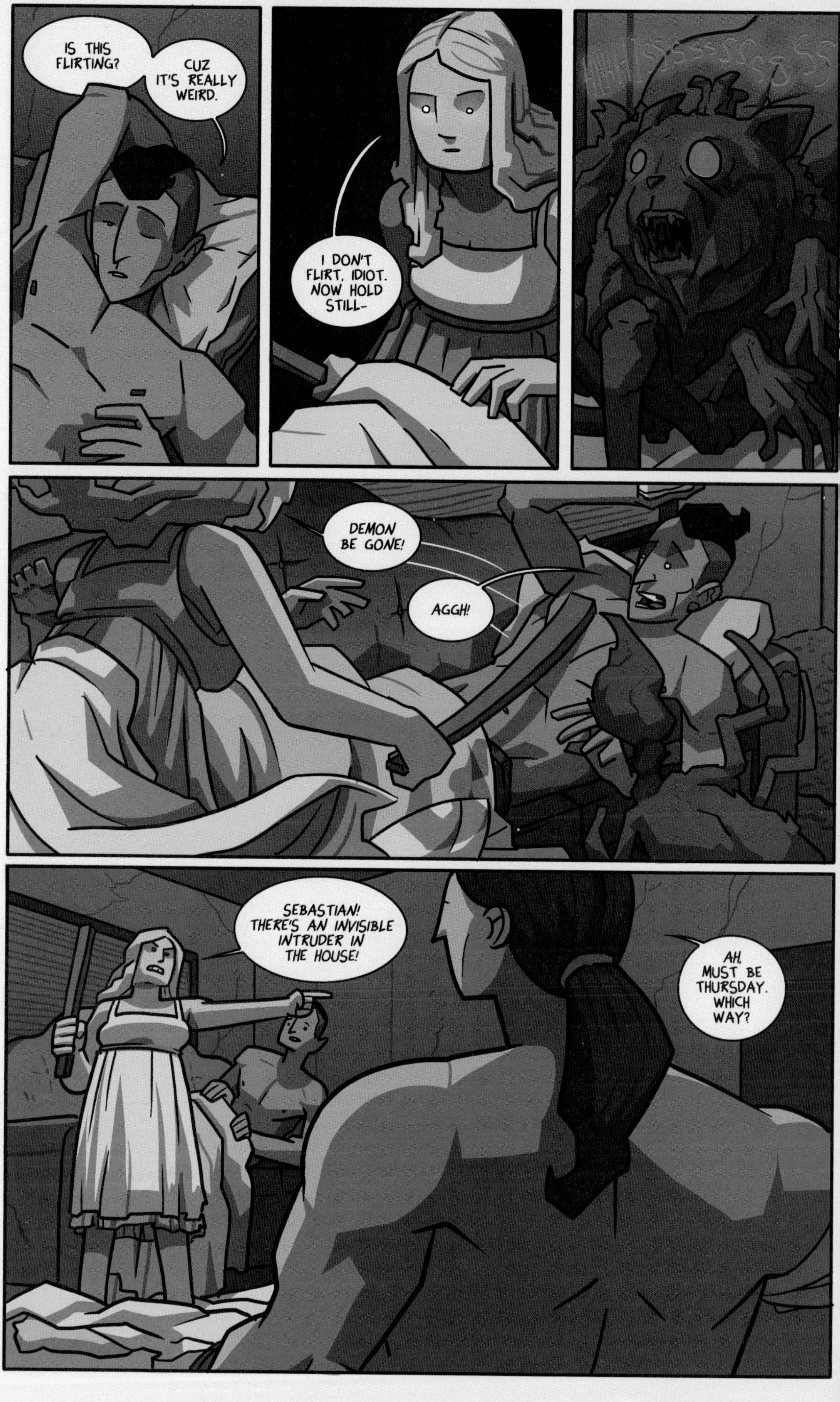
IS THIS FLIRTING?
CUZ IT'S REALLY WEIRD.
I DON'T FLIRT, IDIOT. NOW HOLD STILL-
HHHHISSSSSSSSSSS
DEMON BE GONE!
AGGH!
SEBASTIAN! THERE'S AN INVISIBLE INTRUDER IN THE HOUSE!
AH, MUST BE THURSDAY. WHICH WAY?

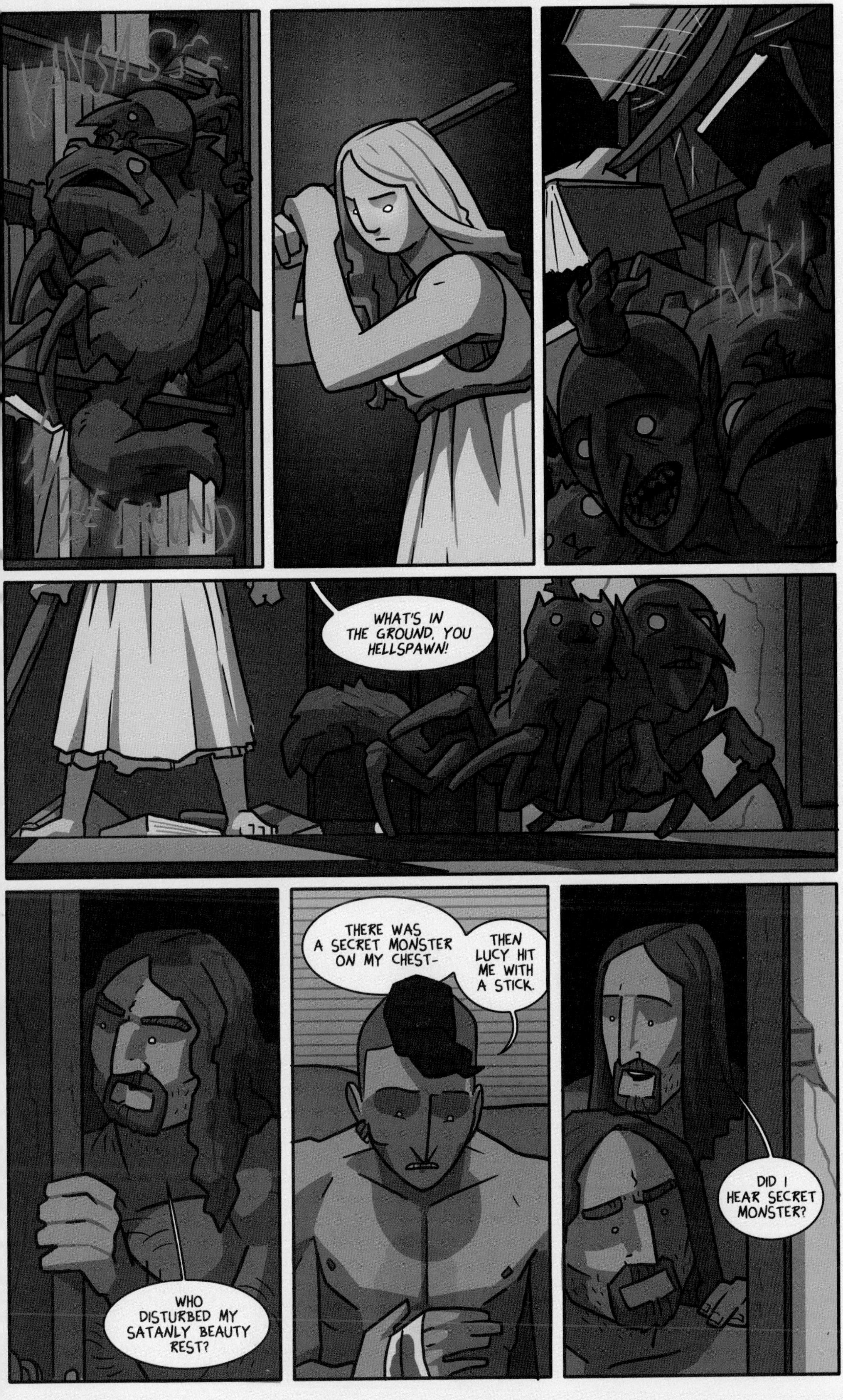
KANSASSS-
IN THE GROUND
ACK!
WHAT'S IN THE GROUND, YOU HELLSPAWN!
WHO DISTURBED MY SATANLY BEAUTY REST?
THERE WAS A SECRET MONSTER ON MY CHEST-
THEN LUCY HIT ME WITH A STICK.
DID I HEAR SECRET MONSTER?

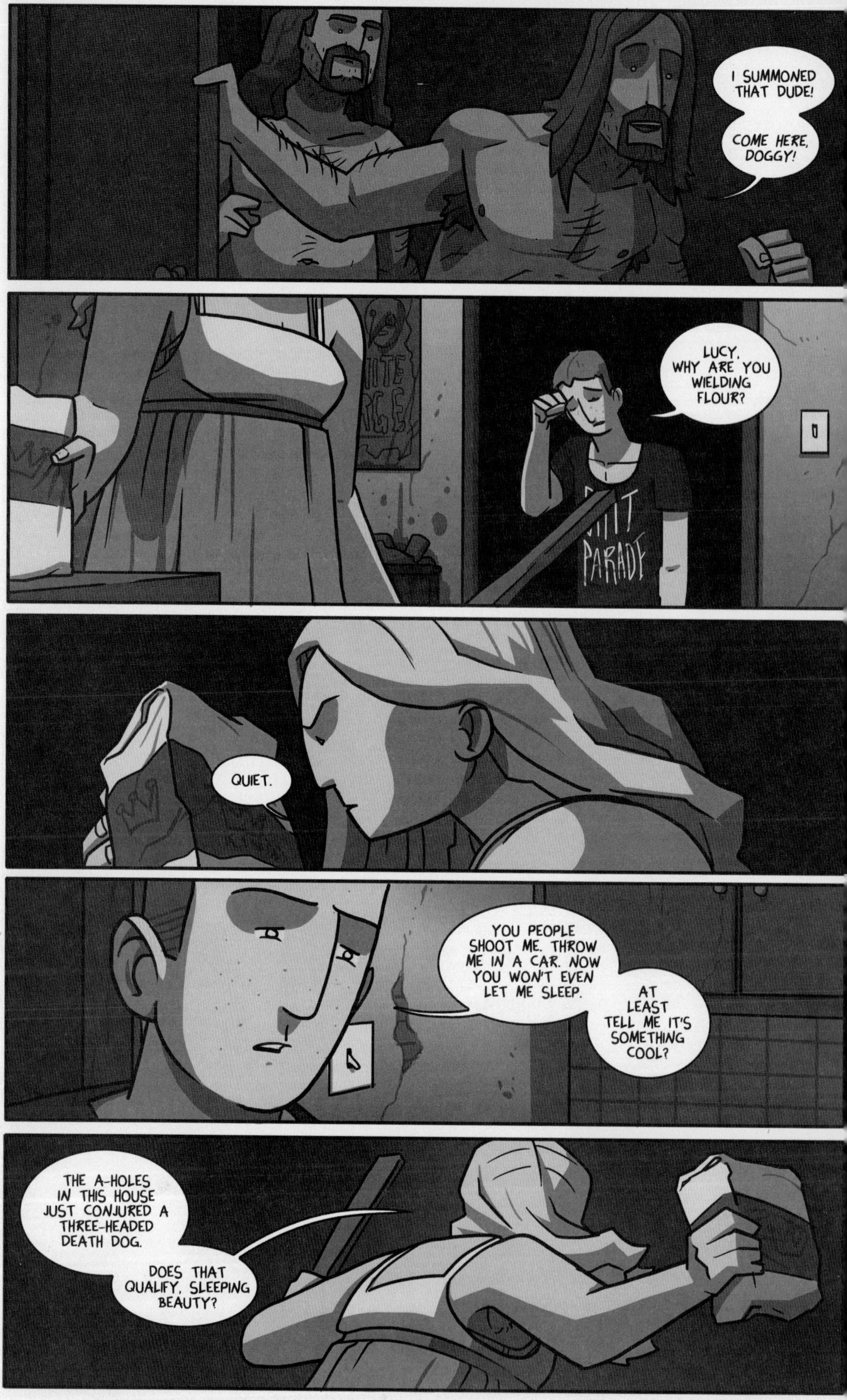
I SUMMONED THAT DUDE!
COME HERE, DOGGY!
LUCY, WHY ARE YOU WIELDING FLOUR?
QUIET.
YOU PEOPLE SHOOT ME. THROW ME IN A CAR. NOW YOU WON'T EVEN LET ME SLEEP.
AT LEAST TELL ME IT'S SOMETHING COOL?
THE A-HOLES IN THIS HOUSE JUST CONJURED A THREE-HEADED DEATH DOG.
DOES THAT QUALIFY, SLEEPING BEAUTY?

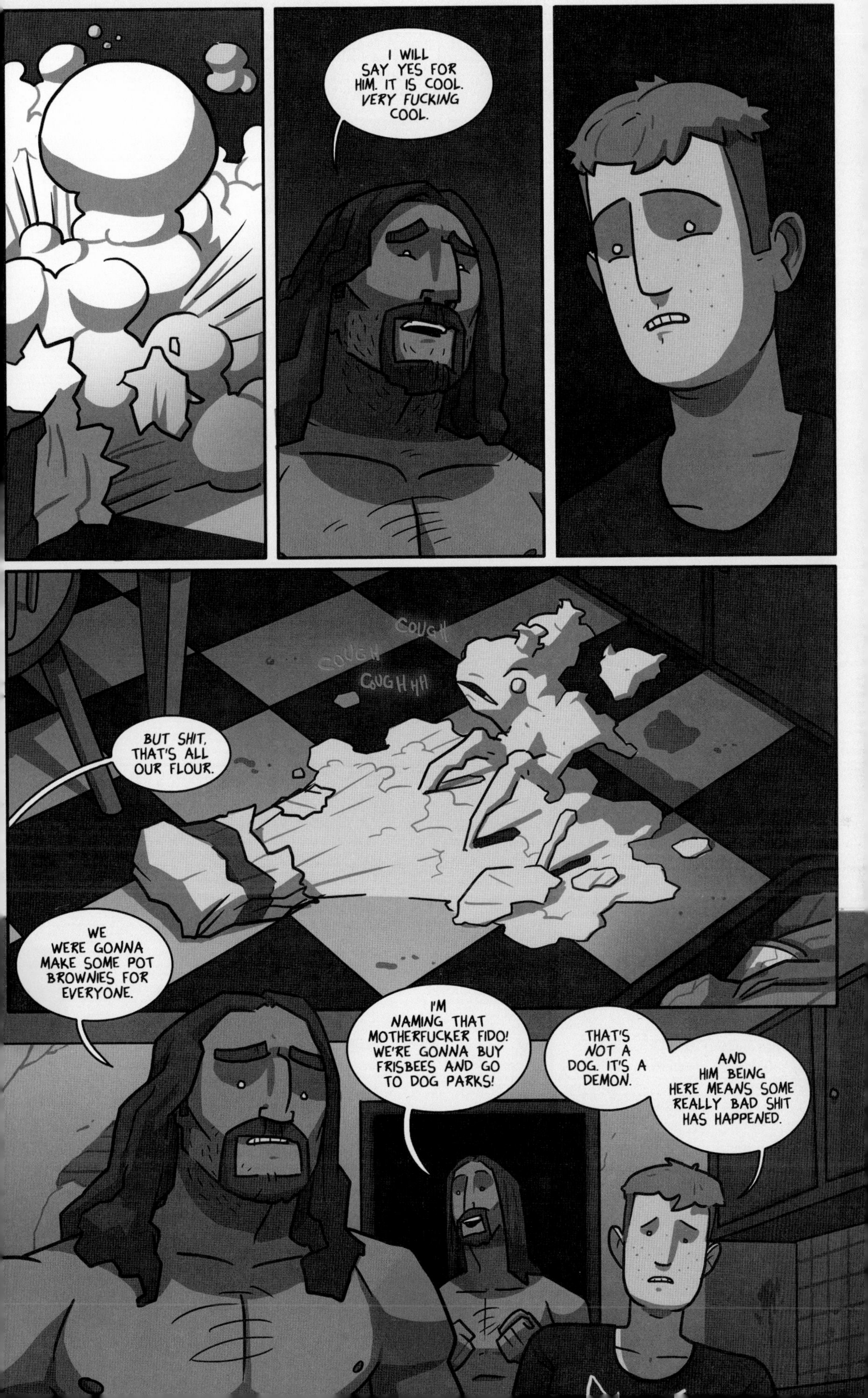
I WILL SAY YES FOR HIM. IT IS COOL. VERY FUCKING COOL.
COUGH
COUGH
COUGHHHH
BUT SHIT, THAT'S ALL OUR FLOUR.
WE WERE GONNA MAKE SOME POT BROWNIES FOR EVERYONE.
I'M NAMING THAT MOTHERFUCKER FIDO! WE'RE GONNA BUY FRISBEES AND GO TO DOG PARKS!
THAT'S NOT A DOG. IT'S A DEMON.
AND HIM BEING HERE MEANS SOME REALLY BAD SHIT HAS HAPPENED.

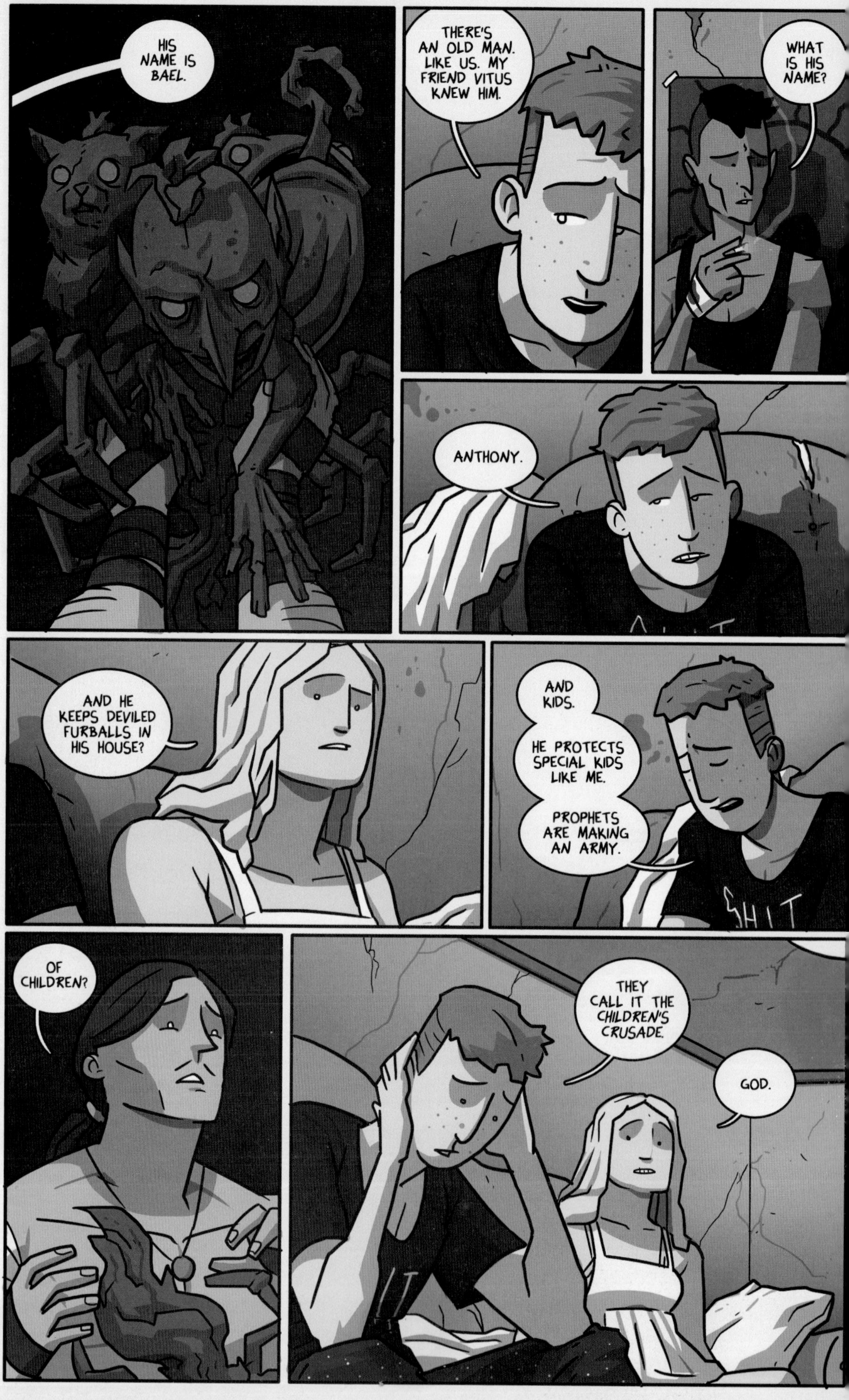
HIS NAME IS BAEL.
THERE'S AN OLD MAN. LIKE US. MY FRIEND VITUS KNEW HIM.
WHAT IS HIS NAME?
ANTHONY.
AND HE KEEPS DEVILED FURBALLS IN HIS HOUSE?
AND KIDS.
HE PROTECTS SPECIAL KIDS LIKE ME.
PROPHETS ARE MAKING AN ARMY.
SHIT
OF CHILDREN?
THEY CALL IT THE CHILDREN'S CRUSADE.
GOD.

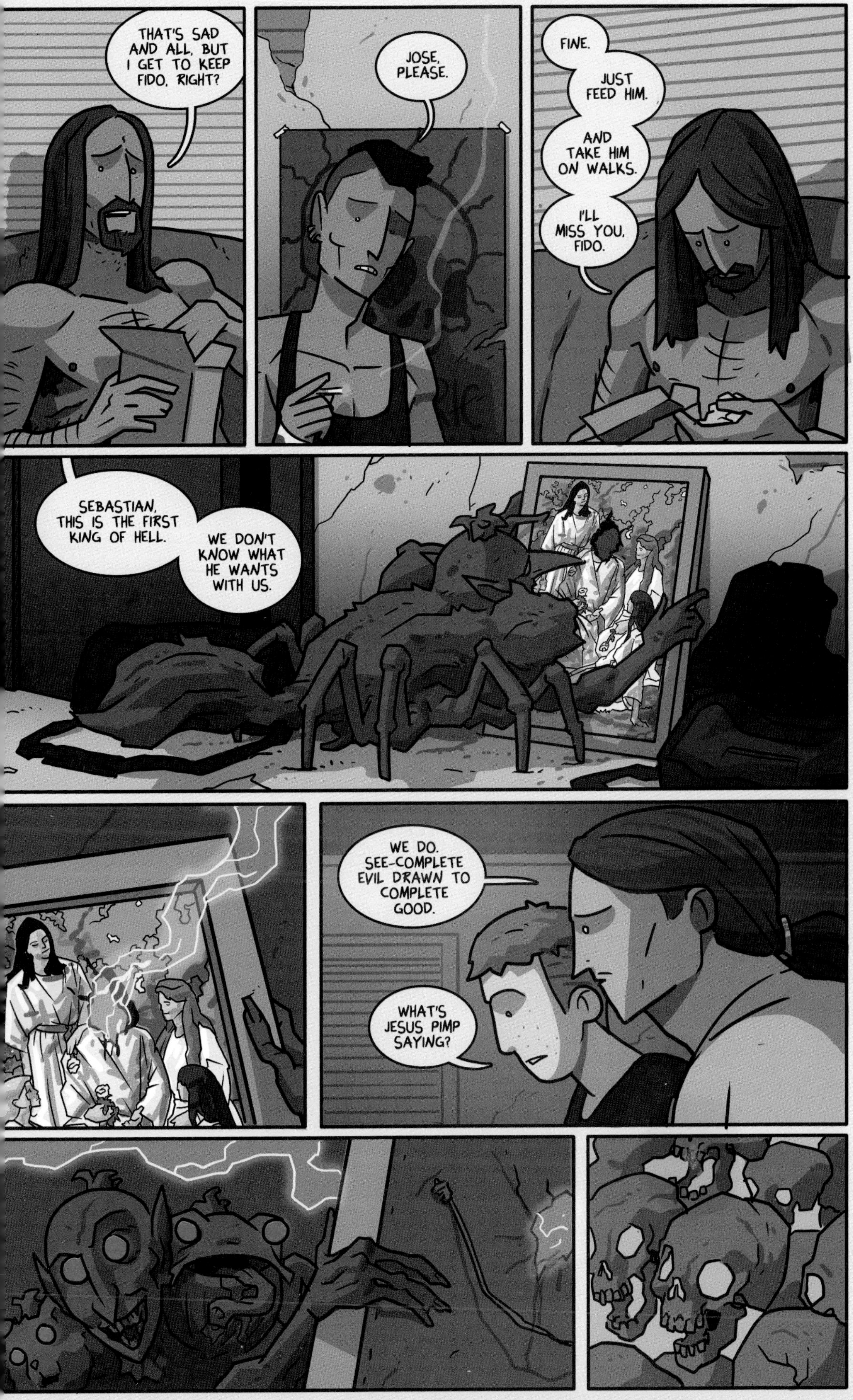
THAT'S SAD AND ALL, BUT I GET TO KEEP FIDO, RIGHT?
JOSE, PLEASE.
FINE.
JUST FEED HIM.
AND TAKE HIM ON WALKS.
I'LL MISS YOU, FIDO.
SEBASTIAN, THIS IS THE FIRST KING OF HELL.
WE DON'T KNOW WHAT HE WANTS WITH US.
WE DO. SEE-COMPLETE EVIL DRAWN TO COMPLETE GOOD.
WHAT'S JESUS PIMP SAYING?

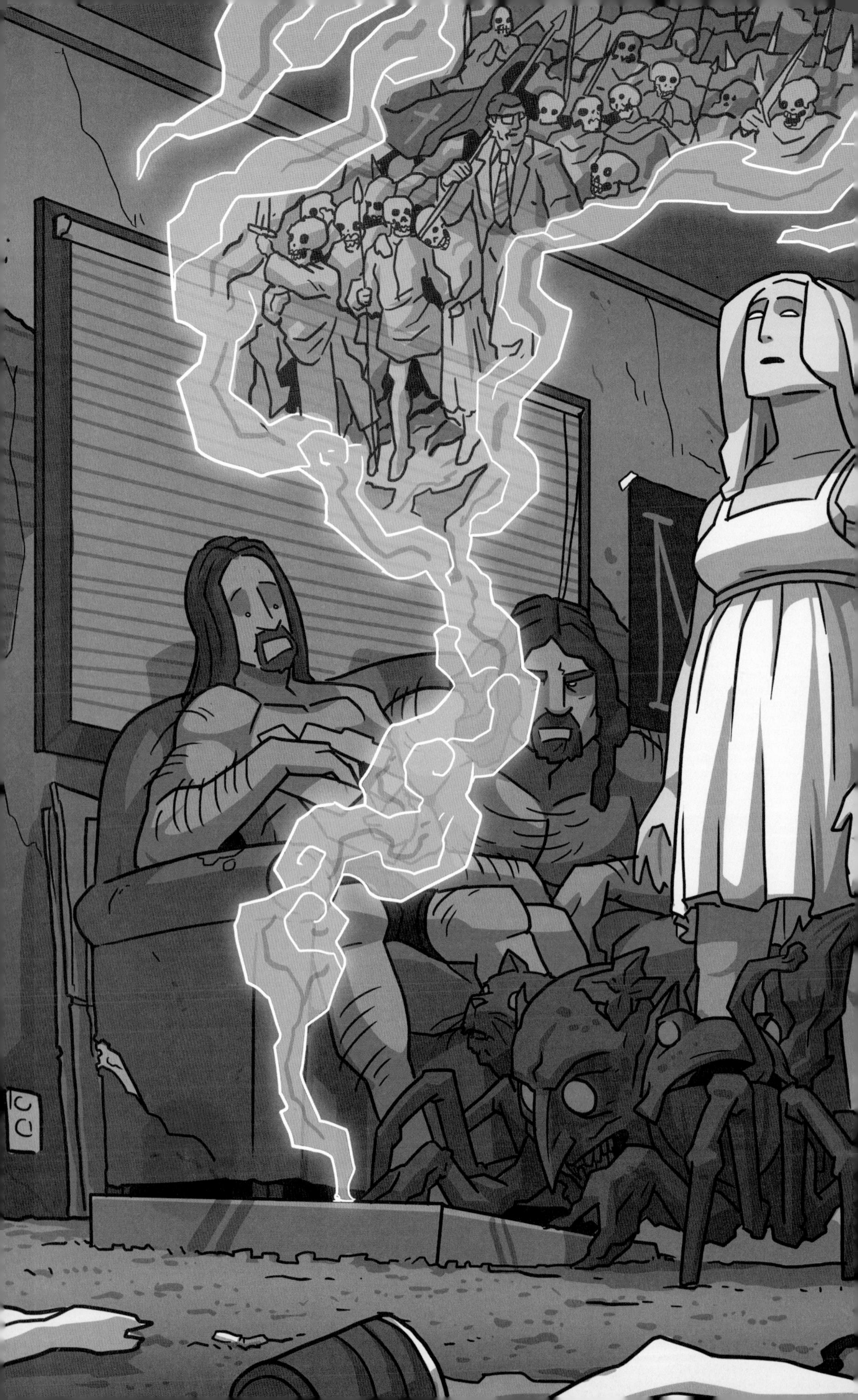

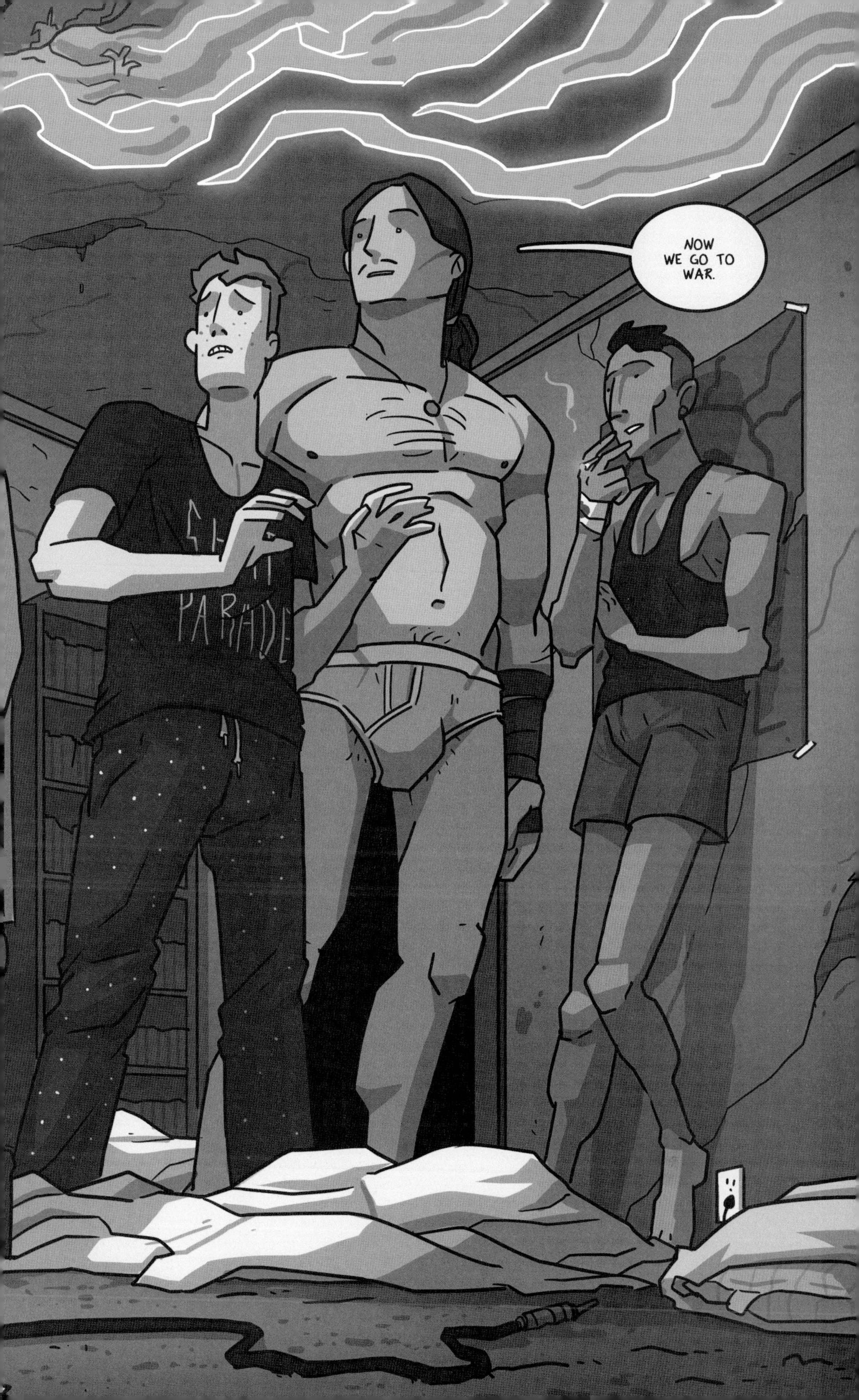
NOW WE GO TO WAR.

V
PILGRIMAGE

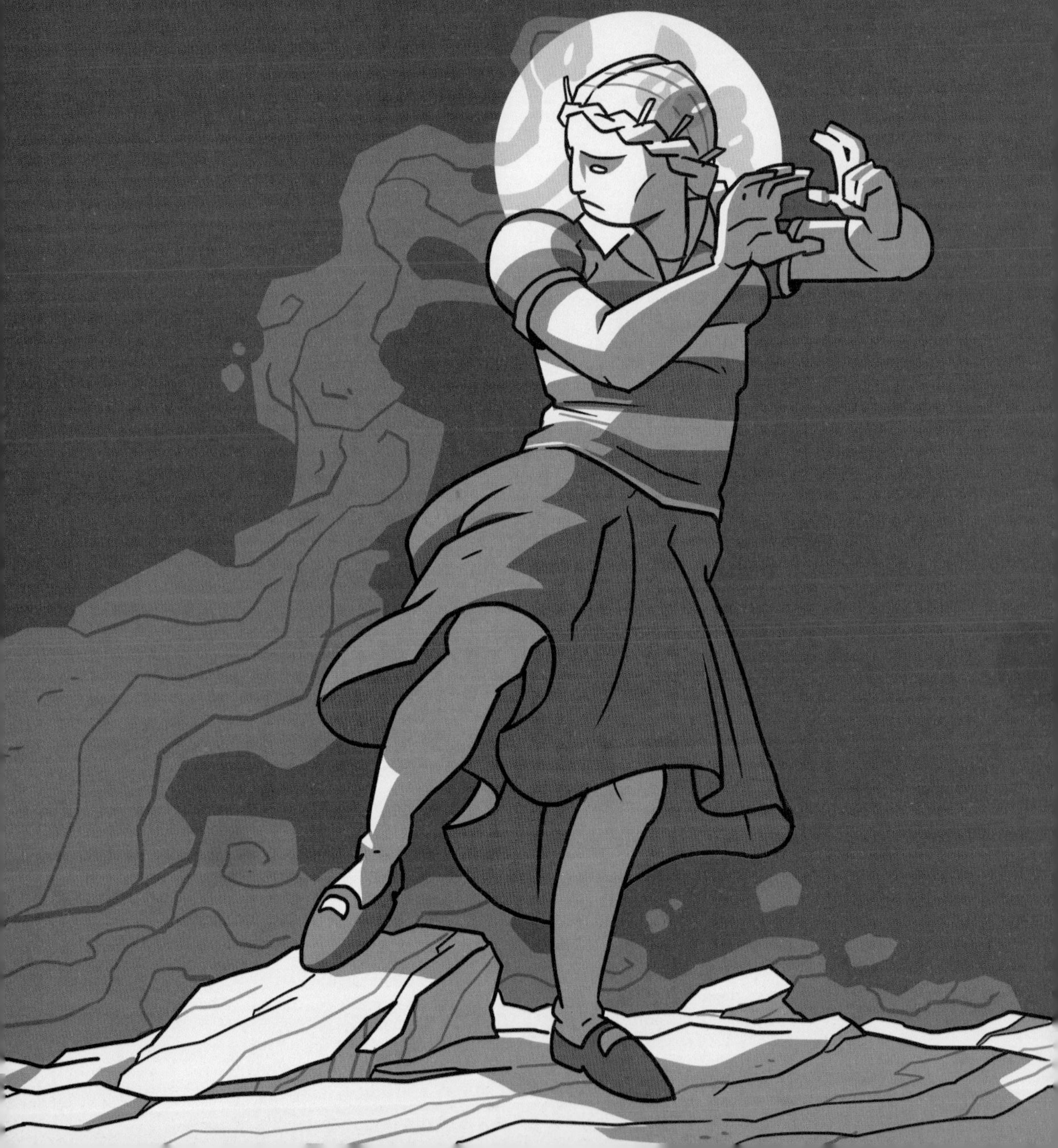

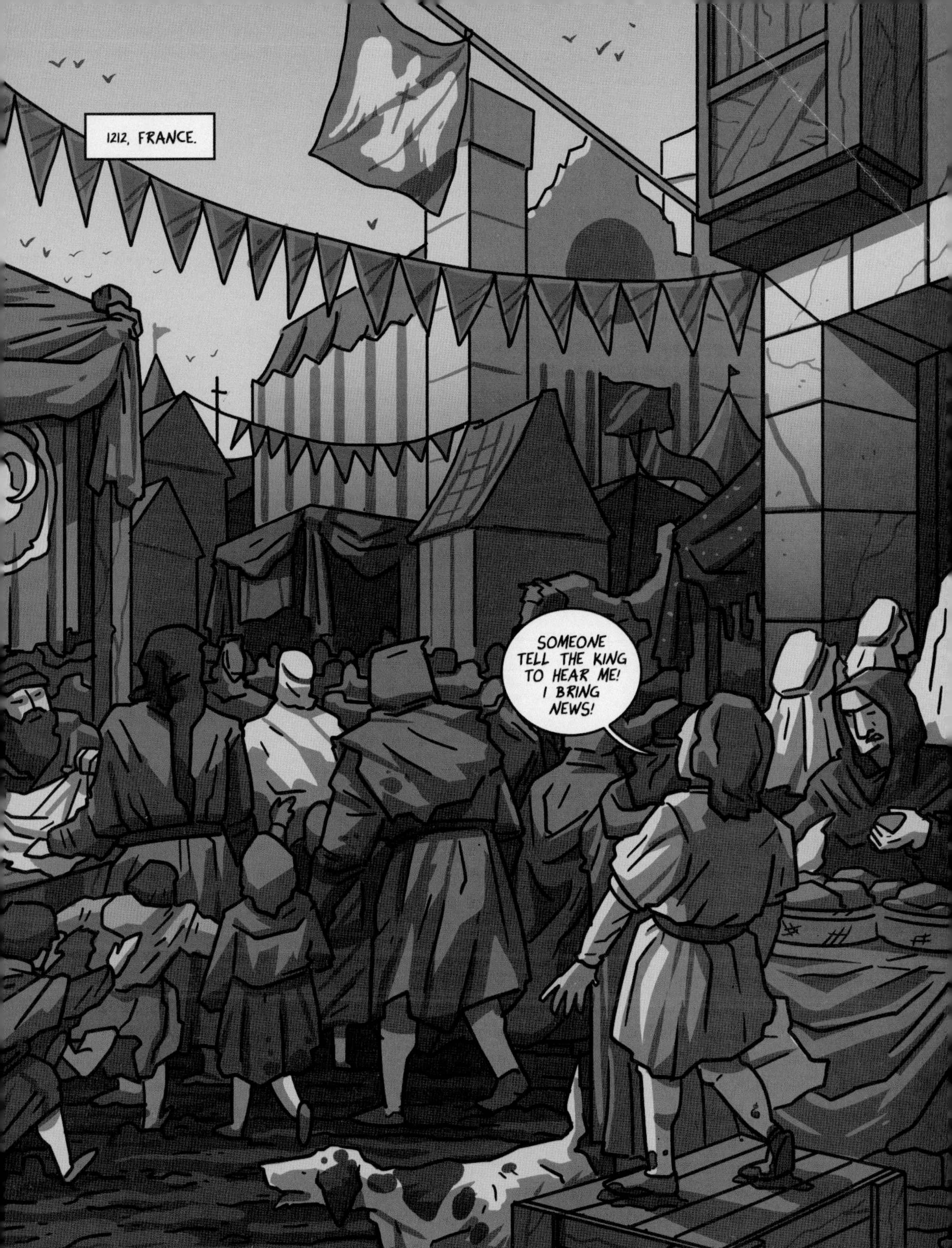
1212, FRANCE.
SOMEONE TELL THE KING TO HEAR ME! I BRING NEWS!

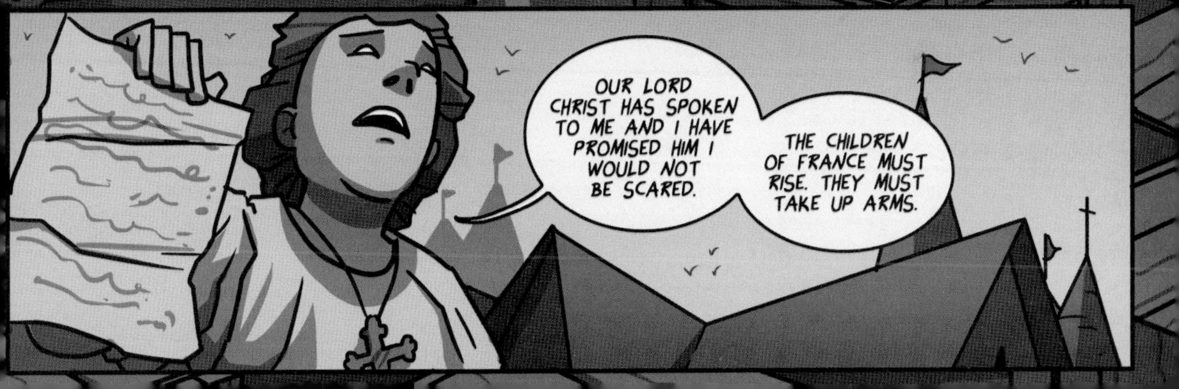
OUR LORD CHRIST HAS SPOKEN TO ME AND I HAVE PROMISED HIM I WOULD NOT BE SCARED.
THE CHILDREN OF FRANCE MUST RISE. THEY MUST TAKE UP ARMS.

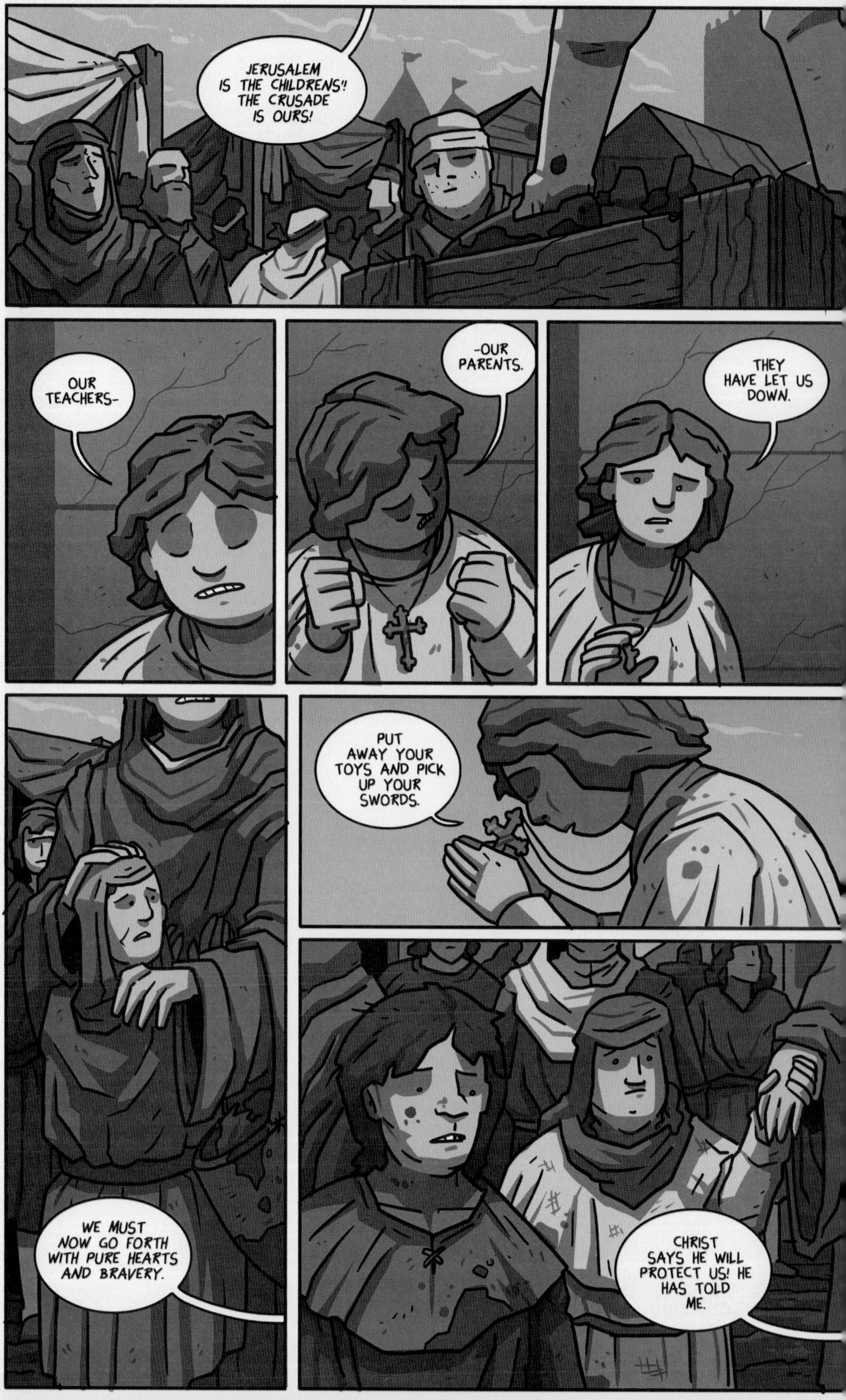
JERUSALEM IS THE CHILDRENS'! THE CRUSADE IS OURS!
OUR TEACHERS-
-OUR PARENTS.
THEY HAVE LET US DOWN.
PUT AWAY YOUR TOYS AND PICK UP YOUR SWORDS.
WE MUST NOW GO FORTH WITH PURE HEARTS AND BRAVERY.
CHRIST SAYS HE WILL PROTECT US! HE HAS TOLD ME.

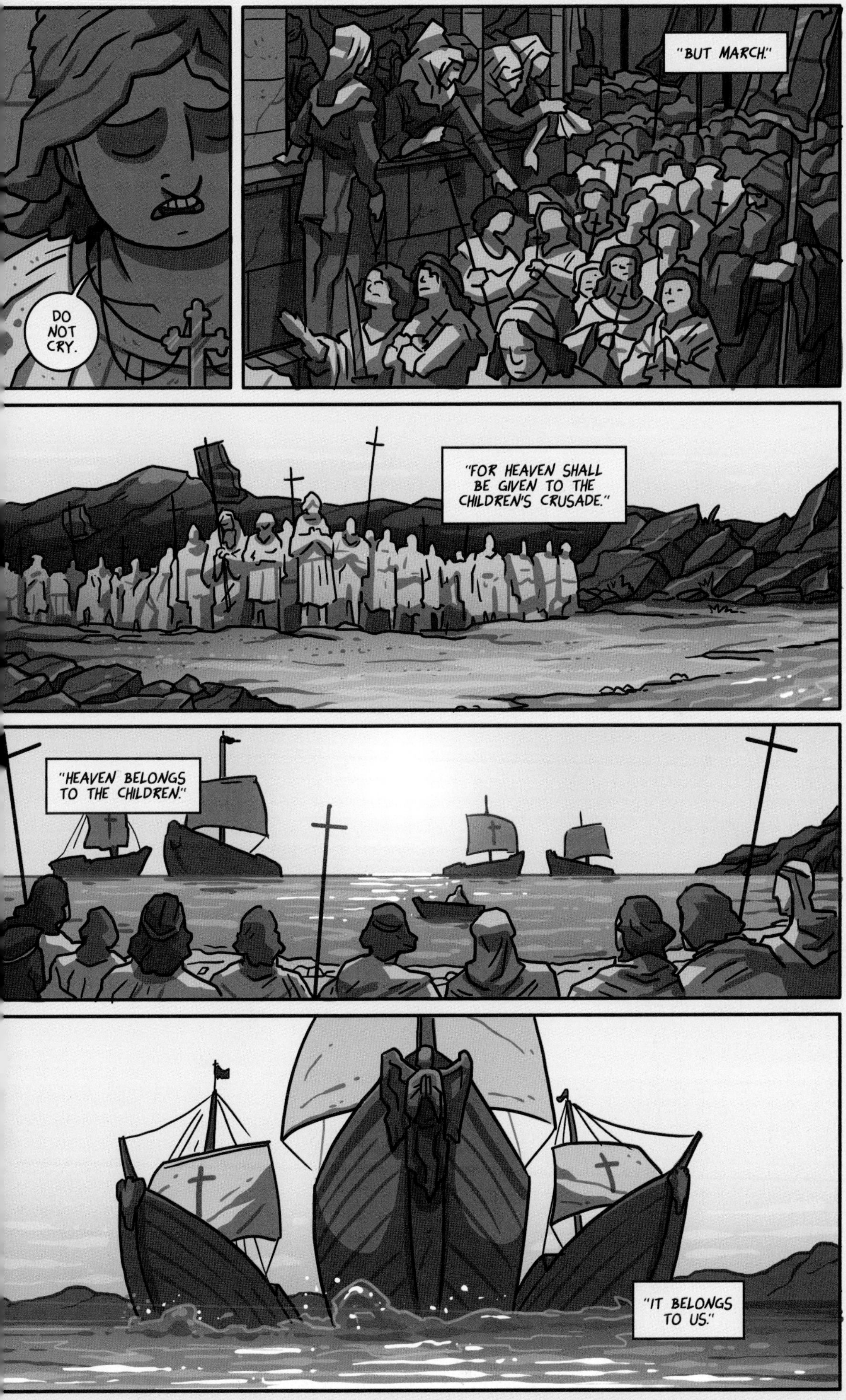
DO NOT CRY.
"BUT MARCH."
"FOR HEAVEN SHALL BE GIVEN TO THE CHILDREN'S CRUSADE."
"HEAVEN BELONGS TO THE CHILDREN."
"IT BELONGS TO US."

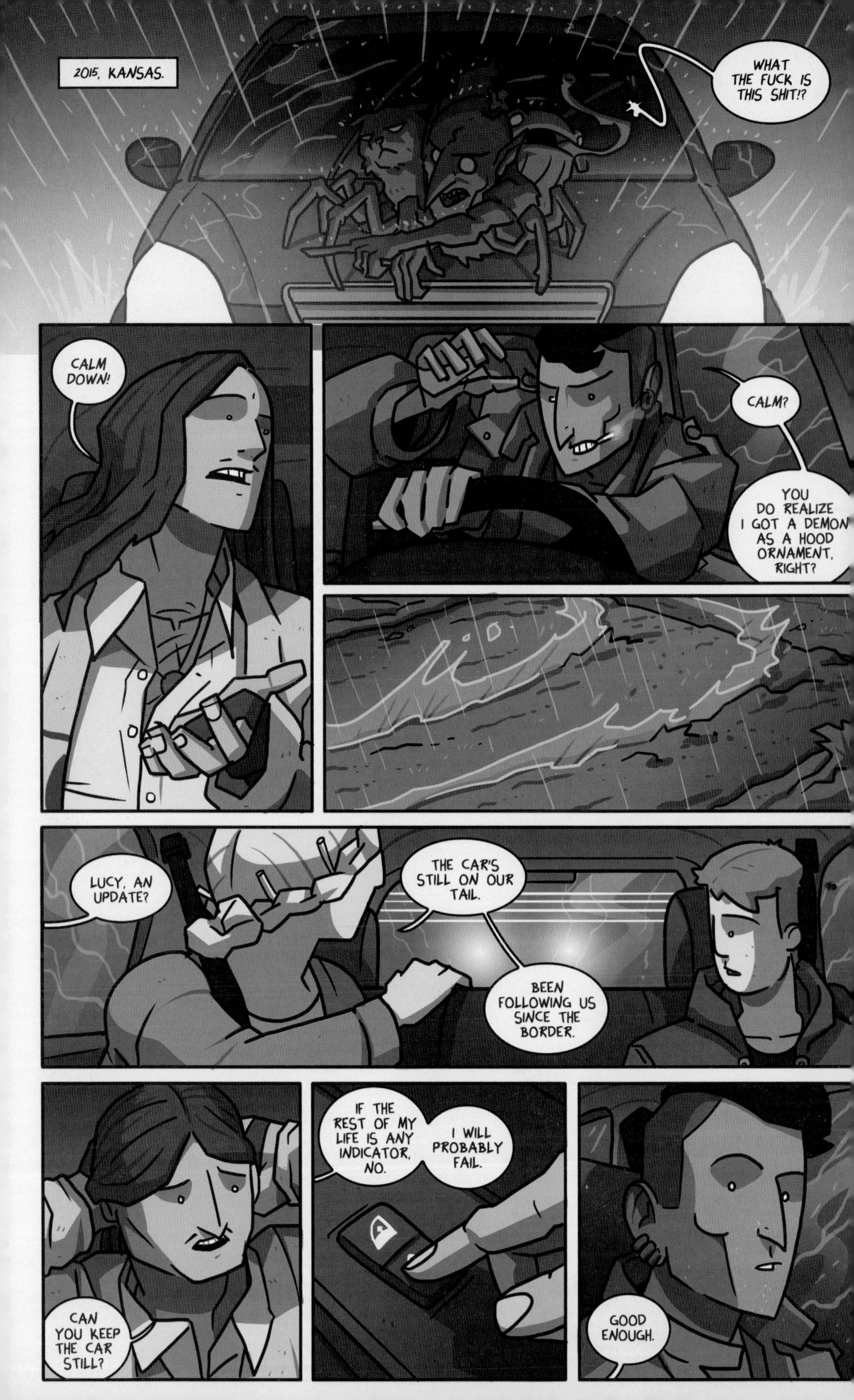
2015, KANSAS.
WHAT THE FUCK IS THIS SHIT!?
CALM DOWN!
CALM?
YOU DO REALIZE I GOT A DEMON AS A HOOD ORNAMENT, RIGHT?
LUCY, AN UPDATE?
THE CAR'S STILL ON OUR TAIL.
BEEN FOLLOWING US SINCE THE BORDER.
CAN YOU KEEP THE CAR STILL?
IF THE REST OF MY LIFE IS ANY INDICATOR, NO.
I WILL PROBABLY FAIL.
GOOD ENOUGH.

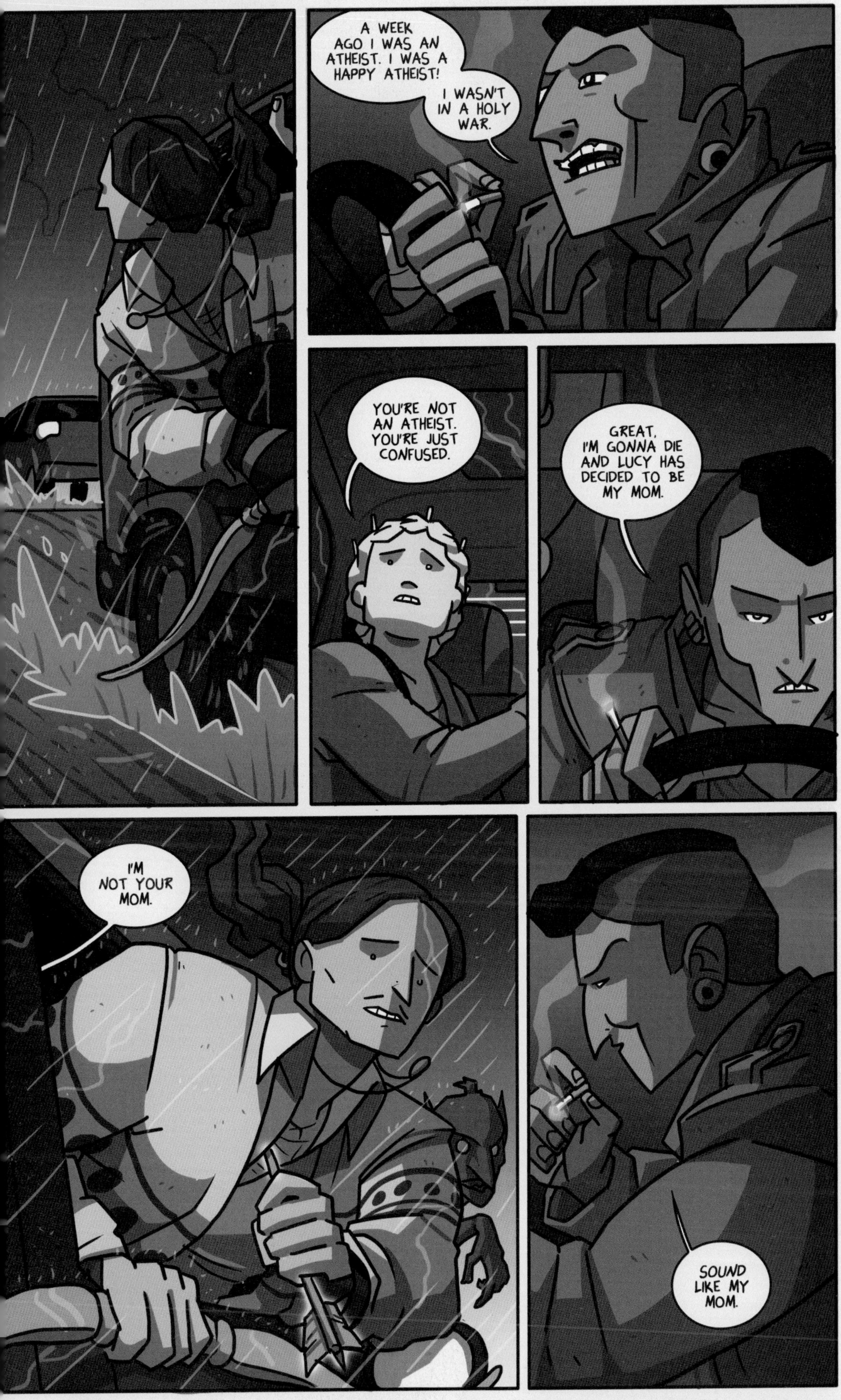
A WEEK AGO I WAS AN ATHEIST. I WAS A HAPPY ATHEIST!
I WASN'T IN A HOLY WAR.
YOU'RE NOT AN ATHEIST. YOU'RE JUST CONFUSED.
GREAT, I'M GONNA DIE AND LUCY HAS DECIDED TO BE MY MOM.
I'M NOT YOUR MOM.
SOUND LIKE MY MOM.

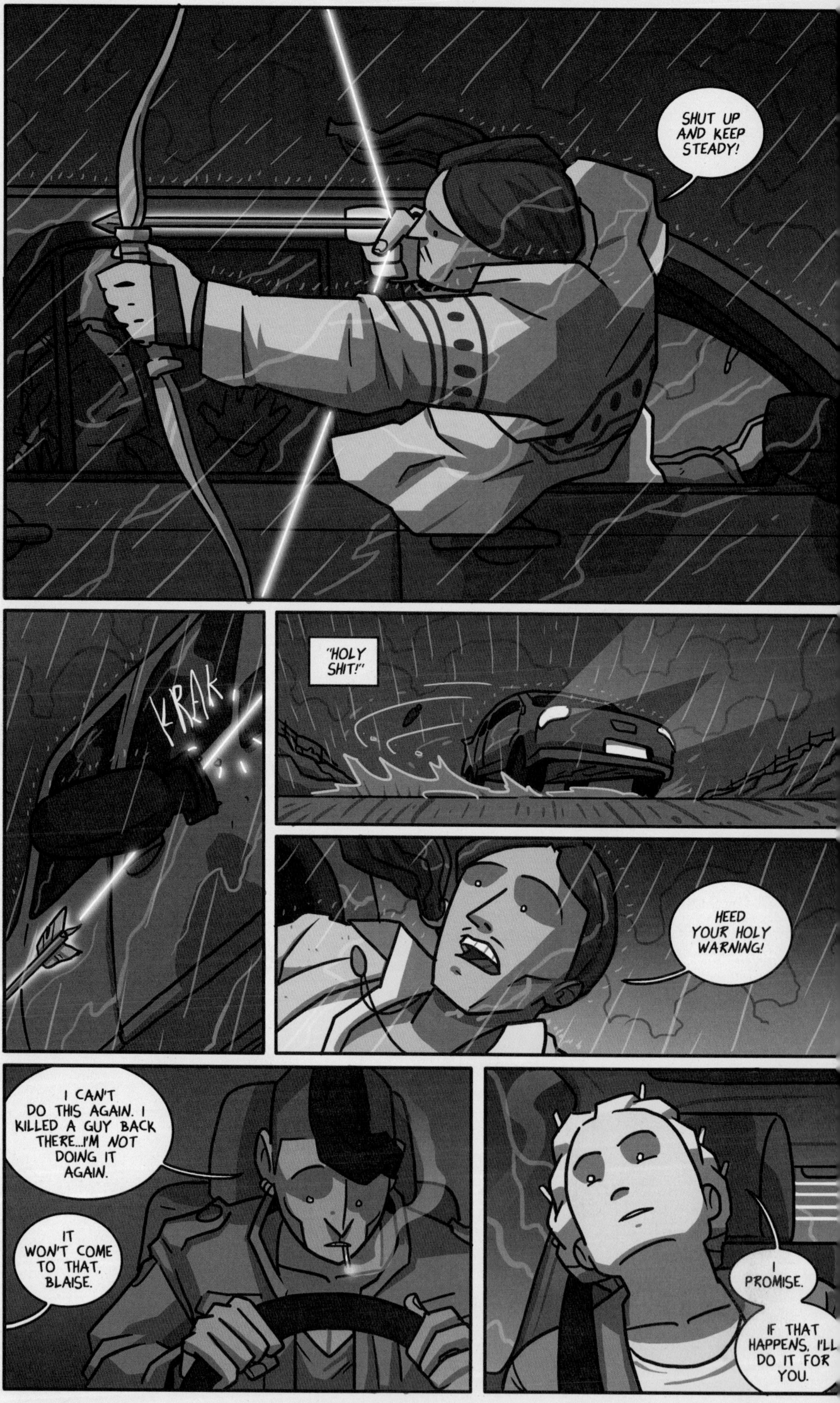
SHUT UP AND KEEP STEADY!
KRAK
"HOLY SHIT!"
HEED YOUR HOLY WARNING!
I CAN'T DO THIS AGAIN. I KILLED A GUY BACK THERE...I'M NOT DOING IT AGAIN.
IT WON'T COME TO THAT, BLAISE.
I PROMISE.
IF THAT HAPPENS, I'LL DO IT FOR YOU.

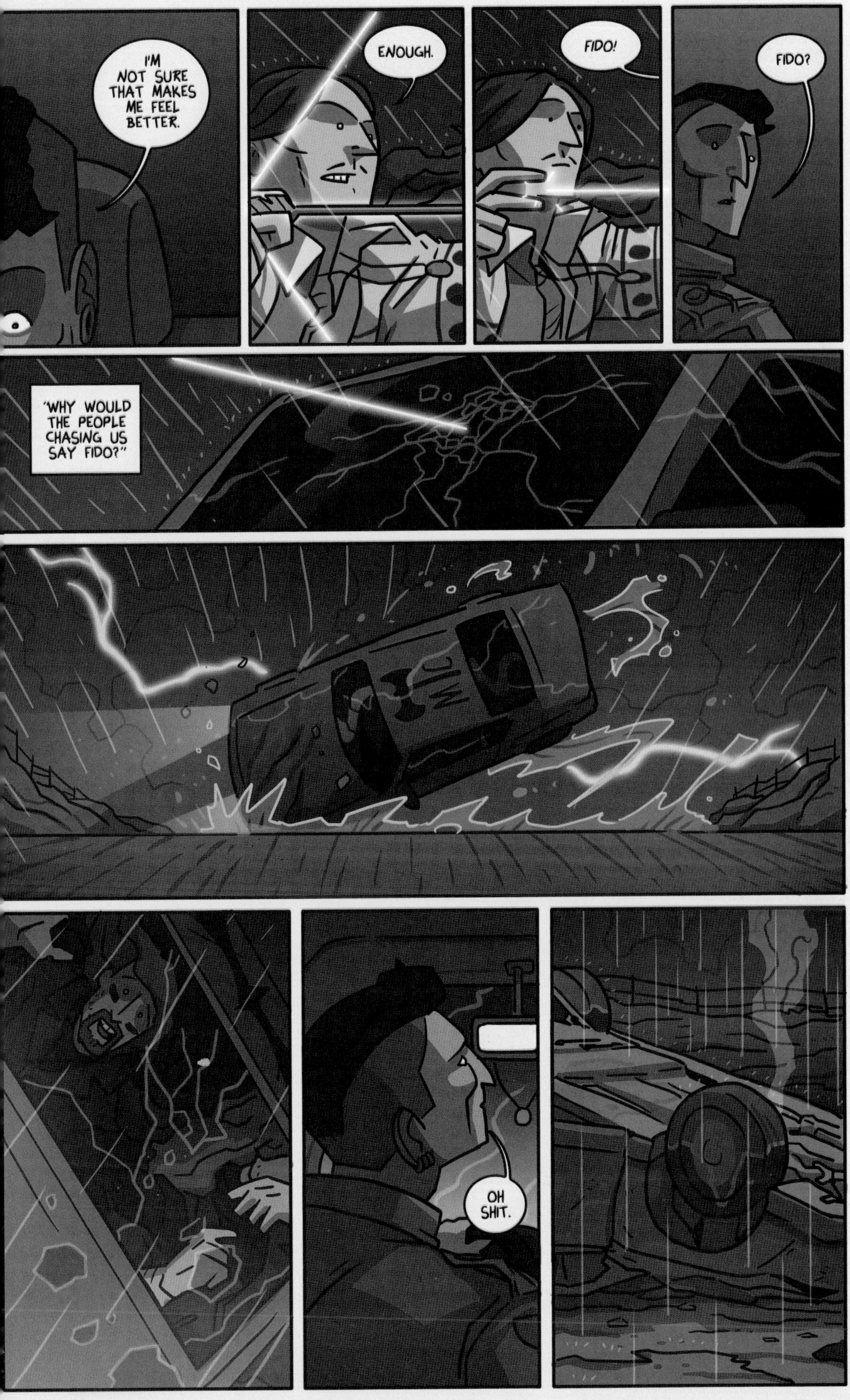
I'M NOT SURE THAT MAKES ME FEEL BETTER.
ENOUGH.
FIDO!
FIDO?
"WHY WOULD THE PEOPLE CHASING US SAY FIDO?"
OH SHIT.

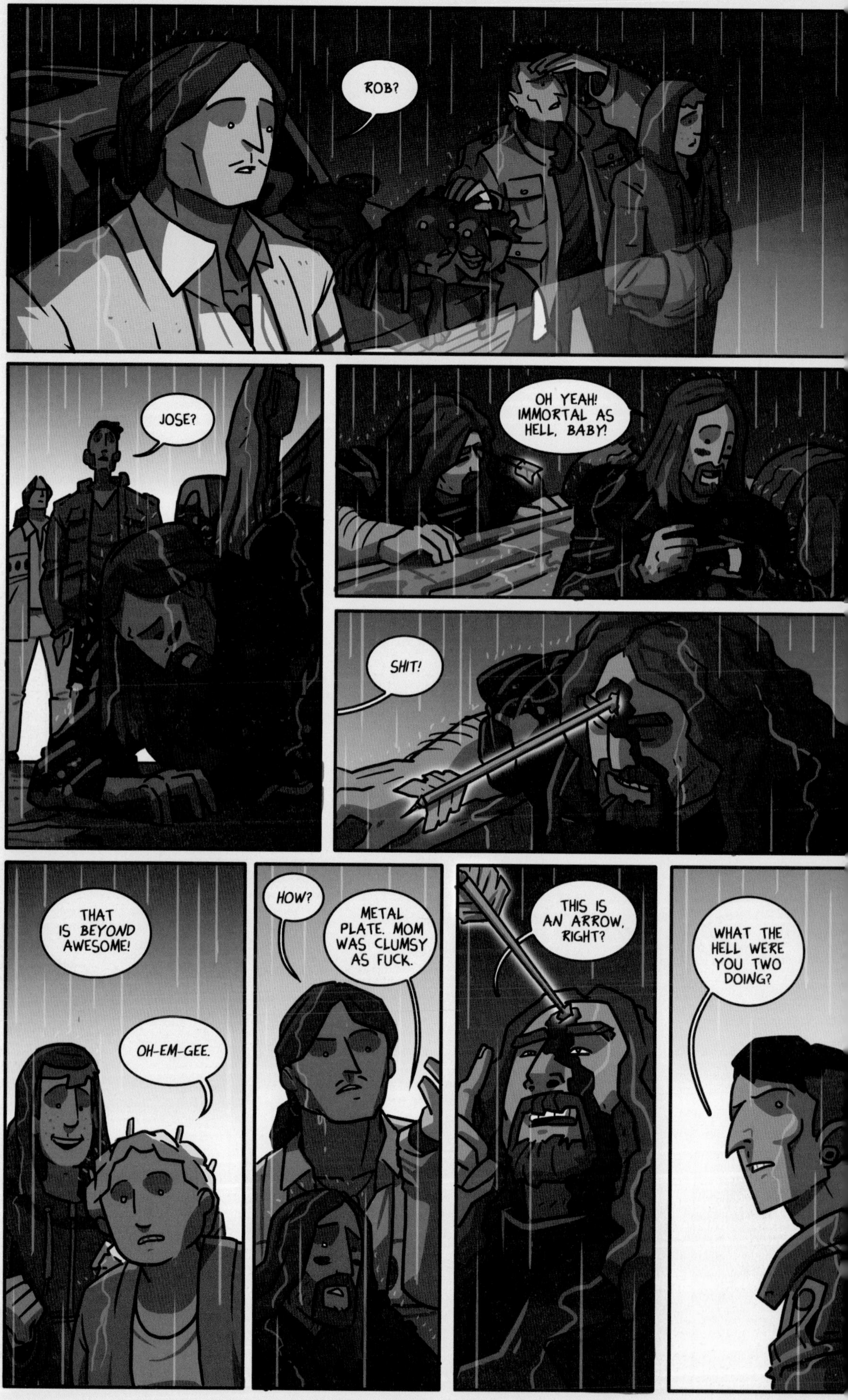
ROB?
JOSE?
OH YEAH! IMMORTAL AS HELL, BABY!
SHIT!
THAT IS BEYOND AWESOME!
OH-EM-GEE.
HOW?
METAL PLATE. MOM WAS CLUMSY AS FUCK.
THIS IS AN ARROW, RIGHT?
WHAT THE HELL WERE YOU TWO DOING?

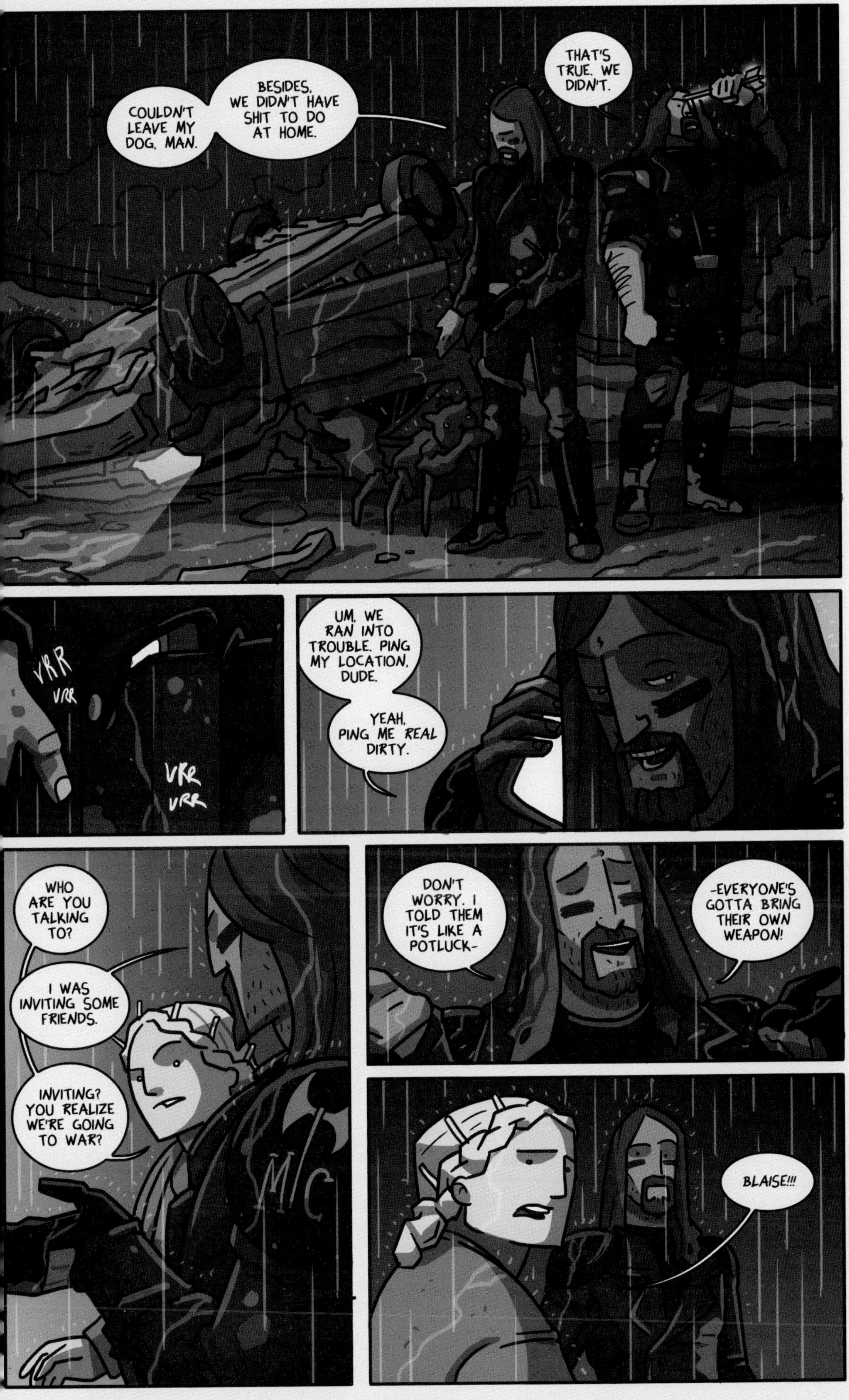
COULDN'T LEAVE MY DOG, MAN.
BESIDES, WE DIDN'T HAVE SHIT TO DO AT HOME.
THAT'S TRUE. WE DIDN'T.
VRR
VRR
VRR
VRR
UM, WE RAN INTO TROUBLE. PING MY LOCATION, DUDE.
YEAH, PING ME REAL DIRTY.
WHO ARE YOU TALKING TO?
I WAS INVITING SOME FRIENDS.
INVITING? YOU REALIZE WE'RE GOING TO WAR?
MC
DON'T WORRY. I TOLD THEM IT'S LIKE A POTLUCK-
-EVERYONE'S GOTTA BRING THEIR OWN WEAPON!
BLAISE!!!

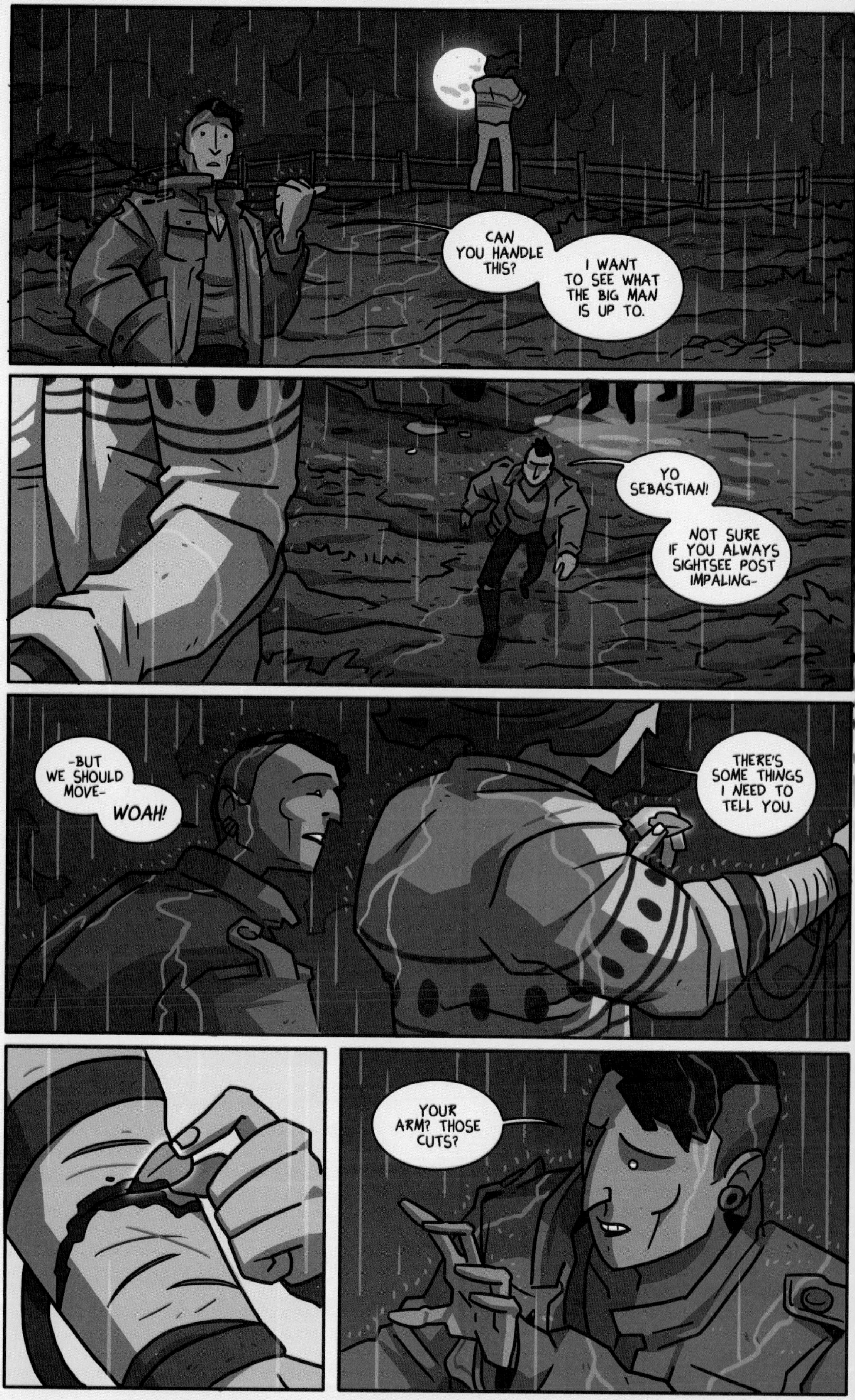
CAN YOU HANDLE THIS?
I WANT TO SEE WHAT THE BIG MAN IS UP TO.
YO SEBASTIAN!
NOT SURE IF YOU ALWAYS SIGHTSEE POST IMPALING-
-BUT WE SHOULD MOVE-
WOAH!
THERE'S SOME THINGS I NEED TO TELL YOU.
YOUR ARM? THOSE CUTS?

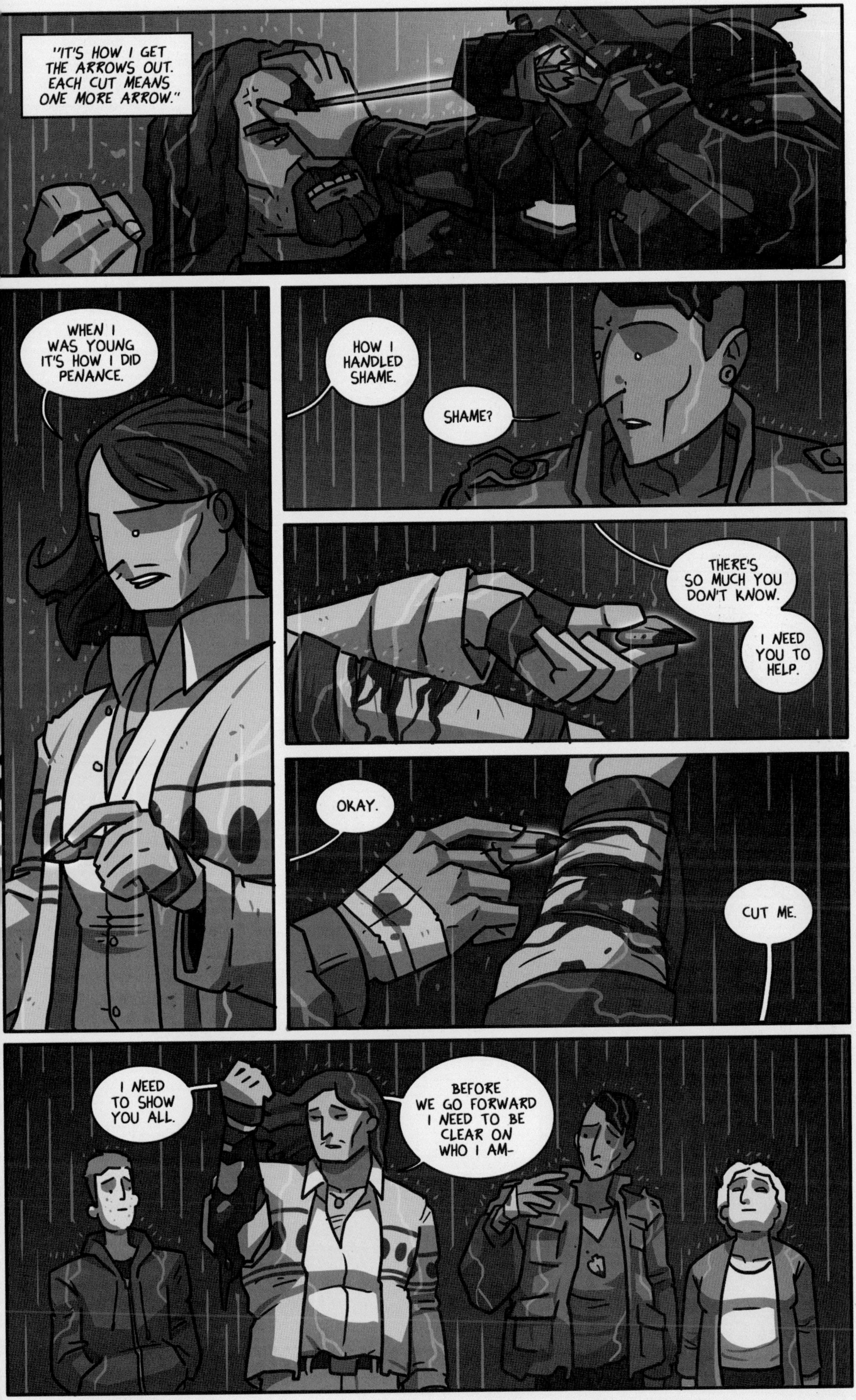
"IT'S HOW I GET THE ARROWS OUT. EACH CUT MEANS ONE MORE ARROW."
WHEN I WAS YOUNG IT'S HOW I DID PENANCE.
HOW I HANDLED SHAME.
SHAME?
THERE'S SO MUCH YOU DON'T KNOW.
I NEED YOU TO HELP.
OKAY.
CUT ME.
I NEED TO SHOW YOU ALL.
BEFORE WE GO FORWARD I NEED TO BE CLEAR ON WHO I AM-

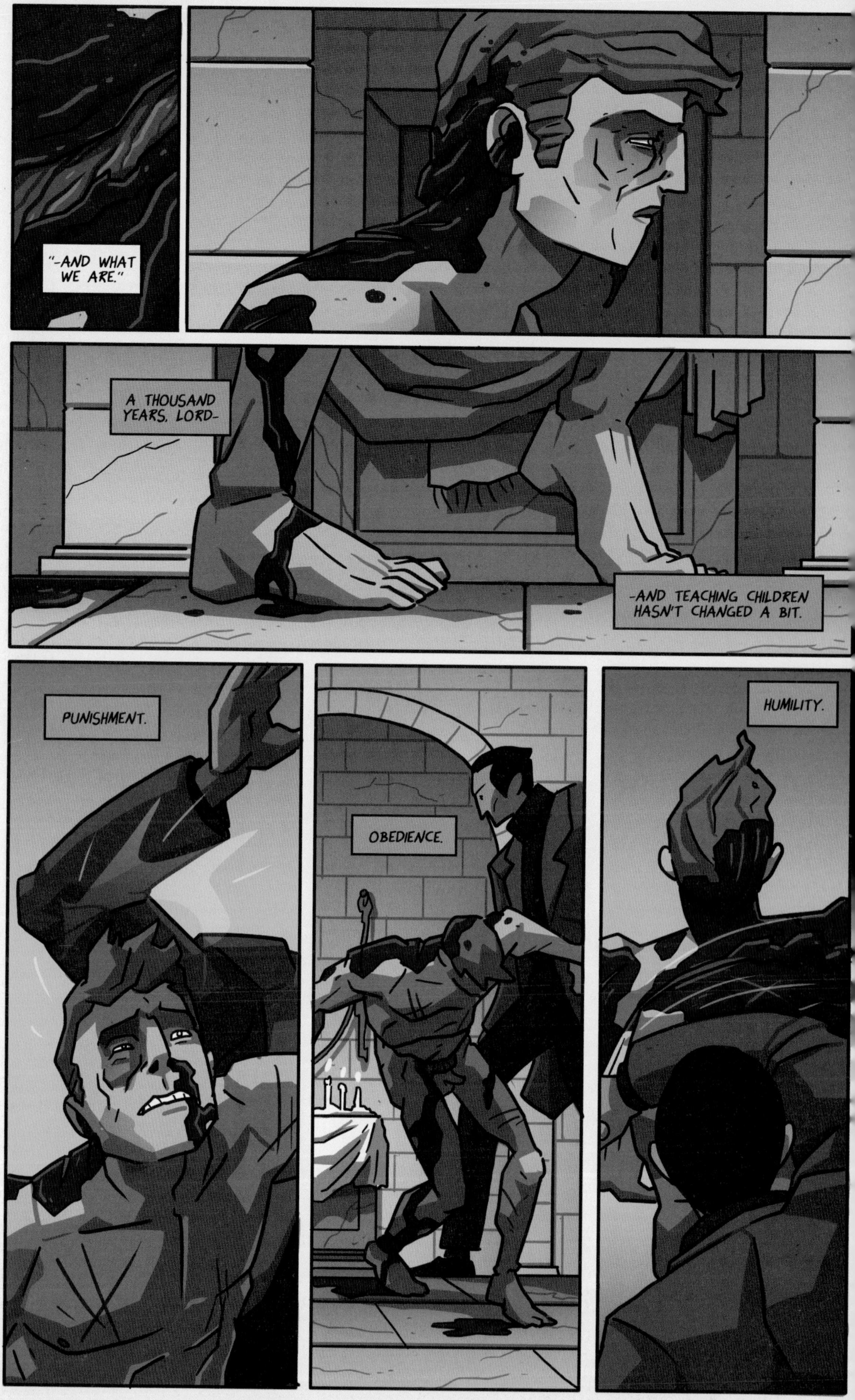
"-AND WHAT WE ARE."
A THOUSAND YEARS, LORD-
-AND TEACHING CHILDREN HASN'T CHANGED A BIT.
PUNISHMENT.
OBEDIENCE.
HUMILITY.

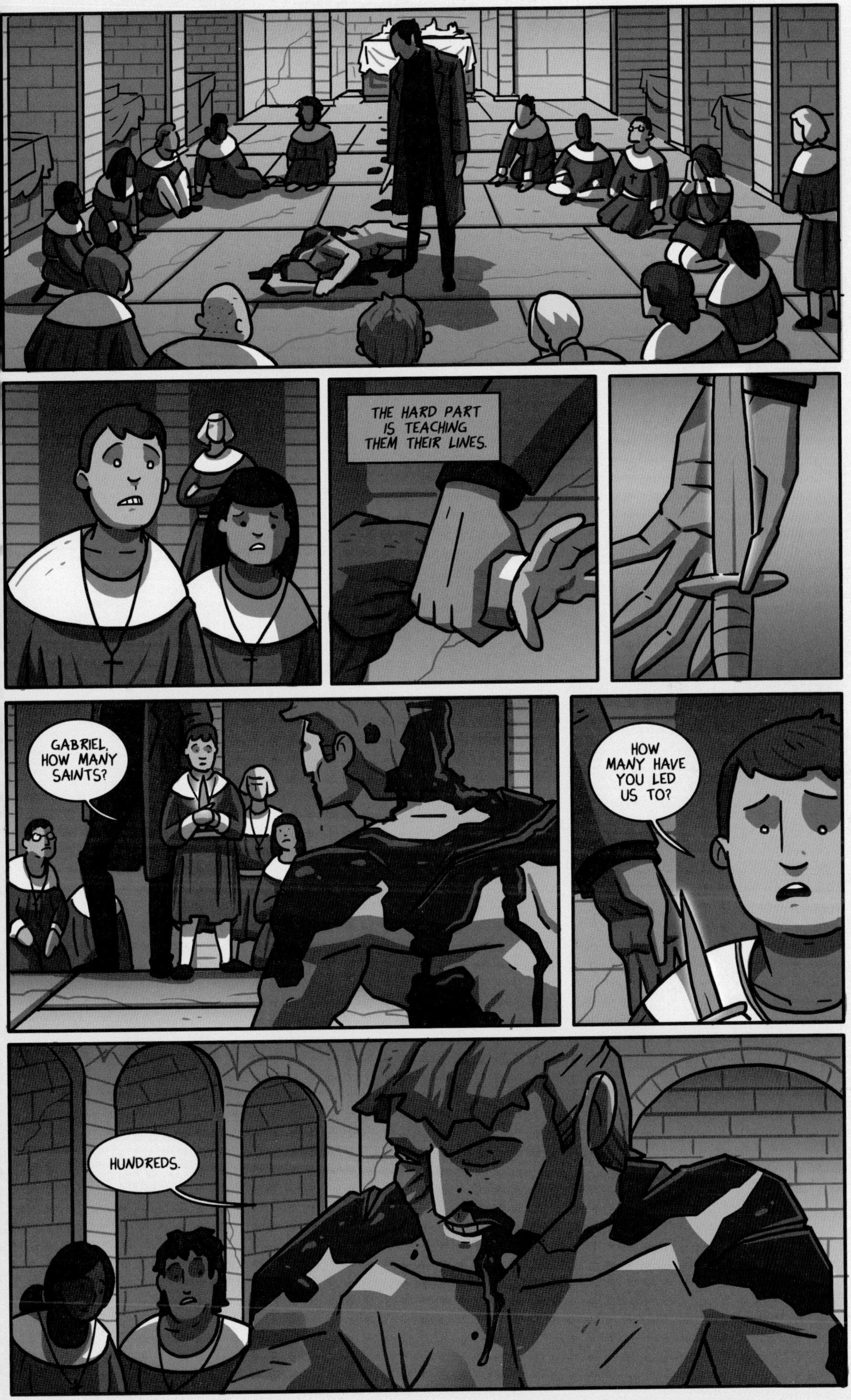
THE HARD PART IS TEACHING THEM THEIR LINES.
GABRIEL, HOW MANY SAINTS?
HOW MANY HAVE YOU LED US TO?
HUNDREDS.

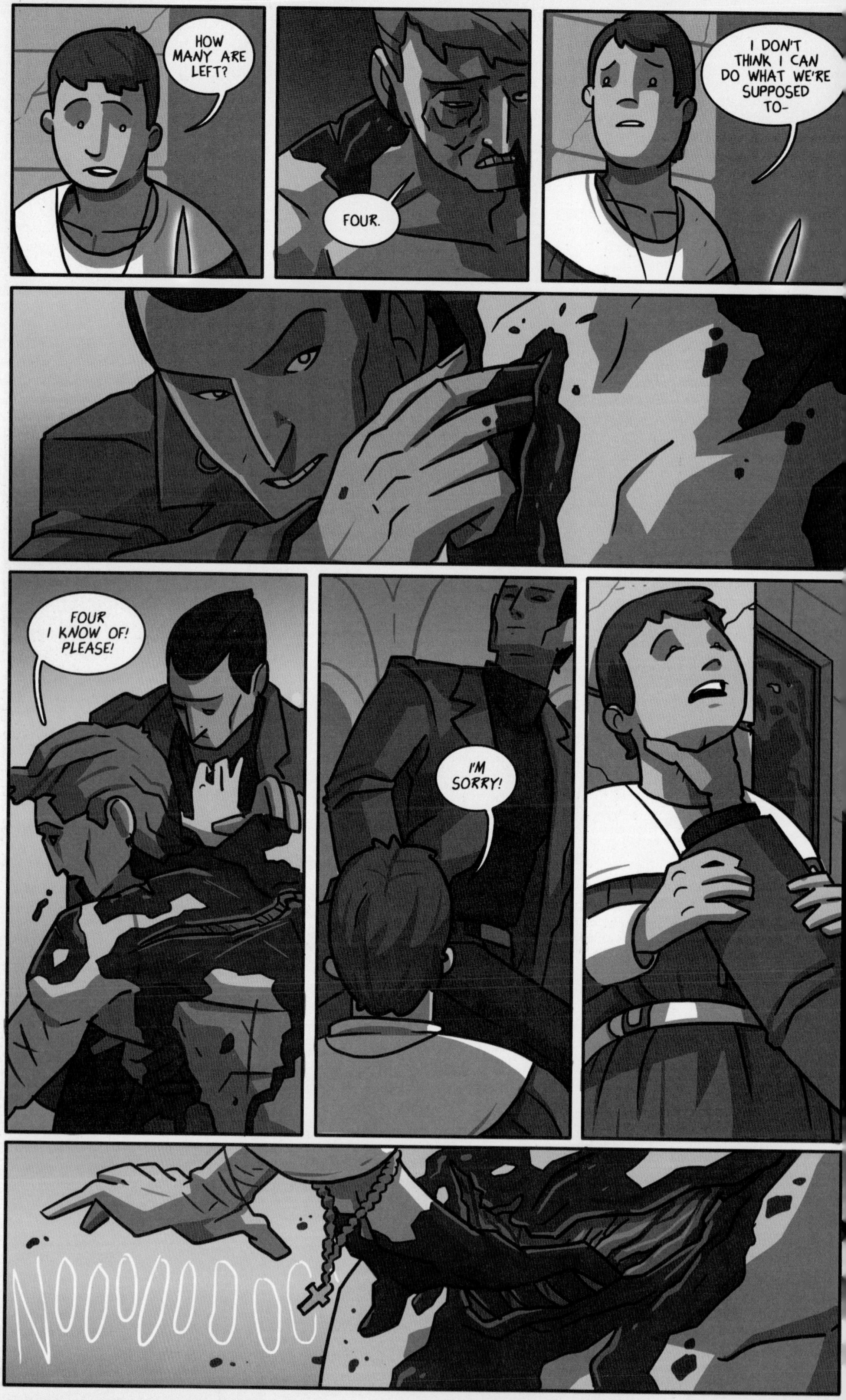
HOW MANY ARE LEFT?
FOUR.
I DON'T THINK I CAN DO WHAT WE'RE SUPPOSED TO-
FOUR I KNOW OF! PLEASE!
I'M SORRY!
NOOOOOOOO

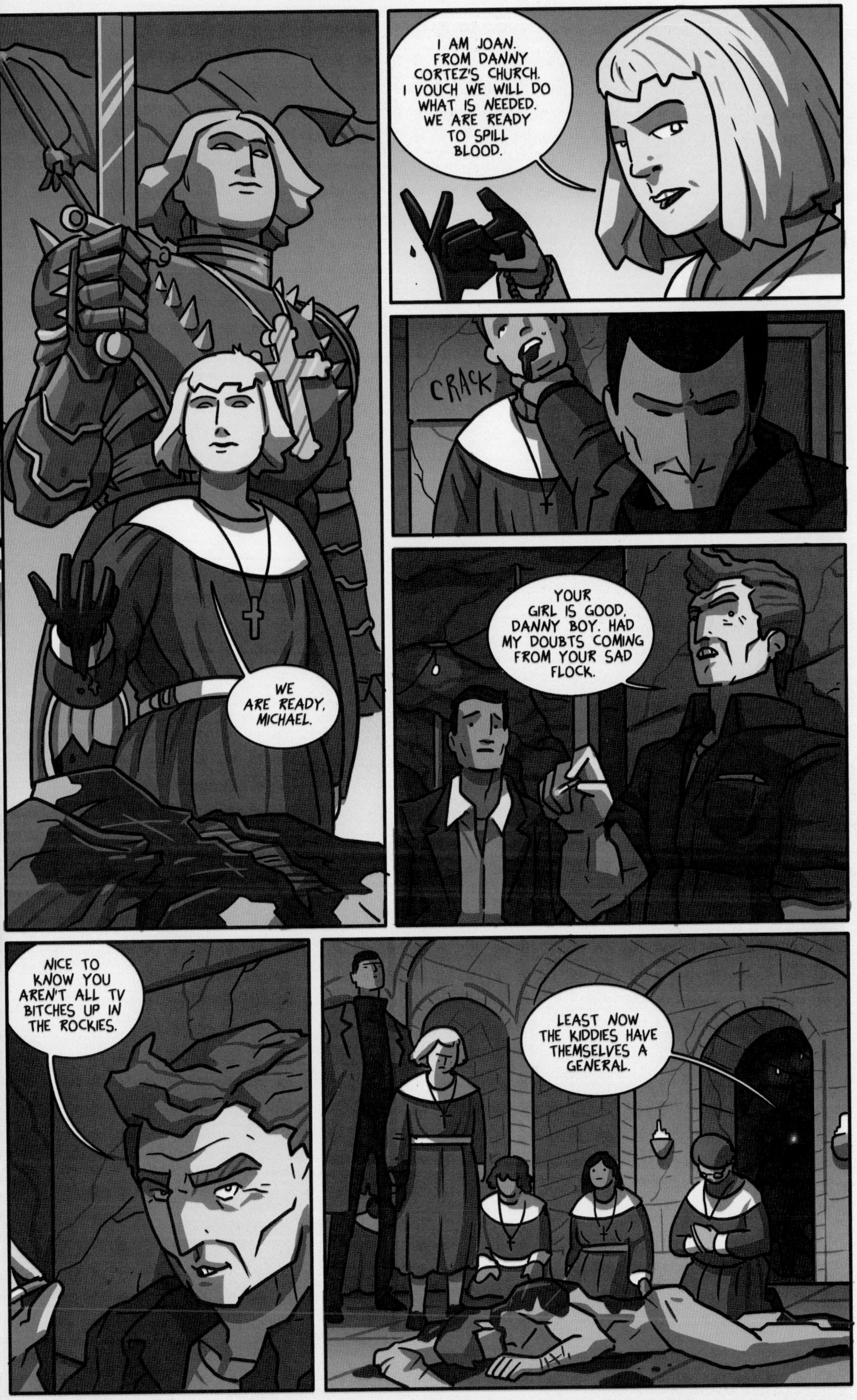
WE ARE READY, MICHAEL.
I AM JOAN. FROM DANNY CORTEZ'S CHURCH. I VOUCH WE WILL DO WHAT IS NEEDED. WE ARE READY TO SPILL BLOOD.
CRACK
YOUR GIRL IS GOOD, DANNY BOY. HAD MY DOUBTS COMING FROM YOUR SAD FLOCK.
NICE TO KNOW YOU AREN'T ALL TV BITCHES UP IN THE ROCKIES.
LEAST NOW THE KIDDIES HAVE THEMSELVES A GENERAL.

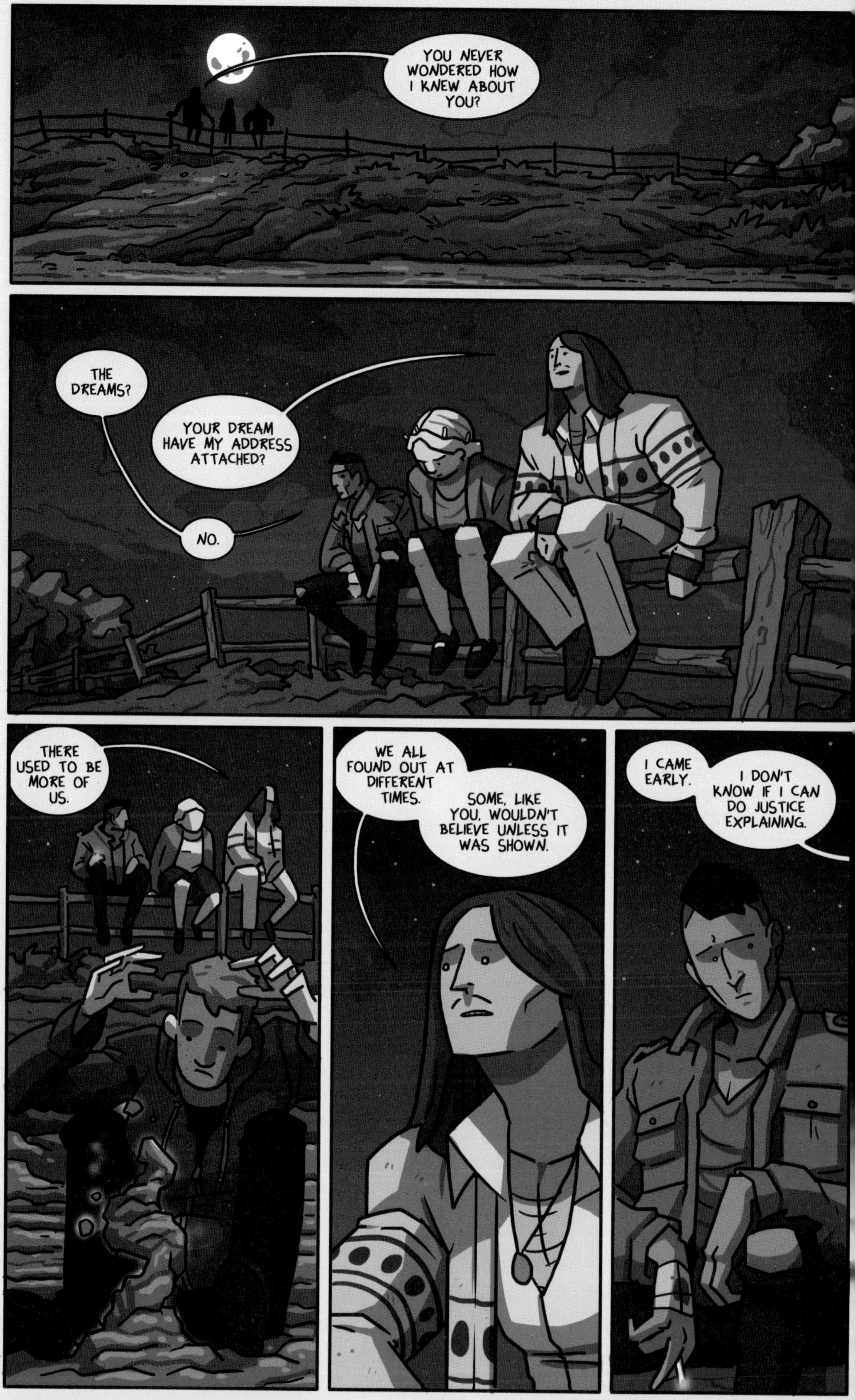
YOU NEVER WONDERED HOW I KNEW ABOUT YOU?
THE DREAMS?
YOUR DREAM HAVE MY ADDRESS ATTACHED?
NO.
THERE USED TO BE MORE OF US.
WE ALL FOUND OUT AT DIFFERENT TIMES.
SOME, LIKE YOU, WOULDN'T BELIEVE UNLESS IT WAS SHOWN.
I CAME EARLY.
I DON'T KNOW IF I CAN DO JUSTICE EXPLAINING.

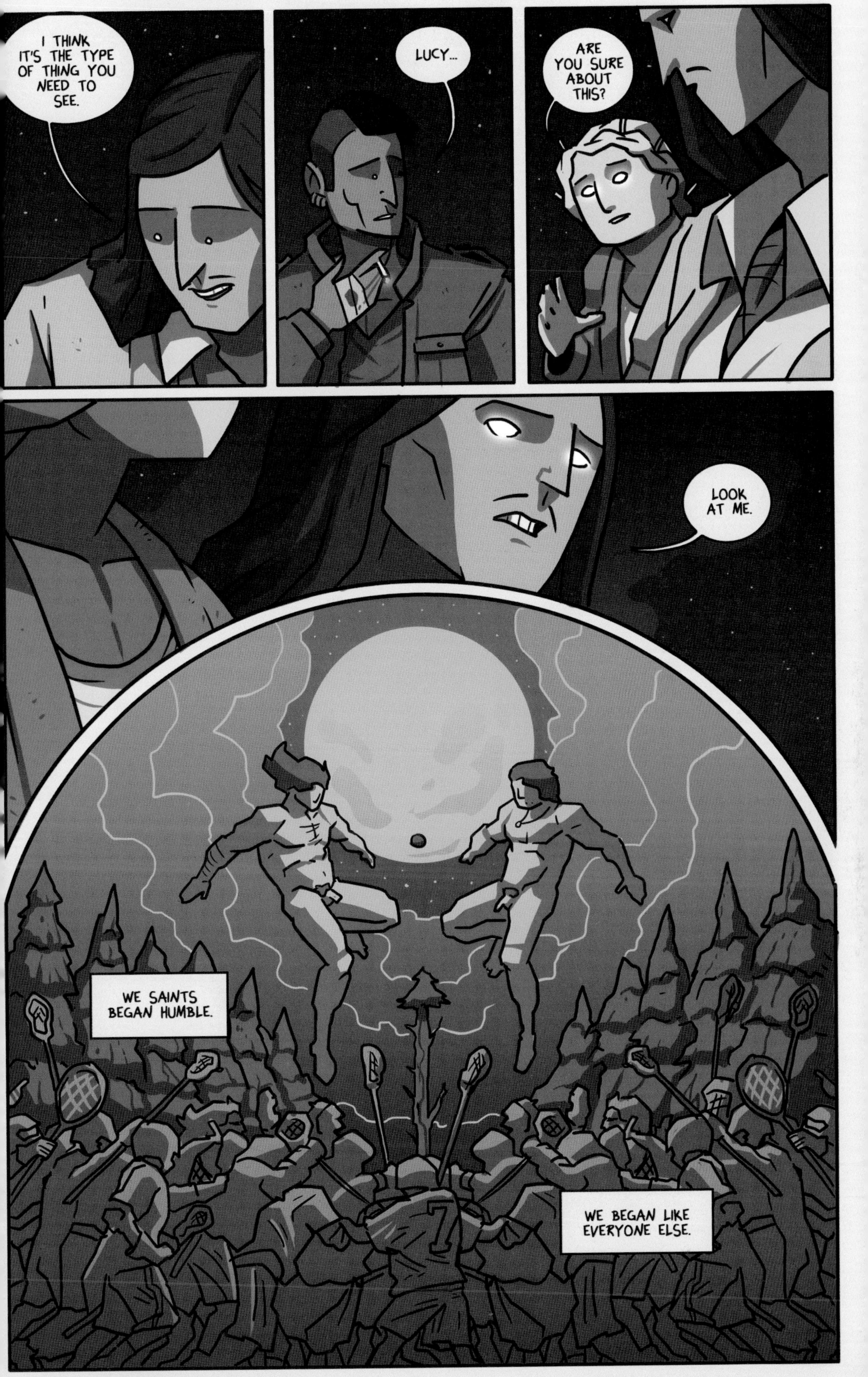
I THINK IT'S THE TYPE OF THING YOU NEED TO SEE.
LUCY...
ARE YOU SURE ABOUT THIS?
LOOK AT ME.
WE SAINTS BEGAN HUMBLE.
WE BEGAN LIKE EVERYONE ELSE.

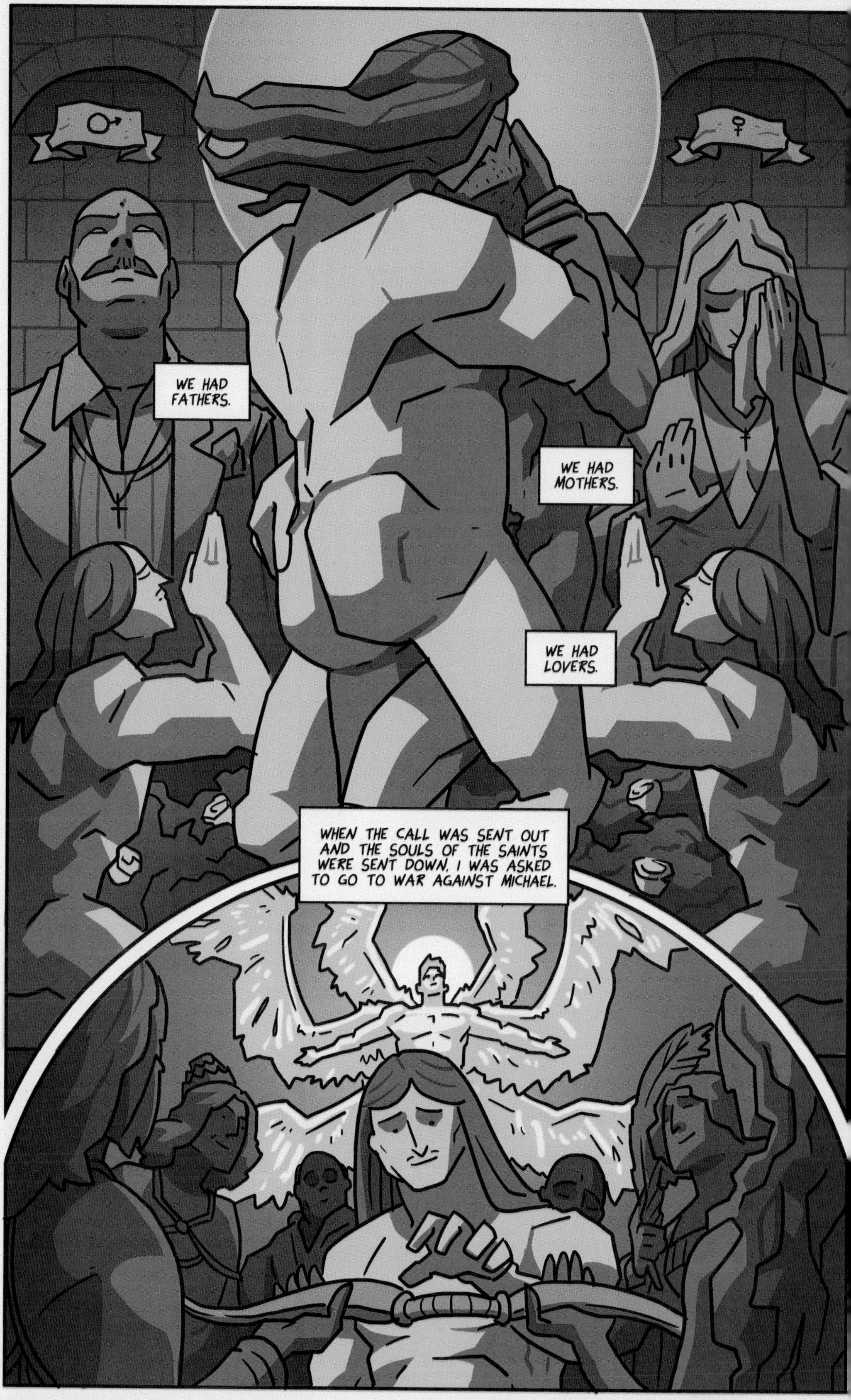
WE HAD FATHERS.
WE HAD MOTHERS.
WE HAD LOVERS.
WHEN THE CALL WAS SENT OUT AND THE SOULS OF THE SAINTS WERE SENT DOWN, I WAS ASKED TO GO TO WAR AGAINST MICHAEL.

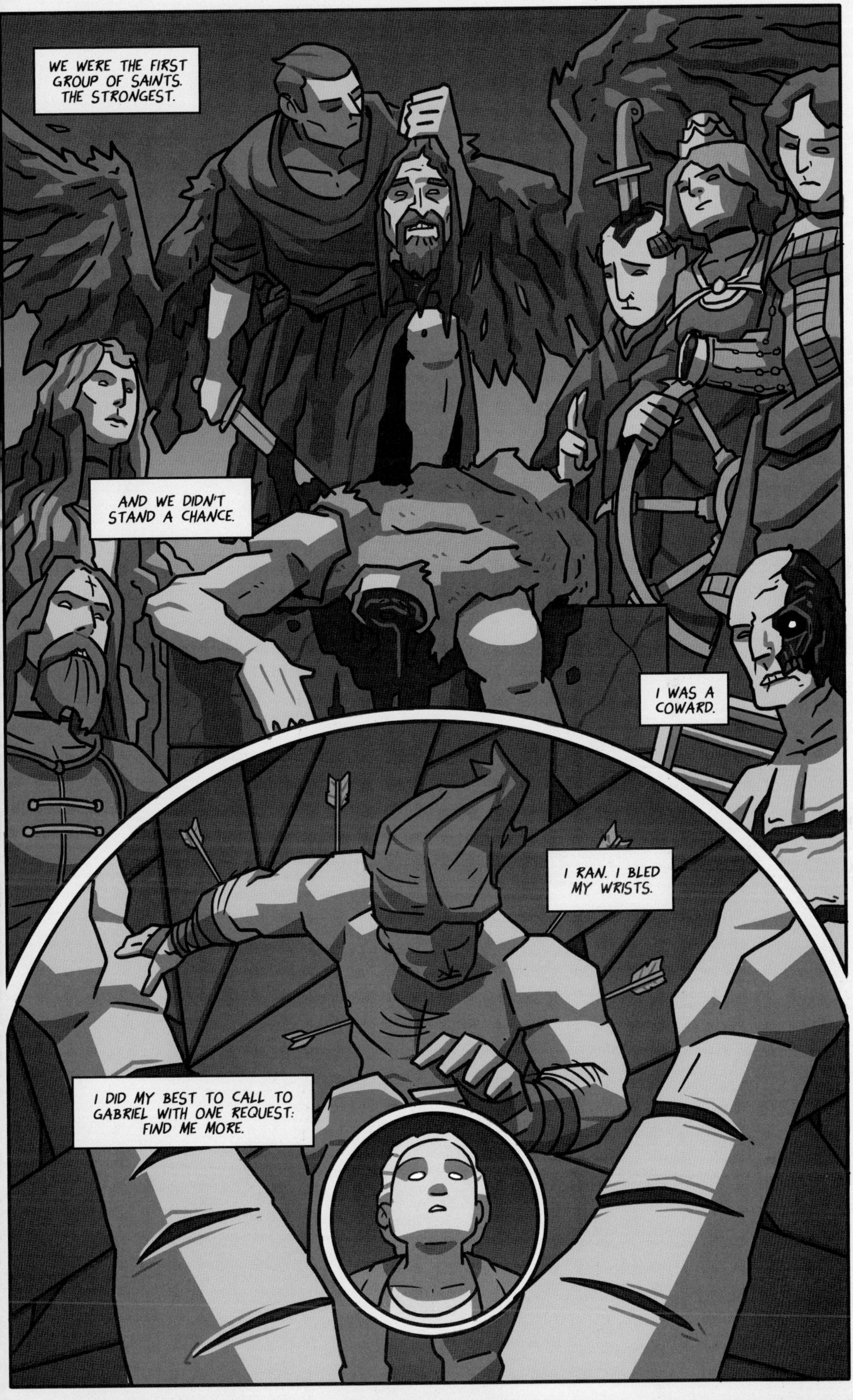
WE WERE THE FIRST GROUP OF SAINTS. THE STRONGEST.
AND WE DIDN'T STAND A CHANCE.
I WAS A COWARD.
I RAN. I BLED MY WRISTS.
I DID MY BEST TO CALL TO GABRIEL WITH ONE REQUEST: FIND ME MORE.

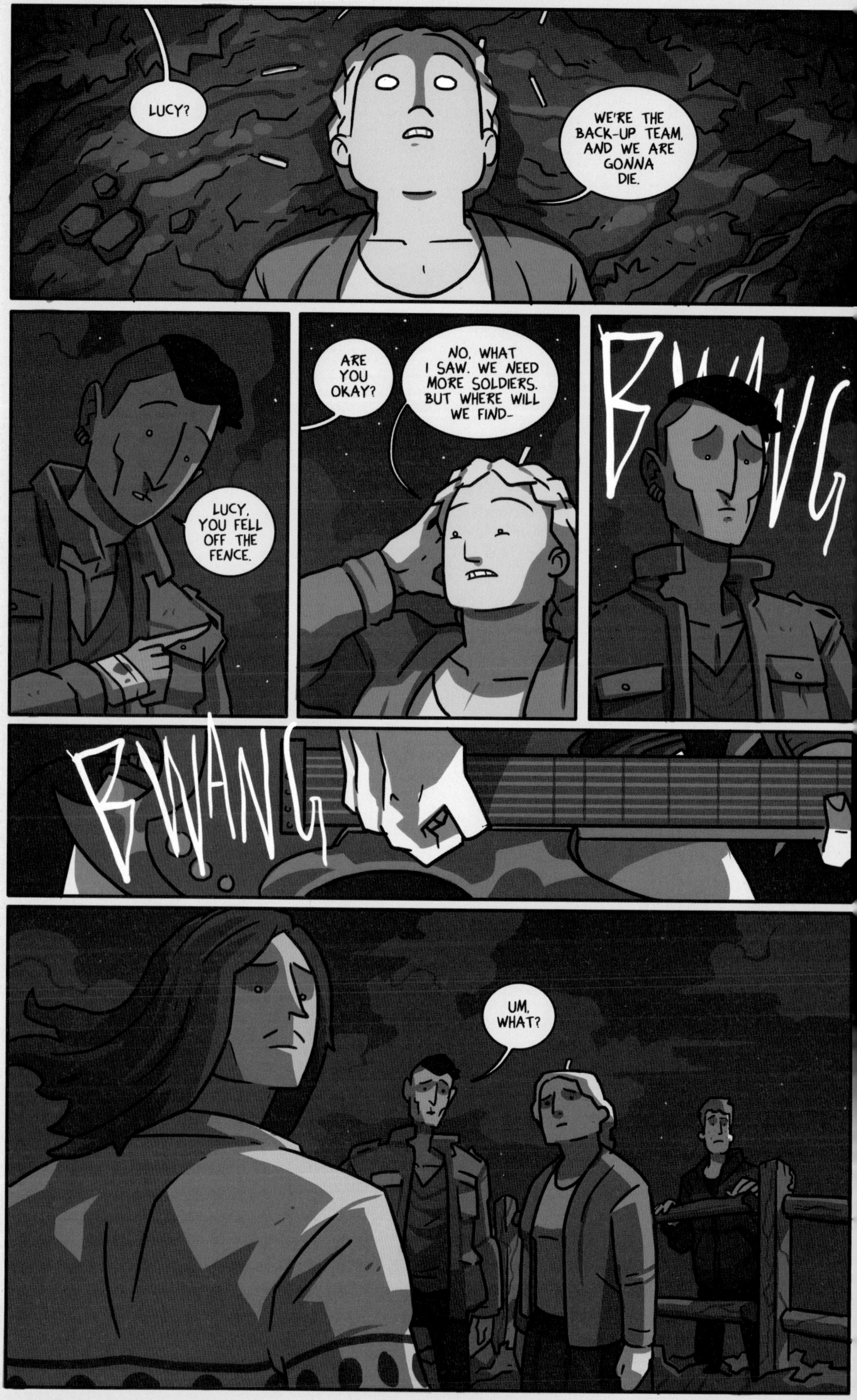
LUCY?
WE'RE THE BACK-UP TEAM, AND WE ARE GONNA DIE.
LUCY, YOU FELL OFF THE FENCE.
ARE YOU OKAY?
NO, WHAT I SAW. WE NEED MORE SOLDIERS. BUT WHERE WILL WE FIND–
BWANG
BWANG
UM, WHAT?

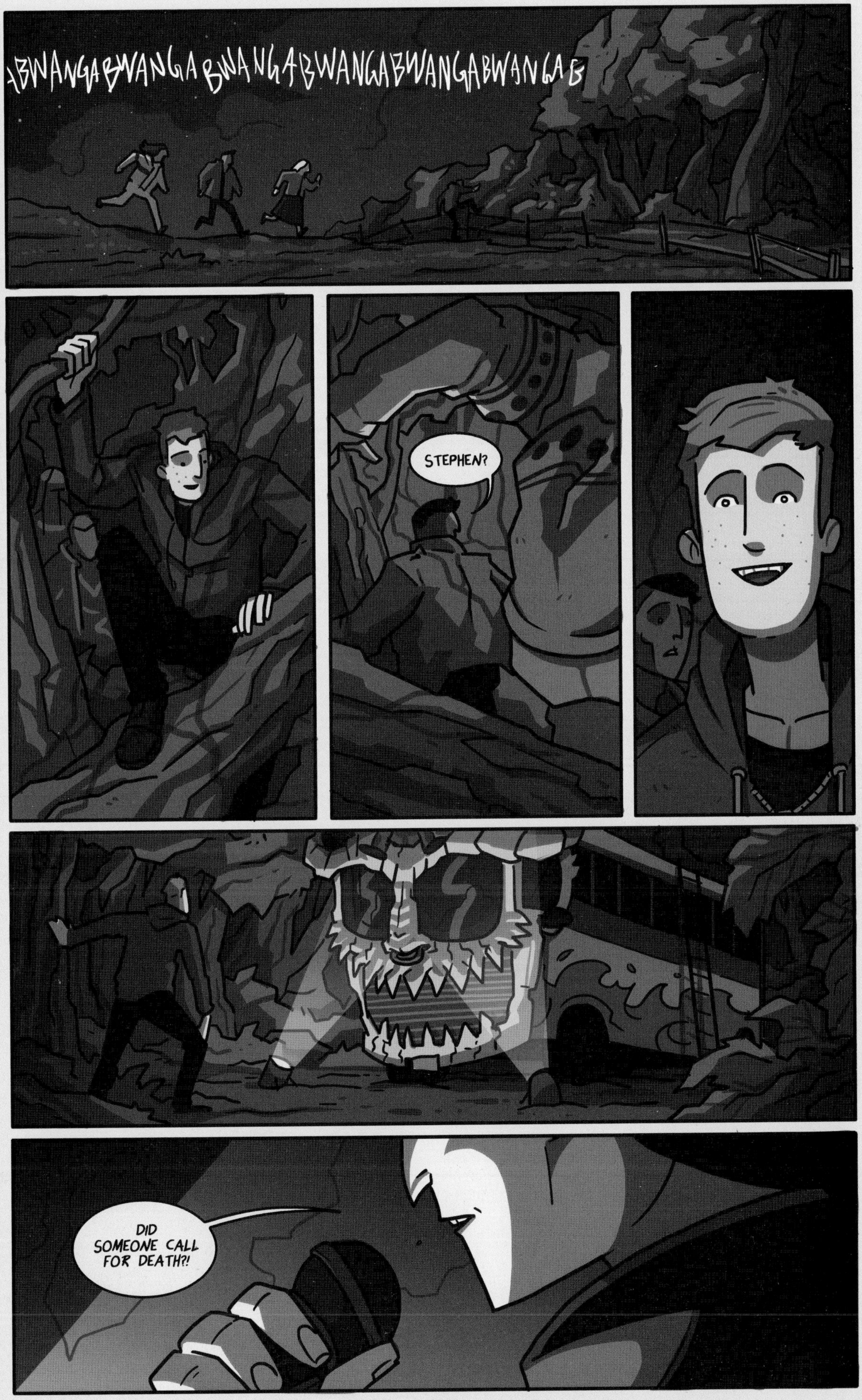
BWANGABWANGABWANGABWANGABWANGABWANGAB
STEPHEN?
DID SOMEONE CALL FOR DEATH?!

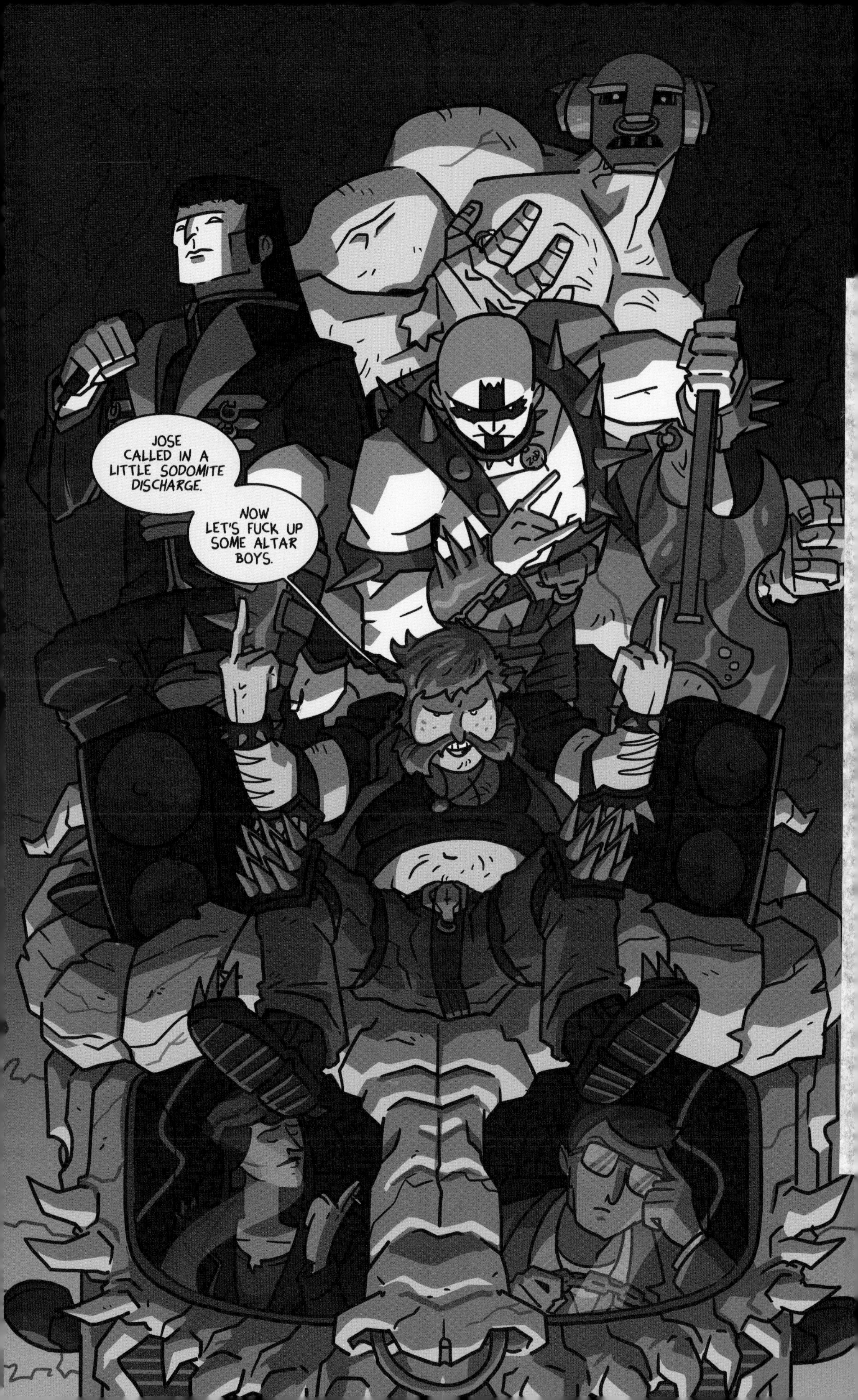
JOSE CALLED IN A LITTLE SODOMITE DISCHARGE.
NOW LET'S FUCK UP SOME ALTAR BOYS.

VI
BABYLON

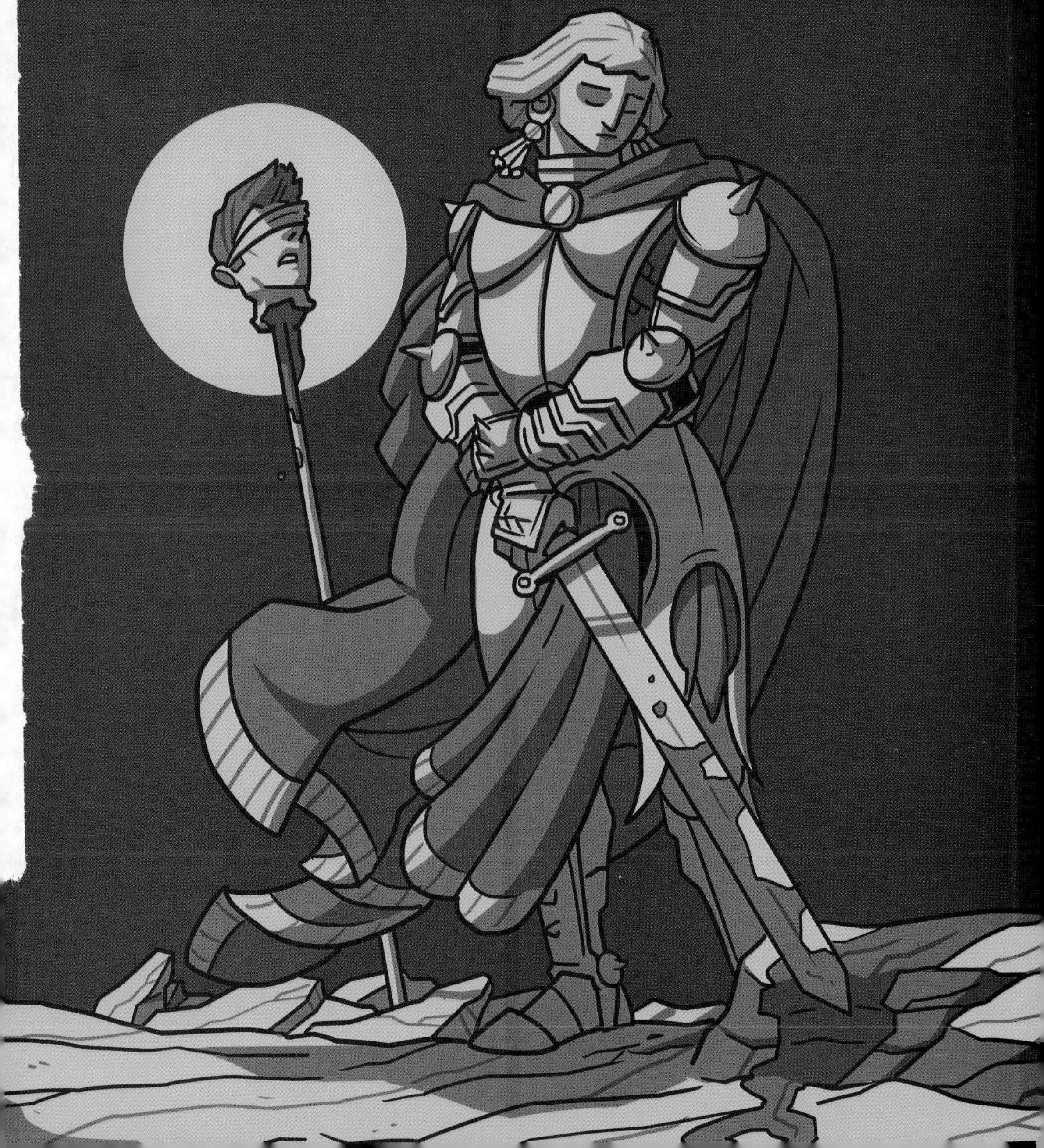

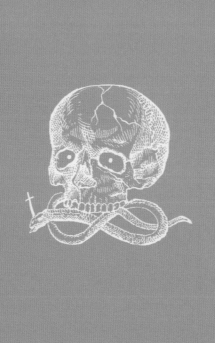

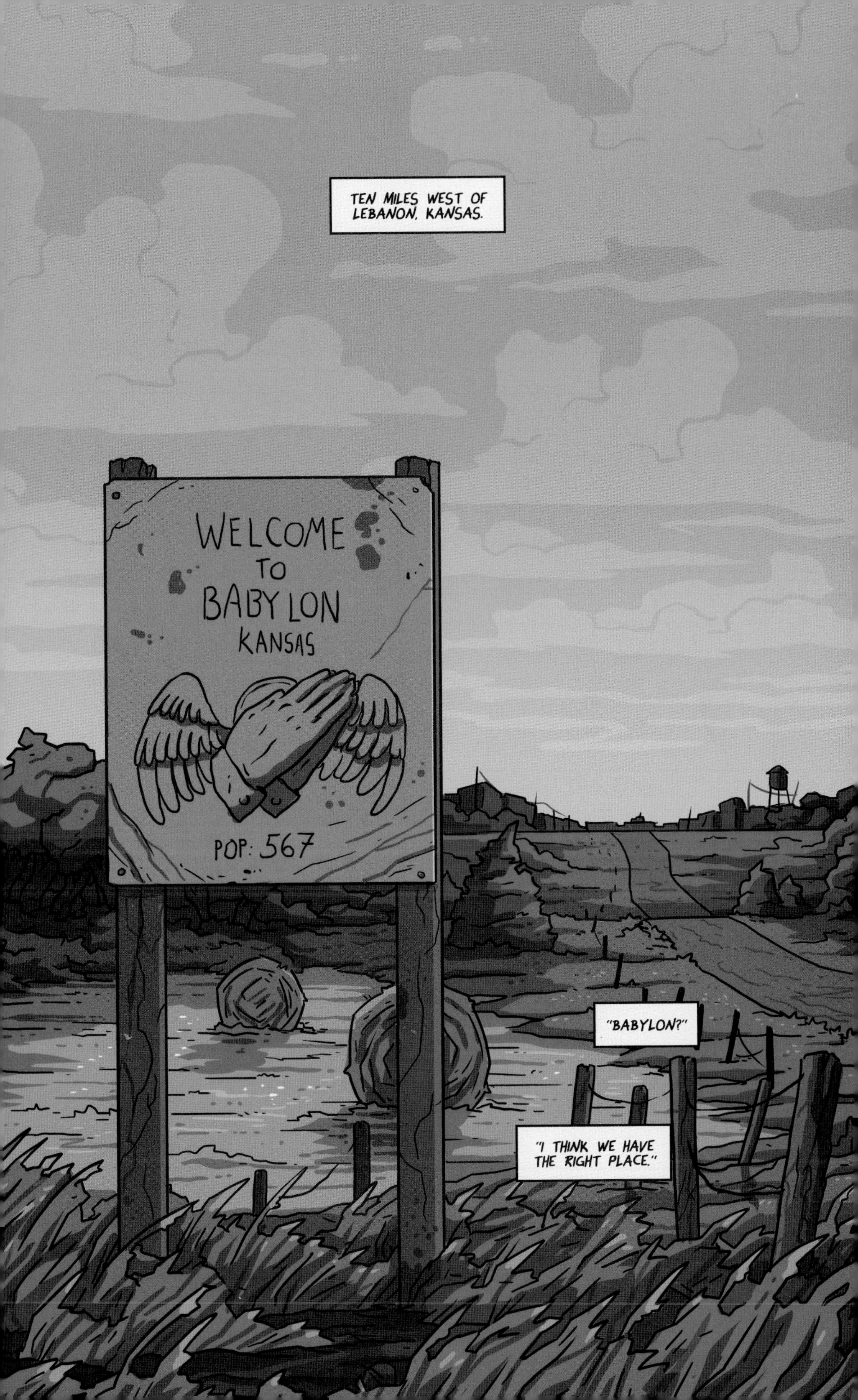
TEN MILES WEST OF LEBANON, KANSAS.
WELCOME TO BABYLON KANSAS
POP: 567
"BABYLON?"
"I THINK WE HAVE THE RIGHT PLACE."

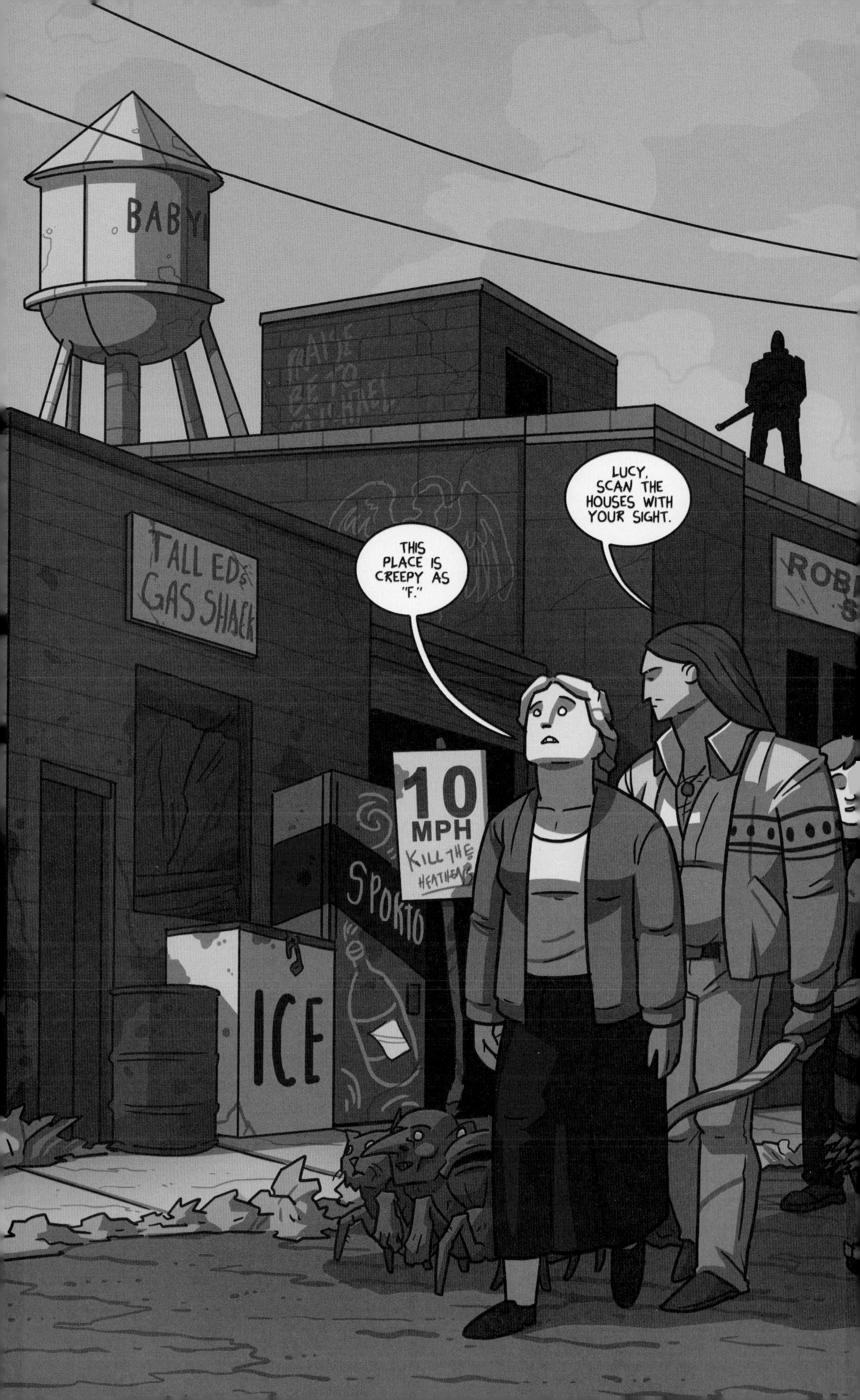
BABY
TALL ED'S GAS SHACK
THIS PLACE IS CREEPY AS "F."
LUCY, SCAN THE HOUSES WITH YOUR SIGHT.
10 MPH
KILL THE HEATHENS
SPORTO
ICE

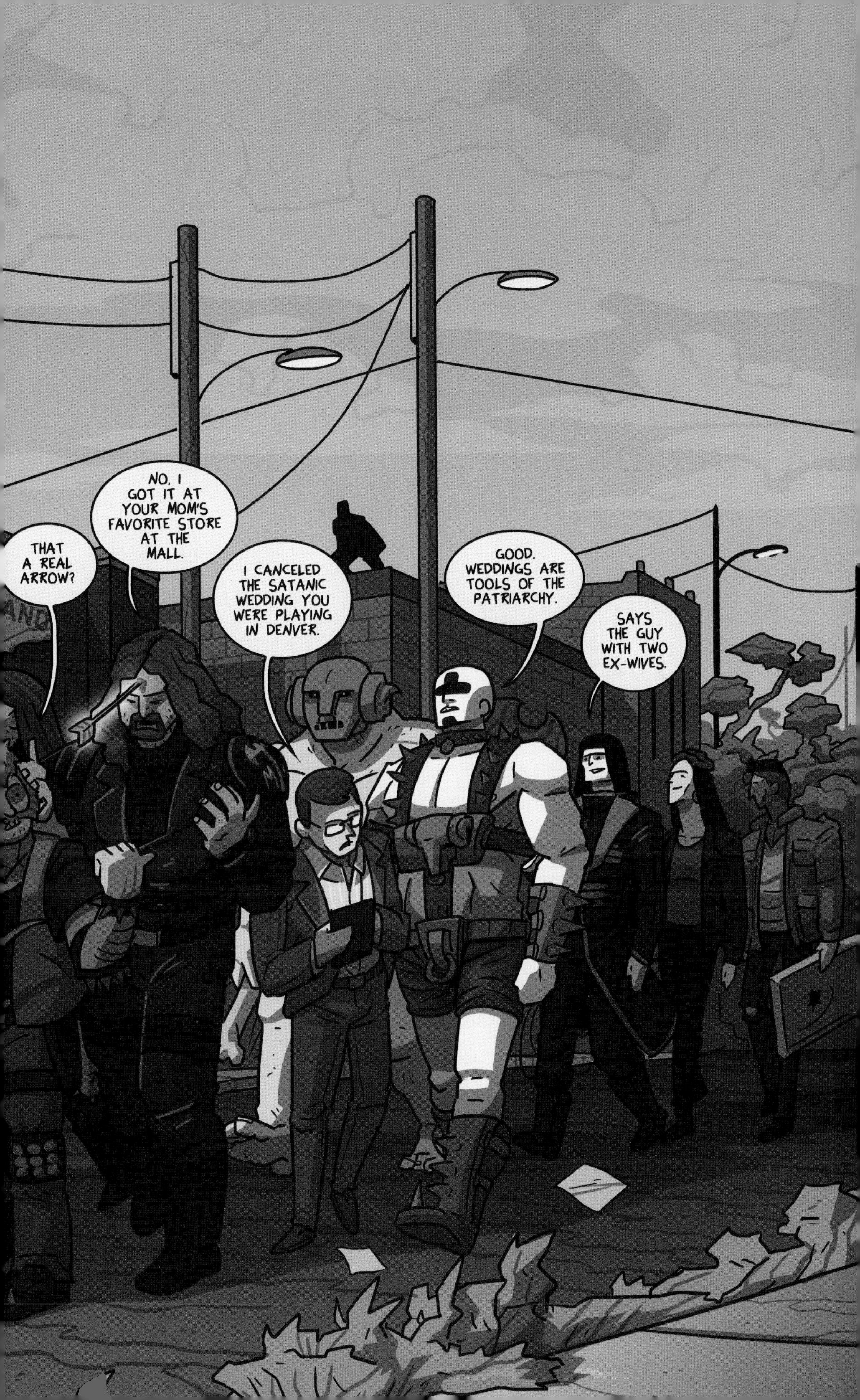
THAT A REAL ARROW?
NO, I GOT IT AT YOUR MOM'S FAVORITE STORE AT THE MALL.
I CANCELED THE SATANIC WEDDING YOU WERE PLAYING IN DENVER.
GOOD. WEDDINGS ARE TOOLS OF THE PATRIARCHY.
SAYS THE GUY WITH TWO EX-WIVES.

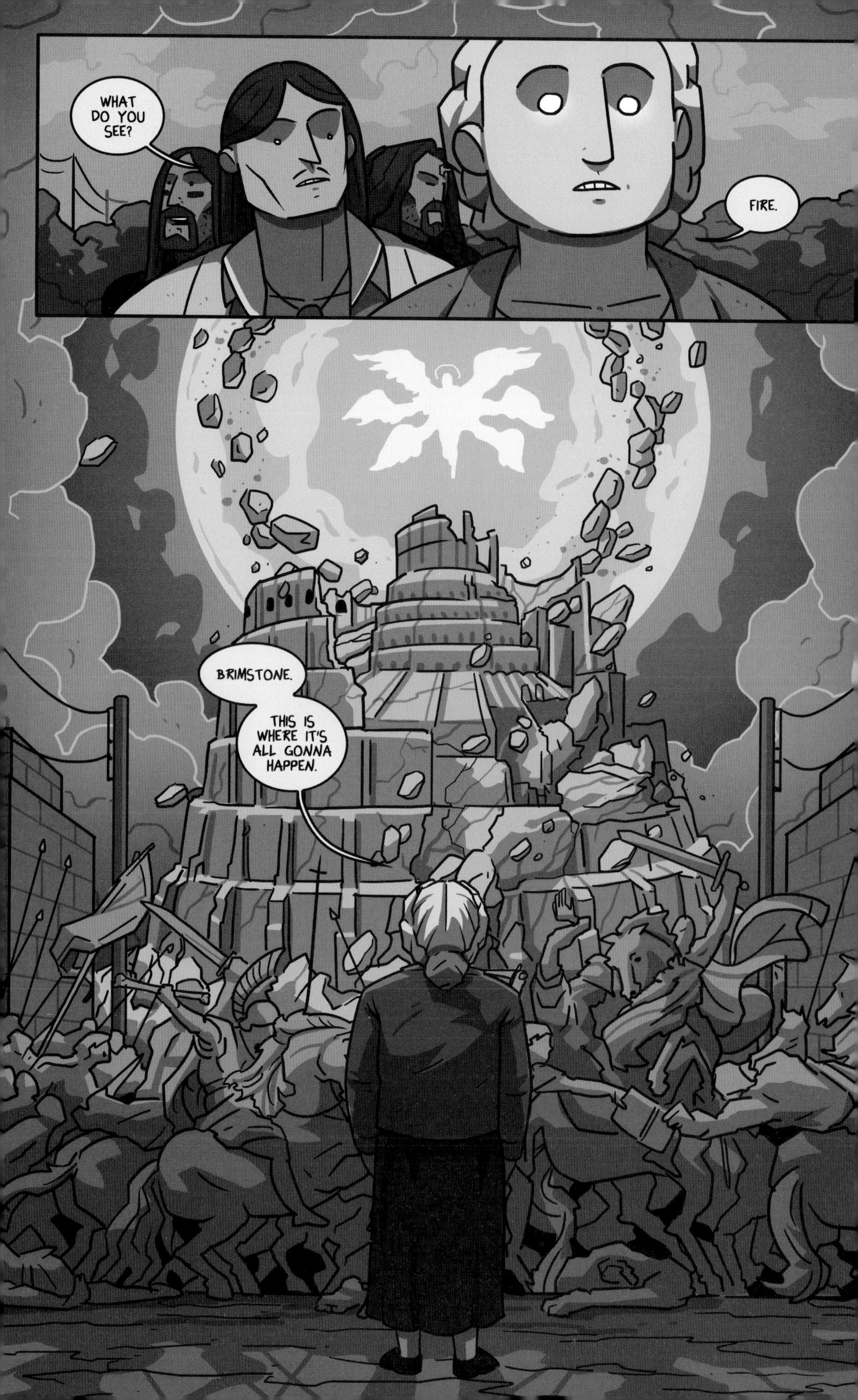
WHAT DO YOU SEE?
FIRE.
BRIMSTONE.
THIS IS WHERE IT'S ALL GONNA HAPPEN.

ALL WHAT'S GONNA HAPPEN?

YOU HEARD OF CUSTER'S LAST STAND?

SURE.

I LOVE CUSTARD. WHY? DID SOMEONE BRING A PIE?

THIS IS OURS.

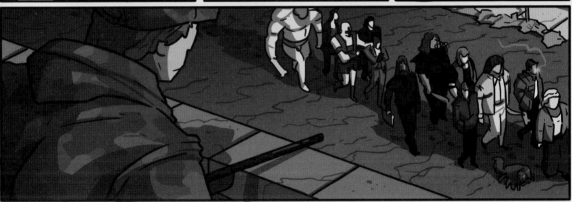

JAMES, THEY JUST ARRIVED.

THANK YOU.

PREPARE FOR ABSOLUTION, YOU ANIMALS.

THE PEOPLE'S CHURCH OF THE ARCHANGEL MICHAEL.

Dear Mr. and Mrs. Martin,

Your daughter Joan is well. She is excelling far beyond our expectations. The We are taking good care of her for her. We will have most glorious plans for her.

...appreciate your ...planted in the Church. As you ...hey will take on a life ...coming lord, and he wi? ...day is at hand, and he wi? ...shall truly bless those he ...stay strong in Christ. donati?

AHEM. GENTLEMEN—

—THE SAINTS ARE HERE.

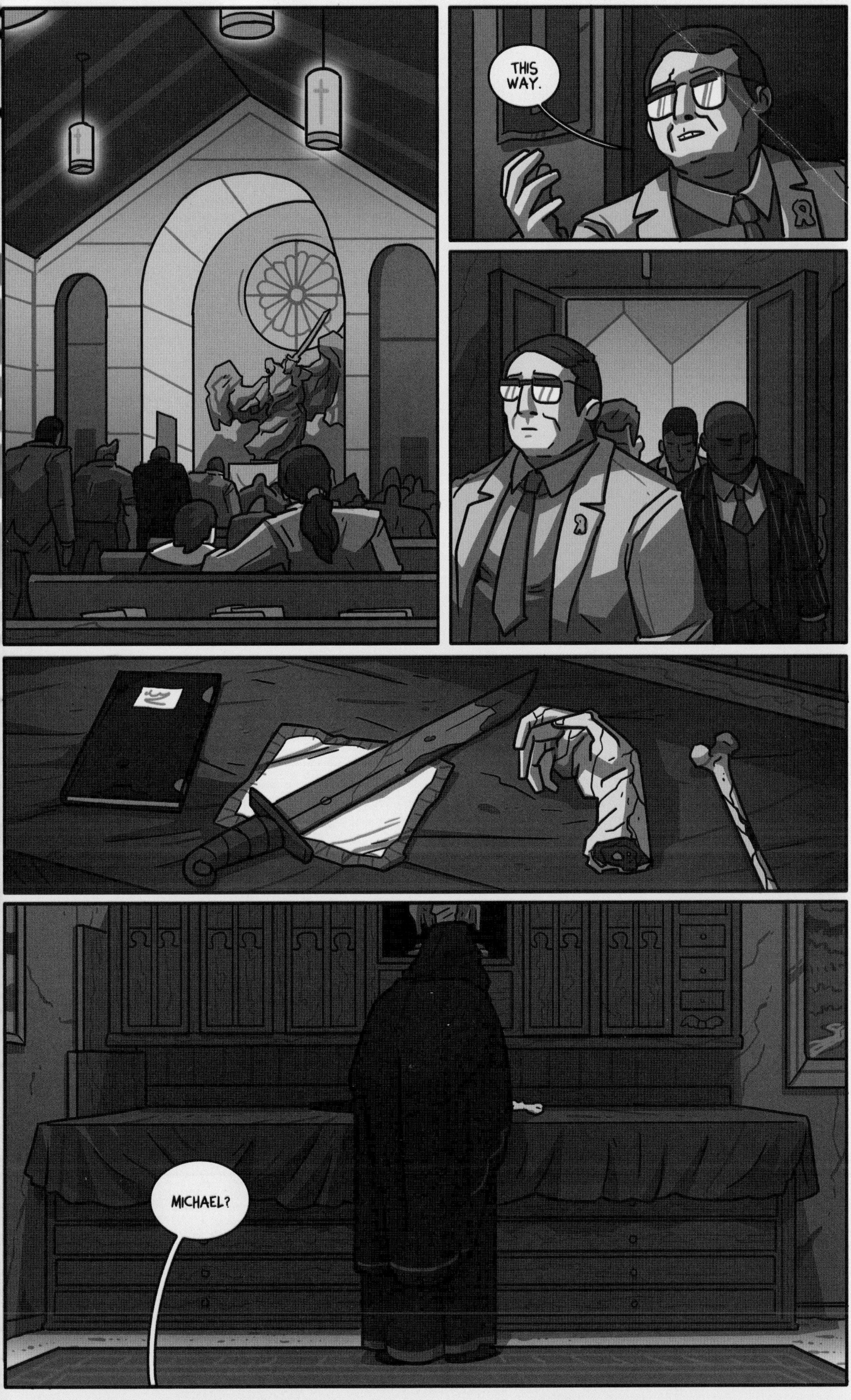
THIS WAY.
MICHAEL?

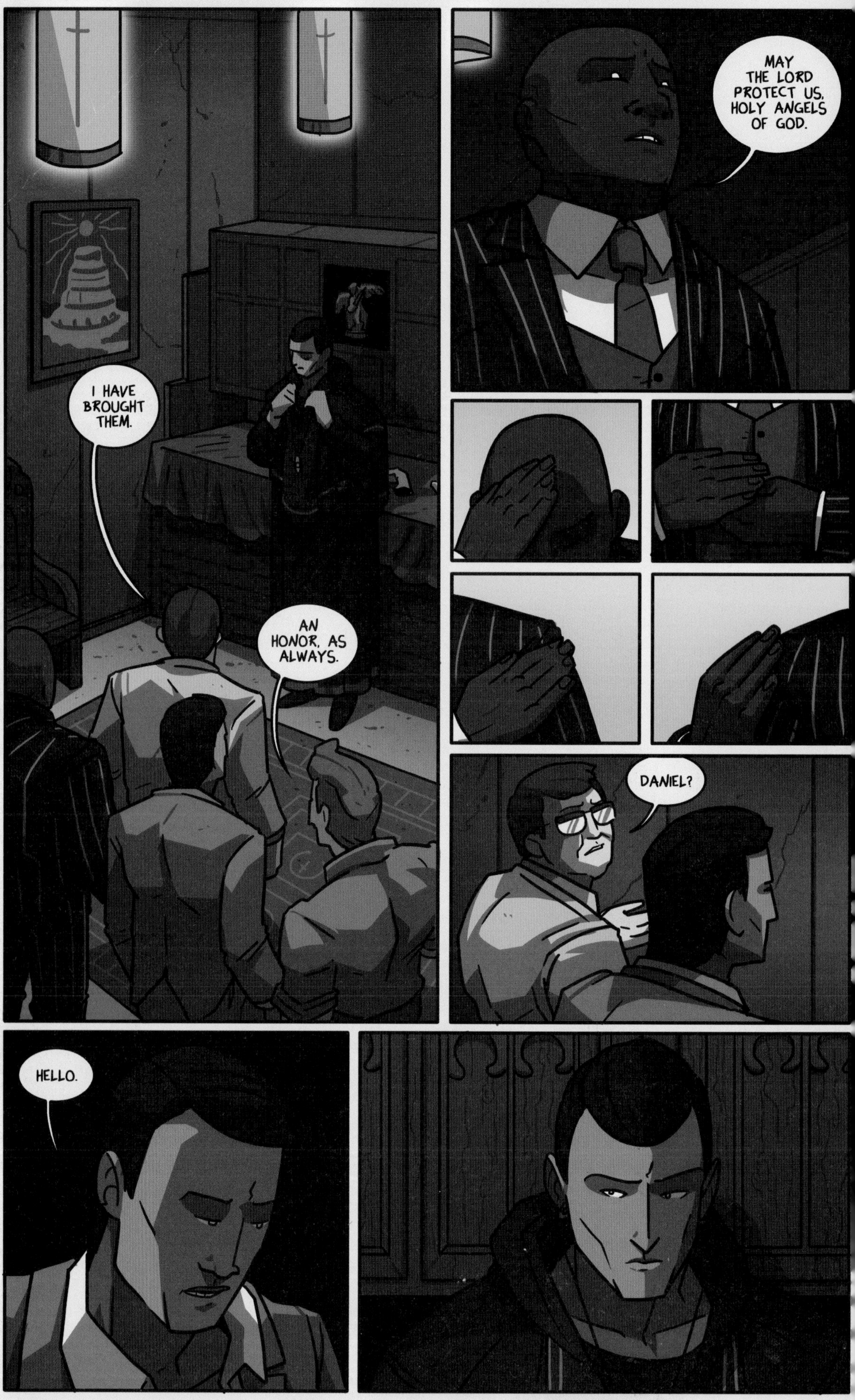
I HAVE BROUGHT THEM.
AN HONOR, AS ALWAYS.
MAY THE LORD PROTECT US, HOLY ANGELS OF GOD.
DANIEL?
HELLO.

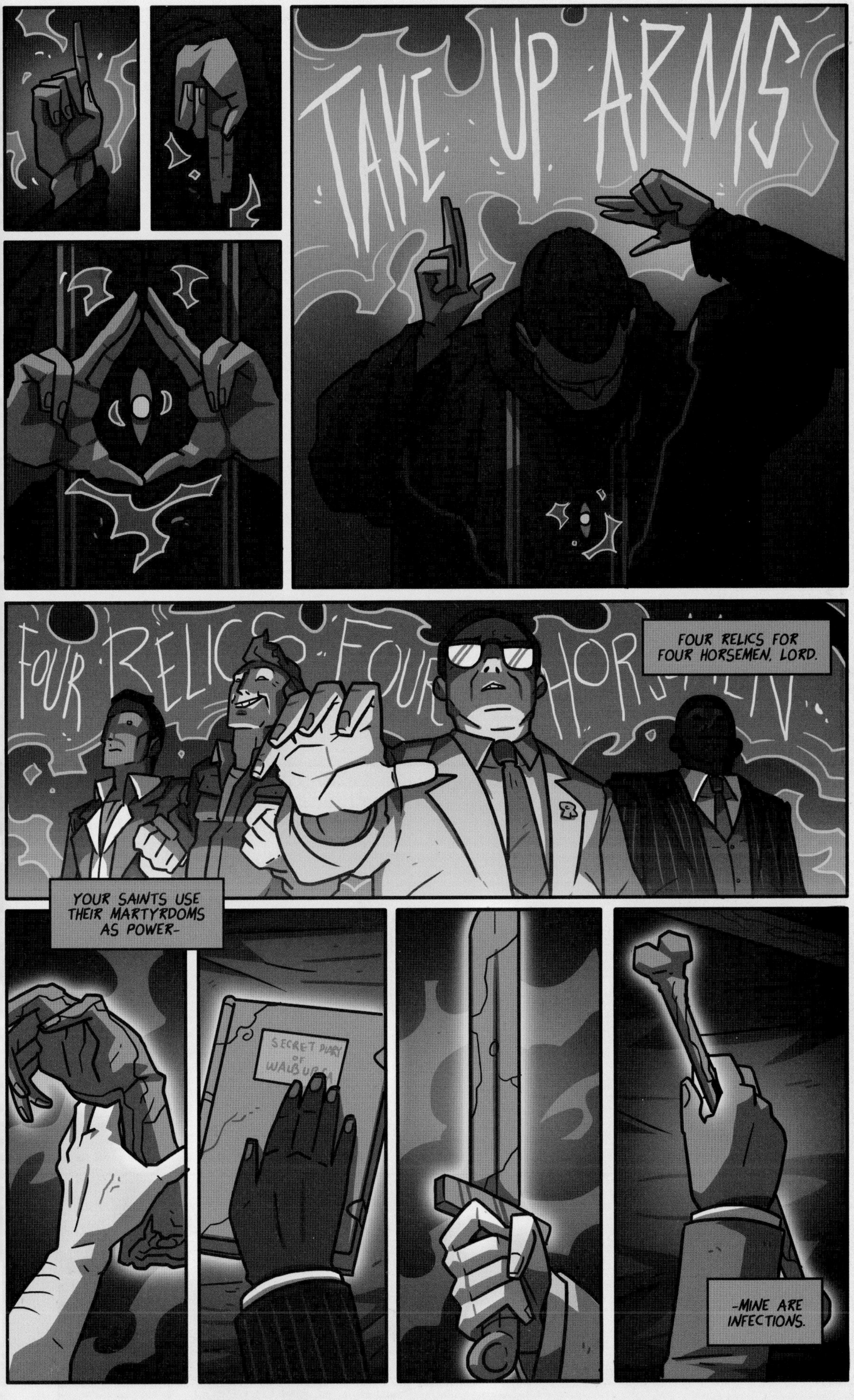
TAKE UP ARMS
FOUR RELICS FOUR HORSEMEN
FOUR RELICS FOR FOUR HORSEMEN, LORD.
YOUR SAINTS USE THEIR MARTYRDOMS AS POWER-
SECRET DIARY OF WALBURGA
-MINE ARE INFECTIONS.

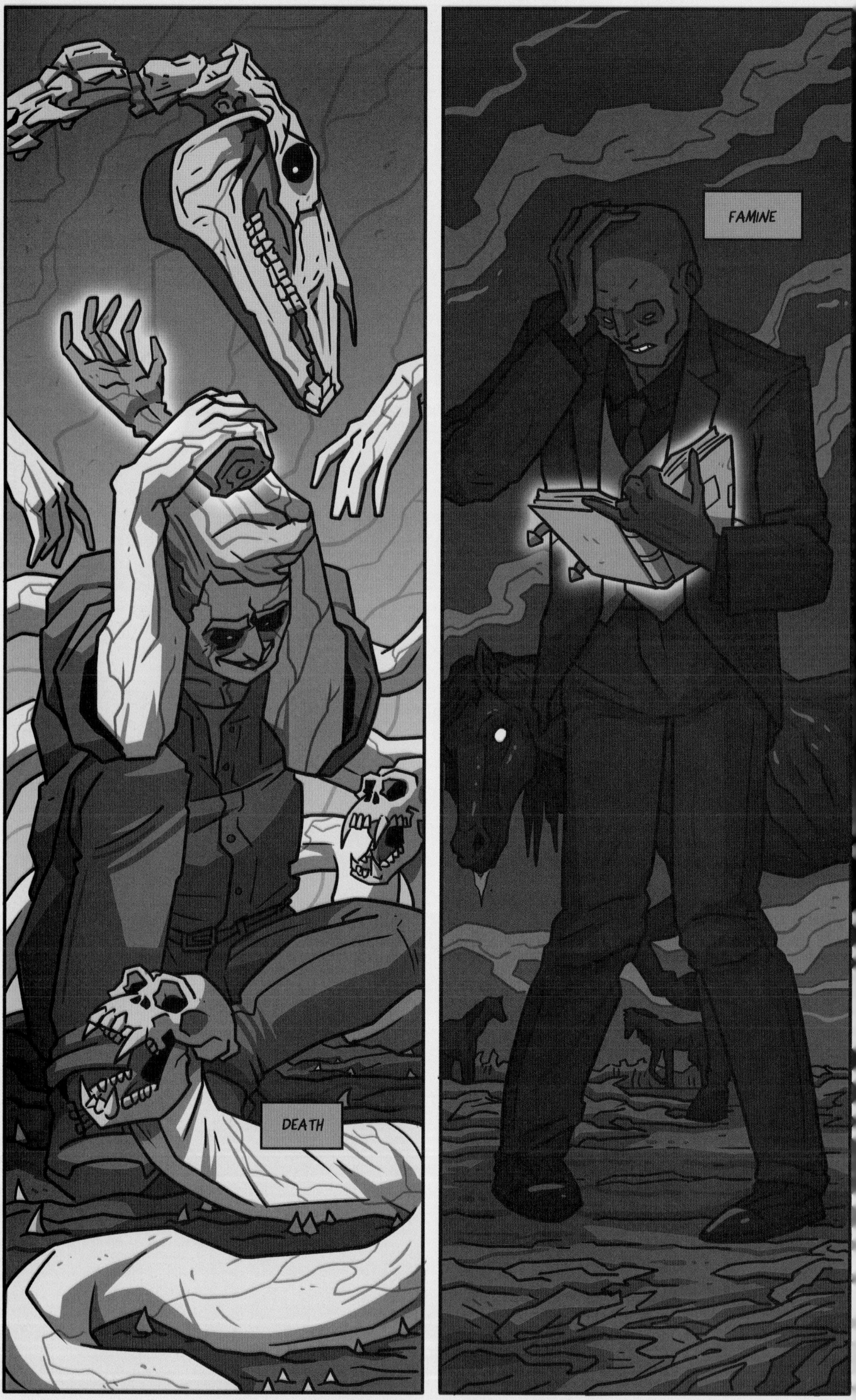
DEATH
FAMINE

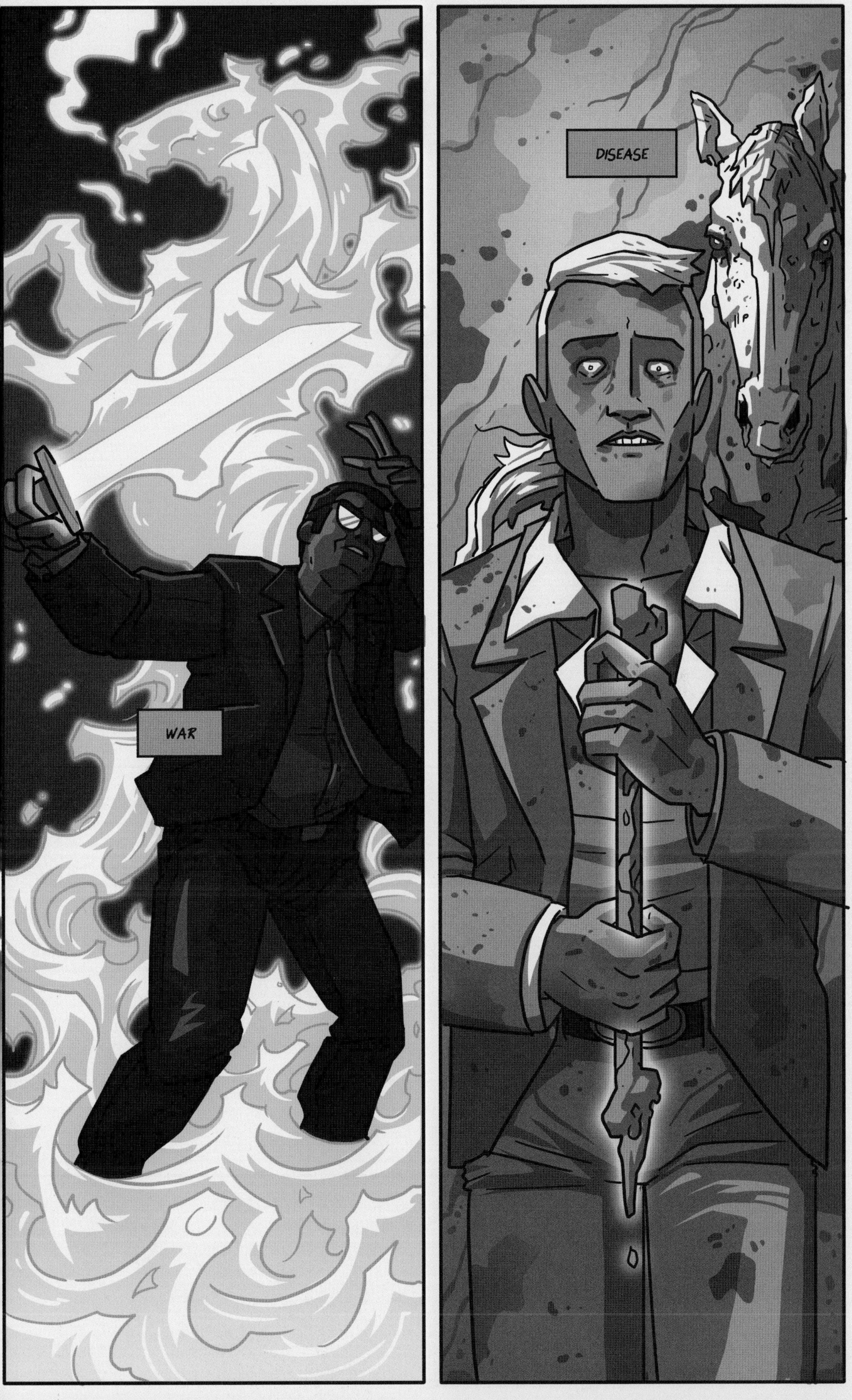
WAR
DISEASE

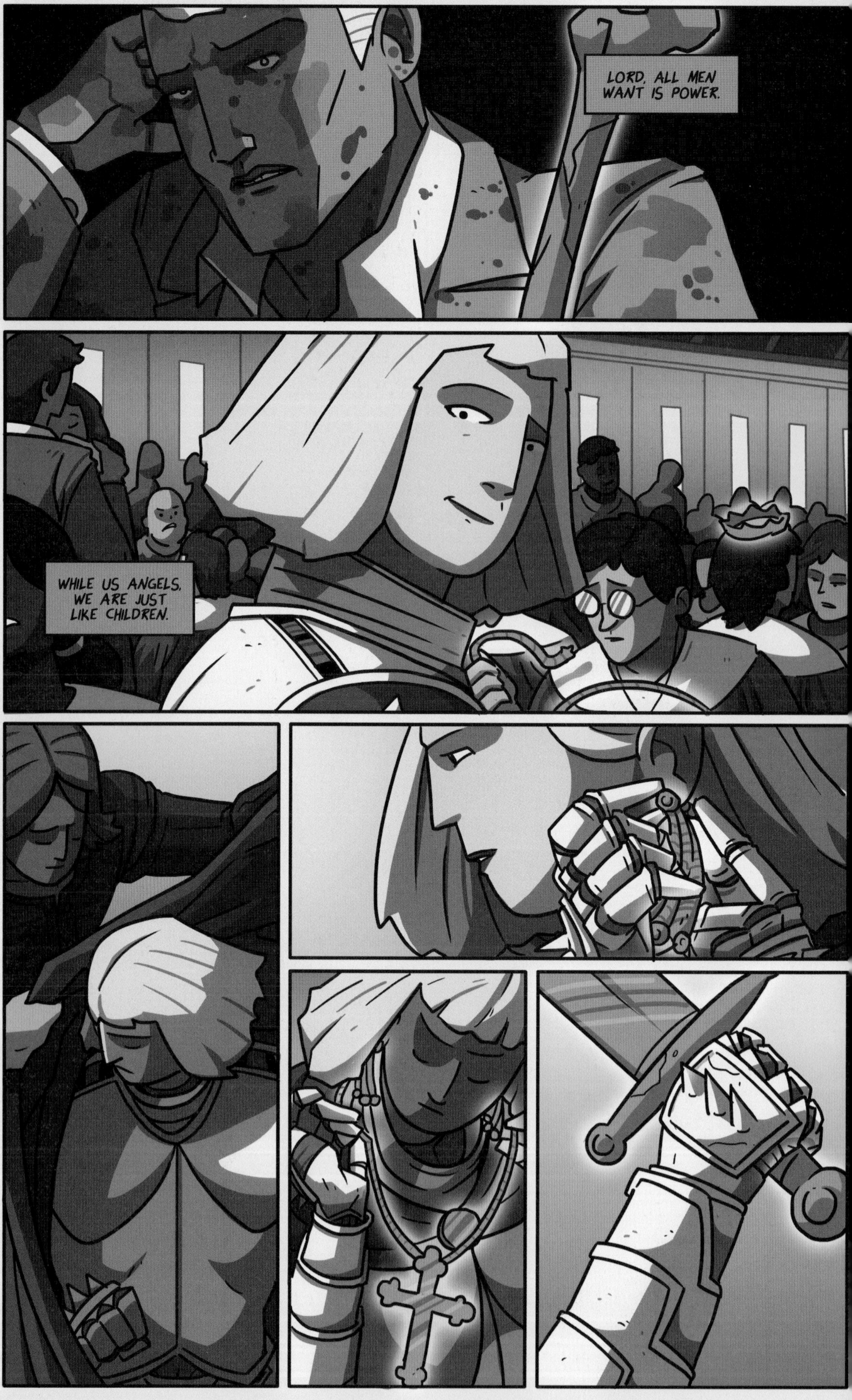
LORD, ALL MEN WANT IS POWER.
WHILE US ANGELS, WE ARE JUST LIKE CHILDREN.

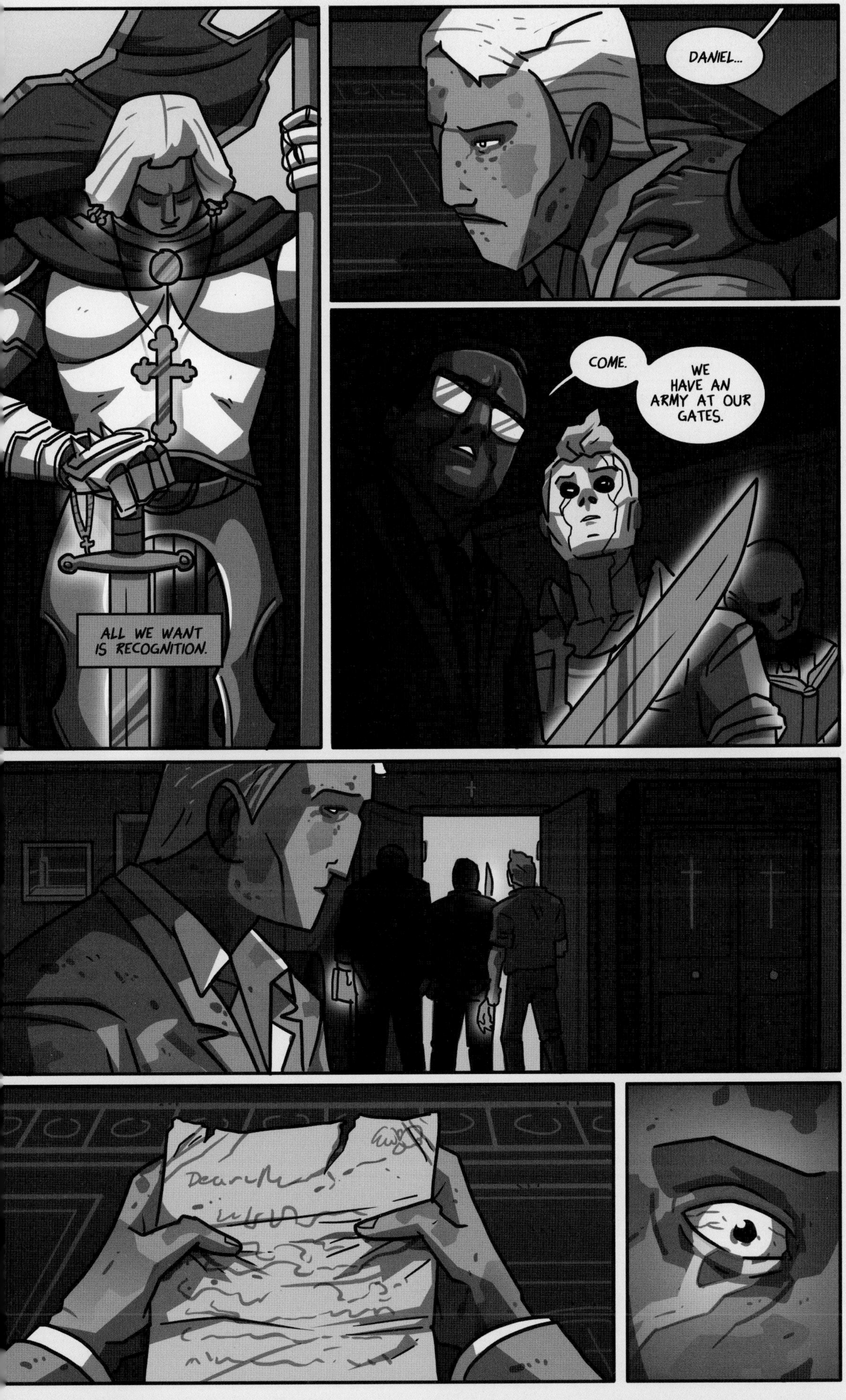
ALL WE WANT IS RECOGNITION.
DANIEL...
COME.
WE HAVE AN ARMY AT OUR GATES.

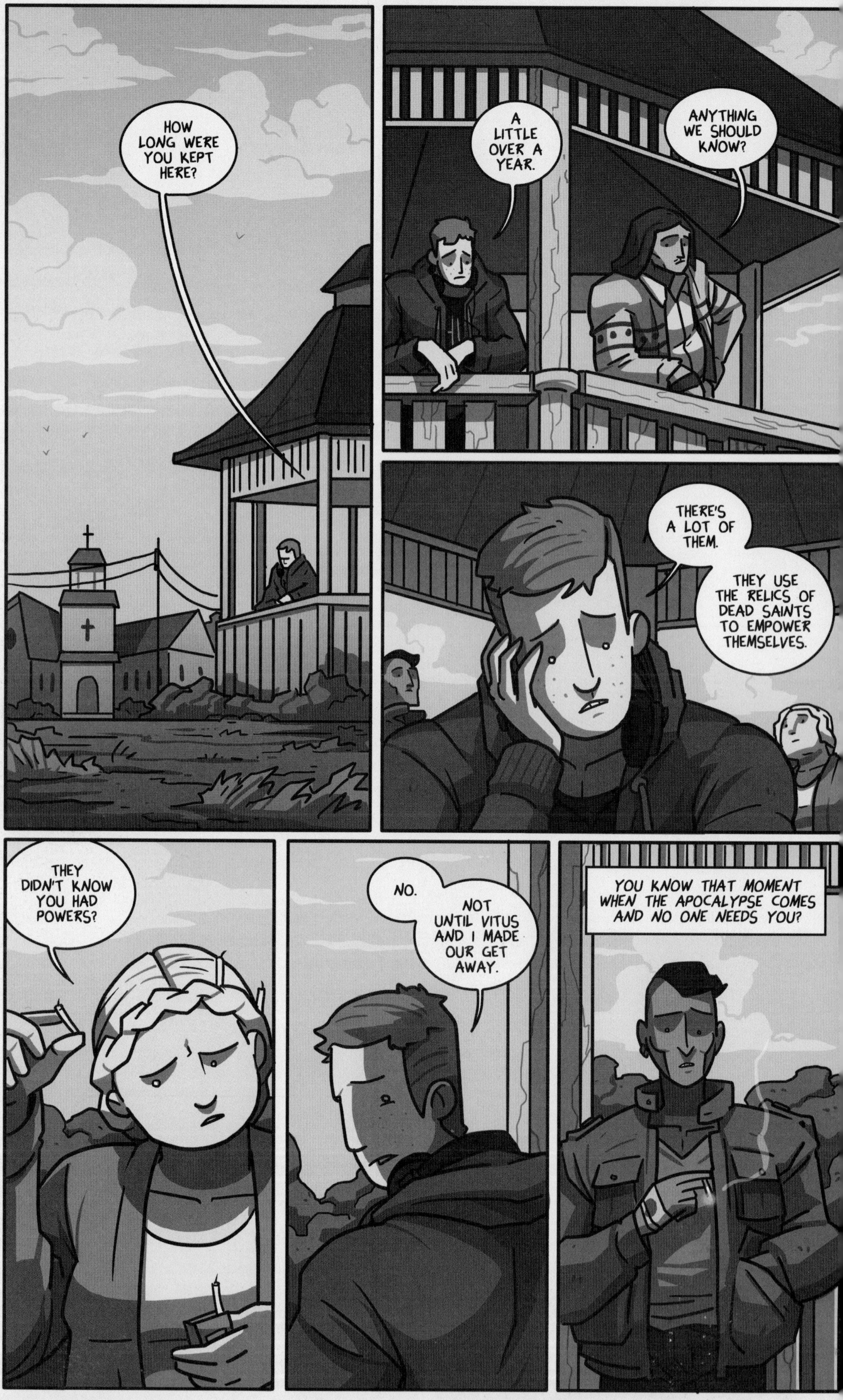
HOW LONG WERE YOU KEPT HERE?
A LITTLE OVER A YEAR.
ANYTHING WE SHOULD KNOW?
THERE'S A LOT OF THEM.
THEY USE THE RELICS OF DEAD SAINTS TO EMPOWER THEMSELVES.
THEY DIDN'T KNOW YOU HAD POWERS?
NO.
NOT UNTIL VITUS AND I MADE OUR GET AWAY.
YOU KNOW THAT MOMENT WHEN THE APOCALYPSE COMES AND NO ONE NEEDS YOU?

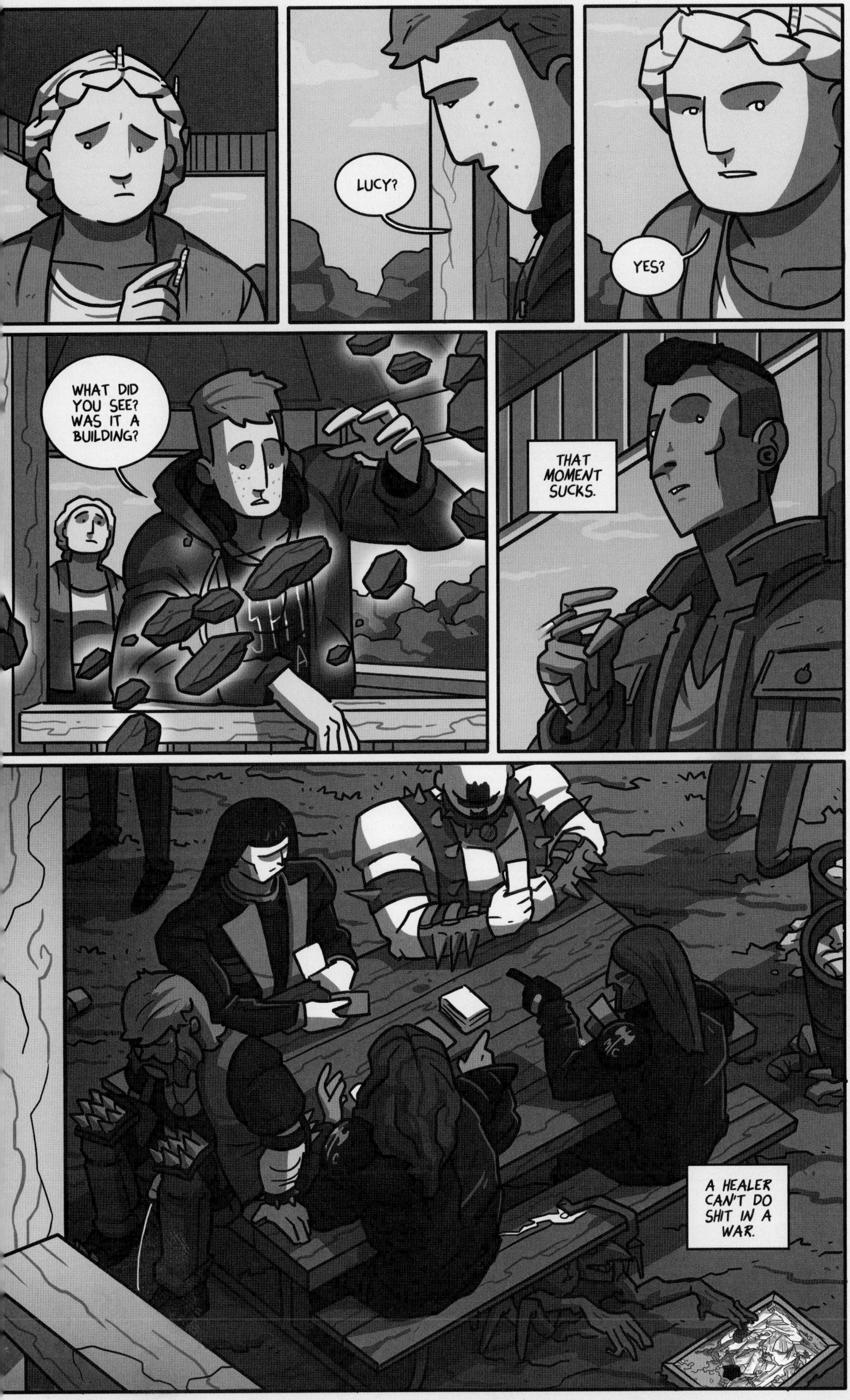
LUCY?
YES?
WHAT DID YOU SEE? WAS IT A BUILDING?
THAT MOMENT SUCKS.
A HEALER CAN'T DO SHIT IN A WAR.

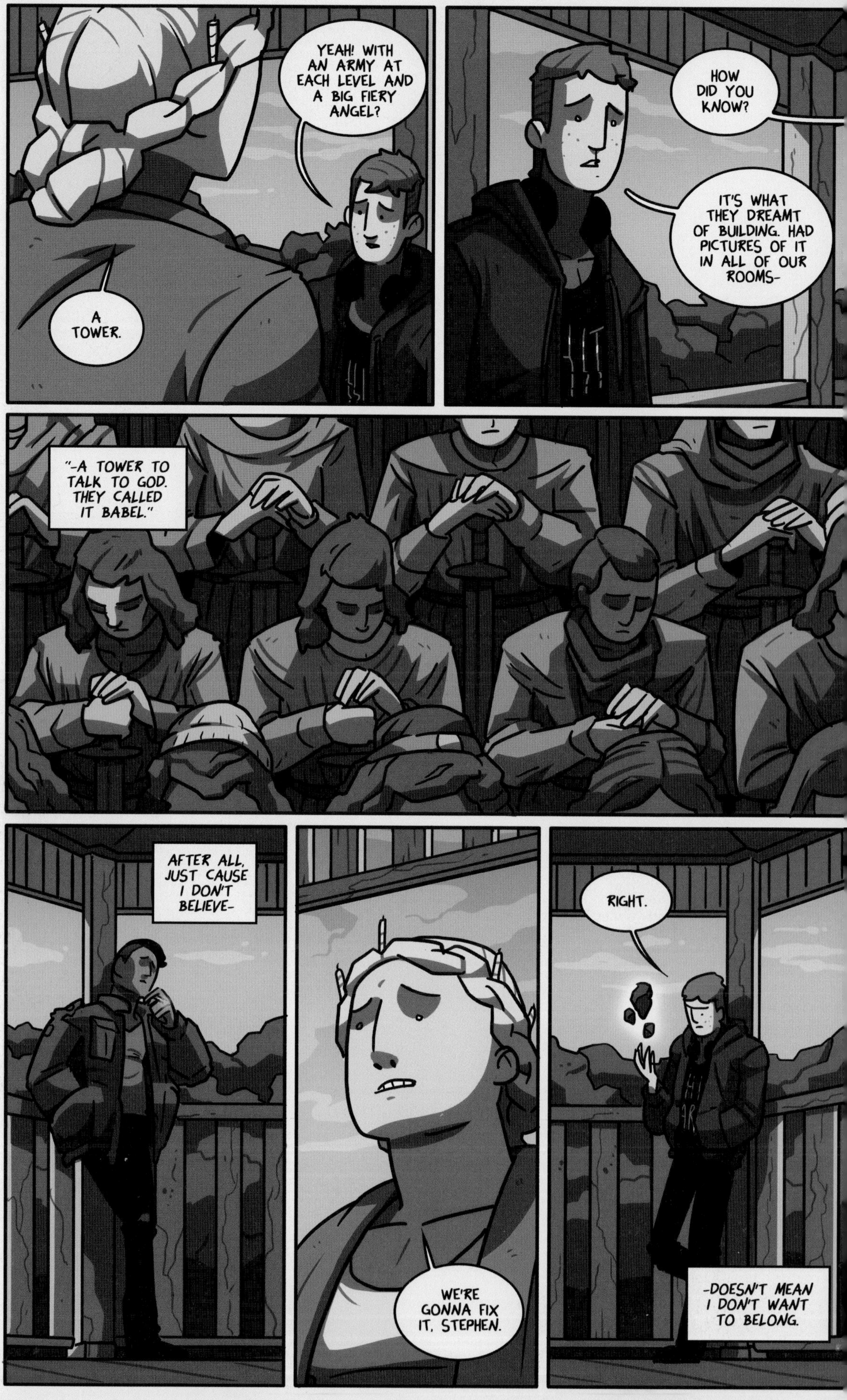
YEAH! WITH AN ARMY AT EACH LEVEL AND A BIG FIERY ANGEL?
A TOWER.
HOW DID YOU KNOW?
IT'S WHAT THEY DREAMT OF BUILDING. HAD PICTURES OF IT IN ALL OF OUR ROOMS-
"-A TOWER TO TALK TO GOD. THEY CALLED IT BABEL."
AFTER ALL, JUST CAUSE I DON'T BELIEVE-
WE'RE GONNA FIX IT, STEPHEN.
RIGHT.
-DOESN'T MEAN I DON'T WANT TO BELONG.

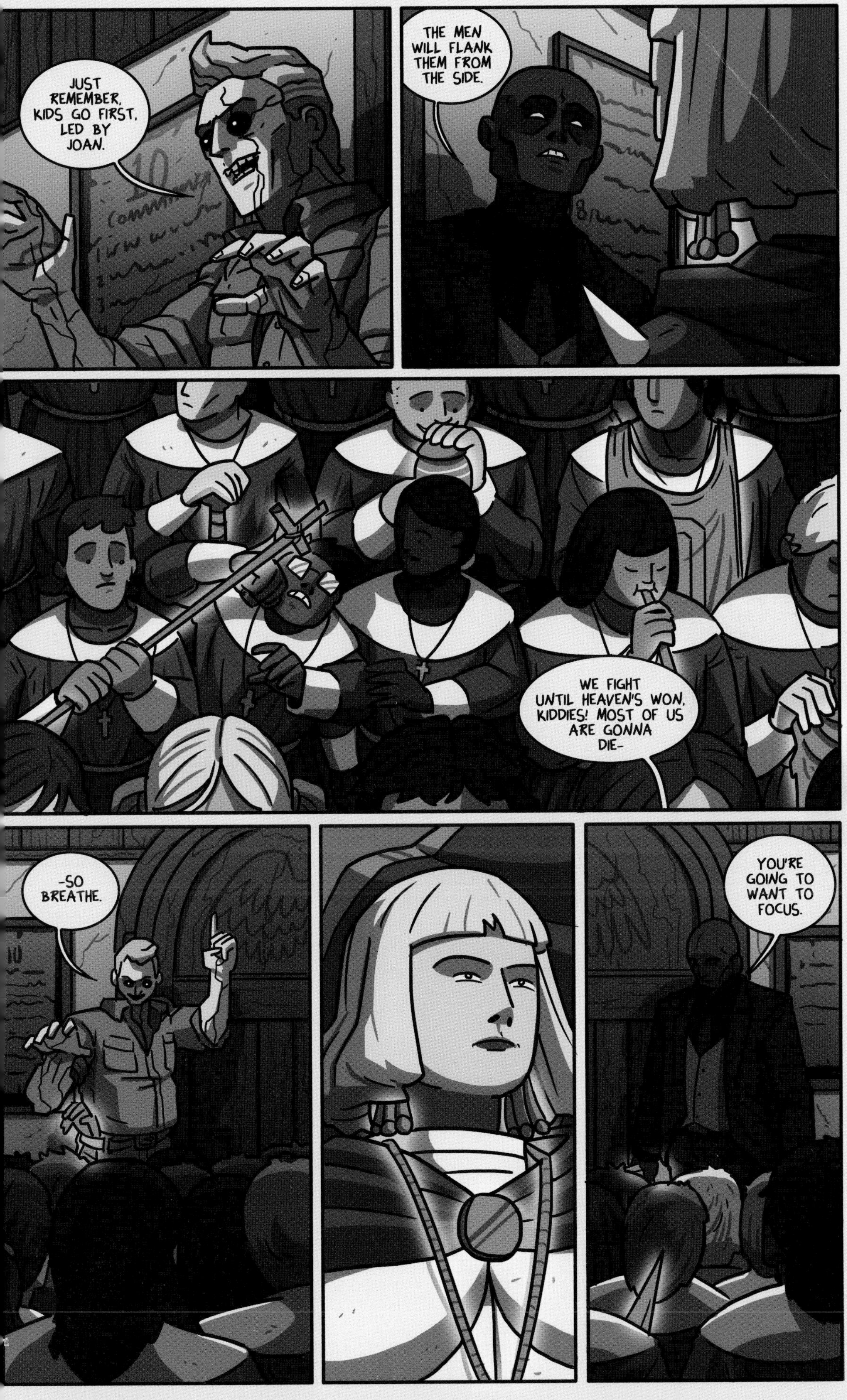
JUST REMEMBER, KIDS GO FIRST, LED BY JOAN.
THE MEN WILL FLANK THEM FROM THE SIDE.
WE FIGHT UNTIL HEAVEN'S WON, KIDDIES! MOST OF US ARE GONNA DIE-
-SO BREATHE.
YOU'RE GOING TO WANT TO FOCUS.

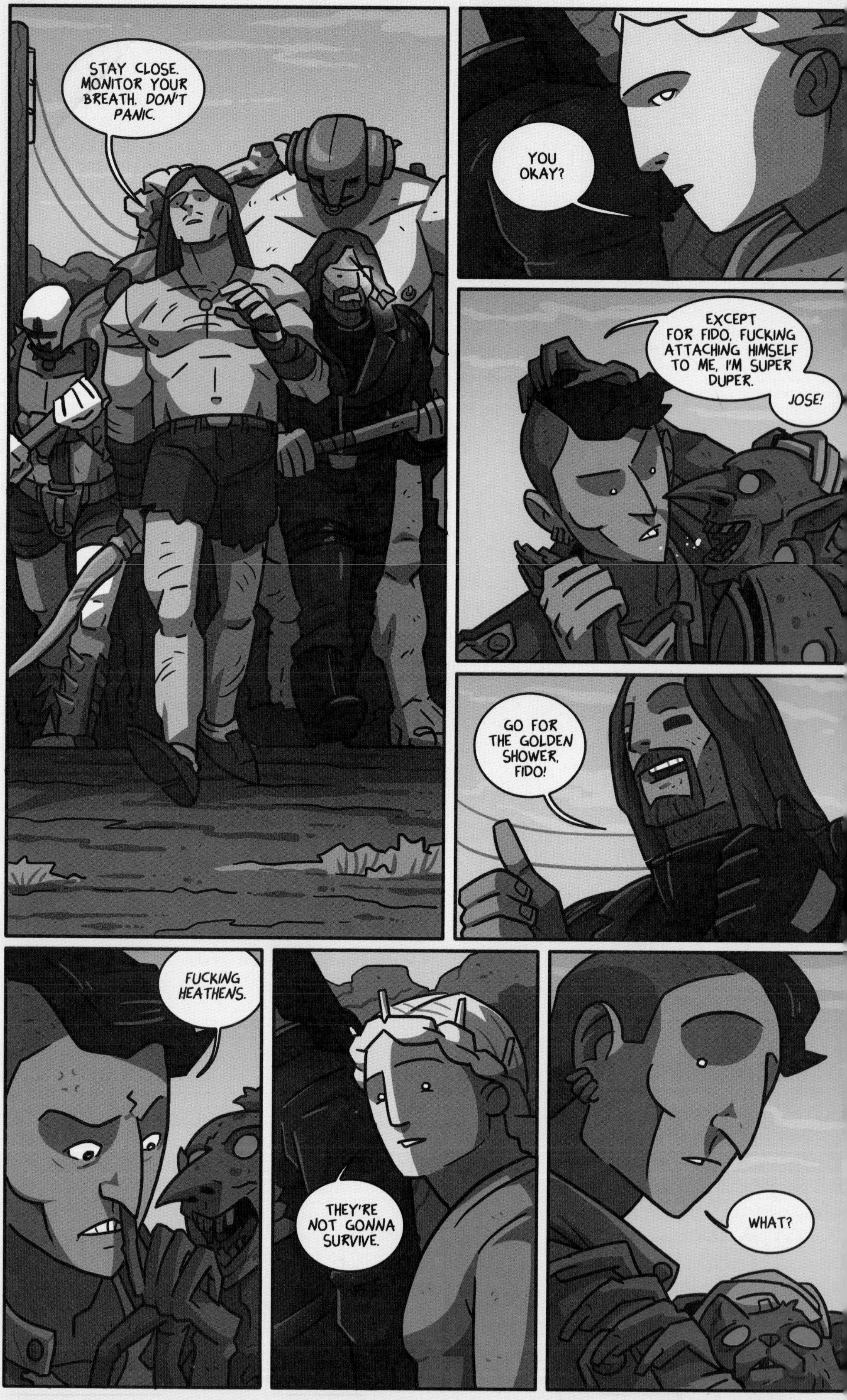
STAY CLOSE. MONITOR YOUR BREATH. DON'T PANIC.
YOU OKAY?
EXCEPT FOR FIDO, FUCKING ATTACHING HIMSELF TO ME, I'M SUPER DUPER.
JOSE!
GO FOR THE GOLDEN SHOWER, FIDO!
FUCKING HEATHENS.
THEY'RE NOT GONNA SURVIVE.
WHAT?

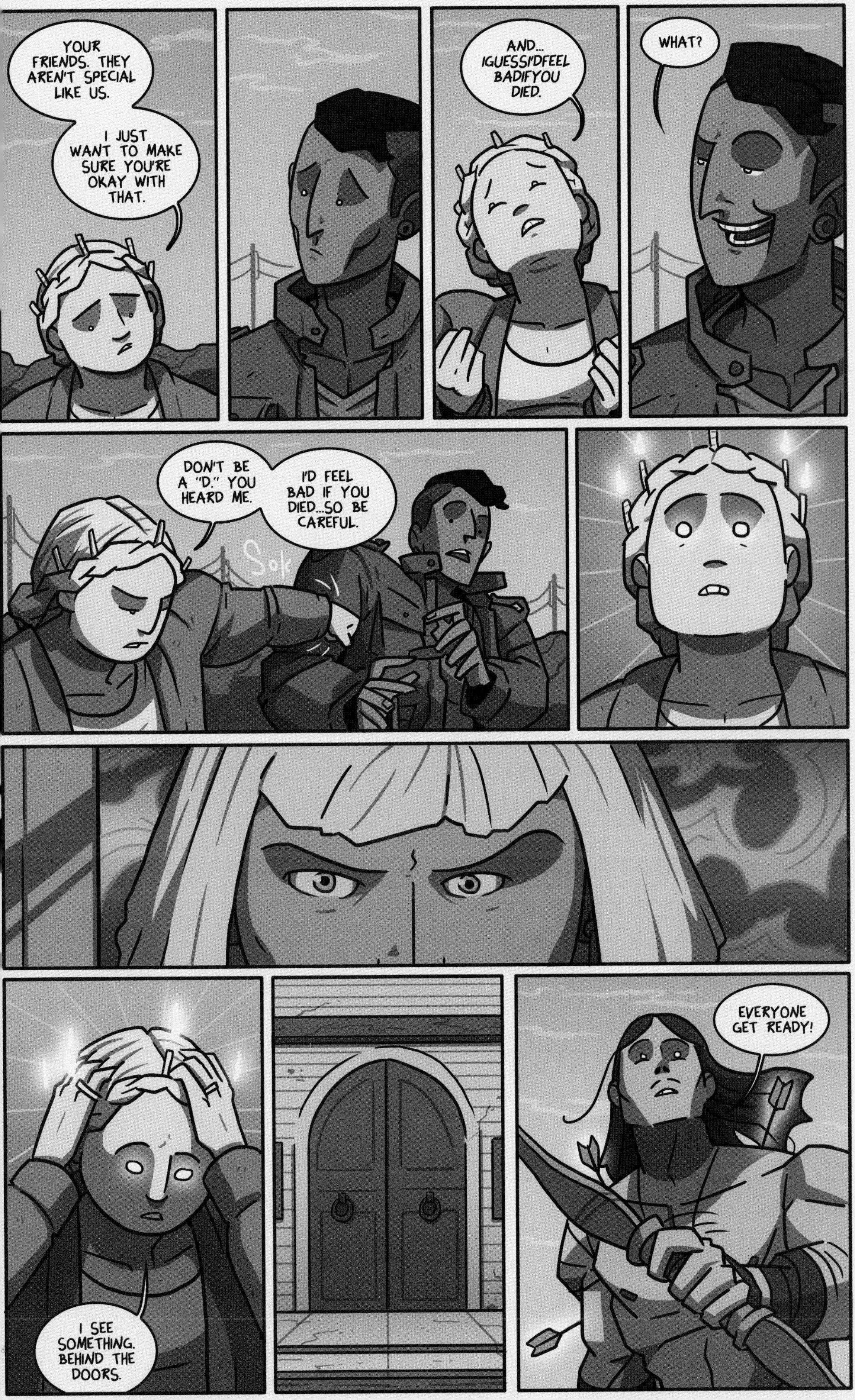
YOUR FRIENDS. THEY AREN'T SPECIAL LIKE US.
I JUST WANT TO MAKE SURE YOU'RE OKAY WITH THAT.
AND... IGUESSI'DFEEL BADIFYOU DIED.
WHAT?
DON'T BE A "D." YOU HEARD ME.
I'D FEEL BAD IF YOU DIED...SO BE CAREFUL.
Sok
I SEE SOMETHING. BEHIND THE DOORS.
EVERYONE GET READY!

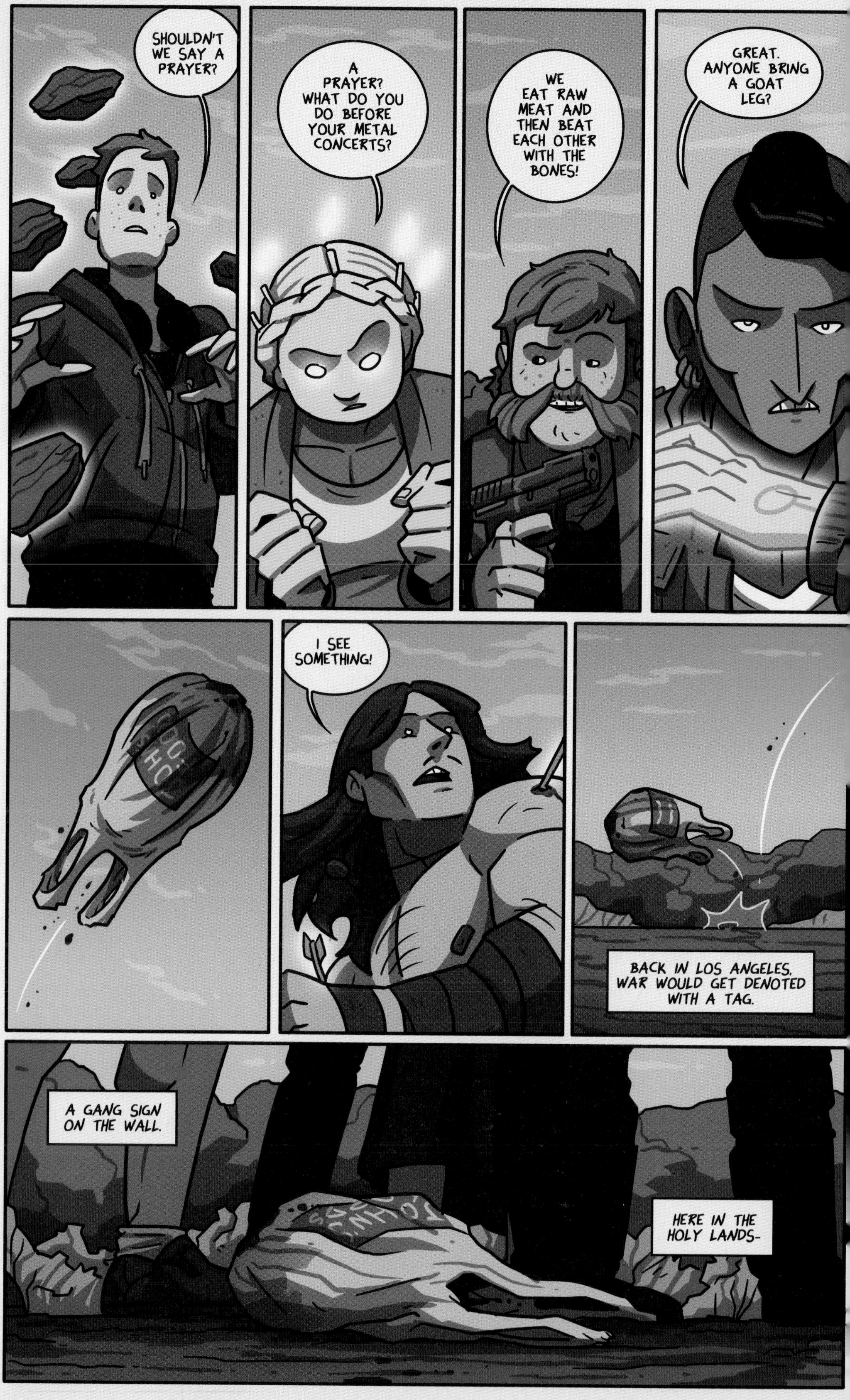
SHOULDN'T WE SAY A PRAYER?
A PRAYER? WHAT DO YOU DO BEFORE YOUR METAL CONCERTS?
WE EAT RAW MEAT AND THEN BEAT EACH OTHER WITH THE BONES!
GREAT. ANYONE BRING A GOAT LEG?
I SEE SOMETHING!
BACK IN LOS ANGELES, WAR WOULD GET DENOTED WITH A TAG.
A GANG SIGN ON THE WALL.
HERE IN THE HOLY LANDS-

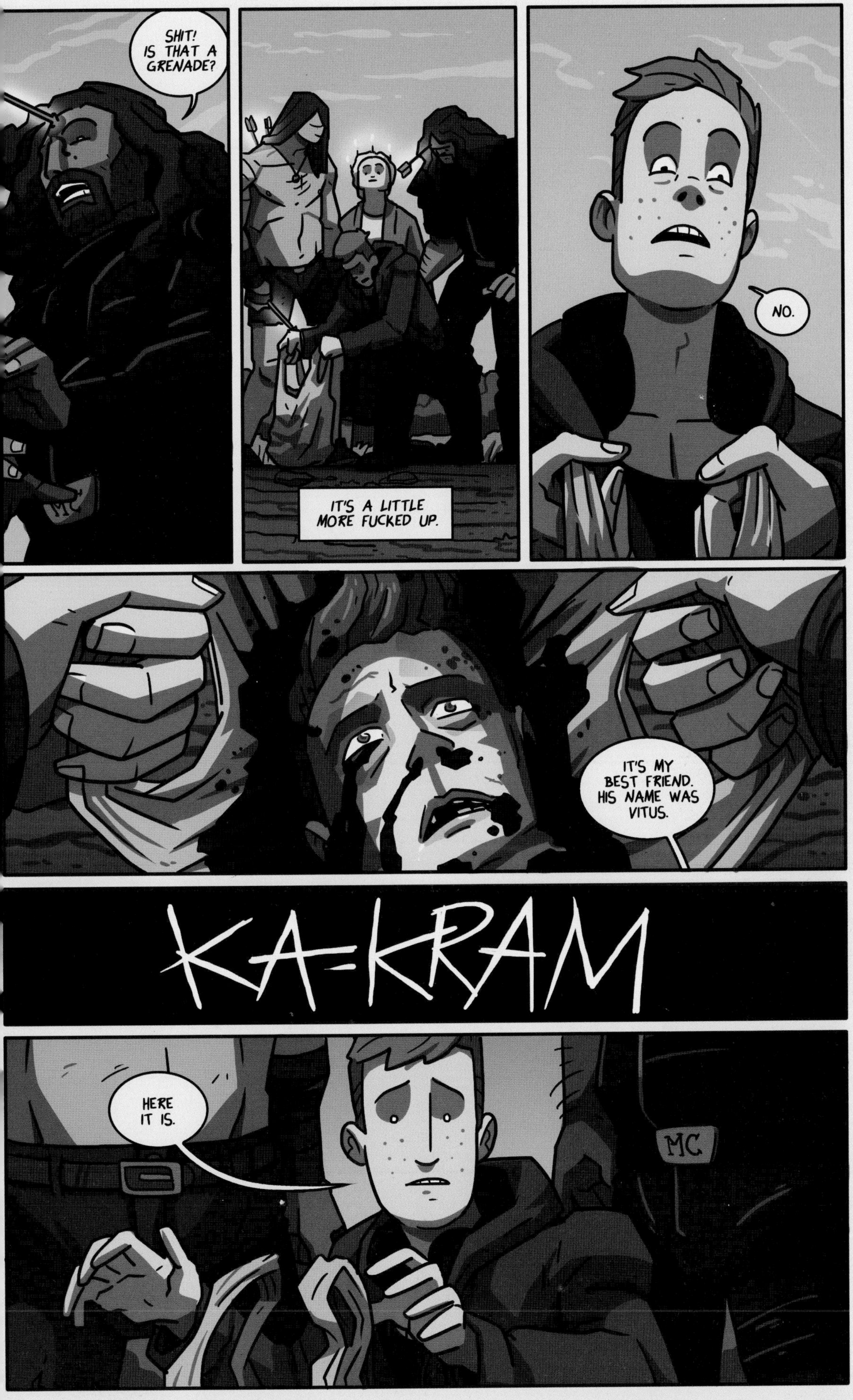
SHIT! IS THAT A GRENADE?
MC
IT'S A LITTLE MORE FUCKED UP.
NO.
IT'S MY BEST FRIEND. HIS NAME WAS VITUS.
KA-KRAM
HERE IT IS.
MC

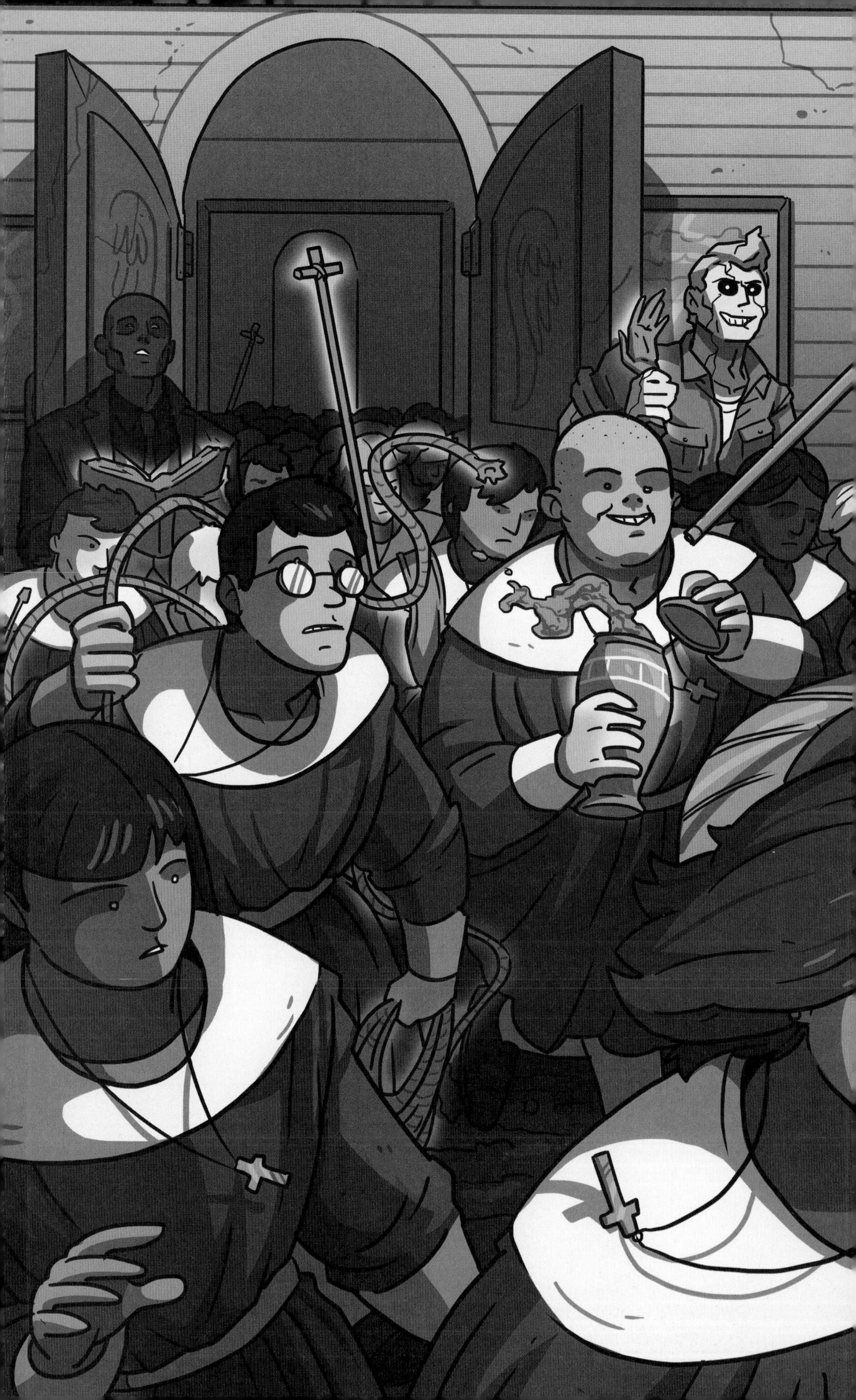

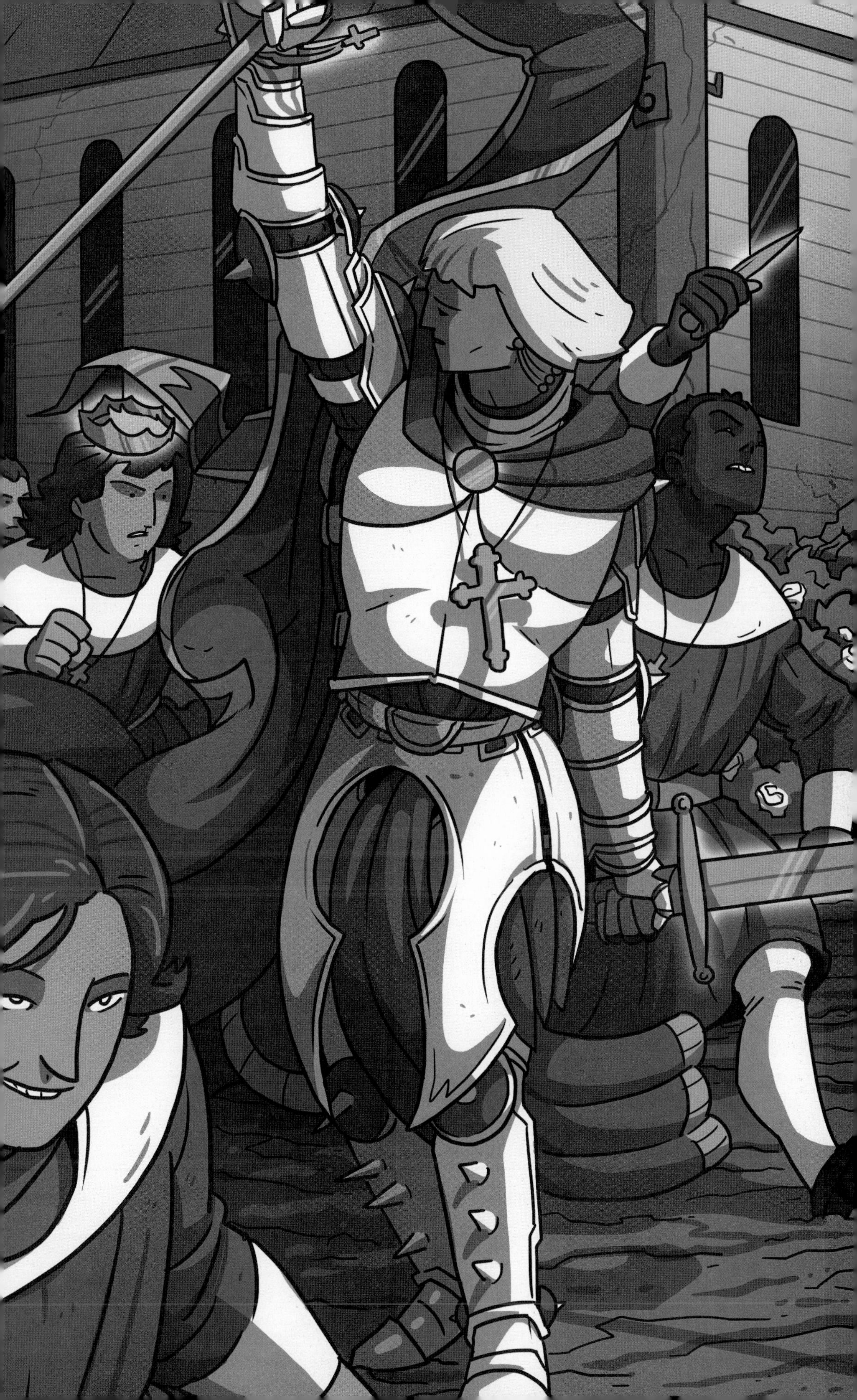

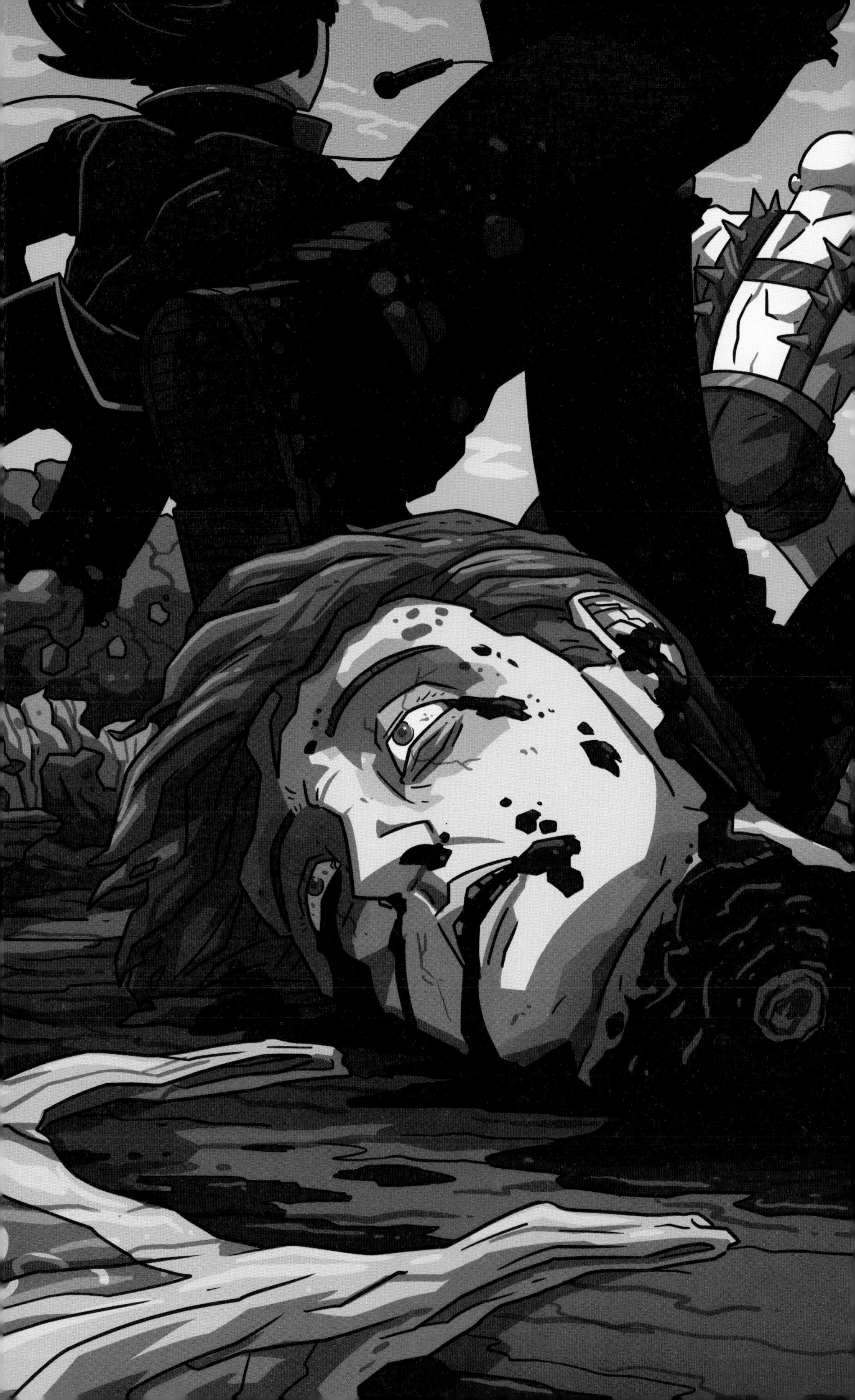

VII

EDEN

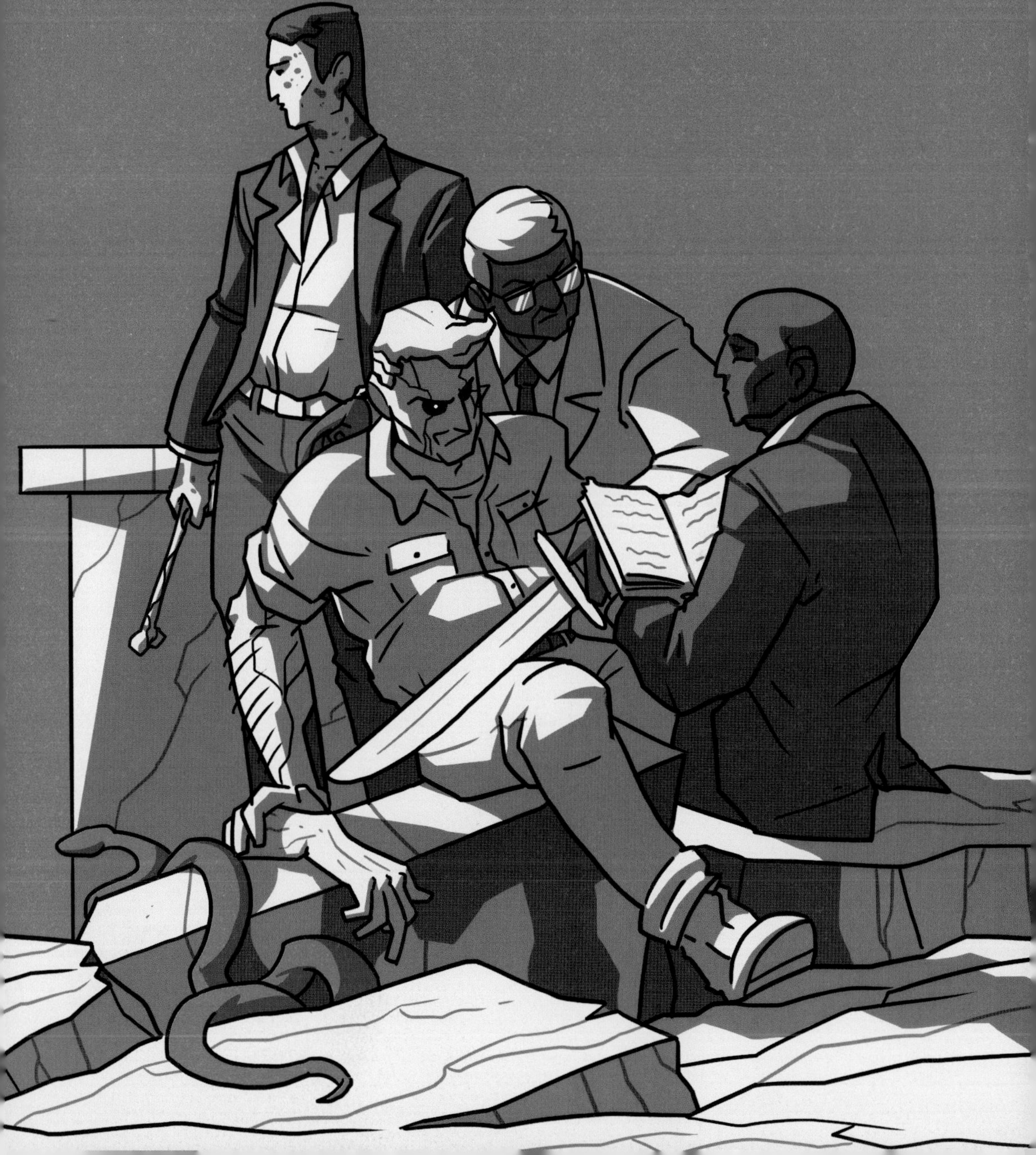

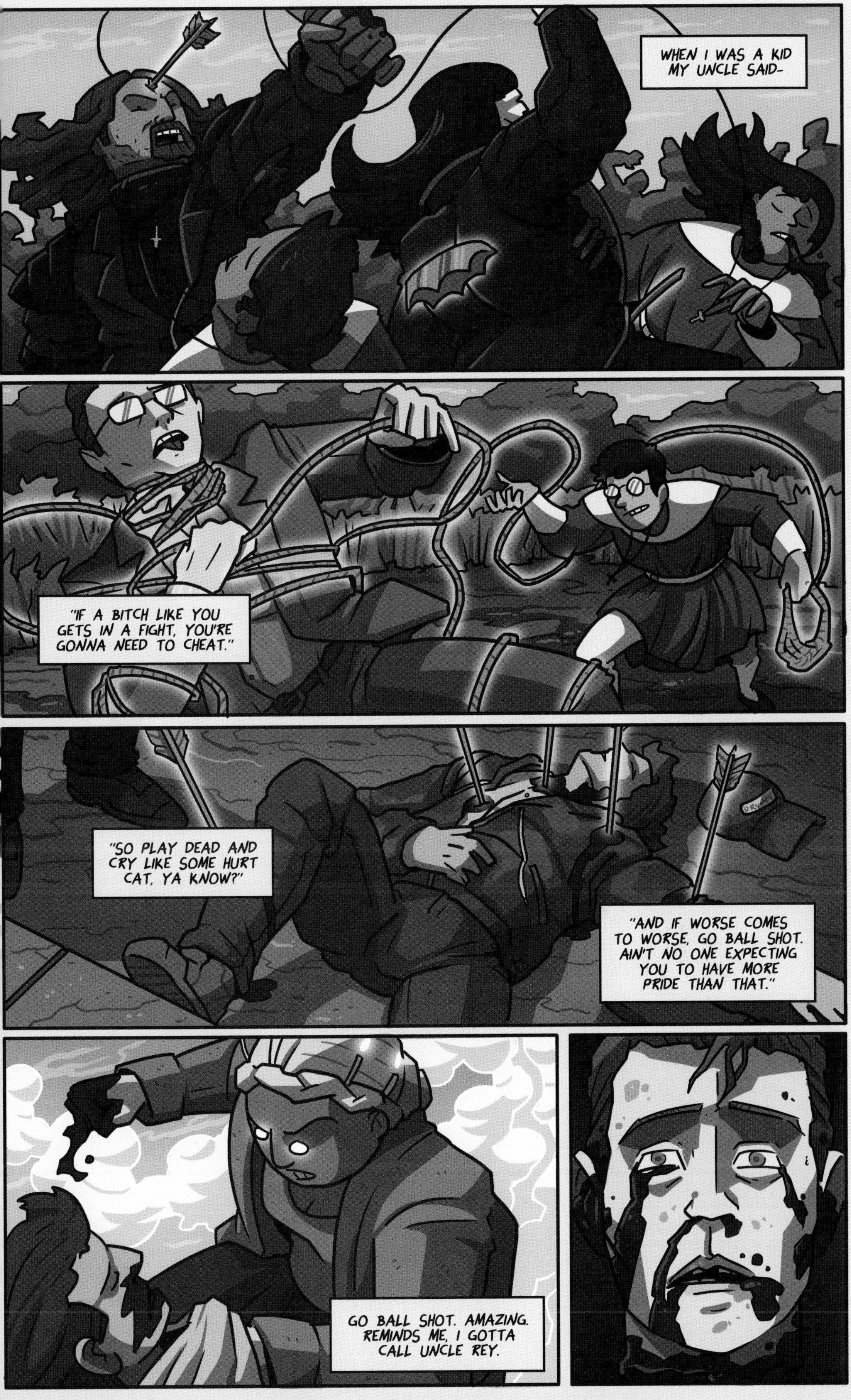
WHEN I WAS A KID MY UNCLE SAID-
"IF A BITCH LIKE YOU GETS IN A FIGHT, YOU'RE GONNA NEED TO CHEAT."
"SO PLAY DEAD AND CRY LIKE SOME HURT CAT, YA KNOW?"
"AND IF WORSE COMES TO WORSE, GO BALL SHOT. AIN'T NO ONE EXPECTING YOU TO HAVE MORE PRIDE THAN THAT."
GO BALL SHOT. AMAZING. REMINDS ME, I GOTTA CALL UNCLE REY.

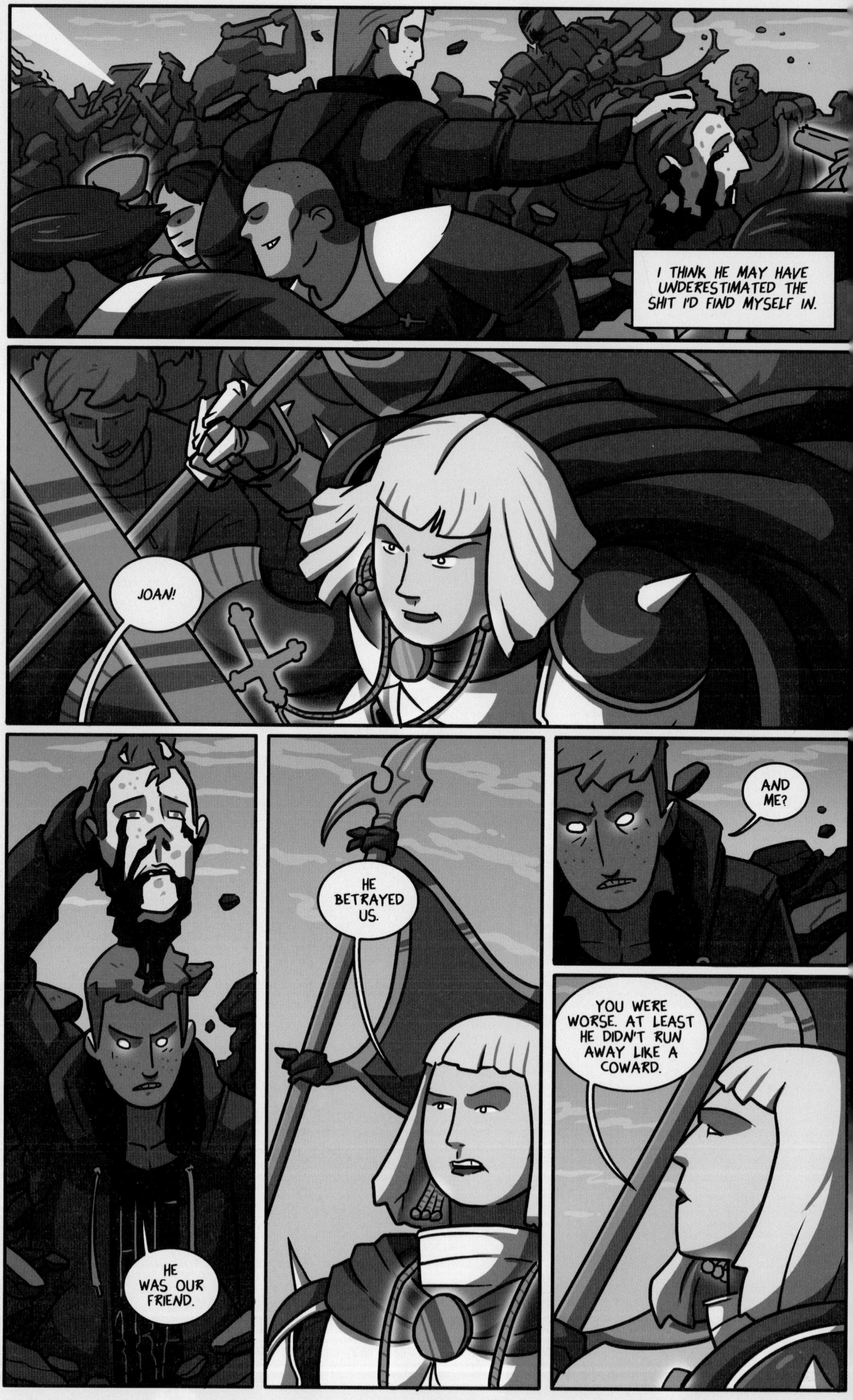
I THINK HE MAY HAVE UNDERESTIMATED THE SHIT I'D FIND MYSELF IN.
JOAN!
HE WAS OUR FRIEND.
HE BETRAYED US.
AND ME?
YOU WERE WORSE. AT LEAST HE DIDN'T RUN AWAY LIKE A COWARD.

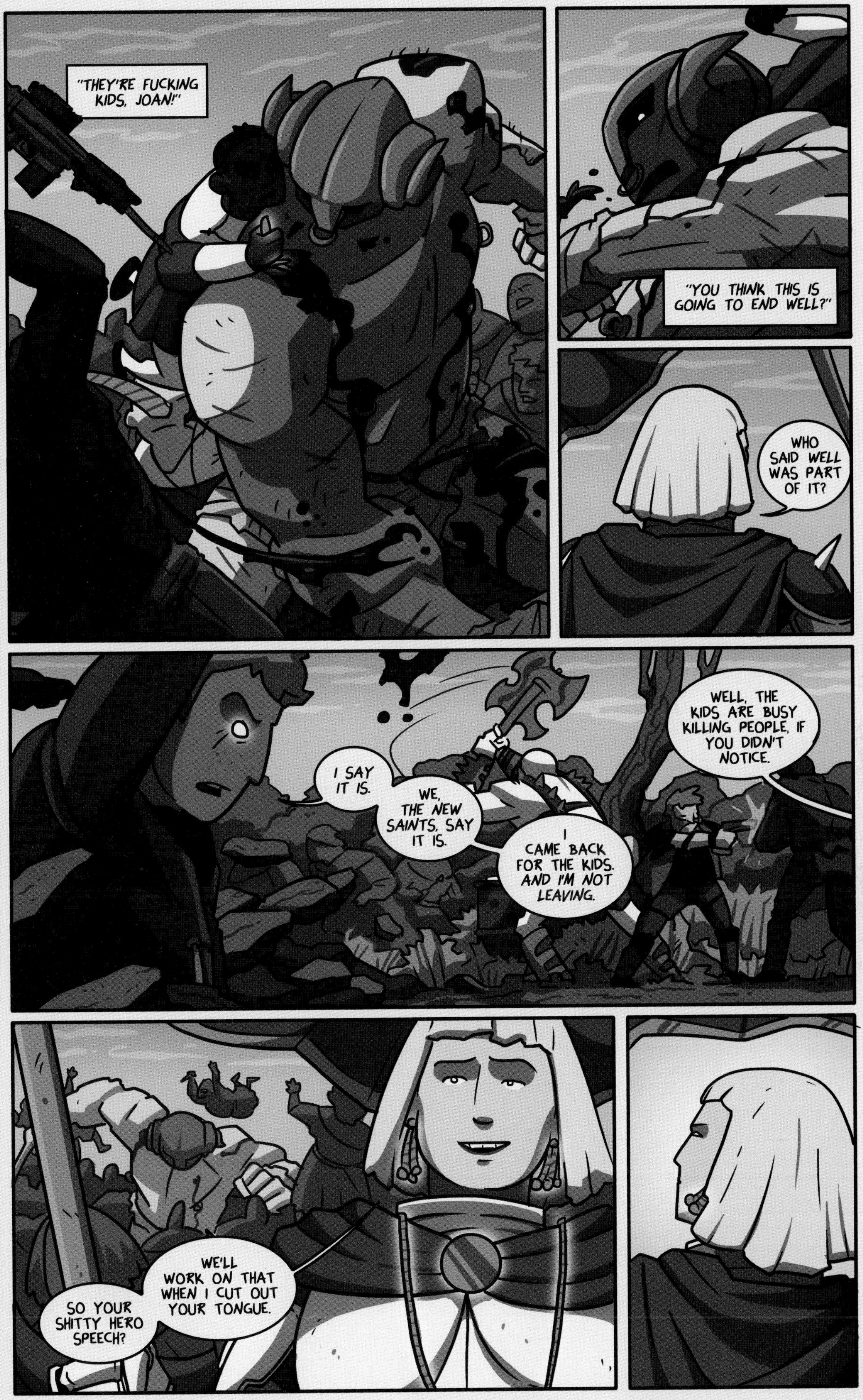
"THEY'RE FUCKING KIDS, JOAN!"
"YOU THINK THIS IS GOING TO END WELL?"
WHO SAID WELL WAS PART OF IT?
I SAY IT IS.
WE, THE NEW SAINTS, SAY IT IS.
I CAME BACK FOR THE KIDS. AND I'M NOT LEAVING.
WELL, THE KIDS ARE BUSY KILLING PEOPLE, IF YOU DIDN'T NOTICE.
SO YOUR SHITTY HERO SPEECH?
WE'LL WORK ON THAT WHEN I CUT OUT YOUR TONGUE.

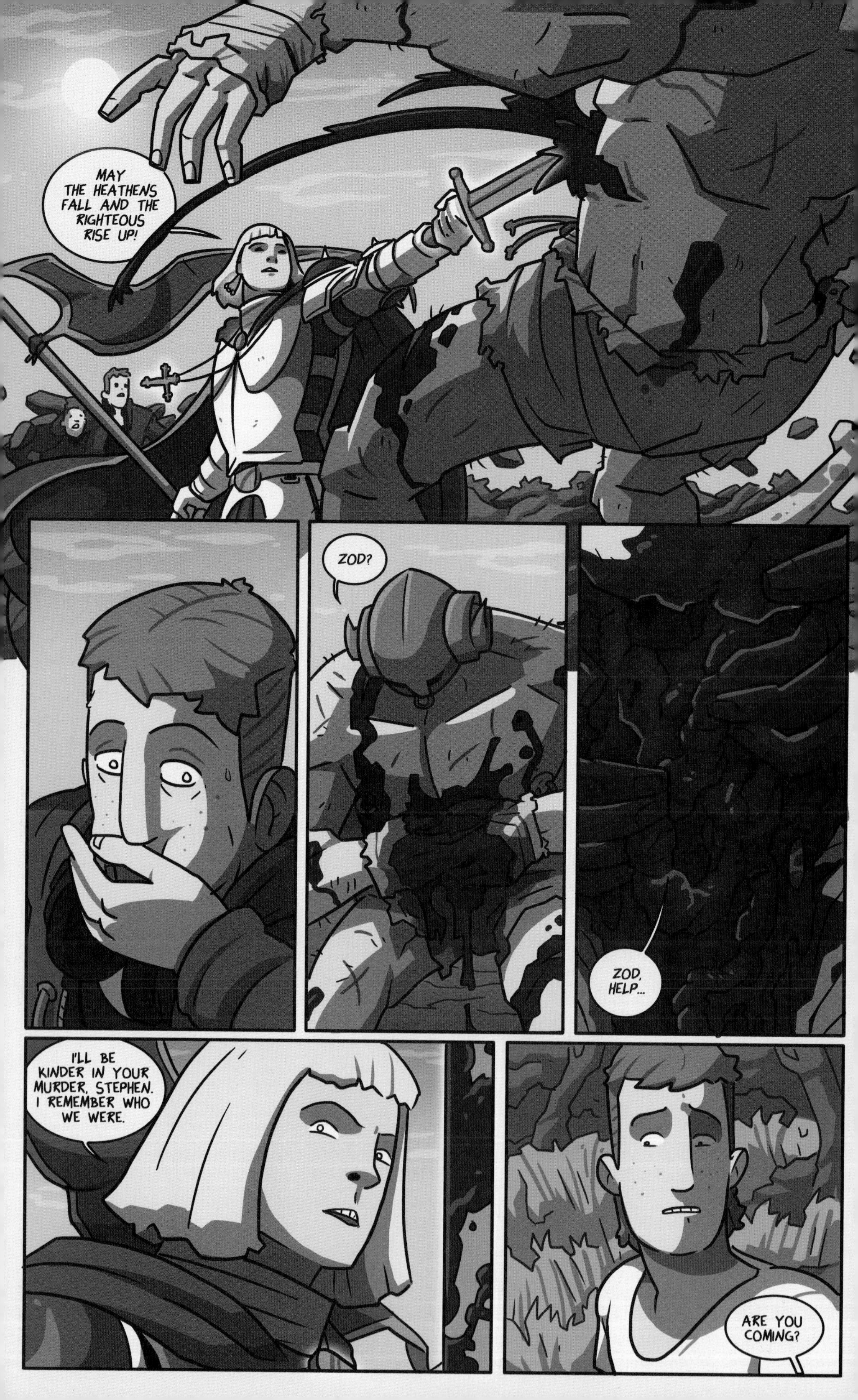
MAY THE HEATHENS FALL AND THE RIGHTEOUS RISE UP!
ZOD?
ZOD, HELP...
I'LL BE KINDER IN YOUR MURDER, STEPHEN. I REMEMBER WHO WE WERE.
ARE YOU COMING?

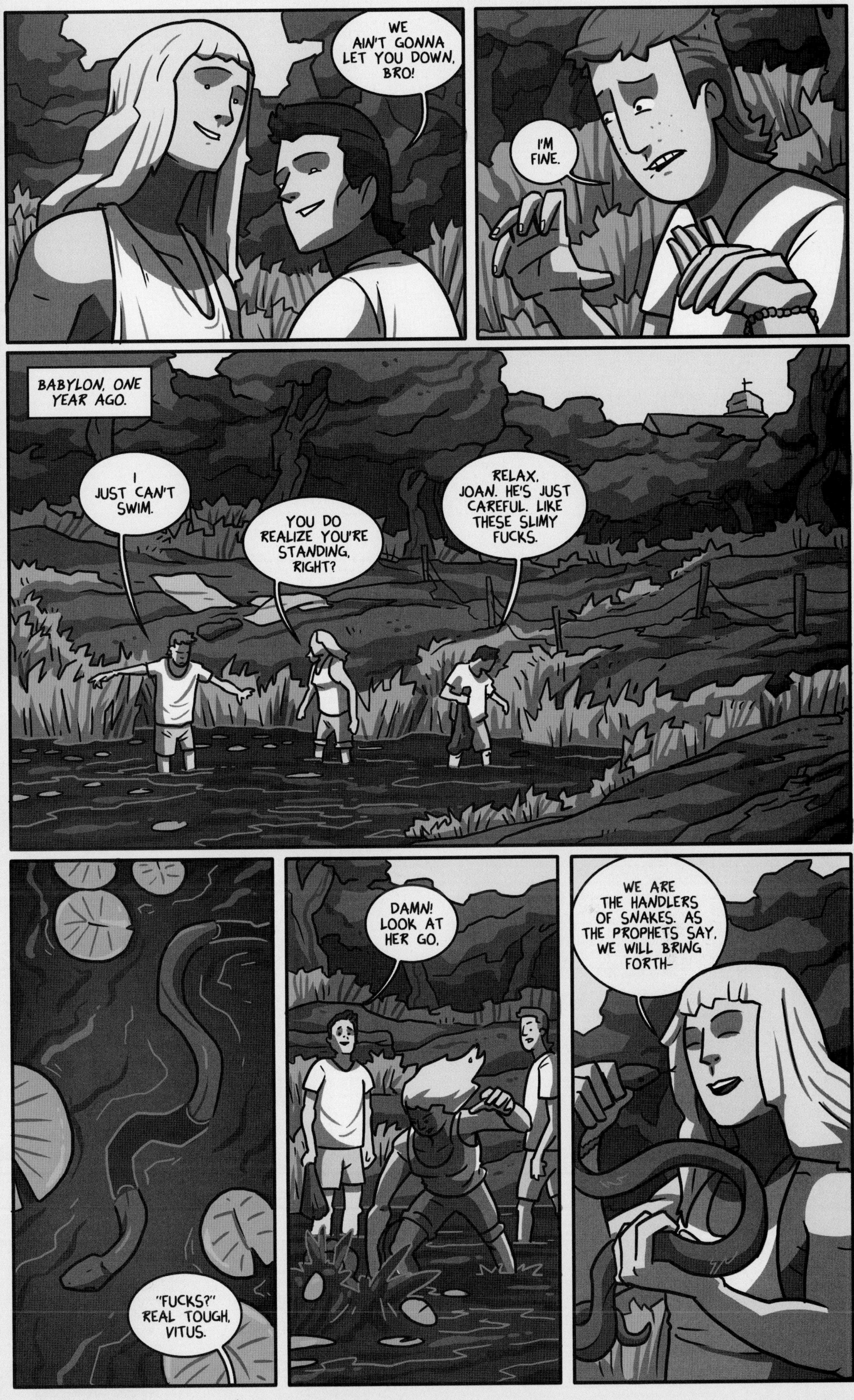
WE AIN'T GONNA LET YOU DOWN, BRO!
I'M FINE.
BABYLON, ONE YEAR AGO.
I JUST CAN'T SWIM.
YOU DO REALIZE YOU'RE STANDING, RIGHT?
RELAX, JOAN. HE'S JUST CAREFUL. LIKE THESE SLIMY FUCKS.
"FUCKS?" REAL TOUGH, VITUS.
DAMN! LOOK AT HER GO.
WE ARE THE HANDLERS OF SNAKES. AS THE PROPHETS SAY, WE WILL BRING FORTH-

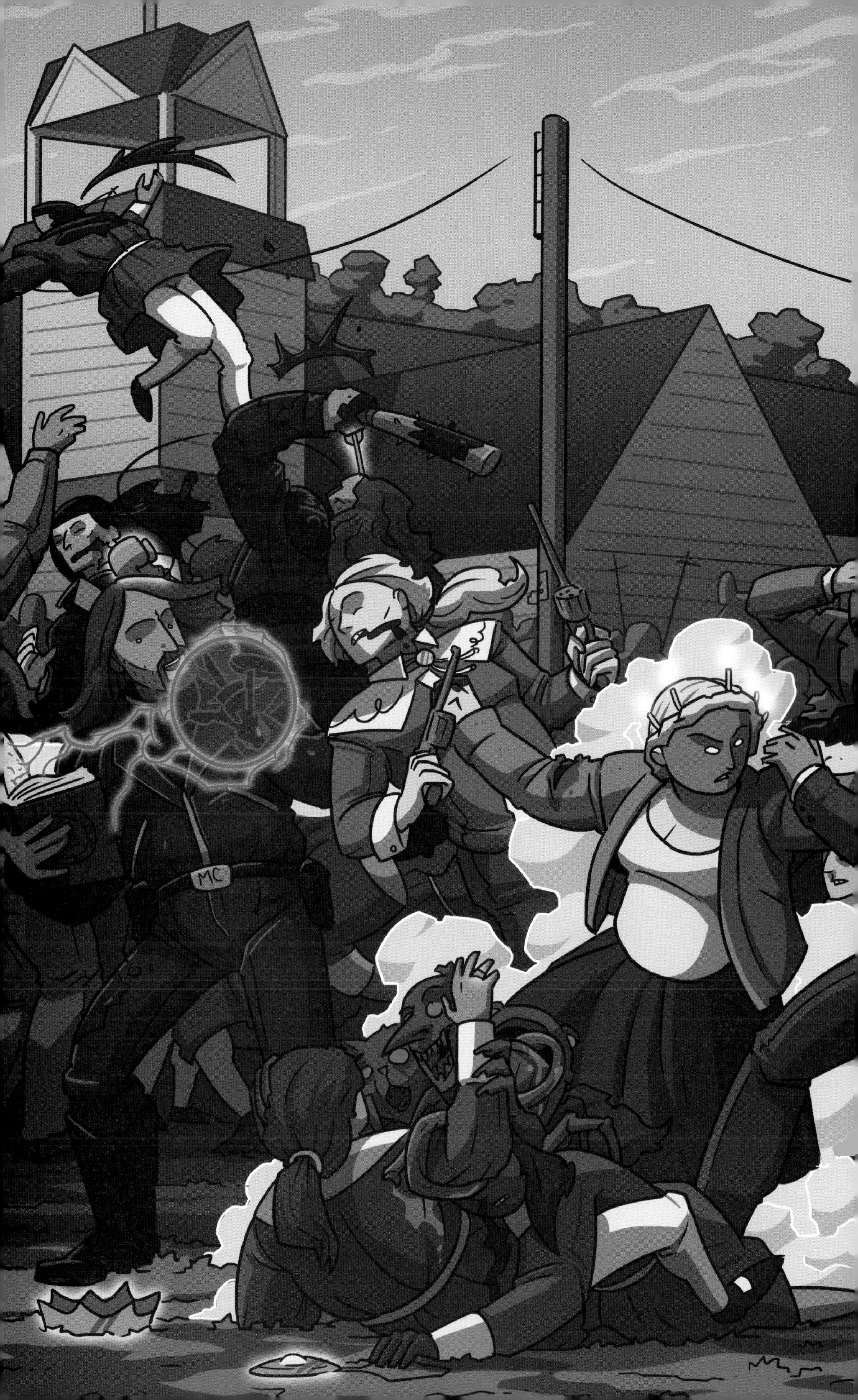
MC

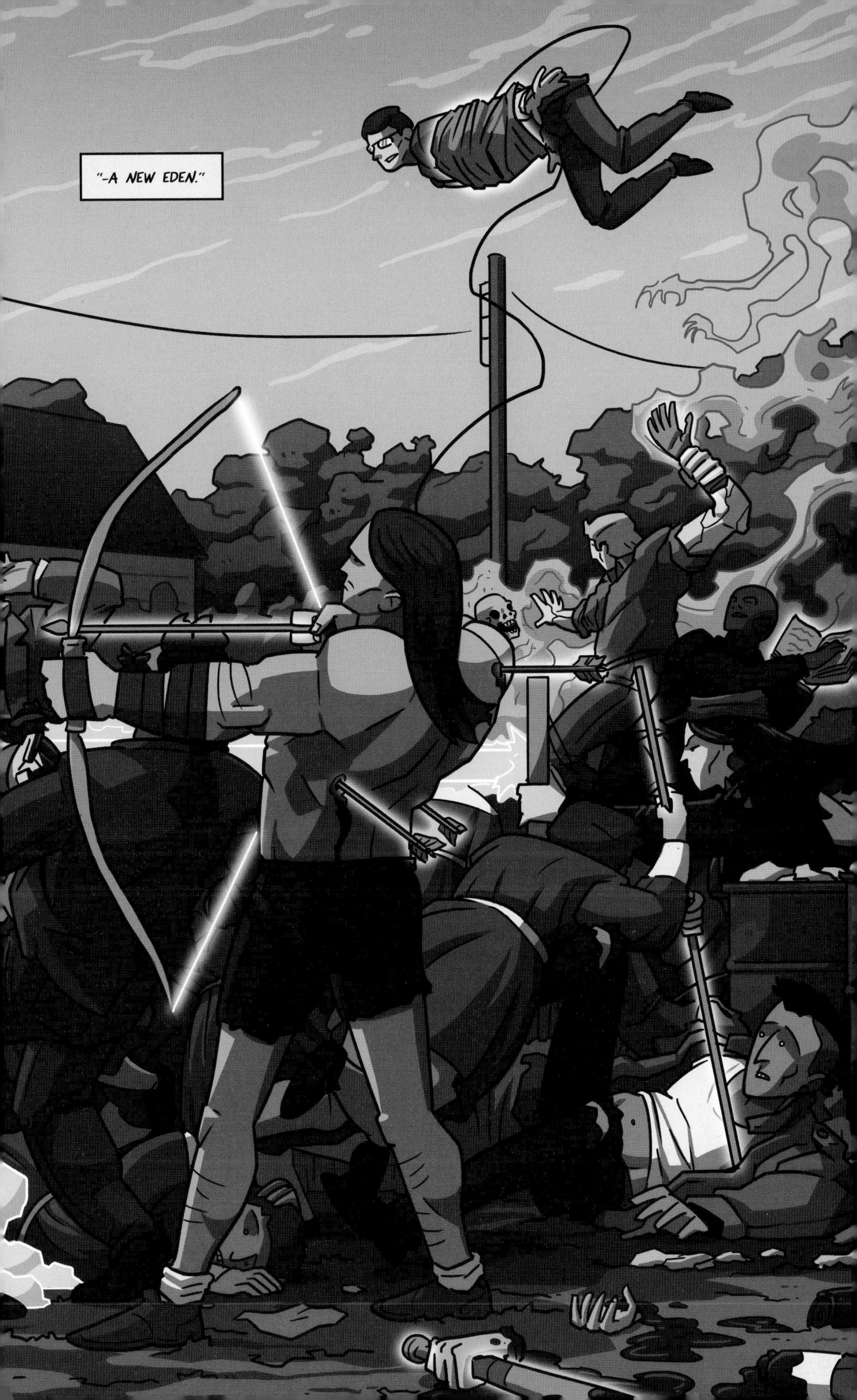
"-A NEW EDEN."

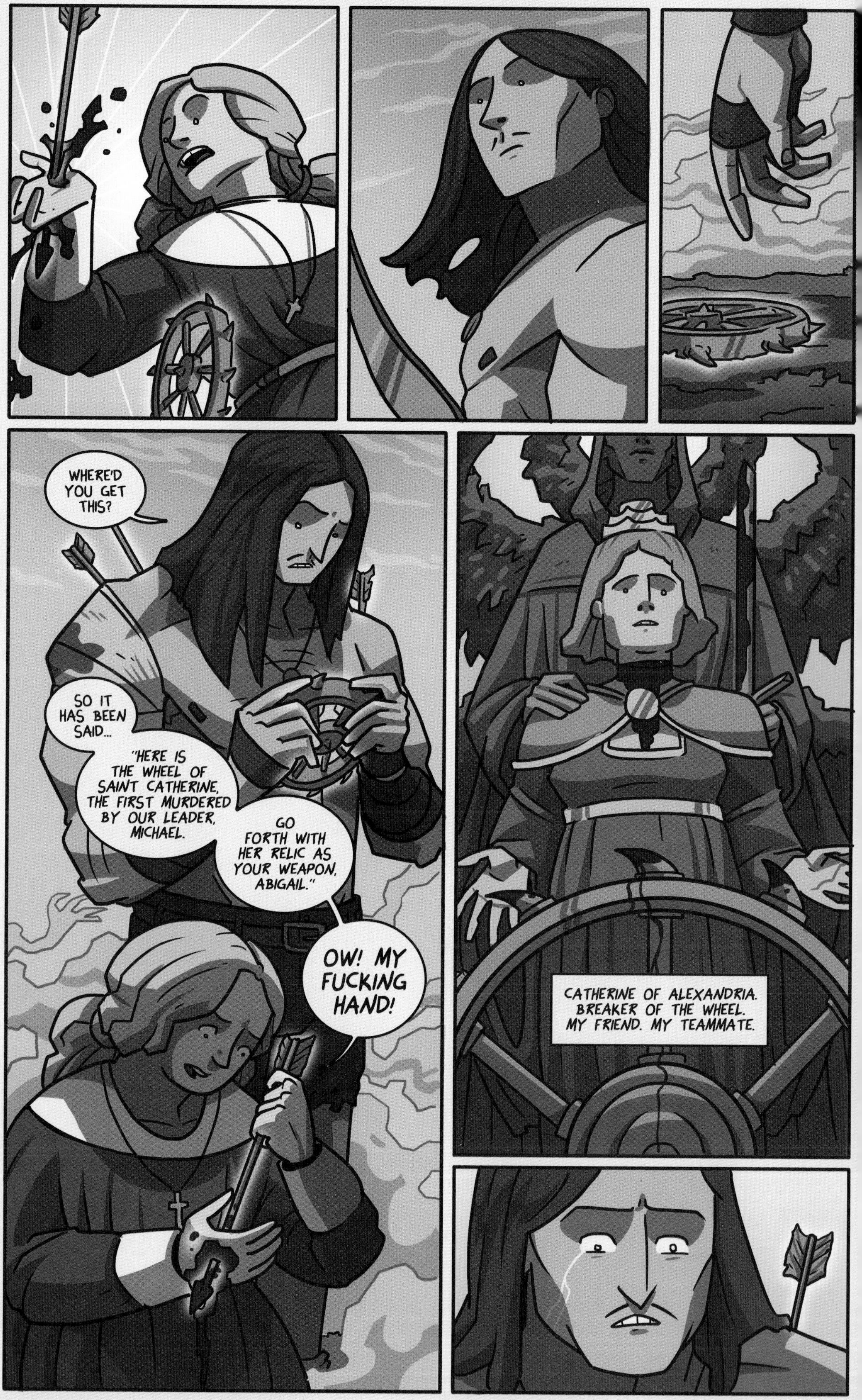
WHERE'D YOU GET THIS?
SO IT HAS BEEN SAID...
"HERE IS THE WHEEL OF SAINT CATHERINE, THE FIRST MURDERED BY OUR LEADER, MICHAEL.
GO FORTH WITH HER RELIC AS YOUR WEAPON, ABIGAIL."
OW! MY FUCKING HAND!
CATHERINE OF ALEXANDRIA. BREAKER OF THE WHEEL. MY FRIEND. MY TEAMMATE.

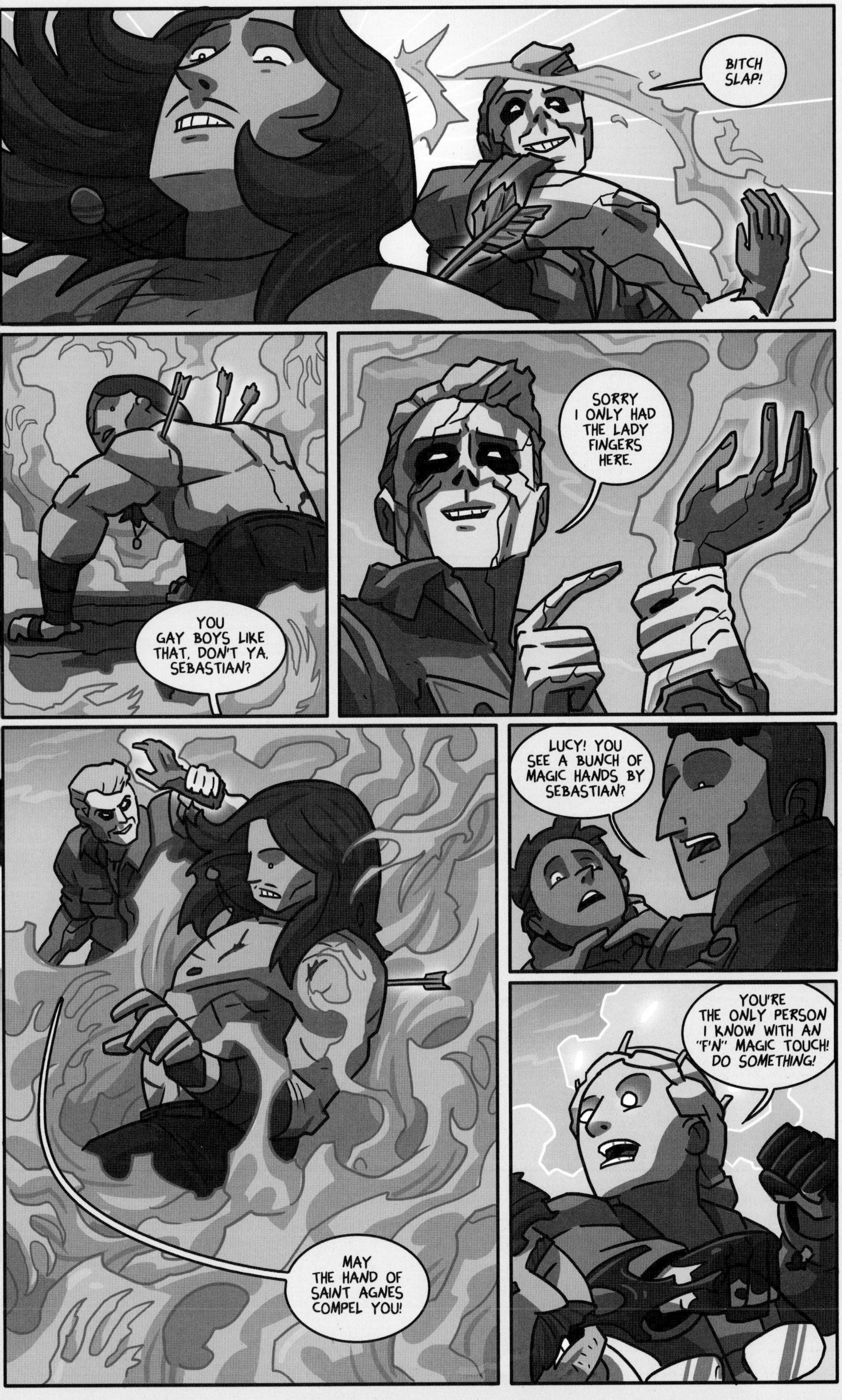
BITCH SLAP!
SORRY I ONLY HAD THE LADY FINGERS HERE.
YOU GAY BOYS LIKE THAT, DON'T YA, SEBASTIAN?
MAY THE HAND OF SAINT AGNES COMPEL YOU!
LUCY! YOU SEE A BUNCH OF MAGIC HANDS BY SEBASTIAN?
YOU'RE THE ONLY PERSON I KNOW WITH AN "F'N" MAGIC TOUCH! DO SOMETHING!

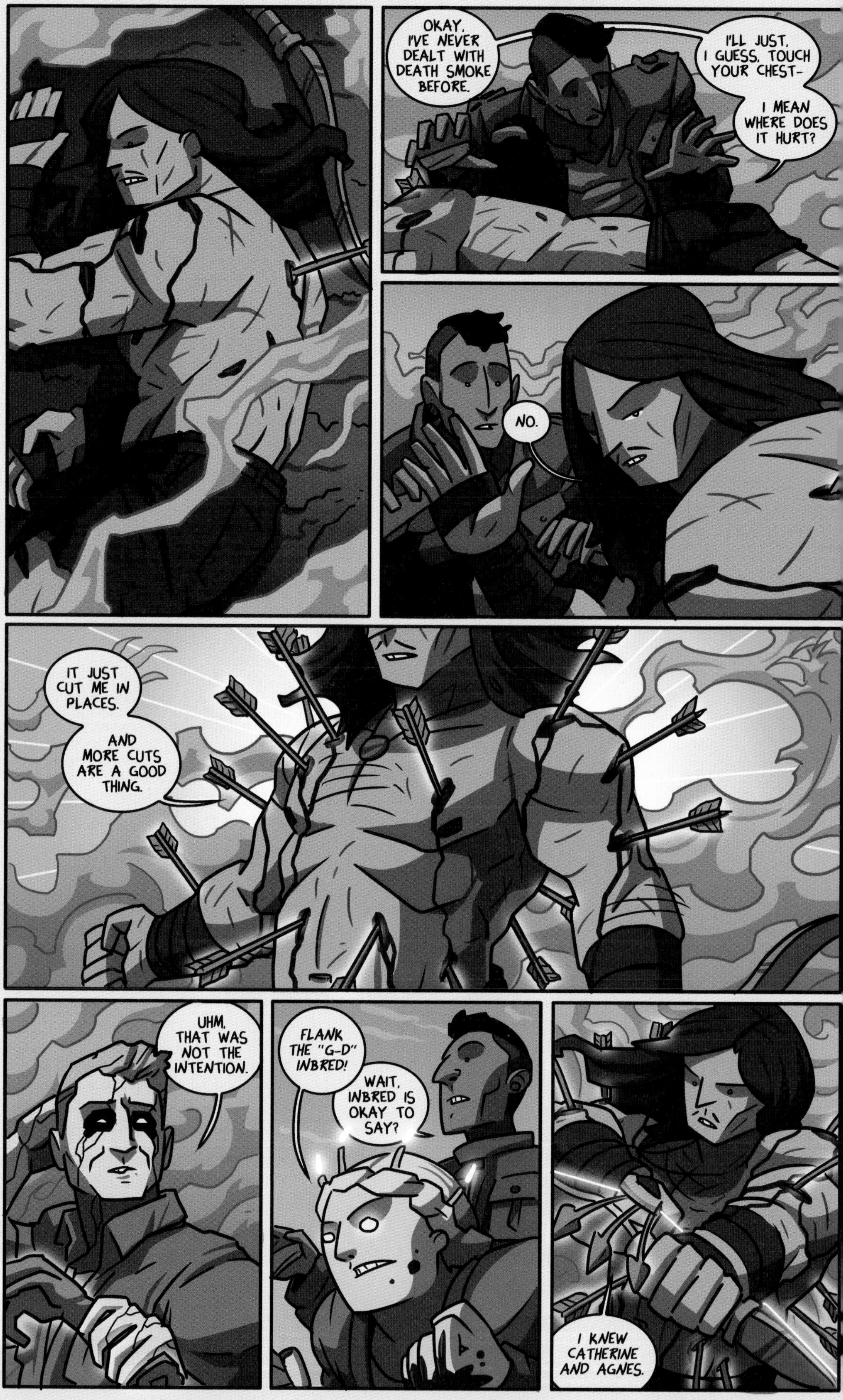
OKAY, I'VE NEVER DEALT WITH DEATH SMOKE BEFORE.
I'LL JUST, I GUESS, TOUCH YOUR CHEST-
I MEAN WHERE DOES IT HURT?
NO.
IT JUST CUT ME IN PLACES.
AND MORE CUTS ARE A GOOD THING.
UHM, THAT WAS NOT THE INTENTION.
FLANK THE "G-D" INBRED!
WAIT, INBRED IS OKAY TO SAY?
I KNEW CATHERINE AND AGNES.

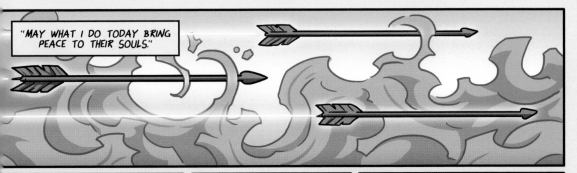

"MAY WHAT I DO TODAY BRING PEACE TO THEIR SOULS."

I DID SAY FLANK, DIDN'T I? FLANK?

HE'S GOT A VENDETTA LUCY. YOU GOTTA ROLL WITH IT.

I AM DEATH!

I AM THE END!

I AM THE—

"HHRK!"

YES. YES YOU ARE.

AND ME?

I'M READY FOR A "M-F'ING" FIGHT.

SNATCH

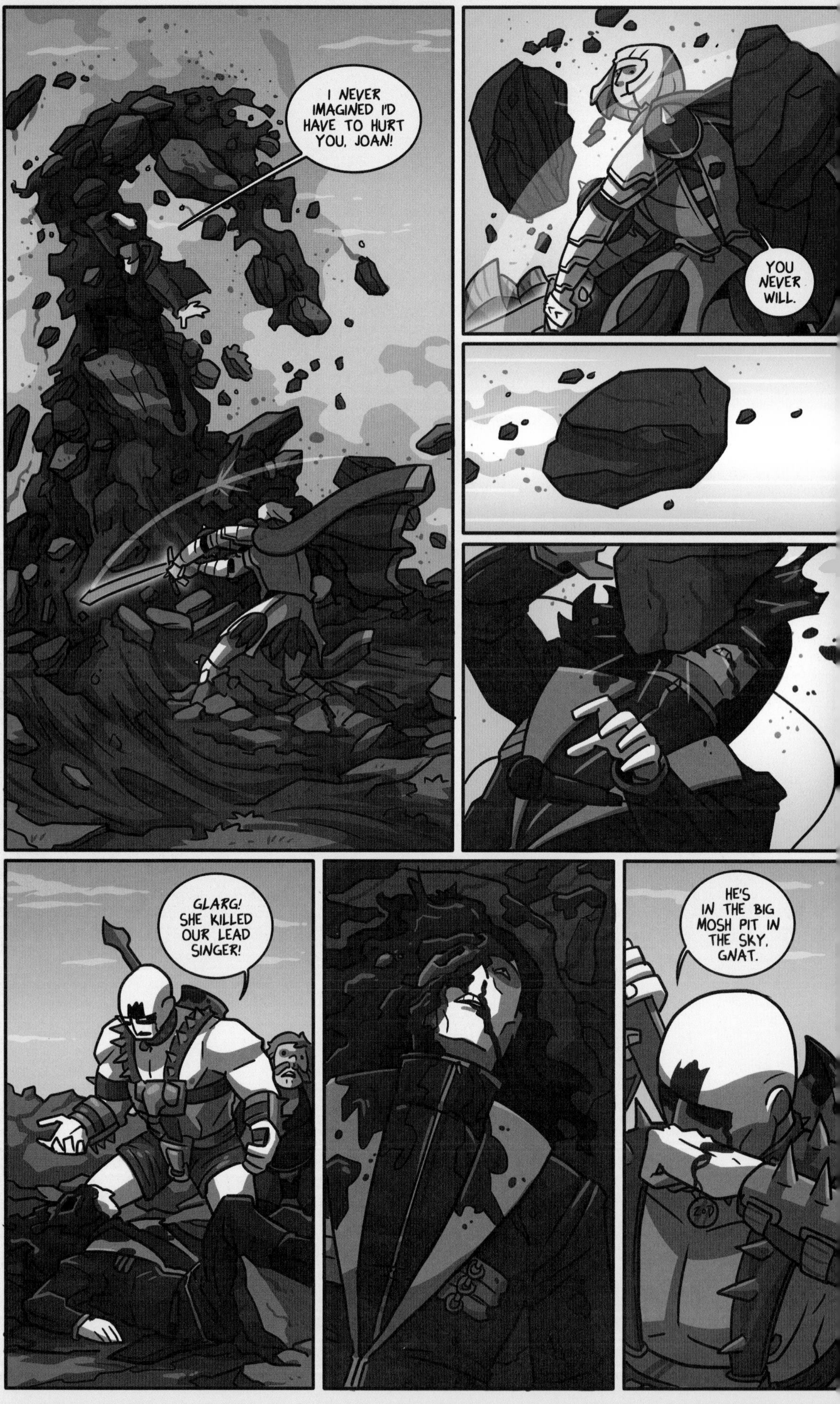
I NEVER IMAGINED I'D HAVE TO HURT YOU, JOAN!
YOU NEVER WILL.
GLARG! SHE KILLED OUR LEAD SINGER!
HE'S IN THE BIG MOSH PIT IN THE SKY, GNAT.

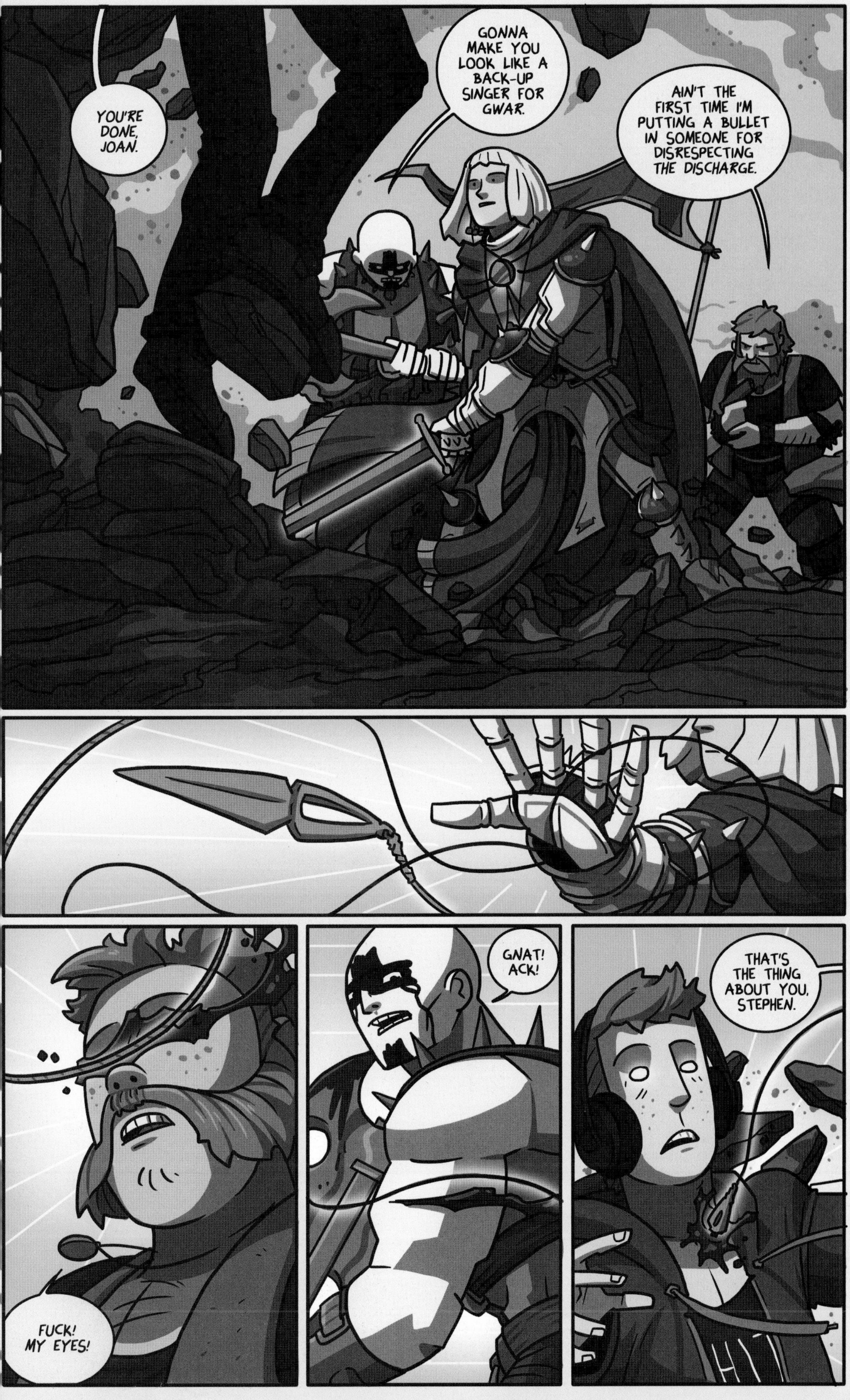
YOU'RE DONE, JOAN.
GONNA MAKE YOU LOOK LIKE A BACK-UP SINGER FOR GWAR.
AIN'T THE FIRST TIME I'M PUTTING A BULLET IN SOMEONE FOR DISRESPECTING THE DISCHARGE.
FUCK! MY EYES!
GNAT! ACK!
THAT'S THE THING ABOUT YOU, STEPHEN.

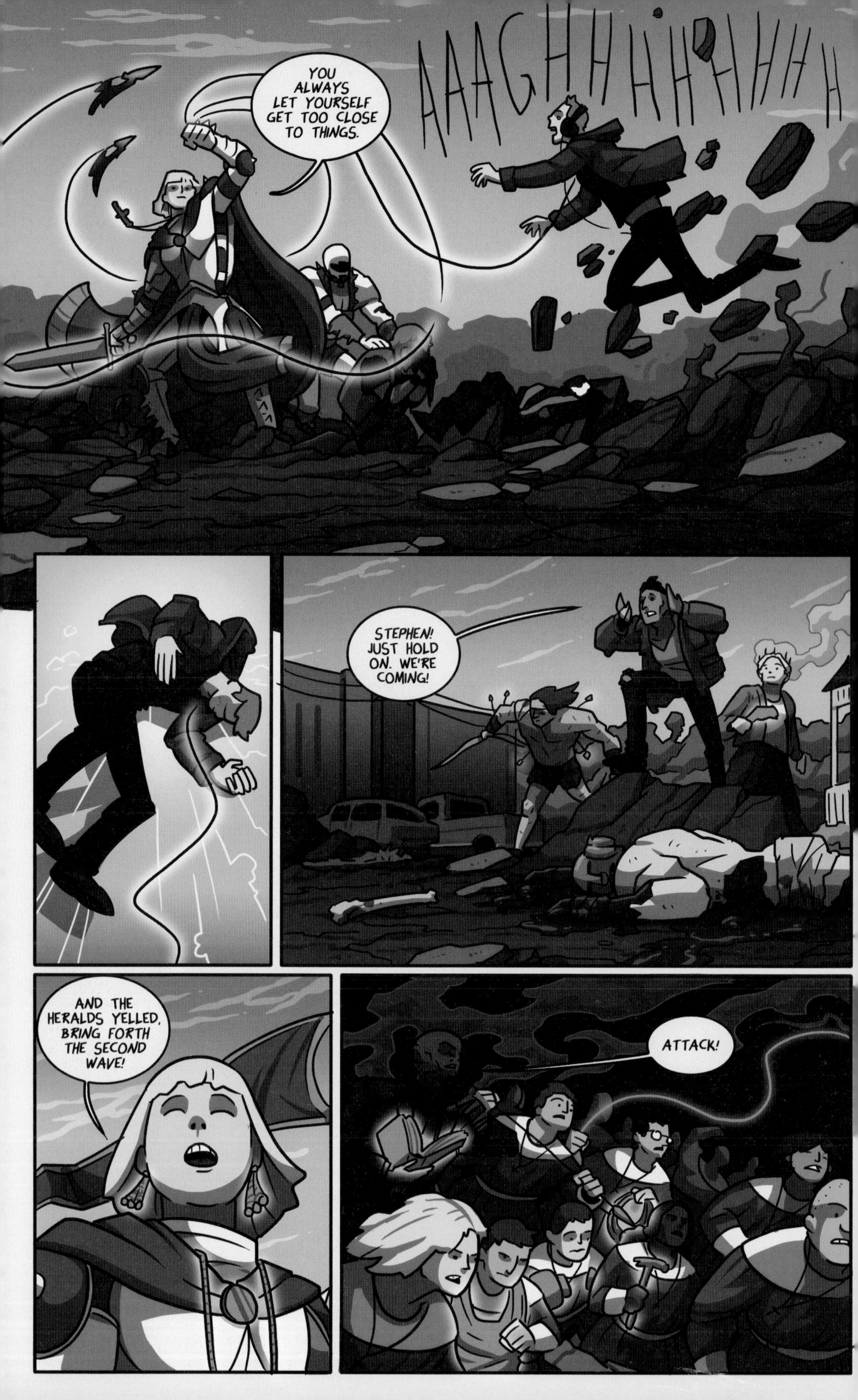
YOU ALWAYS LET YOURSELF GET TOO CLOSE TO THINGS.
AAAGHHHHHHHHHH
STEPHEN! JUST HOLD ON. WE'RE COMING!
AND THE HERALDS YELLED, BRING FORTH THE SECOND WAVE!
ATTACK!

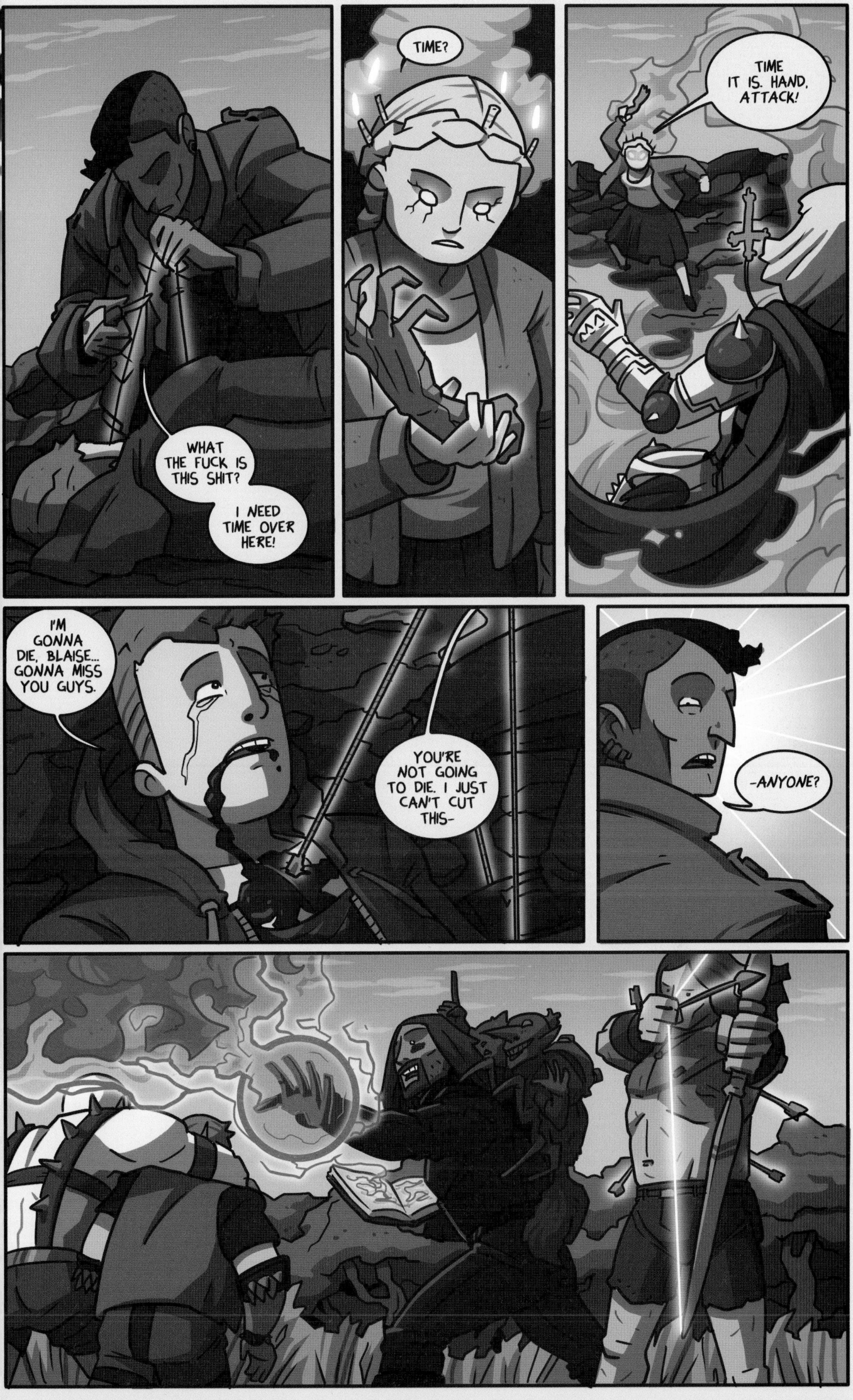
WHAT THE FUCK IS THIS SHIT?
I NEED TIME OVER HERE!
TIME?
TIME IT IS. HAND, ATTACK!
I'M GONNA DIE, BLAISE... GONNA MISS YOU GUYS.
YOU'RE NOT GOING TO DIE. I JUST CAN'T CUT THIS-
-ANYONE?

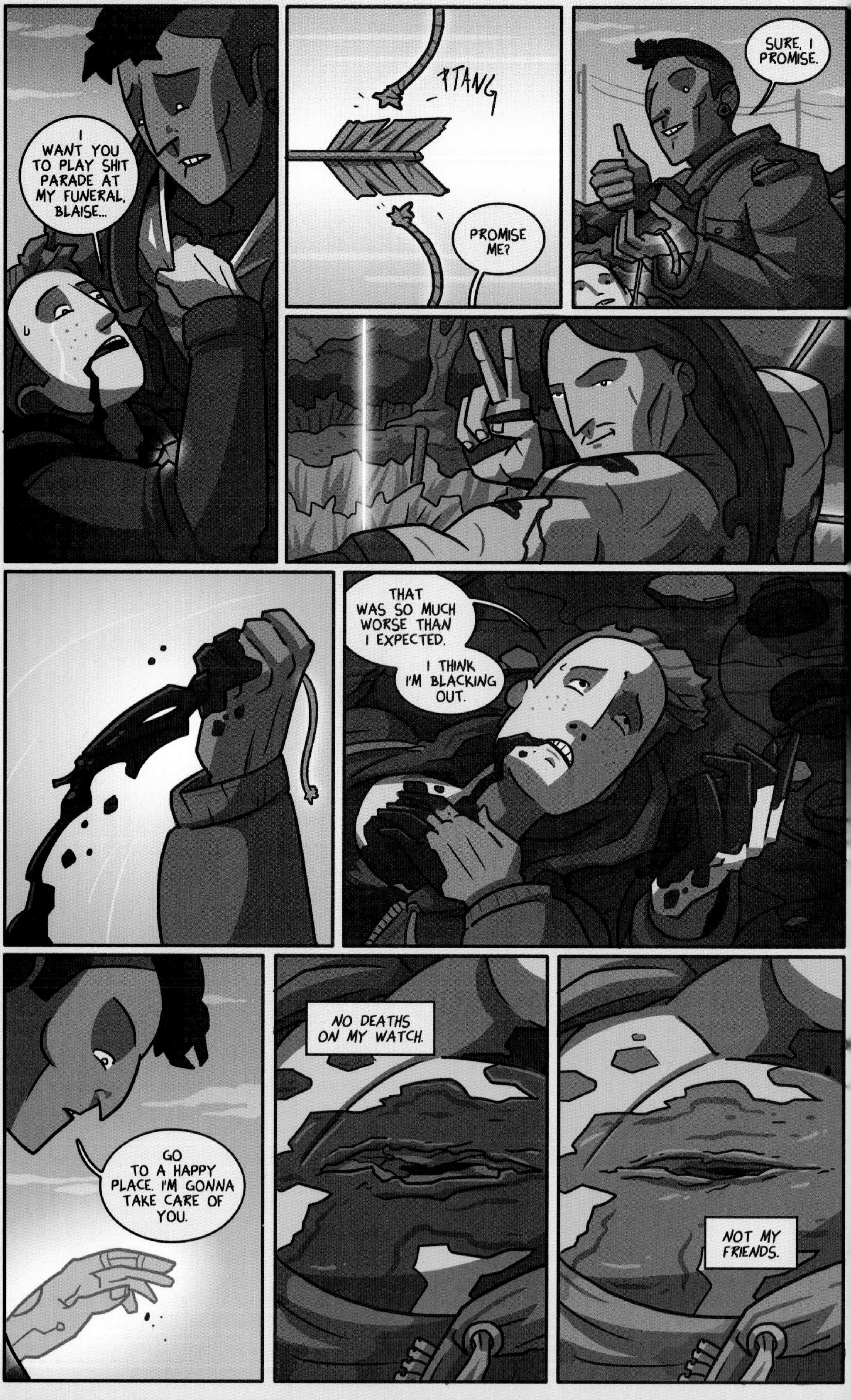
I WANT YOU TO PLAY SHIT PARADE AT MY FUNERAL, BLAISE...
PTANG
PROMISE ME?
SURE, I PROMISE.
THAT WAS SO MUCH WORSE THAN I EXPECTED.
I THINK I'M BLACKING OUT.
GO TO A HAPPY PLACE. I'M GONNA TAKE CARE OF YOU.
NO DEATHS ON MY WATCH.
NOT MY FRIENDS.

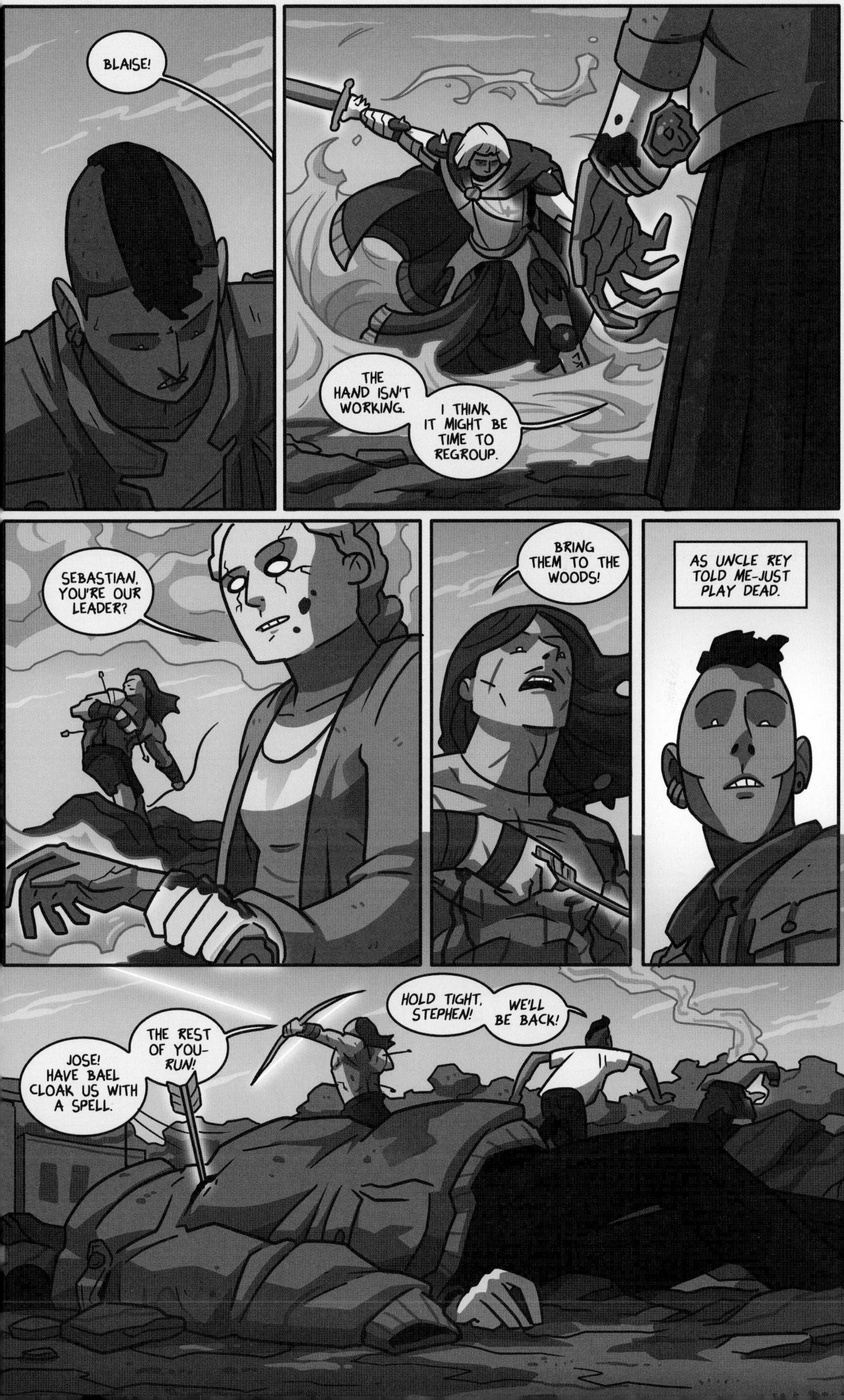
BLAISE!
THE HAND ISN'T WORKING.
I THINK IT MIGHT BE TIME TO REGROUP.
SEBASTIAN, YOU'RE OUR LEADER?
BRING THEM TO THE WOODS!
AS UNCLE REY TOLD ME-JUST PLAY DEAD.
JOSE! HAVE BAEL CLOAK US WITH A SPELL.
THE REST OF YOU- RUN!
HOLD TIGHT, STEPHEN!
WE'LL BE BACK!

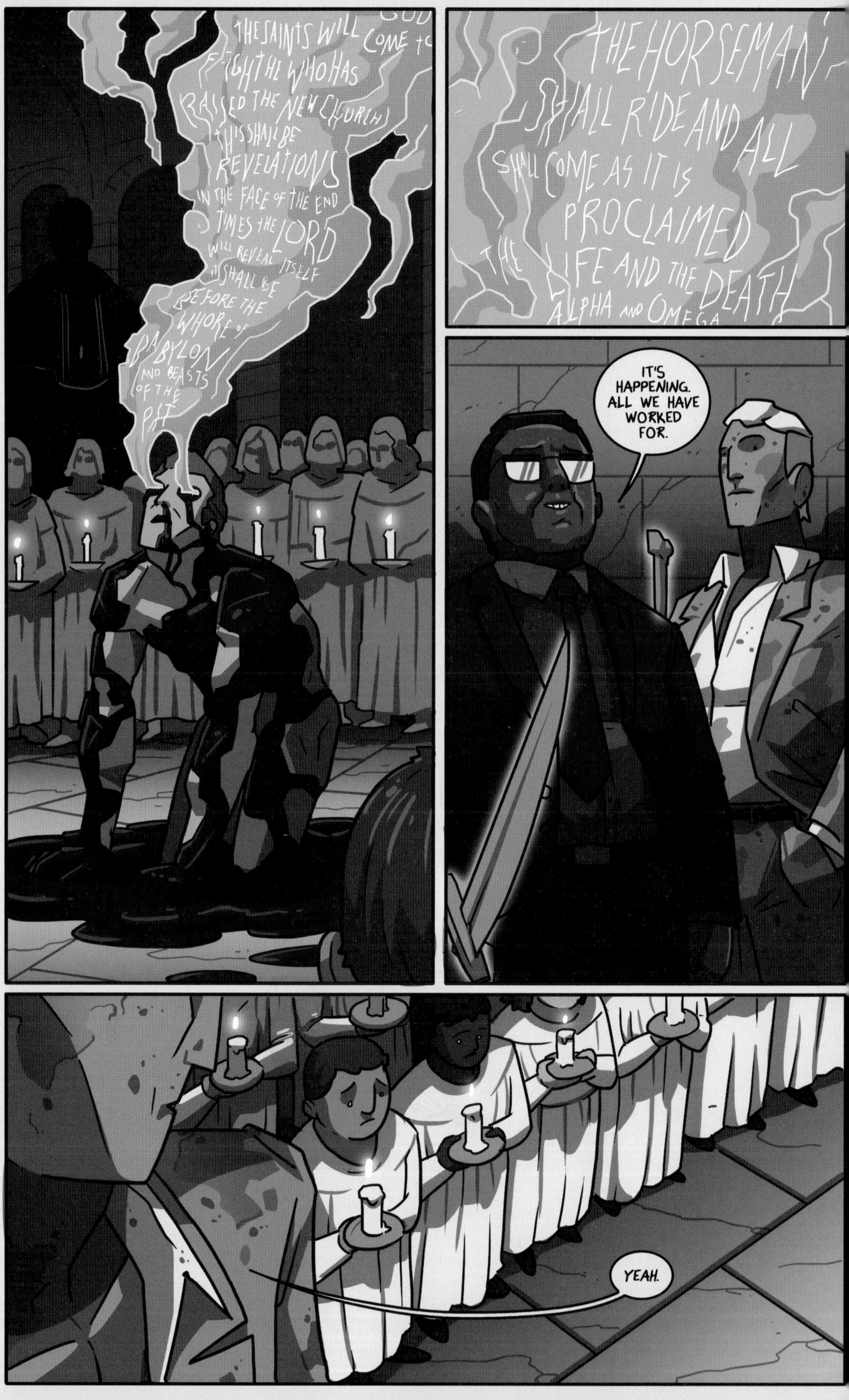
GOD
THE SAINTS WILL COME TO
FIGHT THE WHO HAS
RAISED THE NEW CHURCH
THIS SHALL BE
REVELATIONS
IN THE FACE OF THE END
TIMES THE LORD
WILL REVEAL ITSELF
IT SHALL BE
BEFORE THE
WHORE OF
BABYLON
AND BEASTS
OF THE
PIT
THE HORSEMAN
SHALL RIDE AND ALL
SHALL COME AS IT IS
PROCLAIMED
THE LIFE AND THE DEATH
ALPHA AND OMEGA
IT'S HAPPENING. ALL WE HAVE WORKED FOR.
YEAH.

IT SHALL BE US, DANNY. WE'LL ALL BE THE KINGS WHO SAVED THE WORLD!

IT'LL BE US WHO SENT THESE KIDS TO THEIR DEATHS.

"FOR HIM."

WHAT ARE YOU DOING, DANNY?

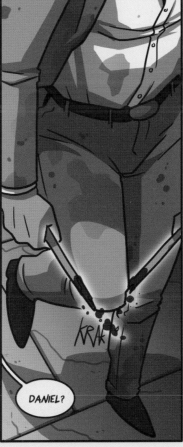

KRAK

DANIEL?

TO MY ANGEL I HUMBLY OFFER—

—THE DISEASE YOUR RELIC HAS GIVEN ME!

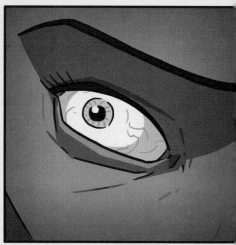

MAY PESTILENCE BURN THROUGH YOUR SOUL!

MAY LOCUST RISE IN YOUR BREATH!

MAY YOU DIE AND MAY THE LORD FORGIVE ALL I HAVE STUPIDLY DONE!

DISEASE

SICKNESS

PLAGUE

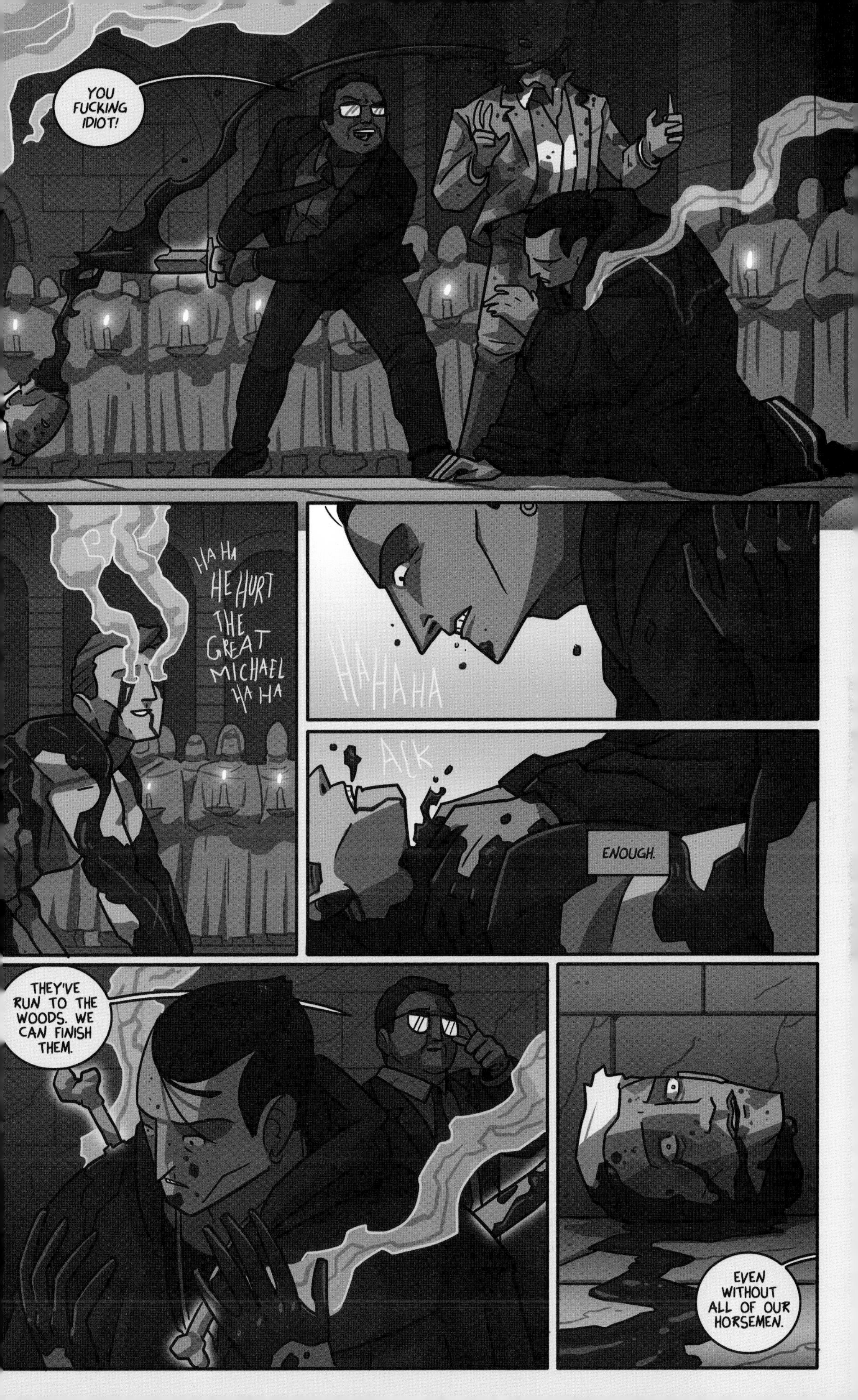

YOU FUCKING IDIOT!
HA HA HE HURT THE GREAT MICHAEL HA HA
HAHAHA
ACK
ENOUGH.
THEY'VE RUN TO THE WOODS. WE CAN FINISH THEM.
EVEN WITHOUT ALL OF OUR HORSEMEN.

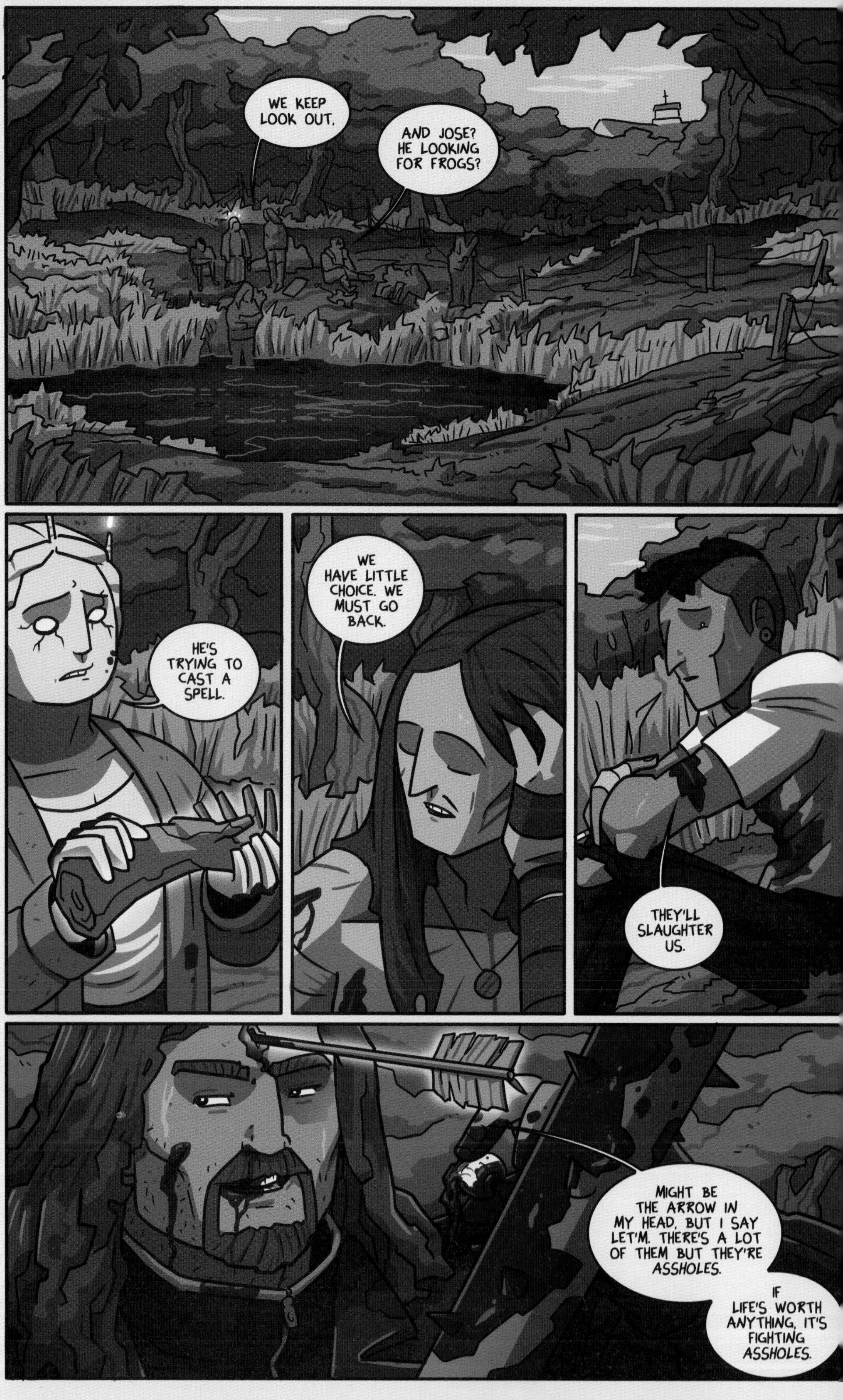
WE KEEP LOOK OUT.
AND JOSE? HE LOOKING FOR FROGS?
HE'S TRYING TO CAST A SPELL.
WE HAVE LITTLE CHOICE. WE MUST GO BACK.
THEY'LL SLAUGHTER US.
MIGHT BE THE ARROW IN MY HEAD, BUT I SAY LET'M. THERE'S A LOT OF THEM BUT THEY'RE ASSHOLES.
IF LIFE'S WORTH ANYTHING, IT'S FIGHTING ASSHOLES.

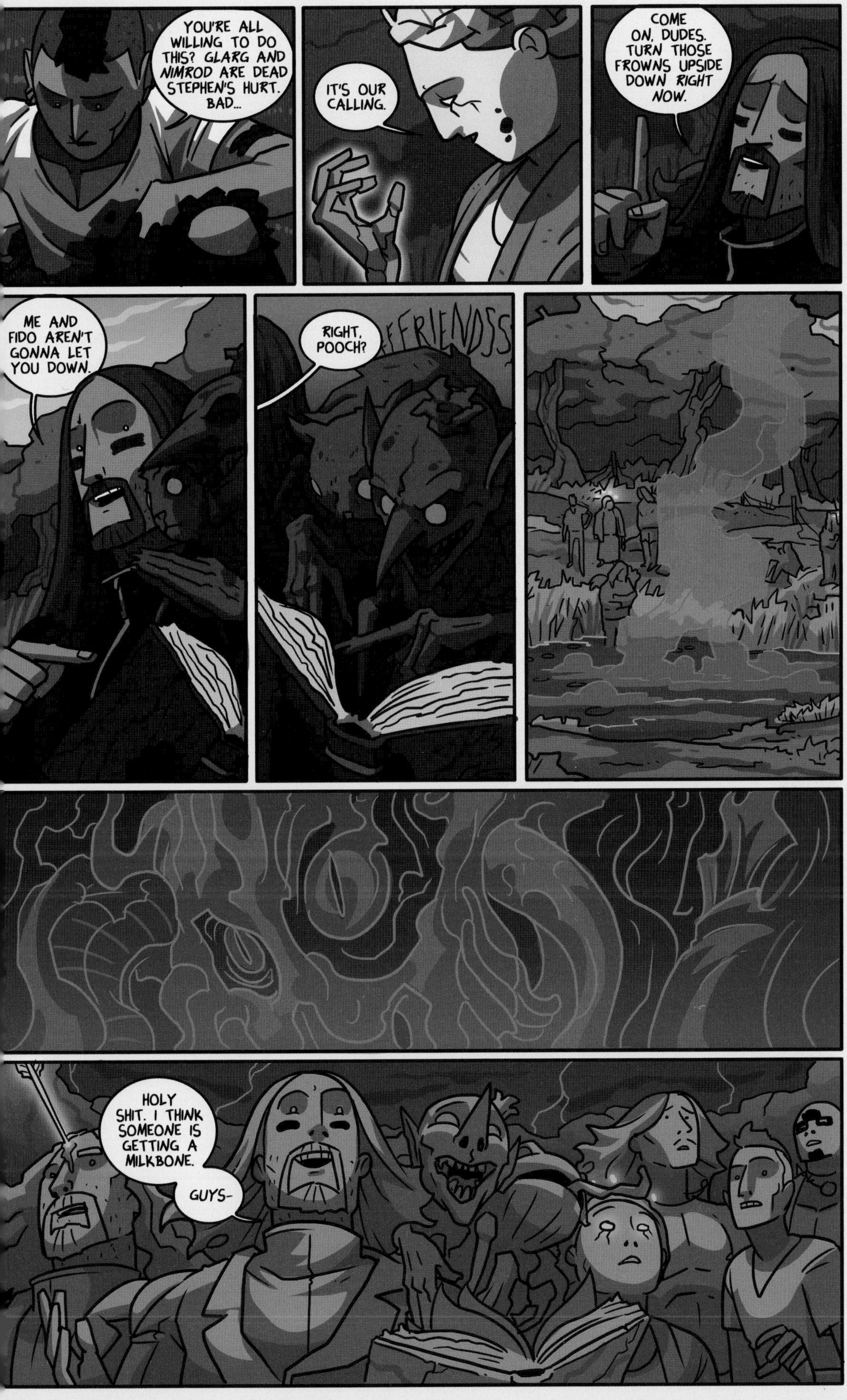
YOU'RE ALL WILLING TO DO THIS? GLARG AND NIMROD ARE DEAD STEPHEN'S HURT. BAD...
IT'S OUR CALLING.
COME ON, DUDES. TURN THOSE FROWNS UPSIDE DOWN RIGHT NOW.
ME AND FIDO AREN'T GONNA LET YOU DOWN.
RIGHT, POOCH?
FRIENDSS
HOLY SHIT. I THINK SOMEONE IS GETTING A MILKBONE.
GUYS-

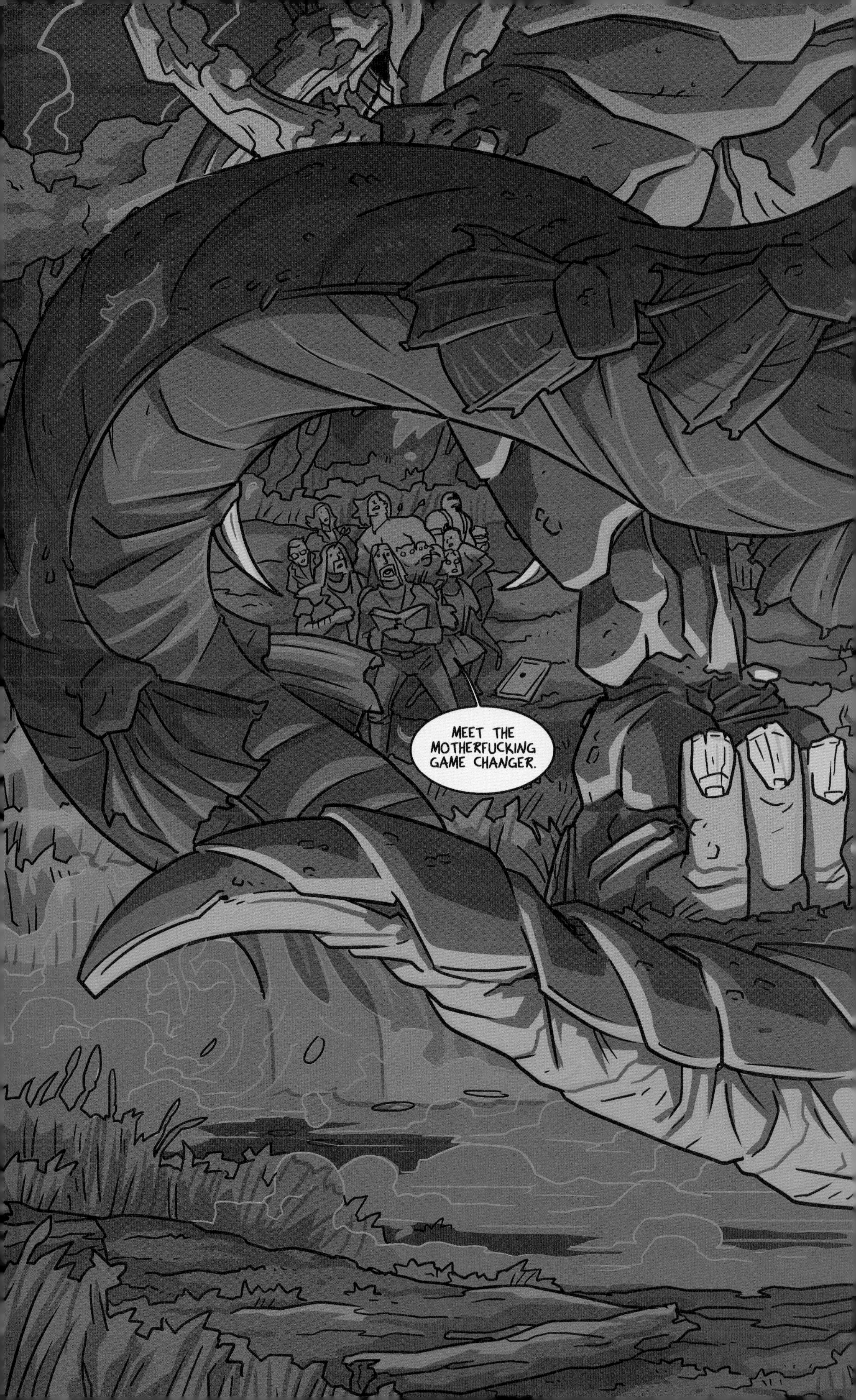
MEET THE MOTHERFUCKING GAME CHANGER.

VIII
TRANSFERENCE

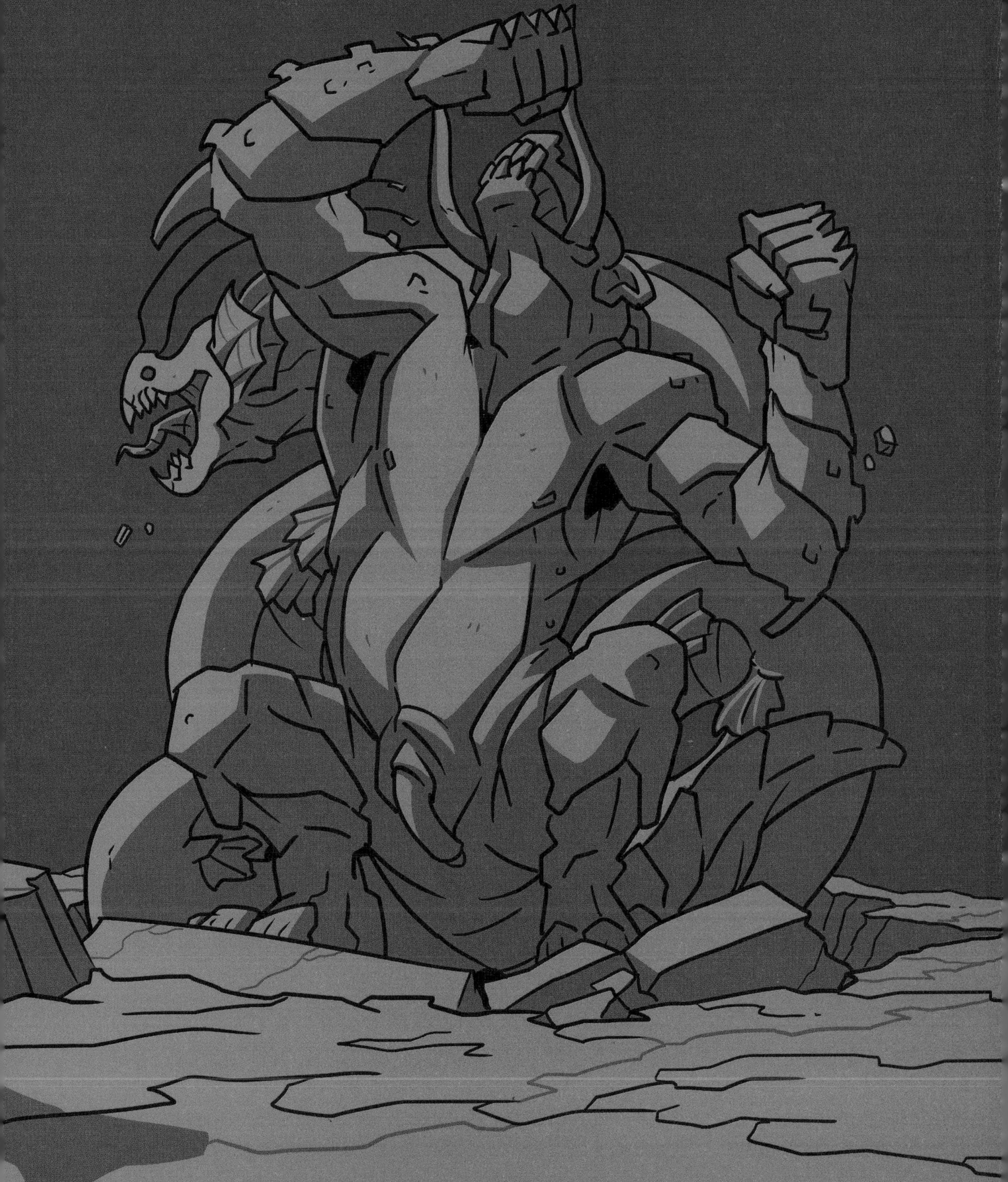

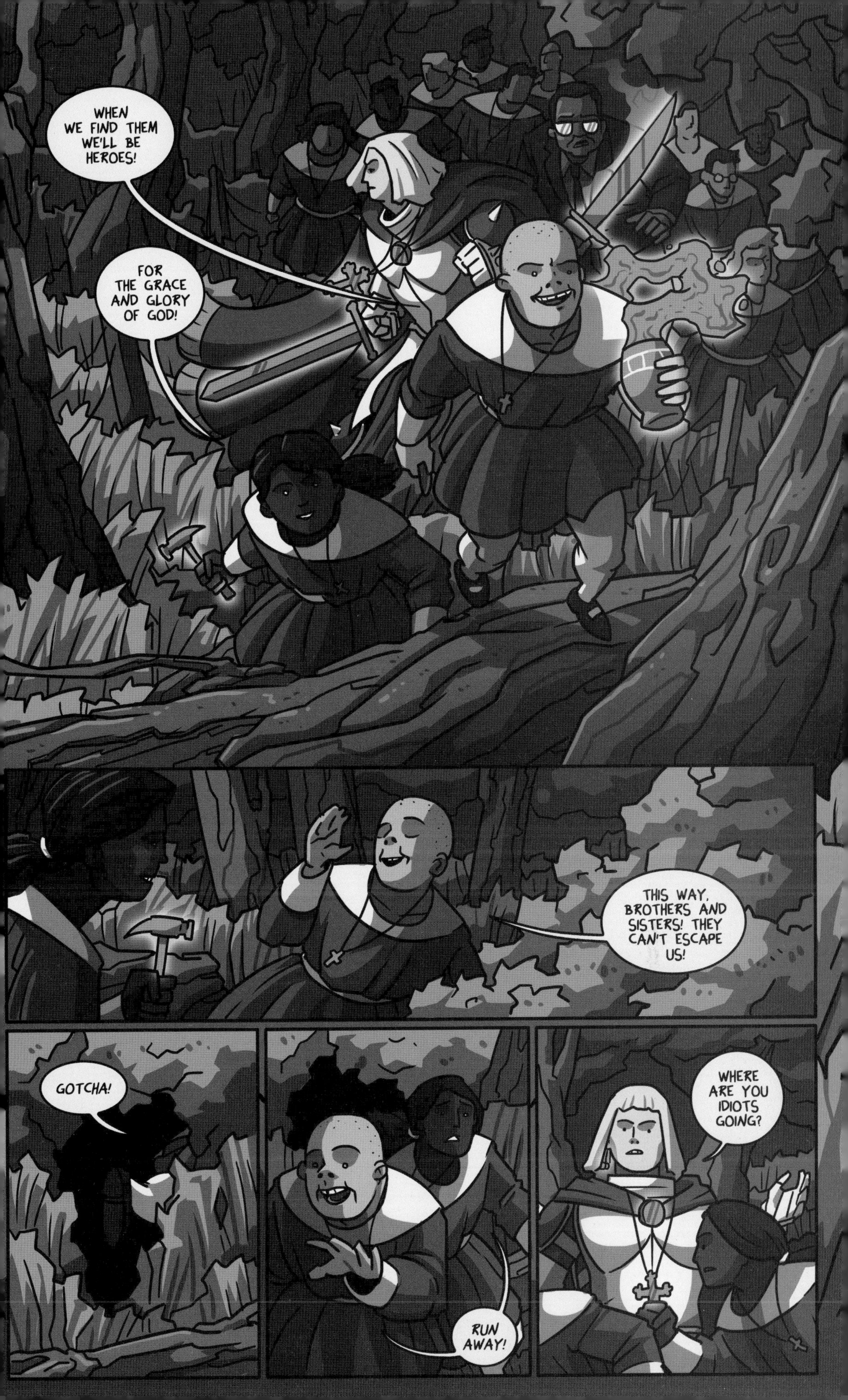
WHEN WE FIND THEM WE'LL BE HEROES!
FOR THE GRACE AND GLORY OF GOD!
THIS WAY, BROTHERS AND SISTERS! THEY CAN'T ESCAPE US!
GOTCHA!
RUN AWAY!
WHERE ARE YOU IDIOTS GOING?

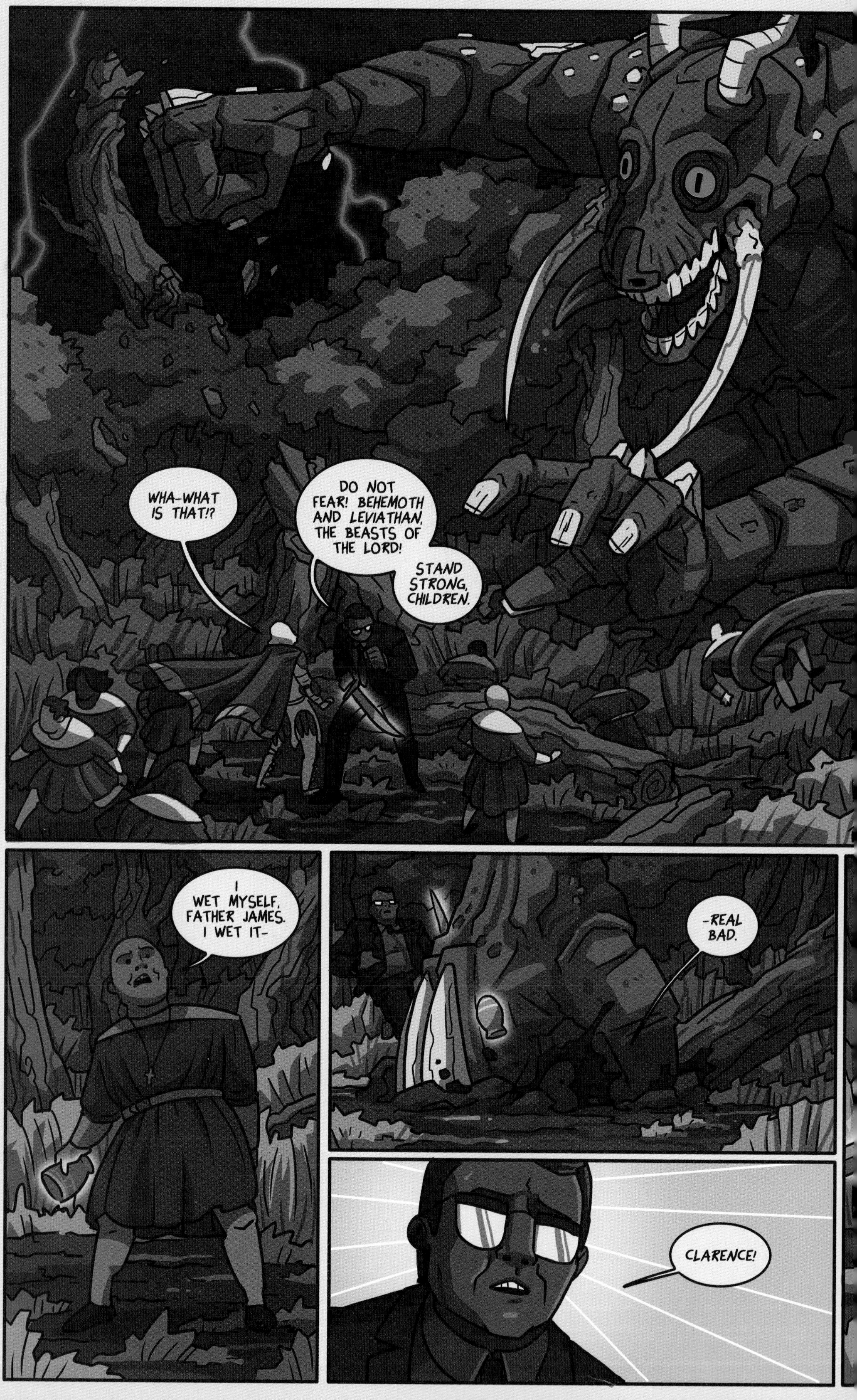
WHA-WHAT IS THAT!?
DO NOT FEAR! BEHEMOTH AND LEVIATHAN, THE BEASTS OF THE LORD!
STAND STRONG, CHILDREN.
I WET MYSELF, FATHER JAMES. I WET IT-
-REAL BAD.
CLARENCE!

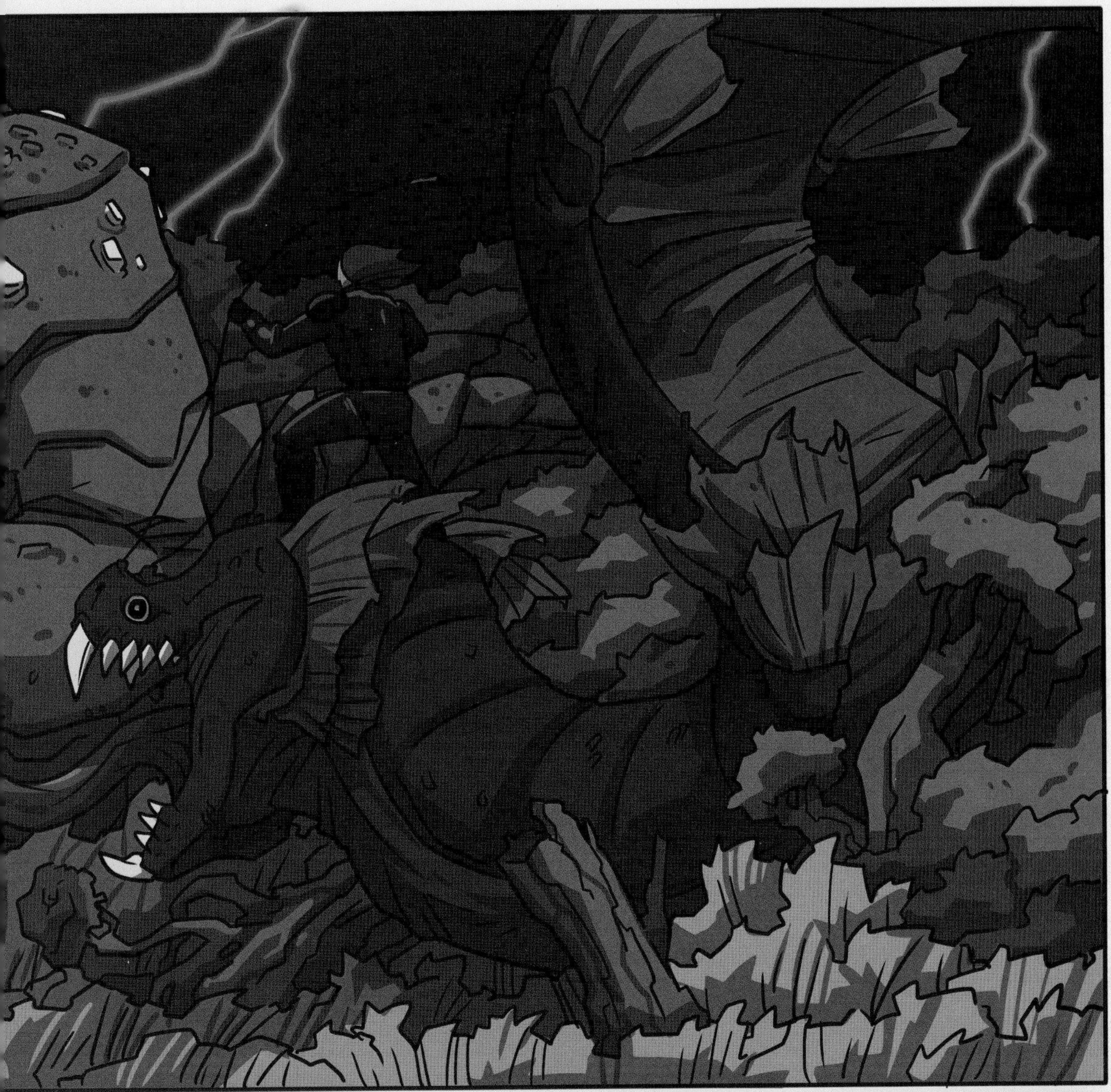

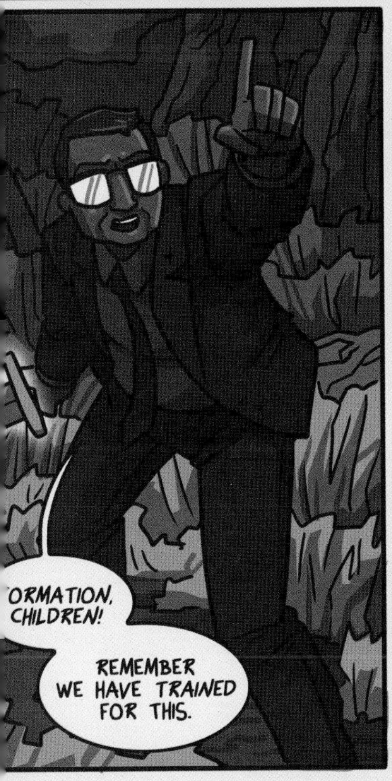
ORMATION, CHILDREN!
REMEMBER WE HAVE TRAINED FOR THIS.

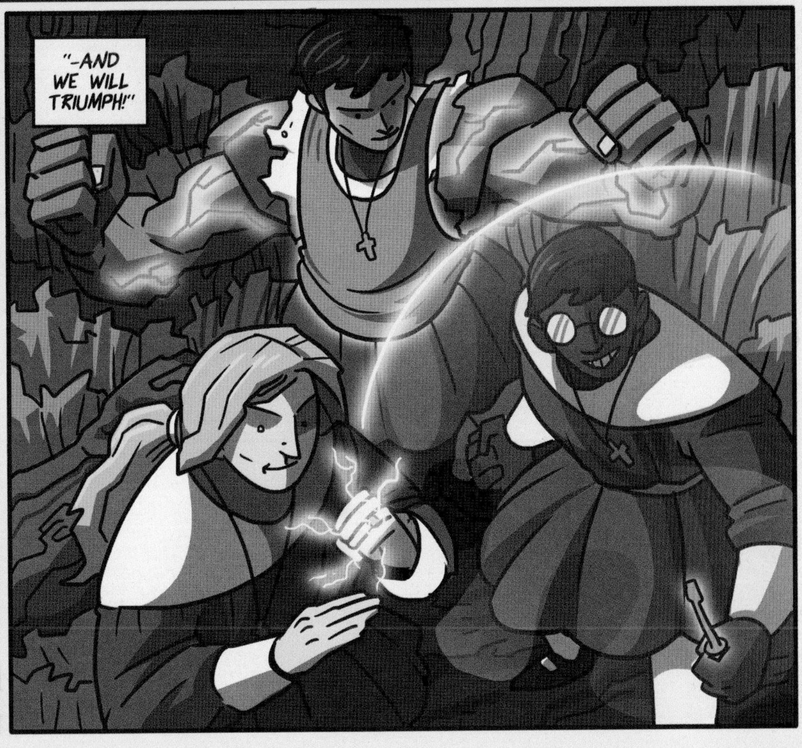
"-AND WE WILL TRIUMPH!"

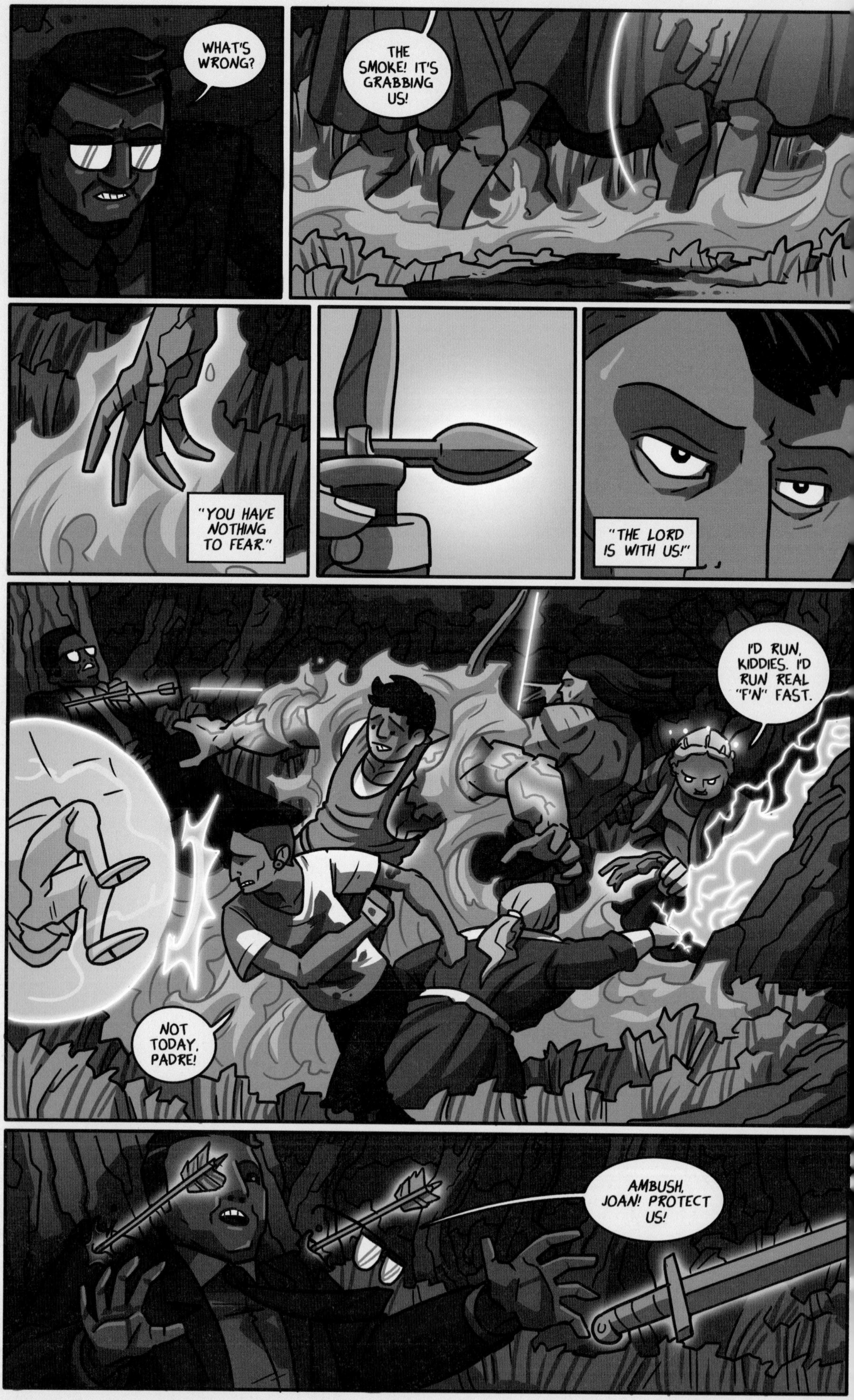
WHAT'S WRONG?
THE SMOKE! IT'S GRABBING US!
"YOU HAVE NOTHING TO FEAR."
"THE LORD IS WITH US!"
I'D RUN, KIDDIES. I'D RUN REAL "F'N" FAST.
NOT TODAY, PADRE!
AMBUSH, JOAN! PROTECT US!

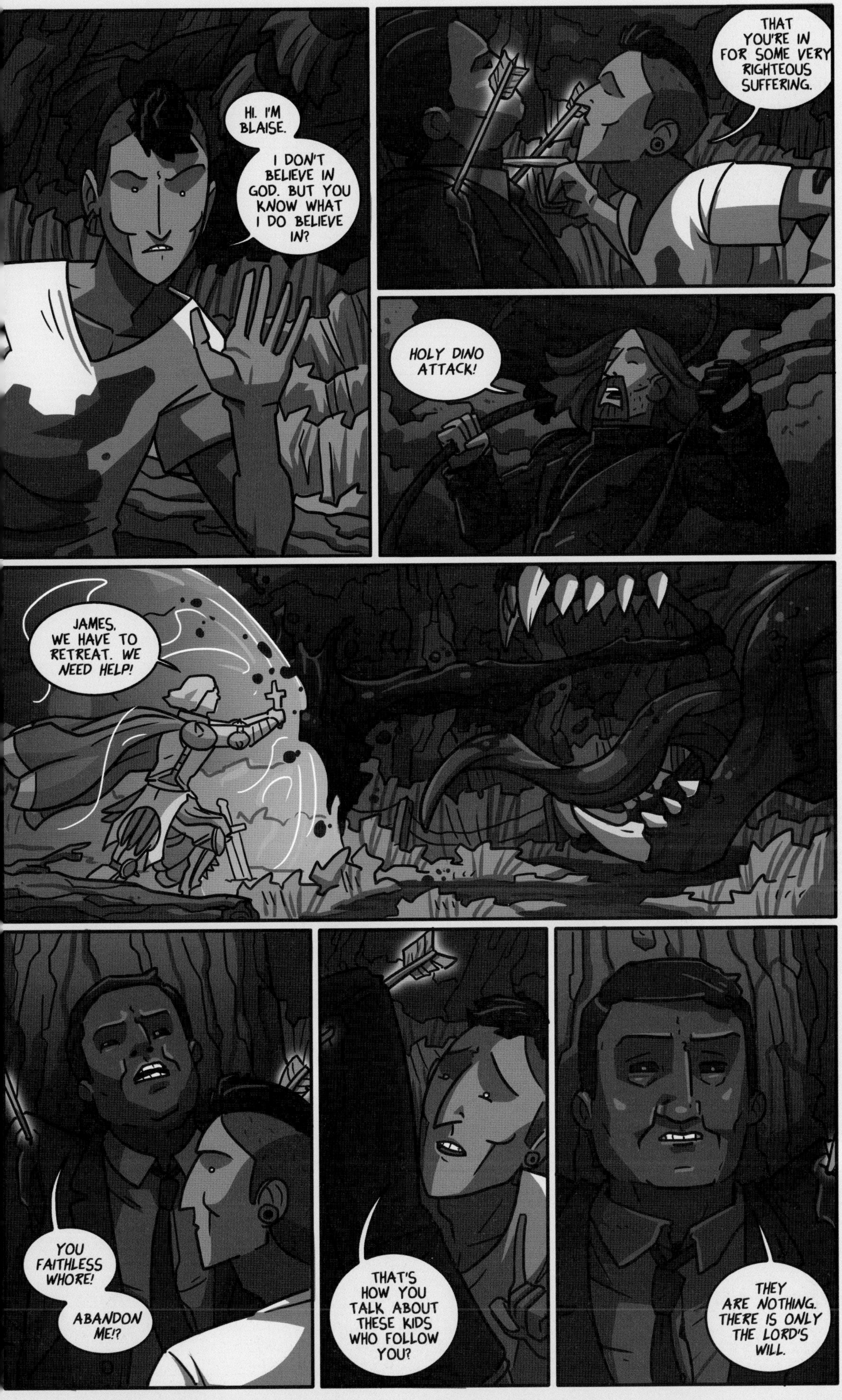
HI. I'M BLAISE.
I DON'T BELIEVE IN GOD. BUT YOU KNOW WHAT I DO BELIEVE IN?
THAT YOU'RE IN FOR SOME VERY RIGHTEOUS SUFFERING.
HOLY DINO ATTACK!
JAMES, WE HAVE TO RETREAT. WE NEED HELP!
YOU FAITHLESS WHORE!
ABANDON ME!?
THAT'S HOW YOU TALK ABOUT THESE KIDS WHO FOLLOW YOU?
THEY ARE NOTHING. THERE IS ONLY THE LORD'S WILL.

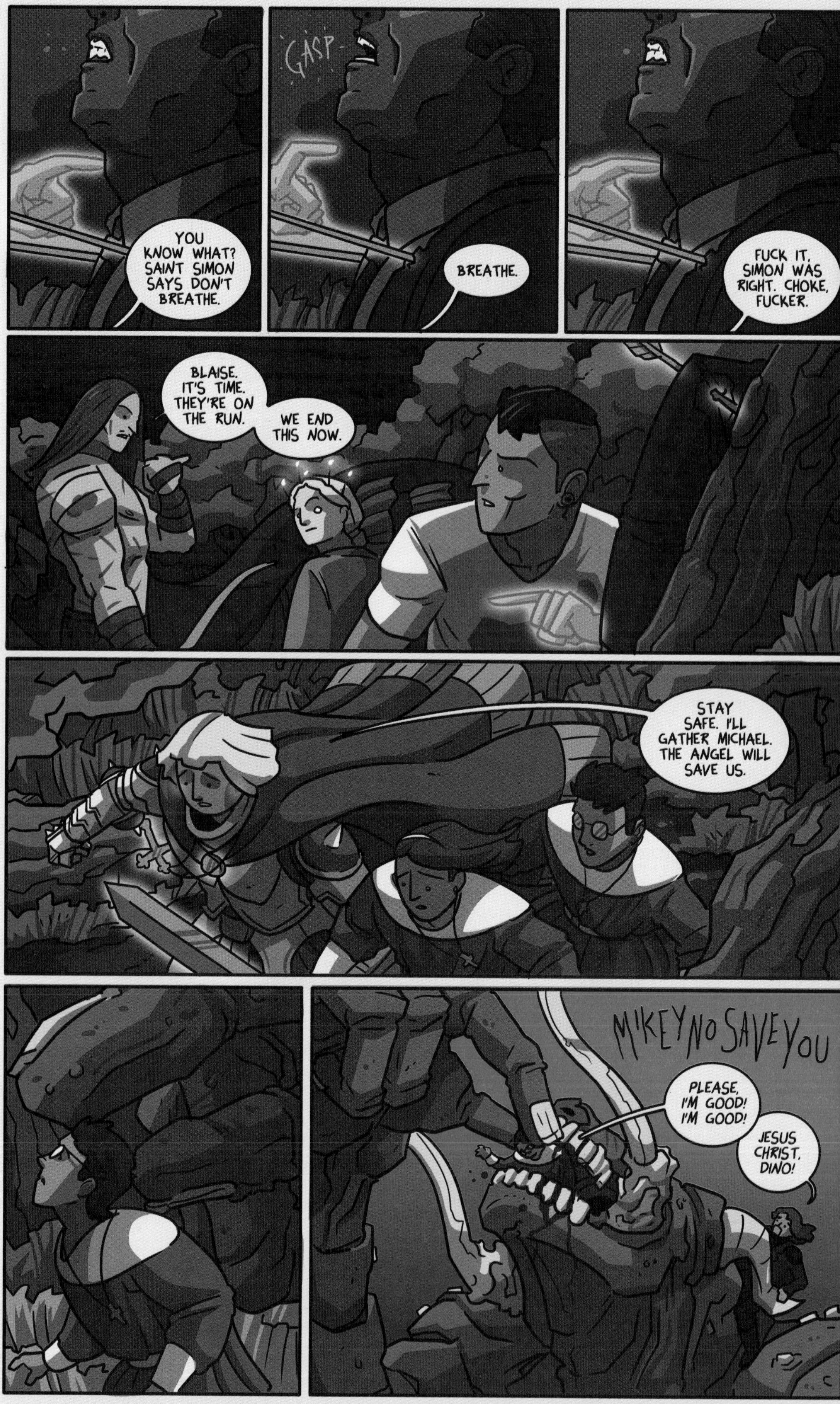
YOU KNOW WHAT? SAINT SIMON SAYS DON'T BREATHE.
GASP
BREATHE.
FUCK IT. SIMON WAS RIGHT. CHOKE, FUCKER.
BLAISE. IT'S TIME. THEY'RE ON THE RUN.
WE END THIS NOW.
STAY SAFE. I'LL GATHER MICHAEL. THE ANGEL WILL SAVE US.
MIKEY NO SAVE YOU
PLEASE, I'M GOOD! I'M GOOD!
JESUS CHRIST, DINO!

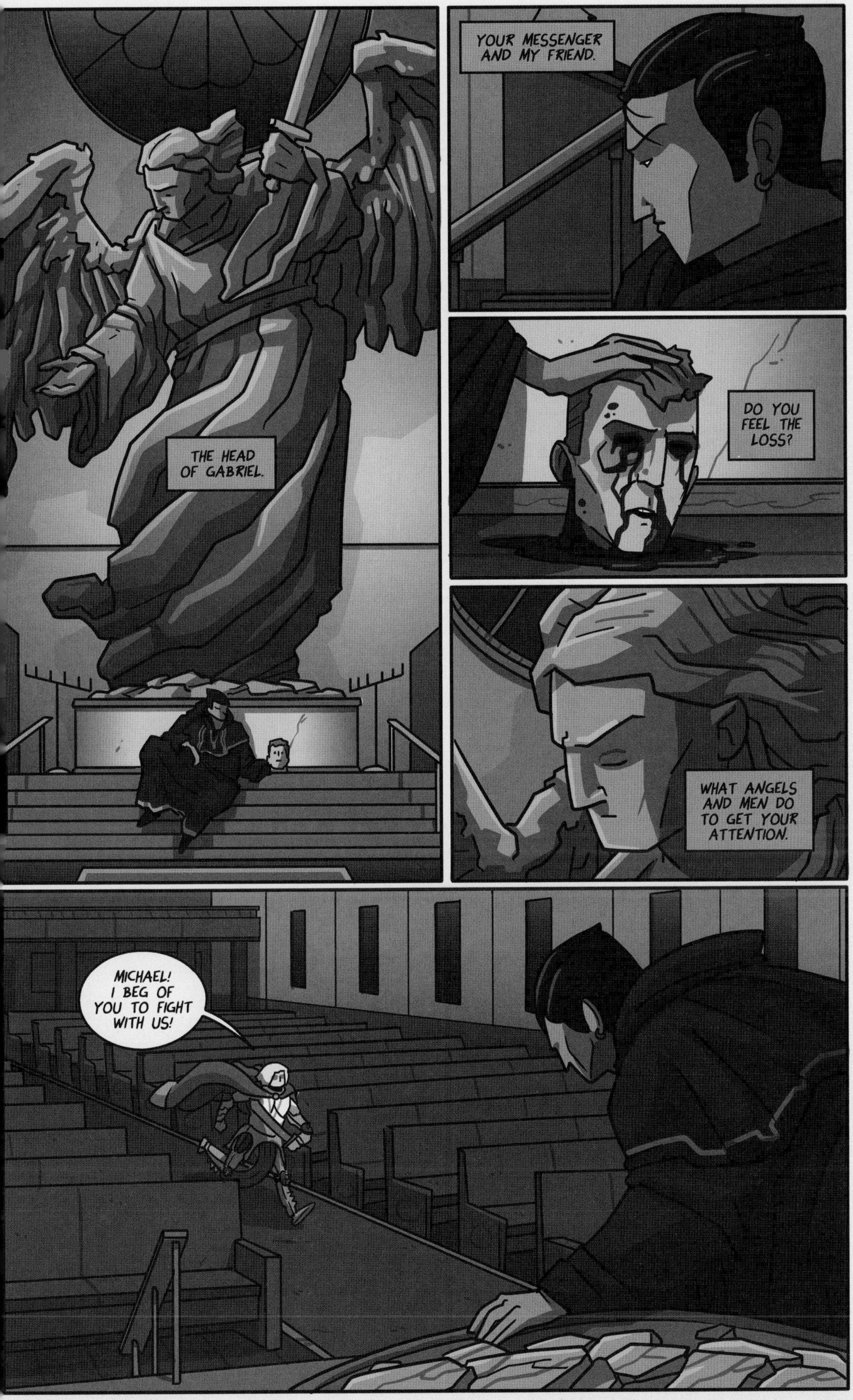
THE HEAD OF GABRIEL.
YOUR MESSENGER AND MY FRIEND.
DO YOU FEEL THE LOSS?
WHAT ANGELS AND MEN DO TO GET YOUR ATTENTION.
MICHAEL! I BEG OF YOU TO FIGHT WITH US!

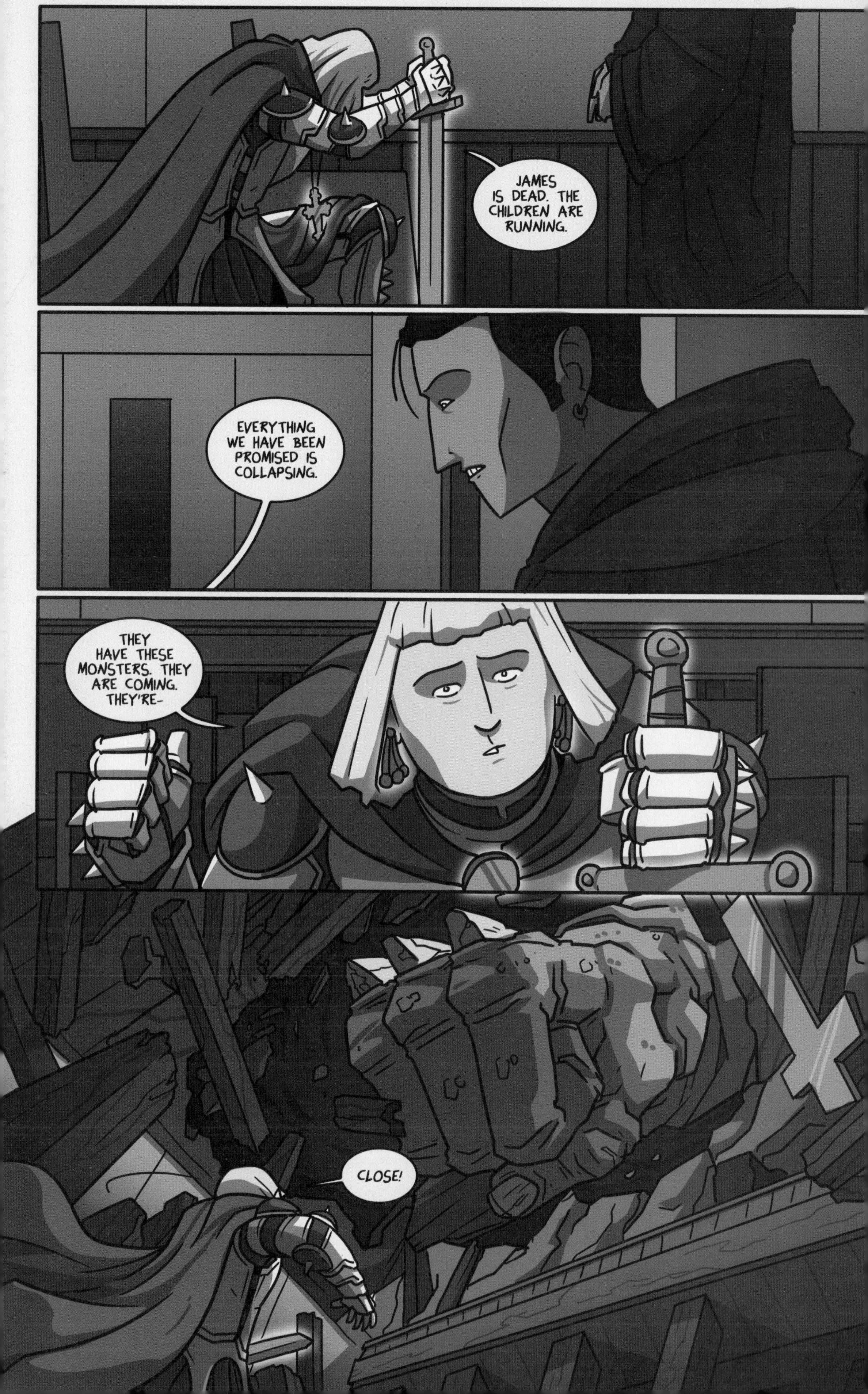
JAMES IS DEAD. THE CHILDREN ARE RUNNING.
EVERYTHING WE HAVE BEEN PROMISED IS COLLAPSING.
THEY HAVE THESE MONSTERS. THEY ARE COMING. THEY'RE-
CLOSE!

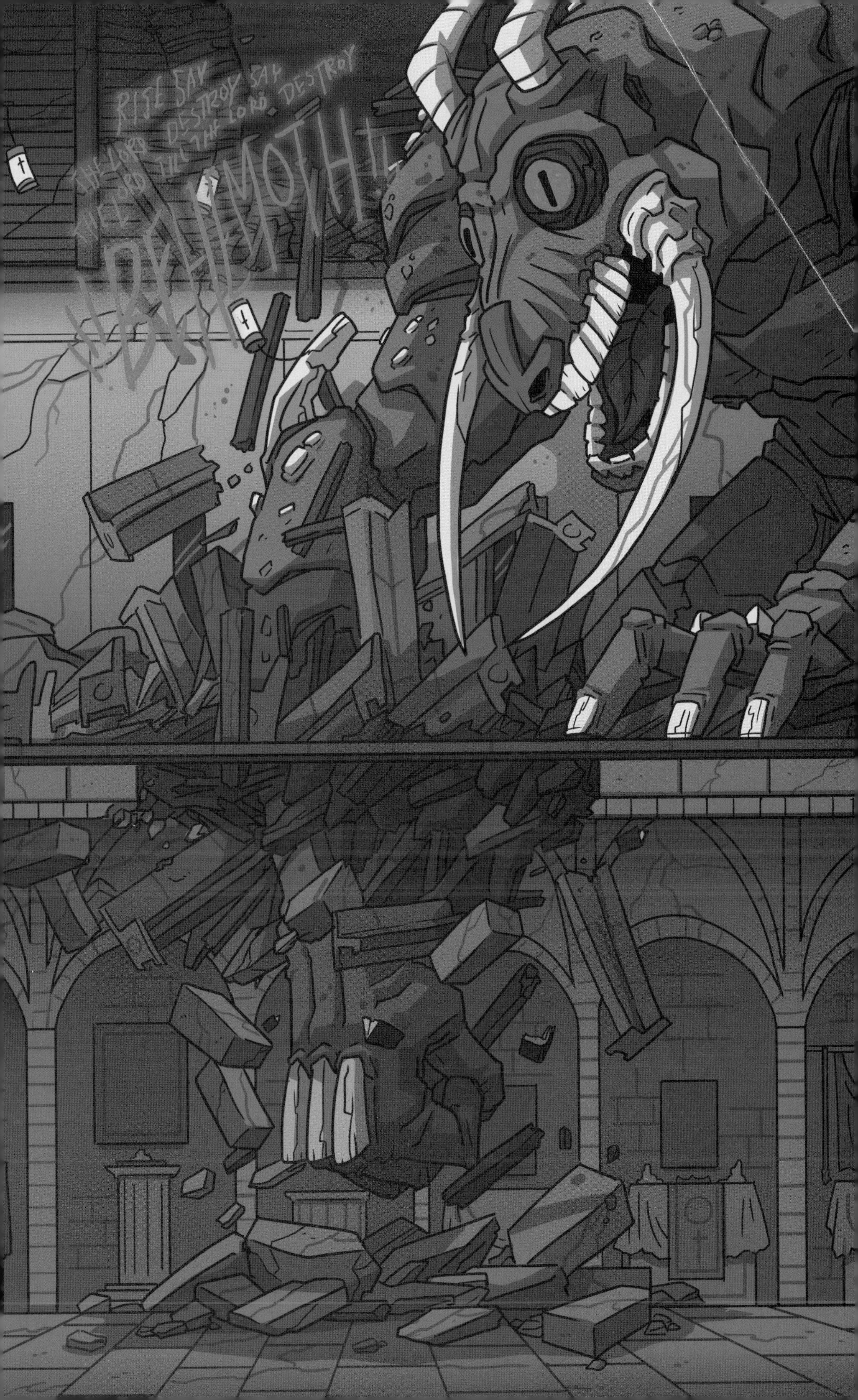
RISE SAY
THE LORD DESTROY SAY
THE LORD TILL THE LORD. DESTROY
BEHEMOTH!!

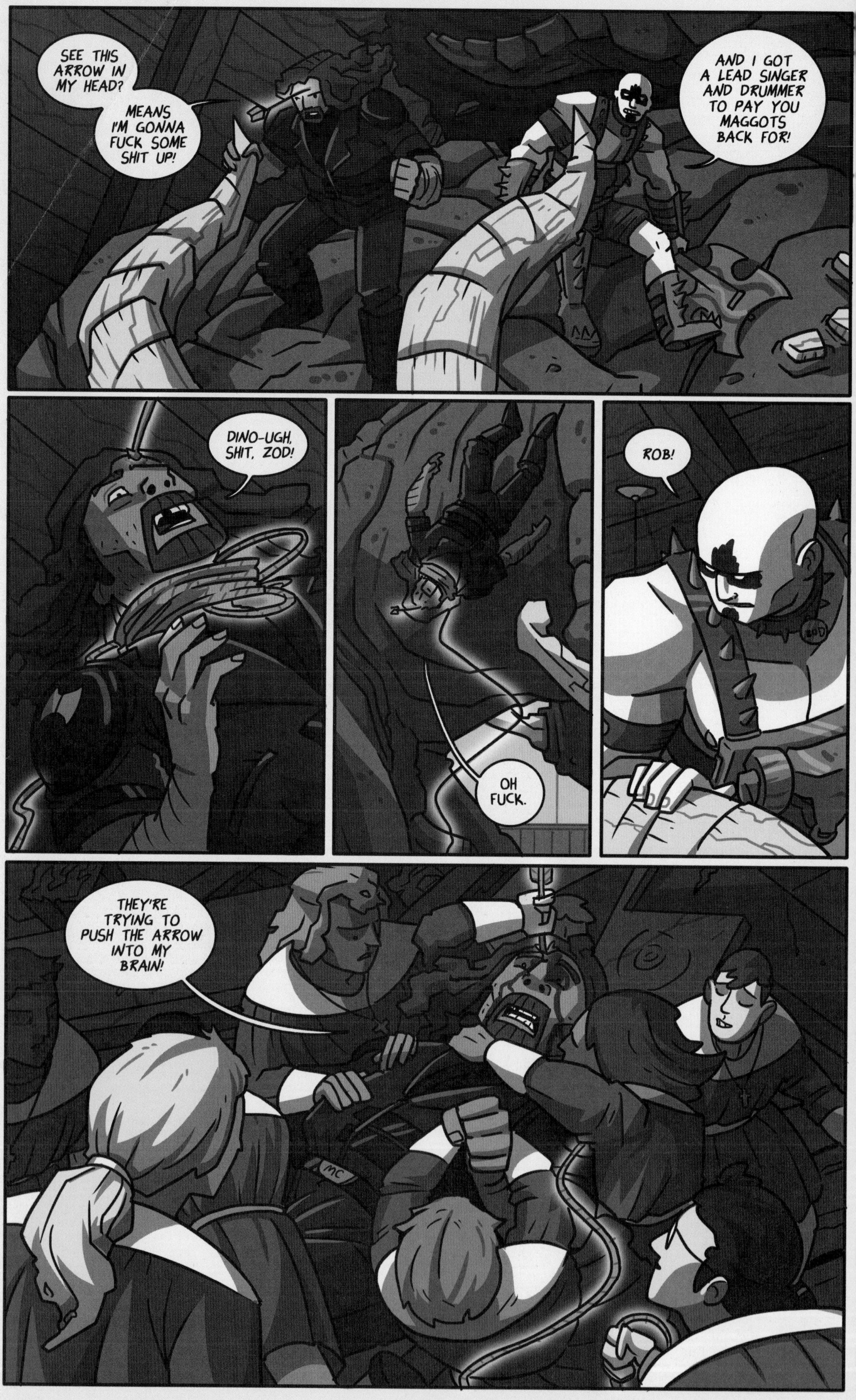
SEE THIS ARROW IN MY HEAD?
MEANS I'M GONNA FUCK SOME SHIT UP!
AND I GOT A LEAD SINGER AND DRUMMER TO PAY YOU MAGGOTS BACK FOR!
DINO-UGH, SHIT, ZOD!
OH FUCK.
ROB!
THEY'RE TRYING TO PUSH THE ARROW INTO MY BRAIN!

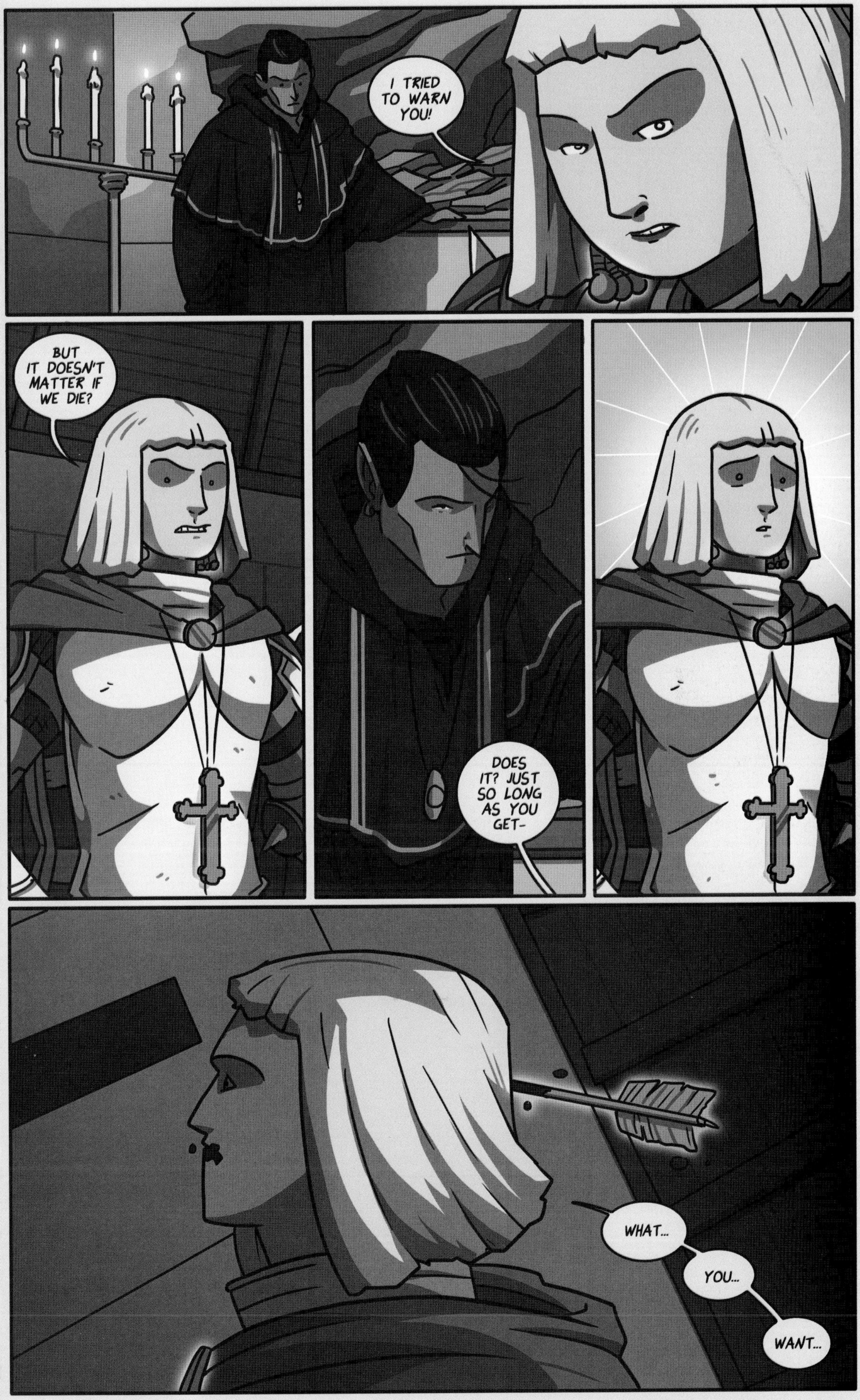
I TRIED TO WARN YOU!
BUT IT DOESN'T MATTER IF WE DIE?
DOES IT? JUST SO LONG AS YOU GET-
WHAT...
YOU...
WANT...

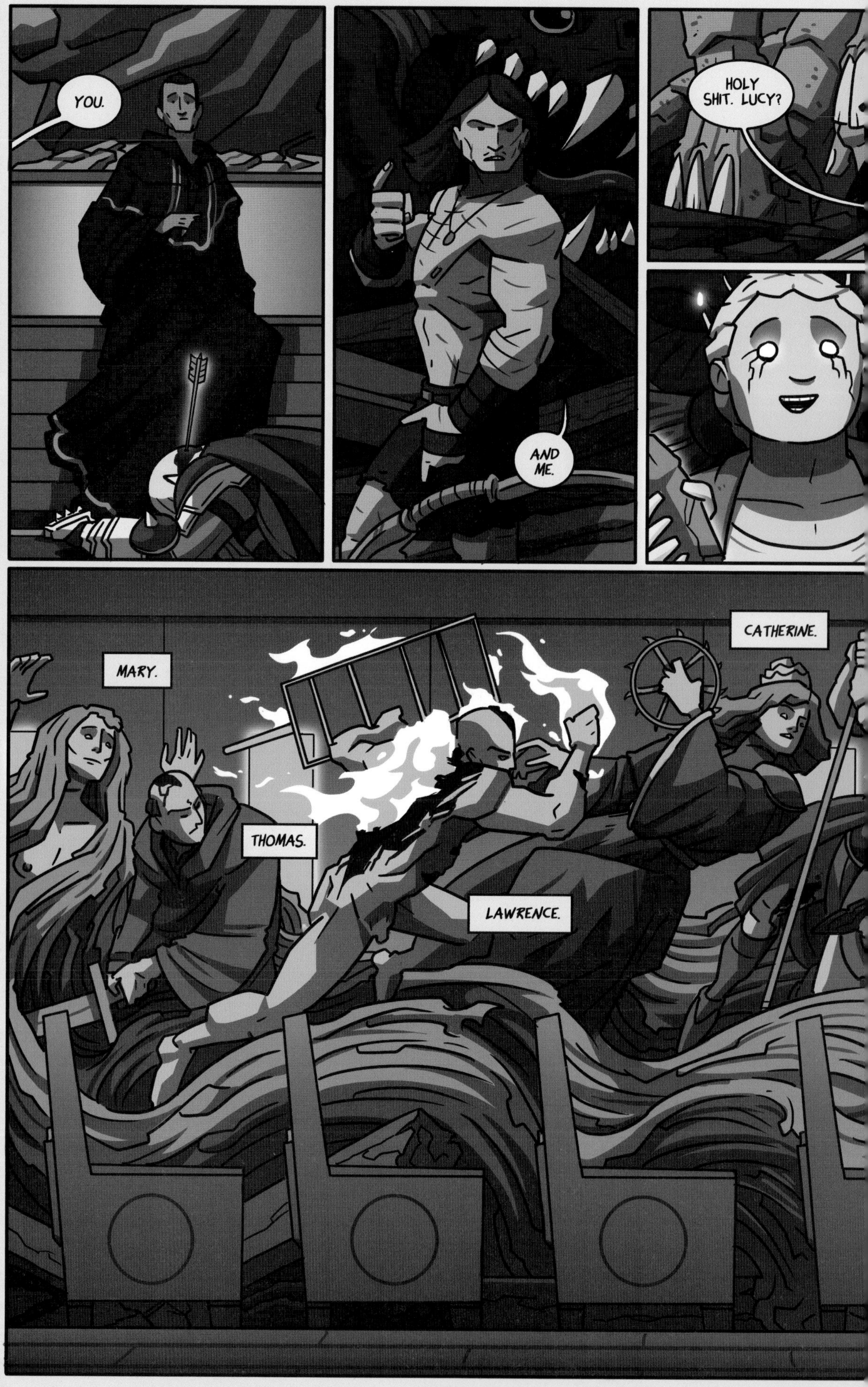
YOU.
AND ME.
HOLY SHIT. LUCY?
MARY.
THOMAS.
LAWRENCE.
CATHERINE.

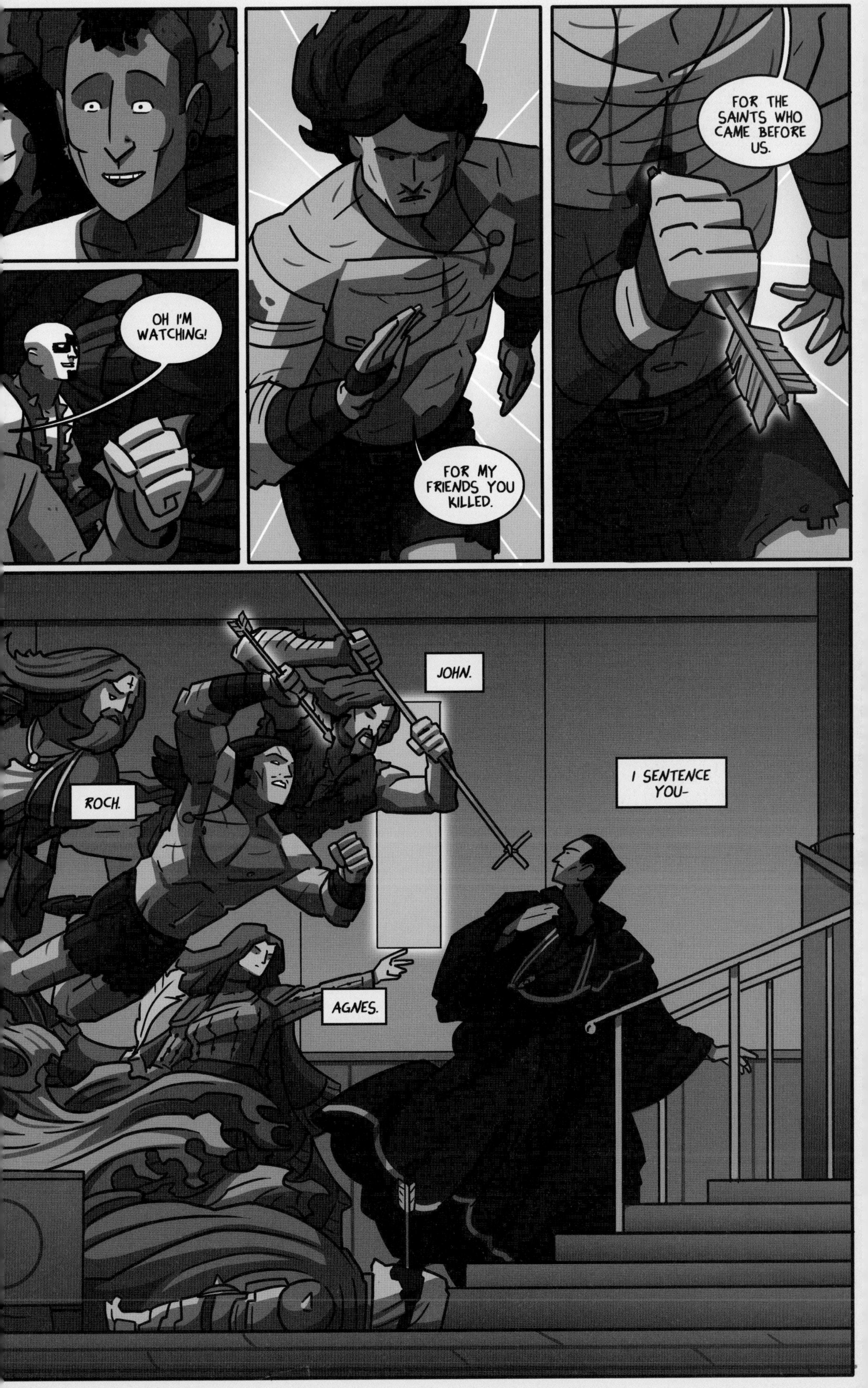

OH I'M WATCHING!
FOR MY FRIENDS YOU KILLED.
FOR THE SAINTS WHO CAME BEFORE US.
JOHN.
ROCH.
AGNES.
I SENTENCE YOU-

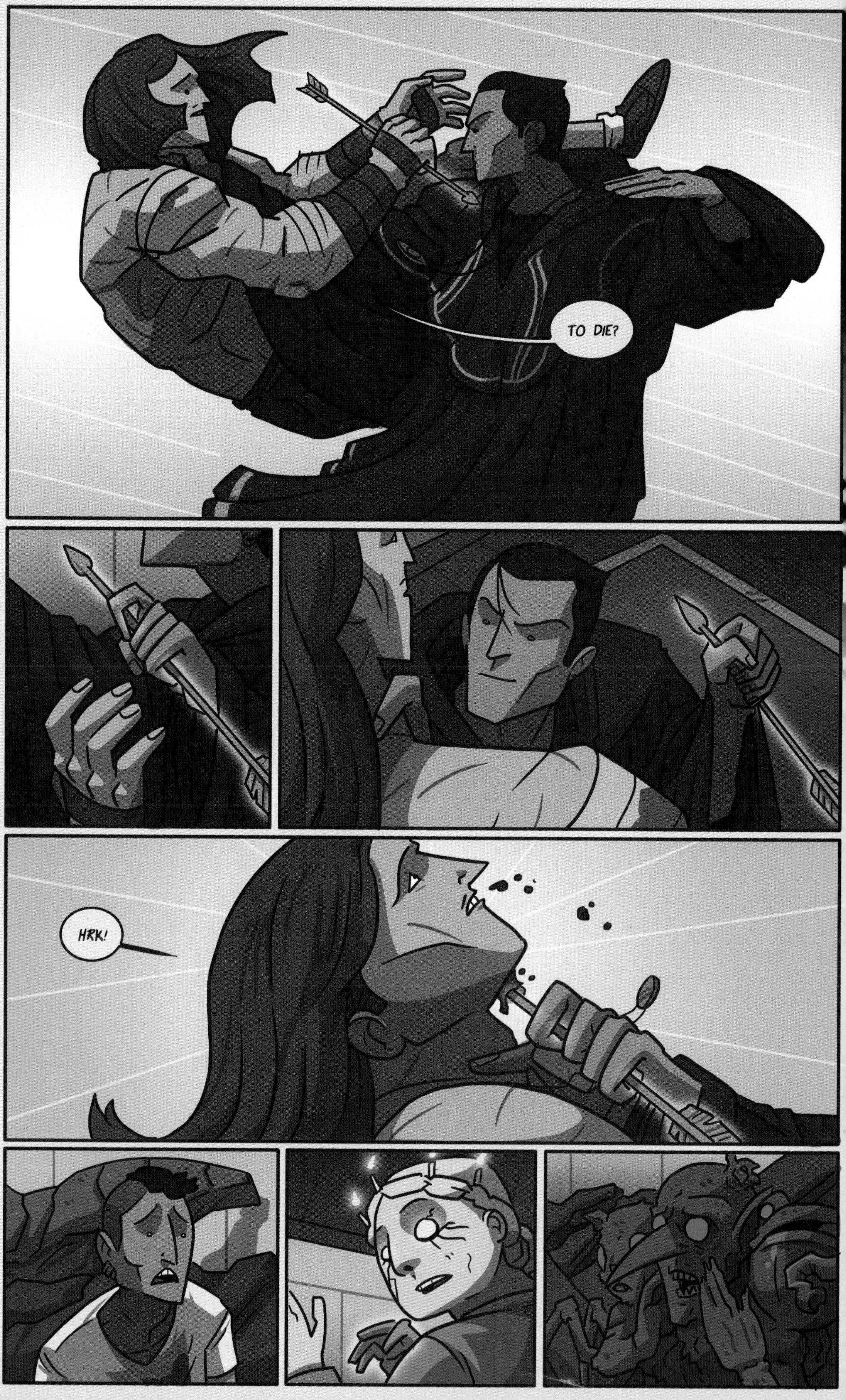
TO DIE?
HRK!

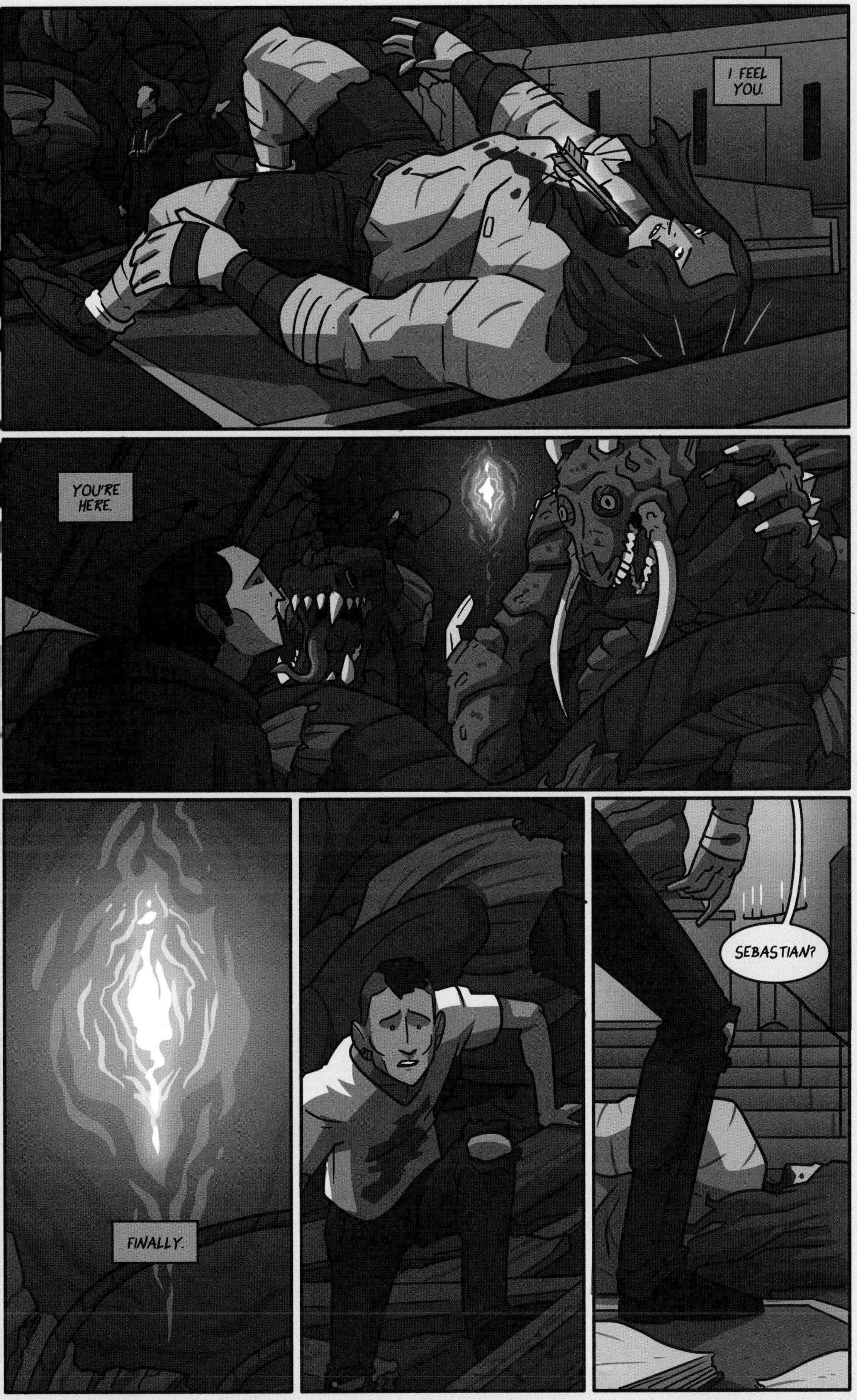
I FEEL YOU.
YOU'RE HERE.
FINALLY.
SEBASTIAN?

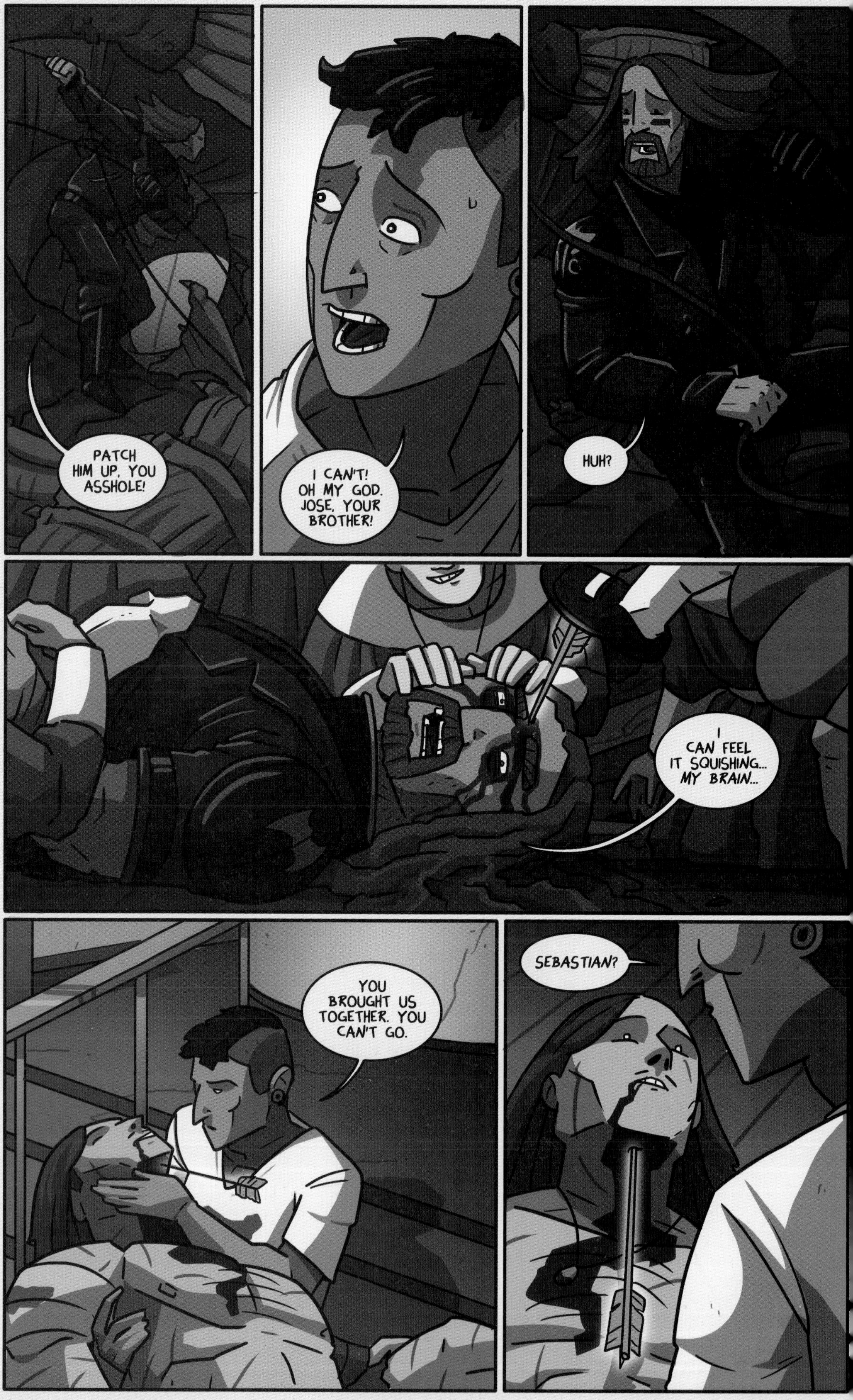
PATCH HIM UP, YOU ASSHOLE!
I CAN'T! OH MY GOD. JOSE, YOUR BROTHER!
HUH?
I CAN FEEL IT SQUISHING... MY BRAIN...
YOU BROUGHT US TOGETHER. YOU CAN'T GO.
SEBASTIAN?

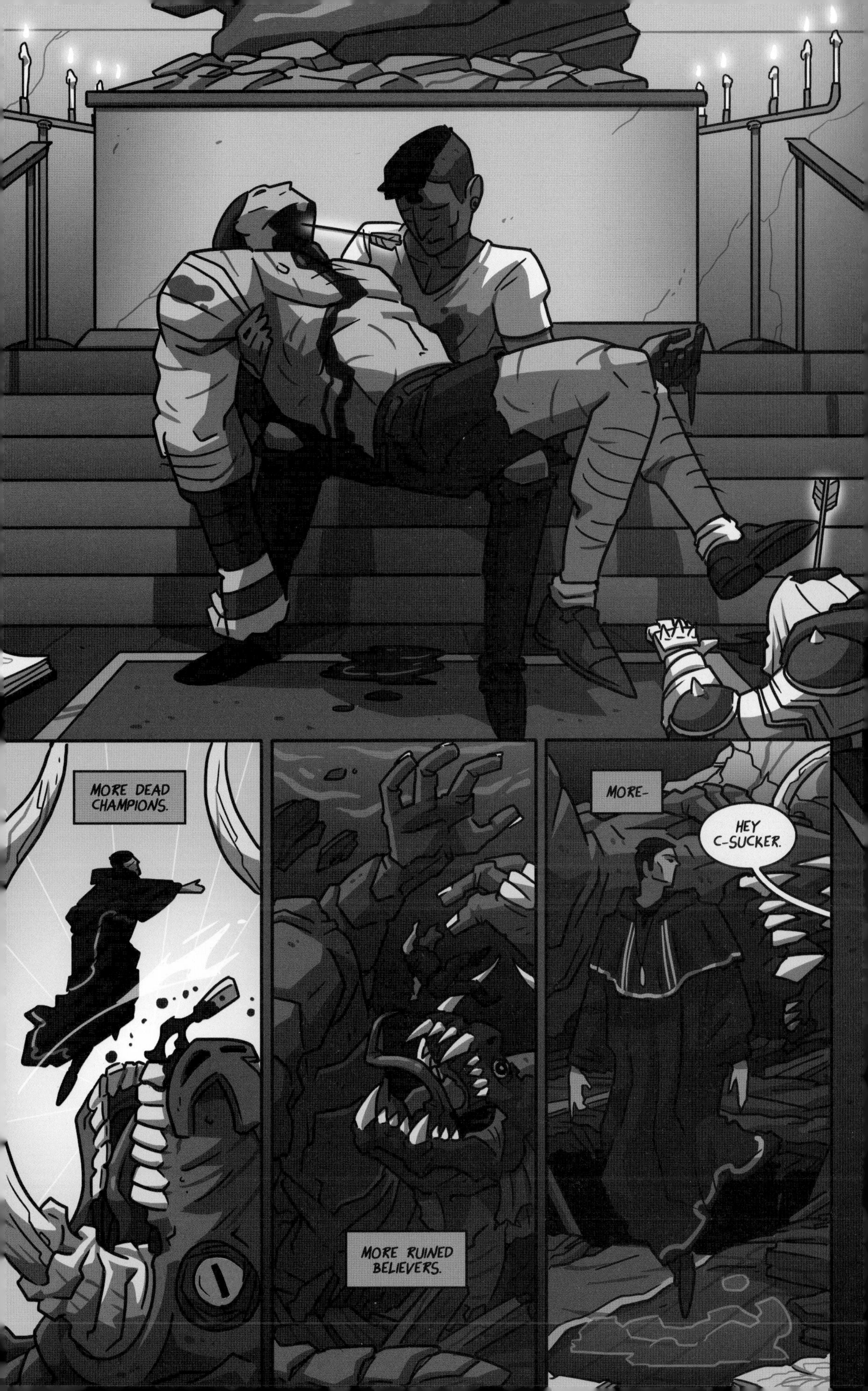
MORE DEAD CHAMPIONS.
MORE RUINED BELIEVERS.
MORE-
HEY C-SUCKER.

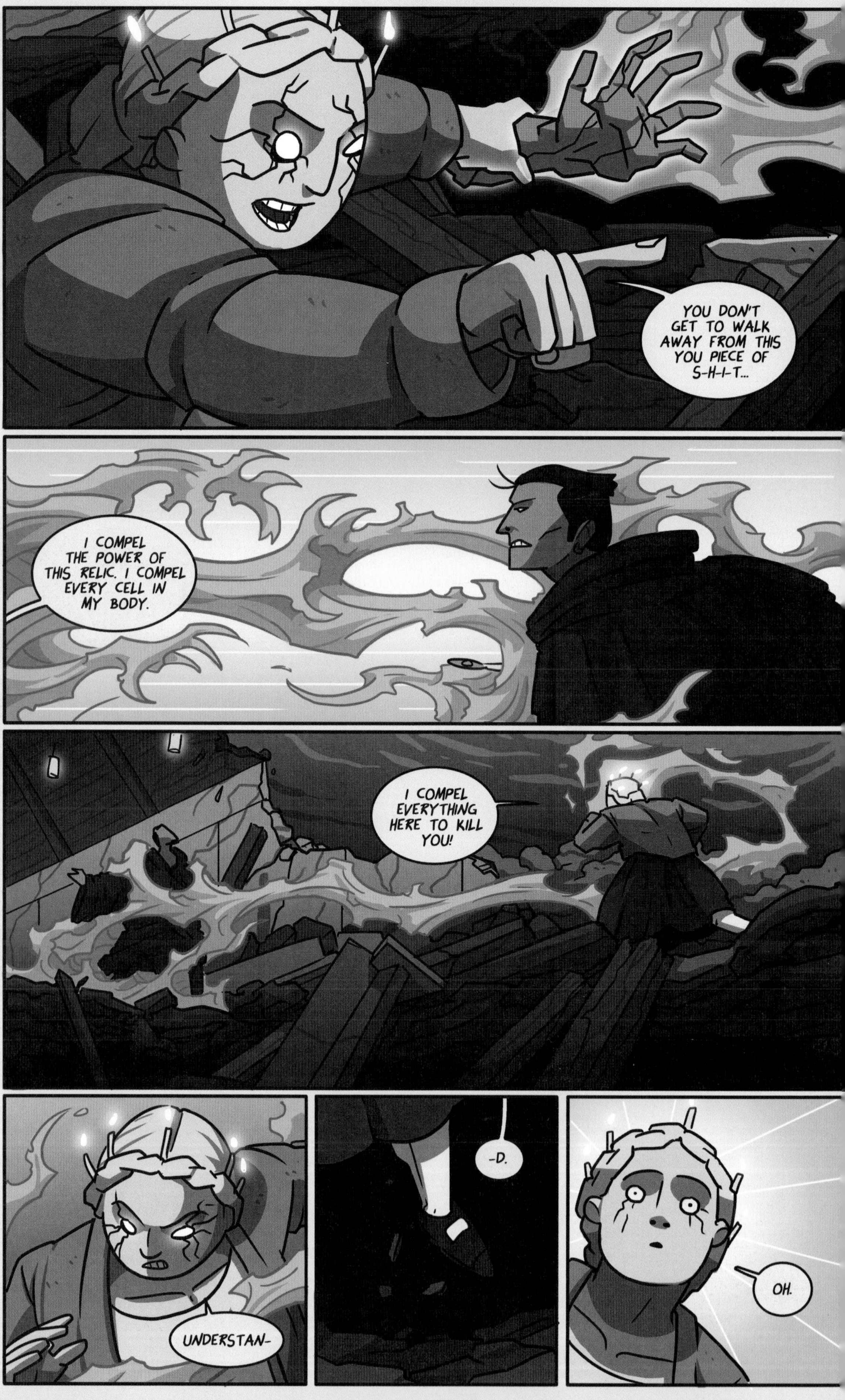
YOU DON'T GET TO WALK AWAY FROM THIS YOU PIECE OF S-H-I-T...
I COMPEL THE POWER OF THIS RELIC. I COMPEL EVERY CELL IN MY BODY.
I COMPEL EVERYTHING HERE TO KILL YOU!
UNDERSTAN-
-D.
OH.

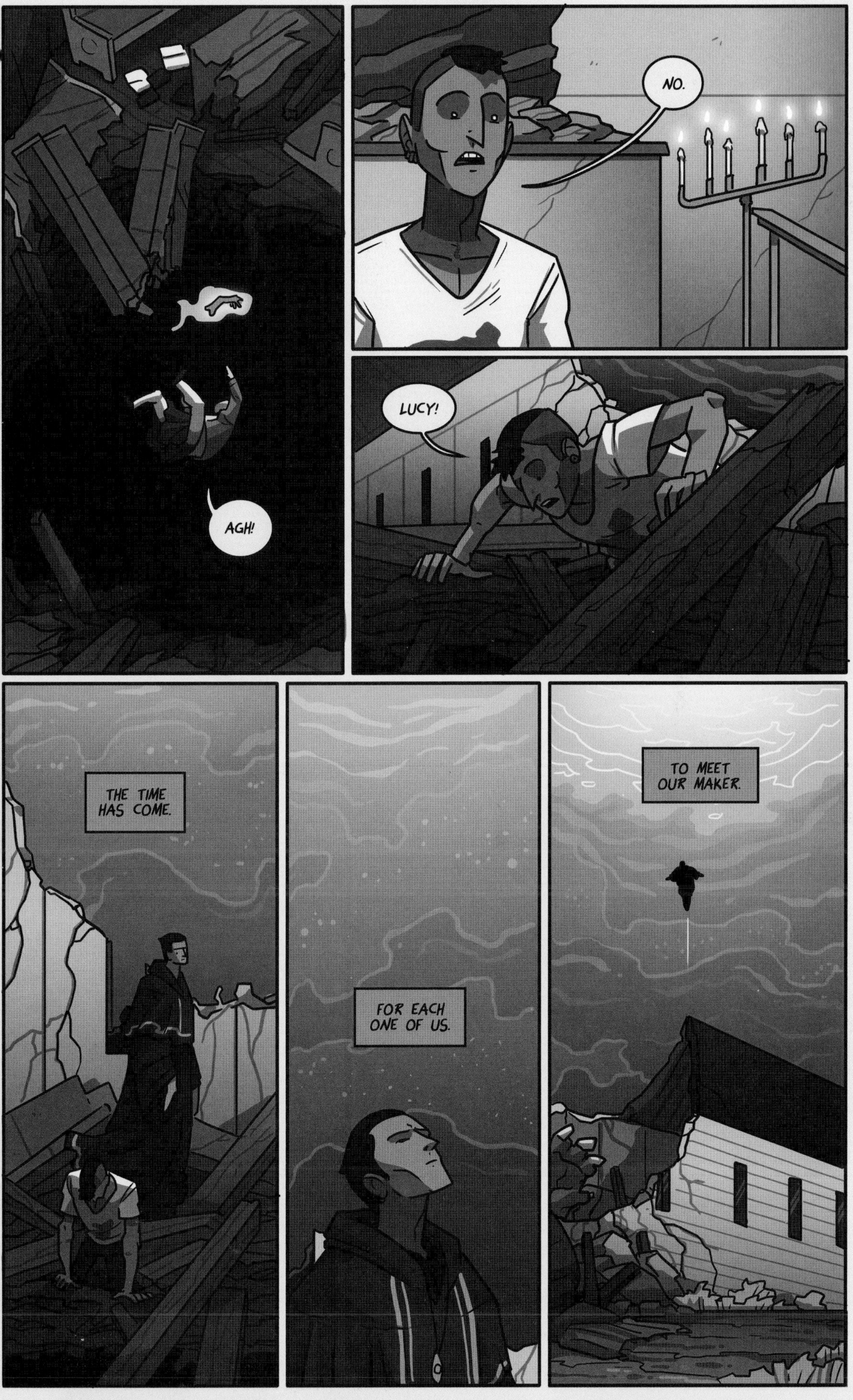
AGH!
NO.
LUCY!
THE TIME HAS COME.
FOR EACH ONE OF US.
TO MEET OUR MAKER.

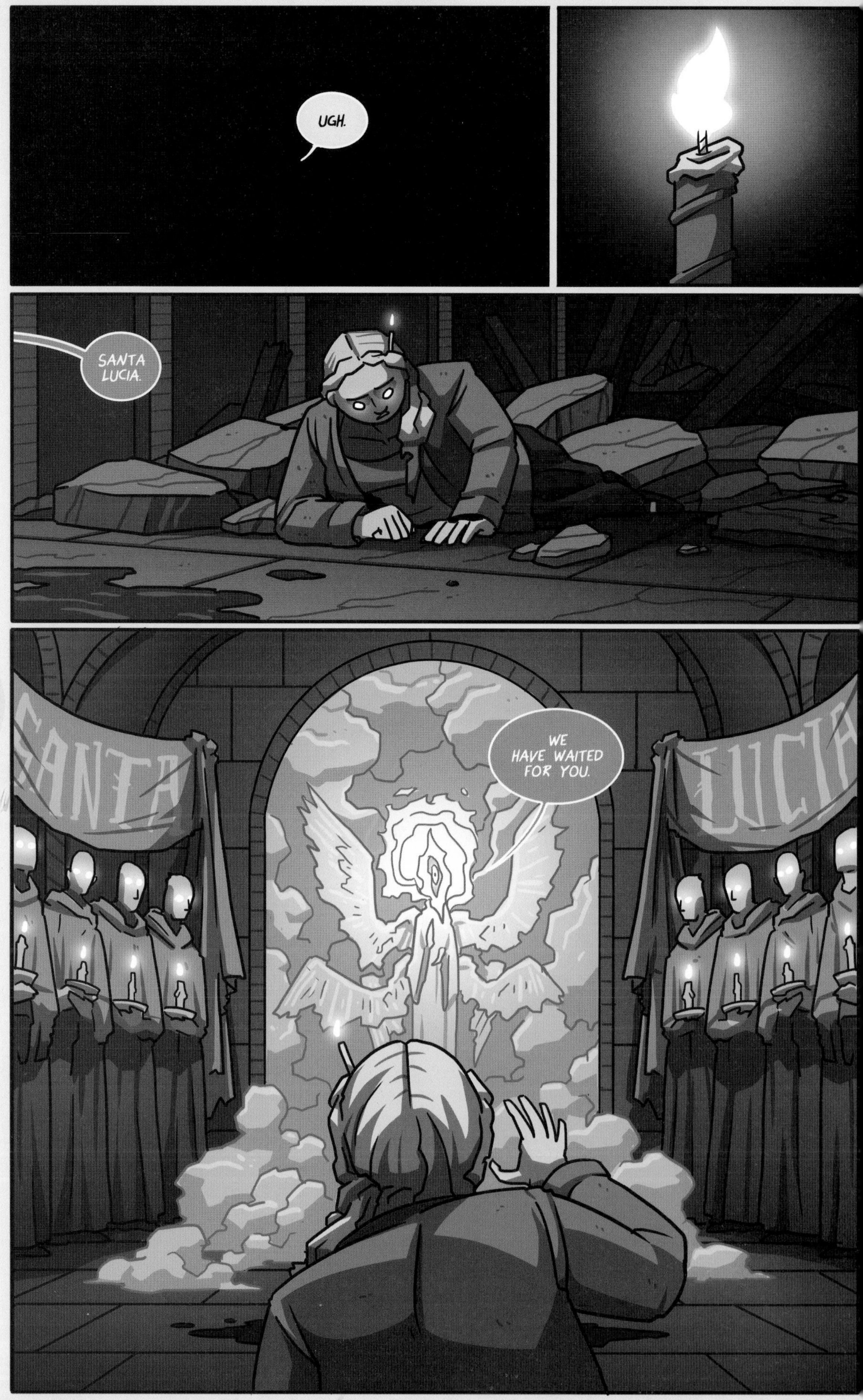
UGH.
SANTA LUCIA.
SANTA
LUCIA
WE HAVE WAITED FOR YOU.

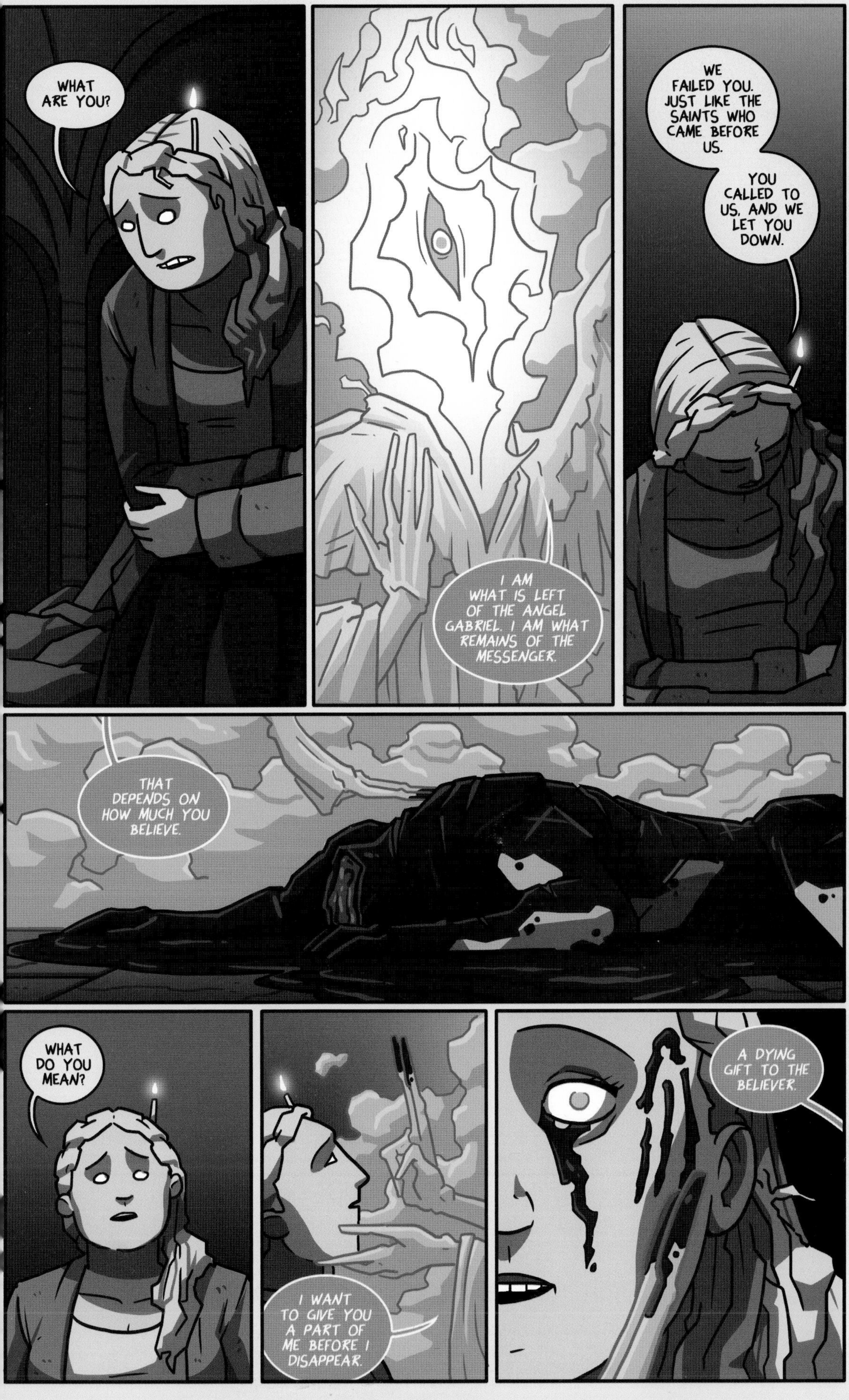
WHAT ARE YOU?
I AM WHAT IS LEFT OF THE ANGEL GABRIEL. I AM WHAT REMAINS OF THE MESSENGER.
WE FAILED YOU. JUST LIKE THE SAINTS WHO CAME BEFORE US.
YOU CALLED TO US, AND WE LET YOU DOWN.
THAT DEPENDS ON HOW MUCH YOU BELIEVE.
WHAT DO YOU MEAN?
I WANT TO GIVE YOU A PART OF ME BEFORE I DISAPPEAR.
A DYING GIFT TO THE BELIEVER.

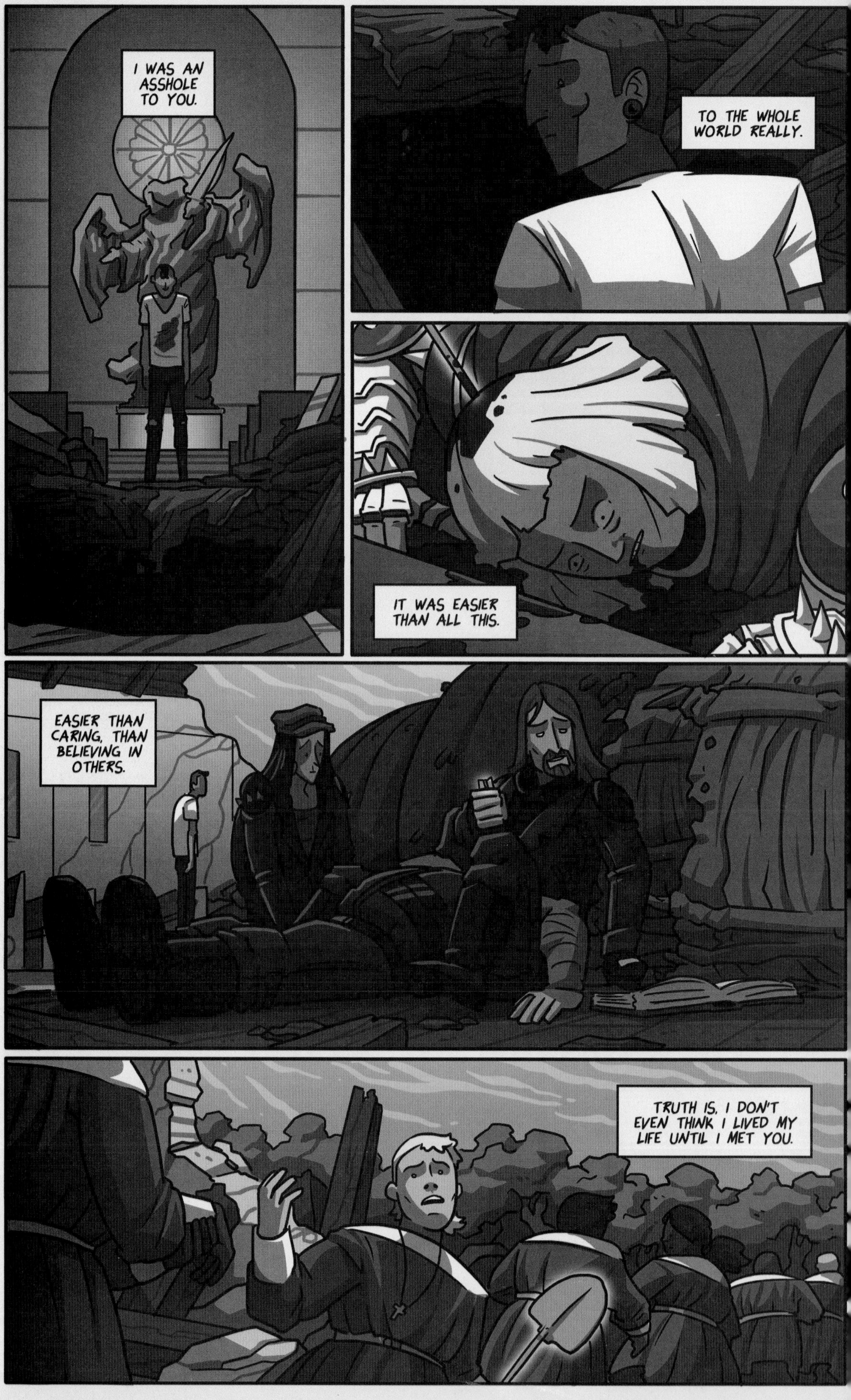
I WAS AN ASSHOLE TO YOU.
TO THE WHOLE WORLD REALLY.
IT WAS EASIER THAN ALL THIS.
EASIER THAN CARING, THAN BELIEVING IN OTHERS.
TRUTH IS, I DON'T EVEN THINK I LIVED MY LIFE UNTIL I MET YOU.

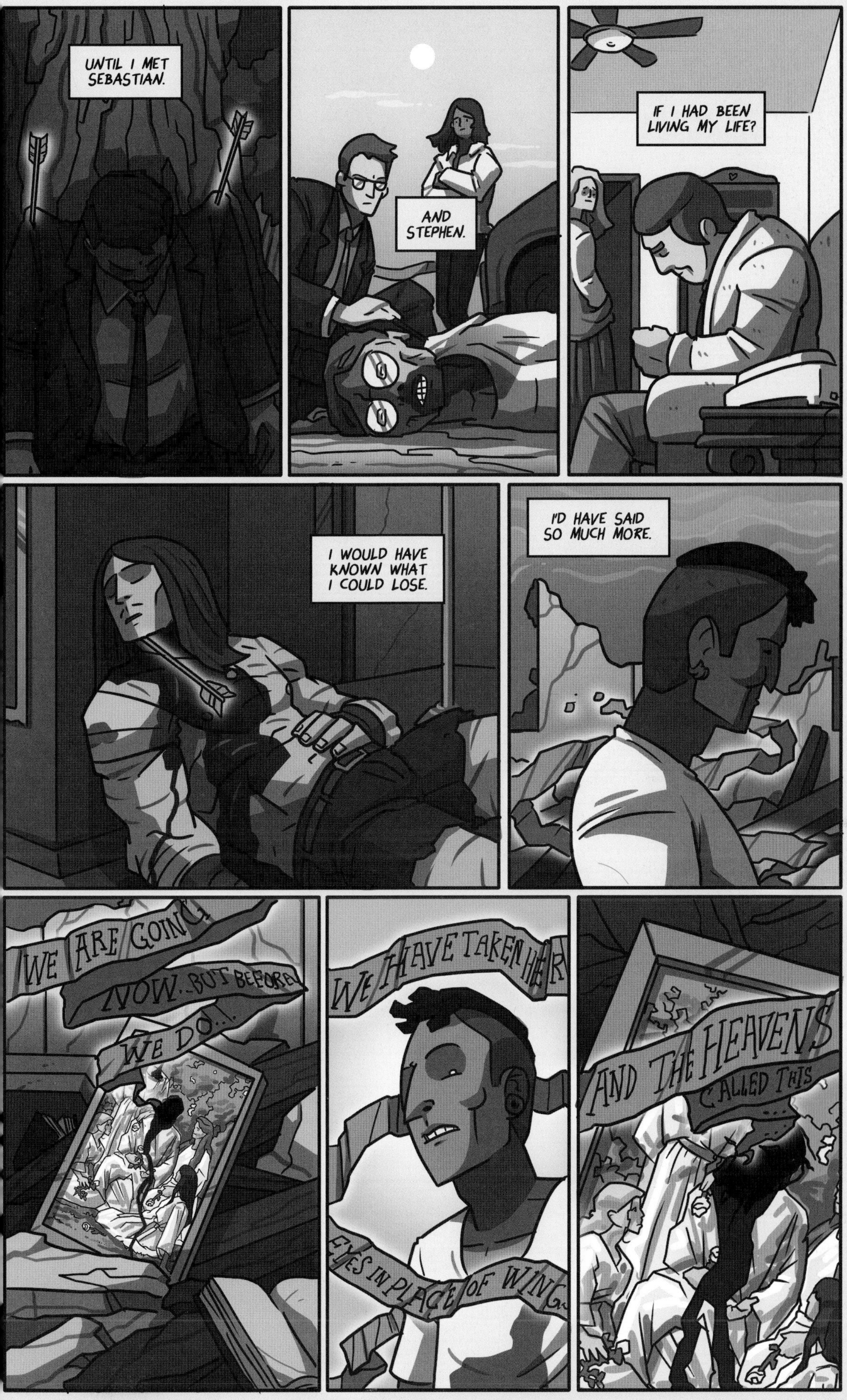
UNTIL I MET SEBASTIAN.
AND STEPHEN.
IF I HAD BEEN LIVING MY LIFE?
I WOULD HAVE KNOWN WHAT I COULD LOSE.
I'D HAVE SAID SO MUCH MORE.
WE ARE GOING NOW...BUT BEFORE WE DO...
WE HAVE TAKEN HER
EYES IN PLACE OF WING
AND THE HEAVENS CALLED THIS

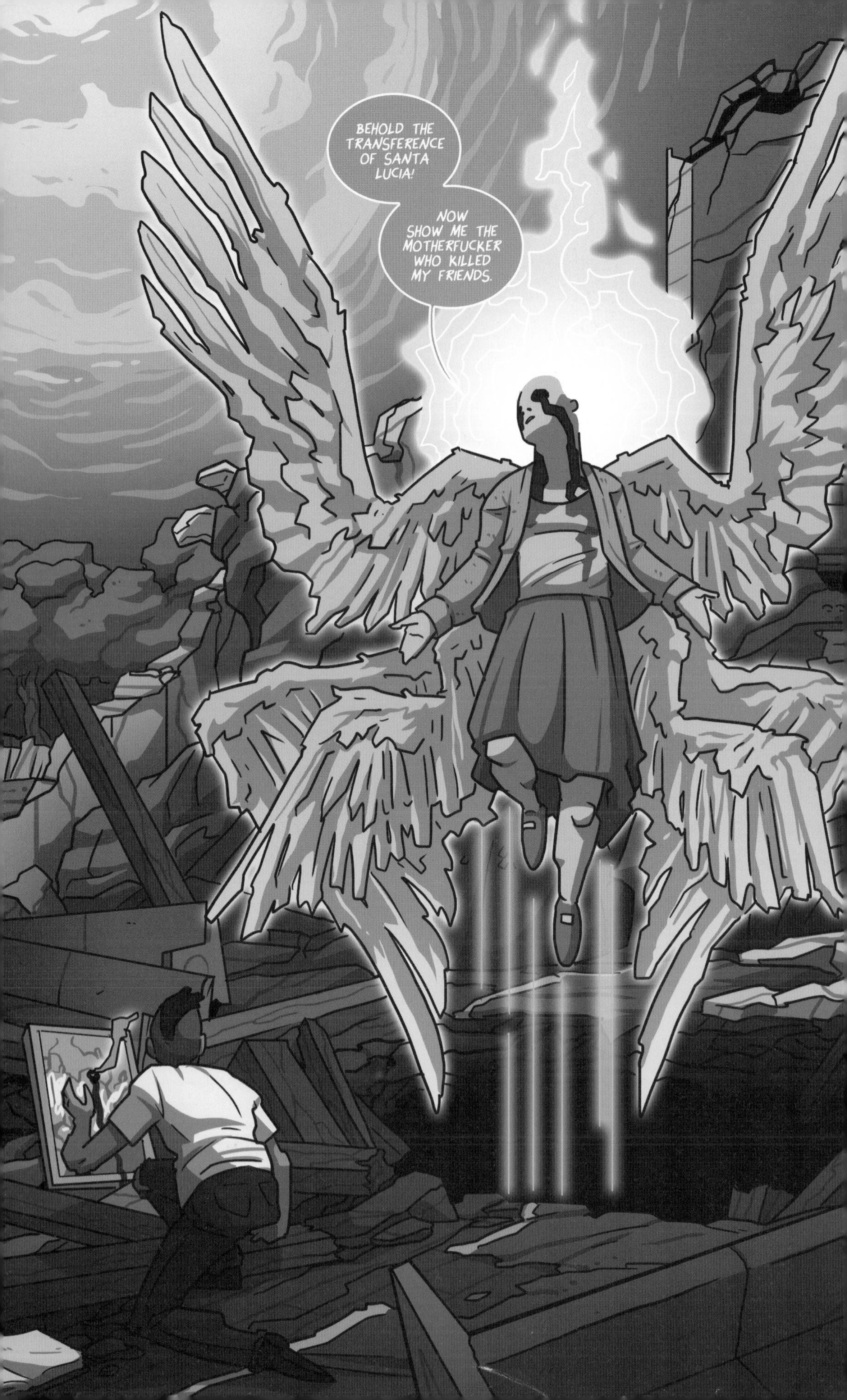
BEHOLD THE TRANSFERENCE OF SANTA LUCIA!
NOW SHOW ME THE MOTHERFUCKER WHO KILLED MY FRIENDS.

IX

ASCENSION

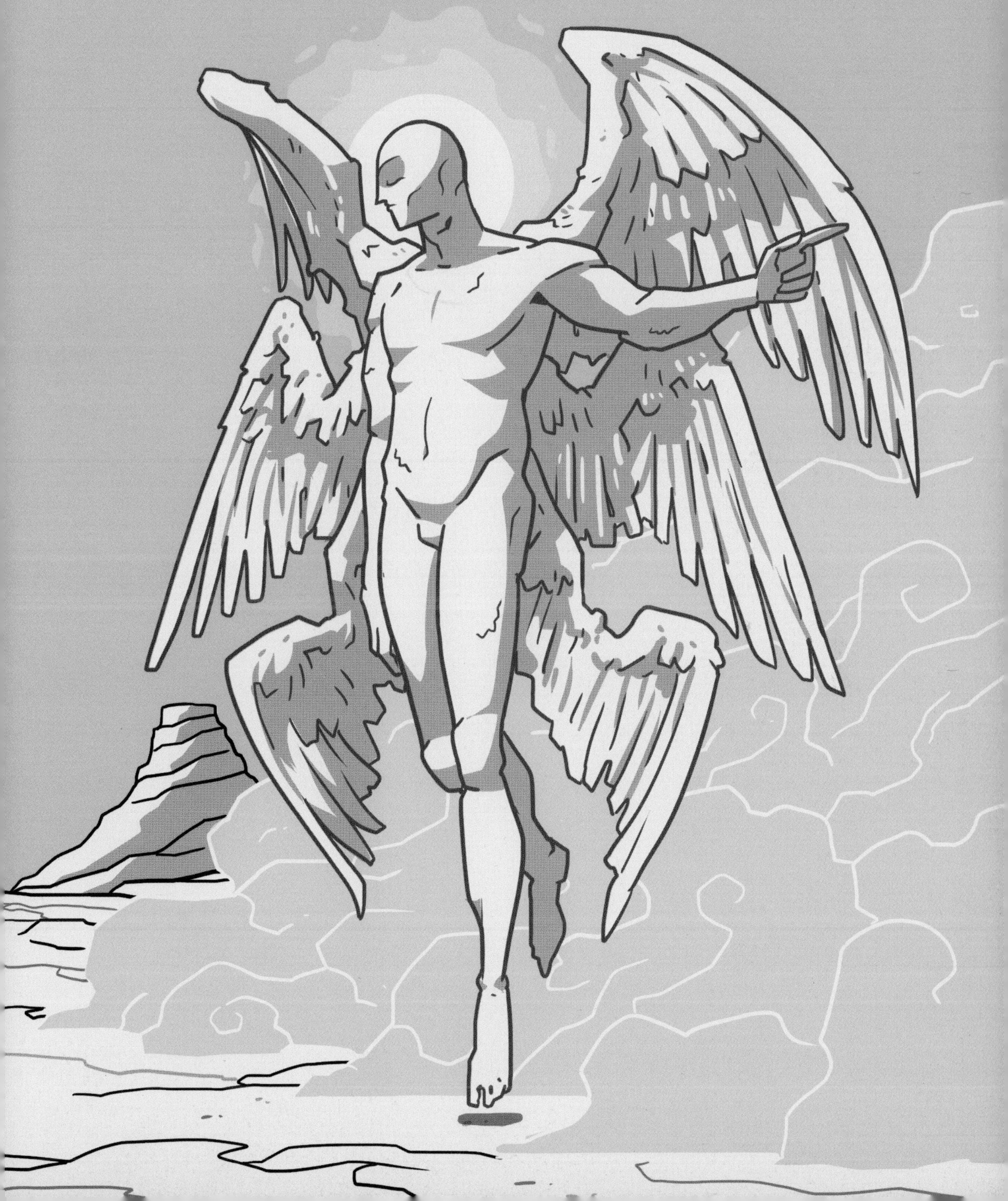

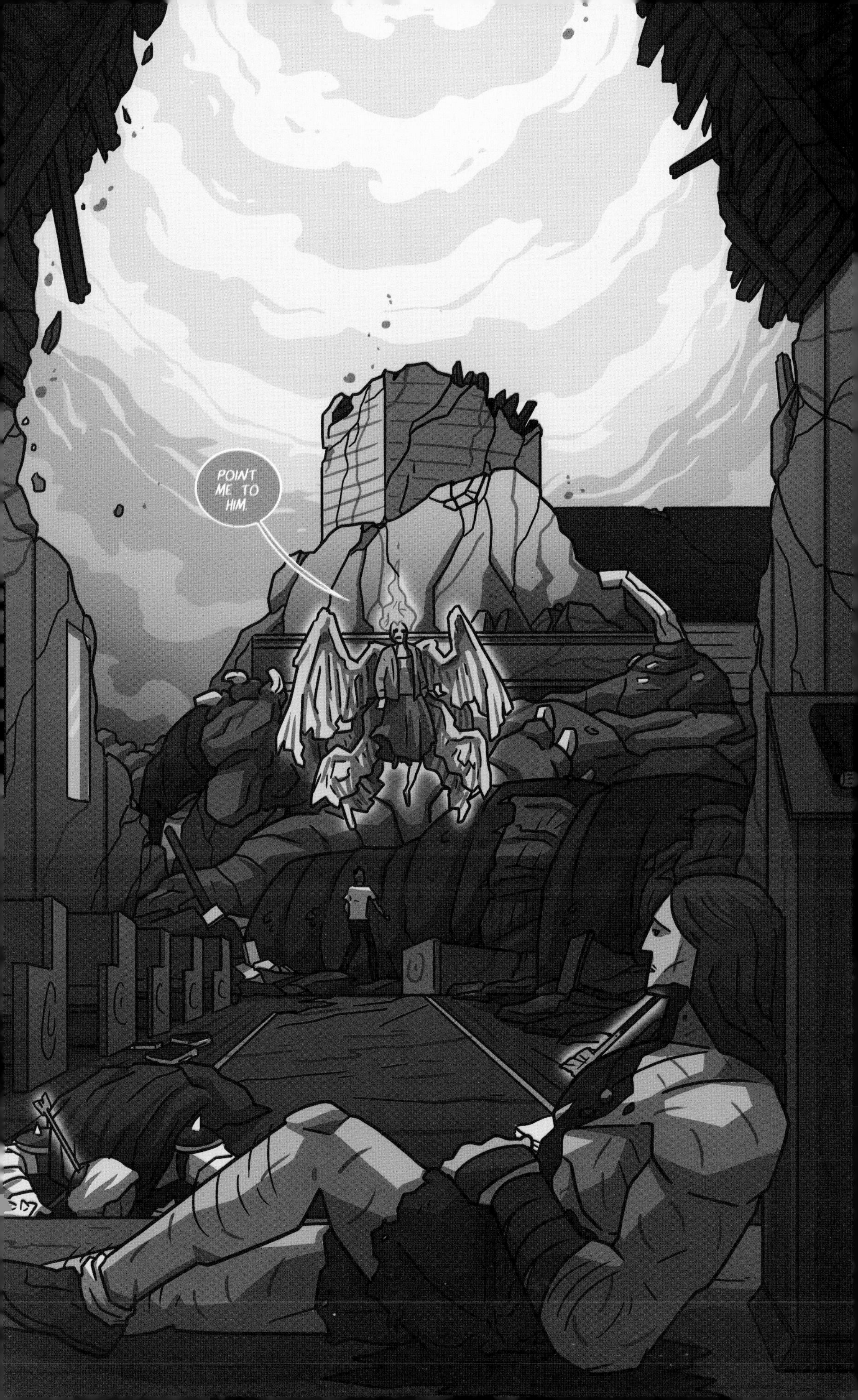
POINT ME TO HIM.

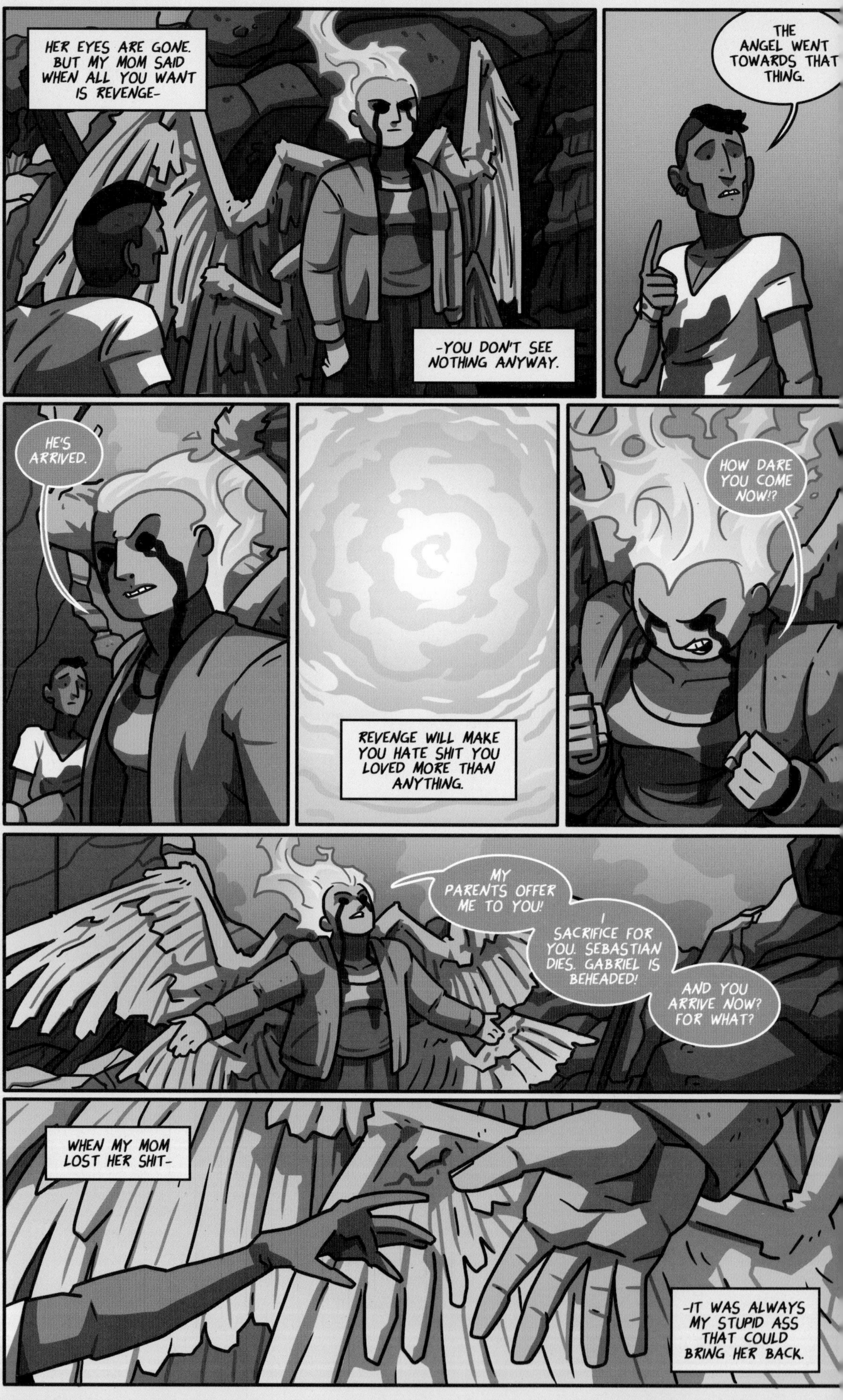
HER EYES ARE GONE. BUT MY MOM SAID WHEN ALL YOU WANT IS REVENGE-
-YOU DON'T SEE NOTHING ANYWAY.
THE ANGEL WENT TOWARDS THAT THING.
HE'S ARRIVED.
REVENGE WILL MAKE YOU HATE SHIT YOU LOVED MORE THAN ANYTHING.
HOW DARE YOU COME NOW!?
MY PARENTS OFFER ME TO YOU!
I SACRIFICE FOR YOU. SEBASTIAN DIES. GABRIEL IS BEHEADED!
AND YOU ARRIVE NOW? FOR WHAT?
WHEN MY MOM LOST HER SHIT-
-IT WAS ALWAYS MY STUPID ASS THAT COULD BRING HER BACK.

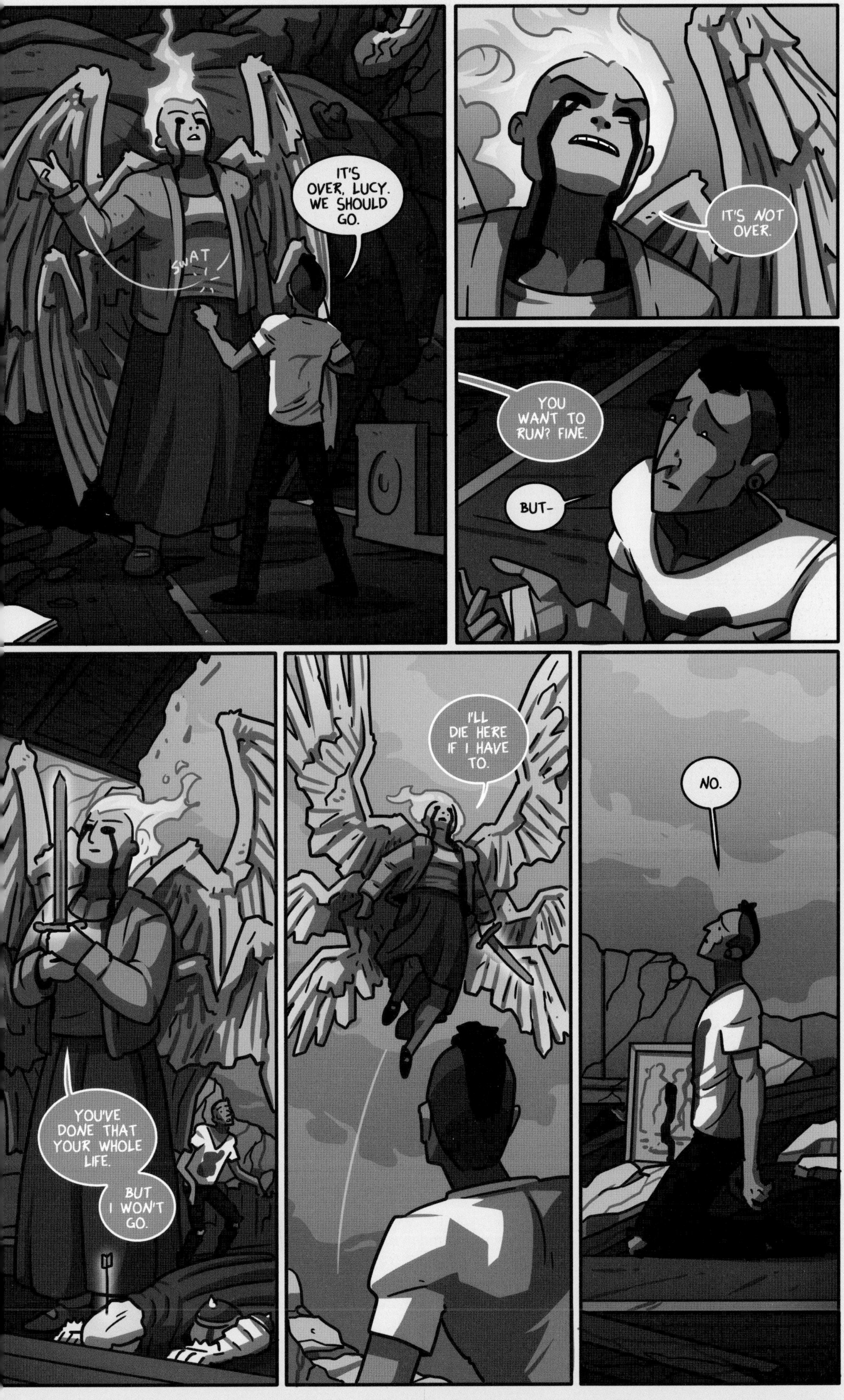
IT'S OVER, LUCY. WE SHOULD GO.
SWAT
IT'S NOT OVER.
YOU WANT TO RUN? FINE.
BUT-
YOU'VE DONE THAT YOUR WHOLE LIFE.
BUT I WON'T GO.
I'LL DIE HERE IF I HAVE TO.
NO.

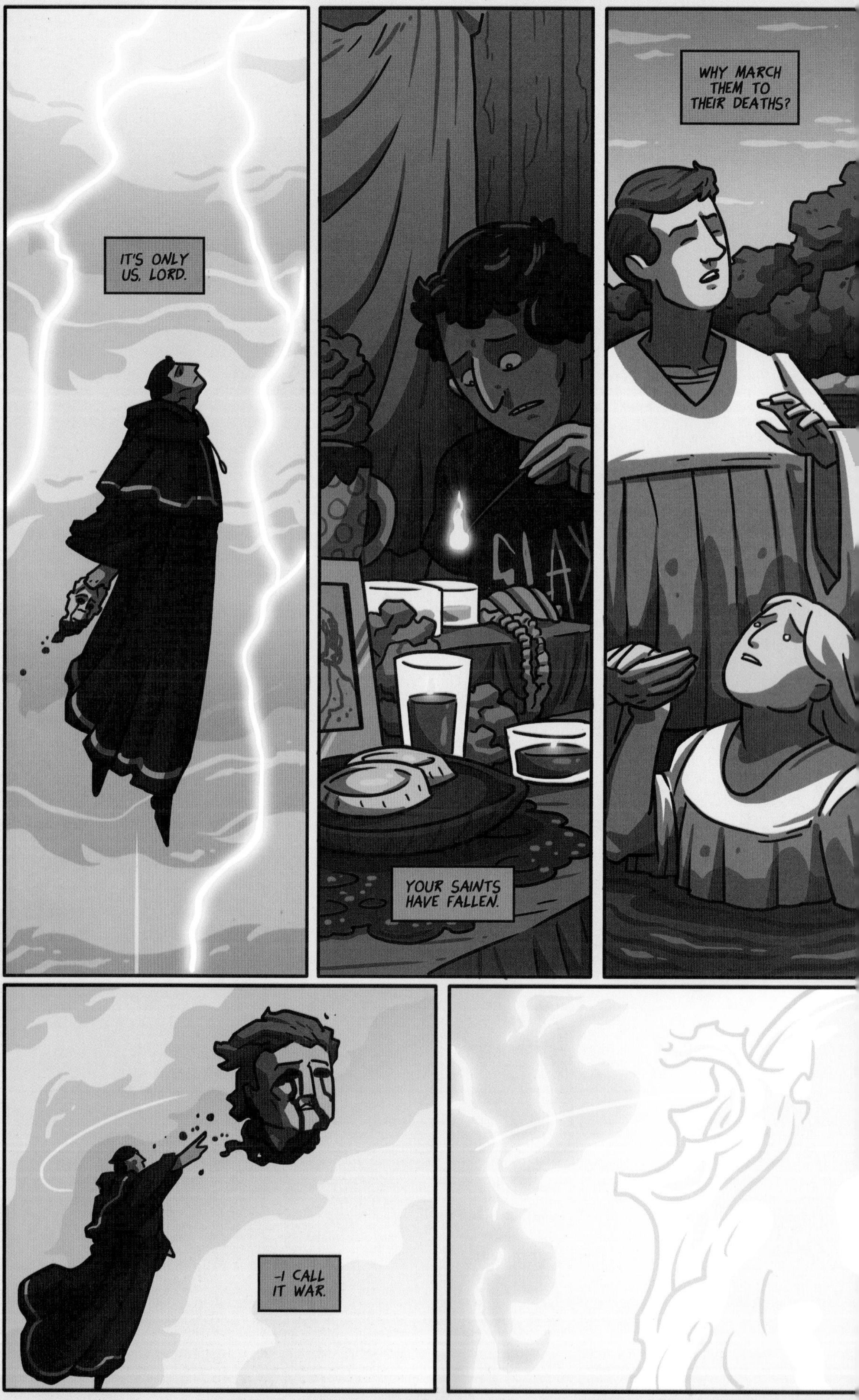

IT'S ONLY US, LORD.
YOUR SAINTS HAVE FALLEN.
WHY MARCH THEM TO THEIR DEATHS?
–I CALL IT WAR.

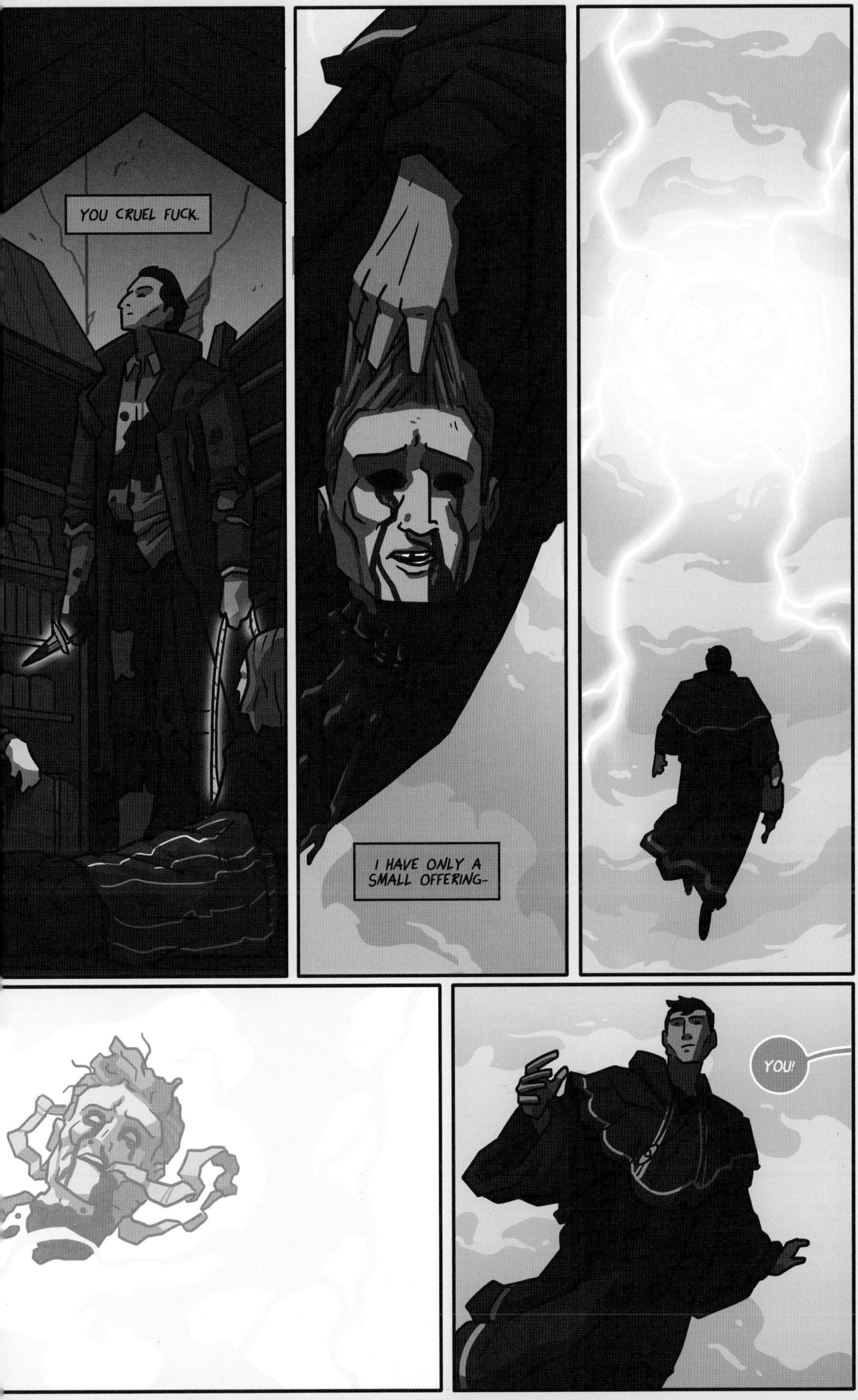

YOU CRUEL FUCK.
I HAVE ONLY A SMALL OFFERING-
YOU!

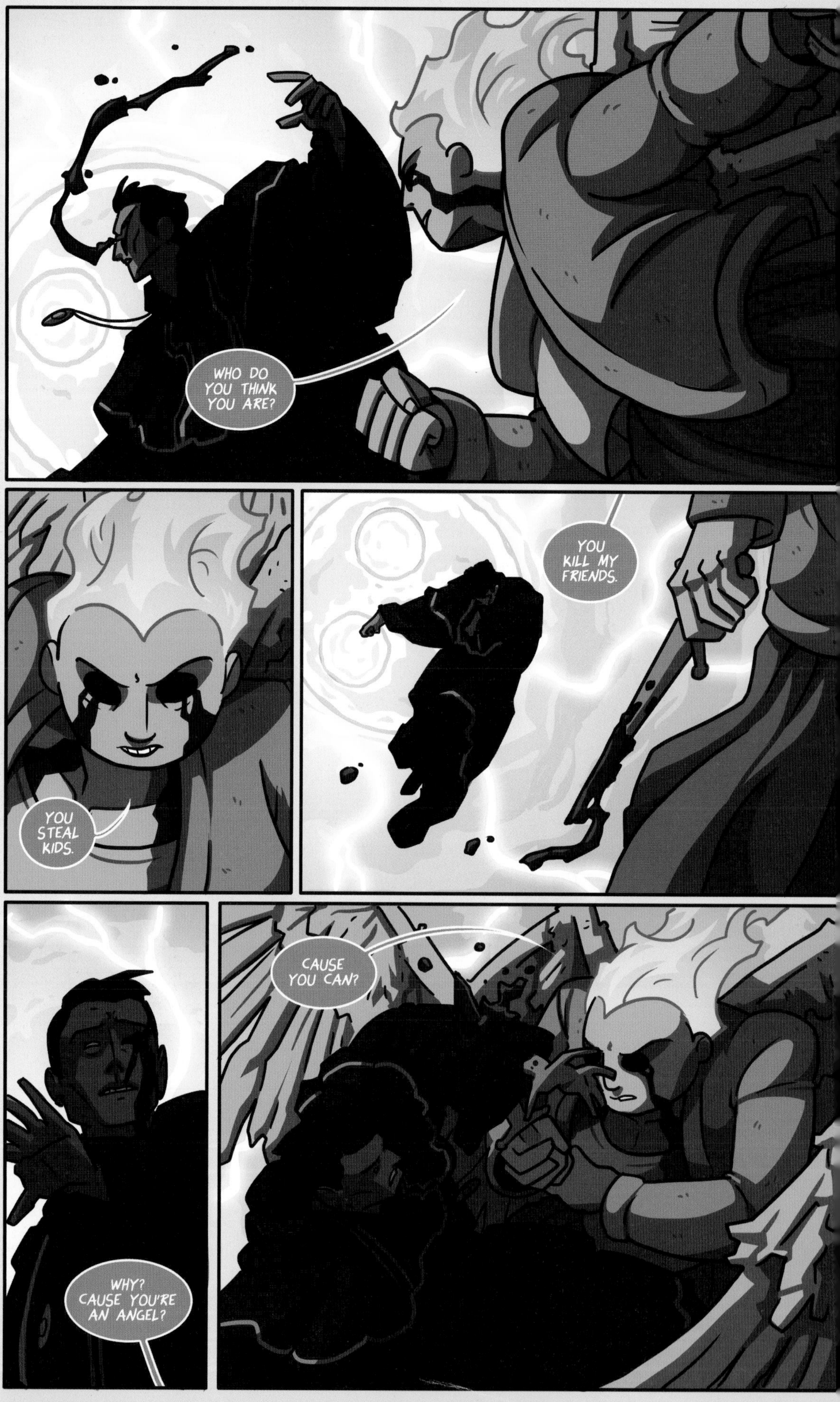
WHO DO YOU THINK YOU ARE?
YOU STEAL KIDS.
YOU KILL MY FRIENDS.
WHY? CAUSE YOU'RE AN ANGEL?
CAUSE YOU CAN?

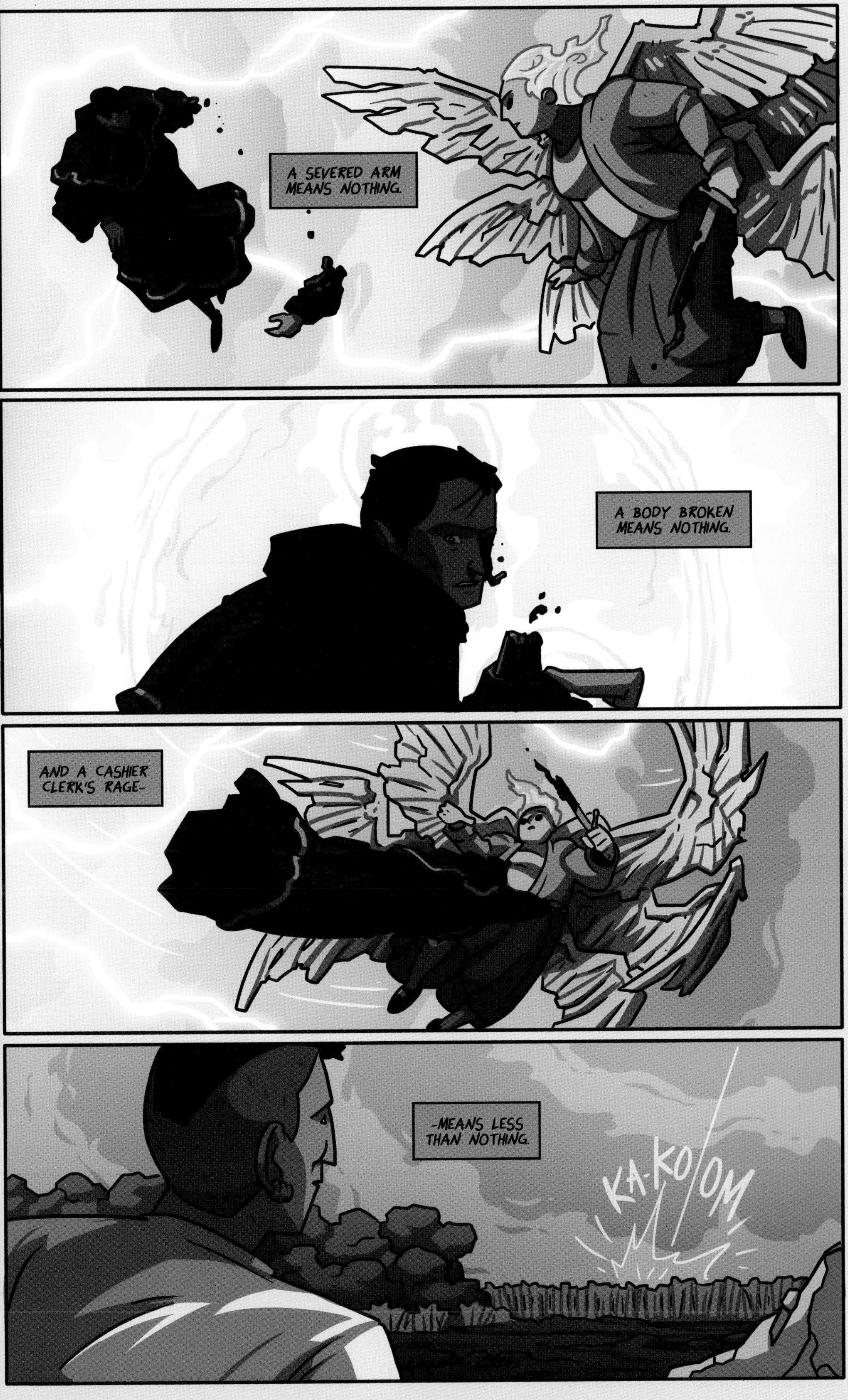
A SEVERED ARM MEANS NOTHING.
A BODY BROKEN MEANS NOTHING.
AND A CASHIER CLERK'S RAGE-
-MEANS LESS THAN NOTHING.
KA-KOOM

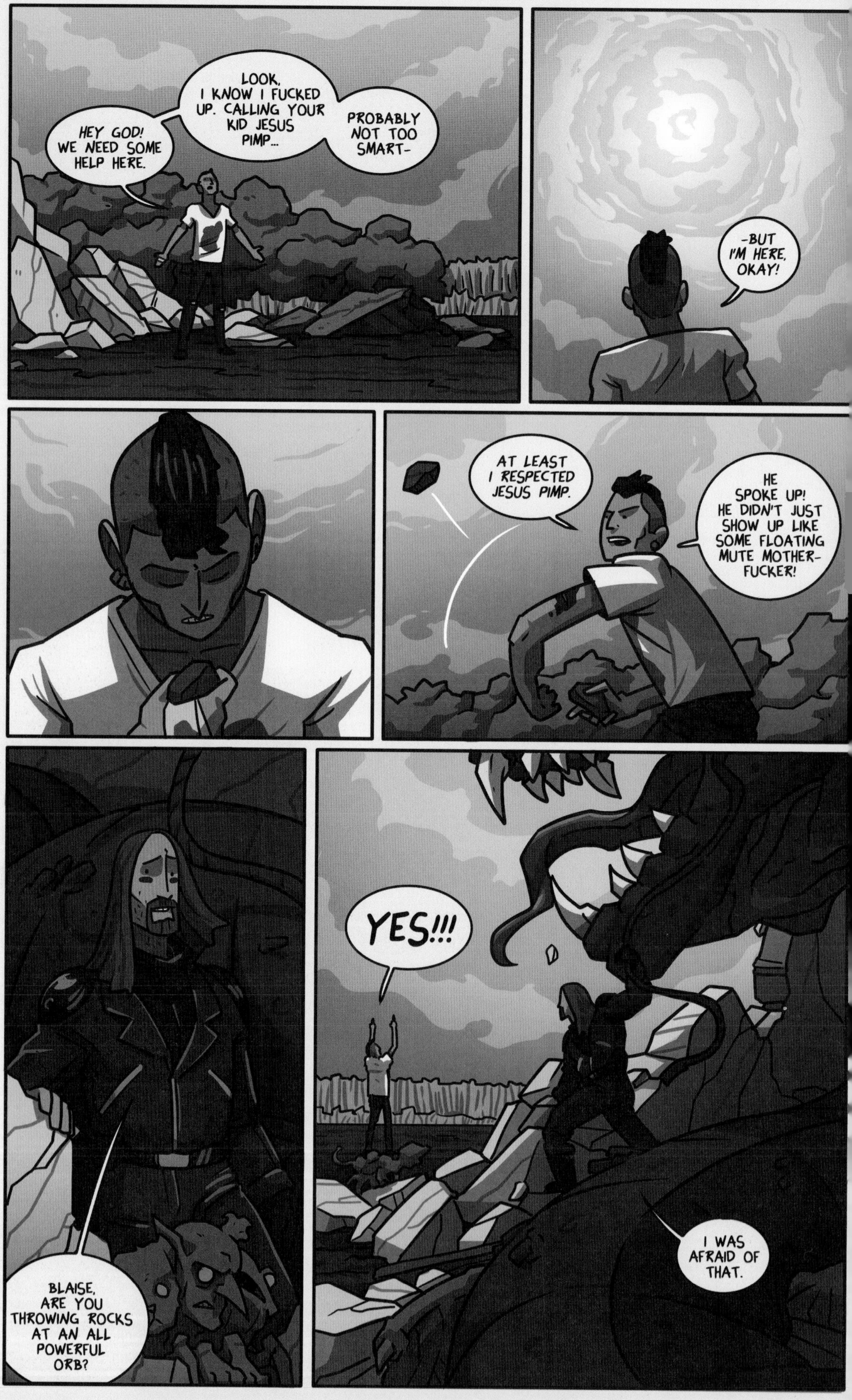
HEY GOD! WE NEED SOME HELP HERE.
LOOK, I KNOW I FUCKED UP. CALLING YOUR KID JESUS PIMP...
PROBABLY NOT TOO SMART-
-BUT I'M HERE, OKAY!
AT LEAST I RESPECTED JESUS PIMP.
HE SPOKE UP! HE DIDN'T JUST SHOW UP LIKE SOME FLOATING MUTE MOTHER-FUCKER!
BLAISE, ARE YOU THROWING ROCKS AT AN ALL POWERFUL ORB?
YES!!!
I WAS AFRAID OF THAT.

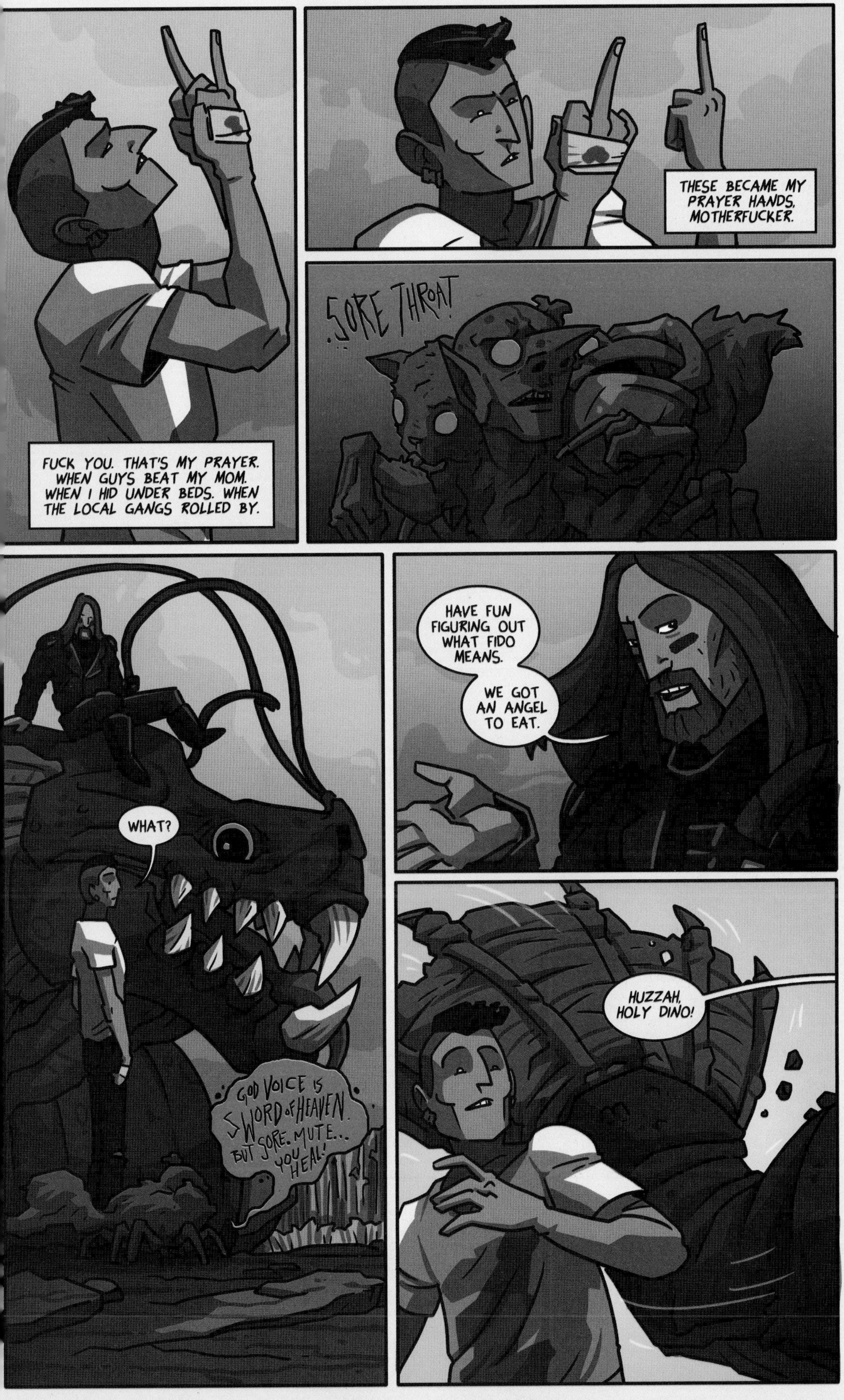
FUCK YOU. THAT'S MY PRAYER. WHEN GUYS BEAT MY MOM. WHEN I HID UNDER BEDS. WHEN THE LOCAL GANGS ROLLED BY.
THESE BECAME MY PRAYER HANDS, MOTHERFUCKER.
SORE THROAT
WHAT?
GOD VOICE IS SWORD of HEAVEN. BUT SORE. MUTE... YOU HEAL!
HAVE FUN FIGURING OUT WHAT FIDO MEANS.
WE GOT AN ANGEL TO EAT.
HUZZAH, HOLY DINO!

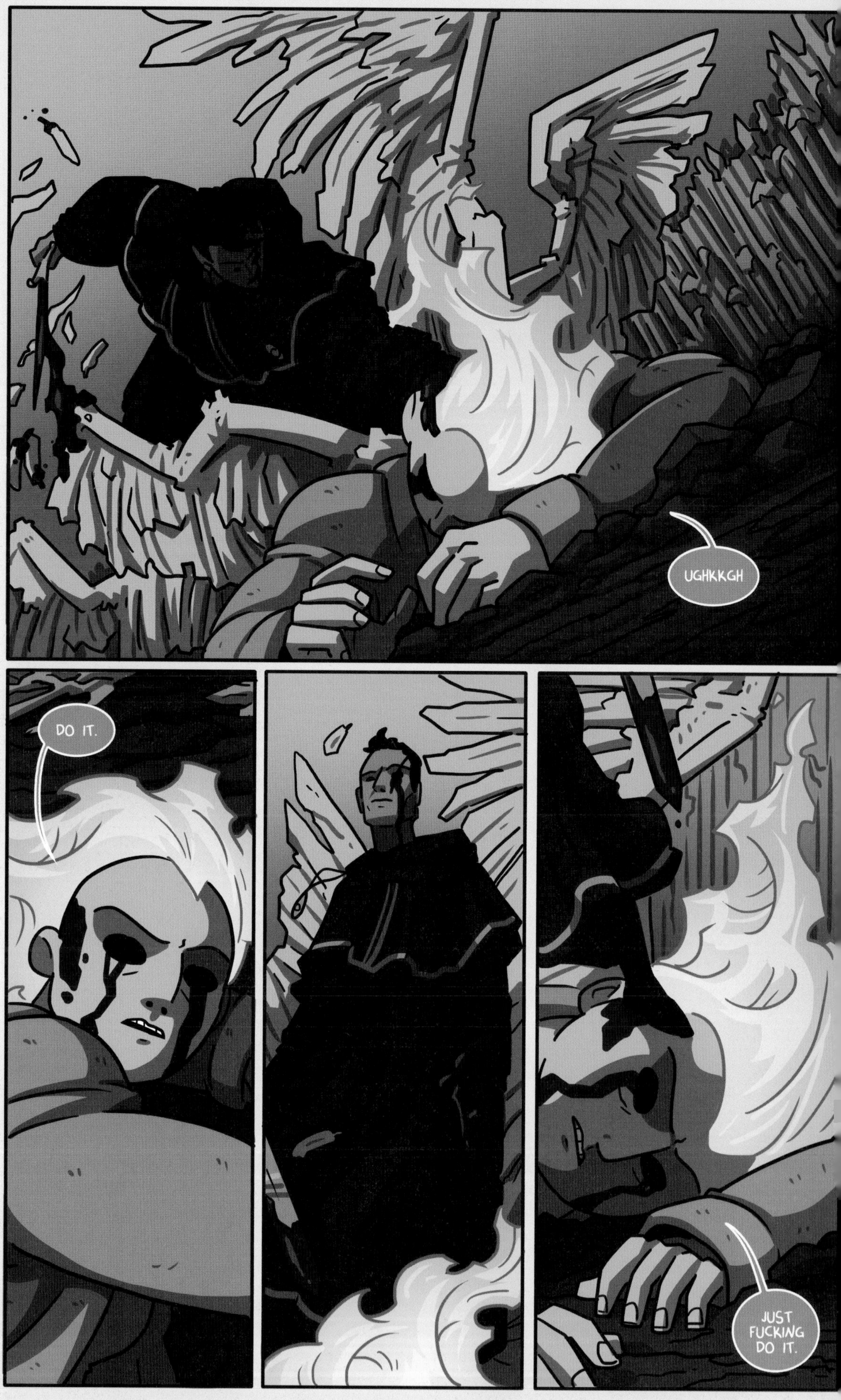
UGHKKGH
DO IT.
JUST FUCKING DO IT.

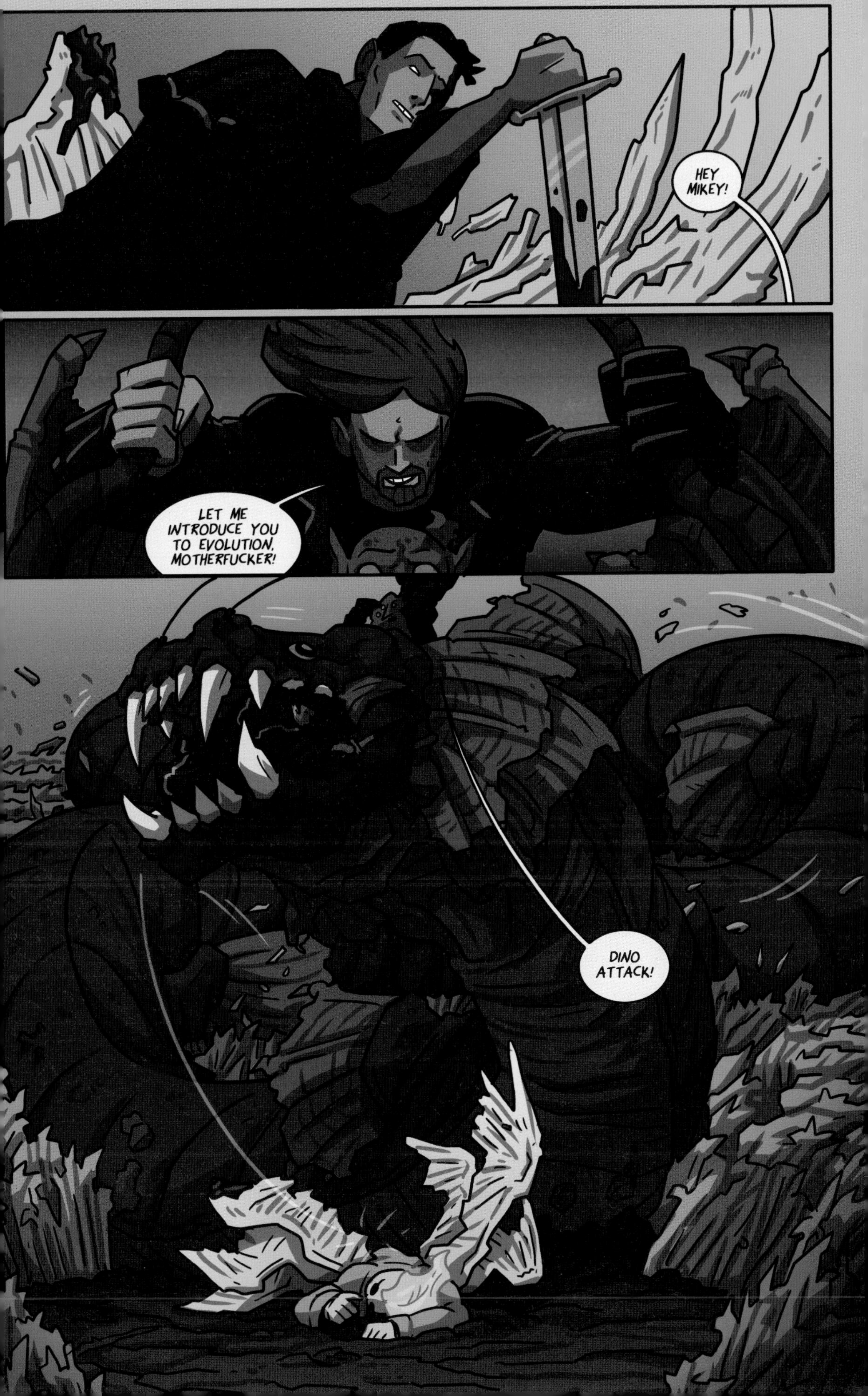
HEY MIKEY!
LET ME INTRODUCE YOU TO EVOLUTION, MOTHERFUCKER!
DINO ATTACK!

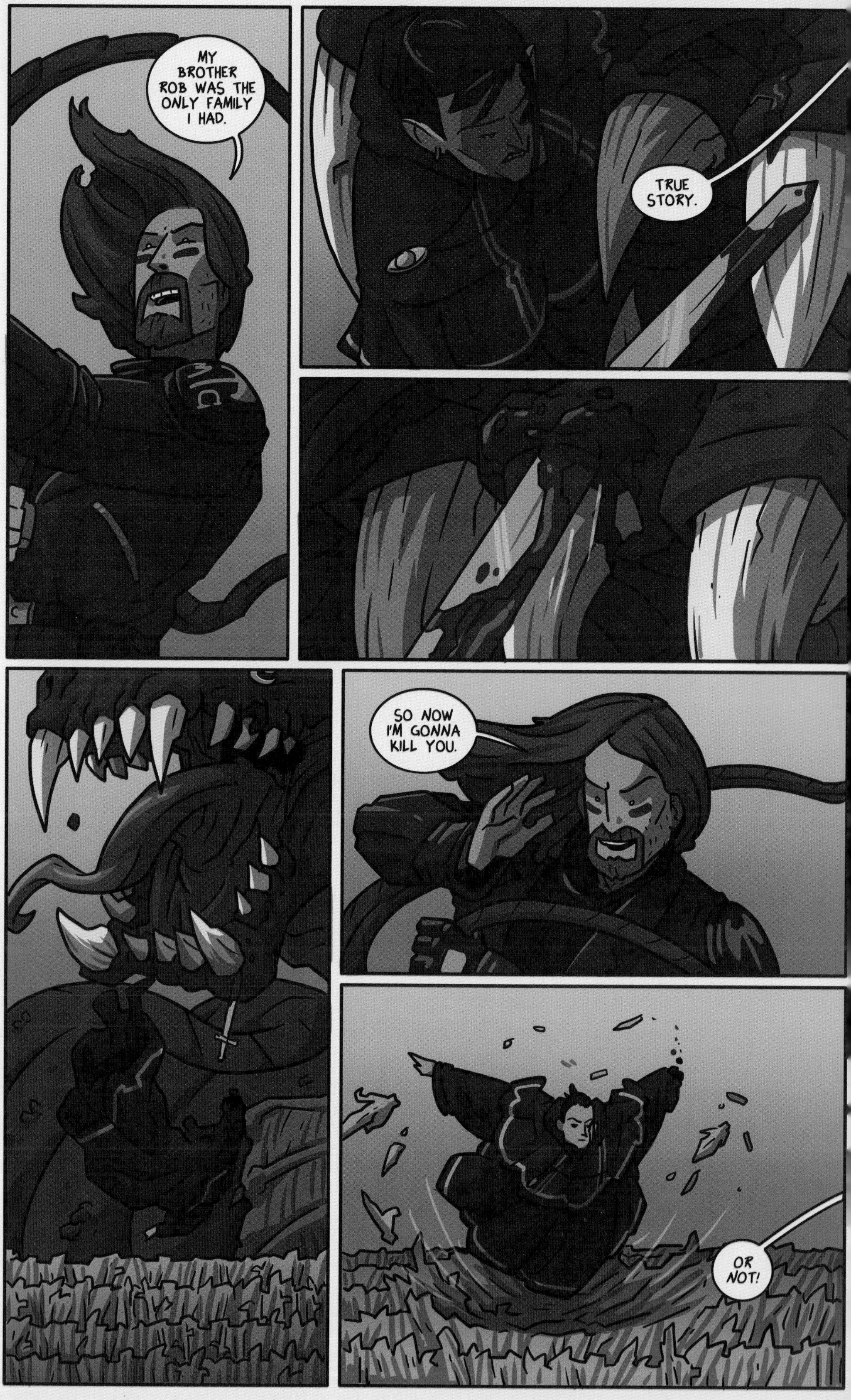
MY BROTHER ROB WAS THE ONLY FAMILY I HAD.
TRUE STORY.
SO NOW I'M GONNA KILL YOU.
OR NOT!

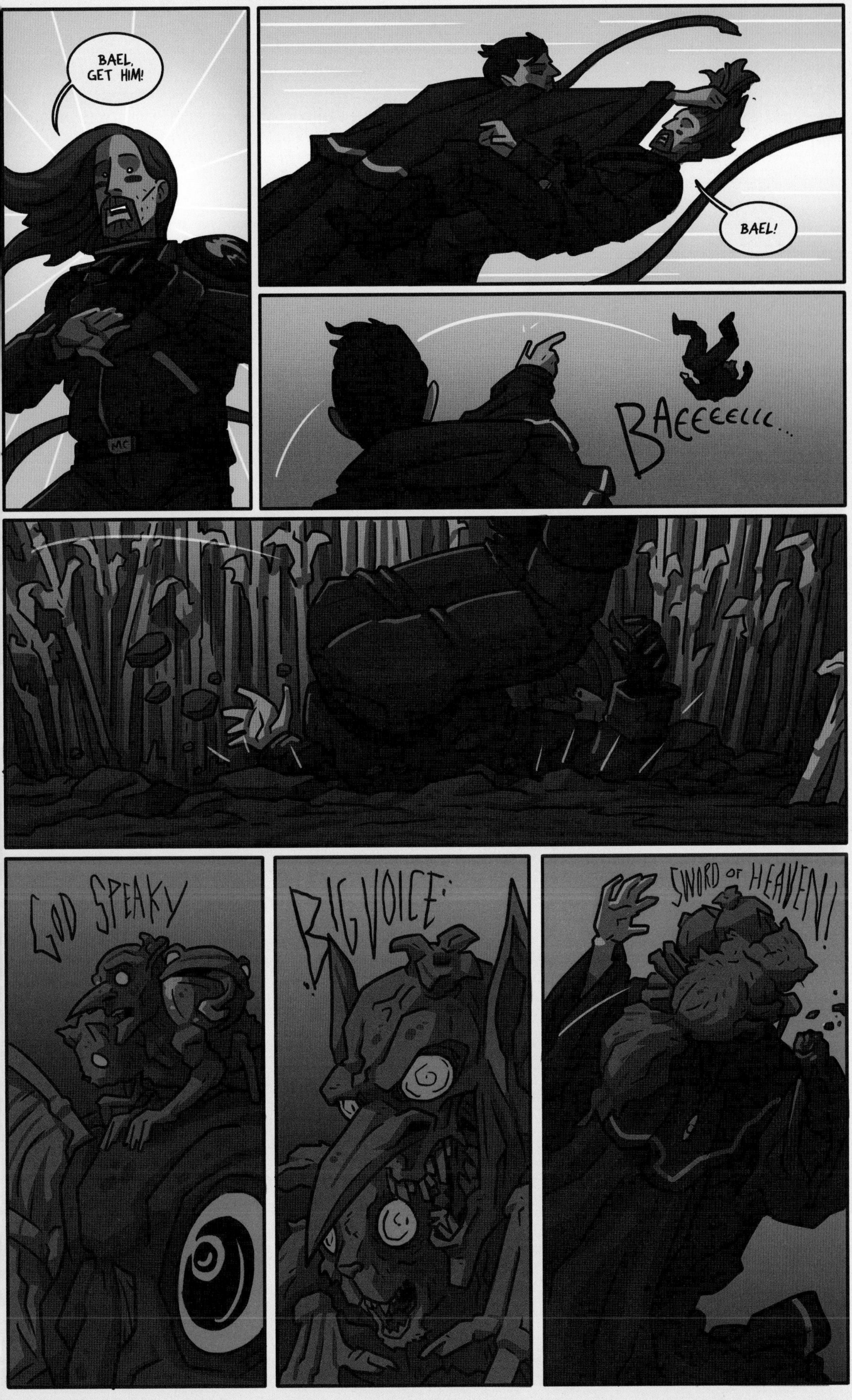
BAEL, GET HIM!
BAEL!
BAEEEELLL...
GOD SPEAKY
BIG VOICE:
SWORD OF HEAVEN!

COME ON, JP! BAEL SAYS I GOT TO GIVE YOUR DAD A VOICE.

TELL ME WHAT THE FUCK THAT MEANS, MAN!

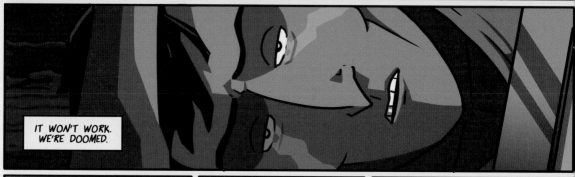

IT WON'T WORK. WE'RE DOOMED.

BLAISE?

WE GOTTA KEEP GOING, MONSTER.

AIN'T NEED EYES TO KNOW THIS PARY IS OVER!

BLAISE, WHAT IS THIS THING?

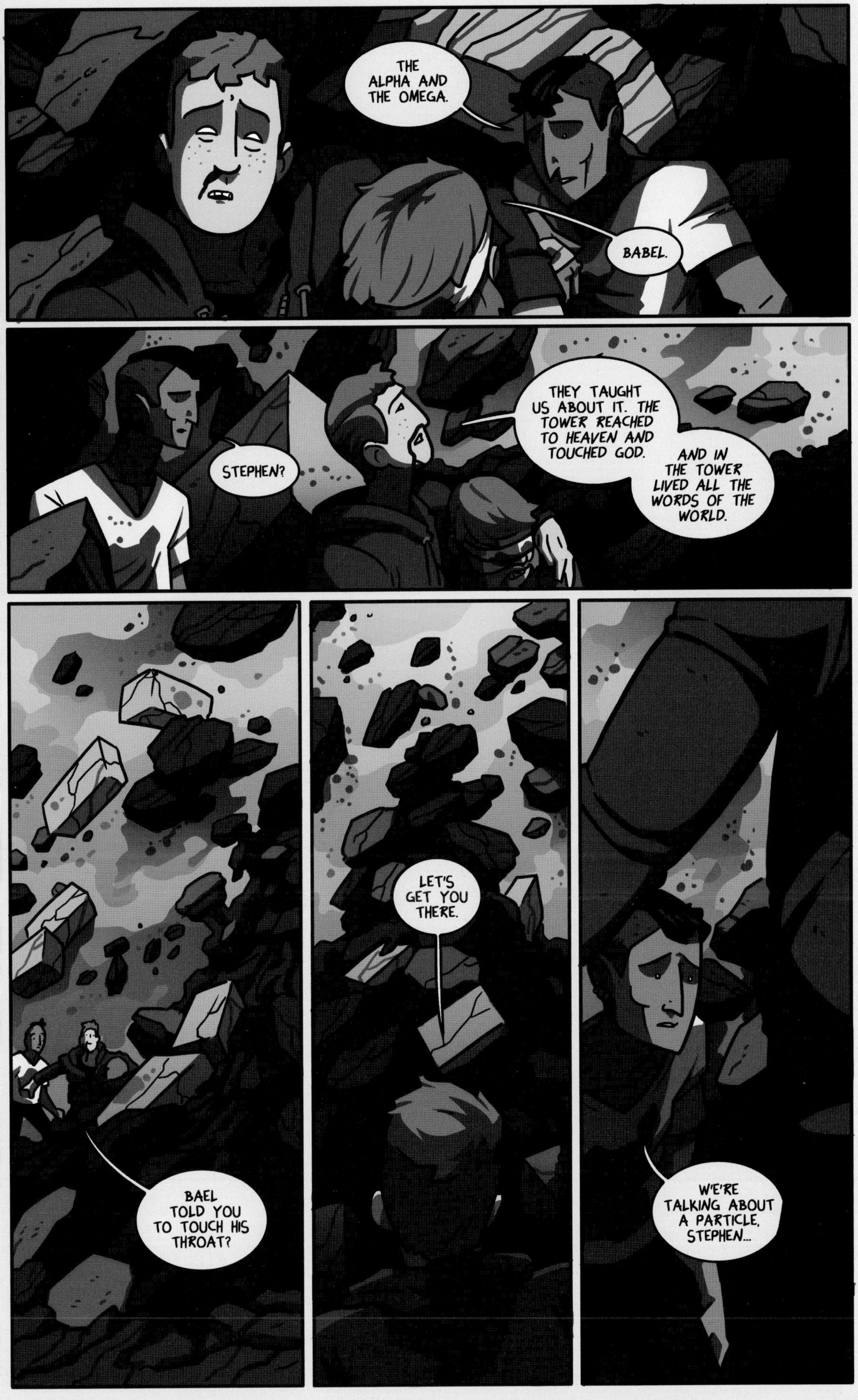
THE ALPHA AND THE OMEGA.
BABEL.
STEPHEN?
THEY TAUGHT US ABOUT IT. THE TOWER REACHED TO HEAVEN AND TOUCHED GOD.
AND IN THE TOWER LIVED ALL THE WORDS OF THE WORLD.
BAEL TOLD YOU TO TOUCH HIS THROAT?
LET'S GET YOU THERE.
WE'RE TALKING ABOUT A PARTICLE, STEPHEN...

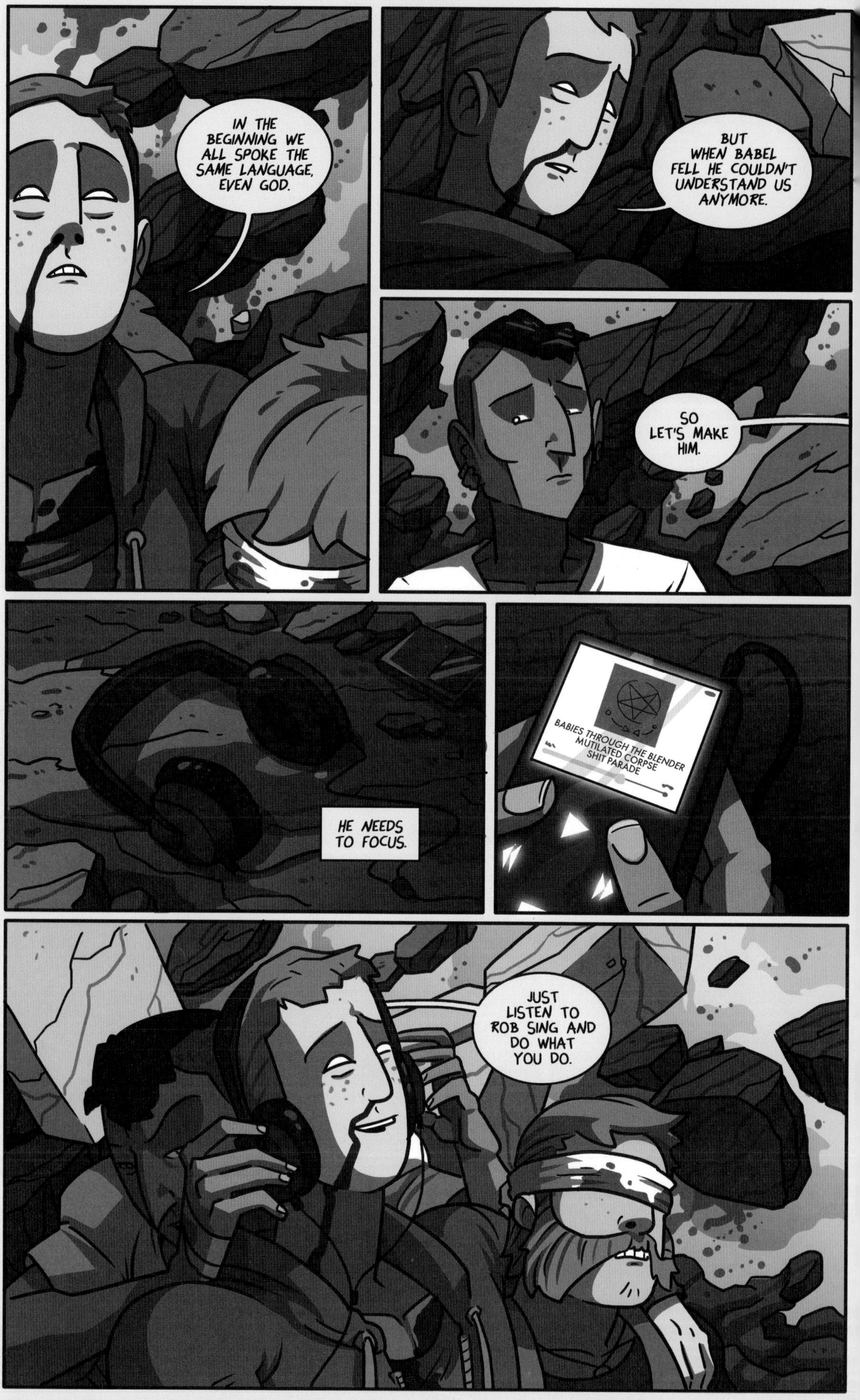
IN THE BEGINNING WE ALL SPOKE THE SAME LANGUAGE, EVEN GOD.
BUT WHEN BABEL FELL HE COULDN'T UNDERSTAND US ANYMORE.
SO LET'S MAKE HIM.
HE NEEDS TO FOCUS.
BABIES THROUGH THE BLENDER
MUTILATED CORPSE
SHIT PARADE
JUST LISTEN TO ROB SING AND DO WHAT YOU DO.

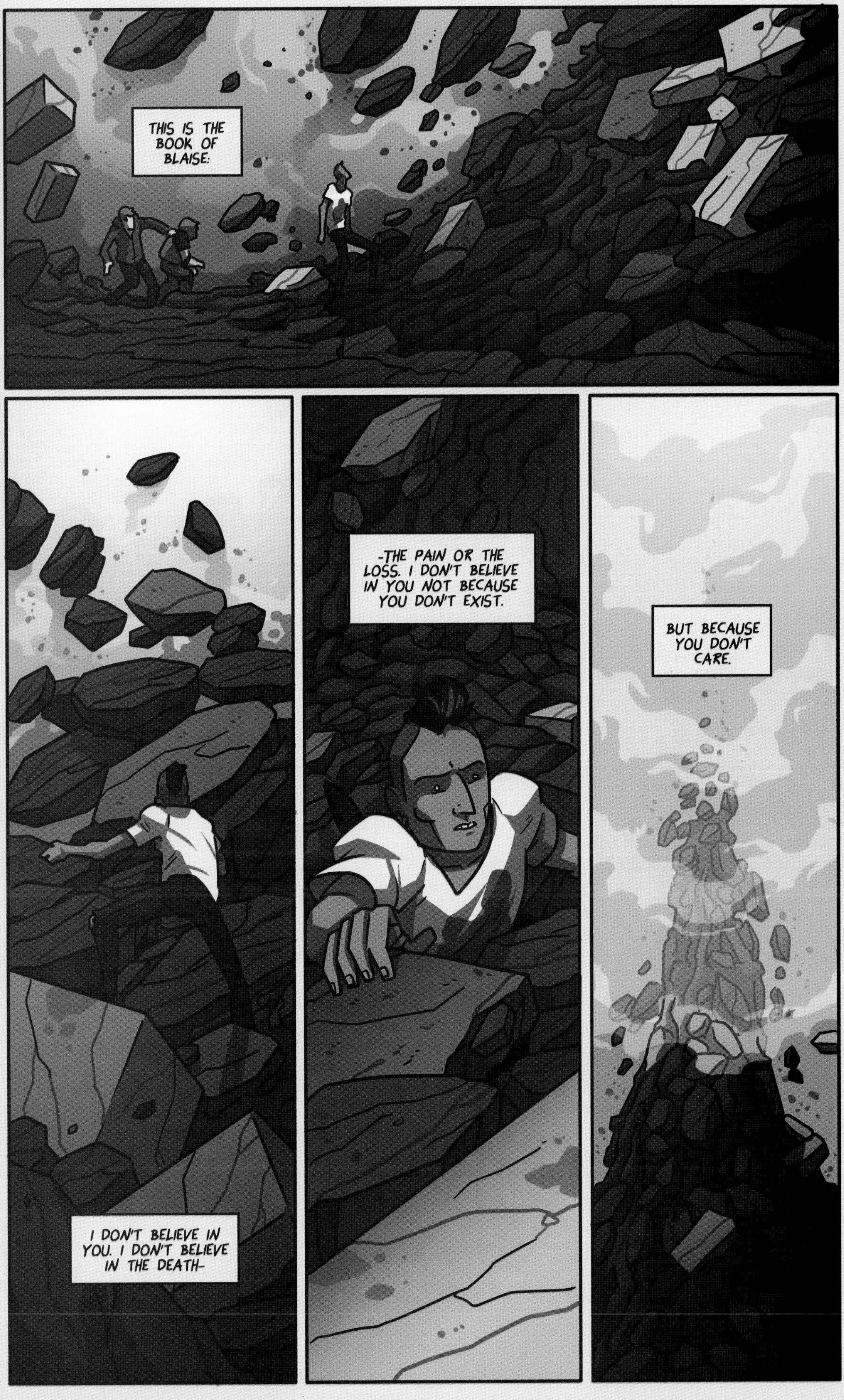
THIS IS THE BOOK OF BLAISE:
I DON'T BELIEVE IN YOU. I DON'T BELIEVE IN THE DEATH-
-THE PAIN OR THE LOSS. I DON'T BELIEVE IN YOU NOT BECAUSE YOU DON'T EXIST.
BUT BECAUSE YOU DON'T CARE.

BUT LUCY, SEBASTIAN—

—STEPHEN—

—ROB, JOSE, AND BAEL.

THOSE ASSHOLES IN SODOMITE DISCHARGE—

UGH...

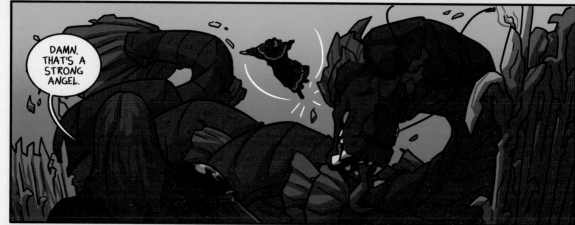

DAMN, THAT'S A STRONG ANGEL.

DINO!

—I BELIEVE IN THEM.

I HAVE TO.

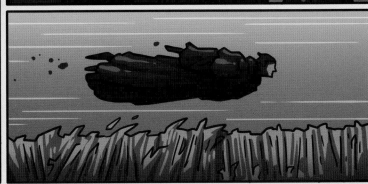

THIS ENDS HERE, MICHAEL!

BECAUSE THEY ARE LOVE.

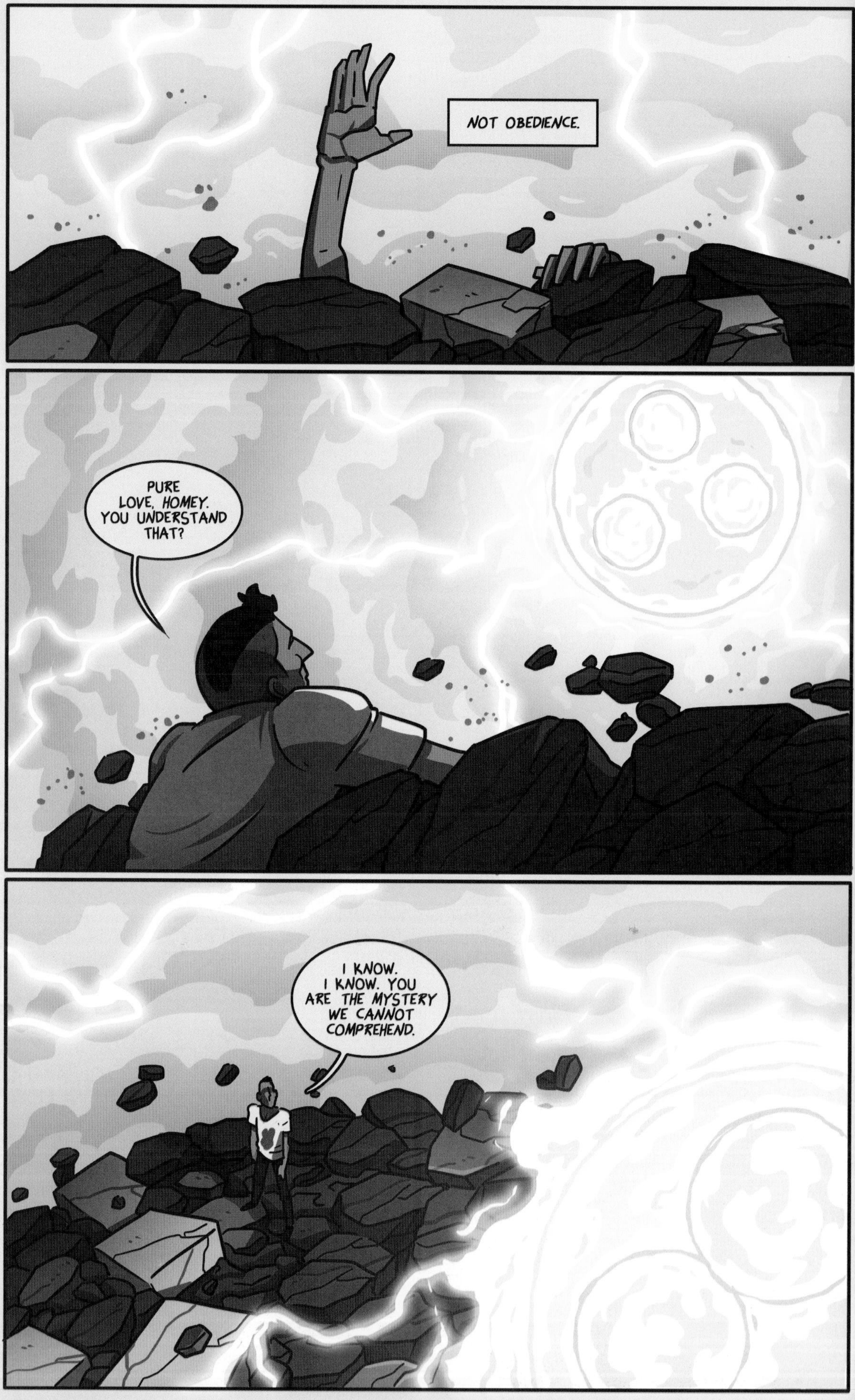
NOT OBEDIENCE.
PURE LOVE, HOMEY. YOU UNDERSTAND THAT?
I KNOW. I KNOW. YOU ARE THE MYSTERY WE CANNOT COMPREHEND.

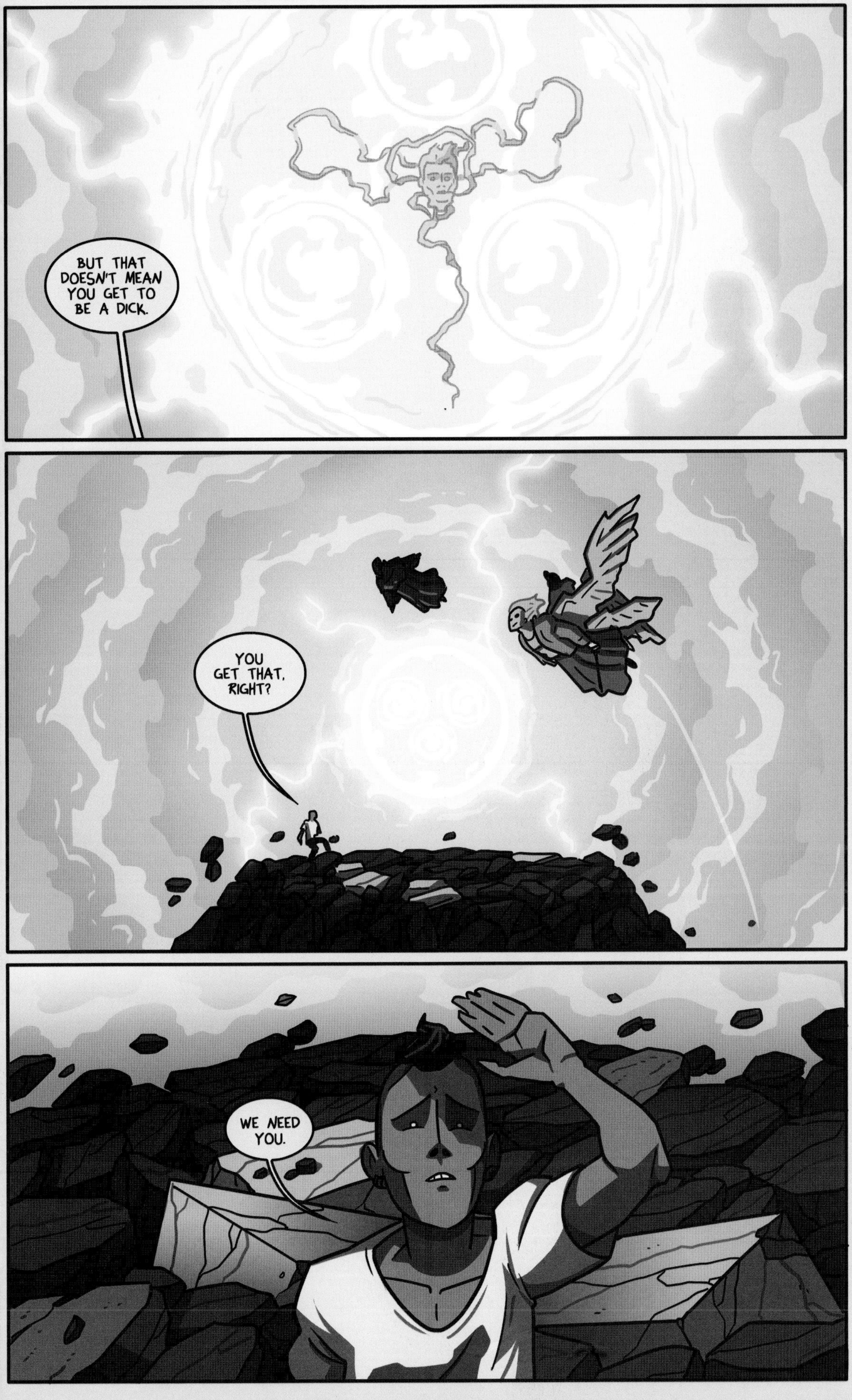
BUT THAT DOESN'T MEAN YOU GET TO BE A DICK.
YOU GET THAT, RIGHT?
WE NEED YOU.

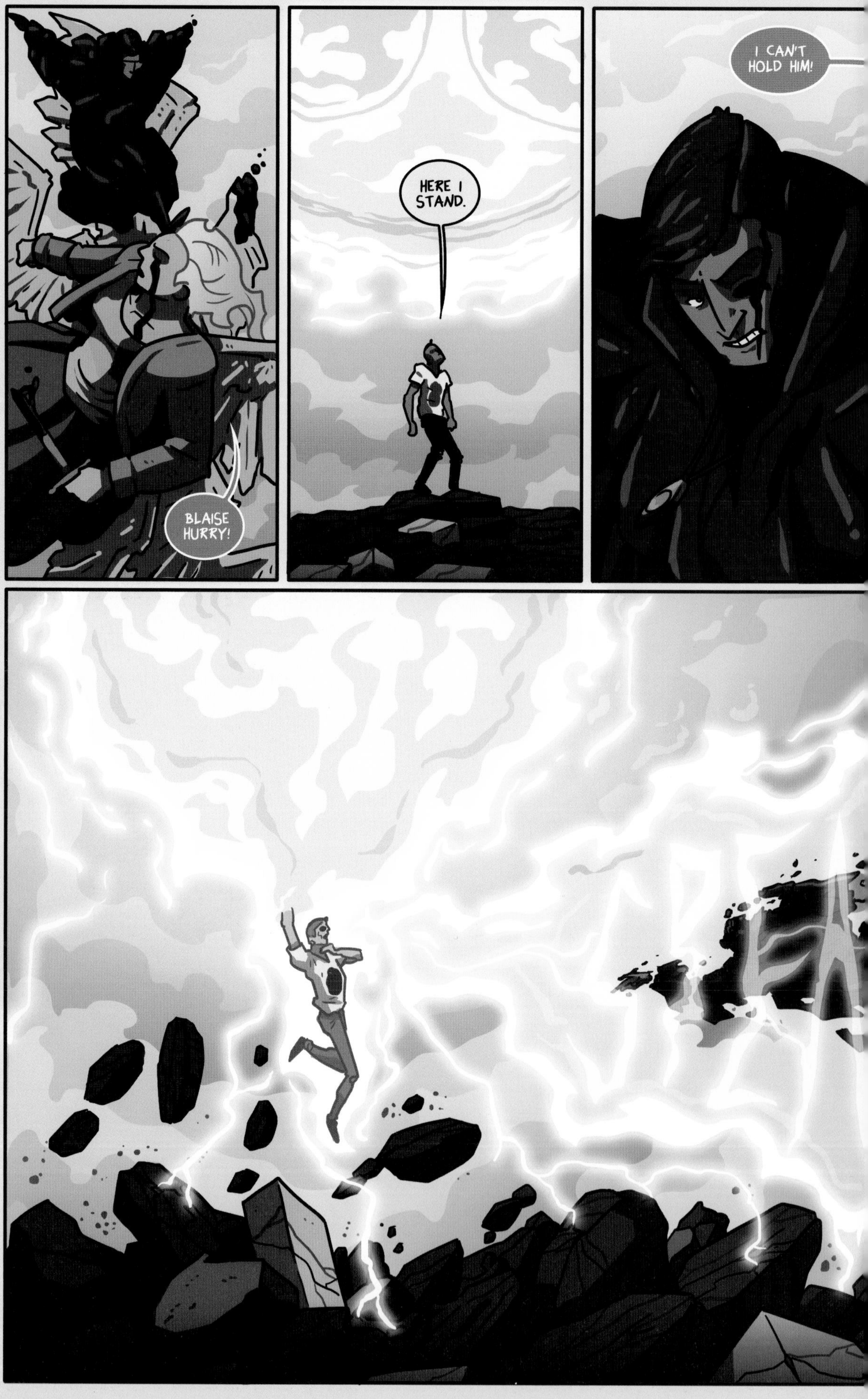
BLAISE
HURRY!
HERE I
STAND.
I CAN'T
HOLD HIM!

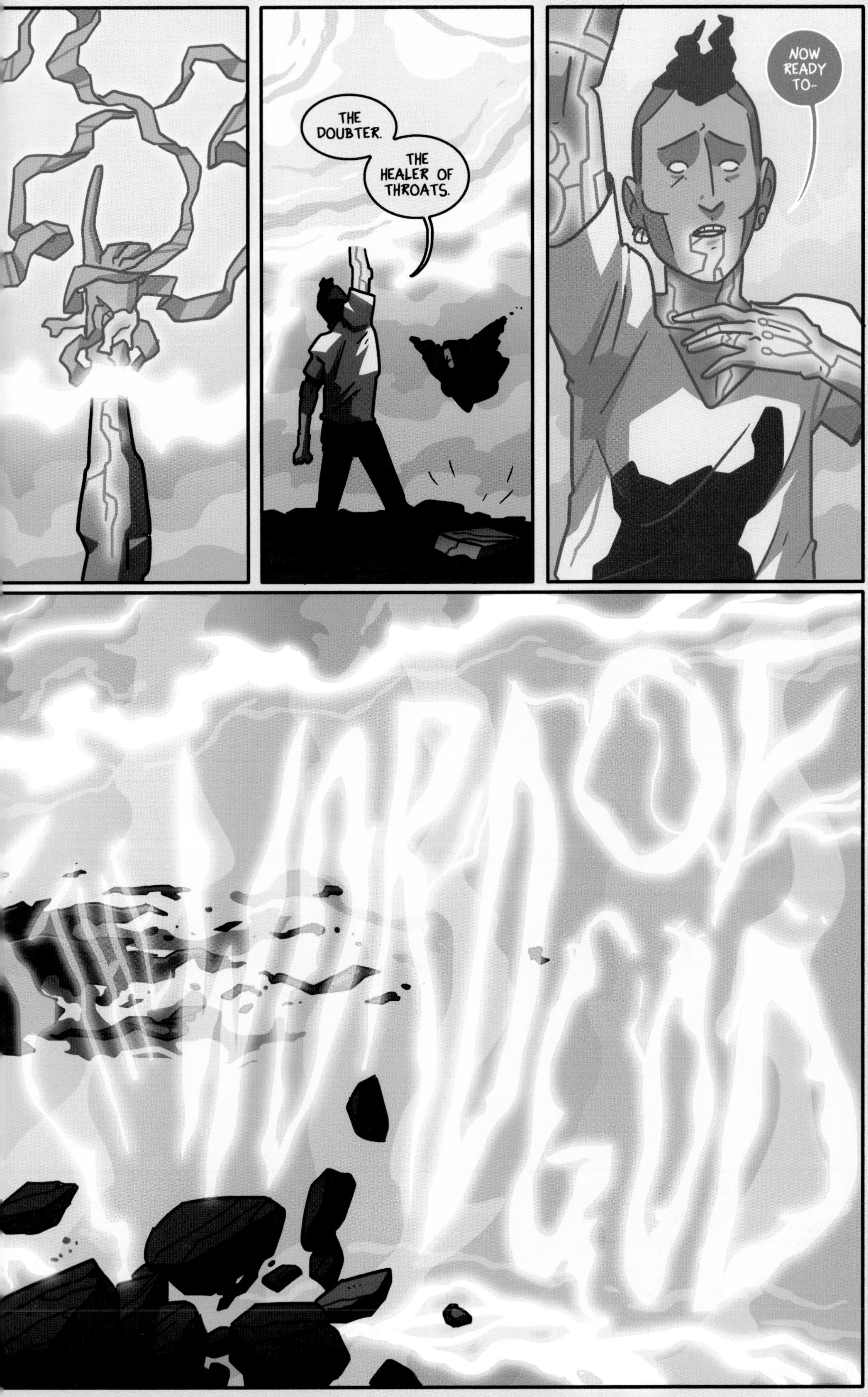
THE DOUBTER.
THE HEALER OF THROATS.
NOW READY TO-

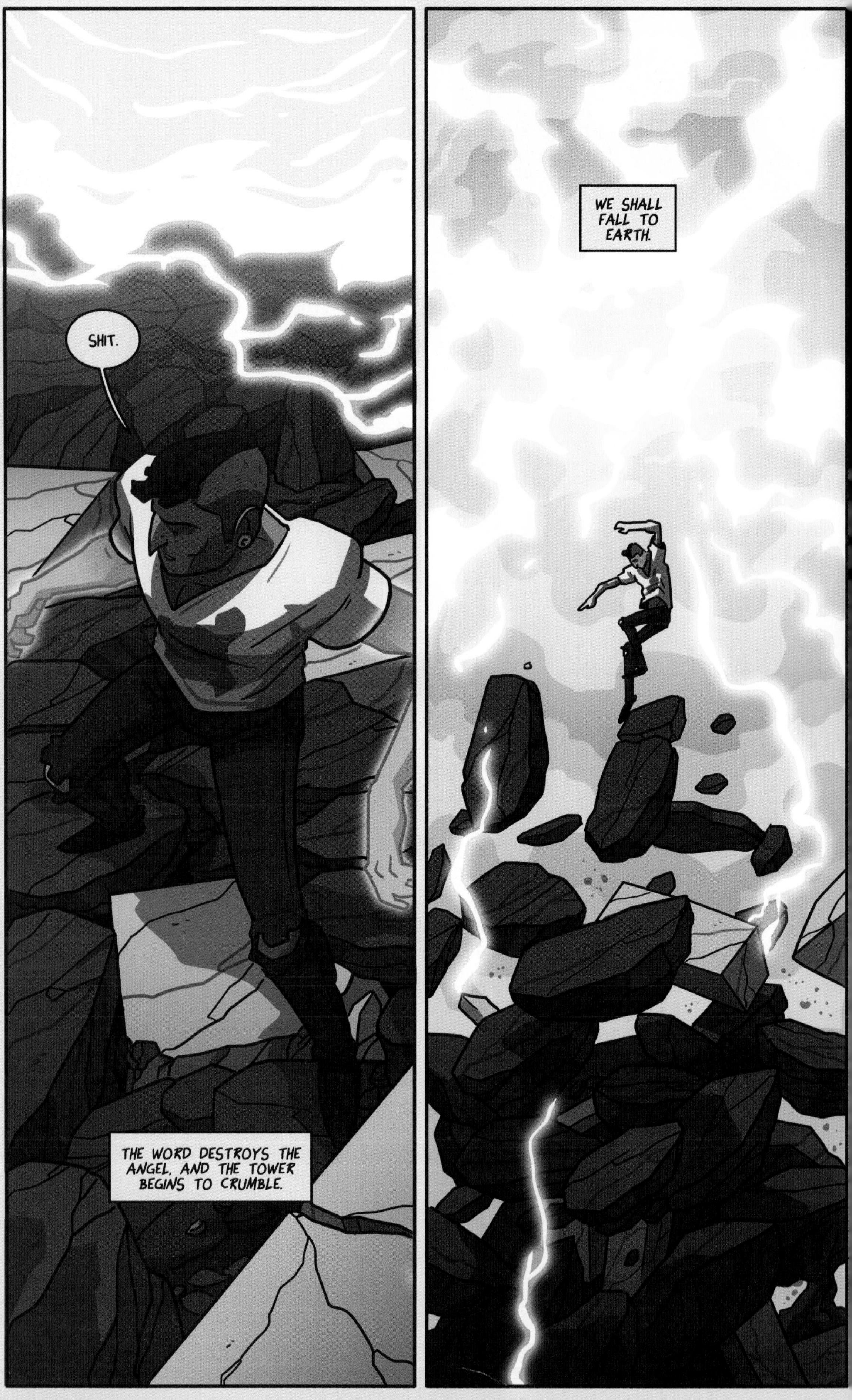
SHIT.
THE WORD DESTROYS THE ANGEL, AND THE TOWER BEGINS TO CRUMBLE.
WE SHALL FALL TO EARTH.

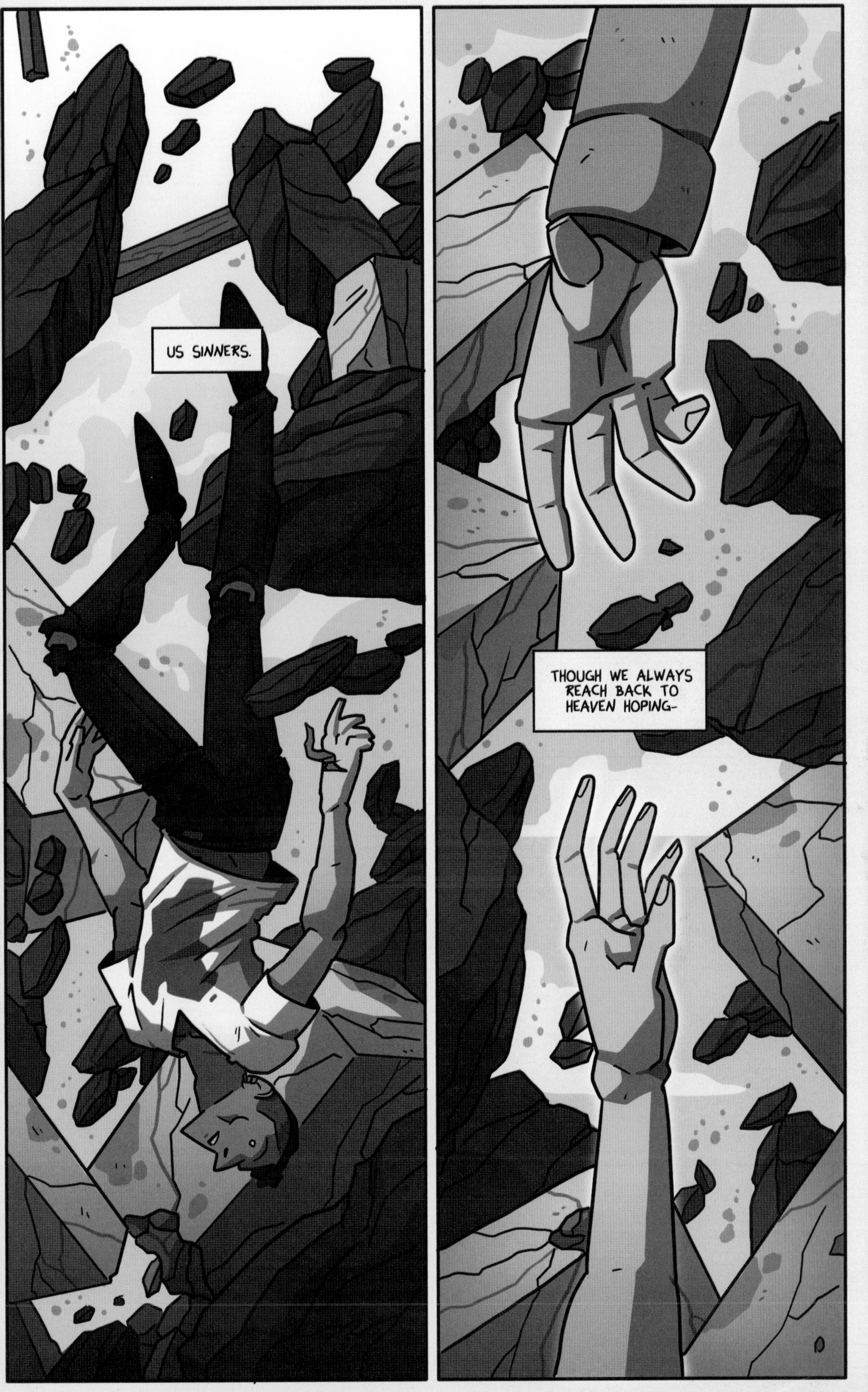
US SINNERS.
THOUGH WE ALWAYS REACH BACK TO HEAVEN HOPING-

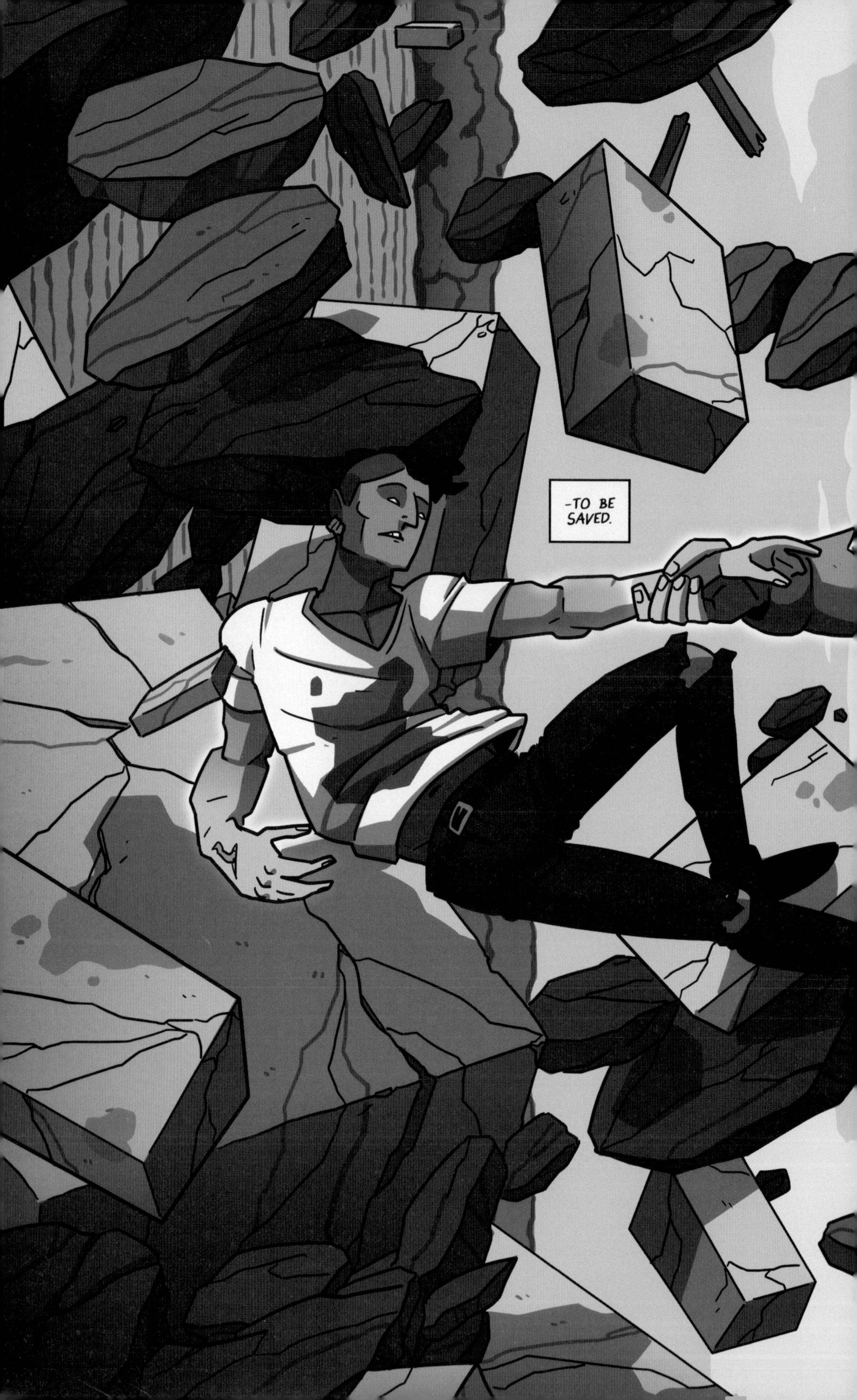
-TO BE SAVED.

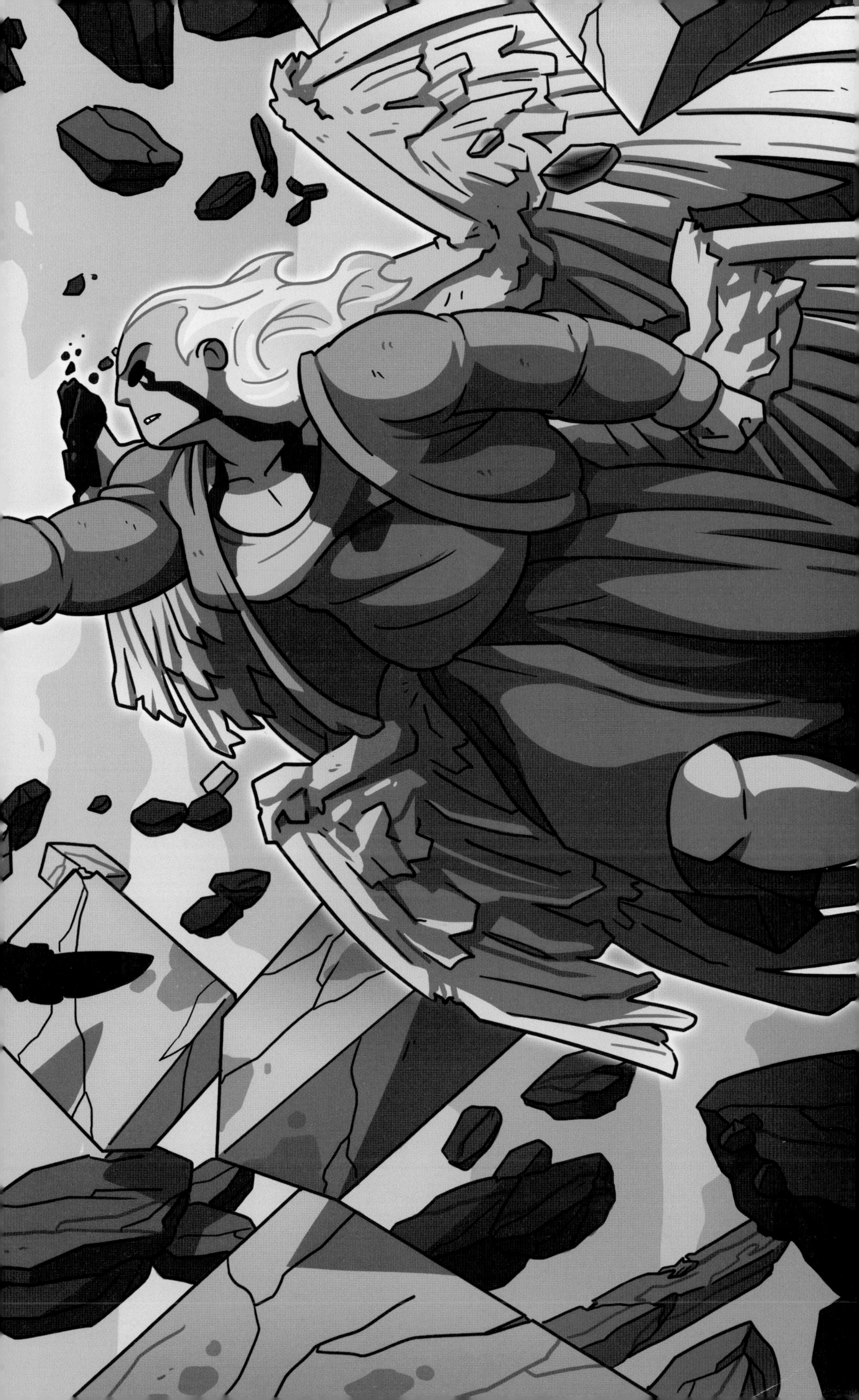

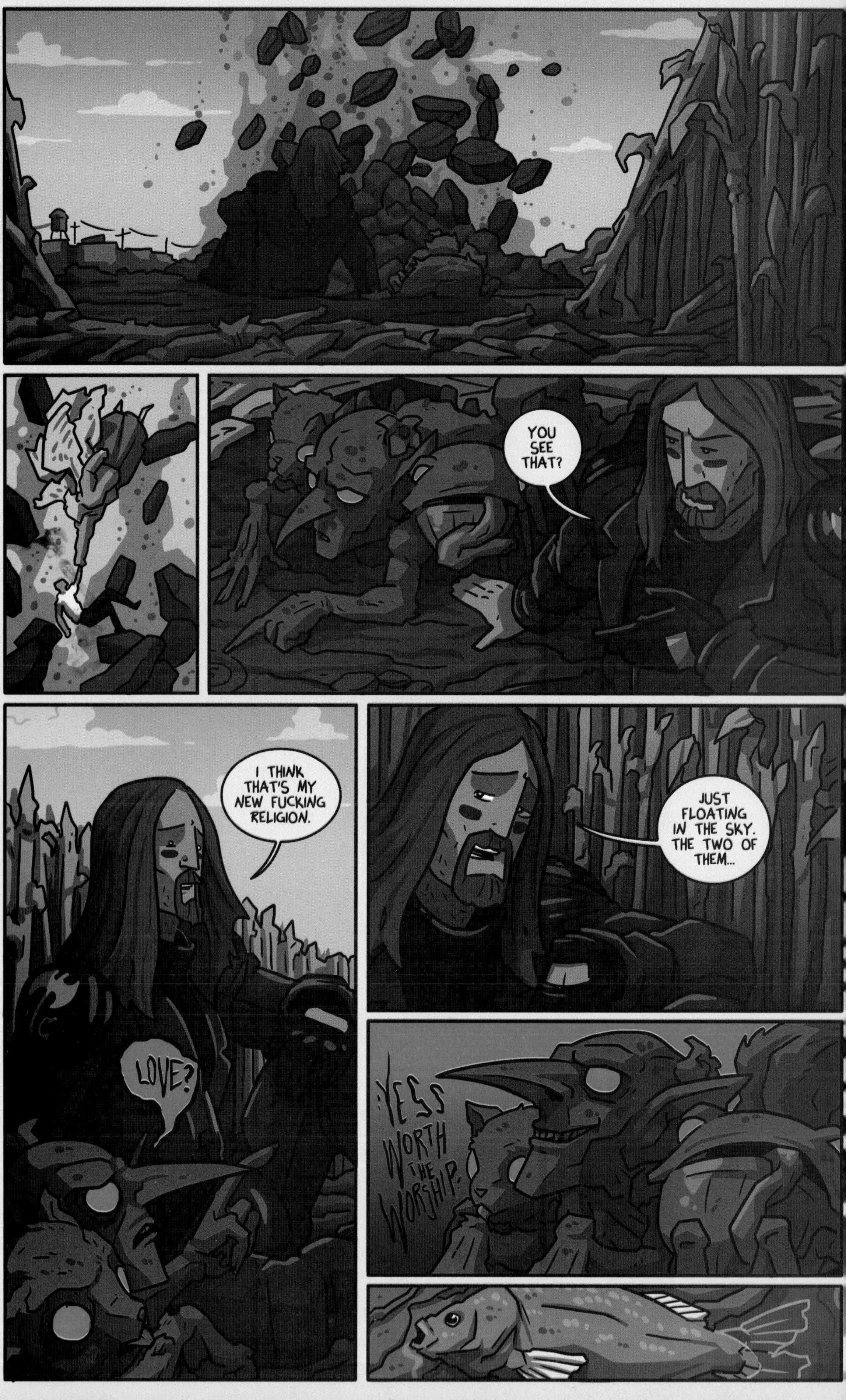
YOU SEE THAT?
I THINK THAT'S MY NEW FUCKING RELIGION.
JUST FLOATING IN THE SKY. THE TWO OF THEM...
LOVE?
YESS WORTH THE WORSHIP.

THE PUNKS AND OUTCASTS
CAME BEFORE THE LORD,
SCREAMING TO BE HEARD.

THEY WENT HOARSE, 'TIL A
NON-BELIEVING BASTARD AND HIS
FRIENDS HELPED THEM MAKE A NOISE.

AND ALL AGREED
IT WAS "F'N" GOOD.

AMEN.

-BLAISE 1:1

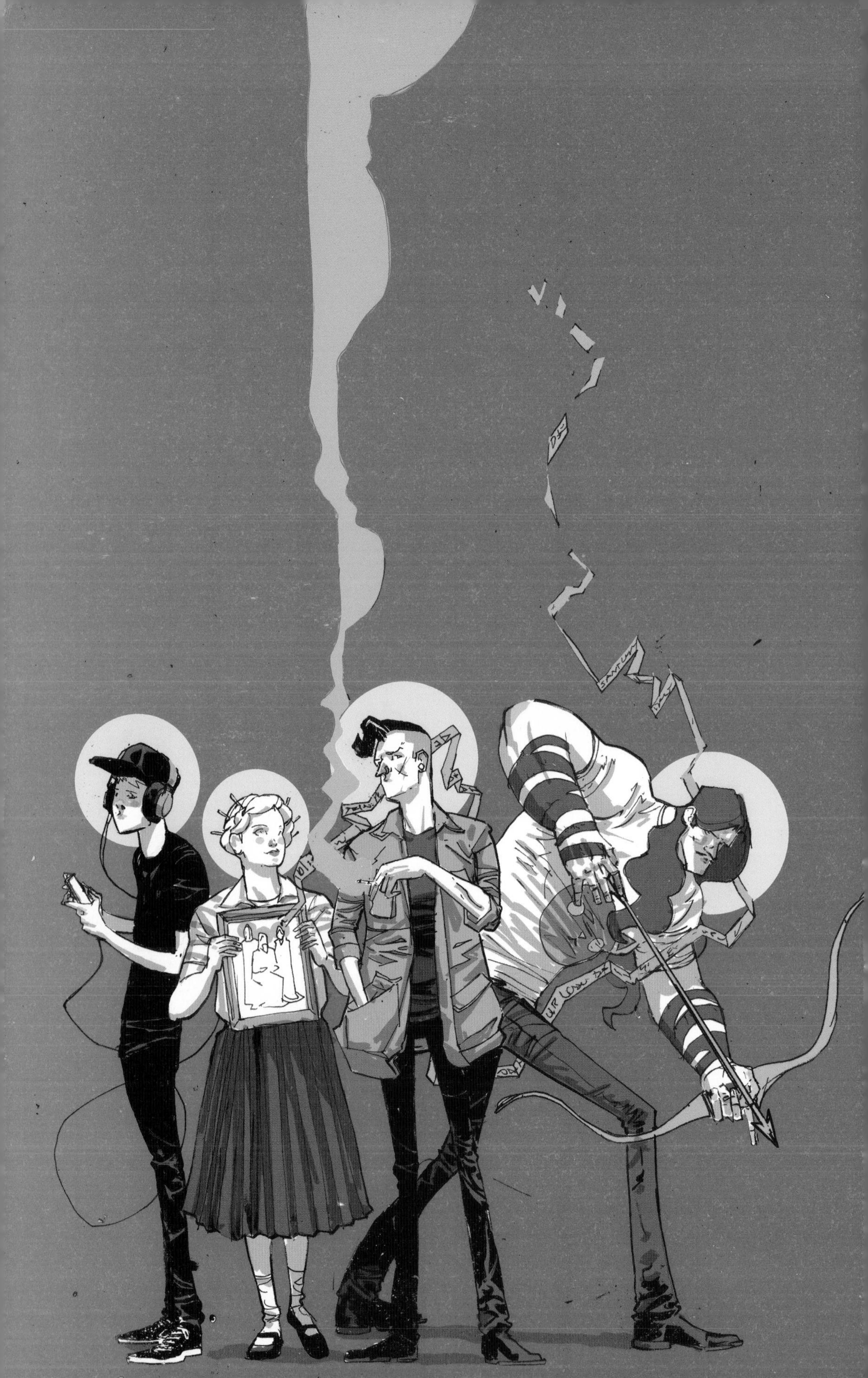

art by riley rossmo